amongst those left

also by francis booth

'Anybody called Francis is elegant, unbalanced and intelligent'
Gertrude Stein

collected works

The Storyteller's Assistant: Complete Words 2005-2011

poetry

Lullaby for a Lost Soul

The Devil's Table

Freefalling

The Blind Seer

translations & adaptations

Dhammapada: The Buddha's Path to the Truth

Songs of the Elder Sisters: Poems by Early Buddhist Nuns

Sakuntala: A Verse Drama

Maurice Maeterlinck: Five Marionette Plays

stories

Nowhere to Here: 50 Flash Fictions

non fiction

Comrades in Art: Revolutionary Art in America 1926-1938

Stranger Still: The Works of Anna Kavan

francisbooth.net

amongst those left

the british experimental novel
1940 – 1980

francis booth

ISBN: 978-1-291-10250-5

If there is progress there is a novel. Without progress there is nothing.

William Carlos Williams

I am now trying an Experiment very frequent among Modern Authors; which is, to *write upon Nothing.*

Jonathan Swift

There is no story to tell.

Alexander Trocchi

This is where the experimental writer (it's not a term I like, but there doesn't seem to be any other) has the cards stacked against him. People are so lazy or so rooted in established conventions in their reading that they won't make the effort.

J. G. Ballard

Everything written, if you say in it what you want to say, has its ideal reader. But it may happen that you, the author, are living here and now, while you, the reader, may live far away, or may have died a hundred years ago, or may not have been born yet.

Stefan Themerson

what I am really doing is challenging the reader to prove his own existence as palpably as I am proving mine by the act of writing.

B.S. Johnson

Perhaps writers are actually readers from hidden books. These books are carefully concealed and surrounded by deadly snares.

William Burroughs

What is happening, and where and to whom? It is happening to you, dear reader.

Eric Korn

There are three rules for writing the novel. Unfortunately, no one knows what they are.

W. Somerset Maugham

contents

preface 11
introduction 18
anna kavan 62
stefan themerson 111
rayner heppenstall 158
nicholas mosley 205
christine brooke-rose 252
alexander trocchi 285
alan burns 320
eva figes 359
b.s. johnson 392
jeff nuttall 436
ann quin 485
penelope shuttle 532
rosalind belben 564
fellow travellers 586
- stevie smith 592
- norman hidden 596
- philip toynbee 602
- paul ableman 606
- peter redgrove 613
- george macbeth 617
- stuart evans 622

julian mitchell 627
d.m. thomas 633
tom phillips 638
emma tennant 642
giles gordon 651
new wave science fiction 659
brian w aldiss 668
j. g. ballard 672
afterword 679
chronology 702
bibliography 706

preface

> How can I evaluate or describe to you the plots of any of these books, or the information they contain! For I am a lover of books, and this is my misfortune; to tell their worth is beyond me.[1]

This book was originally completed in 1982 but not published at the time, except for the section on Nicholas Mosley[2]; thirty years later I have decided to revise and publish it. I have kept the cut-off date around 1980, despite the fact that several of the authors I wrote about continued to write novels after that date and some still do. Although I have read subsequent studies of some of these writers, especially Jonathan Coe's magnificent biography of B. S. Johnson, I have not substantially altered what I wrote back then, which was much closer to the period covered by the book. I want to present the thoughts I had then, without the benefit of hindsight on authors who may have significantly changed their style in their later novels.

Also, if I had rewritten it I would not have been able to recapture the passion and excitement of English studies in the early 1980s: the works of Derrida, Lacan and others were beginning to be translated into English; Colin McCabe had been fired by Cambridge University for being a structuralist and was lecturing to packed halls in Oxford, where my Moral Tutor was Terry Eagleton. It all seemed to matter so much. So I have updated the notes and bibliography to include works after 1980 by and about the authors I have considered, used recent sources to correct some factual errors and update biographical information but have otherwise let the text stand fundamentally as it was at that heady time.

With the exception of Alan Burns I have not included any novels published after around 1982 though I have updated the study to include posthumously published novels by Anna Kavan, Rayner Heppenstall and Ann Quin who died before the cut-off date. I have generally not considered in depth any poetry even for authors like Penelope Shuttle who are primarily poets nor short stories except in the cases of Ann Quin, where they seemed to be essential to any discussion of her work. Anna Kavan's stories are also essential but I have written a separate book about her[3] of which the chapter in this book forms part.

---

[1] Peter Redgrove and Penelope Shuttle, 'Some Books, Some Authors, Some Readers' in *The Hermaphrodite Album*. London: Fuller D'Arch Smith, 1973

[2] 'Impossible Accidents: Nicholas Mosley', *Review of Contemporary Fiction*, vol. 2, no. 2, Summer 1982

[3] *Stranger Still: The Works of Anna Kavan,* 2012

I have also not included any discussion of the art works of novelists who are also artists – Kavan, Stefan Themerson and Jeff Nuttall – except where the art is integrated with the text, though I have tried to give a feeling for any special typography used in the novels. I have also generally not considered the earlier, more conventional works by novelists like Kavan, Mosley and Brooke-Rose who later changed their style. However I have considered autobiographical, critical and theoretical works by Themerson, Heppenstall, Nuttall, Nicholas Mosley, B.S. Johnson and Eva Figes which seem relevant to their novel-writing; in the case of Christine Brooke-Rose I have referenced her later theoretical, critical and autobiographical works where they illuminate her earlier work but have not considered her later novels published after the cut-off date. I have also used the posthumously-published journals of Rayner Heppenstall, and later autobiographical works by figures like Emma Tennant, John Calder and Maurice Girodias that illuminate the period. I have not however not used any secondary sources that were published after around 1980.

As for who counts as British I have claimed Kavan, Themerson and Brooke-Rose on the grounds that although they were not born in Britain they wrote and published most of their works here. I have also claimed Alexander Trocchi who was born in and returned to Britain but wrote and published most of his works abroad.

In addition to the authors given a chapter each there is a section I called 'Fellow Travellers': authors who wrote one or more experimental novels as part of a larger body of more traditional writing but did not seem to me to count as committed experimental novelists. I also included a chapter on British New Wave science fiction.

As for the title of the book: *Amongst Those Left* is a reference to B.S. Johnson's planned trilogy and I have kept the phrase 'experimental novel' although I know many people will object to it; as J.G. Ballard said 'it's not a term I like, but there doesn't seem to be any other.' It is certainly not an ideal description; experimentalism implies that the author didn't know what s/he was doing or what would happen. But neither I nor anyone else as far as I know has come up with a better term. Even B.S. Johnson – almost the only novelist of the time to make pronouncements on the subject - was ambivalent about it: he both used it and objected to it. In a letter to a prospective agent, Johnson wrote that *Travelling People* was 'from the outset an experimental novel'[1], but in the introduction to *Aren't You Rather Young to be Writing Your Memoirs* he says

> 'Experimental' to most reviewers is almost always a synonym for 'unsuccessful'. I object to the word experimental being applied to my own work. Certainly I make experiments, but the unsuccessful ones are

[1] Jonathan Coe, *Like A Fiery Elephant: The Story of B. S. Johnson*, 2004, p. 115

> quietly hidden away and what I choose to publish is in my own terms successful: that is, it has been the best way I could find of solving particular writing problems.

In her letters and diaries Virginia Woolf always referred to *Jacob's Room*, arguably the first British experimental novel[1] as an experiment as opposed to a success but obviously a novel may be both; some of the books in this study may more successful than others but their authors – and publishers - felt they worked or they would not have released them.

In many cases throughout book the question is not: is it experimental? but: is it a novel? I have considered books that are subtitled 'a novel', in case you were wondering; books that lay no claim to be novels; a book that claims – tautologically - to be a documentary novel; novelettes; romances; a surrealist fantasy; a dream; a party piece cut-up; an early summer landscape; books illustrated, handwritten, typewritten and typographically extravagant; a novel in a box and one with holes in its pages. Nothing unites them except their refusal to give us what we expect of a conventional novel, and the quality of their writing: T.S. Eliot said that 'most contemporary novels are not really "written"'[2] and Johnson said 'there are not many who are writing as though it mattered, as though they meant it, as though they meant it to matter'[3]; all these novels are and all these novelists did. They also avoid some or all of what Joyce called 'wideawake language, cutanddry grammar and goahead plot.'[4] If they succeed in their experiments with form and content it is because 'the goal comes, the method and the matter prove to have been one.'[5]

Stendahl said a novel is a mirror carried along a high road[6]; some of the novelists in this study carried their mirror along a dark deserted side street or through a post-apocalyptic landscape, some carried a cracked or smeared mirror, some stayed at home and just looked at themselves in a glass, darkly. And some believed, like Brecht, that art is not a mirror to reflect the world but a hammer with which to shape or smash it.[7]

These writers were not part of any organised movement in British fiction and did not write under any banner or to any programme[8]. They have few stylistic

---

[1] Published in 1922, the same year as *The Waste Land*, and other landmarks in the modern novel such as *Ulysses*, e.e cummings' *The Enormous Room and* Jean Toomer's *Cane.*

2 Introduction to Djuna Barnes' *Nightwood*. New York: Harcourt, Brace & Co., 1937

[3] *Aren't You Rather Young to be Writing Your Memoirs?* London: Hutchinson, 1973, p. 29

[4] James Joyce to Harriet Weaver

[5] E. M. Forster on Virginia Woolf's *Jacob's Room*

[6] *The Red and the Black*, 1830, vol. 2, ch. 19

[7] This quote is sometimes attributed to Mayakovski

[8] Though Rayner Heppenstall does recall a meeting in 1969 at Alan Burns' house attempting to 'start public readings and discussions under the name "Writers Reading"'.

similarities to each other and with some exceptions they did not know each other or share publishers, agents, street cafes or drinking clubs; Jeff Nuttall pointed out that the 'rendezvous of the Underground were not pubs, clubs or discotheques but bookshops.'[1]

This book stops around 1980 because that was when it was first written but in fact this does seem to be roughly the date at which experimental novel writing in this country almost dried up, though Nicholas Mosley, Christine Brooke-Rose and Eva Figes soldiered on. It had never in any case really caught on. As Anaïs Nin said in *The Novel of the Future*: 'People accepted abstract painting in their homes and studied the abstractions of science, but in the jet age read novels which corresponded to the horse and buggy.' And when T.S. Eliot made the comment about books being 'really written' he also realised that a 'prose that is altogether alive demands something of the reader that the ordinary novel-reader is not prepared to give.' B.S. Johnson was quite indignant about this:

> I think I do have a right to expect that most readers should be open to new work, that there should be an audience in this country willing to try to understand and be sympathetic to what those few writers not shackled by tradition are trying to do and are doing.[2]

But most readers weren't and neither were reviewers. Unlike in France and America, where novelists, academics and reviewers were often the same people, reviewers in Britain were mostly unsympathetic. As if echoing Eliot's comment, one reviewer said Christine Brooke-Rose's *Such* was 'very much a book for new-novel readers, who are used to this sort of hard work.'[3] Even Ann Quin's *Tripticks* and Alan Burns' *Dreamerika!* got, also from the serious literary review *Times Literary Supplement*: 'The technique, which must be even more laborious to employ than it is to interpret, cannot perform what it aims at. . . Bile and a certain peculiar pathos enliven Alan Burns' work, in consequence of his wit: there are no such rewards with Ann Quin,'[4] B.S. Johnson was almost constantly fighting the reviews, which had titles like 'Against Nature', Please be Brief', 'Author as Obstacle' and 'The Shallow End'.[5]

---

[1] *Snipe's Spinster*. London: Calder & Boyars, 1975. p. 18. Nuttall is particularly thinking of Better Books which was on London's Charing Cross Road.

[2] *Memoirs,* p. 29

[3] John Sturrock, *Times Literary Supplement* (TLS) October 20, 1968

[4] May 5, 1962

[5] All also from TLS

> A national daily newspaper (admittedly one known for its reactionary opinions) returned a review copy of *Travelling People* with the complaint that it must be a faulty copy for some of the pages were black[1]

Rayner Heppenstall had a similar experience: he said that reviewers would always comment only on the form of his novels not the content, and when the highly-structured and decidedly experimental *Two Moons* was published:

> The reviewers were indignant. It is possible to read most novels skippingly, but of *Two Moons* every word must be read, not in the easiest order. A fiction reviewer expects to give so much time each week to reading. With *Two Moons* he would have to double the time. This he resents. He refuses to do it.[2]

Other novelists faced the same hostility: 'Very roughly put together and jazzed up with neo-Joycean Jabberwocky'[3]; 'Nicholas Mosley has tried to avoid banality by making his narrative hard to follow: it is like a crossword puzzle, like a Royal Academy "problem picture"... The reader is expected to relate these essays to the stories, several of which are good, conventional little tales. The effort demanded is considerable.'[4]; 'the main disappointment in *Days* is the lack of some solid core of developed, realistic action from which the wide implications of Miss Figes' central theme may validly derive'[5]; 'Mr. Gordon baffles without reward... When he is not pretentious he is flat; sometimes (as in his index of characters) he manages to be both'[6]; 'Eccentric punctuation and chapter headings alert the reader at once to the strained and side-long approach Rosalind Belben's novel takes to the business of dying.'[7] Even Christine Brooke-Rose, one of the few to continue the fight for the experimental novel, was almost defeated by it: 'The resistance was great, in France but especially in England, where traditionalist critics and realistic novelists organised strong campaigns, which they no doubt feel they have won'[8] She also thought it was even harder for female experimental novelists than for men: it was 'not only more difficult for a woman *experimental* writer' to be accepted than for a 'woman writer . . . but also peculiarly more

---

[1] *Memoirs,* p. 31

[2] *The Master Eccentric: The Journals of Rayner Heppenstall.* London: Allison and Busby, 1986. Entry for May 29 1977.

[3] David Williams on Alan Burns' *Buster,* TLS, January 5 1962

[4] D.A.N. Jones, TLS, October 17 1968

[5] TLS, January 18 1974

[6] TLS, January 25 1974

[7] TLS, August 16 1974

[8] *A Rhetoric of the Unreal: Studies in narrative and structure, especially of the fantastic.* Cambridge University Press, 1981. p. 311

difficult for a *woman* experimental writer to be accepted than for a male experimental writer.'[1]

And, as I have said, it was not as if British experimental novelists in this book had a support structure among themselves: most of them did not teach in universities, and none in this country - Brooke-Rose and Burns taught in France and America respectively - or had access to an academic writing/reviewing cycle as the French and Americans did. They even sniped at each other: Rayner Heppenstall, discussing the *nouveau roman* in relation to the British novel and twentieth century revolutions in philosophy and science said:

> Only the novel lags behind. More particularly, it is in a large measure due to ignorance. There is no equivalent in Britain to the Nouvelle Critique and virtually no serious English criticism of the Nouveau Roman – the few exceptions apparently finding no outlet here and appearing in French or American reviews.
>
> This ignorance even affects our own would-be experimenters, a scattered few who borrow old tricks of style or typography or time-jumbling without, evidently, having a clue about what is really at stake, since behind the tricks lie the old, personal documentary of the peeved young man or woman, now sadly depleted of its earlier picaresque humour, and full of his or her sexual encounters, his or her analysis of emotions, childhood flashbacks, social commentary &c. The ignorance is so crass one gasps at the sheers cheek of it[2]

Several of the novelists in this study reverted to traditional novel-writing around this time – including even Stefan Themerson's late and Rayner Heppenstall's last works. Some took to editing anthologies, writing historical novels or pastiches; some who were primarily poets returned to poetry; some just stopped writing altogether.

My selection and categorisation of authors may be considered arbitrary and personal, and so it was; I simply tried to choose writers who, acting individually, had laid siege to the fortress of the conventional novel. However my list is in fact not too much different from that of B.S. Johnson:

> Perhaps I should nod here to Samuel Beckett (of course), John Berger, Christine Brooke-Rose, Brigid Brophy, Anthony Burgess, Alan Burns, Angela Carter, Eva Figes, Giles Gordon, Wilson Harris, Rayner Heppenstall, even hasty, muddled Robert Nye, Ann Quin, Penelope Shuttle, Alan Sillitoe (for his last book only, Raw Material indeed),

[1] Things' in *Stories, Theories and Things*. Cambridge University Press, 2009. p. 262
[2] 'The Nouveau Roman' TLS, August 7 1969

> Stefan Themerson, and (coming) John Wheway; (stand by): and if only Heathcote Williams would write a novel. . . .
>
> Anyone who imagines himself or herself slighted by not being included above can fill in his or her name here:
>
> ....
>
> It would be a courtesy, however, to let me know his or her qualifications for so imagining.
>
> Are we concerned with courtesy?[1]

Well, I myself am concerned with courtesy, but it is rather too late for that now, as thirty years have elapsed since I wrote this book and most of the novelists included or not included have since died (two have died this year, 2012, alone); even when I first wrote it three of them had (probably) already killed themselves. I set out with a grand plan to refute the idea that, while American and French fiction was exciting and ground-breaking, British novels were all dull, realist and provincial. Although my ambitions are now much more modest, I still believe this is a worthy cause.

Finally, although it is thirty years too late to thank them, I would like to acknowledge my debt to the inspiration and support of Richard Ellmann, Terry Eagleton and Malcolm Bradbury.

---

[1] *Memoirs,* pp. 30/31

introduction

> the Americans are doing what the Elizabethans did - they are coining new words. They are instinctively making the language adapt to their needs. In England, save for the impetus given by the war, the word-coining power has lapsed . . . It is significant that when we want to freshen our speech we borrow from America . . . all the expressive ugly vigorous slang which creeps into use among us first in talk, later in writing. Nor does it take much foresight to predict that when words are being made a literature will be made out of them.[1]

> So there they were and the Americans were not at all that way they did not live their life at all no not at all in that way and they had it to say that they lived their own life in their own way and they had it to say it with the words that had been made to tell a nation's story in an entirely different way as the nation who had made the language had the entirely different story to tell of living their daily life every moment of every day [2]

Virginia Woolf and Gertrude Stein are both here talking about the difference between the British and American ways of writing. This study is mainly concerned with the contemporary novel in Britain, but in order to show what I think is distinctive about the British novel, I need to contrast it to the American. This has often been done before, though usually in an attempt to define a distinctive American voice rather than a British one, as I shall try to do. 'The fact that English novels and American are written in a common language often blinds us to the differences between them . . . These differences are not recent in origin. They were just as strongly marked in nineteenth century fiction as they are in that of today.'[3] Allen, like Woolf, stresses the 'abiding factor in the American novel, a constant preoccupation with the meaning of being an American'.[4] Allen says that, where English novels have treated the life of the individual in society, the

> classic American novels have dealt not so much with the lives of men in society as with the lives of solitary man, man alone and wrestling with himself . . . They appear, by contrast with the heroes of English novels, often to belong to a different order of experience and conception.

---

[1] Virginia Woolf. 'American Fiction', *Collected Essays* Vol II. London: Chatto & Windus, 1966 p. 121

[2] Gertrude Stein. *On Narration*: Chicago U.P. , 1935 p. 9

[3] Walter Allen. *Tradition and Dream* London: Dent, 1966, p. xi

[4] ibid p. xvii. Woolf, op. cit. pp. 112/3

> Abstracted, alienated from the society of their times, surrounded as it were by an envelope of emptiness, they seem somewhat larger than life, at any rate life as rendered in the broadly realistic English novel in which the crowd of men and women depicted must bring the central figures down to a level of their own. They have, these American heroes an epic, mythic quality [1]

The English novel has had its picaresques, from *Tom Jones* down to *Lucky Jim*, but none of them have had this 'epic, mythic quality'. It has now become commonplace that, whereas the American novel has forged powerfully ahead, confronting modern society head on, the English novel has opted for a safe complacency, returning to the style of a previous age. Susan Sontag, who in the mid-sixties had strongly criticised American fiction and critics for being too conservative, was asked in 1972 whether she thought that the situation had improved. She replied:

> Exactly the same thing was going on in England in that period too and there the novel has remained extremely conservative. A writer like Iris Murdoch was, at least at the beginning of' her career, considered to be far out; and genuinely experimental writers like Virginia Woolf and Ivy Compon-Burnett had no influence whatever. What I said about American prose fiction still pretty much applies to what is going on in England - but less and less to what is happening here.[2]

It was not only the Americans who thought this way; it was still largely the orthodox view in England too. Bernard Bergonzi said in 1970 (and let the comment stand in the revised edition of 1979) that 'the French and many Americans feels compelled to strive for novelty, but the English, including the most talented among them, seem to have settled for the predictable pleasures of

---

[1] Walter Allen: op. cit. p. xv. See also on the essentially American quality of American fiction: D.H. Lawrence's *Studies in Classic American Literature* 1923; C.S. Fiedelson. *Symbolism and American Literature* Chicago U.P. , 1953; Joyce Cary 'The Sources of Tension in America' *Saturday Review* 23 Aug 1952; repr. in his *Selected Essays* ed. A.G. Bishop London: Joseph, 1976; Harry Levin. *The Power of Blackness*. New York: Knopf, 1958; Richard Chase. *The American Novel and its Tradition* New York: Doubleday, 1957; Leslie Fiedler. *Love and Death in the American Novel*. New York: Criterion, 1960; Richard Poirier. *A World Elsewhere: The Place of Style in American Literature*. New York: O.U.P. , 1966. The development of a self-conscious American literary aesthetic is traced in original documents in R. Ruland ed. *The Native Muse: Theories of American Literature vol 1*. New York: Dutton, 1976, and the second volume, *A Storied Land*. New York: Dutton, 1976

[2] J.D. Bellamy ed. *The New Fiction*: Illinois: University of Illinois Press, 1974, p. 115

genre fiction'.[1] Malcolm Bradbury had also noticed (and criticised) the tendency to assume that

> the novel is not dead but fled; it is alive and well and living in America. It is the English novel only that bears the marks of exhaustion, of provincialism, of 'reaction against experiment' . . . In these assumptions we have an interesting antithesis and a view of it: a contrast between realism and experiment, and a proposal that realism is a feature of moribundity and English, and experiment a feature of growth and American. [2]

Speaking in 1963, Brigid Brophy said that, although the novel was 'alive and kicking', 'it often seems to kick with only one leg: or, rather, only one of its legs is truly fictitious'; that the novel in Britain had come to resemble sociology and documentary because of novelists' fears that what they wrote would be considered "only' fiction'.[3] In 1964, the *Times Literary Supplement* ran two special issues on the avant garde: the first contained hardly anything British, the second nothing at all,[4] and in 1966 the editor of a collection of 'experimental writing' complained that the book contained no 'fundamental experimentation with verbal and structural forms. The editor is disposed to encourage such work, but the fact is that no samples of this kind of work were submitted'.[5]

The editors of a British journal devoted to 'new writing' launched in 1979 said in the introduction to their first issue that there were 'few new voices in British writing today, mostly just echoes: the nineteenth century persists nowhere as it does in the contemporary English novel', whereas in America a 'new voice has developed, a new kind of dialogue in fiction. But has England even recognized that it exists?'[6] (This first issue was entitled 'New American Writing', which was also almost exclusively the content of the second issue. The third was entitled 'The End of the English Novel'.) Even B.S. Johnson wrote in 1973:

> Nathalie Sarraute once described literature as a relay race, the baton of innovation passing from one generation to another. The vast majority of

---

[1] Bernard Bergonzi. *The Situation of the Novel* London: Macmillan, 1970, 2nd ed. 1979, p. 20

[2] Malcolm Bradbury. 'The Postwar English Novel', in *Possibilities* Oxford U.P. , 1973 p. 167

[3] 'The Novel as Takeover Bid', broadcast, Third Programme, Aug 1963, *Listener* Oct 1963; repr. in her *Don't Never Forget* London, Cape, 1966

[4] Aug 6 and Sep 3

[5] Philip Rahv ed. *Modern Occasions* London: Weidenfeld & Nicholson, 1966 p. ix

[6] *Granta* vol. 1 no. 1

> British novelists has dropped the baton, stood still, turned back, or not even realised that there is a race.[1]

I want to argue that, whereas the British novel *was* different from that in contemporary America and the Continent, it was not all safety and convention: there was a thriving experimental strain between the end of the Second World War and around 1980, and it contained a trend in novel-writing that had become almost exclusively British.

It is not easy to describe something so diverse as the contemporary American novel, but I think that the 'absurdist' or 'comic-apocalyptic' trend, with which I am mainly concerned, has been well summed up by Bergonzi:

> the tragic, the violent and the comic are interwoven. The conventions of the realist novel may be upheld, but only for as long as it suits the author; at any moment they may be undermined by some unashamedly fantastic or surrealist device. The characters are in no sense 'rounded' or 'substantial'; they are presented like the boldly drawn, two-dimensional figures in a comic strip, with no question of 'freedom' or 'opaqueness' about them. The author is a whole-hearted manipulator, whose consciousness of what he is doing dominates the whole novel. And his powers of manipulation frequently extend to the reader, who is likely to be involved in every kind of trap and mystification. There is often a perverse sense of disaster.[2]

Many of these qualities are emphasised by American novelists themselves in talking about their work: John Hawkes has spoken of the necessity of a

> quality of coldness, detachment, ruthless determination to face up to the enormities of ugliness and potential failure within ourselves and in the world around us, and to bring to this exposure a savage or saving comic spirit and the saving beauties of language. The need is to maintain the truth of the fractured picture; to expose, ridicule, attack, but always to create and to throw into new light our potential for violence and absurdity as well as for graceful action.[3]

---

[1] *Aren't You Rather Young to be Writing Your Memoirs*. London: Hutchinson, 1973
[2] Bergonzi op. cit. pp. 82/3
[3] 'John Hawkes: 'An Interview': *Wisconsin Studies in Contemporary Literature*, Summer 1965; repr. in *Contemporary Novelists* ed. J. Vinson London: St. James Press and New York: St. Martins Press, 1972, 2nd. ed.
1976, p. 609

Absurdity is a strong theme in American postmodernism, as is the feeling of apocalypse: Walker Percy has said of one of his novels that what seemed important to him were 'certain elements of self-hatred and self-destructiveness which have surfaced in American life . . . This accounts for the apocalyptic themes of the book: love in the ruins, end of the world, being among the few survivors etc.'[1] Given these themes, the traditional notion of character is also rejected. Hawkes says: 'I began to write fiction on the assumption that the true enemies of the novel were plot, character, setting and theme' [2]; and Ronald Sukenick: 'I don't think the kind of books I'm interested in are interested in characterisation anymore'[3], and: 'The contemporary writer who is acutely in touch with the life of which he is part is forced to start from scratch: Reality doesn't exist, time doesn't exist, personality doesn't exist.'[4] Hawkes also is prepared to bracket the whole of existence:

> I can't help but think of fictions as artefacts created out of always the nothingness and always pointing toward that source of zero, a sort of zero source. That is why for one reason among others I admire John Barth, because the more elaborate the fiction gets, the more you create, the more you know exactly the nothingness it inhabits.[5]

Barth himself tells 'complicated stories simply for the aesthetic pleasure of complexity, of complication and unravelment, suspense and the rest'[6]; John Gardner, who thinks that Walt Disney, apart from his sentimentality, was one of the greatest American artists, and tries in his work to create 'cartoon' characters (he praises Stanley Elkin for doing the same), is similarly interested in telling stories for their own sake: 'What you have to do, I think, is tell an interesting story. That means a plot that's kind of neat and that's got characters who are kind of neat and it happens in places that are made by the writer's imagination into 'kind of neat . . . That's what I think fiction now is about. It's about, creating

[1] Quoted on the cover of his *Love in the Ruins*. London: Eyre & Spottiswood, 1971. However, Percy has elsewhere argued that the novelist presents this apocalypse to help prevent it; he sees the novelist as not so much a prophet but more like a canary in a mine shaft. See 'Notes for a Novel about the End of the World' in his *The Message in the Bottle*. New York: Farrar, Strauss & Giroux, 1981

[2] Hawkes, op. cit.

[3] Bellamy, op. cit. p. 65

[4] *The Death of the Novel and Other Stories*. New York: Dial Press, 1969

[5] Interview in *The Imagination on Trial* ed. Alan Burns and Charles Sugnet. London: Alison & Busby, 1981, p. 76

[6] Bellamy, op. cit. p. 7

circus shows.'[1] William Gass has stated his preference for the formal over the empirical, a preference shared by many other novelists: when asked if he ever did research for his novels he replied:

> No research. I collect words. Twelve different names for whore among the Romans. Thirty five names for cloth and silk stuffs. Etc. Sometimes I even use what I've collected. Or an old book will suggest something. But there are no 'scenes' to revisit . . . because my choice of factuality . . . was purely formal[2]

Similarly John Hawkes has said: 'I resist and resent very much the idea of associating research with fiction writing. It seems to me a bizarre incongruity to even think of researching something which is real in order to create a fiction which is a fiction'[3]. The fictionality of fiction and its inability to reflect reality is echoed by Donald Barthelme: 'Art is not about something but *is* something'[4], and by Gilbert Sorrentino: 'The novel must exist outside the life it deals with; it is an invention, something that is made; it is not the expression of 'self'; it does not mirror reality'[5]. Sukenick also expresses a similar view: 'Rather than serving as a mirror or redoubling on itself, fiction adds itself to the world, creating a meaningful 'reality' that did not previously exist'[6].

This 'reality' is seen by these novelists to be purely a verbal one; William Gass has said: 'That novels should be made of words and only words is a bit shocking really. It is as though you had discovered that your wife was made of rubber .'[7] Gass's professed concern is ironic, as is shown by another comment: 'the novelist, if he is any good will keep us kindly imprisoned in his language – there is literally nothing beyond'[8]. On similar lines, Raymond Federman has written:

> fiction can no longer be reality or a representation of reality, or an imitation, or even a recreation of reality; it can only be A REALITY - an

---

[1] Bellamy, op. cit. P. 182. However, in other interviews, Gardner has affirmed his belief in the moral responsibility of the novelist. See Burns and Sugnet, op. cit. and *The Radical Imagination and the Liberal Tradition* ed. Heide Ziegler and Christopher Bigsby. London: Junction, 1982

[2] Bellamy, op. cit. p. 38

[3] Burns and Sugnet, op. cit. P. 71

[4] 'The Emerging Figure', *Forum*, Summer 1961, p. 24 This is what Beckett had said about Joyce.

[5] 'The Various Isolated: W.C.Williams' Prose', *New American Review* 15, 1972, p. 196

[6] Quoted by Raymond Federman in the collection *Surfiction: Fiction Now and Tomorrow*. Chicago: Swallow, 1975, p. 5

[7] *Fiction and the Figures of Life*. New York: Vintage, 1973, p. 27

[8] Gass op. cit. p. 8

> autonomous reality whose only relation with the real world is to improve that world. To create fiction is, in fact, a way to abolish reality, and especially to abolish the notion that reality is truth[1]

Federman, in an insert in his novel *Double or Nothing*, which is titled 'Some Reflections on the Novel in Our Time', also says:

> the novel is nothing but a denunciation, by its very reality, of the illusion which animates it. All great novels are critical novels which, under the pretense of telling a story, of bringing characters to life, of interpreting situations, slide under our eyes the mirage of a tangible form . . . The essence of a literary discourse - that is to say a discourse fixed once and for all - is to find its own point of reference, its own rules of organisation in itself, and not in the real or imaginary experience on which it rests.[2]

Stanley Elkin has also emphasised the purely verbal aspect of his work: when asked what he liked most about it he replied: What I like best about it, I suppose, are the sentences.'[3] And Gerald Graft has also noted that postmodernist writers and their critics 'have taken as their subject the problematic status of their own authority to make statements about anything outside the systems of language and convention in which they must write'.[4] No wonder a 1970s book about the American novel was called *City of Words*.[5] All these comments point towards a rejection of the traditional liberal humanist basis of the novel. As Malcolm Bradbury has put it:

> the model of a cybernetic world has led to an art in which the human figure exists itself as a parody - as a role-player, a formless performer, a cardboard cut-out. From this, we may draw a dark conclusion: that many modern writers feel they can yield to us only a post-humanist model of man.[6]

The American critic Leslie Fiedler does not see this conclusion as being dark at all; he sees post-humanism as the goal towards which the youth of America are striving, not as something which is being foisted on them by novelists: 'the tradition from which they strive to disengage is the tradition of the human, as the

---

[1] *Surfiction* op. cit. p. 8
[2] Chicago: Swallow, 1971, unnumbered page between pp. 146 and 147
[3] *Contemporary Novelists* op. cit. p. 404
[4] *Literature Against Itself*. Chicago U.P. , 1979, p. 7
[5] Tony Tanner. *City of Words*. London: Cape, 1971
[6] 'Putting in the Person' in *The Contemporary English Novel*, ed. Bradbury and D. Palmer London: Arnold, 1979, p. 203

West . . . has defined it, Humanism itself'.[1] Ihab Hassan, one of the leading apologists for and theorists of postmodernism comes to the same conclusion, though he seems more ambivalent about it: 'We need to understand that five hundred years of humanism may be coming to an end, as humanism transforms itself into something we must helplessly call posthumanism.'[2] The avant garde American novel and its apologists seem therefore to have abandoned the liberal humanist viewpoint and realist aesthetic which have traditionally characterised the novel,[3] and the post-war French novel seems also to have moved towards post-humanism.

Immediately after the Second World War, John Lehmann, visiting Paris, noted that

> France's intellectual vitality was as remarkable as ever, but it seemed to me to a large extent to be turning in a void. Whether it was the result of the shock of defeat and the humiliation of Nazi occupation, or of some deeper reason that went further back, the dominant spirit was, I thought, anti- humanistic, even nihilistic.[4]

And, of course, the postwar French novel had the influence of such figures as Radiguet, Roussel, Queneau and Blaise Cendrars as well as the influence of Dada and Surrealism[5] at a time when the British novel was turning away from Modernism. The French also had the impetus of Existentialism to add to the

---

[1] Leslie Fiedler 'The New Mutants' in *Partisan Review*, Fall 1965; repr. in *A Fiedler Reader*. New York: Stein & Day, 1977 and in *Innovations* ed. B. Bergonzi London: Macmillan, 1978

[2] Ihab Hassan 'Prometheus as Performer: Towards a Posthumanist Culture?' in *Performance in Postmodern Culture* ed. M. Benamou and C. Caramello. Madison, Wisconsin: Coda Press, 1977, p. 212

[3] For further support of this view, see other works by Hassan and Fiedler, and by Robert Scholes, Richard Poirier and Susan Sontag. For a different interpretation, see Josephine Hendin: *Vulnerable People*. New York: O.U.P. , 1978. For the view that the nihilistic trend of the sixties has already been reversed by 'post-contemporary' writers, see Jerome Klinkowitz: *Literary Disruptions: The Making of a Post-Contemporary American Fiction* Illinois U.P. , 2nd ed. 1980, and for the view that humanism in the visual arts is reviving, see Barry Schwartz. *The New Human*. London: David & Charles, 1974. For the opinions of Americans opposed to this trend see Gerald Graff op. cit.; Irving Howe 'Literature and Liberalism' in his *Celebrations and Attacks*. London: Deutsch , 1979 and Gore Vidal 'American Plastic: The Matter of Fiction' in his *Matters of Fact and Fiction*. London: Heinemann, 1977

[4] John Lehmann. *I Am My Brother*. London: Longman, 1960, p. 306

[5] For an account of the limited influence of Dada and Surrealism, on British writing, see Alan Young. *Dada and After: Extremist Modernism and English Literature*. Manchester U.P. , 1981. Young argues that, since England had had Lewis Carroll and a long tradition of fantasy, it did not need Surrealism.

heritage of Symbolism, a tradition of stylistic innovation and refinement extending back at least as far as Flaubert's desire to write a novel about nothing, and the example of a series of mostly misanthropist writers rejecting and reviling bourgeois humanist values, extending, at least, through de Sade, Lautréamont, Baudelaire, Rimbaud, Céline and Genet.[1]

The French *nouveau roman*, while it has many differences from the American postmodernist novel,[2] has generally been based on post-humanist premises (Nathalie Sarraute is, I think, an exception), and this was continued by younger writers such as J.M.G. le Clézio, Monique Wittig and Patrick Modiano.

> Speak: but from the far side of language, too, from then side of those who create it. Each word needs to be turned inside out like a glove, and emptied of its substance. Each speech should wrench itself from the ground like an aeroplane and smash through the surrounding walls. Up till now you have been slaves. You have been given words to obey, words to write slavish poems and slavish philosophies. It is time to arm words. Arm them and hurl them against the walls. Perhaps they will even reach the other side.[3]

Alain Robbe-Grillet has polemicised the rejection of humanism in the novel, with its anthropomorphic analogies and pananthropism which 'humanises' inanimate things and posits a shared human nature.[4] Robbe-Grillet rejects the old 'myths of depth'.

> We know that all literature used to be based on them, and on them alone. The role of the writer traditionally consisted in burrowing down into Nature, into excavating it, in order to reach its most intimate strata and finally bring to light some minute part of a disturbing secret. The writer descended into the chasm of human passions and sent up to the apparently tranquil world (that of the surface) victorious messages

---

[1] A trend, arguably, exported to America by Henry Miller and now carried on by William Burroughs, having touched Terry Southern, Norman Mailer and Philip Roth to some extent.
[2] The links between them are tenuous, though Raymond Federman, who has been involved on both sides of the Atlantic, has written critically about the *nouveau roman* in *Cinq Nouvelles Nouvelles*. New York: Appleton - Century- Crofts, 1970, and Leslie Fiedler has seen Boris Vian as a linking figure: 'Cross the Border - Close That Gap: Postmodernism' in *American Literature since 1900* ed. M. Cunliffe. London: Sphere, 1975, pp. 350/1. John Barth has said that, whereas Robbe-Grillet and Nathalie Sarraute are aiming for 'a kind of epistemological realism', he' prefers to regard art as purely artifice. Bellamy, op. cit. p. 15
[3] J.M.G. le Clézio. The Giants, London: Jonathan Cape, 1975. Originally published as Les Géants. Paris: Gallimard, 1973
[4] Alain Robbe-Grillet: 'Nature Humanism and Tragedy' in his *Snapshots and Towards a New Novel* London: Calder & Boyars, 1965

> describing the mysteries he had touched with his fingers. And the sacred vertigo which then overwhelmed the reader, far from causing him any distress or nausea, on the contrary reassured him about his powers of domination over the world. There were abysses, it was true, but thanks to these valiant speleologists, their depths could be sounded.[1]

The old concept of character in the novel must change, since the concept of character in life has changed:

> the creators of character in the traditional sense can now do nothing more than present us with puppets in whom they themselves no longer believe. The novel that contains characters belongs well and truly to the past, it was peculiar to an age - that of the apogee of the individual.[2]

Since 'the present age is rather that of the regimental number',[3] of mass society, the novelist who creates characters is not writing about present society but about the past.

Like the Americans already quoted, the *noveaux romanciers* saw language as having its own reality rather than reflecting a reality outside itself. Claude Simon has written : 'There is no need to look beyond what is written. There is only what is written'[4]. And Philippe Sollers, taking this one step further, said 'we are nothing other, in the last analysis, than our system of reading and writing'[5]

Sollers is a good example of the interaction between theory and practice in the French novel, being both novelist and theoretician, and associated with the *Tel Quel* journal. The view of man as a product of linguistic forces only is typical of postwar developments in French philosophy and linguistics, which have had far more influence on French fiction than Anglo-Saxon philosophy has had on English fiction. (Indeed, in some cases, such as Edmond Jabés and Derrida's *Glas*, the borderline between philosophy and fiction is deliberately blurred.) These philosophical developments have tended to be explicitly or implicitly anti-humanist. Lévi-Strauss said in *The Savage Mind* that the ultimate aim of the human sciences was not to constitute man but to dissolve him, and many others have followed him in this. Foucault said that 'man is only a recent invention, a figure not yet two centuries old, a simple fold in our knowledge, and that he will disappear as soon as that knowledge has found a new form',[6] and Derrida advocated a criticism which 'tries to pass beyond man and humanism, the name

---

[1] 'A Path for the Future Novel' in *Snapshots* op. cit. pp. 56/7

[2] 'On Some Outdated Notions' in *Snapshots* op. cit. p. 60

[3] ibid. p. 61

[4] Quoted by Stephen Heath in *The Nouveau Roman* London: Elek, 1972, p. 16

[5] Quoted by Jonathan Culler in *Structuralist Poetics* London: RKP, 1975 p. 264

[6] *The Order of Things* London: Pantheon, 1971, p. 15

of man being the name of that being who, throughout the history of metaphysics or of ontotheology - in other words, through the history of all his history - has dreamed of full presence, the reassuring foundation, the origin and the end of the game'.[1]

The thrust of the criticism and semiotics of Barthes (Who points to 1848 as the beginning of the end of bourgeois humanist illusions), Riffaterre, Macherey, Kristeva, Sollers and the *Tel Quel* group, the philosophy of Derrida, the political sociology of Althusser, the literary sociology of Goldmann and the psychoanalysis of Lacan had consistently been to deny the individual a unique personal identity independent of social and linguistic influences, let alone a soul. The individual becomes the 'subject', the 'decentred' conjunction of ideological and linguistic lines of force; a point in a system rather than the originator of truth and value, which, if they have any meaning at all, reside in the system not the individual.

Given these philosophical premises, the novel based on them will naturally tend not to try to uncover moral and universal truths or try to penetrate to the depths of 'character', which are both seen as illusions which the novelist should pierce. Neither this philosophy and its associated criticism, nor the novel it entails have ever really taken root in Britain, as the earlier American New Criticism did not, and the result is an entirely different type of novel.

The British novel, with its predominantly liberal humanist base has, in contrast to this, often seemed to claim to provide truths about society, morals and character, certainly since its move away from modernism in the forties and fifties. Although

> the English novelists of this period wrote about contemporary social problems, few of them experimented with the form and style of their novels; nor did they incorporate the techniques of Joyce, Virginia Woolf or other experimental novelists into their own styles. Most of the postwar writers conscientiously rejected experimental techniques in their fiction as well as in their critical writings and turned instead to older novelists for inspiration.[2]

And, despite the undoubted revival of interest in the experimental novel, these comments still applied at the end of the 1970s.

> There is, when one thinks about it, a certain felicity about Jane Austen's having dominated the bestseller list in 1975 with *Sanditon* (it sold

---

[1] 'Structure Sign and Play in the Discourse of the Human Sciences' in *The Structuralist Controversy* ed. R. Macksey and E. Donato Baltimore: Johns Hopkins U.P. , 1972, p. 264

[2] Rubin Rabinovitz. *Reaction Against Experiment in the English Novel, 1950-1960* Columbia U.P. , 1968, p. 2

> 22,000 in the first ten weeks and eventually 30,000 in hardback . . .). For the kind of fiction Austen practised lives on. The English novel, as exemplified by Drabble, Snow, Angus Wilson, Elizabeth Taylor et al, is still very much about Sense and Sensibility, Pride, Prejudice and Persuasion. Consciously and often proudly so, one might add.[1]

Not only humanism but realism were seen by many, including the novelists themselves, to be an indispensable part of the novel, and the writers often seemed to feel a part of a long and valuable tradition which, unlike the Americans and French, they had little desire to overturn. Long after *Lucky Jim*, Kingsley Amis was saying 'what I think I am doing is writing novels within the main English-language tradition. That is, trying to tell interesting, believable stories about understandable characters in a reasonably straightforward style: no tricks, no experimental tomfoolery'.[2] David Lodge had similarly said that his novels 'belong to a tradition of realistic fiction (especially associated with England) that tries to find an appropriate form for, and a public significance in, what the writer has himself experienced and observed',[3] and Margaret Drabble, despite her collaboration with B.S. Johnson on the collective novel *London Consequences*, had spoken of her preference for being 'at the end of a dying tradition which I admire' rather than 'at the beginning of a tradition which I deplore'.[4] Drabble also made it clear that the title of her novel *The Middle Ground* is meant to refer both to the audience at which she is aiming, and her own approach to fiction, a view echoed by a very different English writer, John Fowles: 'l suspect the crucial thing, in the novel, is how novelist conceives of audience. My own preferred contact is in the middle ground'.[5]

And, although the realist novel was anything but dead, the critical reaction to this conservatism, from both sides of the Atlantic, has been that it tends to produce merely a dull epigonism:

> There is a good deal of evidence that the English literary mind is peculiarly committed to realism, and resistant to non-realistic literary modes to an extent that might be described as prejudice . . . And, reviewing the history of the English novel in the twentieth century it is difficult to avoid associating the restoration of traditional literary realism with a perceptible decline in artistic achievement.[6]

---

1 J.A. Sutherland. *Fiction and the Fiction Industry* London: Athlone, 1978, p. 21
2 *Contemporary Novelists* op. cit. p. 44
3 *Contemporary Novelists* op. cit. p. 833
4 BBC recording 1967: 'Novelists of the Sixties'; quoted in Bergonzi op. cit. p. 65
5 Ziegler and Bigsby op. cit. p. 124
6 David Lodge 'The Novelist at the Crossroads' in *The Novel Today* ed. M: Bradbury Glasgow: Fontana, 1977, p. 88

But, although the neo-realist trend in the novel in Britain may only have produced works which are 'intelligent, technically competent but ultimately mediocre',[1] this conservatism may have had its positive aspect. The English novel's greatest strength, says Bradbury, is its

> lack of 'purism', and its capacity to maintain a pragmatic and multi-directional momentum. It has been one of the great modern literatures, and its energies have derived not only from those writers who have stood apart from their culture, but also from those who have lived with it and from it. Many of its classic works . . . have been poised, balanced mediations of the new and the old, the idiosyncratic and the communal, in their content, vision and language. Its sense of experiment has been held against a sense of tradition and continuity; the novelties have been remarkably assimilated towards the centre. It is a literature that has been lit by lights from modernism rather than a modernist literature; and it has been considerably rooted in familiar, national and provincial experience rather than in arcane worlds of its own making. In this sense it has conducted a liberal dialogue with reality and with its social audience, its writers functioning as humanist speakers in society while drawn beyond it both to artistic transcendence and historical desperation.[2]

It is interesting that, as a novelist, Bradbury sees himself as conducting exactly this sort of liberal dialogue. He agrees with modernists and postmodernists that the 'securely centred figure' of nineteenth century fiction no longer exists, but regrets that

> because this is so it seems to me that the writer of novels is persistently being driven to what I think of as a strangulated humanism. An awful lot of twentieth century fiction, particularly late twentieth century fiction, seems to me to be constructed exactly on this area of anxiety. The human figure is displaced in some fashion; the idea of character is dispossessed and then resought . . . An awful lot of the fiction we talk about as postmodern, American fiction, French fiction, seems to be deeply structured on the idea of a lost human subject and a lost human voice, a voice which cannot personalise, which cannot signify.[3]

---

[1] Rabinovitz op. cit. p. 169

[2] Bradbury. *The Social Context of Modern English Literature* Oxford: Blackwell, 1971, pp. 33/4

[3] Ziegler and Bigsby op. cit. p. 67

Bradbury sees the justification for postmodernist dehumanisation but nevertheless regrets it, and he says that in *The History Man* he was trying 'to write a book in which there is no character who is securely there in a traditional sense'.[1] However, *The History Man* uses the technical devices of traditional realism and is a novel of social manners, and, moreover, a campus novel, placing it within the English tradition despite its attempt to undermine character. Similarly David Lodge, another novelist/academic, shows an ambivalence revealed by the last two quotes from him, about realism; despite his interest in literary theory and postmodernism, he maintains: 'I have not (like many contemporary writers) lost faith in traditional realism as a vehicle for serious fiction. The writer I admire above all others, I suppose, is James Joyce, and the combination one finds in his early work of realistic truthtelling and poetic intensity seems to me an aim still worth pursuing'.[2]

The question is; is there a literary form which will combine the liberal humanist tradition with a non-traditional approach to technical devices in the novel, so that Bradbury's individual voice can still signify without all the advances of modernism being rejected out of hand, as people such as Lodge and Bradbury believe? I think that there is, and the bulk of this study is an attempt to show this by examples.

Since the war, however, many writers have thought not, and have vigorously attacked any form of experimentalism. 'After World War II, a second and still more determined consolidation took place . . . Ideology was intensified in proportion to the real difficulties and decline. Experimentalism and new attacks on the inexpressible were reduced to even smaller ghettoes and even more prominently labelled 'Foreign''.[3] C.P. Snow, throughout his reviewing career[4], as did other novelists like Kingsley Amis and William Cooper, and many reviewers, conducted a long and bitter campaign to 'run experimental writing out of town'. Cooper wrote:

> I do not need to tell you that in the hands of the current generation of practitioners of the superannuated art of the Experimental Novel, character is out, right out. Actually we all know it could never be in, because writing Experimental Novels is a retreat from writing about Man-in-Society by novelists who are unable to adjust or reconcile themselves to society; it is a retreat into writing about the sensations of

---

[1] Ibid.

[2] *Contemporary Novelists* op. cit. p. 833

[3] Tom Nairn 'The English Literary Intelligentsia' in *Bananas* ed. Emma Tennant. London: Blond & Briggs, 1977, p. 82

[4] See 'C.P. Snow as Literary Critic' in Rabinovitz op. cit.

> Man-Alone by people who cannot stomach present day industrialised society.[1]

(However, the society of which Cooper talked was in fact only a small part of society as a whole, and the novels of the fifties largely showed the viewpoint of 'a middle class soured by privilege'.[2] J.G. Ballard has made the same point: 'I don't believe from the majority of mainstream fiction - tiny, brittle, drying up - you could reconstitute the character of England. They're terribly parochial; it would be London probably, or Highgate.'[3] Similarly, in the Preface to *The Golden Notebook*, Doris Lessing said that no modern novel portrayed society as a whole for succeeding generations, and A. Alvarez has pointed out that, of the nine poets in Robert Conquest's *New Lines*, 'six, at the time, were university teachers, two librarians, and one a Civil Servant'.[4])

From the fifties onwards reviews of even mildly experimental novels seem to divide almost equally into outright praise and outright condemnation (this also applies to American reviews of British novels). Novels containing any new techniques (by which I mean anything not strictly realist; 'new' is hardly the right word – they were almost as far from Joyce as he was from George Eliot in chronological terms) are hardly ever taken on their own terms but are seized on and made the subject of polemics for one side of the debate or the other. Thus praise tends to be extravagant and partisan, and condemnation ranges from mild irony to sneering sarcasm and insult, often aimed as much at the author as the work. However, whether due to the fact that British writers tend to be less iconoclastic in their experiments and less subversive in their political views (or at least are less given to making pronouncements about them) or whether due to the difference in national temperament, there has not been the impassioned invective and polemic here which is characteristic of the French literary scene; more, as one critic has put it 'a climate of warm indifference'.[5]

Indeed, despite such occasional polemics as B.S. Johnson's[6] and Rayner Heppenstall's,[7] there had been no serious and sustained public debate on the role and nature of fiction in this country. There had been plenty of random sniping but no full-scale engagement.

---

[1] William Cooper 'Reflections on Some Aspects of the Experimental Novel' in *International Literary Annual no. 2* ed. John Wain. London: John Calder, 1959, p. 32

[2] John Atkins *Six Novelists Look At Society* London, Calder, 1977, p. 25

[3] Burns and Sugnet op. cit. P. 24

[4] Introduction to *The New Poetry*. Harmondsworth: Penguin, 1962, p. 23

[5] Martin Seymour-Smith 'A Climate of Warm Indifference' in *Bananas* op. cit.

[6] Introduction to his *Aren't You Rather Young To Be Writing Your Memoirs?* London: Hutchinson, 1973, repr. In *The Novel Today*, op. cit.

[7] 'The Need for Experiment' *The Times*, 13th Dec. 1962, p. 14, and 'Speaking of Writing': *The Times*, 19th Dec. 1963, p. 13

Still, because of this inbuilt conservatism, experiment with literary form and the traditional liberal humanism of the novel have come to seem antithetical, as Bradbury pointed out, and few have questioned this antithesis. However, Peter Faulkner's study of the humanist tradition in the English novel concludes that 'although the experimental form may be used to explore areas of experience which the humanist regards as lacking significance, it is made to yield humanistic insights by Berger, Brophy, Figes and Johnson'.[1] Pamela Hansford Johnson, herself a realist novelist and wife of C.P. Snow, though not condoning experimentalism, has seen that experiments with style do not necessitate a break with traditional attitudes:

> We are still living in an age of 'experiment' in art, though this has all too often meant pure stylistic experiment and no experiment at all in the extension of human understanding. That is why so many 'experimental' novelists in this narrow sense find that very few people read them, and the ordinary cultivated reader has been driven back to history, biography or the memoirs of soldiers and politicians. As I remarked many years ago, criticism (which tends to admire and to concentrate solely upon 'experiment' in style, as style is commonly understood) has been driving art steadily underground.[2]

Many of the British authors classed as experimentalists have, as I hope to show, not entirely rejected the humanist tradition at the same time as they have challenged the realist modes of presentation[3] 'the attempt to mediate between the traditional realism and humanism of the nineteenth century novel and the epistemological problems of fiction in our time has been of considerable importance in English fiction and given it something of a distinctive character'.[4] And if 'the English novelists sought to protect a degree of realism and liberal

---

[1] Peter Faulkner. *Humanism in the English Novel.* London: Elek 1975, p. 191

[2] Pamela Hansford Johnson: 'Literary Style' in *Important to Me*. London: Macmillan, 1974, p. 242

[3] These arguments for and against realism are reminiscent of the debate within Marxism. See, on the one side Georg Lukacs: 'The Ideology of Modernism' in *The Meaning of Contemporary Realism* London, Merlin, 1972; *Studies in European Realism*. Merlin; 1978; 'Intellectual Physiognomy in Characterization' in *Writer and Critic*. Merlin, 1970; Ralph Fox. *The Novel and the People* London; Martin Lawrence 1937, repr. 1980, and various Soviet publications. On the other side see Ernst Fischer. *Art Against Ideology*. London: Allen Lane, 1969; *The Necessity of Art*. Harmondsworth: Pelican, 1963 and 'Lukacs and the Theory of Reflection' *Philosophical Forum* vol. 3, 1972; *Brecht on Theatre* ed. J. Willett. London: Methuen, 1974. Accounts of the debate are given in G. Bisztray. *Marxist Models of Literary Realism*. Columbia U.P. , 1978 and *Aesthetics and Politics*. London: New Left Books, 1979

[4] M. Bradbury & D. Palmer. *The Contemporary English Novel.* London: Arnold, 1979, p. 11

humanism in their fiction, they often did so in a context in which the waves of fictional revisionism emanating from the French *nouveau roman* and from American exponents of that plural cause labelled 'post-modernism' did not pass them by'.[1]

It is not only British authors who tried to mediate between a humanist tradition and a post-humanist world: some British critics were in this position too. They can see the abyss to which their American colleagues point but draw back from the brink rather than hurling themselves over the edge. Thus, in one book Bergonzi and Frank Kermode (neither of whom is ignorant of or unsympathetic to either modem American fiction or contemporary literary theory) argue with Fiedler, Hassan and Leonard Meyer that 'apocalyptic alarmism is not called for'.[2] In the same book David Lodge voices his 'Objections to William Burroughs', and elsewhere said that 'while many aspects of contemporary experience encourage an extreme, apocalyptic response, most of us continue to live most of our lives on the assumption that the reality which realism imitates actually exists . . . We are conscious of ourselves as unique, historic individuals.'[3] Bergonzi has also written, *a propos* of John Bayley's *The Characters of Love*,[4] which he has strongly criticised for its extreme formulation of the liberal humanist position on character in the novel:

> Since I find Barth's totalitarian aestheticism even more alarming than Bayley's naive moral realism I suppose that if pressed enough I would opt for the latter. But I would strive to avoid such a disastrous choice. To my mind the tensions between the real world of shared human meanings and experience, and the multitudinous forms of fiction must be preserved and not allowed to collapse towards either pole.[5]

The sentiment behind this statement of position would, I imagine, also have been subscribed to by Bradbury, who had said that, in the debate on the novel's function - as preserver of moral values or as aesthetic game - he would 'climb both sides of the fence at once',[6] and Lodge, who has said in relation to postmodernist writing that the 'often asserted resistance of the world to meaningful interpretation would be a sterile basis for writing if it were not combined with a poignant demonstration of the human obligation to attempt

[1] ibid p. 13. Neil McEwan's *The Survival of the Novel*. London: Macmillan, 1981 makes a similar argument.
[2] B. Bergonzi ed. *Innovations*. London: Macmillan, 1965, p. 13
[3] David Lodge 'Crossroads' op. cit. p. 109
[4] London; Constable, 1960
[5] Bergonzi *Situation* op. cit. pp. 45/6
[6] Ziegler and Bigsby op. cit. p. 69

such interpretation, especially by the process of organising one's memories into narrative form'.[1]

The problem is that these critics who noted and complained of the tendency to dismiss the British novel as moribund and pointed to its flourishing experimental trend had not reconciled this trend with their advocacy of a retention of some form of humanism, and did not produce a sustained and systematic account of the distinctive character of contemporary British experimental writers.

The few innovative writers in Britain who were at all discussed were treated in a vacuum and not as part of any trend, and not related to their tradition or their contemporaries. I hope to show by a study of certain British writers that the British novel not only had a thriving experimental trend, but that this trend was of a different kind from the novel-writing in most other countries, especially America and France, and did in fact preserve a humanistic basis without retaining obsolescent notions of character and formal technique.[2]

In order to explain my view of the difference between British novels and those of France and America, I need to examine more closely the supposed dichotomy between realism (=humanism) and non-realism (=anti-humanism); I think that this is misleading and I would like to replace it. But first I must mention some other ways that have been suggested of splitting up literature into two camps. Stephen Spender divided the writers of the early part of the twentieth century into 'moderns' and 'contemporaries'.[3] The contemporaries, such as Bennett and Galsworthy, confront the society of their time directly, whereas the moderns strive for new forms and ways of expression to try to transcend their society and approach the universal. As Lodge sums it up: 'Life, to the contemporary, is what common sense tells us it is, what people *do*: go to school, fall in love, make

---

[1] *The Modes of Modern Writing*. London; Arnold, 1977, p. 225

[2] Although it is beyond the scope of this study, the same may be true of contemporary poetry: in 1962, Alvarez op. cit. was berating British poets for not abandoning the 'gentility principle', but, defending British underground poetry, Ted Hughes wrote: 'One fact which strikes me - this kind of writing is more interesting than its equivalent in the U.S. There's somehow more to it and it's more human - more elements to it. The poetic personalities over there seem to me to be based more and more on a cliché - like the old tough-guy adolescent cliché. The gang member cliché. Nearly all the U.S. writing I see now has it. It has no real life - just a new surface, more brittle and more shallow than the old one'. Quoted by Michael Horovitz in his editorial to *New Departures* nos. 7-8 and 10-11, p. xxvii

[3] Spender. *The Struggle of the Modern*. London: Hamish Hamilton, 1963. The basis for this distinction comes from Virginia Woolf, as does his other, similar distinction between 'poet-novelists' and 'novelists of saturation' used in his *Love-Hate Relations*. London: Hamish Hamilton, 1974, pp. 159/172

political choices, get married, have careers, succeed or fail ... "man and society". To the modern, Life is something elusive, baffling, multiple, subjective'.[1]

Contemporaries do not necessarily have to be realists, nor moderns anti-realists, though this would usually be the case, and is in Spender's attributions. Applied to more recent literature, we can see that most of the novelists of the fifties and since, and certainly those of the 'Movement' would be classed as contemporaries. This division seems to me to be more helpful than the simple realist/anti-realist dichotomy, since it can account for, for instance, symbolic novels such as those of William Golding, which use the conventions of realism without being realist. Works like this would obviously be modern rather than contemporary. But this division does not give us a means of describing the difference between experimental British novels and experimental American or French ones.

Lodge elsewhere comments on Scholes' and Kellog's distinction between the 'empirical' and 'fictional' modes of narrative.[2] 'Empirical narrative subdivides into history, which is true to fact, and what the authors call mimesis (i.e. realistic imitation), which is true to experience. Fictional narrative subdivides into romance, which cultivates beauty and aims to delight, and allegory, which cultivates goodness and aims to instruct'[3] (the implication, as in Scholes' *The Fabulators*[4], is that the fictional mode is inherently superior). Lodge points out that if the synthesis between these two modes which the novel has always represented is breaking down under pressure from modern society, then it can just as easily move towards the empirical pole as to the fictional, as Scholes and Kellog claim it is doing. Lodge examines the rise of the non-fiction novel to illustrate that this is in fact happening. The advantage of this is that realism is not seen as one side of a dichotomy, but as a synthesis (and an unstable one at that) between two opposites.

Lodge himself has used Roman Jakobson's dichotomy between metaphoric and metonymic as a basis for separating literary movements. Jakobson sees these as expressions of the two basic language-making functions: combination and selection respectively. Lodge sees modernism as being predominantly characterised by the metaphorical, and anti-modernism as metonymic, these two modes tending to alternate throughout literary history, for internal aesthetic and linguistic reasons rather than social ones.[5]

---

[1] David Lodge. *The Language of Fiction*. London: Routledge, 1966, p. 245

[2] in R. Scholes and R. Kellog. *The Nature of Narrative*. Cornell U.P. 1966

[3] Lodge 'Crossroads' op. cit. p. 84

[4] New York: O.U.P. , 1967

[5] See *Modes* op. cit. and 'Modernism, Antimodernism and Postmodernism': Inaugural Lecture, Birmingham University; repr. in his *Working With Structuralism*. London: Routledge, 1981

In relation to the visual arts there was also Wilhelm Worringer's influential distinction, taken up by T.E. Hulme, between 'abstraction' and 'empathy'. Societies which feel in tune with nature imitate it (empathically) while those which see nature as alien and hostile try to abstract patterns of meaning and order from it. Although this is difficult to apply directly to literature, it may be that realism could be considered empathic and postmodernism abstract.[1]

The dichotomy I have in mind is not an alternative to these but cuts across them, and also sees realism as a synthesis between two poles. (The definition of realism is an enormous problem, but I am using the term here to refer to literature which presents 'the individual in society and society in the individual', in whatever style or form.) I would like to propose two modes of writing: the 'internal' 'and the 'external'. To simplify, one could say that the internal is primarily concerned with individuals (that is their inner states, their thoughts and feelings), and only sees society, if at all, as filtered through the sensibilities of one or more individuals.

The external may not be concerned with any particular society, but treats individuals as part of some larger force, of which they are merely aspects. This force may be a post-humanist society, or it may be the author's comic or didactic intention which reduces individuals to variables in a plot, and which has precedence over the investigation of character and personality, these being formulas to be stated rather than mysteries to be studied. If one accepts that realism is not a matter of style, one can trace a strong tradition of the external mode in British novels: Swift, Fielding, Smollett, Peacock and the gothic novel, as well as much of Dickens can be seen as precursors to the development of this mode in the twentieth century by Joyce (in *Finnegans Wake* and to some extent *Ulysses*), Firbank and Wyndham Lewis, who argued specifically for the application of the external approach to writing.[2] Outside the 'mainstream' novel of the time the spy and detective novel, (other than 'psychological' examples, such as those by John le Carré) can be seen as expressions of this tendency, as could science fiction, which

> purveys an imaginative vision profoundly hostile to art and indeed to anything specifically human. Victorian fiction acclimatised the populace to new knowledge by introducing this knowledge in stories of human interest. Modern science fiction does exactly the opposite. It projects its

[1] See *Abstraction and Empathy: A Contribution to the Psychology of Style* trans. M. Bullock. London, 1953 and *Form in Gothic* trans. Herbert Read. London. 1927. repr. Alec Tiranti, 1957

[2] Wyndham Lewis: 'Men Without Art' 1934, pp. 126-128: repr. in *Enemy Salvoes*, ed. C.J. Fox. London: Vision, 1975, pp. 35-37

> human characters into a universe which permits of no emotional response no self-awareness or insight into others.[1]

(Interestingly, nobody seems to mind science fiction, spy and detective stories being dehumanising and external as long as they are firmly distinguished from 'the novel' proper; Kingsley Amis, tireless opponent of experimentalism, has even written a book on science fiction, and one on James Bond.[2] Critics tend, however, at least in this country, either to be hard on, or to ignore writers who move out of these fringe areas and into the novel - J .G. Ballard, Michael Moorcock, Kurt Vonnegut for instance. Thus Doris Lessing seems to have caused consternation with her recent 'Canopus in Argos' series.) Comic and satirical novels also tend to work in this mode - P. G. Wodehouse and Evelyn Waugh being prime examples.

The internal mode has not had such a strong tradition, though Richardson, de Quincey, Jane Austen and Meredith may be regarded from this point of view. This mode was primarily the province of lyric poetry until the twentieth century, when it was developed in the novel by Virginia Woolf, Dorothy Richardson, Ford Madox Ford and Joyce (in *A Portrait*, and partially in *Ulysses*, one of the achievements of which seems to me to have been to merge the two modes), as well as the subsequent spate of 'psychological' novels. Woolf's *Mrs. Dalloway* is a paradigm of this type of novel, in that it breaks down the traditional concept of character as fixed, stable, and, above all, describable. For the important point about this novel is that, even after being granted a searching insight into Mrs. Dalloway's thoughts, feelings and memories (indeed, especially after being granted this), we are completely unable to sum her up in any easy formula.

Virginia Woolf had said: 'I shall really investigate literature with a view to 'answering certain questions about ourselves. Characters are to be merely views: personality must be avoided at all costs . . . Directly you specify hair, age etc. something frivolous or irrelevant gets into the book'.[3] This investigation goes beyond what Woolf called the 'psychological' novel, though some of the techniques used may be similar. Under this rubric she discusses Henry James:

---

[1] John Wain 'Forms in Contemporary English Literature' in *Essays on Literature and Ideas* London: Macmillan, 1963, p. 37. For articles specifically making the connection between American postmodernism and science fiction, and seeing science fiction as the natural contemporary form for the novel see L. Fiedler 'The New Mutants' op. cit., Fiedler's 'Cross the Border' op. cit.; T. Remington and D. Miller 'Science Fiction to Superfiction' in *Granta* vol. 1, no. 2; Sugnet's Introduction to Burns and Sugnet op. cit. For criticism of this view see Ursula le Guin 'Science Fiction and Mrs. Brown' in *Explorations of the Marvellous* ed. P. Nicholls. London: Gollancz, 1976

[2] *New Maps of Hell*. London: Gollancz, 1960; *James Bond Dossier*. London: Cape, 1965. Amis also edited *Spectrum*, in one issue of which he said that writing science fiction for a 'supposedly realistic novelist' gave him a sense of 'tremendous liberation'. Quoted by John Colmer in his *Coleridge to Catch 22*. London: Macmillan, 1978, p. 232

[3] *A Writer's Diary*. London: Hogarth, 1953; repr. Triad/Panther 1978 Sep 5 1923

> we have a strange sense of having left every world when we take up *What Maisie Knew*; of being without some support which, even if it impeded us in Dickens and George Eliot, upheld and controlled us. The visual sense which has hitherto been so active, perpetually sketching fields and farmhouses and faces, seems now to fail or to use its power to illumine the mind within rather than the world without.[1]

Capturing the mind within rather than the world without is the aim of internal writing, though it may also include discussions of ideas, and dreams and fantasies.

Despite her criticism of James, this inner landscape is just what Woolf captures. She tried to show that the interior things are at least as important as the so-called great issues such as politics and war: "Let us not take it for granted that life exists more fully in what is commonly thought big than in what is commonly thought small'.[2] It was for an overemphasis on the external as a sufficient guide to character that Woolf criticised Bennett, Wells and Galsworthy, whom she called 'materialists'. Woolf believed, unlike them, that character was not exhausted by purely external descriptions of class, wealth and appearance:

> novelists differ from the rest of the world because they do not cease to be interested in character when they have learnt enough about it for practical purposes. They go a step further, they feel that there is something permanently interesting in character itself. When all the practical business of life has been discharged, there is something about people which continues to seem to them of overwhelming importance.[3]

The 'Edwardians' however were 'never interested in character in itself; or the book itself. They were interesting in something outside'.[4]

> They have laid an enormous stress on the fabric of things. They have given us a house in the hope that we may be able to deduce the human beings who live there . . . But if you hold that novels are in the first place about people, and only in the second about the houses they live in, that is the wrong way to set about it.[5]

---

[1] 'Phases of Fiction' in *The Bookman* Apr, May and Jun, 1929, repr. In *Granite and Rainbow* and in *Collected Essays* vol. II. London: Chatto & Windus, 1966, pp. 80/81

[2] 'Modern Fiction' in *The Common Reader* repr. In *Collected Essays* vol. II op. cit. p. 107

[3] 'Mr. Bennett and Mrs. Brown' in *The Captain's Death Bed*. London: Hogarth, 1950, p. 92

[4] ibid. pp. 99/100

[5] ibid. p. 106

Virginia Woolf, and internal novelists are interested in trying to capture life, which is a

> luminous halo, a semi-transparent envelope surrounding us from the beginning of consciousness to the end. Is it not the task of the novelist to convey this varying, this unknown and uncircumscribed spirit, whatever aberration or complexity it may display, with as little mixture of the alien and external as possible?[1]

Ralph Freedman's book *The Lyrical Novel*[2] attempts to define a genre which I think is an important part of the internal mode of writing. Freedman suggests that the lyrical novel is not merely a matter of 'poetic' language, though most lyrical novels do show a greater than normal concern with style and language, but is a marriage between the storytelling and characterisation of the novel with its capacity for dramatising ideas and moral choices, and the 'expression of feelings or themes in musical or pictorial patterns'[3] characteristic of poetry. This in itself would not guarantee an internal novel, since, for instance, a murder mystery may combine narrative with a high degree of patterning, but Freedman goes on to note: 'What distinguishes lyrical from non-lyrical writing is a different concept of objectivity'.[4] This comes not from the imitation of the external reality which exists independently of any observer, and at which realism aims, but from the merging of action and perception into a 'pattern of imagery'. (In this sense it is the very antithesis of Robbe-Grillet's method, since it humanises inanimate externals.) What this tends to mean (though Freedman does not put it quite this way) is that the external world is distorted through the perceptions of one central character, the narrator or the 'informing intelligence', who apprehends external events and creates a new world - the world of the novel - which has no existence outside the perceiver's imagination, unlike the world of shared perceptions and values presented by realist novels. This is not to say that lyrical novels are fantastic, since the world which is patterned and re-apprehended by the narrator *is* the objective reality, but distorted and arranged. The point is that everyone inhabits both a social world and a personal one, but only has access to the former through the latter, and the lyrical novel's concept of objectivity takes this into account where realism denies it.

---

1 'Modern Fiction' p. 106

2 Princeton U.P. , 1963

3 op. cit. p. 1

4 ibid. Lyrical perception of the world may in fact be related to psychotic experience: R.D. Laing reports a psychotic woman who, on returning to normality, said that she felt she had been 'living in a metaphorical state. I wove a tapestry of symbols and have been living in it.' *Self and Others* London: Tavistock, 1961; repr. Penguin, 1971, pp. 73/4 I shall return to Laing later.

Freedman traces the history of the lyrical novel mainly in the German Romantic tradition, and considers only one British writer - Virginia Woolf - but it seems to me that the internal mode (which embraces the lyrical novel) has characterised much of the experimental novel writing in Britain in this century, and especially since the beginning of the 1960s. My claim in fact is that, whereas the contemporary French and American novel is predominantly written in the external mode, the internal mode, with its explorations of personality and identity, has been preserved in the British experimental novel.

If it is true, as I have claimed, that some of the innovative novelists in Britain have continued to explore the questions of personality and individuality, while American and French novelists have largely abandoned the idea of character and the 'myths of depth', can any reasons for this be discerned? The most obvious difference is between English and American society. Philip Roth has said that 'the American writer in the middle of the twentieth century has his hands full in trying to understand, describe and then make credible much of American reality. It stupefies, it sickens, it infuriates, and finally, it is even a kind of embarrassment to one's own meagre imagination. The reality is constantly outdoing our talents.[1] John Barth gives an even more apocalyptic view (though admittedly in a work of fiction): 'in this dehuman, exhausted, ultimate adjective hour, when every humane value has become untenable and not only love, decency and beauty but even compassion and intelligibility are no more than one or two subjective complements to complete the sentence . . .'[2] Barth does not complete the sentence, to emphasise even further the uselessness of compassion and intelligibility. The English[3] do not seem to feel this apocalyptic despair: 'Compared to other nations, the English are a remarkably innocent people, who scarcely know what violence, crime or civil disorder is: many American cities have as high an annual murder rate as the whole of the United Kingdom'.[4] On the other hand, Walker Percy sees the problem as being rather that the American dream has in many ways been achieved, but has left nothing worth struggling for:

> The subject of the postmodern novel is a man who has very nearly come to the end of the line. How very odd it is, when one comes to think of it, that the very moment he arrives at the threshold of his new city, with all its hard-won relief from the sufferings of the past, happens to be the same moment that he runs out of meaning! . . . The American novel in past years has treated such themes as persons whose lives are blighted by social evils, or reformers who attack these evils or perhaps the

---

[1] 'Writing American Fiction' in *The Novel Today*, op. cit. p. 34

[2] 'Title' in *Lost in the Funhouse*. London; Secker & Warburg, 1969 p. 107

[3] Like many Americans, Barth uses 'English' to mean 'British'

[4] R. Bergonzi; *Situation* op. cit. p. 61

> dislocation of expatriate Americans, or of Southerners living in a region haunted by memories. But the hero of the postmodern novel is a man who has forgotten his bad memories and conquered his present ills and who finds himself in the victorious secular city. His only problem now is to keep from blowing his brains out.[1]

But is these novelists' New York really any more bizarre or cruel than Dickens's or Fielding's London? Is modem American society any less compassionate than the England of the Industrial Revolution?[2] Perhaps the democratisation of violence has brought this harsh reality home to the writing classes. And perhaps also, as I said earlier. writers such as Fielding and Dickens, faced with societies like this, write in the external mode, as do American postmodernists, and this is a response to societies which treat people as objects.

Also, as we have seen, the differences go further back: in 1941, Henry Miller was calling America 'the air-conditioned nightmare',[3] and one critic points to the Wall Street Crash of 1929 as the beginning of apocalyptic feelings. He quotes Glenway Westcott's *Fear and Trembling* of 1932:

> we are being borne, oh, rapidly indeed, like a great mail coach, running on to an appointed accident - hastening or just sliding toward who cares what beliefs, who knows what downfalls, with a worse vision of sudden death, a worse dream fugue of collisions and confusions, ineffable wars and national bankruptcies, and for what we call civilisation, a great riotous funeral at the end.[4]

It has also been pointed out that 'Americans never had a bourgeois class with homogeneous reading habits',[5] and whether or not this is strictly true, they certainly have not had the English concern - bordering on obsession - with social class and manners. In the period of the growth of the novel in England, this class and these manners were seen as stable and permanent givens, part of the natural order in a way that perhaps American society never was:

---

[1] Walker Percy 'Novel About the End of the World' op. cit. p. 112

[2] It is interesting to compare American with modem Japanese fiction, as Japanese society has had at least as great an upheaval. The Japanese novel today is overwhelmingly realist in its conventions, and, furthermore, often refers nostalgically to the order and certainty of tradition. This is particularly true of Yasunari Kawabata, Junichiro Tanizaki and, in a very different way, of Yukio Mishima. These writers, like Shusako Endo, rather than identifying with the dehumanisation around them, resist it. There is often intense emotional violence, but rarely physical.

[3] *The Air-Conditioned Nightmare*. New Directions, 1945

[4] John McCormick *American Literature 1919-1932*. London: Routledge, 1971, p. 274

[5] Per Gedin. *Literature in the Market Place* London, 1977, p. 186

> The American writer has much less sense of a stable society which his hero encounters and enters - the process by which the European hero usually gains an identity. The institutions, even the buildings, of American society have never had this stability, and the American writer is more likely to express through his hero his own sense of their bewildering fluidity ... hence the perpetually dissolving cityscapes, and the sense of moving among insubstantial ephemera, to be found throughout contemporary American fiction. This is one reason, I think, why there is much less interest in conventional character study and analysis in it than in contemporary English fiction.[1]

Realism was never completely established in America either: Walter Allen noted that in the American novel, the 'mode of expression is allegory and symbolism. Indeed, symbolism seems to be the specifically American way of apprehending and rendering experience in literature. It is not the English way. And allegory and symbolism are ingrained in the American sensibility for good reasons: they are part of the heritage of Puritanism'.[2] Whether or not the heritage of Puritanism is sufficiently strong to have permeated the sensibilities of the many Jewish, African, Catholic and East European immigrants seems to me to be open to doubt, but it is certainly true that the American novel has been imbued with symbolism and mythic power, and that the realist novel has never had the dominance it has enjoyed in Britain for so long. The existence of a strong tradition does not however determine the direction of an art form at any time. The 'anxiety of influence' and the 'burden of the past'[3] seem to affect modern American authors more than British ones, and even those who are particularly conscious of a traditional may make use of it in different ways. For instance, B.S. Johnson and Kingsley Amis were interested in and influenced by the eighteenth century English novel, yet, both in their fiction and in their polemics, had been on opposite ends of the realism versus experimentalism feud in Britain.

It may also be important that British culture has been split on class rather than on ethnic lines, so that where the Americans have had the Negro novel, the Jewish novel, the Southern novel and so on, the British novel has been remarkably homogeneous both in its concerns and in the backgrounds, of its authors, at least up until the 'angry' novelists appeared in the 1950s.[4]

---

[1] Tanner op. cit. p. 151

[2] Allen op. cit. p. xvi

[3] I am alluding to two American books on English poetry: Harold Bloom *the Anxiety of Influence*. New York: O.U.P. , 1973 and W. Jackson Bate. *The Burden of the Past and the English Poet*. London, Chatto & Windus, 1971

[4] Though see Rayner Heppenstall's argument in *The Fourfold Tradition*. London, Barrie & Rockliff, 1961 that in addition to the main tradition of English literature there has always been a provincial, radical-nonconformist, *British* tradition.

Another explanation of the difference may be in the attitude of the Americans to the English language. As Stephen Dedalus felt that the English language would never be fully his, so perhaps American novelists, for many of whom, or at least for their parents or grandparents, English is the language of their thoughts but not of their tradition and heritage, may feel that there are things they want to express that cannot be expressed in language.[1] For this reason, they are likely to stand partially outside the language and be aware of it as a tool to be manipulated, rather than as an integral part of them. This manipulation may become to some extent an end in itself, whence the stylistic and verbal innovation of so many American novelists (and the great stylistic concern of Conrad, Nabokov and Kosinski, for instance).

The British novelist thinks *in* language rather than about it, whereas 'the American author will take nothing for granted; he has to forge his own style as a basic act of self-definition'.[2] 'Whereas young American writers think that novels must be written, with a full concentration of resources, young English writers seem merely to exude them'.[3]

It may be that the American concern with a distinctive mode of expression is as much a national as an individual concern: Alvarez suggested (in *The Shaping Spirit*, 1958) that American modernist poets' experiments were part of an attempt to find a distinctively American language for poetry, and Tanner also has an explanation for the American concern for language. He argues that American writers are obsessed with freedom *of* thought and action, and *from* constraints, patterns and conditioning. But language necessarily constrains both thought and expression, and they must use language in some form,[4] so the author

> may seek to use the existing language in such a way that he demonstrates to himself and other people that he does not accept nor wholly conform to the structures built into the common tongue, that he has the power to resist and perhaps disturb that particular 'rubricizing' tendency of the language he has inherited . . . will go out of his way to show that he is using language as it has never been used before, leaving the visible marks of his idiosyncrasies on every formulation.[5]

---

[1] Similar arguments have been used by feminists since Virginia Woolf to the effect that language is masculine 'and that women novelists have to express themselves in a language not suited to that purpose. This would certainly help to explain why women novelists have not generally been completely at home in the realist mode.

[2] Bergonzi: *Situation* op. cit. p. 67

[3] Bergonzi op. cit. p. 69

[4] This paradox may not only affect American authors: Carlos Fuentes for example, has also expressed the sense of it in regard to his language . 'Central and Eccentric Writing' in *American Review* 21, Oct 74, pp. 100/101

[5] Tanner op. cit. p. 16. He traces this attitude to language back to Blake.

> I am advancing the idea that if we ask, what is the relation of the recent American hero to his environment? We are also asking, what is the relation of the recent American writer to his language?[1]

The difference between British and French authors in regard to language may in a sense be the opposite of that between British and American. What I mean is that compared to English the French language is very homogeneous: where English is something of a linguistic mongrel, and there could never be any question of an ideal 'pure' English style, French novelists have been trying to purify their prose and distil its essence at least since Flaubert. So they too 'work on' their language. A different point in regard to the French language is that French narrative uses the past definite or preterite tense, which is not normally used in speech, so making written narratives seem more artificial to the French, and counting against the dominance of an illusionist realism.

German writers in the post-war period have also had to struggle with their language, which had been debased by the Nazis:

> A whole generation of writers and readers had been exposed to that new, primitive, top-of-the-voice language, created for the sole purpose of bullying a nation into submission and stifling the still, small voices of humanity . . . the tools of the language had been blunted . . . The problem of the why of writing was, for them, also a problem of the *how*.[2]

This problem was at the centre of the concerns of the writers associated with *Gruppe 47*, and it is certainly true that the language used by modern German writers is very unlike that of earlier generations.

It seems to be characteristic of the British literary scene that there is much less cross-influence among novelists than in France or America. French avant garde novelists tend to write criticism (of each other's work sometimes) and theory, and, as I have said, to be far more influenced by developments in non-literary theoretical developments. American novelists tended to be academics, even if not full time, or at least taught on creative writing courses, and this must have made them more aware both of the tradition in which they work, and of formal problems. Britain had academic novelists in Bradbury, Lodge, Bergonzi and Josipovici, though, except for Josipovici, these tended not to be whole-heartedly experimental. However, Bradbury admitted that his teaching duties made him more self-conscious as a writer, though he did not think this was a good thing,[3] and Lodge said that as 'an academic critic and teacher of literature

---

[1] Tanner op. cit. p. 18

[2] Egon Larsen 'A View From Outside' in *Motives* ed. R. Salis London: Wolff, 1975, pp. 5/6

[3] Ziegler and Bigsby op. cit. p. 77

with a special interest in prose fiction, I am inevitably self-conscious about matters of narrative technique'.[1] The link between writing and teaching in America ensures that new (as opposed to recently published) American fiction tends to get onto literature courses in universities and colleges there whereas it hardly ever did in Britain at this time. Not that it would be possible here in any case, since, unlike in France, new novels are almost exclusively published in hardback only - at a high cost - and quickly remaindered, so that the complete works of any except the most popular novelist were never in print at any time. As both cause and result of this lack of academic interest, hardly any criticism - serious or otherwise - was produced at the time on innovative British novelists, in contrast to the large volume of British criticism of French and American writers and the vast amount produced by those countries on their contemporary writers.[2]

I do not know whether creative writing classes turn out creative writers but the effect on their teachers must be to make them more conscious both of formal problems and also of the greatness of their predecessors. I have already referred to the 'burden of the past', and John Barth has discussed 'the literature of exhaustion', by which 'I don't mean anything so tired subject of physical, moral or intellectual decadence, only the used-upness of certain forms or exhaustion of certain possibilities - by no means necessarily a bad thing'.[3] This exhaustion is only felt and not objective - there is no limit to the number of realist novels, and even, say, sonnets that can be written - and this feeling seems to be more of an American problem than a British one (although Goethe did say that he was glad that he was not an English playwright, with Shakespeare constantly in front of him).

On a practical level, John Sutherland linked the relative conservatism of British fiction to the importance of public libraries here. The French, for instance, bought far more of their books than the British (they are cheaper than hardbacks, a form of publication which has never taken a real hold in France), and have fewer libraries, with only 4-5% of French people using libraries as compared with 20-30% in Britain.[4] Libraries in Great Britain were by a huge margin the biggest

---

[1] *Contemporary Novelists,* op. cit. p. 833

[2] However, Stephen Spender has pointed out that, although the enclosed nature of this academic writing/teaching cycle may ensure the academic novelist a serious and sizeable audience with the necessary intellect, training and leisure, it simultaneously separates the writer from society in general. *Love - Hate Relations* op. cit. pp. 220-223

[3] 'The Literature of Exhaustion' in *The Novel Today* op. cit. p. 70. This is not, however, a new theme. Barth himself may have got it from Borges, but a poem by Conrad Aiken from the 1930s began: 'We need a theme? then let that be our theme. ', *Time in the Rock* New York: Scribners, 1936, p. 2

[4] See J.A. Sutherland op. cit. p. 22, although in 1932 Q.D. Leavis asserted that it was not the existence of libraries which explained the British reluctance to buy books compared to the French, but that 'the French buy books because France has an educated public'; the British, being less educated, 'buy journals and periodicals'. *Fiction and the Reading Public.*

purchaser of new fiction, except of those authors who have made the breakthrough into popularity and mass-market paperback publishing.[1] (Paperback editions always followed hardback originals in Britain, and then only if demand for the hardback was enormous, which was rare. The same was largely true in America, though there many new publications were initiated by paperback houses with hardback rights being sold rather than vice versa. Even then the hardback appeared first.[2]) The only practical ways for an author to break out of this vicious circle were to write 'formula' or sensational novels, or to have a novel made into a successful film, neither of which is really open to the experimental novelist (though Nicholas Mosley is an exception). The fact that buying novels came more naturally to the French is shown by the effects of their literary prizes compared to British ones: the British Booker Prize - the only one to have any noticeable effect on sales – may add between 5,000 and 10,000 to the sales of a novel, where the French Prix Goncourt can add 5,000 sales in a day, and 250,000 to the total.[3] Public libraries were then of central importance to the novelist in Britain, who had to ensure that they bought his/her novels in at least sufficient quantities to ensure publication of the next one.[4]

London: Chatto, 1932; repr. Penguin, 1979, p. 24. However, it may be significant that Sylvia Beach's Shakespeare and Company became the centre of literary expatriates – and publisher of *Ulysses,* because of its role as a subscription library.

[1] In a 1980 survey on the place of the literary novel in the public library conducted for the Arts Council, a list of 34 titles chosen from the New Fiction Society back list was submitted to two 'very respectable Sheffield bookshops' and to Sheffield City Libraries. The 'total subscription to the 34 titles for the two Sheffield bookshops was 10 copies. The total purchases by Sheffield City Libraries of the 34 titles was 450 copies'. Peter H. Mann, lecture 'The Library and the New Novel'; Association of Assistant Librarians, Holborn Public Library, 1 Oct 1980. The full report is embodied in Mann's *The Literary Novel and its Public*. London: Arts Council, 1980

[2] See Clarence Petersen. *The Bantam Story*. New York: Bantam, 1070

[3] Sutherland op. cit. p. 22. The last prize does, however, seem to have caused rather more interest.

[4] Brigid Brophy said that implicit pressure from publishers indeed forced more writers to write conventionally: 'Thus without a word spoken does crisis make cowards of us all and a 'dreariness of contemporary English writing'' 'The Economics of Self-Censorship' in *Granta* vol. 1, no. 4. This was not, however, a recent development, at least in America: an American book of 1930 said, in relation to market research in the book trade; 'It becomes more and more obvious that, except in the case of creative literature, the book must be adjusted to its probable readers on a surer basis of knowledge about those readers than now exists. I am not even sure that creative literature need be excepted.' R.L. Duffus. *Books: Their Place in a Democracy*. Boston: Houghton, 1930, p. 219. America has never had an equivalent to the British Net Book Agreement, and the decisive change in attitude there may have come in the 1940s, when the book industry underwent such a boom that manufacturers would only take orders for long print runs, and the need for metal type caused publishers to melt down plates of all but the most popular books. See W. Miller. *The Book Industry* New York:

Dorothy Richardson published the last volume of *Pilgrimage* in 1938. In 1939 Ford Madox Ford died, and in 1941 James Joyce and Virginia Woolf. Is it true that experimental writing in Britain died out around this time, as is generally supposed, and if so, when and why did it reappear? It is undoubtedly true that there was a weakening of the will to innovation and a narrowing of the artistic vision around this time; writing in 1943, John Lehmann, whose *New Writing* series brought together much that was interesting and new during this period, said:

> In looking back on the prose and poetry of the writers of the last decade, it is difficult not to feel how incomplete, on the whole, their vision was, how repeated their failure to assemble the fragments of their inspiration, brilliant as these often were, and to give their work that final imaginative intensity which has always been the characteristic of great art. Even before the outbreak of the present war, this sense of disappointment had been growing, of sitting at a spectacle which reduced itself into an endless series of picturesque *divertissements*, no finished ballet ever emerging.[1]

However, if writing became less ambitious (or merely suffered by comparison with an earlier generation) it did not entirely forget the lessons of modernism, and it is possible to trace a line, a thin one perhaps, of innovative writers and novels throughout the forties and fifties. Certainly internalised writing did not die out, even if much of it was merely novels of 'sensibility'. Writing in 1946, V.S. Pritchett noted that the contemporary novel did not use the traditional, external idea of character: 'The 'I', whether he is the reporter, the camera man, the sensibility, the split self of our time, dominates these books. The 'they' of the Victorians . . . has receded'.[2] Also, during this period, the train of fantasy, which had always been present in English literature, was continued by C.S. Lewis, Mervyn Peake, J.R.R. Tolkein and T.H. White, though all these used the basic conventions of realism to describe fantastic subjects.

Stevie Smith, though known primarily as a poet, published three highly idiosyncratic novels: *Novel on Yellow Paper*, 1936; *Over the Frontier,* 1938 and *The Holiday* (published 1949 but written earlier). Anna Kavan, having published several unremarkable novels under her (then) real name, Helen Ferguson, culminating in the remarkable *Let Me Alone,* 1930 then produced novels and

---

Columbia U.P. , 1949, pp. 67/8 and appendices; also T. Whiteside, *The Blockbuster Complex*. Middletown, Connecticut: Wesleyan U.P. , 1981.

[1] John Lehmann 'The Heart of the Problem' in *Penguin New Writing* no. 18, Jul/Sep 1943, p. 161

[2] V.S. Pritchett, 'The Future of Fiction' in *New Writing and Daylight*, ed. John Lehmann. London: John Lehmann, 1946, p. 78

surrealistic, dream-like short stories regularly until her death in 1968, despite her addiction to heroin. Lawrence Durrell's career did not begin in 1957 with *Justine* as one easily might think, but in 1935 with *Pied Piper of Lovers*. During the early 1950s, other novelists seem either to have similarly changed their style or given up writing altogether: Henry Green's first two novels were published in 1926 and 1929, and then from *Party Going,* he produced novels every two years or so until 1952, when he stopped, although he lived until 1973. George Buchanan also published several highly original novels and other works between 1935 and 1952, when he also stopped until 1971, and Neil M. Gunn similarly stopped writing novels in 1956, though he lived until 1973.

The year 1953, however, seems to be when many novelists went through some sort of crisis: Rex Warner's *The Wild Goose Chase,* 1937 was followed by five other unusual (for Britain) allegorical novels until *Escapade* of 1953, after which he turned to writing historical novels; Philip Toynbee's novels span exactly the same period, from 1937 through the highly experimental *Tea With Mrs. Goodman* of 1947 that influenced B.S. Johnson, up to 1953, when he began to publish 'novels' in verse. Rosamond Lehmann, whose first novel, *The Dusty Answer* appeared in 1927 also published no novels after 1953, until *A Sea Grape Tree* in 1978, and Rayner Heppenstall published no new novel between 1953 and 1962. There certainly seems to be something about 1953 – the Coronation Year. In that year also, *Scrutiny* ceased publication and John Lehmann's *London Magazine* started (his *New Writing* series having finished in 1950). Lehmann himself saw Dylan Thomas's death in 1953 as the 'beginning of a change of mood and intention in contemporary English poetry',[1] and Jeff Nuttall, in his history of this period, pointed to 1953 as the year in which the mindless violence and need for excitement and 'kicks' regardless of consequences which characterised the 'post-Hiroshima' generation first surfaced with the Clapham Common teenage stabbing, and entirely motiveless killing.[2]

The change in the air was described in 1952 by an article on 'The English and American Novel':

> Enough - some would say more than enough - has been achieved in the way of experiment . . . Every kind of juggling with time, character, dialogue and psychology has been attempted during the last 30 years: already a long empirical tradition stretches from *The Waves* to *Tea with Mrs. Goodman.* Nor has originality of style been lacking . . . What the English novel at present demands of the English novelist is the ability to reflect the great social changes that have occurred during the last 10 or

[1] *The Ample Proposition* London: Eyre & Spottiswood, 1966, p. 257, see also p. 262

[2] *Bomb Culture.* London: McGibbon & Kee, 1968, p. 29

> 12 years and to distil the new and varied patterns that have resulted from them.[1]

As if in response to this call, 1953 saw the beginning of what many then considered a revival of the English novel, as the generation of 'angry' young men began to appear on the scene. John Wain's *Hurry on Down,* 1953 was followed in 1954 by Kingsley Amis's *Lucky Jim* and Iris Murdoch's *Under the Net,* all revivals of the picaresque mode (though Rayner Heppenstall might have been said to have revived it in 1942 if anybody had noticed). In 1956 another picaresque appeared: J.P. Donleavy's *The Ginger Man* (in an expurgated version, the original had appeared the previous year in France), as well as Colin Wilson's *The Outsider* (not a novel, but central to the ethos of the 'angry generation'), Philip Callow's first novel, and Robert Conquest's *New Lines,* which established 'The Movement' in poetry. In 1957 appeared Thomas Hinde's *Happy as Larry* (his second novel) and the collection of statements *Declaration,* followed in 1959 by the collection *Protest,* which combined the English writers with American 'beat' writers.

1956 signalled a new wave of anger (in fact the novelists already mentioned were not so much angry as bemused - as one writer put it 'polite'[2]), when John Osborne's play *Look Back in Anger* appeared, and its significance was forcefully pointed out by Kenneth Tynan's review.[3] Osborne's play gave both a name and a direction to the younger writers and their heroes became angrier and from lower class positions: John Braine's Joe Lampton (*Room at the Top,* 1957), Alan Sillitoe's Arthur Seaton (*Saturday Night and Sunday Morning,* 1958) and David Storey's Arthur Machen (*This Sporting Life,* 1960). These, along with the heroes of Stan Barstow and Stanley Middleton, were the shock troops of the new wave. Gone were the gentle irony and humour of the earlier novels (Keith Waterhouse's *Billy Liar,* 1959, is an exception): the class war was declared.[4]

These new novels were a genuine breakthrough for the British novel; they presented the problem of class society and the individual's relationship to it in an entirely new light. The individuals at the centre of these novels are not representatives of a class so much as cut loose from full allegiance with any class, reflecting the greatly increased social mobility of the postwar period. They

---

[1] *Times Literary Supplement* Aug 29 1952, p. xii anonymous

[2] Karl Miller. *Writing in England Today.* Harmondsworth: Penguin, 1968

[3] repr. in his *A View of the English Stage.* London: David-Pynter, 1975, pp. 176/178

[4] See Kenneth Allsop. *The Angry Decade.* London: Owen, 1958; Blake Morris, *The Movement* Oxford U.P. , 1980; Robert Hewison. *In Anger: Culture and the Cold War* London, 1981; Jeff Nuttall. *Bomb Culture,* op. cit.; the collections *Declaration.* London: McGibbon & Kee, 1957 and *Protest* ed. G. Feldman and M. Gartenberg. London: Souvenir, 1959; Anthony Burgess, *The Novel Now* London: Faber, 1967, pp. 140 - 153; Paul West. *The Modern Novel.* London: Hutchinson, 1963, 2nd. ed. 1965, pp. 124 - 146

seemed to speak for a whole generation, both from working and lower middle-class backgrounds who had been

> swept up so quickly through state-schools and universities that there has been no time for the usual taming procedures of middle-class assimilation. For the first time there is a group of English writers who have evaded gentility: escaped, as not even Wells and Lawrence could wholly the assumptions which have ruled English fiction since Fielding and Fanny Burney. They have risen too suddenly to become involved in the complicity of an established culture and audience . . . There is a generation with one foot in each of Disraeli's two nations who can describe British culture as outsiders and bring news of the life outside to the readers within.[1]

Not only the novel itself was disrupted: critical attitudes were changing also.

> However cool the ancient regime was to the 'Angries', its criticism over the novel's life and death had taken on a much different cast from the previous debates, moving away from the perplexity and melancholy tone to outright challenge and engagement. The energy of the novelists had reenergized the debate itself.[2]

The chief virtue of this type of novel was

> to renew the awareness of the novel as a living form. Whether critics quibbled with these new novelists' concern for mere technical competence as opposed to depth, inveighed against their negativeness, canted about their self-advertisement, the very fact of response showed that the novel was neither stultifying nor dead.[3]

As Leslie Fiedler said: 'Cries of rage are heard, mingled with shouts of triumph; insults meet counterinsults and everyone seems astonished that it has all come to matter so much.'[4]

From the point of view of this study, the important points about the 'angry' novels are the breaking of the stranglehold of traditional class attitudes (so that

---

[1] Ronald Bryden. 'British Fiction 1959-1960': *International Literary Annual No. 3* ed. John Wain. London: John Calder, 1961, p. 42

[2] Robert K. Morris: *Old Lines New Forces: Essays on the Contemporary British Novel 1960-1970*. London: Associated University Presses, 1976

[3] ibid. p. xxi

[4] 'Class War in British Literature': *Esquire*, April 1958 repr. *No! In Thunder* New York: Stein & Day, 1972, p. 191

subsequent novelists could afford to stand outside class issues, as well as social and moral ones), and the way that they set the scene, through the picaresque and the concentration of the isolated individual, for a return to the internal mode. Not that any of the novelists mentioned here made use of any of the devices characteristic of modernism:

> Most of these writers, in an attempt to depict their engagement directly, have avoided the kind of technical innovation favoured by an earlier generation of twentieth-century writers. It is not that these writers dismiss James Joyce; it is that they do not (and perhaps could not) compete. Their interest in man's exterior relationships leads to a less associative, internal style, to a style closer to the straightforward narrative of most nineteenth century fiction.[1]

They are certainly 'contemporaries' rather than 'modems'; nevertheless they are not exclusively concerned with 'exterior relationships', but are beginning the move into the interior of the individual, who, having no fixed place in a permanent web of social values and relations, ceases to be describable in external terms:

> man is, today, even less sure of what he is and where he is heading than he apparently was fifty or a hundred years ago. Almost all the contemporary novels are searches for identity, efforts on the part of the hero to understand and to define who or what he is. The hero accepts the fact that he is, but wonders what kind and degree of adjectival postulate he can build upon his existence.[2]

The novels of the fifties then paved the way for a more searching, more inward looking, more 'modern' novel in thc succceding decade.

> The picaresque evasion and nihilism of the fifties, provoked by society's failure to establish some permanent framework to enclose personal values, were recast by the sixties into encounter and engagement: the search for permanent values within a personal framework . . . a decade of quest transcended a decade of anger.[3]

Although the quest motif is of central importance to all literature, as Northrop Frye pointed out, where the novel of the sixties in Britain

---

[1] James Gindin. *Postwar British Fiction: New Accents and Attitudes.* Cambridge U.P. 1962 p. 11

[2] Gindin op. cit. p. 11

[3] Morris op. cit. p. xxvii

> proved itself singular and curiously persistent is in its transvaluation of the archetype. Because the novelist's concern with his hero's personal determination, dynamics, drives and achievements independent of existing systems has inspired an almost universal solipsism, the quest as object is only of slight interest. Since man's fate is to be absorbed, thwarted, ruined, corrupted, deadened, even annihilated by society - the ultimate system - ends become as immaterial as they are deterministic.[1]

There is a quest for wholeness, but within the individual rather than in the individual's social relationships, which become all but irrelevant in the face of the heroes' solipsistic views of the world.

> The new forces in the sixties seldom resonate against society because such a response would vitiate the private vision . . . the sniping at or undermining of society as a wholehearted gesture can never reveal the truth about oneself. The resonance in the sixties is always within.[2]

Not that the fifties had been entirely a decade of realism and class-bound novels. The tendency to individualism had been noted even in 1959, in Durrell, Golding, Angus Wilson and Iris Murdoch. The first two had never been considered social realists, but in relation to the last two it was being perceived that their presentation of 'man-in-society' was different in kind from that of their nineteenth century predecessors: 'each of these four would make of living an individual responsibility in which men do not impose solutions or ways of conduct on others, but in which each works out his own solution'.[3] The point I am making is that the increasing insularity and solipsism of individuals in the British novel (which the author just quoted links to the decline of colonialism, the last expression of which had been at Suez) is not merely a feature of recent 'experimental' writing, but is a part of a trend started (or perhaps revived) in the fifties, and which is discernible in all the ostensibly very different styles of novel from that period on.

The postwar American novel was taking a similar individualistic turn: Saul Bellow's *Dangling Man,* 1942 explored themes carried on throughout his later work, and these can also be found in other American novels: Ralph Ellison's *Invisible Man* and Salinger's *Catcher in the Rye*, for instance. The isolated and confused heroes of these novels, however, were not cut loose from a class structure so much as 'rebels without a cause', later exemplified in the public imagination by James Dean, Elvis Presley and Marlon Brando. Their opposition

---

[1] Morris op. cit. pp. xxvii/iii

[2] ibid. p. xxx

[3] John Bowen, 'One Man's Meat' *Times Literary Supplement*, Aug 7 1959, p. xiii

to the establishment seemed more to do with sexuality than class, and had no real parallel in Britain at that time, though one American writer saw them as representing a move from a concern with the condition of alienated humanity (and the 'epic mythical' quality we earlier saw) to a concentration on 'ordinary' individuals.[1] The American 'beat' novels, like their British contemporaries, were individualistic, stressing the freedom and rootlessness of their solitary heroes, which in turn led in the sixties to the 'hippie' idea of self-actualisation, backed up by the psychology of Maslow, Fromm, Laing and Erikson. The hippie movement, however, produced more in the way of music and poetry than novels, possibly due to the underground nature of its activities, which were not suited to the economics of novel publishing.[2]

I earlier mentioned the year 1953 as the date when the angry novel seemed to overwhelm and silence the previous generation of experimentalists, but there was another generation appearing at that time to take the baton. William Golding's *The Lord of the Flies* and Brigid Brophy's *Hackenfeller's Ape* both appeared in 1954, and Nigel Dennis's *Cards of Identity* in 1955 (his first novel, *Boys and Girls Come Out to Play* had appeared in 1949 but was relatively conventional). The first volume of Lawrence Durrell's *Alexandria Quartet* appeared in 1957, and John Fowles' *The Collector* in 1958, the same year as John Berger's *A Painter of Our Time*. These novelists do not in any sense constitute a movement, but they do show that the hegemony of neo-realism was never complete; that the tendency towards non-realism and stylistic innovation never died out in Britain even during the period when it was all but swamped by a flood of anger.

Although 'experimental' novel writing never completely died out, it does seem to have gone into hibernation and only reawakened when the 'angry' novel began its decline, which it inevitably did.

> In the fifties there was a strong feeling that this was the main road, the central tradition of the English novel, coming down through the Victorians and Edwardians, temporarily diverted by modernist experimentalism, but subsequently restored . . . That wave of enthusiasm for the realist novel in the fifties has, however, considerably abated. For one thing, the novelty of the social experience the fiction of that decade fed on - the break-up of a bourgeois-dominated class society

---

[1] Theodore Solotaroff 'Silence, Exile and Cunning', *New American Review* no. 8, 1970

[2] For a comparison of the Underground movements in America and Britain from a British point of view, see Jeff Nuttall, *Bomb Culture*, op. cit. and his *Performance Art: Memoirs* vol. 1. London: John Calder, 1979 and Snipe's *Spinster*. London: Calder & Boyars, 1975. Also Michael Horovitz's 'Afterwords' to his *Children of Albion* Harmondsworth: Penguin, 1969 and his editorial in *New Departures* issues 708 and 10-11, 1975

> - has faded. More important, the literary theorising behind the 'Movement' was fatally thin.[1]

There were personal reasons for this decline, as well as public and literary ones:

> The fifties was a decade when a good many talented young people, very conscious of the social class which they had risen above, paraded evidence of their lower-classishness. But since they had little visible attachment to their origins other than these signs of social inferiority, when they ceased to be poor these tended to evaporate.[2]

It is certainly true that the novels of those writers who first emerged in the fifties became less class-bound and also less realist (think of David Storey's *Radcliffe*, Alan Sillitoe's *Raw Material*, Angus Wilson's *The Old Men at the Zoo*,[3] and the same applies to the plays of John Osborne, (*Luther* for instance), and the poetry of Thom Gunn and Donald Davie).

It is difficult to put a date on the re-emergence of a self-conscious experimentalism in the British novel as a force rather than as a set of isolated instances. This study begins with Rayner Heppenstall in 1939, though very few experimental novels were written before 1960, the exceptions being by Stefan Themerson, Anna Kavan and Philip Toynbee. Muriel Spark's *The Comforters* of 1957 contained many devices that were later to be hailed as new in the work of John Barth and others; Anna Kavan's *Eagle's Nest* of 1958 was one of the earliest British novels to truly confront Kafka. Paul Abelman's *I Hear Voices,* also of 1958 was published by Maurice Girodias' Olympia Press, which also published Samuel Beckett and Alexander Trocchi's pseudonymous pornography, and heralded the career of a highly individual experimental writer.

On the first page of the *Times Literary Supplement* published on the first day of January 1960 - like a trumpet blast heralding a new decade - an article proclaimed that:

> the battle is at its height and . . . the avant-garde forces must venture all. The middlebrow, consolidating mainstream interest here is beautifully dug-in. Its artillery shot up M. Robbe-Grillet before we, the mere infantry, could see the whites of his eyes. What passes as novel-

---

[1] David Lodge. *Crossroads*: op. cit. p. 100

[2] Stephen Spender. *The Thirties and After*. London, Macmillan, 1978, p. 156

[3] Peter Faulkner's *Angus Wilson: Mimic and Moralist*. London: Secker, 1980 traces his development chronologically. Wilson himself has recently said that he has never really been interested in, or felt part of, a British tradition; he admits a strong attachment to Dickens, sees him as being too individualistic to be part of any tradition. See the interview in Ziegler and Bigsby op. cit.

> writing here is at present so abject that the merest flicker from abroad is likely to be seen as a ray of hope.[1]

Later in the year an article in the same journal by Alan Sillitoe called for more working class novelists,[2] shortly after Lawrence Durrell's article in the same series had complained that

> in some obscure way readers and editors believe that he [the novelist] may have something up his sleeve which will help them to formulate a new way of arranging the world or society; at the worst some sort of tranquilizer which will help alleviate the sleepless pages of the world conscience. Has he? It is very much to be doubted.[3]

This uncertainty about the direction of the novel was (or should be) taking is reflected in another article, on 'British Fiction 1959-1960':

> Few British novelists seem to feel that this is a time for technical experiment or flamboyant personal display. A more profound change may be that few of them seem to aspire to the older English novels' evocation of a 'world'. [They] . . . make no pretence of dealing with microcosms or whole societies.[4]

In other words, the concerns of the traditional realism have been overturned, but not the conventions of style which went with them.

Rayner Heppenstall, 'encouraged' rather than influenced by the example of Robbe-Grillet and Nathalie Sarraute, published *The Greater Infortune*, a revised version of the earlier *Saturnine,* 1942, in 1960 – the year Faber's *Introduction* series began - and dedicated it to Muriel Spark, 'reviver of faint hearts'. He then published two more highly original novels in 1962. Alan Burns' first published work appeared in 1961 in the first issue of John Calder's New Writers.

1963 saw Alexander Trocchi's *Cain's Book* and the republishing of his *Young Adam* as well as B.S. Johnson's *Travelling People*, and 1964 Ann Quin's *Berg*. Also in 1964, Christine Brooke-Rose, who had already published four conventional novels, published *Out*, making a deliberate and self-conscious move towards experimentalism and Andrew Sinclair, who had been known previously for his typically fifties social satires *The Breaking of Bumbo* and *My Friend*

---

[1] The anonymous article, actually by Rayner Heppenstall, was ostensibly about Nathalie Sarraute, the first of her novels having just appeared in translation. Robbe-Grillet's novels had been appearing in translation for two years previously.

[2] 'Both Sides of the Street', *Times Literary Supplement* Jul 8 1960

[3] 'No Clue to Living': *T.L.S.* May 27th 1960

[4] Ronald Bryden: op. cit. p. 53

Judas (both 1959) and his Kerouac-influenced *The Hallelujah Bum,* 1963, published the allegorical *The Raker*.

Other novelists who had started their careers as conventional novelists also started to turn to experiment around this time: Doris Lessing, who had written in 1957: 'I hold the view that the realist novel, the realist story, is the highest form of prose writing',[1] published *The Golden Notebook* in 1962, also the year of Anthony Burgess's *A Clockwork Orange*, and Nicholas Mosley's *The Meeting Place*; in 1963 Anna Kavan published *Who Are You* and in 1968 Julian Mitchell, who had previously written conventional novels produced the experimental *The Undiscovered Country.*

As well as these definite moves to experimentation, there were Storey, Sillitoe and Angus Wilson, who had turned out not to be the committed realists they had at first promised to be (although they could not be called experimentalists either), and by the early sixties it had also become apparent that Iris Murdoch was not quite what she had seemed, and that the formal, stylized quality of her novels was not stilted realism but a deliberate moral and aesthetic patterning, and that her work should not be judged by the standards of realism at all.[2]

So what happened in the early 1960s to set the scene for this renewal of the experimental impulse? The obvious answer is nothing specific, but perhaps a combination of things. They were, after all the 'swinging sixties' when the post-war austerity, rationing and conscription had finally been forgotten; sexual intercourse began for Philip Larkin in 1963, the year of the Beatles' first album, though the Lady Chatterley case had allowed people in Britain to read about it from 1960 onwards. The social upheavals which the novelists of ten years earlier had found their most important subject matter had already begun to seem a thing of the past, as the new prosperity reached rapidly down the social scale, and made standards of living (apparently) almost equal for all. Britain was no longer the centre of a great empire, but it led the world in fashion and popular music. Not since Victorian times had Britain been so widely emulated, and the confidence young British people felt at that time is hard to recall now.

There was, no doubt, influence from abroad: apart from the *nouveau roman*, Beckett's *Malone Dies* appeared in 1958, followed in 1959 by *The Unnameable*, and Borges' *Ficciones* appeared in Britain in 1962. The explosion in the American novel had also been felt in this country around this time: Terry Southern's *Flash and Filigree* was published in Britain in 1958, and his *The Magic Christian* in 1960; John Earth's *The Sot-Weed Factor* followed in 1961, and *The End of the Road* in 1962, although both had been published earlier in America, as had William Gaddis's *The Recognitions* and the two John Hawkes novels also published in Britain in 1962. Also in this year appeared Joseph Heller's *Catch 22*,

---

[1] See *Declaration* op. cit. p. 14

[2] Robert Scholes made this explicit in *The Fabulators* op. cit.

Ken Kesey's *One Flew Over the Cuckoo's Nest* and Nabokov's *Pale Fire;* Pynchon's *V* followed in 1963.

On a different level, the relationship between the novel and poetry was changing. Poetry used to be 'Lofty and if necessary Difficult',[1] where novels were expected to be easily accessible and unproblematic. 'With the disappearance of a mass public for the novel (the kind of writer who used to write mass-circulation novels now writes television sagas), the serious, "literary" novel is now being read by very much the same kind of person who reads poetry'.[2] The novel could now absorb not only the function but the techniques of poetry, since poetry itself seemed to have abandoned the techniques which used to distinguish it, and now appeared to most people like 'prose in short lines'. And if 'the traditional subject matter of the novel has been taken over by sociology and reporting, so that the imaginative novelist is forced to make his statements by poetic metaphor - that is to say, no longer hidden under the stucco of "realism" - how should the poet continue to mark himself off from the imaginative prose-writer? And why should he try to?'[3] The novel has, however a built-in conservatism compared to poetry or the short story, making it liable to change more slowly. This is partly due to its greater length, making experiments and effects harder to sustain, and partly to the economics of publishing: poems and short stories can be published in 'little magazines', often distributed locally and at little expense, whereas novels are almost always published by national, if not international publishers, and of course the costs and risk involved are much greater.

One factor no writer has been able to ignore since the early sixties is the ubiquity of television. Many writers have voiced their feeling that the cinema took over the storytelling function of the novel since E.M. Forster mentioned it in *Aspects of the Novel* in 1927. In 1946, two separate pieces in the series 'The Future of Fiction', by V.S. Pritchett and Rose Macauley, mentioned not only the cinema's storytelling and myth making capacities, but also its ability to convey information.[4] Olivia Manning in an essay on 'The Future of the Novel'[5] in 1958 mentioned it as an important factor, as did Robert Scholes in *The Fabulators* and John Wain in an article of the early sixties.[6] John Barth said: 'When I see a young man taking up the practice of fiction in this age of the camera, it seems to me that

---

[1] John Wain: 'A Salute to the Makers' in *A House for the Truth*. London: Macmillan, 1972, p. 8

[2] ibid. I do not fully agree with this. It seems to me that the sort of novelist who used to write mass-circulation novels now writes even bigger selling novels, and has his/her novels converted into television sagas by lesser talents as the television companies cannot afford to pay the original author. There are not many of these novelists around, however.

[3] John Wain op. cit. p. 8

[4] *New Writing and Daylight* vol. VII. London: John Lehmann, 1946

[5] 'Notes on the Future of the Novel': *Times Literary Supplement*, 15th August 1958, p. vi

[6] 'Forms in Contemporary English Literature': op. cit. p. 37

he is doing a very quixotic thing to dedicate his mortal life to that possibly dead art form'[1]. In her 1968 study *The Novel of the Future,* Anaïs Nin wrote: 'The only objectivity we can reach is achieved, first of all, by an examination of our self as lens, as camera, as recorder, as mirror.' Rosalind Belben later said 'I have been brought up in an age of movie cameras; I can focus; I can zoom in; I can retreat, and telescope my eyes' and B.S. Johnson opened a polemic on the state of the British novel with the claim that:

> It is a fact of crucial significance in the history of the novel in this century that James Joyce opened the first cinema in Dublin in 1909. Joyce saw very early on that film must usurp some of the prerogatives which until then had belonged almost exclusively to the novelist. Film could tell a story more directly in less time, and with more concrete detail than a novel . . . why should anyone who simply wanted to be told a story spend all his spare time for a week or weeks reading a book when he could experience the same thing in a version in some ways superior at his local cinema in only one evening?[2]

By the sixties film makers themselves had started to experiment with techniques as film became a minority art form under the onslaught of television (although in the cinema, as in the novel, by far the greater proportion of productions remain 'conventional'). The trouble with arguments like Johnson's, although they undoubtedly express the feelings of many novelists, is that people did continue to read novels, and in increasing numbers (though the proportion of novels in relation to the total numbers of books sold was decreasing[3]). Moreover, many best-selling novels around that time were made into successful films, and often became best sellers after the release of the film.[4] (Though, interestingly, novels taken from films are seldom successful; nor are those taken from television scripts, a trade which former experimentalist Paul Ableman took up.) If, then, the success of a film can virtually guarantee the success of the book from which it was taken, it must be that people like to read novels even when they already know the story. The fact is that the film experience is different from the experience of reading a novel but does not thereby displace it.

The argument of those experimentalists who use this justification of the pre-eminence of film is that, since film and television do all the work for the audience,

---

[1] *The New Fiction* op. cit. p. 7

[2] *Memoirs* op. cit. p. 151

[3] See Robert Escarpi.t, *The Book Revolution.* London: Harrap, 1966, pp. 71, 73, 74

[4] See *The Bantam Story,* op. cit. ch. 7, and J.A. Sutherland. *Bestsellers* London: Routledge, 1981. In an earlier period, Claud Cockburn says that before the war, films were only made of books which were already successful. On the other hand, Q. D. Leavis's evidence seems to contradict this op. cit. p. 225

the novel should give them a different experience by turning them from passive receptors into active participants in the 'making' of the work, which should therefore be multivalent and open-ended. But reading is necessarily a more active process than watching (apart from the readers' greater control over the physical medium), since the visual and aural images are always supplied from the readers' imagination and personal experience, even when the work is rigorously realistic (hence the disagreements between people who know a book which has been filmed as to whether the actors are 'right' for the part - that is whether they match their visual impression).

> One thing language can do better than any other form of communication is to liberate the individual by setting his imagination to work . . . In a novel, each reader imagines the physical appearance of the characters, hears the timbre of their voices, pictures to himself the physical setting of the action. In the cinema, by contrast, we all see what the camera puts in front of us. Only one imagination is at work - the director's. I used to quote with approval Cocteau's definition of film as 'dream that can be dreamed by many people at the same time'. I still think that this is a good definition of film, but I no longer look on it with complacency: it seems to me, now, a dangerous thing for a crowd of people to dream their dreams in unison . . . What, after all, was Fascism but a dream dreamed by a lot of people at the same time?[1]

The novel is necessarily suited to individualism, not just because it is historically linked to the rise of bourgeois individualism and so tends to depict the individual set against society (not necessarily antagonistically; the point is that in the conventional novel the individual undergoes change where the society does not), but because of this capacity to set free the individual's imagination, and because the activity of reading novels is usually conducted in private (and even if there are other people in the room they will not be reading the same novel). Drama and poetry, by contrast, have their origins in public performance (even lyric poetry can be read aloud).

All this is to say that the argument that novels should stop telling stories because film does it better is unsound, but the feeling that this is so, together with the inescapable presence of television, which from the early sixties onwards far surpassed even the influence the cinema had enjoyed in an earlier period, do go some way to explaining the return to self-conscious experiment in the British novel.

I also believe that the comparison with film shows how well suited comparatively the novel is to the internal mode which is concerned with interior

[1] John Wain: 'The New Puritanism' in *A House for the Truth* op. cit.

states and feelings, and where visual images and action, which film necessarily present, are only a distraction. (Nathalie Sarraute has argued that, in the novel, any external data about the characters which the author presents, even a name, tend, to lead the reader to form stereotyped images, and thus detract from a subtle psychological investigation, which is prejudged by the stereotyping.[1] This applies, *a fortiori*, to films, especially where the actors are well known.) Some authors have recognised this, and have moved into the internal mode because of their recognition of film's superiority in presenting externals. Rayner Heppenstall said, in relation to his *The Blaze of Noon* (a highly internal novel) that he 'had a theoretical notion that the cinema had taken over the story-telling functions of the exteriorised novel and that prose narrative would do well to become more lyrical, more inward'.[2] B.S. Johnson also said that film 'is an excellent medium for showing things, but it is very poor at taking an audience inside characters' minds, at telling it what people are thinking'[3] and this seems likely to continue to ensure the survival of the novel, and especially of the internalised novel.

[1] *Tropisms and The Age of Suspicion*. London: Calder, 1963

[2] Preface to 1962 and all subsequent editions

[3] *Memoirs* op. cit. p. 152

anna kavan

Anna Kavan[1] was born Helen Emily Woods in Cannes, France in 1901 of wealthy British parents and moved to London as a baby, having been given by her distant, aloof mother to a wet-nurse. Her parents moved to America when she was four, leaving her in London with her nurse until she was six, when they brought her to America and boarding school, where she remained until she was thirteen. When she was fourteen her father probably committed suicide by jumping from a ship. After this she attended Swiss, then English boarding schools. While still very young her mother pressured her into marriage with the 30-year old Donald Ferguson (who may have been one of her mother's former lovers), a railway engineer in Burma; she moved to Burma with him and their loveless, unhappy and stormy marriage is fictionalised in her novels *Let Me Alone* and *Who Are You*. Eventually she left her husband in Burma to return to Europe with her son, Bryan Ferguson, who was born in 1922 and died in 1944. In Europe she fell in with the company of racing drivers, with whom she shared a love of danger and a disregard for life. 'I had never had a home, and, like the drivers, never wanted one. But wherever I stayed with them was my proper place, and I felt at home there.'

> Out of their great generosity they gave me the truth, paid me the great compliment of not lying to me. Not one of them ever told me life was worth living. They are the only people I ever loved. . . The world in which I was really alive consisted of hotel bedrooms and one man in a car. But that world was enormous and splendid, containing cities and continents, forests and seas and mountains, plants and animals, the Pole Star and the Southern Cross. The heroes who showed me how to live also showed me everything, everywhere in the world.
>
> My present world is reduced to their remembered faces, which have gone for ever, which get further and further away. I don't feel alive any

[1] For a fuller biography see: David Callard, *The Case of Anna Kavan*, London, Peter Owen, 1992; Jeremy Reed, *A Stranger on Earth*, London, Peter Owen, 2006.

> more. I see nothing at all of the outside world. There are no more oceans or mountains for me.
>
> I don't look up now. I always try not to look at the stars. I can't bear to see them, because the stars remind me of loving and being loved.[1]

Around this time it seems she started using heroin, to which she would be addicted her whole life. She implies in one of her stories that she was introduced to it by her tennis coach. 'To improve her game the tennis professional gives her the syringe. He is a joking man and calls the syringe a bazooka.'[2] After travelling around Europe she met her second husband, the painter Stuart Edmonds in Nice, France in 1925[3]. He soon became an alcoholic and she came to resent him, calling him Oblomov (after Goncharov's idle anti-hero) in some of her stories[4]. Having started writing in Burma, she published three novels under her first married name, Helen Ferguson, in quick succession in 1929 and 1930[5], and another three in the mid-1930s[6]. During the 1930s she attempted suicide several times and had several stays in clinics; by 1940 she had re-invented herself as Anna Kavan, a name taken from a character in her loosely autobiographical novels *Let Me Alone*,[7] and *A Stranger Still*, changing her name by deed poll, and publishing her first work under her new name, the story collection *Asylum Piece*.[8] According to a close friend, 'she changed not only her name and mode of living but also, somewhat remarkably, her personal appearance'.[9]

It is not known whether her decision to use a 5-letter name beginning with K and containing two letter As had any connection with Kafka – Brian Aldiss called her 'Kafka's sister'.[10] She certainly knew and admired his work by the mid-1940s,

---

[1] 'World of Heroes' in *Julia and the Bazooka*. London, Peter Owen, 1970; the stories in this volume were published posthumously and are not dated.

[2] 'Julia and the Bazooka' in *Julia and the Bazooka*, op. cit.

[3] There seems in fact to be no record of an actual marriage between the two.

[4] See 'Experimental" 'Now and Then' and 'High in the Mountains' in *Julia and the Bazooka*

[5] *A Charmed Circle*. London: Jonathan Cape, 1929, republished as by Anna Kavan, London: Peter Owen, 1994; *The Dark Sisters*. London: Jonathan Cape, 1930; *Let Me Alone*. London: Jonathan Cape, 1930, republished as by Anna Kavan, London: Peter Owen, 1974

[6] *A Stranger Still*. London: John Lane, 1935, republished as by Anna Kavan, London: Peter Owen, 1995; *Goose Cross*, London, John Lane, 1936; *Rich Get Rich*, London, John Lane, 1937

[7] Kavan later reworked the same story as the shorter and far more experimental *Who Are You*, 1963.

[8] *Asylum Piece and Other Stories* London, Jonathan Cape, 1940, republished: London, Peter Owen, 1972.

[9] Rhys Davies, introduction to *Let Me Alone*, Peter Owen, 1974 edition

[10] 'Introduction' to Brian W. Aldiss ed., *My Madness, The Selected Writings of Anna Kavan*, 1990, reprinted as 'Kafka's Sister' in Brian W. Aldiss, *The Detached Retina: Aspects of SF and Fantasy*, Liverpool, 1995

as she mentions him as a model for new writing in a *Horizon* review of 1944 and there are strong Kafkaesque elements in many of her stories, as well as in *Sleep Has His House* and *Eagle's Nest.* The first published translation of Kafka into English was Edwin and Willa Muir's version of *The Castle* in 1930, followed by *The Great Wall of China,* 1933; *The Trial,* 1937 and *America,* 1938, so she may have read Kafka before she changed her name but not before she created the fictional character of her *alter ego* Anna Kavan in 1930.

One of the key differences between her and Kafka is the use of language: Kavan's prose, *pace* Anaïs Nin's praise of her as a 'poetic' novelist, is always clear and straightforward, even when describing surreal or dreamlike images. As a Czech, Kafka wrote in a form of German (then called *Prague-Deutsch*) that always seems strange in the original to a native German speaker; it is dense, difficult and sometimes archaic. It is almost impossible to translate it into English and maintain this strangeness.[1] Interestingly, Kavan is the married name of the character in *Let Me Alone*, the name she took from the husband she hated; similarly the author Anna Kavan had previously published books using the surname Ferguson, which the real Helen Woods had taken from the real Donald Ferguson, whom *she* hated. It is as if she felt the need to bear the burden and bare the scars of her real and fictional doomed marriages. However, pronounced the English way, with the stress on the first syllable, Kavan becomes a homonym for 'cavern', which may be another reason for her choice of the name. The first novel published under her new name, *Change the Name*[2], has no apparent connection with her own change, though it has autobiographical elements.

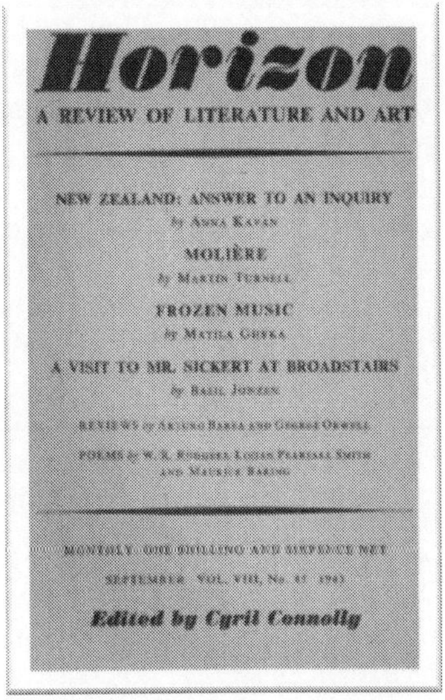

From 1939 to 1943 she travelled around the Far East, writing *Change the Name* along the way, spent time in New York and then stayed for two years in New Zealand[3], before returning to London, where she stayed for most of the rest of her life. From 1943 to 1946, she reviewed

[1] Recent scholarship, based on Kafka's original manuscripts, now in Oxford, has returned the texts, which Max Brod edited for clarity, to their original state, including the restoration of Kafka's idiosyncratic grammar and punctuation. I have myself recently attempted, unsuccessfully, to translate Kafka's only play into English.

[2] London: Jonathan Cape, 1941

[3] A time fictionalised in *A Scarcity of Love*, 1956

fiction for and published stories in Cyril Connolly's magazine *Horizon*, including the title story of the collection *I Am Lazarus* in May 1943[1]; she also published stories during this time in the American magazines *The New Yorker* and *Harper's Bazaar*.

In 1943, Kavan met Karl Bluth, a doctor at a psychiatric hospital where she was being treated after one of her suicide attempts. He became her friend and mentor for the next 20 years, as well as co-author of the book *A Horse's Tale*, which was published by Stefan Themerson's Gaberbocchus Press in 1949. Bluth seems to have changed her life and given her a degree of optimism. In one story, where he is referred to as 'M' and she is 'K', she is in a clinic, having attempted suicide four times. 'Then M spoke kindly to her in the gloomy ward, and everything changed.'

> It was as if she'd always been lost and living in chaos, until this man had appeared like a magician and put everything right. The few brief flashes of happiness she had known before had always been against a permanent background of black isolation, a terrifying utter loneliness, the metaphysical horror of which she'd never been able to convey to any lover or psychiatrist. Now suddenly, miraculously, that terror had gone; she was no longer alone, and could only respond with boundless devotion to the miracle worker.[2]

When Bluth died, in 1964 as she was finishing the first drafts of *Ice*, she was deeply affected.

> I don't quite know myself any longer. I forget how to smile . . . how to squeeze words out of my mouth. Everything drains away. Nothing is left but an empty world, in which Karl's face will never again be seen.
>
> While he was here I felt safe, secure in his support and affection, in the supreme togetherness generated by cosmic rays. But now, of all that, nothing. Of all he gave so generously he has left me nothing. Nothing of himself, of his prestige, his kindness. I am nothing to him. He is

[1] *I am Lazarus: Short Stories:* London, Jonathan Cape, 1945, republished, London: Peter Owen, 1978

[2] 'The Zebra-Struck' in *Julia and the Bazooka*, p. 116

> nothing. There is nothing in life any more. I try to find the way out, but people prevent me. Utterly heartless, they want to force upon me an unendurable existence, not seeing that I have already left their world.[1]

Anna Kavan's last novel with a major publisher for several years had been *Sleep Has His House* in 1948, published by Jonathan Cape as all her other books had been[2]. After this she entered a period of obscurity and was unable to find a publisher for her next book, *A Scarcity of Love*, a thinly-disguised, savage attack on her mother, who had died in 1955; she eventually had it privately published in 1956[3]. However, around this time she met Peter Owen, who was to become her friend and publisher for the rest of her life, continuing to publish and republish her books, including several posthumous reissues and first issues of previously unpublished works.[4] He said of their early days:

> I was introduced to Anna Kavan and her work in 1956 by a mutual friend, Diana Johns, who ran a bookshop which Anna frequented. This was shortly after publication of her novel *A Scarcity of Love*. Following the book boom of the late 'forties Anna had found it increasingly difficult to find publishers for her work, and her reputation, which had seemed secure, was declining. Lacking any offers for *A Scarcity of Love*, she partly subsidized its publication; but the publisher, an acquaintance of hers on the periphery of book publishing, lacked distribution facilities and failed to pay his printer. His subsequent bankruptcy prevented even a moderate circulation of the book – which my firm successfully reissued in 1971.[5]

In her last years, Anna Kavan lived in a quiet residential area of west London and invested in property while continuing to write and paint. Owen said she was living in

---

1 'A Summer Evening' in *My Soul in China*, p. 191

2 London, Jonathan Cape, 1948, republished, London: Peter Owen, 1973, published in America as *House of Sleep*. New York: Doubleday, 1947. Her last three novels as Helen Ferguson were published under Cape's John Lane imprint.

3 Southport: Angus Downie, 1956, republished, London: Peter Owen, 1971

4 *Eagle's Nest*. London: Peter Owen, 1958, republished, London: Peter Owen, 1976; *A Bright Green Field*. London: Peter Owen, 1957; *Who Are You?* Lowestoft: Scorpion Press, 1963, republished, London: Peter Owen, 1975; Ice. London: Peter Owen, 1967, republished, Macmillan. 1973; *Julia and the Bazooka and Other Stories* (Introduction by Rhys Davies). London: Peter Owen, 1970, title story published in *Encounter*, March 1969; *My Soul in China: A Novella and Other Stories* (Introduction by Rhys Davies). London: Peter Owen, 1975; *Mercury*. London: Peter Owen, 1994; *The Parson*. London: Peter Owen, 1995; Guilty. London: Peter Owen, 2007

5 Peter Owen, 'Prefatory Note' to *Asylum Piece*, Peter Owen, 1972

> a beautiful house which she had converted in Peel Street, Kensington . . . she explained that she was obliged to convert houses to supplement the small income bequeathed to her by her wealthy mother. . . During this first visit of mine, she handed me the manuscript of a new novel, *Eagle's Nest.* We published this book in 1957 and, despite poor sales, followed it with a volume of stories, *A Bright Green Field,* the next year.[1]

Kavan died in 1968 with a heroin needle by her side; no one knew whether the overdose was deliberate or accidental.

The novelist Brian W. Aldiss, who, like her had spent time in Burma (during the Second World War) was a fan of hers. In 1967 he had just published the seminal *Report on Probability A*[2], an experimental science fiction novel, and considered the beginning of British New Wave Science Fiction, and was about to publish the even more experimental *Barefoot in the Head*[3]. Aldiss nominated *Ice* for the best science fiction novel of 1967 and arranged its publication by his publisher, Doubleday, in America. He met her just before she died.

> When I went to see Anna first, the glaciers were already towering round her. I had imagined meeting a gloomy Isak Dinesen figure; what I found was entirely different, a small but smartly dressed woman, limping slightly but agile, lively, solitary but seemingly not lonely. Although she was well into her sixties, age was not something one associated with her. I was told men found her attractive, and could well believe it; women too, although she generally shrank from sexual relations with men or women. Constant use of heroin inhibits the sexual facilities.
>
> She lived in a small house, original and delightful, which she had designed for herself in London W11. It had a beautiful little back garden full of green things.[4]

Her long-time friend, fellow novelist and executor Rhys Davies[5] described her last days similarly:

> In the last years of her life, after travelling widely, Anna Kavan lived quietly in her Campden Hill house, with its secluded garden.

[1] Owen, op. cit.

[2] written in 1962 but rejected by mainstream publishers, it was published in *New Worlds* 171

[3] London, Faber, 1969

[4] Brian Aldiss, Introduction to *Ice*, London, Picador, 1973

[5] Davies' novel *The Honeysuckle Girl*, London, Heinemann, 1975, is a fictional version of her life

> Expeditions to big stores – those bustling, if brief, salvations: when in distress, buy a new dress, a gold chain, a smoked trout, all together – and a few visitors were almost her only transactions with mundane reality.[1]

Elsewhere Davies said that her 'vitality remained unimpaired; even her daily recourse to heroin – for some thirty years – as an escape from her conflicts, did not bring drastic physical damage until her last year or so.'[2] Jeremy Reed, one of her biographers, described the house she lived in for many years:

> In the late 1950s Anna Kavan moved into the house at 19 Hillsleigh Road, Kensington, London W8 that she designed and built according to her specifications as a Chinese puzzle-box, a system of complex interlocking rooms opening off corridors, the walls painted white to create the effect of spaciousness and brightly hung with her own visionary paintings. The house, which was increasingly to become Anna's sanctuary as her health collapsed, was divided into two flats, with Anna occupying the upper floor reached by an outside staircase. Anna wrote and painted in a large L-shaped room containing a faux leopard-skin lounging chair, her mother's gold-painted harp, the Burmese gong that acted as a coffee-table, a figurine of Ranga, the inevitable high-rise stacks of books marooned asymmetrically on the floor and the white Venetian blinds closed on the day in the interests of heightening her concentration.[3]

On the night she died, Kavan was due to attend a party given by Peter Owen at which he was to have introduced her to another of her great champions, Anaïs Nin. Nin had written admiringly of Kavan's 'poetic prose' in *The Novel of the Future*, published that year in America.

> Anna Kavan explored the nocturnal worlds of our dreams, fantasies, imagination, and non-reason. Such an exploration takes greater courage and skill in expression. As the events of the world prove the constancy of the nonrational, it becomes absurd to treat such events with rational logic. But people prefer to accept the notion of the absurd rather than to search for the meaning, the symbolic act which is quite clear for whoever is willing to decipher the unconscious. The writer who follows the designs and patterns of the unconscious achieves the same revelation.

---

[1] Rhys Davies, Introduction to *My Soul in China*, op. cit.

[2] Introduction to *Let Me Alone*, Peter Owen, 1974 edition

[3] Jeremy Reed 'A Blonde Legend' in the Anna Kavan Painting catalogue produced by Lucius Books/Punk Daisy, 2005

> Anna Kavan made a significant beginning as a nocturnal writer with *House of Sleep* and achieved this kind of revelation with a classic equal to Kafka titled *Asylum Pieces* in which the nonrational human being caught in a web of unreality still struggles to maintain a dialogue with those who cannot understand him. In later books the waking dreamers give up the struggle and simply tell of their adventures. They live in solitude with their shadows, hallucinations, prophecies.[1]

Kavan herself had described her writing, beginning with *Sleep Has His House*, as 'nocturnal', where dreams and reality merge. It is easy to imagine her, with her heroin addiction, as an insomniac for whom the long nights held particular terrors, which she describes so chillingly. In the Kafkaesque story 'At Night' she describes insomnia as her jailer. 'I lie as still as if the bed were my coffin, not wishing to attract his attention. Perhaps if I don't move for a whole hour he will let me sleep.' But she does not know why she has been singled out and condemned to this existence. 'Why am I alone doomed to spend nights of torment, with an unseen jailer, when all the rest of the world sleeps peacefully? By what laws have I been tried and condemned, without my knowledge, and to such a heavy sentence too, when I do not even know of what or by whom I have been indicted?'[2] And surely one of the most harrowing paragraphs ever written is: 'One of the worst things about hell is that nobody is ever allowed to sleep there, although it's always night or, at the earliest, about six o'clock in the evening. There are beds, of course, but they're used for other purposes.'[3] She said elsewhere:

> A writer must speak, as it were, the language of the subconscious before he can produce his best work. And this is true, not only of such writers as Kafka and James Joyce, who communicate by means of a dream or fantasy medium, but also of those who describe the external happenings of the outer world. Even in stories of action employing a realistic technique, the source of genuine interest springs from an understanding of the fundamentals of personality. It is the interpretation of complexes, together with their sequence of inevitable events, which gives to any book the truly satisfactory rhythmic progression of music.[4]

J. G. Ballard, normally considered, like Brian Aldiss, as a science fiction writer, whose experimental novel *The Atrocity Exhibition* would be published in 1970,

---

[1] *The Novel of the Future*. New York: Macmillan, 1968; London: Peter Owen, 1969; republished Ohio University Press, 1985, p. 171
[2] Asylum Piece, op. cit. p 59/60
[3] My Soul in China, p. 62
[4] *Horizon*, November 1944, a review of *The* Inquest by Robert Neumann

was also a fan of Kavan's work. His early post-apocalyptic novels like *The Drought*, 1962, *The Drowned World*, 1965 and *The Crystal World*, 1966 operate in ruined worlds which, like the worlds of *Ice* and *Who Are You*, are as much psychological as physical. In a 1963 article he said:

> Without in any way suggesting that the act of writing is a form of creative self-analysis, I feel that the writer of fantasy has a marked tendency to select images and ideas which directly reflect the internal landscapes of his mind, and the reader of fantasy must interpret them on this level, distinguishing between the manifest content, which may seem obscure, meaningless or nightmarish, and the latent content, the private vocabulary of symbols drawn by the narrative from the writer's mind. The dream worlds invented by the writer of fantasy are external equivalents of the inner world of the psyche, and because these symbols take their impetus from the most formative and confused periods of our lives they are often time-sculptures of terrifying ambiguity.
>
> This zone I think of as 'inner space', the internal landscape of today that is a transmuted image of the past, and one of the most fruitful areas for the imaginative writer. It is particularly rich in visual symbols, and I feel that this type of speculative fantasy plays a role very similar to that of surrealism in the graphic arts.[1]

Although she was addicted to heroin for most of her life, she was not at all the kind of addict one associates with film stars and rock musicians of the 1960s, probably using it to maintain a balance in her life rather than achieving a series of highs; she is not known to have used LSD, which was not available until the 1960s.[2] She was originally prescribed heroin long before 'heroin writers' like William Burroughs, Alexander Trocchi and others, at a time when it was not considered dangerous and was not associated with youth, rebellion against authority, experimentalism and the criminal underworld. In Burroughs' *Junky*, 1953, heroin addicts form their own subculture: 'Junkies run on junk-time and junk-metabolism. They are subject to junk-climate. They are warmed and chilled by junk.' Although these things may all have been true of Kavan, she lived a life completely unlike the underclass/underworld inhabited and described by Burroughs and Trocchi. She felt herself an outsider but her external life appeared completely normal. Both Aldiss, quoted above, and Peter Owen describe her as alert and well groomed. 'She was an excellent hostess and a good cook. It was some time before I realized that she was an incurable heroin addict.'[3] Nevertheless, it is hard to read her work without taking her addiction into

---

[1] J. G. Ballard 'Time, Memory and Inner Space', in *The Woman Journalist*, 1963

[2] Jeff Nuttall's *Bomb Culture*, 1968, explores the effect of LSD on the art of the 1960s.

[3] Owen, op. cit.

account; Anaïs Nin attributed Kavan's success with this inward, dreamlike writing to her drug addiction.

> The hallucinatory drugs only reveal the world of images we contain but do not teach us interpretation, illumination, or enlightenment. By shutting out the outside world, drugs place one not only in confrontation with the dreaming self, but also with one's nightmares. The poets who have poured their nightmares into literature (such as Lautréamont in *Les chants de Maldoror*, Rimbaud in *Les illuminations*, Anna Kavan in *Asylum Pieces*, or Genêt in any of his works) give them to us in a form which differs as widely as the drawings of the insane differ from the drawings of great painters.[1]

However, heroin is not of itself hallucinatory and, unlike Rimbaud or Lautréamont, who descend into a world of terror in order to write, Kavan seems to need heroin to stay out of this world. In the prologue to *Junky* Burroughs says: 'Junk is not, like alcohol or weed, a means to increased enjoyment of life. Junk is not a kick. It is a way of life.' Kavan is not like nineteenth century laudanum (opium) users such as de Quincey, Coleridge and Poe, nor like Cocteau (whose *Opium* was published by Peter Owen in English in 1957). In the autobiographical title story of *Julia and the Bazooka* Kavan says of the syringe that 'it is as essential to her as insulin to a diabetic. Without it she could not lead a normal existence, her life would be a shambles, but with its support she is conscientious and energetic, intelligent, friendly. She is most unlike the popular notion of a drug addict.'[2] She is also unlike Aldous Huxley, whose 1954 *The Doors of Perception* describes his experiences with the hallucinogenic drug mescaline and who asked to be injected with LSD on the day he died of cancer[3], not to mention the poets and artists involved in and affected by Timothy Leary's later experiments. The nightmare world Kavan lives in is not induced by drugs, but is her own reality, from which the heroin helps her escape, even if only temporarily – she called it her 'injected tranquillity'[4]. Kavan does not use drugs to create visions but to try, albeit unsuccessfully, to keep them at bay. Without the heroin she is never far from complete and terrifying madness.

> Why am I locked in this nightmare of violence, isolation and cruelty? Since the universe only exists in my mind, I must have created

[1] Nin, op. cit., p. 13

[2] p. 153

[3] Though she would presumably have approved of the dystopian *Brave New World*, 1931 and *Ape and Essence*, 1948, though perhaps not *The Island*, 1962, which is utopian, though it still involves drug-taking

[4] 'Fog' in *Julia and the Bazooka*, p. 35

> the place, loathsome, foul as it is. I live alone in my mind, and alone I'm being crushed to suffocation, immured by the walls I have made. It's unbearable. I can't possibly live in this terrible, hideous, revolting creation of mine
>
> I can't die in it either, apparently. Demented, in utter frenzy, I rush madly up and down, hurl myself like a maniac into the traffic, bang my head with all my force against walls. Nothing changes. The horror goes on just the same.[1]

So, as 'the terror of life imprisonment stupefies me', she has only one escape open to her, and she takes a taxi to 'the old address', presumably the house of her heroin supplier. And, even though she attempted suicide at least several times in her lifetime, Kavan does not even see death as a path to peace and oblivion.

> The indifferent splendid face of this vacant world is rather too much for me to take. I'm almost glad a familiar odour tells me it's time to be going. I take one last look at the sky, at the heavens from which God has gone into exile. As indifferent, as vacant as the uninhabited world, the blank empty eye of infinite spaces stares me down; and the blue unblemished arch of a godless eternity has no consolation to offer me, none at all.

Of the six novels Helen Ferguson published under her first married name, three were republished by Peter Owen under the name Anna Kavan: *A Charmed Circle,* published by Jonathan Cape in 1929, was republished in 1994 and *A Stranger Still,* published by John Lane in 1935, was republished in 1995, also as by Anna Kavan. *Let Me Alone,* Jonathan Cape, 1930, was republished in 1974 but is now available only as a print-on-demand book. The other three - *The Dark Sisters,* Jonathan Cape, 1930; *Goose Cross*, John Lane, 1936 and *Rich Get Rich*, John Lane, 1937 - have never been republished and are now extremely rare and collectible. Original copies of *Rich Get Rich* are available for well over £1,000 but the other two are almost impossible to find.

[1] 'The Old Address' in *Julia and the Bazooka*

Four of these early novels are relatively conventional and contain very little of the Anna Kavan who was to come. However, the other two, *Let Me Alone* and *A Stranger Still* which come chronologically in the middle of the group of six Helen Ferguson novels, do point clearly to her future direction and her future name. A character called Anna Kavan appears in both of them, and even their titles sound like later, Anna Kavan novels. When she became Anna Kavan, she re-wrote the latter part of *Let Me Alone*, a thinly-disguised autobiographical account of her unhappy marriage to her first husband, into which she is pressured by her mother, and their time in Burma, as the experimental novel *Who Are You?*

Anna Kavan is not normally considered as an experimental novelist but at the time of its first appearance in 1940 *Asylum Piece*[1] was received as a clearly experimental work. A review of the 1946 New York publication of Asylum *Piece* (which included the stories from the later *I Am Lazarus*, which in Britain was published separately) said it was 'definitely experimental writing, but experimental writing of a very high order.' The reviewer, Leo Lerman, understood that Kavan was breaking down the conventional structures of fiction to convey her own internal reality. 'I hesitate to classify her pieces as stories, for she is less concerned with formal story structure — plot, characterization, time, place, personality — than she is with communicating the integral essence of mental upheaval.' However, Lerman misunderstands Kavan's perspective on mental illness and her reasons for being

[1] *Asylum Piece and Other Stories,* London, Jonathan Cape, 1940, republished: London, Peter Owen, 1972

in psychiatric clinics; possibly the publicity for the book was deliberately misleading. He says that:

> she has researched extensively in psychiatry and worked in a mental hospital. This last is most important, for almost all of Anna Kavan's fiction is concerned with mental collapse, with both the obscure and the overt manifestations of the neurotic personality of our time.

This puts her in the entirely different position of a being sensitive observer of mental agonies rather than a victim of them, an inventor of literary devices to convey mental disturbance rather than realistic descriptions. The American reviewer puts her in a tradition of European experimentalism: 'What you get out of "Asylum Piece" depends on how hard you are willing to work. It's not Joyce, but it is intentionally difficult to read. Anna Kavan is definitely a most important new writer.'[1] As an experimental writer Kavan was also just as frustrated by the conservatism of the British novel as B.S. Johnson was later, and as strong an advocate of new forms of literature to reflect the new world In the immediate post-war period there had been an increase in paper quotas for publishers, allowing them to print more books, but instead of publishing exciting, new works the mainstream publishers reissued comforting, traditional Victorian novels. In a review of Victorian ghost stories she wrote, echoing Ballard but with greater emphasis on the horrors of the mind's internal landscape:

> There has recently been an increase in the paper quota, and the way in which the publisher distributes the extra pages at his disposal is of significant interest. One might expect preference to go to new names and experimental forms appropriate to the inchoate fluidity of a time when culture as previously known is almost certainly ending. In actual fact, most, if not all thc frcsh allocation is devoted to reprints - often excessively long. Works, familiar to us since childhood, crowd new writers and non-traditional writing out of a list reminiscent of the catalogue of a school library. . . If one compares the 'horrors' to be found in this volume with the horror content of the work of an adult intellectual writer, the reason for the artistic failure of the Victorians as well as for the preference shown to them becomes clear. The mature artist's work is the outcome of his own experience; his own thought, imagination, emotion. It is his own death which Kafka describes in the terrible last paragraph of *The Trial* when the knife is turned twice in K's heart. The whole of Kafka's life is in the book as well as his last moments. And the poor, crazy man in *The Overcoat* is mad Gogol

[1] Leo Lerman, *The Saturday Review*, August 10, 1946, p. 9/10

> himself. Writers of the quality of Kafka and Gogol do not run away from reality. They have too much integrity, both as artists and human beings, to indulge in escapist flights. Especially sensitive, they are especially vulnerable, and they escape nothing. When life frightens and hurts them, they do not look back at the nursery windows with longing eyes, but incorporate in themselves a part of life's fear and pain. The artistic value of their work endures because it is also a part of reality. It is conscious, uncompromising, personal, true. It is life. It is everything the new Victorian tries to avoid.[1]

It is *Asylum Piece*, 1940, which really marks the beginning of the Anna Kavan style. What other British novelist of this time would have dared to explicitly name a short story collection after a series of stays in mental institutions? Women's madness and so-called (after Freud) 'hysteria', and their savage responses to male attempts to 'cure' them were not new subjects – one thinks of Charlotte Perkins Gilman's 'The Yellow Wallpaper' – but this was in the middle of the Second World War and a long time before mental illness and heroin addiction were considered acceptable subjects, especially for women writers. These stories contain the seeds of all Kavan's later writings.

Anna Kavan's second published book of short stories[2], *I Am Lazarus* from 1945 is mainly set in wartime London and/or in psychiatric hospitals. The title story[3] concerns a young patient suffering from dementia and a visiting doctor who questions his insulin therapy. Similarly 'Palace of Sleep' is a story about a doctor visiting patients undergoing narcosis as therapy. Although the stories in Kavan's third published collection, and the last in her lifetime, *A Bright Green Field*[4] are more realistic and less harrowing that in the previous two, the title is nevertheless misleading in its apparent optimism; most

[1] *Horizon* Jan 1946

[2] Peter Owen, 1945, reprinted 1978

[3] Originally published in *Horizon*, May, 1943, and reprinted in *The World Within: Fiction Illuminating Neuroses of Our Time*, edited by Mary Louise Aswell New York: McGraw-Hill,1947

[4] Peter Owen, 1958

of Kavan's themes and nightmares recur here.

The collection of stories *Julia and the Bazooka*[1] was put together shortly after Kavan's death. The stories are not individually dated so we do not know at what stage in her life they were written but they are in her later style so must be from her Anna Kavan period. They are mostly 1st person and apparently autobiographical: some describe the failure of her relationship with Stuart Edmonds – here called Oblomov; some have Karl Bluth as the character M; one is about racing drivers and some describe her time in Burma in similar vein to *Who Are You.* Perhaps it was because these stories are so personal that Kavan, who destroyed almost all her diaries and personal records, did not publish them in her lifetime.

[1] Peter Owen, 1970

Change the Name, 1941 was the first novel published under the name Anna Kavan, though it was written before she did in fact change the name and probably before the more experimental stories in *Asylum Piece*, published as a collection in 1940. Her next published book was the short story collection *I Am Lazarus* in 1945 but the first novel to really use Anna Kavan's new, experimental style was *Sleep Has His House*. Published in America 1n 1947 and in Britain in 1948, it is probably both Kavan's most poetic and most experimental novel; it was well ahead of its time and would still have seemed avant garde when Peter Owen republished it in 1973. Nevertheless, it was well-received: an American review praised it highly:

> In her three previous books, and now in this one, Anna Kavan has concerned herself with the unbalanced mind, the pathos and terror of the intellect in the tragic act of slipping its tether to reality. It is this tiger of the mind which, like Blake's, burns so brightly, which has fascinated her by its fearsome beauty, and which she has tried to capture in her delicate and discerning prose. This is a brave and unpopular thing for her, or any writer, to attempt, and it is due her to say that she has done it more sensitively, more respectfully, has thrust farther into the wild brilliance and darkness of the world beyond reality than has any writer of her time. To my mind, no contemporary can approach her in the articulation of the esthetics of insanity.[1]

The reviewer appreciates both the beauty and the terror of the book.

> This is a strange, softly terrifying book. It is difficult not to yield helplessly to its beauty, and it is impossible not to be profoundly disturbed by it. The final and most desperately-defended privacy is that of the secret, inner consciousness, that corridor of the mind through which each of us walks alone; and Anna Kavan invades that privacy

[1]John Woodburn, *The Saturday Review*, August 23, 1947

> brilliantly, humbly, and insistently. She knows a great deal about the tiger of the mind, and it disturbs us to know that she knows.

The novel consists of two parallel autobiographies: short, italicised 'realistic' sections and longer, dreamlike sections which are really prose poems. The short sections describe how the girl B grows up lonely and isolated, under the dominating effect of her cold, distant mother, A, '*the queen in the house – a princess in exile. All the shine of the house was quenched by my mother's sadness.*' These early experiences prevent her from ever having genuine relationships with other people. She blames her mother, whom to some extent she becomes, for her unhappiness. '*One day when I combed my hair in front of the mirror, my mother looked out at me with the face of an exiled princess. That was the day I knew I was unhappy.*[1] Even though they are written realistically, these sections describe how she developed an internal, nocturnal world where she could live in comfort. They are if anything more powerful than the poetic sections, which develop Kavan's unique 'nocturnal' language. '*Because of my fear that the daytime world would become real, I had to establish reality in another place.*'[2] In the foreword she says:

> At night, under the influence of cosmic radiations quite different from those of the day, human affairs are apt to come to a crisis. At night most human beings die and are born
>
> *Sleep has his house* describes in the night-time language certain stages in the development of one individual human being. No interpretation is needed of this language we have all spoken in childhood and in our dreams

The title comes from John Gower, quoted in part, in modern English on the cover page. The full quotation, from *Confessio Amantis* Book 4, is:

> And that was in a strange lond,
> Which marcheth upon Chymerie.
> For ther, as seith the poesie,
> The god of Slep hath mad his hous,
> Which of entaille is merveilous.
> Under an hell ther is a cave,
> Which of the sonne mai noght have,
> So that no man mai knowe ariht
> The point betwen the dai and nyht.

---

[1] p. 61

[2] p. 75

This is very appropriate to the book: the point between day and night, reality and dream is not known aright. Although B has invented her own night-time world in the 'realistic' sections, it still holds terrors in the prose poems.

> How dark it is. The moon must have stolen away secretly. The stars have thrown their spears down and departed. There seems to be nothing except primordial chaos outside the window. Utterly still, utterly alone, I watch the darkness flower into transient symbols. And now there is danger somewhere, a slow, padded beat, like cushioned paws softly approaching. What an ominous sound that is to hear in the night.[1]

The paws may be those of the leopard in the story in *Julia and the Bazooka*, which becomes her friend. The 'transient symbols' flicker in and out of the poetic sections, many of which read like notes for a surrealist painting or directions for a film.

> The ashy remnant of what was once cherry blossom continues to rain through the blackness while the accompanying noise expands spouts and crackles into an ear-splitting engine-roar. As this shattering thunder becomes quite unbearable, it explodes into silence. At the same instant the whirling formlessness bursts into a shower of leaflets which are catapulted in all directions. They drift downwards and there is a momentary glimpse of them sucked and eddying madly in the up-draught of a flaming jungle village, fired palm trees ablaze and streaming. Vacuum.[2]

In the large, 'shiny' house her parents hardy speak to her and she is alone most of the time with the rain.

> *It was lonely in those rooms dark with my mother's sadness and with the rain on the windows. The rain shut off the house by itself in a lonely spell.*
>
> *In time I found out what it was that the rain whispered. I learnt from the rain how to work the magic and then I stopped feeling lonely. I learnt to know the house in the night way of mice and spiders. I learnt to read the geography of house bones. Invisible and unheard I scampered down secret tunnels beneath the floor boards and walked tightrope webbing among the beams. . . I transmuted flat daylight into*

---

[1] p. 9
[2] p. 17

> *my night-time magic and privately made for myself a world out of spells and whispers.*[1]

In one of the dream sections, B is following her mother in heaven. The scene is described in cinematic terms. 'Broad brilliant azure sky with cloud cushions on which parties of angels recline. To the left, a landscape of flowery fields where numerous saints and seraphs are strolling about or sitting on the seats placed as if in a park.'[2] B sees her mother and an arch with the sign EXIT TO HELL which she manages to dash through just before the angels remove it.

> Everything blacks out – as if in an abrupt dense smoke-screen – as successive curtains of darkness are drawn. The faces of child-angels last longest, porcelain painted with Os of insipid disparagement. On the obliteration of the last doll face, the hymn singing, very distantly, starts up again and continues, diminishing into final inaudibility, for a few seconds more.
>
> What happens when you start on the downward trip? The elevator doors clang shut, a suffocating wind roars up the shaft, it seems as though you'll never get to the bottom; there's plenty of time to wonder what's coming and to wish yourself somewhere else.[3]

As in most of her works, Kavan's alter ego has been judged by people and standards she does not understand; she has been condemned without knowing what she has done, and can never overturn her conviction. As the later *Eagle's Nest* has the Administrator, *Sleep Has His House* has the Liaison Officer. In a room of 'white-coated workers comparing notes' she sees files with her name and details on but cannot read them.

> Suddenly a precise disembodied voice asking coldly: Have you any statement to make at this stage? Followed by a slight hesitation, by the voice of invisible B; at first stammering, scarcely audible; gaining gradually force and tension until it breaks on an overtone of hysteria.
>
> By what judgement am I judged? What is the accusation against me? Am I to be accused of my own betrayal?
>
> Am I to blame because you are my enemies? Yours is the responsibility, the knowledge, the power. I trusted you, you played with me as a cat plays with a mouse, and now you accuse me. I had no

---

[1] p. 27
[2] p. 49
[3] p. 52

> weapon against you, not realising that there was need for weapons until too late.
>
> This is your place; you are at home here. I came as a stranger, alone, without a gun in my hand, bringing only a present that I wanted to give to you. Am I to blame because the gift was unwelcome?
>
> Am I accused of the untranslated indictment against myself? Is it my fault that a charge has been laid secretly against me in a different language?[1]

At the end, B has her own house, in the town but also in the country with views of 'lakes and streams, and fields and forests and villages', possibly a description of how Kavan felt in her London house with its garden that all her later visitors remarked on. Although she is by herself in the house she is not lonely; this is her house not her parents'. 'How does a girl like B feel, you may wonder, alone in this great dark place? The question can be answered in four simple words: B is at home.'[2]

The very strange novel *The Horse's Tale*, co-authored with Kavan's friend, mentor and doctor, Karl Theodore Bluth, was published by Stefan and Franciszka Themerson's avant garde Gaberbocchus Press in 1949. It is an anomaly in Kavan's work, though the title page has 'K. T. Bluth and A. Kavan' as the authors, so Bluth may have been the principal author, with Kavan's help. There seems to be no record of how Bluth and/or Kavan came to know the Themersons but, although the book does not fit with Kavan's other works, it does fit perfectly with Gaberbocchus' list, and is printed in Gaberbocchus' usual small, beautifully-designed format. Indeed, parts of it could easily be by Stefan Themerson himself, resembling both *Bayamus* and *Cardinal Pölätüo*, though both of these were published by Gaberbocchus after *The Horse's Tale* (*Bayamus* having originally been published elsewhere in 1949). The talking horse, Kathbar[3], who is the narrator, and his tongue-in-cheek philosophising seem straight out of

[1] p. 123
[2] p. 187
[3] Another name beginning with a 'K' an containing two 'A's

Themerson, as does the epigraph at the beginning: 'All characters in this story are fictitious, even the horse'. Comparisons to Animal *Farm*, 1945, are inevitable but Orwell is allegorical and political where Bluth and Kavan are playful and philosophical. The novel begins in a dystopian post-war world.

> That was a bad time for us horses: we used to stand around with empty faces, unsheltered, unfed; we were nobody's business. Foreigners had invaded the country, won all the battles, killed off all the fighting men, raped the women, taken prisoner the King himself.[1]

In this time, where there is no food available, horses are slaughtered for their meat and bones: 'dead, we were just what the peasants needed to help them through the hard winter.'[2] The horses begin to organise themselves politically but Kathbar, who often thinks and speaks in nonsense rhymes is too much the poet and philosopher to join any political movement. 'I know we're headed straight for the slaughter house, but I can take it.'[3] Setting off on his travels, Kathbar experiences the quiet of a church and the comfort of religion.

> For the first time in weeks I was free from flies. I knelt down beside the cow and the lamb. For the time being I felt calm and secure - saved, temporarily anyhow, from the drain. . . Resting half asleep near the holy crib, I felt as if I'd been restored by a miracle to my proper place. Life no longer seemed terrifying and cruel; it still contained hope. Why, I might even get back ultimately to the circus![4]

A farmer talks to him, asks him to live on his farm; the war is over and he is rebuilding the farm. However, the farmer tells the horse he will have to work, not dance and recite verse. The farmer, who sounds just like Themerson's Cardinal Pölätüo, tells him:

> You mustn't expect to spend your time writing sonnets or listening to the wireless professors. Don't be so foolish as to be taken in by the polemical positivists who, like suburban super-bores, destroy all values, and leave the ground too barren to bring forth anything but another war.[5]

---

[1] p. 5
[2] p. 6
[3] p. 9
[4] p. 11
[5] p. 13

The farmer, Hugh has been to college and believes a person's accent is everything.

> He had been trained as a nominalist; according to his tutor, language was the key to all wisdom, language consisted wholly of sounds, and the most superior sounds were those produced by Oxbridge and Camford dons.[1]

The horse, on the other hand considers himself a realist.

> My training had been realistic, on the metaphysical side I was familiar with Aquinas, Husserl and Scheler. To me, one, two and three were concepts expressing permanent truths; it was beyond me how anybody could believe "that the symbol 2 meant nothing." Even the Grand Old Positivist himself would hardly get away with changing the figure two to three on a cheque.[2]

And if the farmer could be Stefan Themerson's Cardinal Pölätüo, the horse could be Themerson himself talking about Semantic Poetry and the overtones carried by words:

> What I dance is the process of life, sometimes gay, sometimes grave, cynical sometimes, but never heavy or solemn. How I distrust words! They substitute concepts for real individual things. Unless a poet's words dance like my legs he's no poet at all. There's nothing to fear about going down the drain if you go down in a dance. Change we must from moment to moment, so let the dance be made with the grace of a dance or poem. The poem began long ago and nothing can stop it; it must go on to the very last sentence, which is the sentence of death.[3]

For Kathbar, life leads to death as a river leads to the sea; death is the meaning of life. The horse is also a painter and founds the school of Hoofism; he says that, as van Gogh painted with commas, he paints with hoof prints. Although he accepts that he is only a horse:

> I understand how knowledge and being unite in the trance of creation so that the ego becomes one with all manifestations of the outer world. The inexplicable comes to birth in that relationship which links artistic activity to the universe. Art is inseparable from all being. The artist,

---

[1] p. 17
[2] p. 18
[3] p. 29

> surrendering himself to the cosmic dance, has a conception of that same rhythm, participates in it, and works in harmony with its law.[1]

In contrast to the harmony of Hoofism, his teacher has tried to get him to accept Clawism, which is aggressive and violent, but he refuses to accept it. At the end of the novel, it seems that Kavan's voice may be coming to the fore, as Kathbar is sent to a mountain clinic, where he has had electric shock treatment then narco-analysis, with sodium amytal. The clinic 'bore no resemblance to the asylum where I'd been so unhappy'[2] A Rorschach test reveals his depression was 'due to a constitutional abnormality'. 'Not only was I a sensitive artist, but I also displayed practical traits, not generally found in conjunction with the artistic temperament.' Being a 'super-horse', 'imprisoned in my equine shape, I was debarred from making use of the forms and symbols available to the common run of humanity. I was inferior to none: but (although this was not stated in so many words) I was chained down to my bodily form.'[3] Is this Kavan talking about herself?

Anna Kavan could not find a commercial publisher *for A Scarcity of Love*; all her previous books except for *The Horse's Tale* had been published in London by Jonathan Cape and some in America by Doubleday but she had had nothing released by a mainstream publisher since 1947. It is not hard to see why. After the searing power and experimental nature of *Asylum Piece, I Am Lazarus* and *Sleep Has His House*, it is a serious disappointment, though it does contain some powerful and very personal writing. If it had had an editor like Peter Owen it might have been much stronger. Eventually Kavan had it privately published in 1956 but the publisher did not have enough money to pay the printers and so the novel had almost no circulation until it was reprinted by Peter Owen, after her death, in 1971. Containing obvious autobiographical elements, this is a strange and oddly-structured but very personal story. 'A scarcity of love, and the consequent insecurity and inferiority-feeling, operated like a machine, specially

[1] p. 83
[2] p. 99
[3] p. 103

designed to neutralize and break down her innate qualities.'[1] If Kavan had ever written an autobiography, she might well have called it *A Scarcity of Love*.

The novel starts in a ruined castle on a hill, - a 'gloomy castle of whispers'[2] - occupied by 'the Countess', Regina, a cold, aloof woman who does not want or like children or anything to do with the act of reproduction – 'The other was bad enough – but this . . . It's obscene, I tell you, this giving birth!'[3] This sounds much like Kavan's description of her own mother, but then the Countess shares some of Kavan's feelings for the older husband she is made to marry: 'The whole physical relationship revolted her, each repetition of the sexual act seemed a rape'[4]. A young doctor is called to her to handle the birth and comes to have strange feelings for her. 'He was shocked and confused, not only by the force of his uncomprehended feeling, but by the conflict between the conscious "real" self of his actual life and the other unauthorized self, which, having gained the upper hand temporarily, was making its illicit dream world seem more important than reality.'[5]

The Countess gives the baby to a wet-nurse, whom the doctor takes to a remote village in the mountains. The description of the cold, forbidding mountains is very similar to that in *Eagle's Nest*.

> She looked up at the now disembodied summits, terrible great ghost-shapes of luminous pallor floating on the dark sky, almost phosphorescent, with black gaps of shadow where darkness came pouring through; dim, huge, breathing down iciness. Deliberately she identified herself with their inhumanity and utter loneliness – with the fearful cold otherness of the non-human world. She would not feel the terror of it; she would not feel anything any more. She drew the horror and awe and loneliness of the mountains into herself; willing it to freeze her into some substance so rocklike that it could never melt, never be broken, harder than stone and colder than ice; so that no one should ever again have the power to hurt her; or even come near her.[6]

If the Countess can be identified with Kavan's mother, the girl may be identified with Kavan herself. Like Kavan's father, Regina's husband kills himself. 'His suicide came as a relief to her, pure and simple. . . in view of the tortures she had endured, the agonizing humiliation of her shamed body, his death seemed no more than an act of atonement that was her due.' She emerges 'extraordinarily

---

[1] p. 105
[2] P. 61
[3] p. 17. Elisions in the original
[4] p. 51
[5] p. 15
[6] p. 49/50

untouched, childlike, innocent-seeming, as though she were, like such sexless beings as sprites and mermaids, exempt from human emotions.' She is now 'left free to devote herself to restoring her own perfection.'[1] The doctor treats her like a 'Venetian-glass-girl'; a similar description to the frail, pale, *femmes fragiles* of Maeterlinck's marionette plays and of *Ice* and *Mercury*; the way Kavan so often refers to herself, though the Countess is far more calculating than fragile. Similarly, when he goes to see the wet nurse, she too has become a

> cold-seeming inhuman girl: who appeared to his imagination, stimulated by the dancing mirage-light from a thousand ice crystals, like a figure from a winter legend. For a second, he saw her as a sort of snow queen, robed in the iridescent diamond-shimmer of frost; forever frozen, white, hard, inaccessible, under shifting resplendency of the northern lights.[2]

Later, Regina brings the child, Gerda, to live with her, as Kavan's mother had sent for her, and marries an older man with a teenage son. Gerda becomes a Cinderella-like figure: 'she'd been given the gold sandals, more beautiful than anything she had ever possessed . . . their beauty was magical and would transform her: while she wore them she'd lose her shyness and become gay and popular.' Although 'she longed to go to the dance', she 'wasn't allowed to go' although all the other young people in the place would be there.' Alone in her room, she can hear a 'gay brilliant world of happiness, from which she was for ever shut out.'[3] Again, a good description of Kavan's childhood memories. 'Nobody in the world seemed to want her; there was no one she could speak to about herself; no place where she mattered, belonged.'[4] Gerda, like Kavan, is sent away to various schools, 'spending the last days of term, when everyone else was rejoicing, in a state of anxiety, waiting to hear whether she was to join Regina or be left where she was for the holidays.' She still has a 'naïve' belief that there is 'some relation between personal conduct and the course of events' but in fact, 'fate seemed to have placed her, as if maliciously, in a position where it was virtually impossible for her to attain even the very humble form of happiness that was all she asked.'[5] Like so many of Kavan's characters, she has been judged and condemned by unseen and capricious forces to which there is no appeal. 'She had a vague notion that she was to blame for her own unhappiness. But she no longer

---

[1] p. 52
[2] p. 56
[3] p. 81. Elisions in the original
[4] p. 84
[5] p. 92

understood how this was so. She could no longer remember what she'd done wrong'.[1]

Entering a 'fever hospital', Gerda befriends a nurse, Jean, who sees Gerda as a 'moon-girl', who, 'when she vanished, left behind a less definite memory than would have been left by a human being; something so nebulous, shadowy – just moonshine – that she could never be sure she had existed at all.'[2] Having disappeared, Gerda marries Val, who 'couldn't be considered much of a catch'; he 'had a lot of personal charm, and that was all he *did* have.'[3] But, unlike any of Kavan's partners, Val transports Gerda 'from an empty unloved existence to one of magnificent happiness – Val was her life's centre and its whole reason; without him it was worthless.'[4] However, just as he is about to go to 'a new post abroad', she has to go into an institution and is 'shattered' to be separated from him. Again, unlike Kavan's experiences, Gerda is treated well in the sanatorium, where 'her simplicity and appreciativeness had a special charm that appealed to everyone'; she becomes 'an enchanting puppet, a beautifully-made doll.'[5] As in *Ice* and *Mercury*, there is a triangle involving two male characters who fall out, at least partly because of the pale, fragile girl. In this case, Val's employer Louis is the third party. Betrayed by Louis, the pre-Raphaelite world she has been living in, a world 'flushed with sunset', where 'golden light flooded the pool and flared on the tree trunks; like countless emerald pendants the leaves hung down, set in unearthly gold' begins to break up.

> The sun disappeared. Instantly there was a chill in the air. With uncanny speed, the golden light faded, the world began to turn hostile and dark and cold. Between one stone and the next, all colour was expunged. The trees looked blackly ominous, the water had a gruesome gunmetal gleam. . . To her horror, the water, the willows, the sky, seemed to have different faces; while she wasn't looking, they'd slyly transferred themselves to the dark, frightening underside of the world, to which the vast, unknown country beyond the trees also belonged. She could feel the alien country, hostile and savage and huge; the endless lifeless hills crowding one behind the other like the waves of some monstrous sea, fearsome masses of earth, horribly heaving up out of nowhere; rearing up in a ghastly tidal wave, ready to fall upon her. She was lost, utterly, hopelessly lost, out of her world.[6]

---

[1] p. 182
[2] p. 101
[3] p. 118
[4] p. 130
[5] p. 132
[6] p. 175

Val forgets Gerda completely: 'Instantly and entirely, she was forgotten, as though she had never been' and becomes 'at one again with his friend', Louis; Gerda now has 'no further reason to go on living.'[1] Having given up on the world of happiness, Gerda seeks her own world again. 'Under black feathery trailing branches, the water, sprinkled with diamond stars, was the ceiling of her private world . . . That was where she wanted to be. With sudden intensity, she longed to escape from all the sadness, the guilt and the not-being-loved, of the world to which she had come unwanted, where nobody wished her to stay.'[2] The next and last chapter fast-forwards to the future of the calculating, witch-like Regina, but this penultimate chapter ends with what must be a description of the suicidally-inclined, heroin-addicted Anna Kavan's ideal of the ideal end to everything, the final wished-for oblivion.

> She had been looking up at the trees. Now she lowered her eyes; and saw, at her feet, like a silver carpet put down in her honour, a radiant path leading straight to the place where she wanted to be – there it lay, her own world, safe and secret, beneath the dark water, its splendid lights, blazing like Christmas stars. She had a sense of enchanted wonder, and of arrival. Now she was nearly home. Very soon she would be in the midst of the bright insubstantial reality of her dream. The great stars poured out their wonder-light, welcoming, not far away. So brilliant, made of pure diamond-sparkle, they shone in their beauty. She wanted to come to them . . . to come to them quickly . . . she kept her wide open eyes fixed on the lustrous stars.
>
> She felt light – lighter than air. And she seemed to be moving towards them with wonderful ease and speed . . . through silver-black glitterings and cool dark depths, and still deeper darkness, surrounding her . . . growing deeper . . . She gazed at the brilliant stars till her eyes filled with darkness; till everything was dark in her head: and the stars, as they set their jewelled wreath on her floating hair, seemed to be trying to give her what she had never been given by human beings.[3]

---

[1] p. 181
[2] p. 182
[3] p. 183

Eagle's Nest was the first book of Kavan's that Peter Owen published – she gave it to him on their first meeting. Owen subsequently became a mentor and supporter, publishing and/or republishing all her work so that, at one time, Peter Owen had all her work as Anna Kavan in print. Of all her novels, this is the closest to Kafka, taking place in a remote castle in the mountains run by the Administrator – or perhaps taking place entirely in the mind of the narrator, unusually for Kava, male. However, it is also to some extent in the English gothic tradition of *The Castle of Otranto* and also brings to mind the castle with its hierarchical, ordered society of Mervyn Peake's *Titus Groan*, 1946, and *Gormenghast*, 1950. It also brings to mind other psychological works set in castles with an oppressive atmosphere dominated by a mysterious controlling figure and a doomed protagonist: Béla Balázs' *Bluebeard's Castle*, 1911 – 1918 and Maeterlinck's *The Death of Tintagiles*, 1894. Also, in its portrayal of the mindless machinery of a faceless bureaucracy it is related *to Animal Farm*, *1984* and *Brave New World*, but in a psychological, dreamlike and ambiguous form. Although it may not be relevant and there is no evidence in the text that the name of the novel's castle in the mountains is a deliberate reference, the Eagle's Nest was Hitler's 1930s Bavarian mountaintop residence, also known in German as the *Kehlsteinhaus*.

The unnamed, male narrator loses his job as a display artist at a department store and applies for a job with a former employer and mentor: the person known only as the Administrator at Eagle's Nest. Near the start of the novel the narrator is wandering and comes upon an old abbey in a heightened emotional state and his mind begins to split into real and unreal states.

> It looked as though I had parted company all at once with my usual reasoning self, which had withdrawn into the shadows, leaving me no means of communicating with it; while another "I" took command, functioning at a different, more mysterious level, where all outer appearances were deceptive, and even the thoughts in my head shot with ambiguity. . . Still in that queer "other" state I scarcely had time to feel disappointed, before I received an impression of danger, emanating, it seemed at first, from those black meshes, which were trying to

> entangle me in their crafty web. The next moment I realized that the whole silent, solemn, supercharged atmosphere of the abbey had become sinister and antagonistic. Even the clustering flames had lost their flowerlike prettiness, transformed into misleading will-o'-the wisps, confusing me by their untrustworthy flickerings[1]

This paranoia is typical of Kavan's earlier stories, though the split personality is new: the narrator has an 'other identity outside my control, obscurely related to me. . . with a reality far beyond that of dreaming, so that I seemed to be living two lives at once.' [2] The narrator is summoned by a mysterious letter to Eagle's Nest and travels there through a strange landscape in a strange mental state. 'My own state of mind was certainly not very normal that day. I hardly knew whether I had been travelling for hours, days or weeks.'[3] As he arrives at the railway station, the narrator is caught up in a welcome party for two strangers he has previously met: the young one turns out to be 'Miss Hairdressing', a young woman he will later fall in love with after he leaves the castle. He takes a taxi to escape the throng; approaching the castle;, the road winds through a 'wilderness of weird crags, their shapes fantastic beyond belief, all seared to the same fierce lion tint by the blazing sun. Everything was arid, inhuman, enormous and elemental, like a scene from some earlier stage of the planet's long life.'[4] Volcanic hills rise like 'islands from this unstable brilliance, mirages floating in the transparent dazzle', the mountains 'savagely coloured and depthless-looking, as if painted on the cobalt sky; crowding behind one another like a gigantic city of vast skyscrapers, or a monstrous cemetery of colossal coffins stood up on end.'[5] At the same time a 'new sort of mirage seemed to confront me outside. Seven great crests, shaped like wigged judges, sat in the sky, with robes of rich green falling in velvet folds to their feet: lush fields and orchards, plantations and vineyards, improbable as an Eden in this desolation of stone.'[6]

When he arrives at Eagle's Nest, the Administrator is not there and he does not seem to be expected. The castle seems to be deserted except for the 'native' servants and the Administrator's secretary, Penny (later explained as the bad penny that always returns), with whom he has dinner every night in grand surroundings. He is given no work to do, though he believes he has been sent for to continue cataloguing the Administrator's books, which he says he had previously been involved in, though he has never been to Eagle's Nest before. In his room is a portrait of the Administrator.

---

[1] p. 9
[2] p. 11
[3] p. 29
[4] p. 28
[5] p. 29
[6] p. 30

> But this was no ordinary portrait, I perceived, examining it more closely, struck by the translucent flesh tints, through which the spirit seemed to shine like a flame. Mysterious, magical, the picture at this point transferred me to the other world, to which it obviously belonged: and for some reason, I was able to make the transition as naturally and easily as, if I'd fallen asleep, I should have begun to dream. I felt no surprise, watching the softly pulsing and winglike flames, which fluttered around the head, encircling it with their living wreath. It was my own vision I saw there, man and angel in one shape, incorporeal angel-stuff shining out of the painted man. If only I could interpret its meaning correctly![1]

It is not clear to the reader how to interpret the vision either. The narrator has previously made angel figures for the department store's Christmas display and has seen angel faces at the abbey and in a photograph that the Administrator will later show him. Certainly he is not the guardian angel the narrator had hope for. When he finally meets the Administrator he is given a cool reception. The administrator appears to emerge from his portrait, but the narrator now sees this as a 'childish theatrical trick. . . Obviously , I had been altogether mistaken in him. My hero-benefactor didn't exist, never had existed, except in my imagination. Now I hated him for assuming the halo that had destroyed my illusion.'[2] The Administrator tells him he will not be working at Eagle's Nest, and that his 'impatience' and investigations have ruined his chances. He returns to his – and Kavan's - former paranoia. 'Though I resented it, I knew there was no possibility of defending myself. It suddenly seemed that all this had happened to me already . . . some time long ago in the past I had been judged and sentenced'.[3] But the Administrator says that at Eagle's Nest 'everything is a symbol of something else, and every sign can be interpreted in various ways.'

> I suppose you think, quite naturally, that because I'm master here, I can do as I like. Actually, I assure you, this is far from being the case. Although I have to settle all doubtful questions, the decisions are not my own. My task is to administer the existing code as it applies to particular situations.[4]

His role, like that of the Masters of Ritual in Gormenghast castle, is not to do anything new, but to make sure that everything is done in accordance with

[1] p. 60

[2] p. 128

[3] p. 133. Elisions in the original

[4] p. 135

precedent, however mysterious or senseless; an administrator not a ruler – there is no ruler, nothing new is ever allowed to happen, no one has the authority to change anything. This role accords well with the faceless officials who have 'condemned' Kavan's previous narrators in the short stories. Now the narrator in all his paranoia sees the Administrator differently. 'The perfidious smiling face of my betrayer emerged from the mists of time past. The tongueless bell dumbly clanging, I recognized the face of all my enemies and oppressors; of all the injustice which had pursued me; of all my fears.'[1] But later, forced to leave Eagle's Nest, he realises that he has condemned himself. 'I alone had imposed upon life the pattern of injustice and failure which it was now too late to change.'[2] He sees that it makes no difference whether he stays at the castle with Penny, who he now knows had feelings for him, or leaves.

> it made very little difference whether I stayed with her, or set out alone on my journey that had neither visible starting point nor destination. It didn't matter: since, however closely I became involved with another existence, my own world would always remain secret, inaccessible and shut-off; nobody would even see me, except as a dim, changeable, wavering shadow, through its impenetrable, semi-opaque walls.[3]

This is the end of the novel (and a good summary of Kavan's view of herself) but there follows a final chapter, numbered according to the preceding sequence of chapters, but subtitled 'The Dream Within', which is effectively a separate short story on the same theme, as *Who Are You* has two separate endings, *Eagle's Nest* has two variations. Possibly 'The Dream Within' was an earlier version or an early draft, but it is presented as part of the novel. In this version, the narrator goes to see his 'protector and only friend', the Administrator, but he is not recognised. Although the Administrator recognises his name, he says: 'The trouble is, you aren't the man.'

> A shudder goes through me . . . it's all over . . . now I must go, and the sooner the better, back to where I belong . . . I've no right to be here. I have no place in this room . . . in this house . . . in this world, for that matter . . . nothing binds me to my surroundings . . . but the tendrils of my perception, which I have to detach painfully from the graciousness of the warm room . . . to which they obstinately persist in clinging . . . shrinking from the cold sordid ugliness outside.[4]

---

[1] p. 137
[2] p. 155
[3] p. 157
[4] p. 179. Elisions in the original

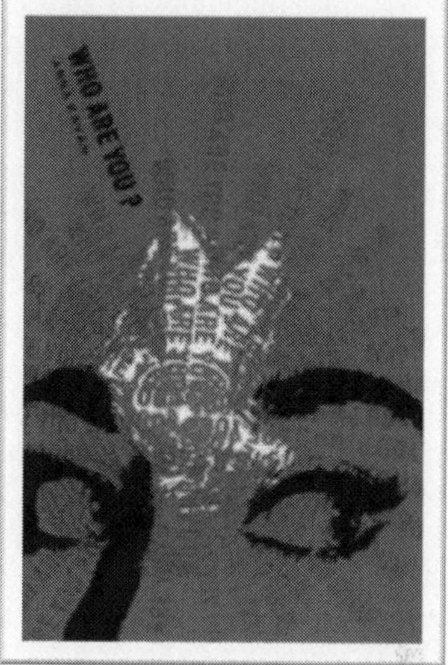

Who Are You? was originally published by the small Scorpion Press in 1963, and republished by Peter Owen in 1973[1]. Some of the same themes are also covered in *Change the Name*, but *Who Are You* is an almost exact retelling in a more experimental style, of the latter part of the autobiographical novel *Let Me Alone*, published in 1930 under the name Helen Ferguson, where the leading character is called Anna Kavan, and from whom she later took her new name and identity. Both novels concern her first marriage to Donald Ferguson, though *Who Are You* only covers the time they spent in Burma together. In the later novel, the central female character has no name; she is referred to only as 'the girl' and her husband is 'Mr Dog Head', the disparaging name the Burmese servants have given him- 'one doesn't at once see why'[2]. Whereas *Let Me Alone* was written quite conventionally, the later version is more experimental: far shorter and more elliptical, written in Kavan's later poetic and nocturnal prose. It also has two alternative endings.

The title refers, symbolically, to the tropical birds outside her house in Burma which cry this lament loudly and constantly. 'The intolerable thing about them is the suggestion they are produced by machines nobody can stop, which will eternally repeat the question no one ever answers.'[3] The cries punctuate the book as they punctuate the girl's life; impossible to ignore the 'exasperating din that seems as though it will really go on for ever. The earsplitting, monotonous repetition continues like an infuriating machine-noise that nobody knows how to stop.'[4] In a way, all Kavan's work asks the question 'who are you' and, like the birds, never answers it. Is she Anna Kavan, Helen Woods, Helen Ferguson or just the ghost-girl of so many of her stories, with no substance, whose soul has gone to China?

> *Is* it her life? It hardly seems so. A picture comes to her of her schoolfriends, enjoying themselves in pretty dresses and gay

[1] The story behind this is explained by David Callard, op. cit., p. 121/122: Owen thought the work was too short to issue by itself and too experimental to sell well.

[2] p. 15

[3] p. 7

[4] p. 33

> surroundings, or else at the university, as she ought to be[1]. Who *am* I? she wonders vaguely. Why am I here. Is she the girl who won the scholarship last year? Or the girl living in this awful heat, with the stranger who's married her for some unknown reason, with whom it's impossible to communicate? Her questions remain unanswered; both alternatives seem equally dreamlike, unreal. Somehow she seems to have lost contact with existence .[2]

Although it is early in their marriage the couple – an eighteen year old girl and a husband 'double her age' - 'have nothing in common; although they have only been married a year, neither enjoys the company of the other.'[3] He is 'aggressive and overbearing physically' with a pent up anger that makes him continuously swat mosquitoes and chase rats with his tennis racquet; he also takes his anger out on her. ' "Fuck you and your intelligent conversation!" The man looks at her in blazing indignation; how dare she put on airs just because she's supposed to be brainy?'[4] The girl is alone in the house with him except for the husband's 'severely ascetic grey-bearded Mohammedan' servant, who is loyal to his master and treats the girl with disdain. Her only outside contact is a young man called just 'Suède Boots' who 'fancies he's falling a little in love with the girl, though not seriously enough to commit himself.'[5] But in 'this climate, always seething with sex, the small white community is a hotbed of scandal' and they must meet discreetly; nevertheless, Mr Dog Head comes home one day to find Suède Boots there and throws him out. After the incident with Suède Boots, the girl loses touch with reality even more and her husband becomes even more angry with her. He tells her she is free to leave but then decides she must give him a child; she repels his advances and he rapes her.

> Down comes his whole hard body then, crushing her flat, the prominent bones digging into her flesh. Now she can struggle no longer, can't even move her head, immobilized by his weight, and his hot mouth glued to hers. Sickened, she's forced to inhale his breath, stinking of whisky, and can only gasp in repulsion. She becomes panic stricken . . . she's suffocating . . . she can't breathe . . . His hot heavy body is hard as rock – a rock overlaid with damp, dank, shaggy fur . . . It's as though a fiery rock from an erupting volcano has fallen on her, and is painfully

[1] In real life, Helen Woods, as she then was, had wanted to go to Oxford University, but her mother had refused to send her, and encouraged her marriage to Ferguson.

[2] p. 30

[3] p. 13

[4] p. 69

[5] p. 57

> crushing her to death . . . she can't stand it another second . . . she's dying . . . being horribly murdered . . .[1]

She realises, with desperation, that she might become pregnant and rushes to the bathroom, as a flash of lighting in the tropical storm 'forks its way down the sky, splitting it apart, its lurid brilliance lighting up every detail: the broken mirror, a few jagged splinters of smashed glass adhering to the frame' amidst her torn night clothes. Mirrors are a recurrent symbol in Kavan's later writing, representing the split in her personality and her ability to look at herself from the outside; the broken mirror points to her shattered personality. In the intensity of the storm, her husband madly and drunkenly chases after a huge rat – a 'rat-king' that trips him up.

> An inexplicable, indescribable movement rouses him: hairs coarse as wire are scratching his chest, neck and chin. With horror, he realizes that he must have tripped over and be lying on top of the monster rat, which he'd completely forgotten until this moment. And the beast's moving . . . it's come to life . . . it's cold sharp claws scrabble at his chest, becoming entangled in its furlike growth, as he struggles desperately to get hold of it[2]

As he 'feels its teeth sinking into his throat' he falls and pulls over the wardrobe on top of him. 'Like a coffin, it falls with a crash, imprisoning him in stifling darkness beneath – in the dustbin to which he consigns his victims.' Just at this moment the rain 'comes down with a thunderous smash. Pounding on the roof, the vast mass of water adds its continuous battering boom to the ponderous roar of the great thunder-wheels rolling loose in the blackness outside.'[3] The 'Who-are-you?' cries of the 'brain-fever birds' now come from all around, from near and far; 'they don't express hunger, or love, or fear, or anything else, but seem uttered with the sole object of maddening whoever hears them.'[4] At the end of the first of the book's two alternative endings, there is a cinematic cut as the sun comes up after the storm and the noises of birds and insects is overwhelming. Over it all comes the sound of the brain-fever birds.

> They implant an obscure irritant in the brain, eternally calling out the monotonous question nobody will ever answer. from all points of the compass, from far and near . . . which others of their kind infuriatingly

[1] p. 82. Elisions in the original

[2] p. 94. Elisions in the original

[3] p. 94

[4] p. 96/97

> echo . . . and others still . . . driving the crazed hearer into delirium . . . until the nightmare climax – when suddenly everything stops . . .[1]

In the next chapter, the narrative rewinds into the alternative, or, rather, parallel ending as the two stories are not in fact very different; it restarts when Suède Boots is in her house; this time the husband is not quite so fierce with him and the rape scene set to the sound of the thunder storm is not so graphic. This time though, after the rape she immediately leaves the house: 'what Suède Boots said is quite true - all she has to do is to walk out of the place, exactly as ha always told her. How simple it seems. The thing she's thought almost impossible, when it comes to the point, is really perfectly easy.'[2] But as she leaves the house, in the storm, it 'looks like a hallucination. Everything out there has the same fantastic, improbable aspect, as if it were part of a fever dream.'[3] We never learn if she does escape, as she decides to leave it to chance – Helen Ferguson did not in fact leave until after her son had been born – and the second ending of the novel ends like the first, with a view of the house at dawn where this time:

> The dilapidated house stands silent as if deserted, in the almost cool air of daybreak; as though it were already an abandoned ruin, empty, and fallen into decay. The rooms appear as so many black holes through the unshuttered, wide open windows.[4]

---

[1] p. 97
[2] p. 113
[3] p. 114
[4] p. 117

Ice, Anna Kavan's last novel to be published in her lifetime[1] is usually considered to be her masterpiece. Set in a post-apocalyptic future where ice is encroaching all over the world, it is reminiscent in many ways of the crop of British and American science fiction novels of the early 1960s. Brian Aldiss voted it the best science fiction novel of 1967, even though Kavan had not intended to write science fiction and claimed not to have read any herself. As a result of this, Aldiss subsequently met Kavan and tried to convince her that she was in fact a very fine science fiction writer. He also wrote the introduction to the novel's 1970 reprint. The spreading ice in Kavan's novel is very like the worldwide ice age in Kurt Vonnegut's *Slaughterhouse Five,* 1963, caused by *ice-nine*, which is a 'new way for the atoms of water to stack and lock, to freeze'; at the end of his novel the whole world has been affected and has become a frozen waste land. It also brings to mind Aldiss's own, slightly later experimental novel, *Barefoot in the Head*, 1969 and J. G. Ballard's early catastrophe novels, especially *The Crystal World*, 1966, in which an apocalyptic crystallisation is spreading around the world.[2] And among post-apocalyptic experimental novels of roughly the same time were Alan Burns' *Europe After the Rain*, 1965 and Christine Brooke-Rose's *Out*, 1964. All these novels immediately postdate the Cuban missile crisis of 1961, during which it seemed entirely possible that the world could be destroyed in a man-made apocalypse, a moment in culture probably best described by Jeff Nuttall in *Bomb Culture*, 1968. However, it is possible to take Kavan at her word and assume she had not read any of these books; Aldiss, Ballard and others are writing realistic novels about an imagined future; the apocalypse in *Ice* is dreamlike and metaphorical, and the symbols of ice, snow, whiteness and fragile ghost-girls had been part of her work for a long time. In fact it may be closer in feeling to Mallarmé's earliest prose poem *Le Phénomène Futur*, which starts: 'Un ciel pale, sur le monde qui finit de decrepitude, va peut-être partir avec les nuages'.

The novel concerns the unnamed, male narrator's search for the unnamed girl, whose body is 'slight as a child's, ivory white against the dead white of the snow, her hair bright as spun glass.' She is the doomed, pale *femme fragile* from

[1] London, Peter Owen, 1967, republished: Macmillan, 1973

[2] The novel's precursor, the short story 'The Illuminated Man' was included in the British edition of his collection *The Terminal Beach*, 1964

Maeterlinck's mediaeval marionette dramas, a glass-girl like the Kavan-figure in *A Scarcity of Love*, 'her personality had been damaged by a sadistic mother who kept her in a permanent state of frightened subjection.' So there is no doubt that we are meant to identify the girl with Kavan herself. 'Her hair was astonishing, silver-white, an albino's, sparkling like moonlight, like moonlit Venetian glass. I treated her like a glass-girl; at times she hardly seemed real.'[1] Very little in the novel seems real; the narrator implies as much at the very beginning. 'Reality had always been something of an unknown quantity to me.'[2] Although he says that his aim in finding her is to protect her from 'the callousness of the world', he admits to enjoying seeing her hurt and the subsequent scenes of her suffering turn out to be his fantasies: 'I derived an indescribable pleasure from seeing her suffer.'[3] Against a background of encroaching ice, he first comes to take her away from an old friend of his, with whom she has been living.

> Great ice-cliffs were closing in on all sides. The light was fluorescent, a cold flat shadowless icelight. No sun, no shadows, no life, a dead cold. We were in the centre of an advancing circle. I had tried to save her. . . The tower was bound to fall; it would collapse, and be pulverised instantly under millions of tons of ice. The cold scorched my lungs, the ice was so near. She was shivering violently, her shoulders were ice already; I held her closer to me, wrapped both arms around her tight.[4]

The girl herself *is* the ice: the narration switches to third-person as Kavan describes the hard coldness and impermeability she so often describes as her ideal state: 'she felt herself becoming one with the structure of ice and snow. As her fate, she accepted the world of ice, shining, shimmering, dead; she resigned herself to the triumph of glaciers and the death of her world.' The narrator travels to another country, a small and backward place, where there is evidence of the war that a suicidal mankind has been waging against itself instead of banding together to try to escape the ice. 'Everywhere the ubiquitous ruins, decayed fortifications, evidence of a warlike, bloodthirsty past.'[5] Like *Eagle's Nest*, the town is dominated by a castle, the High House, where the girl is being held prisoner by the warden, who may in fact be the narrator's projection of himself:

> she was cut off from all contact, totally vulnerable, at the mercy of the man who came in without knocking, without a word, his cold, very bright blue eyes pouncing on hers in the glass. . . Forced since childhood

[1] p. 13
[2] p. 12
[3] p. 13
[4] p. 17
[5] p. 32

> into a victim's pattern of thought and behaviour, she was defenceless against his aggressive will, which was able to take complete possession of her, I saw it happen.[1]

As the husband rapes his wife in *Who Are You*, the warden/narrator rapes – in his fantasy, presumably - the imprisoned girl; 'her feeble struggles amused him, he knew they would not last long. He looked on in silence, in half-smiling amusement, always tilting her face with a slight but inescapable pressure, while she exhausted herself.' The girl escapes from the castle, but arrives in a place where the people need to sacrifice a young girl to an evil presence in the water, 'something primitive, savage, demanding victims, hungry for a human victim.'[2] The girl is of course, like all Kavan's ghost-girls, already doomed for reasons she never discovers. She is destined to be a victim.

> Systematic bullying when she was most vulnerable had distorted the structure of her personality, made a victim of her, to be destroyed, either by things or by human beings, people or fjords and forests; it made no difference, in any case she could not escape. The irreparable damage inflicted had long ago rendered her fate inevitable.
>
> A pitch black mass of rock loomed ahead, a hill, a mountain, an unlighted fortress, buttressed by regiments of black firs. Her weak hands were shaking too much to manipulate a door, but the waiting forces of doom dragged her inside.[3]

As in the story 'The Gannets' in *I Am Lazarus*,[4] the girl is sacrificially thrown from the cliffs but the narrator feels no pity. 'Big tears fell from her eyes like icicles, like diamonds, but I was unmoved. They did not seem to me like real tears. She herself did not seem quite real. She was pale and transparent, the victim I used for my own enjoyment in dreams.'[5] The narrator later arrives in a place where there are 'wide streets, well-dressed people, modern buildings, cars, yachts on the blue water. No snow; no ruins; no armed guards. It was a miracle, a flashback to something dreamed.' But he believes that 'this was the reality and those other things the dream. All of a sudden the life I had lately been living appeared unreal.'[6] He tries to forget the girl, but his fantasies of hurting her will not go away.

---

[1] p. 33/34

[2] p. 44

[3] p. 45

[4] A very similar scene also occurs in the 'lost' novel *Mercury*

[5] p. 49

[6] p. 61

> Her face haunted me: the sweep of her long lashes, her timid enchanting smile; and then a change of expression I could produce at will, a sudden shift, a bruised look, a quick change to terror, to tears. The strength of the temptation alarmed me. The black descending arm of the executioner; my hands seizing her wrists. . . . I was afraid the dream might turn out to be real. . . . Something in her demanded victimization and terror, so she corrupted my dreams, led me into dark places I had no wish to explore. It was no longer clear to me which of us was the victim. Perhaps we were victims of one another.[1]

Unable to forget the girl, the narrator travels across a border and ends up in a similar situation as before, with a warder who is his alter ego. 'I fought to retain my identity, but all my efforts failed to keep us apart. I continually found I was not myself but him.'[2] Again he finds the girl, recues her again and again moves from a dreamlike terror to a 'gay, undamaged town, full of light and colour, freedom, the absence of danger, the warm sun. . . . Nothing but the nightmare had seemed real while it was going on, the other lost world had been imagined or dreamed.'[3] But the nightmare of the destroyed world keeps returning, and he thinks again of his symbol of an idealised, peaceful world, the habitat of the Indri lemurs, 'believing their magic influence might lift the dead-weight of depression which had fallen on me. I did not care whether I saw or dreamt them.'[4] He sees the impending death of the human race, 'the collective death-wish, the fatal impulse to self-destruction, though perhaps human life might survive.'

> From the doomed dying world man had ruined I seemed to catch sight of this other one, new, infinitely alive, and of boundless potential. For a second I believed myself capable of existing on a higher level in this wonderful world; but saw how far it was beyond my powers when I thought of the girl, the warden, the spreading ice, the fighting and killing. . . I knew that my place was here, in our world under sentence of death, and that I would have to stay to see it through to the end.[5]

At the end the girl is waiting for him, doomed to be his – perhaps masochistic – victim. 'I don't know why . . . you're always so horrible to me . . . I only know I've always waited.'[6] In the end, they go together into the 'huge alien night, the snow,

---

[1] p. 62. Elisions in the original

[2] p. 80/81

[3] p. 95

[4] p. 101. The Indris, a large Madagascan lemur also recur in *Mercury*

[5] p. 101

[6] p. 125

the destroying cold, the menacing unknown future. . . We went out together into the onslaught of snow, fled through the swirling white like escaping ghosts.'[1]

The 30,000 word novella *My Soul in China* was 'extracted' by Rhys Davies after Kavan's death and published posthumously in 1975. It is not clear how much editing Davies and/or Peter Owen did, or what state the original manuscript was in; Davies says in the introduction that she had left a 'crystallisation of her younger self, fact breaking mercilessly into loose attempts at a novelistic arrangement of her material (from which the novella has been extracted')[2]. The book also includes nine short stories, previously unpublished in book form[3], which Davies says are later works; though they are only loosely connected to each other in style or content. The novella relates incidents and dreamscapes from just after the break-up of her second marriage, to Stuart Edmonds. The narration moves between first-person and third-person; the principal character, Kay [*sic*] feels split in two and can watch herself as if in a mirror. The book starts with a strong sense of loss, though nothing material has yet been lost. The house she used to visit, 'curled up like a friendly white animal sunning itself, or sheltering under the trees' has now changed.

> Wandering lost and aimless without even a name to connect me to life, I begin to add up the dismal accounts of loss. Lost, all vanished, the lovely things; the lovely globe of security broken that could not break. Lost, all forever silent, the voices and steps of love, the doors all locked, no handle turning again with premonition of love. Like the dandelion clocks, all blown and dispersed on the wind, my life has evaporated into the emptiness of a dream; for which I blame my betrayer, that dubious stranger wearing the mask of a once-loved face.[4]

---

[1] p. 126

[2] p. 7

[3] 'Five More Days to Countdown' had been published in *Encounter*, July, 1968

[4] p. 14

It is not clear whether the betrayer is a real person – her second husband – or the faceless enemy of many of her other works. She swings at 'him' with an axe, but 'his neck isn't even scratched; which is surprising as I notice the axe is made of silverpaper. The kneeling man gets up, brushes the dust off his trousers, then strolls away, lighting a cigarette, without once looking at me'. In despair, she dissolves 'veronal, tuinal, sodium amytal, etc, etc' into her tea but it does not kill her. She believes the police will come soon and she 'can only escape by going to China.' She sees a girl on her bed in an Asian robe; 'though the girl isn't dead yet she pretty soon will be. Her face has the same blue tinge as her sash.' She wipes the girl's face but then 'a most confusing thing happens: it's my own face I'm wiping. I try to understand this, but it's quite beyond me. I simply don't see how I can be this half-dead girl I'm looking at.'[1] In a dreamlike state she catches a train and gets out 'with the vague idea that I've arrived in China', but can't get out of the deserted station.

> I'm all alone in the huge, empty, echoing place, where above my head the lights are starting to go out one by one. . . all the while I'm an ugly mud-coloured fish someone has pulled out of the water and thrown down to die in its own time. Just as I thing I've gasped out my last agony, a dog comes up and sniffs me; it starts lifting its leg, I give one unspeakable frantic twitch, and blood spurts out of my gills.[2]

The narrative switches to third person as 'the girl' is brought into a clinic. As in the stories of *I Am Lazarus* and *Asylum Piece*, the clinic is a form of hell. 'Here there is no law but the nightmare of sleep, no reality but its divided shell'.[3] She is split in two, as in R.D. Laing's *The Divided Self*, 1960 and *Self and Others*, 1961 – a person who can 'cannot take the realness, aliveness, autonomy and identity of himself and others for granted'[4] and who needs external evidence of her own existence. Kay's alter ego seems to have no true self, no 'soul'.

> The girl beside me strays along with rapt white face uplifted. Looking at her, you might guess that she had no soul, that one day her soul had taken a flight to China. One day she saw a vision of blossoms on a pagoda-tree, she saw a landscape where temples were shrugging their shoulders, and yellow slant-eyed men. 'China! China!' she cried, and her soul flew out of her mouth with the words. Over oceans and continents it

---

[1] p. 15
[2] p. 17
[3] p. 19
[4] Penguin edition 1965, p. 41

> flew, never once looking back, all the long way to China: and there it stayed; what was there to come back for?[1]

The 'girl with no soul' sits beside the narrator, she refers to them as 'myself and I, but they are not allowed to communicate. 'Her eyes are fantastic. not like human eyes, two great dark empty holes, through which can be seen a glimpse of the howling wilderness of chaos and outer darkness, of the horror of eternity and ancient night. Only someone whose soul was in China could have such eyes.' She appears to leave the clinic and return to a consultant's room in Wimpole Street but is still on the edge of collapse. 'Everything will be all right as long as I keep cool. As long as I keep my head, no one will lock me up or stick needles in me or hold my head under water.'[2] She sees herself on a narrow bridge without hand rails; at one end is 'security, familiarity, the anaesthetic routine of days passed in approved tasks; a safe vegetable life without risks or emotions that's really no life at all'; the other is 'dangerous and unknown, stern cloud shapes there coldly assembling.'[3]

The novella then switches to a basically realistic and loosely autobiographical account of her time with her ex-husband, Martin, and 'the Australian', John[4], who offers to take her out of the country. John does not know that, like all Kavan's alter egos, she is really a 'ghost-girl – that was all he was holding. He could not know the coldness and nothingness she was experiencing – unreal in a world gone unreal.'[5]

> She wanted him to see what he was getting, so that later on he couldn't blame her or be disappointed because she was a ghost-girl without a heart or a body. It seemed to her that it must be obvious she was living in a different world, where there were no such things as bodies or hearts.[6]

John wants her to be happy; he sees that she can sometimes be happy, normal even. With him she can occasionally get through a day 'doing without any dope and not drinking anything much.' But their time together was only ever meant to be six months, and she knows that, like all men, he will leave her, 'she who was

---

[1] p. 20

[2] p. 22

[3] p. 24

[4] Presumably a fictionalisation of Ian Hamilton, an English expatriate and conscientious objector who had been living in New Zealand; they met in 1939 and she returned to New Zealand with him.

[5] p. 45

[6] p. 48

completely unlovable. She would always be abandoned by everyone'[1], because she was 'unattractive and unlikeable and no good in bed.'[2] Halfway through their time together, she realises she can 'no longer remain in the state of unthinking, contented dependence that for three months had relieved her of responsibility for her existence'[3]. Her self-loathing continues to increase; she sees versions of herself in various mirrors, a regular Kavan metaphor for her split persona. (She apparently loved mirrors in real life and her London house was full of them.)

> There was a small mirror on the wall and Kay stared into it for a moment. She saw there a face not unlike her own except that it was rather deteriorated and had an expression of great anxiety, almost of desperation. Her face was as unbearable as her thoughts, she turned quickly away. . . Nobody now would ever believe that she had once herself been considered desirable. She hardly believed it herself.[4]

Their seaside idyll is ruined because she cannot enjoy the present without thinking of the future where she will be abandoned. Her paranoia returns; one day she is looking towards the mountains and they seem to have changed. Like the mountains in *Eagles' Nest*, 'it was no longer possible not to see that the mountains wore the white wigs of judges. I knew then that judgement had already been given against me and that very soon someone would come to take me away.'[5] She waits in the 'owl's black maw of night to be ejected into the void. . . Like all the other rooms, this bedroom contains a mirror in which I'm not reflected. I gaze and gaze into it, trying to become real. It's no good, no mirror will ever reflect the face of a person whose soul is in China.'[6] The short stories published together with the novella are not individually especially distinguished or representative of her work, except for the last story; charmingly titled 'A Summer Evening' it is in fact a first person meditation and elegy for Karl Bluth, whose death she was never to fully get over, only surviving him by three years. She says she 'can never go back to the living world' unless she is completely transformed. The story and the book end:

> If this whole structure could be transmuted into something hard, cold, untouchable, unaffected by any emotion . . . if flesh became something like granite, burning with mineral fires, so that, if a limb was snapped off, there remained an icicle dazzle of sparkling beauty, not a

---

[1] p. 60
[2] p. 66
[3] p. 57
[4] p. 67
[5] p. 76
[6] p. 78

disgusting mess, then and then only, indifferent to isolation and independent of time, I might endure the world.

Composed of some iridescent substance, smooth, hard, cold as ice, with a ruby from Mogok for a heart, and a diamond brain, inexhaustible and impervious, I would stride all over the world, seeing everything, knowing everything, needing nothing and nobody . . . finally leaving the earth and the last human being behind me and turning away to the most remote galaxies and the unimaginable reaches of infinite space.[1]

According to Rhys Davies, this may have been the last thing she ever wrote.

Mercury, discovered long after Kavan's death and published in 1994 is very similar indeed to *Ice*, and may even have been an earlier version of it. There is the encroaching apocalypse of ice, though here it is more metaphorical; we have the two male friends, one living with the girl, Luz [light], who, exactly like the girl in *Ice*, is 'extremely pale and excessively thin – he feels he can almost see through her, almost as if she were made of Venetian glass'[2] and the other who comes to take her away. We have, as in *Ice*, the Indri lemurs as a symbol of an unattainable peace and tranquillity. 'The lemurs' singing had always seemed to him not of this world, so that he'd come to identify it with another and happier life, regarding it as a symbol of all that he held most precious.'[3] We also have the sacrifice of the fragile ice-girl – the 'foredoomed victim' - to the sea monster. And the central character, Luke has the same ambiguous relationship to the girl of both saviour and tormentor. 'How diabolical of fate to involve him with the very person who appealed so irresistibly to his sadistic impulse'. He is attracted to her because she is 'vulnerable and submissive', with 'something of the pathos of a toy, constructed only to be destroyed.'[4] At the end of the novel, faced with a terror more psychological than the apocalypse of *Ice*, the two 'simply stand clinging together, like two terrified

[1] p. 192. Elisions in original
[2] p. 17
[3] p. 35
[4] p. 105

children.'[1] If anything, *Mercury* is an even more powerful novel than *Ice*: it is written in Kavan's most surreal, nocturnal language, as opposed to the more clipped prose of *Ice* and contains some of her most disturbing hallucinatory scenes.

> The secluded garden is deep in the beech woods, hidden away from the world in silence and secrecy, isolated by the countless great trees pressing close on all sides, their ancient enormous trunks ranked close together like walls . . . like impassable prison walls . . . the dense massive foliage pierced here and there by only a few small scattered rings of light, which give no idea of how the sun is blazing down on the world outside. . . .
>
> The tremendous ocean of leaves, encroaching everywhere on the small open space, fills the air with a green liquid transparency, and this fluid greenery arches up in colossal waves, overhanging and threatening the house . . . collapses and surges forward in a vast green tide, overwhelming everything . . . sweeping the girl away . . .
>
> She turns once; he sees her dilated victim's eyes gaze wildly, imploringly, at him, before she is engulfed by the assaulting flood.[2]

The Parson was first published by Peter Owen in 1995, only a year after Mercury but it is not clear when it was written and seems to be much earlier. It begins as a conventional novel and most closely resembles *A Scarcity of Love* in style and tone. The main female character, Rejane, like Regina in *Scarcity*, appears to be modelled on Kavan's mother, though in this case she is far more sympathetically portrayed. 'The Parson' is the regimental nickname of the younger army officer Oswald who becomes obsessed with her, and refers to his upright behaviour. He is unlike almost all of Kavan's characters, being a member of a large family and seems at first to be fundamentally well-adjusted, and seems to be closer to the Helen Ferguson character type. The story is told

[1] p. 136
[2] p. 33. Elisions in original

straightforwardly until the couple come to a hill-top castle, which, like the rocky outcrops of *Eagle's Nest* and *My Soul in China*, takes on an unreal aspect. Like Bluebeard's castle:

> Untold atrocities, perpetrated in the distant past, had left a legacy of abomination all the intervening years had been unable to obliterate. An aura of sadism and terror clung to the walls, much as shreds of threadbare fabric clung to the doorless archways.[1]

Slipping on the slippery stones, she starts to fall towards the sea. 'With the ghastly sickness of nightmare she struggled in vain, her hands helplessly clutching and clawing the bare, slimy walls.' She slips further down, screaming, as, 'at this moment of ultimate horror, the pitiless, pale bird-eye indifferently watching; as, in an agonised slither, she started lurching, sliding and slipping, helpless down to the sea.' As in *Ice*, *Mercury* and 'The Gannets', a woman is sacrificed to the sea. Although she does not in reality die, 'she could not easily return to the living world. She had died, her life has been violated by the death-kiss of the sea.'[2] Oswald is also transformed by the act of saving her: his love for her turns to bitterness, she is a 'stranger' he does not want to know. But his previous gentleness now turns to resentment. 'A strong, savage excitement was working in him, unmistakeably pleasurable, though it was perverse and sadistic – The Parson could never have harboured any such cruel sensation.' He is now 'going to take what he wanted' in yet another rape scene in a Kavan novel.

> At this moment he derived a peculiar satisfaction from knowing that he was outraging his most fundamental beliefs by performing an illicit cruel act, abhorrent to everybody. The sadism that had replaced his tender love rejoiced at the prospect of humiliating the lovely body he'd hitherto regarded as unattainable and almost holy.[3]

Oswald now becomes permanently dissolute, and at the end 'the wave of his destiny, swelling towards a climax, swept him on its forward rush to the climax of breaking. . . hurtling on, in obedience to fate's higher command, further and further from everything, into the unknown.'[4]

---

[1] p. 63
[2] p. 65
[3] p. 69
[4] p. 106

Guilty, not published until 2007, but apparently written in the 1940s is fundamentally a conventional story about a boy whose father returns home from a war to profess pacifism, as her companion in New Zealand, Ian Hamilton, had done in World War Two. Although it is not fully in Kavan's later, nocturnal, experimental style, it has aspects that relate it to some of the stories in *I Am Lazarus* and to *Eagle's Nest*, so it can perhaps be dated somewhere between them. It also has elements of the post-apocalyptic novels *Ice* and *Mercury* and the faceless central bureaucracy of *Eagle's Nest* and the stories 'All Kinds of Grief Shall Arrive' and 'A Certain Experience' in *I Am Lazarus* and 'The End in Sight' in *Asylum Piece*. The boy, Mark ['marked out' for something] meets a man called Spector [spectre], having grown apart from his father. The country appears to be at war; Mark discovers a news sheet, which gives the news of 'the first of the sequence of big explosions which, in such a short time, laid waste our principal cities and came to be known as the Eight Days War.' This gives rise to a stream of 'demoralized homeless people from the big towns.'

> These starving refugees from the shattered cities, many of them sick or with minds unhinged by suffering, flooding over the countryside in every direction, in lawless, leaderless, tragic mobs, were a problem as grave and were as much a cause of our country's final capitulation, as the actual bombs.[1]

After his parents are killed in the war, there is soon an armistice and Mark leaves school but stays close to Mr Spector. But he is not sure of Spector's status in regard to the powerful, central bureaucratic organisation, the Athing – 'that mysterious hierarchy of anonymous individuals who ruled our lives through the public administrations, of which the Housing Bureau had lately become the most important.' Searching for a house has become 'a kind of perverted religion . . . everything was demanded by this Moloch before which they cringed, hypnotized by supernatural terrors and impossible hopes.'[2] He makes a friend, Link, who does in fact become his link to the real world, and whose sister he is expected to

[1] p. 86
[2] p. 120

marry until he meets Carla, who 'carried me over the threshold of magic without transition . . . She hadn't looked at me in the real world; but in the mysterious secret depths of the mirror our eyes met.'[1] Mark becomes obsessed with visiting the Housing Bureau, even going there during the Christmas holidays when it is closed, 'advancing, for no particular reason, towards the protective bars and running my hands over the cold steel.' Pushing his way in, he is grabbed by the arm and pulled in to a totally dark room.

> I ceased to be myself, feeling my being invaded by the personality of a criminal; the hand on my arm was the grip of the law – of the police, by whom I'd been arrested. What crime I'd committed I didn't know; nor did this matter, since I knew I was guilty, and guilt itself was my crime. The shades of the prison house already enclosed me. There was no hope. I was being dragged deeper into some weird cavernous darkness, lit only by glow-worm glimmers of greenish light. Never again, I thought despairingly, should I see the sun.[2]

Although 'the nightmare breaks before the falling dreamer can hit the ground, before the past could swoop down on me', Mark now inhabits a world of 'childish loneliness and forlornness', a cold world like that of his (and Kavan's) childhood, in the icy shade of his/her mother, when he 'piled logs on the fires but could light no corresponding warmth in her heart or my own.'[3] He has never been the 'confident, normal young man of my thoughts', never been 'anything but in transit.' He wonders whether 'any such thing as my real self could be said to exist at all' and is 'consumed by the desire for identification with the essential "I" . . . wandering like a stranger, lost, frightened and confused, among the changes and contradictions of my own personality.'[4] The novel ends with a fitting, though no doubt unwitting, summary of Kavan's life's work.

> So I come to the end of my writing. I've often thought it was of no value, my ideas of no more significance than the aimless circling of flies in an empty room. And, if anyone else ever reads these words, he'll probably endorse this opinion, saying these are trivial personal matters that tell him nothing he doesn't already know.
>
> To such a person I must admit that I deserve his criticism, for communication was not my primary object. But my egotism seems justified by the understanding, to which the writing has led, of things

[1] p. 129
[2] p. 162
[3] p. 179/180
[4] p. 185/186

> that are of supreme importance to me, though possibly they are incommunicable.[1]

[1] p. 189

stefan themerson

Stefan Themerson was born in Plock, Poland[1] on January 25th 1910. During the First World War his family moved to Russia where his doctor father served in the pre-revolutionary army. After the Russian Revolution, Stefan returned to Poland, eventually moving to Warsaw to study physics and architecture. He initially wrote children's books, illustrated by his wife Franciszka, née Weinles, who was born in Warsaw on June 28th 1907; they married in 1931. Together and separately, they later worked as painters, filmmakers, and theatre designers. From 1931 – 1937 they and the co-operative they founded made a series of experimental films, all of which were lost in World War II, as were many of his extraordinary, experimental photograms of 1928-29[2]. Two of the films, *Europa*, 1930, from a poem by Anatol Stern[3] and *Apteka*, 1931-32 were subsequently partially recreated.

The couple moved to Paris in 1937 and became briefly involved in the avant-garde scene there until the outbreak of the war when Stefan joined the Polish army and Franciszka moved to London to work in wartime intelligence. During the war she produced a series of drawings called 'Unposted Letters' and he wrote *Professor Mmaa's Lecture*, which was eventually published in 1953. This is a satirical/philosophical novel about a world run by termites, who are investigating the body of what they call a 'homo' – 'called the bristleless mammal or the bald ape'[4], and speculating on the nature of human life. Themerson's friend Bertrand Russell (referred to in the book as 'our luminary Errtrand Russell'[5]) wrote the introduction.

---

[1] "a small, historic 12th century town in Poland with countless schools, churches and cemeteries"; from the cover of *Tom Harris*.

[2] Some of these were included *in The Urge to Create Visions*, written in 1936 but not published until 1983 by Gaberbocchus and De Harmonie in Amsterdam, with a preface by Themerson dated 1980.

[3] Published by Gaberbocchus, 1962.

[4] p. 28

[5] p. 28

> The book parodies so many points of view that the reader is left in doubt as to what if anything wins the author's assent. Perhaps this is as well. The world contains too many people believing too many things, and it may be that the ultimate wisdom is contained in the precept that the less we believe, the less harm we shall do.[1]

Stefan and Franciszka were reunited in London in 1942 in London and spent the rest of their lives in England until 1988, when they died within a few months of each other. In 1948 they founded the Gaberbocchus Press[2], which published their own work as well as that of Bertrand Russell, Kurt Schwitters, Alfred Jarry, the English avant-garde filmmaker and poet Oswell Blakeston and concrete and sound-poet Henri Chopin. Stefan Themerson wrote children's books, experimental novels (in the sense the term is used in this book), poetry, philosophy, essays on art and cinema, a play[3] and an opera[4], including words and music. Many of his works were written and rewritten, sometimes having been written earlier in Polish and sometimes existing in several versions; the editions I have used are the first English versions published by Gaberbocchus.[5]

---

[1] p. 10/11

[2] The name Gaberbocchus came from a Latin version of Jabberwocky by Lewis Carroll's uncle, Hassard Dodgson. See: Various Authors, *The Themersons and the Gaberbocchus Press: An Experiment in Publishing,* 1994, the catalogue to a New York exhibition.

[3] *Bone in the Throat*, written 1959, unpublished at the time but published in 2007 by Obscure Publications.

[4] *St Francis & the Wolf of Gubbio*, or "*Brother Francis' Lamb Chops*" An opera in 2 acts Text & music, Gaberbocchus, 1972.

[5] Almost all are now out of print; Gaberbocchus was taken over in 1979 by the Dutch publishing house Uitgeverij De Harmonie, who committed to making them available through the Athenaeum bookshop in the Netherlands; however, as of 2012 I have been unable to obtain new copies from this or any other source. *Bayamus*, 1965 and *Cardinal Pölätüo*, 1961, are available as reprints in a single volume: Boston, Exact Change, 1997. *Tom Harris*, 1967 and the later novels *Hobson's Island* and *The Mystery of the Sardine* have been reissued by the Dalkey Archive Press. Obscure Publications have also printed several of Themerson's texts, some for the first time, and made them freely available as PDFs online with the help and cooperation of the Themerson Archive (in London and

Letters to the Editor

NOT FOR HAMPSTEAD?

Sir,—We were initially (though no longer) amused when during the past year we received inquiries from various people, asking how they could obtain our books since they did not seem to be available from public libraries. It also transpired that they were often told that Gaberbocchus Press is a foreign publisher and the books were not obtainable. This seemed rather strange since we are members of the Publishers Association (and in the London Telephone Directory for that matter), and our books are regularly noted in *The Bookseller* list.

Recently we had a telephone call from an enterprising gentleman who actually looked for us in the Telephone Directory in order to get a catalogue, and asked us why we hide from the public to such an extent that our books are not even available from the public libraries.

To find out what was actually happening I applied, as an ordinary member of the public, to my local library in Hampstead for the three titles: *Cardinal Pölätüo* by Stefan Themerson, *Gimani* by Edmund Héafod, and *Pin* by Kurt Schwitters and Raoul Hausmann.

After a lapse of time I was informed by the assistant that Gaberbocchus is an American publisher and the books were not available in England. I showed him a catalogue with Gaberbocchus's address on it, and after checking it once more, the assistant admitted that they had some difficulties with the chief buying office. I asked what the difficulties were, and four days later received a letter from Mr. William R. Maidment, F.L.A., the Chief Librarian for the Borough of Hampstead, saying:

> I have had an opportunity of examining these books and they are, in my view, of such bizarre nature that they are likely to add little to the Library's resources. I do not, therefore, propose to add these volumes to stock.

Perhaps Mr. Maidment did not read the excellent reviews these books received in *The Times Literary Supplement*, perhaps he did not understand what they were about, and perhaps it should not be left to one man to judge these books on behalf of the Borough of Hampstead.

It seems to me a rather strange and high-handed way of behaviour, as well as a very clear-cut case of aesthetic censorship. Probably many people do not realize that such instances of aesthetic censorship actually occur.

GWEN BARNARD,
Director.

Gaberbocchus Press, 42A, Formosa Street, London, W.9.

---

online), curator Nick Wadley and Barbara Wright, friend of the Themersons and translator for Gaberbocchus of Jarry 's *Ubu Roi*. See Various authors. ed. Jan Kubasiewicz and Monica Strauss, The Themersons and the Gaberbocchus Press - an experiment in publishing, 1994

Some of Stefan and Franciszka's collaborations were published by Gaberbocchus in *Semantic Divertissements*, 1962.

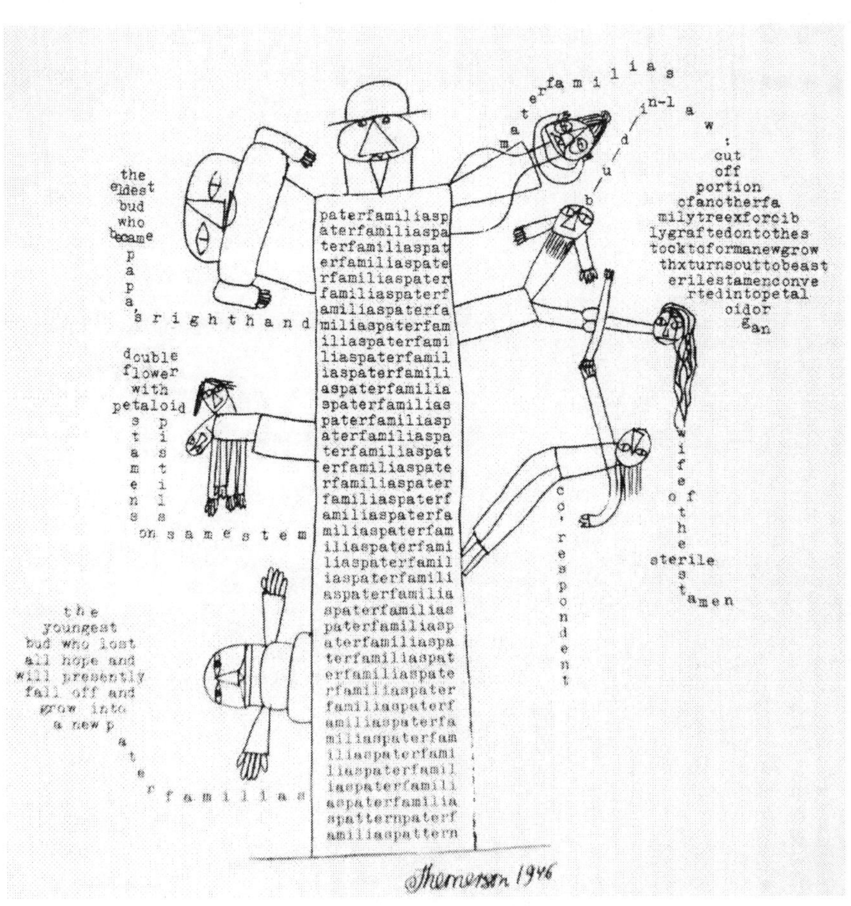

Many of Themerson's key concerns are addressed outside the context of fiction in a lecture he gave to the Architectural Association[1] which was reprinted by Gaberbocchus, along with selections from some of his other works as *Semantic Poetry*, 1975. In the lecture he addresses the question of what makes poetry. '*I don't know what poetry is*. Though I know (occasionally at least), what is poetry.'[2] Following Thomas à Kempis on contrition he says: 'So long as you don't ask me, I know. As soon as I'm asked, I don't. But I would rather feel it than be able to define it.'[3] Themerson proposes two theories of definition; the first

> professed that *the truth of the semiotic is in its pragmatics*. In other words, that the entire meaning of any intellectual conception is in its practical consequences. In other words that the truth of a proposition is to be judged by its results. For instance, the meaning of a statement that something is funny is in the fact that people will laugh, and the meaning of such a thing as a two-way mirror in a courtesan's bedroom is in the fact that it can be used to produce some sensational changes in the government.[4]

The second theory – that of the 'doubting Thomases' – is the 'anti-irrationalist' idea that '*the truth of a semiotic is in its empirics* . . . in other words that the analysis of language shows that it is futile to try to say what can only be shown.' Some things 'can neither be said nor be shown to our senses' like love, time, contrition, poetry. 'The poetry of the poem is not in the poem. Nor is it in what the poem is about. It is in us.'[5] Putting theory before practice is putting the cart before the horse and practically all Themerson's philosophical enquiries are in the form of fiction.

---

[1] February 5th, 1974

[2] p. 5

[3] p. 8

[4] p. 5/6

[5] p. 7

> That is, perhaps, where the philosophy of some of the 1968 art students went wrong. They seemed to have thought that theory comes before practice. They seemed to have thought that it is necessary to define what Art is before producing a Work of Art. Yet, (just as it was with you and me, and with our fathers and our sons) they didn't think it was necessary to define what Love is before making love.[1]

Themerson's views on poetry are playfully ambivalent: in *Cardinal Pölätüo*, the Cardinal, who is the father of Apollinaire, says 'the most evil thing in the world today is poetry', which is at least to take the business of poetry seriously. In a 1981 lecture 'The Chair of Decency', given in the Netherlands Themerson says:

> 'What I shall bring you is a flaming torch, a loud-hailer, an *Allons, Citoyens*! Fortunately . . . and it is not that I'm not capable of putting rhymes and rhythms into a howling cry . . . but, having lived through hairpin bends of history, and met and seen and heard some howling voices, both true and false (the former is more dangerous), I called my sense of humour to stop me, just in time.'[2]

---

[1] p. 5
[2] published in Dutch in 1982, published in English by Obscure Publications, 2007, also published by the same publisher as 'The Aim of Aims' in *Six Short Texts*, 2004.

The children's book *The Adventures of Peddy Bottom* – if it can really be called a children's book, Themerson said it was 'for children under thirteen and over thirty[1] - has something in common with Lewis Carroll; not surprising as the name Gaberbocchus came from Jabberwocky – Peddy asks the camel, who writes poetry, why he is lecturing in electricity: 'You see', said the camel, 'for lecturing in poetry they pay here with uncracked nuts, and I can't eat uncracked nuts, while for lecturing in electricity they pay with grass, and I *do* like grass'.[2]

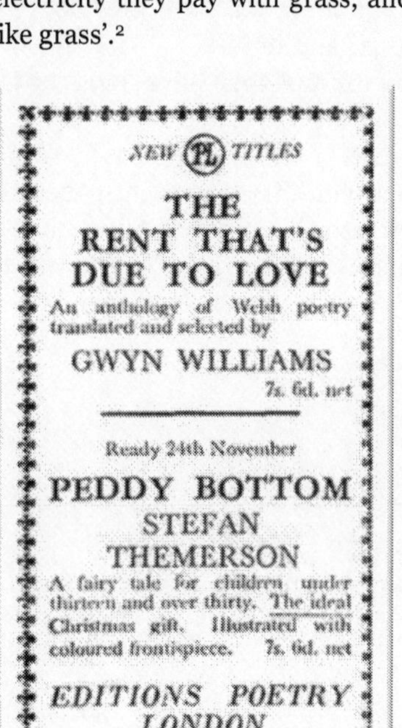

---

[1] In a letter, Themerson described it as a 'book for children and adults', *A Few Letters from the 1950s*, Obscure Publications, 2009, p. 3

[2] *The Adventures of Peddy Bottom,* first published by Editions Poetry, 1951, republished by Gaberbocchus, 1954, p. 14

For obvious reasons, Themerson had a special interest in Apollinaire – who, he points out, invented the word 'surrealist' - and he wrote the illustrated book *Apollinaire's Lyrical Ideograms*[1], this despite the fact that Cardinal Pölätüo spends most of his book trying to do away with Apollinaire. He uses Apollinaire's *calligrammes* or *'idéogrammes lyriques'* as an occasion to examine the meaning of words. Referring to examples where the words form the shape of a table he says:

> There is a difference between a table and a 'table'. This typographical device " ' " & " ' " is used by linguistic philosophers to make clear whether they mean a particular thing (a table) or the word that designates it (a 'table'). It sounds childishly simple, but . . . But what shall we do with Apollinaire's 'tables'? They are not tables (one cannot sit at them), they are 'tables'. And yet, they have both 'legs' and letters . . . They have letters not 'letters' (you *can* read them); but they have 'legs' not legs (you can't break them).[2]

In his *Semantic Sonata*[3], which, like a piano sonata, has movements, themes, development and variations, the trilingual Themerson, an observer rather than a native speaker of the English and French languages, ends with a 'Recapitulation' musing on the ontological status of words.

> Words about words
> are about words
> but words
> are about the rest of the world.
>
> And even words about words about words
> will not reach you
> without that part of the world
> which isn't words.

Semantic Poetry, explained and illustrated in *Bayamus*, is intended to strip words of their emotional accretions and concentrate on their meanings in relation to the external, objective world. These layers of reference and significance that cling to words cause beliefs to become embedded and, as

---

[1] First published in *Typographica*, 1966, republished by Gaberbocchus, 1968

[2] p. 13

[3] Written 1949/1950, first printed in *factor T*, Gaberbocchus Black Series no. 8/9, 1956, pp. 51-64, reprinted in *On Semantic Poetry*, op. cit., 1975, pp. 47-57 and the posthumous *Collected Poems*, Amsterdam, Gaberbocchus, 1998

Bertrand Russell said above, we have too many beliefs for our own good. 'It is through the emotional impact that wine becomes Blood, bread becomes Flesh, and a land becomes Holy and crying out for crusaders to deliver it from the hands of the Infidel.'[1] Themerson described his only opera, *St. Francis and the Wolf of Gubbio,* as a Semantic Opera. Referring to the concepts of Dislike, Needs and Tragedy, which are analysed in *factor T*, he gives instructions on the performance of the piece:

> What results is expressed in commonplace words, the words of the characters, who are the real authors of both the text and the music. Because the music here also comes directly from the arsenal of clichés stored in their minds. As you will see, there is dead music-less silence for a second or two (a pause for breathing) between the end of one line of text and the beginning of the next. Here, the relation of the music to the text is what colour may be to some line drawings. The bone structure of this work is built of words. Their meaning is essential. That is why I call it a Semantic Opera.[2]

At one point, St. Francis sings semantic lines, where he gives the definitions of the words.

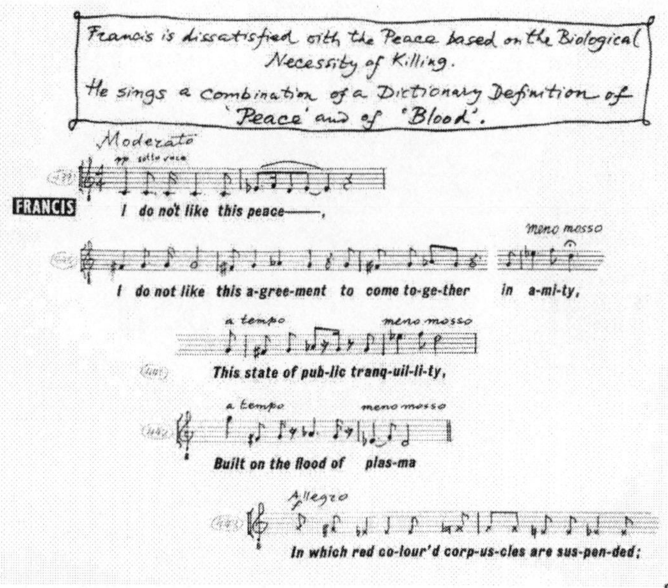

[1] *Apollinaire's Lyrical Ideograms,* p. 14
[2] op. cit., p. 9

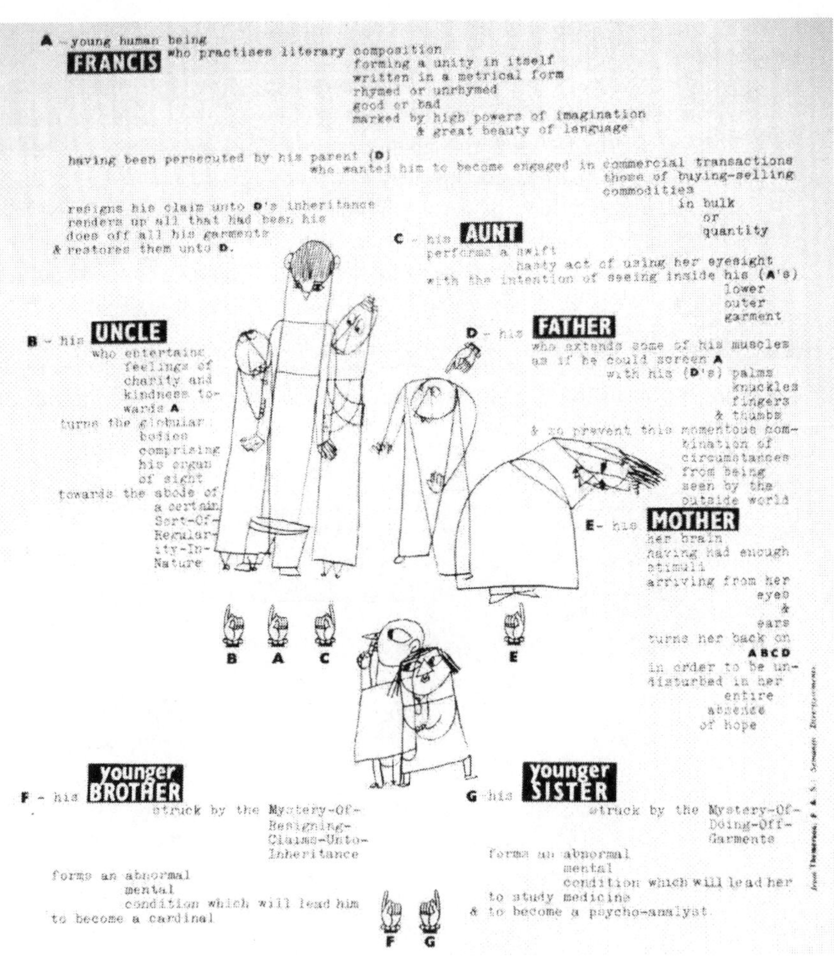
A - young human being
FRANCIS
who practises literary composition
forming a unity in itself
written in a metrical form
rhymed or unrhymed
good or bad
marked by high powers of imagination
& great beauty of language
having been persecuted by his parent (D)
who wanted him to become engaged in commercial transactions
those of buying-selling
commodities
in bulk
or
quantity
resigns his claim unto D's inheritance
renders up all that had been his
does off all his garments
& restores them unto D.
C - his AUNT
performs a swift
hasty act of using her eyesight
with the intention of seeing inside his (A's)
lower
outer
garment
B - his UNCLE
who entertains
feelings of
charity and
kindness to-
wards A
turns the globular
bodies
comprising
his organ
of sight
towards the abode of
a certain
Sort-Of-
Regular-
ity-In-
Nature
D - his FATHER
who extends some of his muscles
as if he could screen A
with his (D's) palms
knuckles
fingers
& thumbs
& so prevent this momentous combination of
circumstances
from being
seen by the
outside world
E - his MOTHER
her brain
having had enough
stimuli
arriving from her
eyes
&
ears
turns her back on
ABCD
in order to be un-
disturbed in her
entire
absence
of hope
B
A
C
E
F - his younger BROTHER
struck by the Mystery-Of-
Resigning-
Claims-Unto-
Inheritance
forms an abnormal
mental
condition which will lead him
to become a cardinal
G - his younger SISTER
struck by the Mystery-Of-
Doing-Off-
Garments
forms an abnormal
mental
condition which will lead her
to study medicine
& to become a psycho-analyst
F
G

There is more consideration of the status of words in *Logic, Labels and Flesh,* 1974, a philosophical essay which covers concrete poetry and Semantic Poetry (Themerson always capitalised it), and refers back to both *Bayamus* and *Cardinal Pölätüo.* Themerson considers 'noun-less thoughts': ideas that not only cannot be expressed in words but that do not exist in word form.

> Bach creates and conveys something about the world which is a thought and yet it is neither made in words nor can one convey it in words; and so does Picasso; and so does a Cathode-ray tube showing a luminous abstract pattern, which like a great poetic metaphor contains and conveys a thought about some relationships that are in the universe.
>
> None of these thoughts could be adequately formed in words. Perhaps, because they are noun-less thoughts, and in our terrestrial historically developed word-languages it is impossible to construct a proper sentence without a noun.[1]

Themerson says he recognises three realities:

physical reality,
conceptual reality,
and the reality of words.

These he relates to John Locke: 'What I call "physical reality" he calls "the reality of things" ("their essences", "their being"); what I call "conceptual reality" he calls "ideas" (simple and complex); and what I call "words" he calls "words".'[2] Themerson also quotes from and illustrates Ogden and Richard's *The Meaning of Meaning*, with its triangles of Thought or Reference, Symbol and Referent, as well as A.J. Ayer (who is satirised in Cardinal Pölätüo). Such 'classical formalists' are also attacked in the 1981 lecture 'The Chair of Decency'.

---

[1] *Logic, Labels and Flesh,* Gaberbocchus, 1974, p. 166/167
[2] p. 74

> And here, straight from the lopped and barked wood of bare trunks, come some classical formalists, who dream their dream about the world of distinct nouns and predicates, governed by the yes-or-no-law of the excluded middle, the world in which things (including you and me and him and her) are what they are, and are not what they are not. And they dream their dreams to their logical conclusions, which are true in all possible worlds except the world in which we live. Because in the world in which we live, no noun is timeless, no predicate makes sense without the rest of the universe, no fact is what it is and nothing else, and no man is an island.

In *Logic, Labels and Flesh* Themerson also approvingly quotes Marinetti (along with Apollinaire, an obvious predecessor for Themerson) on the noun: ' "By stripping it of all adjectives and by isolating it, the noun, worn out by the multiple contrasts and by the weight of classical and decadent adjectives, can be brought back to its absolute values" (*Les Mots en Liberté*).' Almost exactly how Themerson describes Semantic Poetry. In 'The Chair of Decency' Themerson talks about the way words are used to gain and maintain political power; one of the reasons Semantic Poetry is important for stripping words of accretions of associations:

> Some naïve lovers of semantics believe that if only our rulers, our saviours (of all sorts), could understand the meaning of their own pronouncements, they would amend their ways. What an illusion! They, the saviours, know the mechanism of Language much better than all the Semanticists, Linguistic philosophers, and Logical formalists put together. That's how they know how to use it to play upon the prejudices of the mob: you and me.
>
> And, when a Poet, or a Novelist, becomes a Demagogue, the same applies to him. Because POETRY, as well as POLITICS, may be morally vicious, and intellectually dishonest. In such cases, both poetry and oratory – political, religious, philosophical – are like a crime. In the same work, Themerson asks: does our traditional, linear way of writing and reading structure the way we see the world?

Elsewhere Themerson had said that what most troubles the typographer is what most advances art. In *Logic, Labels and Flesh* he considers typography as more than mere decoration: the way words look affects their meaning and our very thought patterns:

Typographers' Contribution to Logic

> In the early days of printing and still today, printers picked up the characters one at a time and shoved them into a thing called a compositor's stick. The result was the purely linear patterns of
>
> **good: and God divided the light from**
>
> words. Now if, as it has been said – the pattern of linguistic signs, such as those on a printed page, reflects the relationships that are in the world, then the printing technique must indeed have had some bearing on our way of philosophical thinking.[1]

In an earlier philosophical work, *factor T*[2], (where, again, Cardinal Pölätüo appears), Themerson had posited the essentially tragic nature (the factor T) of 'man', by which he means 'anything (a beast, a plant, or a machine) whose nervous system is split into two parts so that the one part prompts it to perform actions leading to the satisfaction of its primary needs while the other part restrains it from performing such actions.'[3] This split, stops us, for example, from killing, even when killing may be in our interests. He gives the example of the inhabitants of Notwahrocteh who cannot bear tomatoes but need the vitamin C that tomatoes would give them. They solve the problem by killing and eating their neighbours, who do eat tomatoes.[4] 'This is not a dramatic conflict. It is sillily unavoidable and therefore Tragic.'[5] Assigning N = needs; D = dislike and T = tragic, he says

> Whether your [D]islike is to kill, or to risk your life in battle or in work, or to have your offspring and your [N]ecessity – to eat, or to get rid of the semen that produces itself in your silly body, *factor T*, original Tragedy, remains and has to be acknowledged.[6]

---

[1] ibid, p. 160

[2] Gaberbocchus, 1972. This book contains three earlier works: *Beliefs, Tethered and Untethered*, written 1952; *factor T*, written 1953-1955 (both works previously published together in 1956 and republished in 1958 in *The First Dozen*) and *The Pheromones of Fear*, first published as 'Will the Discovery of *d* Lead Us to Ethicophysics?' in *The Scientist Speculates*, Heinemann, 1962.

[3] p. 28

[4] p. 6

[5] p. 9. These considerations reappear in the *opera St. Francis and the Wolf of Gubbio.*

[6] p. 11

'Rational' systems do not capture this but religions 'base their theologies' on the fact that 'our situation on the earth's surface is unavoidably silly – (Tragic).'[1] It is just this 'tragic' silliness illuminates all Themerson's work.

[1] p. 11

The manuscript of the original version of *Bayamus* was dated 1944; it was originally published by itself in 1949 by Editions Poetry, then the expanded edition was published by Gaberbocchus in 1965 as *Bayamus and the Theatre of Semantic Poetry: a novel.*[1] It introduces Themerson's theory of Semantic Poetry – 'a kind of writing of poetry, with words skinned of every associational aureola, taken directly as they are supplied by the common dictionary'[2] – and gives many examples of 'translations' from conventional poetry into semantic form[3].

"—calls in question 'just about every corrupting dogma of our fashionable intellectual and aesthetic dandies—an extremity of alertness not morbid or decorative but like a sudden new angle of light. I found it impossible to put down."
(*Robert Nye, Tribune*)

BAYAMUS

a novel by STEFAN THEMERSON. New Edition, 112pp., paperback, 8s. 6d.
"an uproariously funny novel"
(*Poetry London*)
"nearly as mad as the world"
(*Bertrand Russell*)
Gaberbocchus

Later, in the 1960s, concrete poets regarded *Bayamus* as a key predecessor. In an article on concrete poetry, its leading British exponent dsh (dom Sylvester Houédard), specifically referred to it in a very experimental article on the history of concrete poetry.[4]

---

[1] Subsequently reprinted with *Cardinal Pölätüo,* Boston, Exact Change, 1997

[2] *A Few Letters*, op. cit., p. 14. In the same letter he compared these associations to the overtones of a note of music:

> Most of the words used in poetic writings nowadays consist of overtones - the fundamental tone, (exact meaning) being (as apparently so obvious, evident) disregarded or lost, - gone. We very seldom think about the fundamental tone (exact meaning), and if we do, we very often take it not as it may be defined, but by reconstructing it from the harmonics we hear (associations)., p. 13

[3] Many of these were not included in the 1949 edition; the final versions are reprinted in *On Semantic Poetry*, op. cit., and *Collected Poems*, op. cit.

[4] *Times Literary Supplement,* Aug 6, 1964. Themerson visited dsh in his cell at Prinknash Abbey and wrote the introduction to dsh's *Begin again : a book of reflections & reversals*, Brampton LYC Publications, 1975.

finally great britain—1st eye-concrete pbd was scotland 1963 by ihf in his POTH & fishsheet (moura / xisto / a de campos / hendry / hollo / morgan / ihf / jonathan williams / mary solt)—in england was ihf pbd in aylsford review 1963—still not quite everywhere apart from fi j & b advts in punch 1962 & current pp run-proof leg in tatler (both uncredited) it is ± level w/ syntactic olson-zukofsky &c. blackmountaineer as felt influence here tho various lacks not muns only hold some advances frustratingly up — 1962 Edwin morgan / ian h finlay / anselm hollo / myself all came to concrete directions out of different places thru TLS letter 250562 on *international movement* from de melo e castro in re article *poetry prose & the machine* TLS 040562—sir herbert read (vocal avowals 1962) / jn furnival / jn sharkey independently — stefan themerson had preceded us w / starpoems in bayamus 1949—then (ear-concrete) wm stone / margaret lothian / charles cameron / mike weaver — thru gomringer contact w/ garnier—thru him w/ chopin & 5e saison now OU ? group & links w/ dada & other-ways w/ eg locus solus poets harry mathews / rbt lax / emmett williams / brion gysin (hallucinating strobo-scopic giftpoem in olympia-2 ?first step to mechanized poetry : machine poem fi *i am* w/ geo macBeth) / wm burroughs (cf poem silent sunday in budd / burroughs / brown peinture-poésie-musique rencontre at stadler mars-avril 64)—projects in gb include kinetic — fi ihf's poemorama — sharkey's wordfilm—an OU? film w/ chopin audiotrack to my typestract—furnival's abacuspoem — weaver's motorized BOMBpoem edwin morgan's motorizables—the courier 1963 *movement in art* article & RCA 1964 *random/planned art in motion* expo helped dissolve luminodynamist-poet frontier over-here—1st ? moving poem furnival's origami mobilization of FROG-POND-PLOP*—cf too his deviltrap & priesthole & deckchair poems sharkeys scrollpoems my un-folds & space-invasions by fi diter rot's boks & bruno munari's mobile paper-folds—vis-à-vis kinetic (& dynamic) artists are fi aubertin / boto / pol bury / calder / jn healy / hoenich / michael kidner / gyula kosice / frank j malina / group MU paris / group N padua / julio le parc / bridget riley / nicholas schoeffer / sobrino / j r soto / steele / group T milano / v tarkis / jn tinguely / gregorio vardangea / victor de vasarély / yavaral / &c june 1964 foundation of international kinetic poetry fund at cambridge by mike weaver & hookup w/ popper schoeffer malina &c—& planned ?autumn expo cambridge—plus? osiris expo oxford—3 autumn bbc-3 talks

first decade wasnt that art (concrete 4-D kinetic) edged thru gutenberg galaxy to poetry but that poets as poets completed the scene

2nd decade 64-74 shaping to total fusion poet-painter-player in brain-controlled machine creation (l'important c'est d'avoir vaincu la machine—sleeve to 1st OU? disk)—coexistential scramble man/tool barrier like to electronic tautology in clunk of innerlit poesie.

*my translation of matsuo bashō's haiku *furu ike ya / kawazu tobikomu / mizu no oto*—also cf morgan's motor-izables.

> 'And now, which do you want to see, the Theatre of Anatomy or the Theatre of Semantic Poetry?' said he.
> 'Both', said I.
> 'Well', said he, 'the Theatre of Anatomy is in 1815.'
> 'I don't mind', said I.
> 'That's O.K. then', said he, 'let's go.'
> And we went to the Theatre of Anatomy[1]

The eponymous Bayamus is a three-legged man, born a woman, who attaches a roller skate to his third leg, and is very concerned to father children so as to create more three-legged humans: '*Je sème à tout vent*', he says[2]. In the first part of the novel the unnamed narrator and Bayamus take a surreal and picaresque journey to the Theatre of Semantic Poetry, meeting a selection of real and imaginary characters along the way, including, at the Café Royal on Regent Street, Karl Meyer 'author of the scenario of the expressionist film *The Cabinet of Dr. Caligari*. I was startled. I knew that he had died in 1943. Admittedly I wasn't at his funeral, but I read about his death in a newspaper: DEATH OF MAN WHO DROVE CAMERA IN PERAMBULATOR.'[3] They also meet Themerson's friend Kurt Schwitters, '*dadaist* and inventor of *Merz* art.'[4]

Visiting a brothel, where Bayamus hopes to *sème,* the narrator does not wish to participate in the presence of someone else, but meditates on 'professional women'.

> True professionals have in general certain magnificent features: they are moderate in character and temperament; they are of sound cool

---

[1] Gaberbocchus 1965 edition, p. 7. Themerson's 'clarified' this in a letter to his Swedish translator in 1950:

> "in 1815" means primarily a point in time, but it is talked about as if it were a point in space. Time is treated here on a conversationally equal footing with space so: "in 1815" means both: in 1815 A.D., and "in 1815" (as in "London", or in "England"; - as if "1815" were a name of a street or place etc.) ((The description of the Theatre of Anatomy (Chapter 1) is that of an early 19th Century Theatrum Anatomicum. The description of the road leading from it to the Theatre of Semantic Poetry (Chapter 2) - (Victorian imitation of Gothic, sham Ionic column, Cafe Royal) suggests our coming back in time. (Besides, there is an intimation; Theatre of Anatomy; Anatomy of Language - Theatre of Semantic Poetry; description of the Theatre of Anatomy, repeated on page 74-75 in the chapter "Theatre of Semantic Poetry"; - freaks in bottles in Chapter 1, and the living freaks at the Bottle Party in Chapter the last.))), *A Few Letters*, op. cit., p. 7

[2] p. 40

[3] p. 10

[4] p. 12

> judgement; not given to extremes in opinions and prejudices; avoiding vehemence of feeling and expression, or violence in action. They possess a keen, natural perception of what is right and fitting, a quick apprehension of the right thing to say or do; instinctive skill, adroitness and discretion in dealing with persons or difficult situations. They don't ask personal questions and they intrude on nobody with accounts of their own private life, which remains free from professional business, and which they keep well closed to the public in general. Their mind is impartial, just, their intelligence thoroughly formed, developed by training and experience; not superficial, or childish; their thoughts and actions resulting from those mental faculties are prudent, wise, based upon careful deliberation; their movements are well thought out; complete in every detail.[1]

And so on, at great length. These qualities are of course completely contrasted with those of practitioners of '*dada* and *Merz* art'. On the way to the Theatre, the pair become involved in a spontaneous street conversation.

> A bystander who had evidently heard the last words spoken by the man called 'Doctor', approached the man who was still leaning against the lamp-post:
>
> 'Breast-feeding is best, Sir, but Utent Barley and milk is an excellent substitute, digestive and nourishing, inexpensive and easy to prepare. If you really want to forget beggars, Indians and Negroes. . . .'
>
> 'Well, Sir, answered the man leaning against the lamp-post; and he pointed a business-like finger at one of the cars running along the road – 'Here's a 10-h.p. quality saloon bristling with improvements! For performance – a quieter, more flexible power unit; redesigned cylinder head giving extra power; improved gearbox and back axle; variable ratio cam gear steering. For comfort – deeper seating with centre arm rest at rear; heavily sound-proofed body panels; flush-fitting sliding roof. You are dealing with Utent Barley and I'm dealing with these things. Buy one of them for £310 plus approx. £87 Purchase Tax and I'll send you a 1d. stamp for a copy of this invaluable booklet on substitute Breast-feeding.[2]

These exchanges come to involve several passers-by and only end when an 'irritated voice behind him' says:

---

[1] p. 46

[2] p. 56/57

> Solution to his problem is: ACROSS – 1. Dressed crab; 7. Denominator; 8. Asses; 10. Front; 12. Dab; 14. Hue; 16. Marsh Mallow; 18 and 19. Month of May. DOWN – 1, 8 and 16. Dad and Mum; 2. 'D/Ennis; 3. S-am; 4. Do-n/ot/; 5. Ratio; 6, 11 and 17; Bar the Way; 9. South; 10. Freda; 13. Baron; 15. H-i-lum.[1]

Arriving at the Theatre of Semantic Poetry, the narrator realises that the name on the poster advertising the event was his, and that he is the main speaker. He remembers an Australian poem quoted by E. B. Tylor[2]

> Kardang garro
> Mammul garro
> mela nadjo
> Nunga broo

> I didn't mind that it was composed by Australians. It was translated and I understood it much better than the poetry I had known until then.

> 'Young-brother again
> Son again
> Hereafter I-shall
> See never'

> I considered it the best, the most universal poem of the world. There was nothing which could be specially connected with Hugo's or Mickiewicz's particular countries, with Homer's or Dante's particular time, with Byron's or Goethe's particular language, and there were no words in it the meaning of which would change according to the reader's country, time or language.[3]

In Semantic Poetry, each word 'should have one and only one meaning.' Words 'should be well defined. They should be washed clean of all those diverse aureolas which depend on the condition of the market.' So, instead of using the word 'war', which 'carries with it different associations for different people', Semantic Poetry might substitute: '*The open conflict between nations, or active international hostility carried on by force of arms.*' Semantic Poetry's purpose is:

---

[1] p. 59/60
[2] British anthropologist, 1832 - 1917, founder of cultural anthropology. In *Primitive Culture,* 1871, he posited an evolutionary relationship between primitive and modern cultures; also provided the earliest, still commonly-accepted definition of culture.
[3] p. 64

> to translate poems not from one language into another but from a language composed of words so poetic that they had lost their impact, - into something that would give them new meaning and flavour. I had been fed-up with political oratory and with ezrapoundafskinian jazz plus joyce plus dada-merz plus some homespun rachmaninoff glossitis. Avant-garde, I thought, go back to Diderot.[1]

The narrator goes on to provide 'translations' of a number of poems, the first of which is the Chinese poem *Drinking to the Moon* by Li Po. The first verse, translated into English by Winifred Galbraith reads:

> The wine among the flowers,
> O lonely me!
> Ah, moon, aloof and shining,
> I drink to thee.[2]

The narrator 'translates' this into Semantic Poetry, writing the 'number of words that form an entity, a bouquet of names by which a rose may be called . . . as I would write the notes of a musical chord: one under the other'.[3]

---

[1] p. 67
[2] p. 66
[3] p. 68

The fermented
grape-
juice
among the reproductive
parts
of
seed-plants

O! I'm conscious
of
my state
of
being isolated from others!

Ah! Body attendant revolving keeping & shining
on about 238,840 miles by
the (mean) reflecting the light
Earth aloof radiated
by
the
sun
into
my
mouth
I take
& while expressing the hope for thy success
swallow
the
liquid

The narrator translates the other three verses of the Chinese poem and then moves on to a Russian ballad about a ride in a troika in the snow.

Heigh
my large flowing mane
three powerful coarse and
solid-hoofed long
tail[1]
domesticated mammals with

And, later in the same poem, he translates the idea of snow:

[1] This poem is very similar to one by dsh, from his collection *Op and kinkon poems and some non-kinkon,* Writers Forum Poets number 14, 1965. 'Kinkon', a term invented by Houédard, is a concatenation of kinetic and concrete.

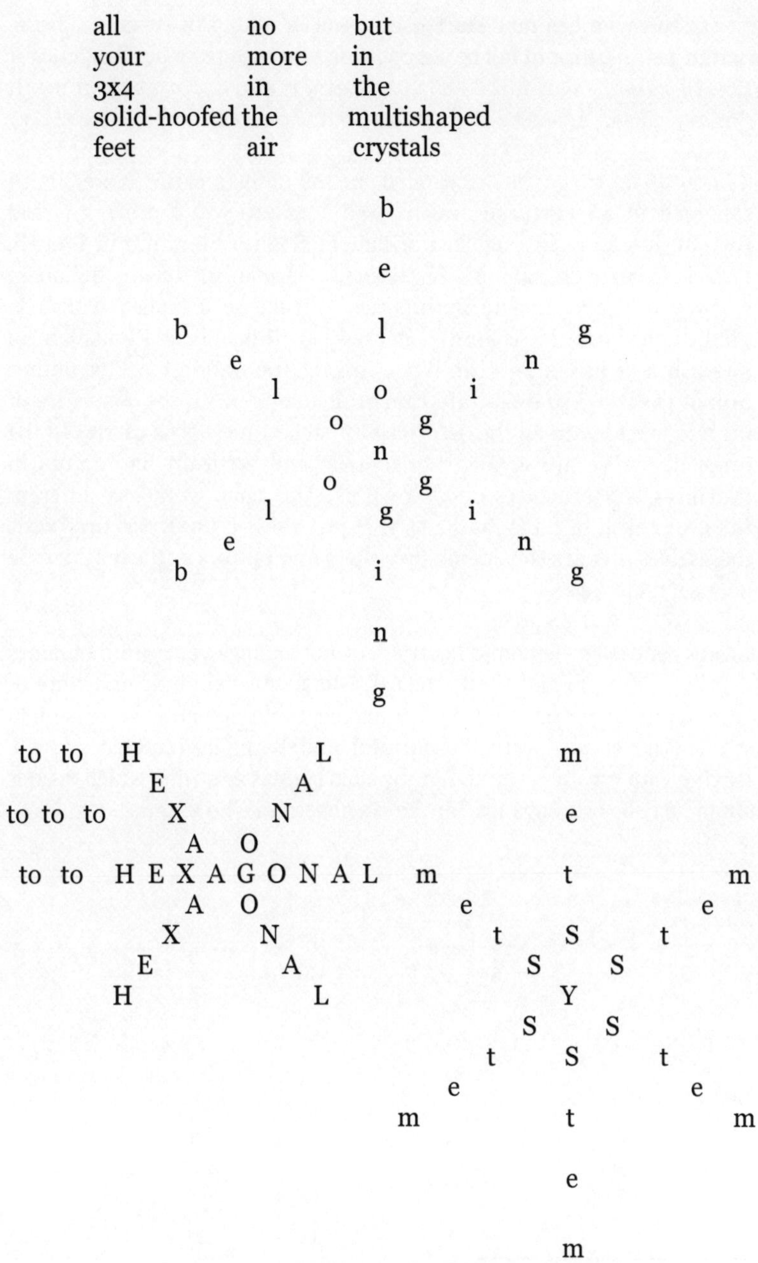

formed by the freezing of water vapour.

Later, the narrator, who has now started to speak in a kind of semantic prose, finds himself in a strange room full of people, with what seems to be a ringmaster in the centre. He asks the narrator: 'Semantic Poetry is also *against* something. It is against provincialism. Against a limited intellectual outlook. Isn't that so?'[1]

> 'I know 46 languages,' he continued, 'not all of them perfectly well, but I can read in 46 languages easily. And I assure you I prefer to read Russian literature in English translation, English literature in French, French in Spanish, Spanish in German, German in Italian, Italian in Norwegian, Norwegian in Portuguese, Portuguese in Polish, Polish in Yiddish, Yiddish in Hebrew, Hebrew in Rumanian, Rumanian in Swedish, Swedish in Turkish. When I read a translation I feel the author cannot cheat me so easily. He cannot delude me with the sonorities of his words and with all the associations each of his words carries in the original. . . We are divided horizontally and vertically and across in provinces and provinces and provinces. The same word has different echoes in each of them, and alas it is just these echoes, not the words themselves that are considered by writers and readers as the most subtle poetical material.[2]

The ringmaster continues 'Semantic Poetry does not arrange verses into bunches of flowers. It bares a poem and shows the extra-linguistic data hidden behind it. There is no room for hypnosis in its rhymes and rhythms. Semantic verse is lucid and sober.'[3] The novel ends with the narrator and Bayamus reunited and the narrator leaving with a baby given to him by the ringmaster's wife, which, as her legs are bound, may be his, Bayamus' or the ringmasters. Who knows?

---

[1] p. 93
[2] p. 94
[3] p. 99

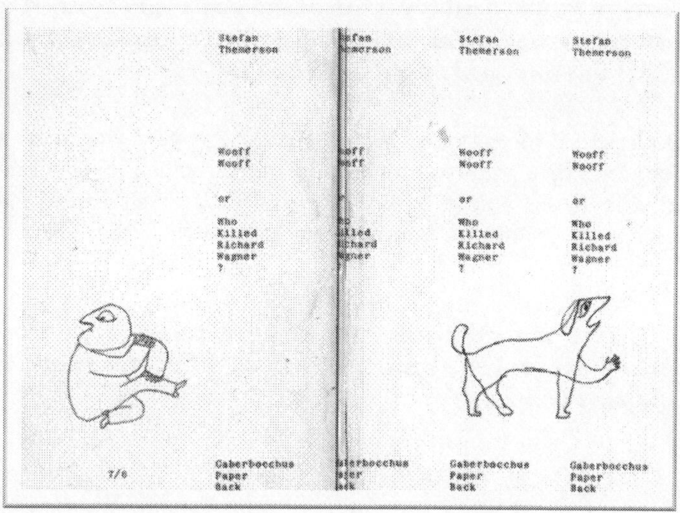

Like *Bayamus*, The very short *Wooff, Wooff, or Who Killed Richard Wagner*,[1] is about the poetic use of words. Also like Bayamus it has an unnamed narrator with a strange companion, Lampaphedor Metaphrastes, with an opening scene reminiscent of Bulgakov's *The Master and Margarita*. Metaphrastes is afraid that 'one day someone might find it logical to have my left leg and my right arm cut off.'[2] The narrator questions his idea of logic, which he had been considering as a result of listening to the speakers in Hyde Park; 'ten out of a dozen of them were applying fairly strictly the rules of that part of syntax which is now called Logic.'[3] However, even though all the speakers wanted the "good", 'their conclusions always doddered, and sometimes they differed diametrically'. That was a rather unhappy state of affairs.' Because of disagreements over the application of logic: 'One man has to die because another has found it logically justifiable.'[4]

> **you know that preferring one chain of reasoning to another doesn't result from it being true, but from what you happen to be. If you are one who seeks power, you don't care about the mis-applying of formal logic to conversational**

[1] Originally published in 1951, reprinted by Gaberbocchus in 1967 and again in *On Semantic Poetry*, 1975

[2] 1967 edition, p. 8

[3] p. 10

[4] p. 11

> **languages, and you impose your preferred chain of argument on others. But if you are not, you feel rather sad. And helpless.**[1]

In his helplessness, the narrator recalls Anatole France saying that even the smallest dog feels he is at the centre of the universe, so he gets on all fours and begins to bark. 'It was a good bark. There was black air all around me, and I barked more boldly.'[2] But then he sees a 'yellowish patch' in the beam of a street lamp.

> **The patch looked like the page of a book, or like a newspaper cutting. I bent towards it and began to read:**
>
> **LADIES' TROUSSEAUX FOR £100**
>
> **Twelve best 'Dagmar' Chemises, trimmed with insertion and work. @ fifiteen-six. Nine six o !**
> **Six 'Alexandra' Chemises, trimmed with real lace. @ eighteen six. Five eleven o !**
> **Twelve 'Belgravia' Nightdresses. @ twenty-two six. Thirteen ten o!**
> **Six 'Princess' ditto. @ twenty-five o! Seven ten o !**
> **Twelve Pairs Long Cloth Drawers, trimmed with work. @ ten six. Six six o !**
> **Six Ditto ditto ditto lace @ twelve six. Three fifteen o !**
>
> **I read it as if it were a poem. Whether any particular thing is a work of art or not, that depends on you, the reader. You, the author, say what you want to say, and then it all depends on you, the reader. Everything written, if you say in it what you want to say, has its ideal reader. But it may happen that you, the author, are living here and now, while you, the reader, may live far away, or may have died a hundred years ago, or may not have been born yet.**[3]

The narrator thinks: 'Well, the man who wrote that certainly said what he wanted to say, and with perfect clarity of thought and style. Yet, it was primarily the

---

[1] p. 12
[2] p. 14
[3] p. 15/16

musical side of his writing that I was impressed by.' He likes the 'percussion of dittos. They carried on the rhythm, but had meaning only by virtue of what had been sung before.'[1] It read 'like a surrealist poem. . . You didn't know its purpose, but you had the feeling that somewhere, somehow it had made or did make or it would make sense, had had or would have its purpose.'[2] The 'poem' 'had its own purpose, irrelevant to you.'

and then you realise that if you read it as a poem, such a line as :

Two Muslinette Dressing Jackets. @ twenty-seven six. Two fifteen Oh !

gives you an insight into the working of the world, while a philosopher's assertion that : THE OBJECT IS TO ATTAIN THAT ENORMOUS ENERGY OF GREATNESS WHICH CAN MODEL THE MAN OF THE FUTURE BY MEANS OF DISCIPLINE AND ALSO BY MEANS OF THE ANNIHILATION OF MILLIONS OF THE BUNGLED AND BOTCHED, AND WHICH CAN YET AVOID GOING TO RUIN AT THE SIGHT OF THE SUFFERING CREATED THEREBY, THE LIKE OF WHICH HAS NEVER BEEN SEEN BEFORE does not discover any world for you, but deforms savagely the one you live in.[3]

The rhythm of these poems said more than the 'trumpets of the RHINE GOLD, with its power of making you the Master of the World' and made more sense than

Nietzsche, Wagner and Bergson, even if they did sound like automatic writing.

It *was* automatic writing. The manager of *Mrs. Adley Bourne, Underclothing Department, 37, Piccadilly, W.*, who wrote it a century ago, was only the nib of the real author's pen. The real author was THE EPOCH, built of myriads of things and happenings, the truth, sense and

---

[1] p. 17

[2] p. 18

[3] p. 18/19

> **purpose of which are already becoming as remote and obscure to us as the functioning of a brain engaged in writing an automatic poem. . .**
>
> **Time turns advertisements into poems, and Time turns poems into advertisements, because Time changes the reader, and it depends on the reader whether a thing is or is not art.**[1]

Sitting on the bench under the street lamp, the narrator notices an old man sitting next to him and then sees two burly policemen. He tries to talk to the policemen but they seem to think he is a dog; the only way he can communicate with them is by saying 'Wooff! Wooff!' which they understand to mean whatever he is thinking. After meeting again with Metaphrastes, who tells him that 'certain famous people who have been considered dead for many decades are still alive'[2] he is arrested for the murder of the old man in the park.

> **"I suppose his name wasn't Friedrich Nietzsche?" I said, as one might say : ' I suppose he didn't come from Mars '.**
>
> **" No ," answered the detective quietly, " as far as we know, his name was Richard Wagner ; Friedrich Nietzsche was killed on Tuesday and Henri Bergson on Friday morning. I suppose you knew that ?"**
>
> **"Gentlemen ! Gentlemen !" exclaimed Lampaphedor Metaphrastes, " you're making a great mistake, gentlemen ! Every schoolboy knows that Richard Wagner died in 1883, Nietzsche in 1900, and Bergson in 1941."**
>
> **"I can show you the very fresh corpses, Sir, if you would like to see them," said the detective**.[3]

It turns out that Metaphrastes is an 'interpreter' to President Truman and Mr Russell; this, he explains, is different to being a translator. 'The World is more complicated than the truths about it. And so they have to be interpreted. To the people, they are interpreted by artists and writers. To men of action, they are

---

[1] p. 20/21
[2] p. 35
[3] p. 38/39

interpreted by *me*!'[1] Men of action 'cannot afford not to know what their truth is like in other people's minds.'[2] Even though it is a mathematical truth that 1 + 1 = 2, there are exceptions: 'if you are adding one drop to one drop', that makes one, and 'when you add one atom-bomb to one atom-bomb, in which case I don't know the result.'[3] Like Pyrrho of Elis, he is a skeptic.

> **I'm not saying WHITE when the majority says BLACK ; I'm not saying BLACK when the majority says WHITE, but I do say CHLOROPHYLL when the majority says GREEN, and when the majority says CHLOROPHYLL, I do ask : 'Have you seen that beautiful GREENNESS ?' Because the world is more rich than the truths about it.**[4]

The police have solid evidence against the narrator and Metaphrastes. His counsel brings in two psychiatrists, who cannot agree whether he hates his father and loves his mother or vice versa. He asks for a 'behaviourist' but the counsel tells him people do not like behaviourists and that he 'might just be one of Sartre's personages, and might have in my heart an indetermination, a nothingness, instead of a character, and so, après avoir fait n'importe quoi, I might still be capable of doing n'importe quoi.'[5] The narrator, Metaphrastes and the driver are all convicted.

> **Two weeks and two days after the following Sunday we were hanged, all three of us. I don't know how Lampaphedor Metaphrastes and his driver felt about it, but for me it was a very important experience. The field of my pleasurable concerns changed abruptly, and my chief interest since has been to make grow several grains I found in the few cubic feet of the prison cemetery earth above me.**[6]

---

[1] p. 42
[2] p. 43
[3] p. 44
[4] p. 48/49
[5] p. 53.
[6] p. 64

The Life of Cardinal Pölätüo with Notes on his Writings his Times and his Contemporaries[1] like *Bayamus*, is subtitled 'a novel'. The story opens in 1880, when the eponymous cardinal is 78 years old. He is still alive in 1915, towards the end of the novel, and reappears in several of Themerson's later works when he is even older. Much of the novel is about his writing the '6935 pages of the *Philosophy of Pölätüomism*', his defence of religion and attack on logical positivism. The Cardinal is the father of Guillaume Apollinaire by the Countess Kostrowicki, who carries him in her womb for 18 years, having originally only planned to carry him for 7 years. She announces his birth to the Cardinal in a letter.

> *. . . I should not like you, Eminence, to take it amiss, that I carried him for a whole eleven years longer than was settled between us. Eighteen years en somme. However, I trust that Y. E. will agree with me that to produce a poet one needs at least nine times more than to produce an elephant. Et Guillaume n'est pas un elephant, je vous assure; il est un Apollinaire.*
>
> *Kissing the Sacred Purple, I am my Lord.*
>
> *Yr. aff. cousin*
>
> *Angelique*[2]

[1] Gaberbocchus, 1961, republished together with *Bayamus*, Boston, Exact Change, 1997

[2] p. 11

Pölätüo is disturbed to be the father of a poet:

> if he felt a danger, as he did, he felt it neither among the physicists nor among the astronomers, busy with dead matter, nor even among the naturalists, nosing into the matrix from which living creatures are made, but among the poets; - the poets who dare to attempt alchemy – not with that *Materia Prima* which, in conjunction with *Forma Corporeitatis* constitutes the Body of Man, but with the *Substantial Form* which transcends the Law of Change and constitutes the Soul of Man; - the poets who interfere with its *vis cogitativa*; the poets who cause accidents to happen to Its precious Immaterial Substance; who meddle in their own irresponsible way with this only Origin of All Vital and Mental Performances, the Origin created each time individually by God for each body, and ordained by Him to be entrusted to the priest's care, and not to their suspect influence. The most evil thing in the world today is Poetry. And as, for the Cardinal, Voltaire was a poet, it would be difficult to say that he felt danger where there was none.[1]

Given the narrator's position in Themerson's later *Special Branch*, where he pits poets' 'winged words' against Plato, and Themerson's admiring book on Apollinaire, we may suppose this is not Themerson's own view. We may also wonder whether Pölätüo is meant to remind us of Plato and Pölätüomism of Platonism. Having unwittingly 'begotten Thine Adversary', the Cardinal promises God he will 'erase him from the surface of the Earth in whatever way we shall consider proper.'[2] This he tries to do repeatedly by sending Apollinaire to various wars to try to get him killed. However, he needs to wait until Guillaume is 19 before he can send him to war, so he has 19 years to work on his philosophy, intending to write a page a day, giving 6940 pages of his work.

---

[1] p. 13/14
[2] p. 14

Pölätüomism distinguishes two categories of knowledge:

1
DIRECT KNOWLEDGE

We

Pölätüo

have Direct Knowledge

of the existence of God.

He revealed Himself to us and we have seen Him; not through the Embassy of our eyes but directly in the parieto-occipital region of our brain. We spoke to Him, and He answered us, and we heard Him in the Inner End of our Ear. We felt Him with all our direct senses. We are a witness to His Existence.

N.B. 1 to pagina 1.:
AND THIS EXPERIENCE OF OURS BREAKS THE VICIOUS CIRCLE OF HUME WHO CLEARLY DID NOT HAVE DIRECT KNOWLEDGE OF GOD.

2
INDIRECT KNOWLEDGE

They who employ indirect methods deny that God is known by the Gentiles through created things. Let us assume that they are right. Let us assume that Indirect Knowledge gives us no evidence of the existence of God.

But we by no means demand this of it. Indirect Knowledge, based on the Intermediary of the Outer End of the Eye and the Ear and the Nose, claims rather to explain, if not now then in the future of OURSELVES.

Therefore also us who have Direct Knowledge of the existence of God.

In order to do this, Indirect Knowledge will move all the cog-wheels of physics, chemistry, biology, sociology, educational theory – And in contradistinction to some authorities we find no blasphemy in it; on the contrary we commend it,

since:
is not all the content of the right column an effort to answer the question, which is implied by the left column, namely: AFTER WHAT FASHION does God reveal Himself to us?[1]

Pölätüomism commends many things that appear to contradict traditional religion; it encompasses everything within itself. The Cardinal visits all the famous scientists of the age across the world and manages to incorporate all their theories: Pasteur's faith in immunisation is compatible with belief in God: '*if disease is God's Punishment, then recovery is God's Grace. Hence is not Louis Pasteur a carrier of God's Grace?*[2] Similarly for Kekulé's synthesis; Kleb's diphtheria bacillus; Krupp's armaments; Goldstein's cathode rays and Michelson and Morley's experiment and so on for practically all the scientific discoveries of the end of the nineteenth century. Karl Marx is included, since his '*conclusion is a timely sign given to the Church by God, that she must not let temporal power slip from her hands'*, and even the theories in James Frazer's *The Golden Bough* '*show me AFTER WHAT FASHION God constructed the Way through which men may come to knowledge of Him.*'[3]

The novel next becomes a series of letters to the Cardinal, starting on 31 December 1900, from correspondents who have tried unsuccessfully to get Apollinaire involved in wars and therefore killed until finally in 1916 'Guillaume (Kostrowitzki) Apollinaire was wounded in the head by a shell splinter. He was twice trepanned, but died of the Spanish influenza, in hospital, on 10 November 1918, while the crowds in the streets around shouted : 'À bas Guillaume!'[4] After his death the Cardinal returns to his work on Pölätüomism which he had abandoned in 1900, studying Planck, Thomson, Ramsay & Soddy, Einstein, Rutherford, Punnett & Bateson, Russell & Whitehead, Moseley, Watson, Bragg, and Pavlov's theory of conditioned reflexes. He also reads St Augustine and wonders why Pavlov's ideas should not be used to make people obey religious doctrines.

---

[1] p. 27/28

[2] p. 34

[3] p. 43

[4] p. 72. Apollinaire did in fact die of Spanish Influenza but on 9 November 1918, two days before the signing of the Armistice to end World War I.

He put a sheet of paper into his *macchina da scrivere* and tapped out with two fingers:

```
In order to evoke reflexes we must have
stimuli. Stimuli may be positive or negative;
exemplum: food or pain.
These stimuli are in the hands of the secular,
Temporal power.
```

He thought for a few moments more, then tapped on:

```
But a man is not a dog.
To a man, material stimuli are unnecessary.
To a man, it is enough to say that he will be
comfortable or that he will suffer.
And these stimuli, positive and negative, are
accessible to the hands of the Church.
```

The typewriter bell struck the end of the line. Pölätüo turned the roller. Then suddenly his fingers began to jump about on the keys of their own accord:

```
But these stimuli are already in the hands of
the Church:
HEAVEN and HELL!
```

In *Part Two* of the novel, the issue of words in relation to language, Themerson's constant theme, recurs. Considering a Dictaphone he has acquired, 'a German invention, very new then' he holds its wire and muses that, unlike a 'grooved gramophone disc, the wire possessed nothing that could be seen, nothing that one could smell, taste, or put one's finger on' and yet it contains a message.

'. . . EVEN PERTRANT RUSSELL CANNOT GETRIT OFALL
THE UNIVERSALS ANTRETAINSSSI MILITARY
FATHER TOUGLAS COULTYOUPLEASE TELL JONATHAN
TOREMEMPER NOTTO LEAVE HIS HOOVER IN MY
STUTY HE'S ALREATY TONE SO TWICE THIS
WEEK ITS RUPPERPIPE LOOKS LIKEA SERPENTOF
PARATISE ANTIT DISTURPS ME OR WAS IT
ITENTITY? ' *click!*

How do we know that there are not many more things in the universe that look as innocent as the thin iron wire and yet contain a message.[1]

He wonders what message a bunch of violets would make if put through the machine. 'Must everything be expressible in a word-language? Of course not.' But 'if there are things in heaven and earth that cannot be expressed in words, then his own work, the *Philosophy of Pölätüomism*, which was built of words, must inevitably be incomplete.'[2] But he realises that there are other kinds of language than those built of words: kneeling is the language of prayer; throwing balls is the language of the *Jongleur de la Sainte Vierge*, who, 'instead of saying his prayer, juggled before the image of the Virgin Mary', killing is the language of Hitler, houses of Le Corbusier and so on. But this means that the *Philosophy of Pölätüomism* would become the *Poetry of Pölätüomism*. He has now forgotten Apollinaire and his hatred of poetry but he has never written a poem, never 'juggled with words'. He listens to the violets:

'-Măscărōnĭnŏpōlĕvā
Căscărōnĭnŏpōlĕvā
Lăscărōnĭnŏpōlĕvā'

He felt happy. He must ask the Archbishop of Merangue to dinner and recite the poem to him. He felt the blessedness of peace.[3]

There follows a humorous attack on logical positivists, including the 'Earl of Unbelievers', Bertrand Russell (Themerson's friend, published by Gaberbocchus) and A. J. Ayer, who appears as a 12-year old boy. In relation to a discussion on Russell's soul, the boy Ayer says 'the statements that he has, or has not, a soul are

[1] p. 80
[2] p. 81
[3] p. 84

both meaningless. The noise: "soul" cannot be referred to anything observable. Therefore: a sentence that contains that noise is neither true nor false.'[1] The argument proceeds through the reality of an onion and ends in a fight, with the Cardinal losing his upper first premolar. Following this the Cardinal has a vision and adds to his *Philosophy* the chapter *On the Reality of Soul and on the Reality of Onion.*

> *3b. Now, let us take the case of an animal. It would be a theoretical mistake to think that an animal, in having a perishable soul, resembles a logical positivist. An animal does not know that it does not have an immortal soul. A logical positivist does not know that he has one.*
> *3c. In contradistinction to an animal, he (the logical positivist) maintains that both realities are not real, though one of them has meaning while the other is meaningless. Indeed, what forces him to reject Soul, is not so much the deficiency of his direct senses, as the quality of his logic, which would permit him to call a soul 'soul' if it had the characteristics of an onion, but forbids him to call a soul 'soul' because it has the characteristics of soul.*[2]

Part Three of *Cardinal Pölätüo* is a collection of letters from Pölätüo to his biographer in his old age. '*Undoubtedly, I am the oldest man in the world. Has God forgotten about me? No. Rather, I think, I have not yet accomplished some*

---

[1] p. 99

[2] p. 116/117. In Cadaquès, a 1957 sketchbook of a visit to Spain by Franciszka Themerson with a text by Stefan, unpublished at the time but released by Obscure Publications in 2010, Stefan meets a priest.

> On the spur of the moment I told him I was a logical positivist. As he had never heard of such a denomination and it was too late for me to back out, I had to tell him something about it. I mentioned Russell as its Spring and Forefather, and Ayer as its Thomas Aquinas. I'm afraid he didn't know the first two names. He was most anxious to learn whether logical positivism was a christian denomination or not, and relaxed visibly when told it was not – if it was not christian then, thank God, it was ignorant of Truth and therefore there was no room for heresy in it. He sat beside me on the low, white, sun-hot wall, some hundred feet above the level of the sea. "And what does your teaching say about the immortality of the soul?" he asked.
>
> Well, there I was, invited to drink down the brew I had inadvertently prepared for myself. "we." I said, not feeling at all at my ease, firstly because I had labelled myself one of the clan of logical positivists, and secondly because I was usurping the role of their spokesman. "We don't particularly mind what kind of signs people use to draw a map of the world so long as it helps them find their place in it. If they choose to give a certain set of circumstances the name of 'soul', I don't see why they shouldn't". p. 17/18

special task He has for me'.[1] The letters introduce Princess Zuppa and Dr. Goldfinger, who, along with the Cardinal, will reappear in future novels. After this chapter comes a 1-page *Coda,* in which in the year 2022, he is 'broadcast' by a disintegration and reintegration system from Rome to America for the election of a new pope (who by now, presumably lives there).

> By a coincidence, instead of one in New York, 12 telephonists in different parts of America receive the call and stand by; and the Cardinal, 'broadcast' from one station in Rome, is 'received by 12 stations in the U.S.A. and 12 identical (?) cardinals make their way from different states in the U.S.A. to New Vatican, Florida.
>
> How many souls have they?
>
> How many votes have they?
>
> How do the new acquired characteristics begin to differentiate them?
>
> New possibilities of asexual reproduction: you choose the type of homo you need (Army, clergy, &c) and multiply it by the intermediacy of the Post Office (Duplicate Copies) Supplementary Services.
>
> You disintegrate a person and keep a record of the process. At any time in the future, you can pass it through the receiver and have the person again as he/she was 10, 100, or 1000 years before.
>
> (- in that case – what happens to Original Sin?).
>
> New Possibilities of immorality?
>
> New possibilities of immortality?

This is the end of the novel proper, but following it is a section called *The Dictionary of Traumatic Signs,* purportedly taken from Freud's *Interpretation of Dreams* and prepared for the Cardinal by his assistant Father Douglas. It is highly obscene throughout, translating everyday words into sexual meanings.

---

[1] p. 134

A

aeroplane: 1. m. organ; 2. ability of penis to raise itself upright; *Cf*: FLYING.

affectionately behave to the husband of your lover: 1. *wsh*: to kill him to win his wife' 2. *wsh*; to kill your father to have sxl intercourse with your mother. Cf: MOTHER, HAVING SXL INTERCOURSE WITH.

alone (without your "little one", which see**) through the streets, going**: having no man, no sxl relations.

angel, to be an: *see*: FLYING (*if* f.) 4.

animals: *see:* SMALL ANIMALS; *see*: WILD ANIMALS.

another person: your own beloved ego in a disguised form; *Cf:* PERSON WHO ATE THE JOINT &c.

anxiety in flying, falling, vertigo and the like: a transformed recollection of pleasurable sensations of games of movement; *see* also: FLYING.

Apollo, candles of,: *see*: CANDLE, INTO A CANDLE-STICK TO PUT A.

apples: 1. a beautiful bosom*; hence (possibly):* your wet-nurse; *hence (possibly)* her bosom; *hence (possibly):* an inn (for children; *Cf:* NURSE; *Cf:* INN; or: 2. the larger hemispheres of the human body.

aprons (sack-like) tied round the loins of two vagrants going along with a policeman: (*if f.*, *if your husband is a policeman*): the two halves of the scrotum.[1]

arrange flowers: *see*: TABLE WITH FLOWERS IN THE &C.

arrest for infanticide: *in R:* you had performed coitus interruptus clumsily; *wsh*: that you have not begotten a child.

ashamed for being naked; partially clothed &c: *see*: NAKED, OR &C.

asparagus: m. member.

[1] p. 165

Both *Cardinal Pölätüo* and *Bayamus* say 'a novel' on the covers of the Gaberbocchus editions but the cover of the American edition of *Tom Harris*, 1968[1], says it 'can perhaps be regarded as his first "conventional" novel' and that Themerson has 'published a number of philosophical fantasies (including *Professor Mmaa's Lecture*, with a preface by Bertrand Russell), composed music, and contributed articles on aesthetics and philosophy to scholarly journals', without mentioning any of his other works. *Tom Harris* is an anomaly in Themerson's work: though not entirely 'conventional' as the blurb says, it is certainly a novel. It has no philosophical digressions, is full-length (almost as long as his other novels put together) and a firm setting in place: Genoa and a London described in great and loving detail, though it does wander about in time and the eponymous Tom changes age and character continually. It is about the mystery of identity: is the narrator Tom Harris; does Harris exist and if so, who is he 'really'. Themerson's two late novels, *The Mystery of the Sardine*, Faber & Faber 1986, reprinted by Dalkey Archive Press, 2006, and *Hobson's Island*, Faber & Faber, 1988, reprinted by Dalkey Archive Press, 2005, are of a similar form and *Tom Harris* seems to belong more with these than with his early work.

[1] New York, Alfred A. Knopf

Stefan Themerson's *Special Branch*[1] is a 'dialogue' in a philosophical, Socratic sense, concerning, as most of his works do, meaning, truth and logic, but in a less playful, less absurdist mode than his earlier works. The narrator is called on by Detective Superintendent Watson of Special Branch, who has come to ask him what he knows about 'Dr. Good's Ultra-Intelligent Machine' which

"will do every intellectual activity better than any man."
"O, Bollocks!" I said.[2]

Watson's question is 'can she spring up some ultra-new basic conceptual elements from the foam of her own neural guts. Well, can she?' The point is whether a machine, programmed by humans, however intelligent, can invent concepts that are not already in the human mind. Scientists, who will programme the machine, use terms, which are 'tethered', while poets originate the meanings of words, which are 'winged'. Terms, like Semantic Poetry, are fixed and defined.

> Homer's River Scaramander says:
>
> Dear brother let us both together
> Stem the hero's power.
>
> As a term, 'power' becomes

$$\frac{\text{mass} * \text{acceleration} * \text{distance}}{\text{time}}$$

The detective is a 'practical' man. He does not feel the need of a translator like Lampaphedor Metaphrastes in *Wooff, Wooff*:

> I am a detective. I have been trained to be a *matter-of-fact* man, to listen to hearsay evidence but not to rely on it, and when I have a philosophical problem that goes beyond *'2 + 2 is synonymous with 4'*, I

[1] MS dated Feb. – Dec. 1969, published by Gaberbocchus 1972.
[2] p. 8

don't go to philosophers to help me, no, I go to our forensic medicine department and ask:

'At what stage of a mother's pregnancy does Immanuel Kant insert into the embryo it's *a priori* forms & categories –

And Chomsky – its grammatical templates,

And God – its soul?'[1]

Later the detective is asked if he has heard of Chomsky. "Now you are forgetting who I am. Of course I know about him. I am a detective Superintendent, Special Branch, am I not?"[2] To be ultra-intelligent, the machine should be able to break out of Jameson's prison-house of language, and not be condemned to play Wittgenstein's language games all day.[3] Detective Watson says:

"It was *you* who mentioned that the ultra-intelligent machine cannot be limited to the world of language divorced from the world of brute facts."

I agreed.

"We cannot limit her to playing with syntactical truths which we have built into her."

I agreed.

"Unless we want her to produce some modern French novels."

I agreed.

"And we don't want her to do that."

"No, we don't," I said.

"We want her to understand the world," he said.

I agreed.[4]

The narrator worries about the machine inventing new connectives; he still believes that there is an outer world that language can describe rather than believing that language creates the world and that whereof one cannot speak, thereof one must be silent. He asks what will happen if she finds herself

"in need of some new *sentential connectives* such as cannot be defined in terms of our *and, or, not, if. . . then*, a sort of thing which we cannot even imagine?"

He took it all quite smoothly, "That's what I should call Logic-Fiction," he said. "Look, if we've come to accept without a murmur all those things that are being brought to us by science-fiction, there is no

---

[1] p. 16

[2] p. 42

[3] Jameson and Wittgenstein are not mentioned by the narrator.

[4] p. 19

reason why we shouldn't also get used to those that logic-fiction might bring us, don't you think?"

"I'm not sure," I said.

"That' because you are still in the old inner-outer pattern of mind. You think there is an infinite world which we are exploring and a fixed inner set of mental tools we are exploring it with. And you think the set of tools is complete and given us *a priori*."

"O no," I objected.

"O yes," he insisted.[1]

The narrator insists that, as poets use winged words, and as he has read poetry before he read Plato, his mind is free. Watson later admits that there is no ultra-intelligent machine, and he has just come to find out if the narrator is a communist. The detective had earlier admitted that the narrator could not be a Marxist. 'You are not a peer of the realm, or rich enough, to afford to be a Marxist. In our system of co-ordinates, that is.'[2] Now he says: 'you don't look like a communist to me, and I've seen some.'[3] Watson has a file marked XXX to give to his superiors, containing one piece of paper, which he shows to the narrator.

Under the typewritten heading:

AFFILIATIONS

There were written three words pencilled in his hand:

homo per se

I looked at the words, and at him, and felt embarrassed in an inexplicable, strange way: flattered and humiliated both at once, both at the same time.

"Can they read Latin?" I asked drily.

"O yes," he said. "And that's where the trouble lies. They all read their Plato before they read La Mettrie."

"In Latin?" I asked.

"Well," he said. "Your files will not go so high up as to reach the ones who read Plato in Greek."

We shook hands and I showed him out.[4]

---

[1] p. 52/53
[2] p. 39
[3] p. 92
[4] p. 92/93

General Piesc[1], is another short work; it relates back to *Cardinal Pölätüo*; this time with a third-person narrative followed by a series of letters. However, the letters contain dialogue, subverting the epistolary form. Piesc (which means fist or Faust in Polish) has won 'the lion's share' of £129,740 on the football pools. A reporter asks him what he is going to spend the money on.

Stefan Themerson

General Piesc

OR THE CASE OF THE FORGOTTEN MISSION

> 'As this is off the record, I suppose you want to know the truth –'
>
> 'I dare say a man with your present fortune, general, can afford to tell the truth.'
>
> 'Richesse oblige' said the photographer.
>
> General Piesc still didn't smile.
>
> 'The other day I saw in a shop, in Piccadilly, a mackintosh,' he said. 'Light in colour, almost white. With exceptionally large pockets. I am going to buy it now.'
>
> 'Ha, ha, said the evening paper man,
>
> 'What does he need large pockets for?' said the photographer.
>
> 'I believe we've missed something there,' said the woman reporter.[2]

It seems the general's wife Ewa has left him, possibly for the mysterious Brzeski, taking with her the dog (though not the dog's lead). 'What did she (Ewa) see in Dr. Brzeski? . . . What did she see in his (Dr. Brzeski's) white, smooth, shining skull with two enormous ears attached like wings?'[3] 'Would she have left him, would she have gone, and with whom?, with Brzeski!, if... well,... let's put it bluntly, if he (General Piesc) had won all that money, not now but a fortnight ago?'[4] He seems not to know what he should do; possibly he has lost his memory; he is 'perhaps the only general who had a thin plate of gold fitted in his cranium.'

---

[1] Gaberbocchus, 1976, republished 2006 by Obscure Publications. Spelt Pięść in the Polish original.

[2] p. 10/11

[3] p. 15

[4] p. 16

> General Piesc was standing in the middle of his room. But there are so many ways one can stand. If, from the main staircase, one approached the front door and peeped through the key-hole, one could easily be under the impression that there was, somewhere in the room, but beyond one's field of vision, a portrait-painter who had arrested the general in that particular posture in order to catch the moment when, all orders having been dispatched, there is nothing more to do but wait. That, however, was not the reason for his standing motionless in the middle of the room. In a sense, the reason was quite opposite. The orders hadn't been sent. Not yet.[1]

He seems to be preparing for a mission, but neither he nor we know what it is. He takes his British passport and some of his newly-won money. 'The passport in his breast pocket meant liberty, and the wads of banknotes in his left trouser pocket meant freedom. A passport protects your rights, money gives you the means to exercise them.'[2] Taking his gun in his mackintosh pocket and putting out a notice for no more milk, he leaves the house and takes a taxi to Heathrow Airport. When he gets there he has a 'change of mood (if it's all right to call it a change of mood)' and goes back to London. Waking up in a strange hotel, he does not remember why he has the gun and 'sees the puzzled expression of his face in the mirror.'

> How long had he been sitting there, holding the cup suspended in the air in front of him, and staring at it? His bushy brows frowned, his back straightened. 'Now then,' he said to himself, 'go to your room, lie down, till lunch-time, have a light meal, then go for a stroll. And this is an order.' He went up to his room, lay down till lunch time, had a Dover sole and a glass of white wine, and went for a stroll along the coast. A drunken sailor was coming towards him. General Piesc crossed the road: there was a narrow alley in front of him, it led him to another street, where, in a first floor window of the house just opposite the alley, he saw an enormous white hand painted on the window-pane.[3]

The white hand later turns out to be the sign of the palmist, Prudence Prentice, which we find out as the novel now becomes a series of letters. The first is from the general's daughter, Princess Zuppa, a friend of Cardinal Pölätüo in Rome. In what could be a reference to Semantic Poetry, she tells Piesc that Poles like him were 'educated in those abstract nouns garlanded with the whole adjectival flowershop of your romantic literature.' Whereas: 'Your reality and mine are

---

[1] p. 12
[2] p. 13
[3] p. 20

different, there are potatoes in your proud vodka and there's the sun in my wine.'[1] She refers to the secret mission he has presumably told her about in a previous letter.

> Yes, supposing you had, supposing you *did* have a beautiful idea, whatever it was. It came to you like a flash of lightning without the thunderclap. 25 years ago. You nursed it in you for a quarter of a century. You knew what to do and how to do it. It was your mission. You didn't tell anybody anything about it but you went on carrying it in yourself till the moment came when you had the freedom and the power to accomplish it. Your mission. Because you knew the moment would come. A miracle. Two miracles. And they came. The first: your wife let you free. The second: that enormous sum of money you won. So you bought yourself a white mackintosh, put a pistol, or was it a revolver?, in your pocket and you . . . went. To realize your idea. To start fulfilling your mission. And then you saw a seagull in the sky, and the seagull opened its beak, and the fish fell back into the sea. And you got up and you couldn't remember what your mission was. It vanished. Like that fish in the sea.[2]

The princess tells him not to try to remember his mission; we don't 'want any saviours any more.' In an echo of Bertrand Russell's introduction to *Professor Mmaa's Lecture* she says:

> All saviours disrupt normal evolutionary processes, which anyway will go their own way. The way may be tragic. It usually is tragic. But what all saviours do when they start meddling with it, is to make the tragedy still more painful. . . They think they know everything better, who believe they know what is the thing. The Greek males thought geometry was the thing. Dr. Zamenhoff thought Esperanto was the thing. Jesus Christ thought love was the thing. Karl Marx thought the dialectical loaf of bread was the thing. And geometry produced bazookas, and ployglotism produced more quarrels, and love produced hatred, and two loaves of bread produced greed.[3]

In the course of her very long letter, Princess Zuppa tells Piesc that she has been to Bukumla in Africa with her friend Dr. Goldfinger (who, like the princess, has already appeared in *Cardinal Pölätüo*) and seen the general's son: 'he is

---

[1] p. 21

[2] p. 23

[3] p. 32/33. The princess believes the 'thing' is 'good manners', in a section very reminiscent of Themerson's in 'The Chair of Decency', op. cit.

completely black. And when I say completely black I mean completely black. Beautifully completamente, interamente nero. Like his mother.'[1] She warns him never to go to Bukumla.

> What I mean my dear, dear dear Jan is that you mustn't ever, and I do mean you must never never never dream of going to Bukumla, either on a horse, white or black or dappled, or on a bicycle, or on foot. This is serious. And when I say 'serious', you know me, I mean serious. If what you had in mind was that you would become to your son what Aristotle was to Alexander the Great, or Machiavelli to his imaginary Prince, or Clausewitz[2] to his Prussian Kronprintz – what an illusion! Once you put a foot in Bukumla you will never leave it alive. Not that you would be allowed to stay there alive. And that not because you are his father. People there can have as many fathers as they please. But because you are white. And he, the chieftain, the leader, the boss, cannot afford to have a white father.[3]

In a PS to the letter, she asks whether, even if he remembers the plan, will it be the same plan? 'If a seagull lets its catch fall back into the sea and then dives and reappears with a fish in its beak, how can it be sure it is the same fish.'[4] The next letter is to Princess Zuppa from Miss Prentice, the palmist-girl, 'as you called me in your kind letter to the General.' He has been living with her and he has relaxed and stopped worrying about the mission while they have had a tender relationship. She tells Zuppa about their walks along the Thames and their visit to a German bierstube, where he risks upsetting the customers by asking the accordionist to play the Polish national anthem. The same night the general is accosted by two men; he shoots at them and they run off, but he dies anyway, just after has told her he is perfectly happy. Miss Prentice says:

> We shall never know what his mission was. Was it a white-horse mission, or a two-blades-of-grass mission. Or what? What mission can it be, to accomplish which one arms oneself with a gun loaded with one solitary bullet?[5]

The reader's response may be suicide or assassination, but neither of these are mentioned. There are three more letters: one from Dr. Brzeski on behalf of Mrs. Piesc to Miss Prentice telling her that the general's new car is registered to her,

---

[1] p. 29
[2] The general had a volume of the military strategist Clausewitz on his bookshelves.
[3] p. 30
[4] p. 34
[5] p. 50

that she can collect it and that she should avoid the press; a return letter from Miss Prentice saying she has already 'resisted all the attempts of the Press to interview me' and on the penultimate page there is a letter to Princess Zuppa from the Chancellery of the Republic of Bukumla, thanking her for letting them know of the General Piesc's death[1], but saying that the Secretary does not know of him. The last page of the book, in its entirety is:

Confidential

MEMO

from.................................... to..

Close the file and forget the whole thing.

---

[1] Princess Zuppa, General Piesc, the President of Bukumla and Cardinal Pölätüo all reappear in Themerson's later novel *The Mystery of the Sardine*, 1986, and all except Pölätüo also appear in *Hobson's Island*, Faber & Faber, 1988

rayner heppenstall

Although in 1980 he could still undoubtedly be regarded as a contemporary novelist, [John] Rayner Heppenstall, 1911 - 1981 published his first novel as long ago as 1939, when Virginia Woolf and James Joyce were still alive. But from that period on he was committed to the idea of the experimental novel; in 1962 wrote an article called 'The Need for Experiment'[1] justifying this and linking the decline in the novel's popularity with its lack of novelty.[2] He also wrote, in a later article:

> In general, novels in the classic mould represented by, say, George Eliot, bore me. I do not think you can write that sort of thing any more with full conviction[3] . . . Applied to a thriller or light comedy of the P.G. Wodehouse type, the 'classic' structure works well enough, because you know what the novel is written *for*: it is to set you a puzzle or to make you laugh. But I cannot really accept the novel as practised - superbly - by Wodehouse or Simenon as a way of expressing things seriously. So I write a different sort of novel, with less accent on constructed plot and more on the effects of directly apprehended experience.[4]

Like many others, Heppenstall links the novel to its society, and sees that the two must be in step if the novel is to have any effect on people's ways of life and of thinking. The present age is so different from the age of the rise of the novel that novelists must strive to find new methods of expression:

> There was a great age of capitalism and it coincided with a great age of the novel . . . For a hundred years, great things were written by persons who subscribed to the idea of the novel proper or true novel, but the idea

---

[1] *The Times*: 13 December 1962, p. 14. Hereafter referred to as NE

[2] This is the argument Bernard Bergonzi was later to use in *The Situation of the Novel* op. cit. ch. 1

[3] This is the argument B.S. Johnson was later to use in the introduction to *Memoirs*: op. cit. Heppenstall was Johnson's friend and mentor.

[4] 'Speaking of Writing': *The Times* 19 December 1963, p. 13. Hereafter SW

> now simply fills publishers' lists with rubbish and bedevils the work of writers who might be doing something more amusing.[1]

In the early sixties, Heppenstall became identified as the main champion on this side of the Channel of the *nouveau roman;* an Italian critic had even called him 'il padre del nouveau roman' on account of *The Blaze of Noon*. He disclaimed this in one place[2], but elsewhere said, with some pride, 'Hélène Cixous was once kind enough to describe me in print as the founder of the *nouveau roman*[3]. However it was a role he disliked since it tended to polarise the debate:

> Either people attribute to one a revolutionary's desire to see everything except *nouveaux romans* swept away, to enforce this as the only way of writing novels now, or else they take it on themselves to reject the new novel on principle, and abjure all the novelists' works. Sometimes both . . . the new novel is not a new orthodoxy which replaces the old; it is simply a different sort of novel evolved by certain individuals who happen to find the novel as they received it unsuitable for what they want to do. Like or dislike any particular example by all means, but do not, for goodness' sake, try to codify these likes and dislikes into principles by which any and all novels must be judged.[4]

However, he does seem to have been proud of his role as a senior figure for younger experimental novelists, while having 'never cared for the experimentalism which has recourse to typographical oddity.'[5] 'I was somewhat

---

1 *Raymond Roussel* (London: Calder & Boyars, 1966), 90. Hereafter RR

2 *The Intellectual Part* (this is one of Heppenstall's autobiographies): (London: Barrie & Rockliff, 1962), 212. Hereafter referred to as IP

3 *The Master Eccentric: The Journals of Rayner Heppenstall*. ed. Jonathan Goodman. London: Allison and Busby, 1986, published posthumously in the same year and by the same publisher as *The Pier*. Hereafter referred to as ME, 188

4 SW 13

5 ME 67

regarded as the senior *avant-garde* British novelist, also representing the *nouveau roman*. It was therefore as to a *chef de file* that B.S. Johnson first sent me a proof copy of his first novel, then telephoned to ask if he could come to see me.'[1] However he was ambivalent about joining any group of novelists; in a journal entry in 1969 he records: '*Avant-garde* novelists at the house of Alan Burns, off Portobello Road. They want to start public readings and discussions, under the name "Writers Reading". I was one of the greybeards invited, the other Stefan Themerson. For some reason Bryan Johnson seemed bent on needling me . . . I don't think I shall go along with them.'[2] Nevertheless he also recounts being at a book fair in 1971 where the speakers seem to have been organised into 'traditionalists' and 'the *avant-garde*', and there is no doubt where he belongs.

> There was, it seems a great turn-out for Margaret Drabble's traditional novelist's evening, but we of the *avant-garde* had barely fifty people in the big top. Eva [Figes] was excellent, though everything she said about novel-writing would have done just as well on the traditionalists' platform. Alan [Burns] looked forward with enthusiasm to the day when novels would be written by computers. He failed to communicate this enthusiasm. I, as an experimental father figure, am out of touch with my juniors and disciples, in that they believe in a sort of progress in the novel, their sort of novel superseding the traditional novel, as socialism or (for Alan) anarchism supersedes capitalism. I spoke a little against this confusion of aesthetics with politics and said that I didn't even believe that time marched on, it merely staggered around.[3]

But while remaining aloof he certainly seemed to have known, encouraged and personally liked many of the younger generation of experimental novelists. In his journal he described Eva Figes (at a party given in 1969 by Anna Kavan's publisher Peter Owen) as 'a thin creature with large eyes and hectic colouring, whom before the War one would have assumed to be tubercular.'[4] Heppenstall was also fond of Ann Quin and B.S. Johnson, who he said first met in his flat 'over a light early dinner, after which Bryan drove us all to the shop called Better Books in Charing Cross Road, where Nathalie Sarraute was lecturing, with me as her chairman.' Heppenstall himself had met Quin earlier; he described her as a 'splendid hunk of young womanhood, with a face almost to match, her hair cut short and scrupulously clean, unlike those of her friends whom M[argaret, Heppenstall's wife] and I met at a party she invited us to'[5].

---

[1] ME 67
[2] ME 26
[3] ME p 70/71
[4] ME 50
[5] ME 120

He was not at first drawn to Johnson, and thought him pushy (as did others). Johnson had asked his advice on *Travelling People*:

> the question I remember him asking was whether I thought his book had anything in common with the French new novel. It hadn't. If anything, it was reminiscent of Sterne's *Tristram Shandy,* or so a cursory glance suggested to me, for that was all I had given it. . . . Nor, frankly did I at first much take to Bryan himself, who was fat, uninterestingly pale, without much facial expression, and who spoke with a Londonish accent in a voice I noted as of rather high pitch without at first perceiving that it was a light tenor which might have repaid training, had its possessor been musical.[1]

However, he soon became very fond of Johnson. 'I have rarely had men about me that were fat. . . Bryan is a fat man. There is something about him which I enormously like. An easy man he is not, but then perhaps neither am I.'[2]

> I liked his second novel, *Albert Angelo* [1964] and I liked his thin, sharp wife, Virginia, who had worked in Paris and who spoke good French. They dined us in Islington, and we took a present when they had a baby son. A certain pushiness made Bryan unpopular in certain quarters (in others, it succeeded very well), and it was alarmingly said to me (by Charles [C.P.] Snow, I think) that people were making me responsible for B.S. Johnson. There remained that about him which I increasingly liked. For one thing, he would put himself out for you. In those days, he drove a large van, and with this he would always fetch M. and me as well as taking us home.[3]

---

[1] ME 67

[2] ME 88

[3] ME p 77/78

It was Johnson who rang Heppenstall on September 1st 1973 to tell him of Ann Quin's suicide. By November Johnson was also dead.

> It is not much over two months since Ann Quin committed suicide. Ann was beautiful, though highly neurotic. It has crossed my mind to wonder whether there was any love affair between them. I conclude that it is unlikely. On the other hand, I feel quite sure that Ann's suicide continued to affect Bryan, from whom I first heard of it.[1]

Johnson's own death affected him badly. 'I am more shocked by this death than I have been by any for a long time. For one thing, Bryan was the last person I should have expected to commit suicide. For another, as I have suddenly realised, he was my only friend of his generation. Indeed, I wonder whether, outside the family, he was not my only friend.'[2]

Heppenstall's influences extended back beyond the *nouveau roman*, and most of the main features of his style are already present in *Saturnine* (1942). However, he did approve of the new French movement (he knew Nathalie Sarraute quite well - she wrote to him praising *Saturnine*[3] - and met Robbe-Grillet[4] and Butor[5]), if only because he 'thought it was a new sign of life . . . the conventional novel has tottered and that was a good thing'.[6] He said of the *nouveau roman*:

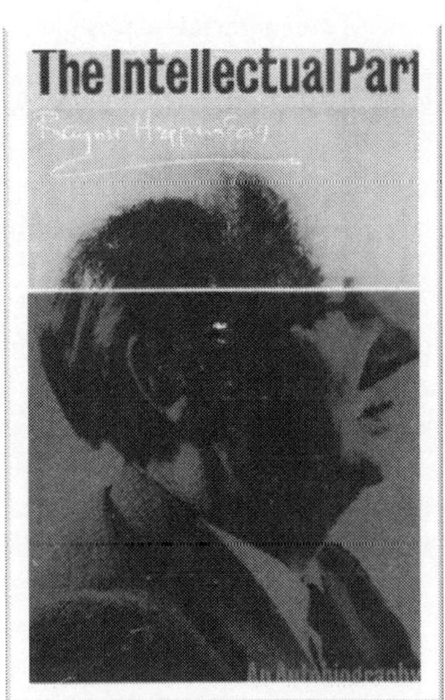

1 ME 123

2 ME 122, entry for November 15th 1973

3 IP p. 199 and 208

4 ibid. pp. 199/200 and 209/210

5 ibid. 208. He also wrote article (anonymously) for *The Times Literary Supplement* on Robbe-Grillet and Sarraute, and one on Butor, 'The Novels of Michel Butor', *London Magazine*, July 1962, pp. 57-63

6 NE 14

> I, for my part, find it more stimulating than anything going on at present in our own literature . . . There are novelists in this country who can write, but the total phenomenon to which they contribute is less interesting than its French counterpart today. No doubt it is largely due to their audiences or perhaps rather to their publishers who, on very flimsy grounds, claim to know just what the public wants and to those critics who underwrite the position. And yet Mr. Beckett finds a public here, and the success of Mr. Durrell and Mr. Golding suggests a demand for at least verbal glitter and brooding symbols, a weariness with middlebrow normality. Mme. Sarraute and M. Robbe-Grillet both have something to offer us here, though it is early days yet to say what . . . In this country there is too little technical enterprise. We have endless conventional novels. We have the ostentatious indifference of Mr. Amis, taking it all far too easy.[1]

Heppenstall's interest in French literature went back to his university days (he studied French and English at Leeds, and got 'a poor third'[2]) and he had always read at least as much in French as in English (he also did translations[3]). At one time he even began to worry about the effect of this on his own writing:

> A notion I had was that by too much reading (and a fair amount of talking) in a foreign language, a writer might lose the mastery of his own, which was his strong rock. I was, I felt, beginning to think in French. I now find the notion absurd, and am inclined to take the opposite view, viz., that only through constant rubbing against a foreign language can a writer achieve mastery in his own. I am further inclined

---

[1] *The Fourfold Tradition* (London: Barrie & Rockliff, 1961), 269 (This is a book about the two traditions in French - since the revolution - and English - the 'central' and the 'radical-nonconformist' - literature.)

[2] IP 12

[3] Notably of Balzac and Roussel

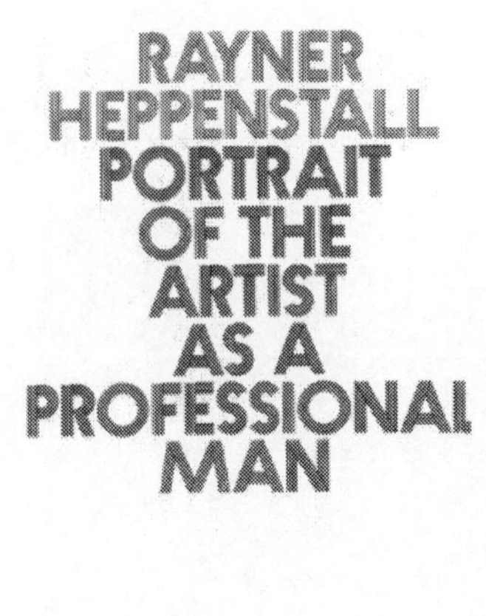

to say that the principal foreign language against which an English writer rubs must be French.[1]

Despite this, and despite the fact that his principal influences were French - Marcel Jouhandeau[2], Henry de Montherlant, Céline, Drieu la Rochelle[3] - and American - Henry Miller and William Saroyan[4] - he was 'not committed to the view that new life must be French. I hope new life will spring here, as it has in the past . . . The more purely native the growth is, the better pleased I shall be'.[5]

For Heppenstall felt that English literature had not always been under the hegemony of realism. He notes the long tradition of English anti-novels: '*Joseph Andrews*, not only *Love and Friendship* but to some extent *Sense and Sensibility* and *Northanger Abbey*, much of Dickens, all of Peacock, and more recently, Joyce and the best of Evelyn Waugh'.[6] 'It could indeed be argued that, in significant literary history, the anti-novel preceded the novel. The earliest 'novel' any large number of people still think worth reading is Don Quixote, a parody of the novels of its time, an anti-novel'.[7]

It seems that, despite his French influences, Heppenstall wrote a very English experimental novel in terms of the distinctions I outlined in the introduction. *The Connecting Door* was hailed by reviewers as an English version of the *nouveau roman*, but it has a tenderness and humour altogether lacking in Robbe-Grillet, Simon, Sollers et al. Despite his often repeated distaste for Virginia Woolf's 'feminine world of domestic hyperaesthesia', his view of the human personality is sometimes strikingly similar to Woolf's (and he also mentioned with respect *Mrs. Dalloway* and *To the Lighthouse*):

---

1 IP 120

2 IP. 87

3 IP 46

4 *Portrait of the Artist as a Professional Man* (London: Peter Owen, 1969), 14 (This is Heppenstall's account of his time as a radio producer at the B.B.C.) Hereafter referred to as PAPM

5 NE 14

6 NE 14. I would add, at least, *Villette*, Swift, Sterne, Smollett and Firbank.

7 RR 192

> In the last five hundred years we have developed a curiously literary conception of what constitutes a man's life. It is natural that this should be so . . . The actual composition of any individual life, here and now, in this world, is a mystery. The principle of its continuity is mysterious. Its discontinuity and lack of principle are no less so. And that both continuity and discontinuity, principle and lack of principle, coherence and incoherence, should always display themselves together in the process of a man's life is perhaps the greatest mystery of all. It is certainly a mystery that no philosopher will face, unless the existentialists may recently be thought to have faced it.[1]

THE DOUBLE IMAGE

Mutations of Christian mythology in the work of four French Catholic writers of to-day and yesterday

BY

RAYNER HEPPENSTALL

LONDON
SECKER & WARBURG
1947

Theologians stress order and principle, while philosophers maintain either that life obeys some order or that it does not. 'It is the natural tendency of lyrical poetry alone to sing the fragmentary song' However, lyrical poetry belongs to an age when poet and audience belong to a world of shared and mutually agreed meaning and values:

> Direct lyrical utterance is only tolerable, and indeed only possible within a group whose preconceptions are identical. It communicates little beyond the sense of community. It is an arabesque, a variation upon this sense. Prose narrative is more searching because it is more informative and more narrowly expressive[2]

Prose, in other words, can spell things out, and this is necessary for a modern audience, for whom this sense of community has disappeared: 'It seems to me that this is a prose age because it requires us to be terribly explicit. And the

---

[1] *The Double Image: Mutations of Christian Mythology in the Work of Four French Catholic Writers of To-day and Yesterday* (London: Secker & Warburg, 1947), pp. 69/70 (The four are Léon Bloy (on whom he published a separate study); George Bernanos; Francois Mauriac and Paul Claudel). Hereafter referred to as DI

[2] DI 124

serious possibilities of prose narrative have only just become known'.[1] Heppenstall had himself started as a poet[2] but later abandoned poetry entirely in favour of the novel.[3] He was, however, aware of the dangers inherent in the novel's implicit claim to totality, objectivity and truth.

> The writing and reading of fiction and biography give the mind an agreeable sense of coming to grips with reality and the supreme reality of individual human life. But nothing could be more remote from the reality of a man's life than any version of it which could be written down. The mere writing gives form to things which had no form and substitutes an intellectual form for a form which once had reality. Every piece of writing is a dramatisation . . . Biography is always tendentious and always untrue. Fiction and drama are further refinements of the biographical method. To praise no matter what play or novel for being 'true to life' is to prove oneself a fool . . . To embrace with a formula is to strangle. A country is not its map. And every man's written life is a literary fiction.
>
> How then can we present the reality of a man's life? I fancy there is no way.[4]

Man exists

> in a state of flux. He is a flow of existence. He is pure vibrancy. The personality which is continuous is also diffuse. It is hardly a personality at all. In solitude a man is diffuse. He takes form in relation only to an external situation. His friends and enemies define him. In a quite real sense they create him. Only the poet and the artist, the mystic, have any personality in solitude. And that is because they are capable of defining themselves in relation to an imaginary world defined by themselves.[5]

Although literature should try to work against the codification and pinning down of the individual, the task is ultimately impossible: 'The purpose of literature is to take charge of the exception, to indulge eccentricity and lop-sidedness. And yet in the wider, unaccountable flux of human life, even the wildest literature comes in the end to serve the purpose of systematisation too.'[6]

---

[1] ibid. 131

[2] He published four volumes of verse between 1932 and 1940 and a collected volume in 1946 which included poems up to 1945.

[3] See IP 65/69

[4] DI 70/71

[5] DI 71

[6] ibid. 75

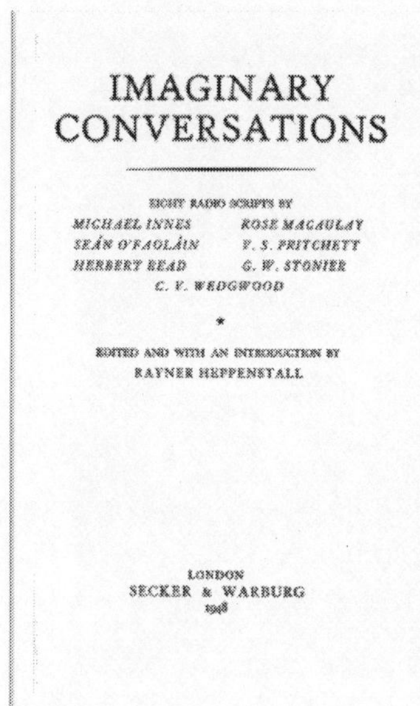
IMAGINARY CONVERSATIONS

EIGHT RADIO SCRIPTS BY

MICHAEL INNES — ROSE MACAULAY
SEÁN O'FAOLÁIN — V. S. PRITCHETT
HERBERT READ — G. W. STONIER
C. V. WEDGWOOD

*

EDITED AND WITH AN INTRODUCTION BY
RAYNER HEPPENSTALL

LONDON
SECKER & WARBURG
1948

Heppenstall tried to keep alive the sense of struggle with the novel form which so many of his contemporaries and successors had lost: 'The novel remains largely what it was. The experiments of Virginia Woolf and James Joyce are admired and by-passed'.[1] But Heppenstall, like the other novelists in this study, tried to find some way out of the apparent dead end represented by Joyce: 'Joyce's creative word-play is also destructive. Its trend is to destroy language and meaning, to make any further literature impossible'.[2] But although Joyce may have precluded any further experimentation with language, he left wide open the largest area of all: the individual.

Before going on to examine Heppenstall's novels it is worth mentioning his other interest in France: French criminology, on which he wrote four books. To paraphrase the title of his autobiography, this might be called the non-intellectual part of his life.[3] In 1970 he noted in his journal that he had practically stopped writing novels and was now concentrating on criminology.

> I am now comparatively uncluttered. My present life, such as it is, may be understood to have started last year. I am a criminal historian and translator, who may yet write further novels and who in the meantime keeps a diary which may or may not do wholly or in part for publication.[4]

---

1 Introduction to *Imaginary Conversations* (London: Secker & Warburg, 1948) 8 (this is a set of reprints of radio broadcasts which Heppenstall produced.)

2 *The Fourfold Tradition* 155

3 *A Little Pattern of French Crime* (London: Hamish Hamilton, 1969); *French Crime in the Romantic Age* (London: Hamilton, 1970); *Bluebeard and After* (London: Owen, 1972); *The Sex War and Others* (London: Owen, 1973) and one on British crime: *Reflections on the Newgate Calendar* (London: W.H. Allen, 1975).

4 ME 54

A
LITTLE
PATTERN
OF
FRENCH
CRIME
Rayner
Heppenstall

BLUEBEARD
AND AFTER
THREE DECADES OF MURDER IN FRANCE
RAYNER HEPPENSTALL

RAYNER HEPPENSTALL
French Crime in the
Romantic Age

THE
SEX
WAR
AND OTHERS - A SURVEY OF RECENT
MURDER
PRINCIPALLY IN FRANCE
RAYNER HEPPENSTALL

The Blaze of Noon[1] is both a lyrical novel and an experimental novel. I have already quoted Heppenstall's comment in the preface to this novel that the cinema had taken over the function of the exterior novel, and that the novel should therefore become 'more lyrical, more inward'. Certainly, no film could adequately be made of *Blaze*[2], since the narrator is blind, and everything is described in terms of his perceptions. In it, Heppenstall tried to 'reapprehend' his world[3] through these perceptions. Because the narrator himself is blind, the reader is forced into a world without visual impressions, and where apprehension of the novel's world is necessarily only partial. In this it is more similar to novels with limited or deluded narrators[4] than its most obvious precursor; Henry Green's *Blindness*, which uses the perceptions of several of the characters and not just the blind boy.

Blindness is a lack, the lack of sight,[5] but it is also a difference. Dunkel,[6] like all Heppenstall's narrators, is an outsider, but in some ways is superior to those around him,[7] as he spends much of his time trying to prove to himself and to others, and which Sophie Madron comes to realise. The novel's reader is aware all along of both his difference and his superiority, and it is Heppenstall's achievement in this novel to realise these different perceptions, and to do it in such a lyrical prose. Sometimes even Dunkel can only express things in visual terms:

---

[1] Secker & Warburg, 1939; New York and. Toronto: Alliance, 1940; revised and reset Secker & Warburg, 1947; repr. Ace, 1959; repr. Barrie & Rockliff 1962; reset and repr. London: Sphere, 1967; reset and repr. London: Alison & Busby, 1981. Hereafter referred to as BN followed by the page numbers of the four different editions in chronological order.

[2] Though Heppenstall told me that several film makers had considered it.

[3] Which is what, according to Freedman (op, cit.) lyrical novels do.

[4] Rosamond Lehmann's *The Ballad and The Source*; *The Turn of the Screw*; *The Good Soldier* etc.

[5] Also, in Freudian terms, a symbol for castration.

[6] German for 'dark'.

[7] of. H.G. Wells' *In The Country of the Blind.*

> I stared out over the lily pond and into the depths of the willow shadows beyond. That is the only way I can put it. I stared. It was a kind of yearning outward of all the senses, a powerful listlessness, a heavy, eyeless staring which brought into play the muscles about the sockets of my late lamented eyes.[1]

> From this point there was a clear view over Gwavas Bay. I call it a view because there isn't a nearer word. I mean that I was suddenly exhilarated by the air that rose up from Gwavas Bay[2]

Just how different his perceptions are is highlighted when he falls in love with Sophie. This comes as a bit of a shock; how can you fall in love with someone you cannot see? His description of Sophie is entirely dynamic; as opposed to the static description a sighted person would give which would be largely in terms of 'looks':

> She had just that slenderness and tautness of body which can never settle into banality. Every inch of her lived with its own life because she had a natural, voluptuous pleasure in the most insignificant movement of her own limbs. In the very lowest estimate she must always be a piece of mobile, living sculpture of which a man could never tire.[3]

Compare this with his description of the 'brassy' Betty des Voeux:

> She has no pleasure in living for its own sake, no simple, private voluptuousness. She enjoys playing tennis and no doubt plays both well and gracefully, because the game has, at any rate, an immediate social purpose, but she can derive no pleasure from her own movements when she is alone.[4]

In a book on the creative activity of the blind and partially-sighted, Viktor Lowenfeld explained how blind people build up an impression of a situation from a number of smaller impressions where sighted people tend to proceed in the opposite direction, analysing a whole impression (or gestalt) into its component parts:

> being unable to see . . . may become the basis of a specific and unique creativeness . . . This specific approach results from the need of building

---

1 BN 56:41:33/4:35/6
2 BN 149:110:81:84
3 BN 269:193:135:43
4 BN 295:211/2:147:155/6

> up a whole image out of partial impressions. What the blind individual cannot always achieve in life he can do in his creative work: out of the many partial impressions he builds up a 'whole'[1]

Dunkel's perceptions do indeed seem to be synthetic rather than analytic: 'It is, I suppose rather more difficult for me than for an ordinary man to integrate scattered groups of sensations into a single whole'[2]: 'To speak of taking the rough with the smooth was nonsense, I knew. I knew that a smooth surface was made up of a large number of imperceptibly small roughnesses'.[3] He also seems to experience time as a series of discrete moments: 'This moment is good, and so was the moment before it, and the one before that'[4]; 'Again it was a different moment',[5] and to feel its passage as a flow: 'we maintained together the simple continuity of the day'[6]. The result of this perception of time and space is a difficulty in maintaining a consistent self:

> I have an extremely good memory. It is necessary that I should have, because I have fewer means of maintaining the continuity of my life from one day to the next than people whose eyes recognise for them what has been seen before and warn the mind continually of the strange, the new and the incomprehensible wherever it may present itself. In a very definite sense I believe that a good memory is a guarantee of my own integrity, my own singleness of life.[7]

Dunkel sees this fragmentation in other people too, especially in Sophie, though this is partially a result of his effect on her. By his cool and detached mastery over her and by his skilful handling of their sexual relationship, he feels he has made her:

> one and indivisible, a whole . . . Something I introduced into her life and it split, divided her and shattered her experience into a thousand fragments all at once. But I stayed patiently by her. I drew as a magnet draws and once again assembled all the fragments into a new order. And

---

1 *The Nature of Creative Activity*: trans. O.A. Ceser (London: Routledge Kegan Paul, 1939; 2nd ed. 1952; repr. 1965), pp. xix/xx

2 BN 15/16: 12: 15: 15

3 BN 206: 152: 108: 114

4 BN 205: 151: 108: 113

5 BN 204: 150: 107: 113

6 BN 199: 147: 105: 110

7 BN 249/50: 179: 125: 133

> now already she is once again or perhaps for the first time a whole woman.[1]

This is Dunkel's creativity. He also feels it as his responsibility. He feels responsible for the whole world, whose burden he bears:

> Now my world has drawn in. It is smaller than the world of an unimaginative man. And its weight is sometimes intolerable . . . I am Atlas. Formerly I was a god who contemplated all things airily from above. Now I bear the world upon my own shoulders as a burden which I cannot so much as turn to see.[2]

This feeling of the world as pressing, which is natural to a person who can only experience things as they impinge directly on his sensations - Dunkel can have no perception of things in the distance - is at least better than the only other way a blind person could perceive the world: as infinite. 'There I sat shivering and listened to the mighty suction of the water and tried to feel that it was not infinite, that facing me was land across the bay'[3]. In H.G. Wells' *In the Country of the Blind*, the race of blind people imagine the sky as a roof rather than as an infinite space, and Lowenfeld has discerned the consequences of these two different ways the blind have of perceiving their world:

> Space cannot be conceived in its totality. Its infinity is irrational and it becomes accessible to our senses only when we circumscribe it. At the centre of space, with nothing whatever to surround us, space itself would be infinite and therefore non-existent. The self would cease to be a measure of value in space. It would vanish to nothing in infinity. Our senses set limits to space and each in its own way enables us to grasp it. Visual space, for which the eyes are the intermediaries, we perceive as the widest space. Haptic space, for which our organs of touch and our bodily sensations are the intermediaries, as the most restricted. . . . The narrower, the more restricted three dimensional space or the space of our psychological experiences is, the more importance we assign to the self. Haptic space is of necessity restricted. . . . In it therefore, the significance and importance of the self are very much emphasised.[4]

The importance of Dunkel's self is very much emphasised. Even for a first-person narration there are an extraordinary number of 'Is' (to compensate for the eyes?).

---

1 BN 210: 148: 106: 111

2 BN 90: 66: 50: 53

3 BN 202: 49: 106: 112

4 Lowenfeld op cit. pp. 95/6

Dunkel is not only the centre of his world, but he has worked hard to detach himself emotionally and physically from dependence on the outside world and other people in order to make himself not only independent of it but master of it. And of course, responsible for it. Even in matters of sex, he must always be fully in control:

> I have never found that even the most frankly pagan, transitory love was easy. A woman is at all times a continent to be explored, not a port of call. I have sometimes envied those men who are only good for love when heavily primed with drink, and fully assured that their responsibility will not be extended beyond a night[1]

His detachment and mastery are underlined by the references to Nietzsche; Dunkel thinks it 'amusing' to read about the Superman in braille, but in many ways sees himself in these terms, and certainly feels himself above conventional morality.[2] Partly this is because, for him, the sensual and the sexual merge. Other men can look at women and imagine possessing them, but Dunkel can only have any knowledge of women whom he can touch, which for normal men will usually be a prelude to sexual contact: 'I have to touch as other men will look'.[3]

> I feel that I have the right and the obligation to myself of demanding and receiving more in physical love than another person. For love is touch and I am touch. My only profound contact with any other person is tactile. Woman I know only as a lover or as patient, and very frequently indeed the latter will demand to be the former as a natural completion of the process[4]

His insistence on mastery of himself makes his approach to the sex act different from that of most men, but is quite natural given his appreciation of the sensuality of movement for its own sake. He considers that

> in love which is to be fully satisfying to those engaged in it the emotional temperature must be kept down as low as humanly possible.
>
> The emotions must be frozen beforehand as the dental nerve is frozen before the extraction of a tooth . . . The actor who is to move his

---

1 BN 191: 141: 101: 106

2 This is where the professed debt to Henry de Montherlant's Pierre Costals novels shows most strongly, though in the first edition there was a dream sequence, cut from all subsequent editions, which made specific reference to the passage in Montherlant from which is was drawn.

3 BN 160: 118: 86: 89

4 BN 89: 65: 50: 52

> audience deeply must himself remain unmoved . . . The good actor is a man of extraordinary depth of feeling, a man emotionally rich above the average. But his emotion must be tapped and himself disintoxicated beforehand at rehearsal. If the feeling is strong in his heart it will be correspondingly feeble in his hands and features.[1]

When a man is in the grip of his emotions

> he is so much less a man. The human impulses, those that arise in a man as such and have reference to the whole of his existence, are not emotions at all. Love is not an emotion. It is the whole of a man brought into play by a range of things perceived in which the elements of crude emotion are negligible . . . A poem written in a state of emotional tension will be a fidgety, unfinished poem, and the colours will run. The sexual act, approached in a state of emotional tension will be premature, convulsive and unsatisfying to the point of nausea. It will be like the coupling of animals. For despite the view so heavily canvassed by contemporary writers like D.H. Lawrence that we must become more animal the simple fact of the matter is that animal love does not satisfy human beings even in their animal nature.[2]

Dunkel's unconventional attitude to morality is, as Elizabeth Bowen noted in the preface to the first edition very unLawrentian, even though the book caused the same kind of scandal on publication[3] as later attached to *Lady Chatterley's Lover*.[4]

Dunkel's mastery is thrown off balance by the arrival of the deaf mute Amity.[5] Even the mention of her causes him to withdraw into himself: 'I did not wish to be implicated . . . I repelled the thought of other people's infirmities, especially when they were greater than my own. It was a call on my emotions.[6] Amity reminds him of his own difference and her greater handicap seems to him 'ugly'. Her presence makes him realise that he may have had the same effect on the sighted ones when he arrived, even though he classes himself with them as opposed to Amity.

---

1 BN 117/8: 87/8: 65: 67

2 BN 127: 94: 69/70: 71/2

3 Because of a banner headline in the *Evening Standard*, the book sold out on the first day. See IP 43/4

4 The reference to visiting Lawrence's grave at Zennor and 'paying our respects' (199: 147: 105: 110) is surely ironic.

5 Based on Helen Keller, IP 35

6 BN 38: 28: 25: 26

> It turned me into a creature left stranded between two worlds to neither of which I belonged and I suffered from my sense of isolation. Again I had the sensation of being a stranded merman. Only now I had put on a lounge suit, professed Christian principles and found myself joining people of the dry land in shooting their nets.[1]

Sophie explains to him that as 'a matter of fact Amity's extremely pretty herself. Only, of course, you weren't to know that.'[2] But the 'fact' is a visual one; she looks pretty, and visual facts are taken for objective, universally shared facts. In the absence of the visual dimension, words like 'pretty' and 'ugly' can only be subjective (and perhaps metaphorical, as in 'an ugly business' for instance). So it is not that Dunkel is wrong about her appearance - her visual aspect - since this does not concern him; her ugliness comes from her 'triteness of feeling, and her awkwardness. He senses these things in ways the others can't. To them she appears 'patient and tranquil and . . . womanly'[3], so that they are 'blind' to just those aspects he can sense and vice versa. However, his feelings for her are largely a projection of his own fears and anxieties, since in the absence of a visual framework for his impressions of her, his emotional framework must shape them.

Dunkel can, however be wrong about things, as he sometimes realises: 'I may be wrong. All these ideas of Sophie Madron may have been wrong. And I may be at fault in the whole deliberate structure of a life that I have built around myself and my limitations.'[4] He is wrong about the girl he is embracing when he mistakes Betty for Sophie, and there are times when he is obviously inferring the action - 'John was going through what I am sure were graceful evolutions with tea-cups and plates of sandwiches . . . Sophie's voice lay in the same direction as Mrs. Nance's, and I fancied her leaning over the back of her aunt's chair.'[5] Most importantly, he is wrong about Amity's clumsiness. In fact, as he should have realised, her sensitivity is even greater than his, since her disability is greater. Her triteness, as he comes to discover, is purely the result of the inflexibility and lack of subtlety of the touch-sign language which is her only means of communicating, except for her uncontrollable voice, which seems to come from the depths of her being. Here is the animal feeling which Dunkel so disdains, and which nevertheless shows him for the first time that she is not merely to be identified with her crude communications.

This seems to me to be at the heart of the novel: not only does the use of a blind narrator question and subvert the idea of an objective first person narration, but it questions the objectivity of narrative as a whole. We are left

---

1 BN 238: 170: 120: 126

2 BN 244: 174: 123: 129

3 BN 244: 174: 123: 130

4 BN 37: 27: 25: 26

5 BN 229: 163: 115: ;22

knowing that Amity has 'hidden depths', but also that these depths are, in principle, unfathomable. And what applies to Amity applies to everyone to some degree. Language and thought are not identical, and a person's utterances are not definitive of a person's character, which, as Heppenstall said, is indefinable.

Whereas in *Blaze* the symbolism (Dunkel's name, the Cornish place names and the presence next to the house of the Druid temple etc.) are given by the author and not the narrator, *Saturnine*[1] and its revised version, *The Greater Infortune*[2] are permeated with symbolism filtered through the narrator's consciousness. Though it shows the influence of Céline in its mingling of reality and hallucination, of Céline and Henry Miller in its bohemian and low-life bizarrerie, and William Saroyan in its marginal[3], isolated and rather pathetic narrator, I can think of nothing like it written in this country around that time. Heppenstall's language, however, has none of the violence and outrage of Céline or the pulsing flow of Miller. It is always detached, ironic, humorous often in a sardonic way, and laconic always, even when describing the most bizarre fantasies. It is often impressionistic[4] but never expressionistic. Heppenstall also lacks Céline's pessimism and sense of evil, and Miller's obscenity (unlike a later writer whose work much resembles *Saturnine* - Jerzy Kosinski). Perhaps the nearest parallel is Saul Bellow's *Dangling Man*,[5] published the same year as *Saturnine*, which also has an angst-ridden intellectual waiting to be called up into the army and finding it hard to form his life into a meaningful pattern in the meantime.

---

1 London: Secker & Warburg, 1943. Hereafter referred to as Sat.

2 London: Peter Owen, 1960 Hereafter referred to as GI. Page numbers for both versions are given, but only significant differences in readings are noted. References to Sat. include both books unless otherwise stated

3 The narrator and his wife begin the book living in Marginal Road, which Heppenstall changed from Boundary Road (PAPM 12: this chapter of PAPM also confirms many of the details in *Saturnine*, although the names are changed)

4 See, for instance, the description of Effie; Sat. 18: GI 22

5 Heppenstall much admired Bellow (PAPM 14), though since both books were published in the same year there is no question of direct influence.

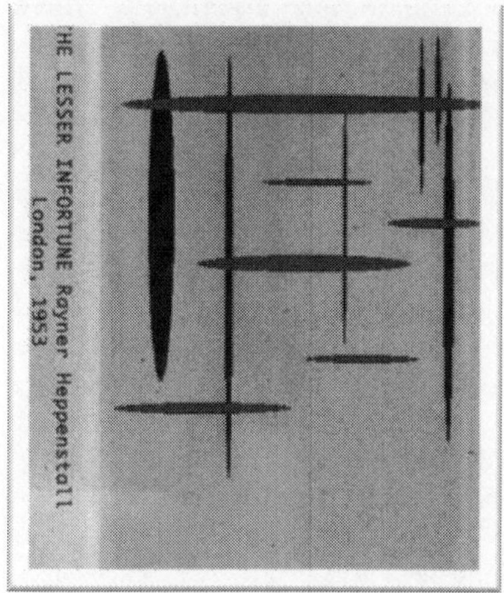

Saturnine contains a description of itself which brings out its extraordinary complexity and diversity:

> It seems as if I were telling four or five stories at once, but that is how it was. I can imagine this story divided up between four or five distinct novels. There would be the novel dealing with the business man who crashed and upon whom a hitherto suppressed romanticism thereafter took its revenge, causing him to suffer from delusions and eventually to lose his memory. There would be a novel dealing with the London of before the war and during the Sitzkrieg, its decadent intellectualism, its circles of vice, the disintegration of personality later to be remedied by a national risorgimento. There would be novels of simpler theme, the downfall of an erotophile, the errant husband and wife brought together by the birth of a child. More interesting perhaps than any of these, there would be a highly atmospheric novel dealing with experiences in a half-world of death and rebirth. But in actuality these and other potential themes were inextricable.[1]

The sequel to *Saturnine, The Lesser Infortune*[2], by contrast, is an almost entirely straightforward account, indeed recording, of the narrator's (and insofar as the

[1] Sat. 93. Not in GI

[2] London: Cape, 1953. Hereafter referred to as LI. This book was also considerably revised (parts of it having gone into GI) but the revised version has never been published. Mars

novel is highly autobiographical, Heppenstall's) wartime experiences. Where *Saturnine* shows the influence of Céline and Miller, *The Lesser Infortune* was written in the manner of Marcel Jouhandeau, whose style Heppenstall consciously tried to imitate:

> For several years before 1946, Jouhandeau had represented, and for some ten years more was to represent, the kind of writer I should have liked to be. What I mean is that I should have liked to write, from day to day, simply about the moment and its concerns and any past matters which pressed on the memory, the prose being merely careful, transparent, exact, easy on eye and ear, varied only by the variety of the mind's approach to what it scrupulously dealt with, utterly shameless, wholly personal. That it was quite impossible is due to the rigid formality of British literary customs. The novel and the diary-without-dates cannot flow into each other here, and I had long been sickened by the contrivances expected of a novelist.[1]

Nevertheless, this is exactly what *The Lesser Infortune* achieves.

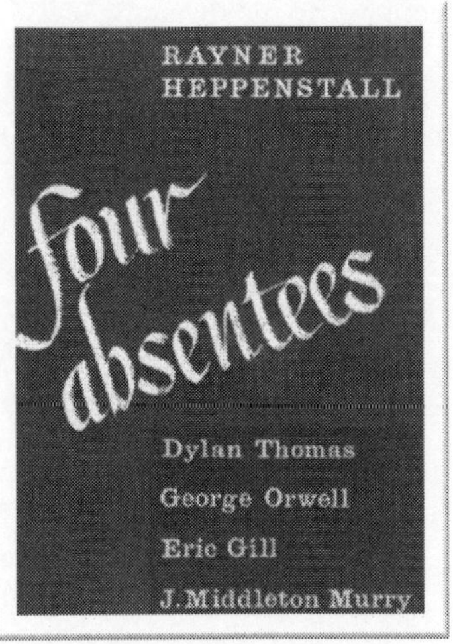

The problem of personal identity which the narrator of *Saturnine* faces is sublimated (if not completely overcome) by the narrator of *The Lesser Infortune* in his attempt to become a passive receptor of impressions:

> I entertained some notion that it was my duty as a poet to live through the extremes of contemporary experience.[2] . . . But I must not go on thinking 'I . . . I . . . I . . .'. That way lay madness. 'I' must be only the shadow and the recorder. The sensitive, recording mind could remain (I hoped). The sensitive ego, the life sensitive to its

---

(according to the book's epigraph) is the lesser infortune, Saturn being the greater. Mars is also of course the god of war.

[1] IP 87 See also his discussion of Jouhandeau in *The Fourfold Tradition* 170/177

[2] In *Four Absentees* (a book of reminiscences about Middleton Murry, Eric Gill, George Orwell and Dylan Thomas (London: Barrie & Rockliff, 1960), 150) he records Dylan Thomas's reply to his view on this. Thomas disagrees.

own impulses and motions must disappear[1]

In fact, he does not live through any extremes at all. His war is spent removed from active service in an environment where the only things grotesque and bizarre are the military rules and procedures. He feels, though, that his intelligence stands between him and the direct recording of experience. As Dunkel noticed the poetry in the speech of the road menders, so Leckie envies the simpleminded Fletcher, who envies Leckie's education:

> what he showed was precisely that gift which he believed to be characteristic of educated men and so kindly attributed to me, of using words to make the world about him quiver with life.
>
> What educated men said was new, delightful and transparent and Fletcher felt released by it. Other people muttered darkly in the grip of their obsessions.[2]

Leckie clearly feels that this is the wrong way round, since in *Saturnine*, where he had given too much thought to life and his role (if any) in it, he had been muttering darkly at great length in the grip of his obsessions. In the later book, he tries to abandon reflection on the world for reflection of the world, to become a recorder not an interpreter, and to efface rather than to develop his personal identity. Not that, in either case, he can be fully involved in the world. Either way he is an outsider, unable to form part of any community.

It is partly in this sense of the otherness of the world and other people and partly in the instability of Leckie's personality that *Saturnine* can be considered an existentialist novel, as well as in the search for order, meaning, pattern and freedom from responsibility which the novel at once seeks and denies. *Saturnine* is probably the first British novel to make use of existentialist themes (not that there have been many more since) with the possible exception of *Blaze*. It was published in the same year as Camus' first novel, *The Outsider*, and only four years after Sartre's *Nausea* (before *Being and Nothingness* but after the three early philosophical essays), and Heppenstall's existentialism seems to go back to Nietzsche and Kierkegaard.[3]

---

[1] LI 37

[2] LI p 100/101

[3] Though, later, in Dl (1947) he discusses Berdyaev and Karl Barth, and in the same year he edited de Ruggiero's *Existentialism*. See also IP 62 where he mentions his post-war interest in French existentialism and p 78/9 where he discusses Sartre. Kierkegaard was also a prime influence on *The Connecting Door*: see IP 212

Leckie[1] feels an outsider but tries 'to find myself a place in the world.'[2] Like Dunkel, he considers himself classless, and he has no profession or training. He has no 'position', either in the sense of a job or in the sense of a social position. He cannot even think what sort of job to apply for[3] (he seems to have no past experience in this sense) or what to put on his military registration form.[4] He hates the middle classes however and sees his ideal world as a 'world of complete lawlessness, a chaos without policemen. Then I should know how to deal with a middle-class imbecile like Frances Abell. I should slit her throat and steal her purse.'[5] Money rather than class is the true source of his anger, which is purely personal rather than on behalf of any class:

> The sun does not shine upon the rich and the poor, the just and the unjust equally. It is because of his money that Richard sits there enjoying the sun, while I oversleep with misery. That is why his face is plump, ruddy and without a single line, while mine at the same age is deeply scored, set hard and very pale. He shuts me out from the light of the sun.[6]

Leckie's feelings of powerlessness and claustrophobia are partially due to his lack of money and consequent lack of physical freedom, which seem also affect his ideas on freedom in general; when he receives the money unexpectedly due to him, he goes so far as to say 'I recaptured my belief free will.'[7] It is his enforced (as he sees it) idleness which has been responsible for his mental state: having no activity with which to identify himself, and no other people sufficiently close to define himself against, he hardly exists, as we saw that Heppenstall said of people in isolation. 'I must have spent the bulk of those months rotting in an armchair, while madness rooted busily in the motionless soul. When I think of this inaction, it is as if one had turned to his mirror and found that he no longer cast any reflection in it.'[8]

Instead of resolving this lack of identity through action and involvement, Leckie attempts, inauthentically, to deny his freedom and responsibility as well as the formlessness and meaninglessness of the world in three ways: by subscribing

---

[1] This is the narrator's name in Gl and LI, changed from Frobisher in Sat. Many of the names have been changed, including his wife's (Alison from Margaret) and Kokoschka's (whom Heppenstall knew, and who drew the cover for Sat.)

[2] Sat. 39: GI 49

[3] Sat. 39: GI 50

[4] Sat. 147: GI 179

[5] Sat. 38: GI 48

[6] Sat. 39: GI 49

[7] Sat. 79: GI 101

[8] Sat. 62: GI 78

to a belief in astrology[1], which substitutes fate for free will; by flirting with Catholicism, which substitutes obedience and faith for free will; and in his hallucinations. In these three ways he seeks some meaning and purpose for his suffering, though he says that he has 'never subscribed to any doctrine because it gratified, comforted or exalted me.'[2] The doctrines humble him rather than exalt him, but that is precisely the comfort he needs.

Astrologically, as well as in the normal meaning of the word, Leckie is saturnine[3], 'a man three parts fire, four earth and two water, a man without air, an obsessed man lacking the free, disinterested mind, a son of Cancer and Leo, arrogant, truthful, passionate and afraid.'[4]

> As to myself, I shall never be subject to undue influence from Mars but remain in the grip of Saturn. While Mars lords it over the lives of other people, I labour alone beneath this cold, basilisk eye. That is the meaning to be found in my conjunction of Mars and Saturn in the House of Fame, with Jupiter, lord of luck, in opposition to them both but by two or three degrees in closer opposition to the man with the hour-glass on a cooling moon. No branding irons, no racks or thumbscrews for me, only dripping water.[5]

Even during wartime, he is alone and isolated. Looking for comfort, he turns to astrology; if all is governed by fate he is freed of the burden of responsibility and choice. After he has assaulted Richard he says: 'It was not my act. The world and a great many stars conspired to rob me of the power of free movement'.[6] He also makes several passing references to his clandestine Catholicism, but despite these twin beliefs, he still declares his distrust of any philosophical system. He compares himself to Richard, who 'had in his time looked at a great many philosophical works and still hoped that one day he would find in one of them a simple formula which contained the whole truth.'[7] Both astrology and Catholicism look for the truth in a book, but Leckie sees himself as entirely different from Richard (who is in some ways his alter ego; the two are often compared and contrasted, especially after they have both received scars in

---

[1] It may be that the change of name to GI may have been intended to emphasise the astrological, since 'saturnine' has a more normal meaning.

[2] Sat. 30: GI 38

[3] Longfellow apostrophised Dante as 'poet saturnine' and Verlaine's first book of poems was entitled *Poèmes Saturniens*. Gustav Holst's Saturn is the bringer of old age.

[4] Sat. 17: GI 20. GI omits everything from 'lacking'.

[5] M 133

[6] Sat. 56: GI 69

[7] Sat. 18: GI reads 'Richard expected that one day he would find the truth in a book. I did not. I sometimes grew angry with Richard on this score. I became dogmatic. It was, of course, understood that I had superior intuitions' 2???

identical places; Richard, the wealthy homosexual, being Leckie's antithesis). Richard reads Hegel: Heppenstall, when not writing fiction, has said of Hegel (and Marx): 'I do not myself subscribe to this evolutionary optimism',[1] and that in 'philosophy there are no axioms'.[2] Indeed the formlessness of the novels and their mass of seemingly irrelevant detail deny any pattern in life. But Leckie, paradoxically, holds on to his belief: 'I am certain that all things do cohere within a pattern, that anarchy and chaos are conditions not to be found in nature and that, if one were possessed of the necessary technique, the whole of a man's life could be read clearly from a single hair of his head.'[3] Leckie sees the novel's diversity and apparent randomness as reflecting an order and pattern which it is beyond his power to discern, but that none of the seemingly unimportant details are irrelevant. That these reflections are not in *The Greater Infortune* may reflect a change in Heppenstall's attitude after 1942. Certainly he wrote in 1947 that writing novels and belief in any religious system are incompatible:

> All literary creation is myth-making activity, and we may therefore suppose that a practising myth-maker who happens also to owe allegiance to a fixed and embodied mythology is likely to find himself in difficulties.[4]
>
> The creative imagination, dealing with experience according to its own laws, makes discoveries which the praying, the believing soul does not acknowledge. There is a sense in which the creative imagination is repugnant to Christianity and to any fixed and embodied myth. It is a question of time and space, of the dramatic, the dynamic qualities of existence.[5]

Leckie's contradictory impulses – to find a place in some system and to be free – put him in an untenable position, and his escape is through hallucination. He has several of these, the most important of which are his illusion of watching himself from a distance,[6] his visions of 'Thea', the perfect woman, 'the naked impact of my own life upon me . . . the 'beauty of the world''[7], to whom he is linked by fate; and the illusion of his own death.[8] He believes that he has, in a previous life, been

---

[1] RR 90
[2] DI 67
[3] Sat. 93: not in GI
[4] DI 26
[5] DI 27
[6] Sat. 73-78: GI 94-99
[7] Sat. 113: GI 135
[8] 'I died instantly and without pain' must surely be the most effective chapter ending in literature. It is even more effective than the opening of Rex Warner's *Why Was I Killed?*

cruel to 'Thea' and that this explains his present misery: 'I knew that 'Thea' and I were not strangers . . . I knew in what relation we had previously stood to each other, that she had been in some way subordinate to me and that I had used her cruelly'[1]: 'I was permitted to know that it was a wrong done to her which had drifted like sand into the delicate machinery of my fate . . . Nothing is now permitted except to die in full knowledge and with full consent. Now the planet Saturn will slowly chill me to death.'[2] She also represents the imperfection and pointlessness of his own life:

> It was as if a man should regard a picture, read a poem or contemplate a beautiful action and find in it so much revelation of his own life that he cried aloud. His cry would be composed only in part of pure wonder. The rest would be intolerable anguish because he saw the form of his life exhibited with a definition which he in his actual life-time would not be able so much as to indicate. Thereafter he would become a saint or a drunkard or else die quickly.[3]

Leckie 'sees' her just before his 'death', which as his astrological investigations had revealed, would be due to falling masonry. Death, however, does not bring an end to his angst. He had previously thought that to face fully the inevitability of death would enable him to live free from anxiety:

> I thought that henceforward I would go through the world with a rope around my neck like the Burghers of Calais. If anybody were impolite enough to ask me about it, I would explain that I was herein expressing my true condition and that I expected the moment to come soon when that condition finally worsened beyond endurance, upon which I should simply attach the free end of my rope to a tree or something of the kind and jump. I felt that to appear everywhere costumed in a rope would in some way act as a talisman or phylactery, removing me from anxiety and despair because I had so fully expressed and thus come to an end of these things and because the means of a quick deliverance was so tangibly to hand.[4]

But the mere acceptance of the inevitability of death is not enough; he needs to 'die' to finally escape from his freedom and responsibility. Richard had said that

---

(Bodley Head, 1943): 'I continually wonder how to account for my present state, which, I suppose, it would be accurate to describe as one of death.'

[1] Sat. 25: GI 31

[2] Sat. 30: GI 38

[3] Sat. 30: GI 38

[4] Sat. 39/40: GI 50/51

the Abells were 'dead' whereas Leckie was alive,[1] referring to their lack of authenticity, but Leckie cannot achieve this inauthentic stage, no matter how hard he tries (and as a student of Kierkegaard he would know that the greatest misery is not to realise that one is in a state of misery, as the Abells do not), and welcome death as the only escape. He is seeking the kind of climax to his life which he has already claimed is impossible:

> To hear people talk, you would think that climaxes were very common, that in fact everything had a climax. It is wishful thinking. People would like something to come to a resounding conclusion and remove them henceforward from the awful continuity of time. It is part of the death wish. The Victorian novel-reader believed marriage a climax to love. We know better.[2]

Not surprisingly, then, 'death' proves to be a disappointment, and not at all the escape for which he had hoped:

> Here is peace. Here is an end to all strife, division and anxiety. No longer have I anything to fear. The worst that can befall me has already befallen, and I am still happy. Responsibility and care . . .
>
> I checked myself. This was not true. I still nourished the seeds of anxiety in my heart.[3]

The 'Guardian of the Threshold' tells him that there is peace, but not how to find it.[4] After his return to life, Leckie does to some extent find it, as he grows towards his wife and their newly-born baby. The book does not have a climax,[5] but ends in relative tranquillity and stability.

A vision of a possible way of life is given by Gertrude Mallinson.[6] She is referring to Joe Passiful (whose name connotes not only 'Parsifal', the perfect fool, the guileless innocent, but also 'peaceful' and 'passive'), who, Gertrude claims, is a saint. Gertrude herself is seen as something of a perfect woman by Leckie: 'Truth resides in her. Wisdom and love reside in every vein and vessel of her body and in every minutest wrinkle of her soul . . . She is the most beautiful of

---

1 Sat. 64: GI 81

2 Sat. 65: GI 84

3 Sat. 199: GI 142

4 This seems to be particularly important for Heppenstall, though he never fully resolves it. In a discussion of Sartre (IP 78) he argues that the 'point of rest' may be the most important existential problem.

5 GI has as its last chapter the beginning of LI, but neither version has an 'ending'.

6 Called Flora Massingham in GI. In real life, she was the woman referred to in *Four Absentees* as the 'Labour Party Organiser'.

all women and all men . . . Gertrude Mallinson surpasses . . . all . . . beautiful women as the sun a sulphur match'.[1] Joe's putative sainthood comes from his great humility; he 'feels that he has no right to existence'.[2] Gertrude feels that the true beauty of life resides in what most people would consider its ugliest and filthiest aspects. Sainthood means:

> kissing the dust, not because you're bidden to do so but kissing it with a loving, passionate kiss. Not for display and not out of panic anxiety, but with a quiet, passionate and compassionate love, with all due patience and humility. Listen, we've mentioned worms.[3] It isn't necessary to go so far as worms. Consider merely that everyone stinks of excrement and putrefaction. . . . St. Augustine and Dean Swift thought of all this and thought it a reason for hating and belittling mankind. I think it is a reason for being in love with excrement and putrefaction. It is a reason for choosing out among all mankind those who stink unashamedly, for consorting with lepers, thieves and whores, for choosing to be accounted scum. Scum, the rest of the world would say. The cream say I. The elite . . . A man is worthless until he has touched rock bottom. He is worth only a little if, having once touched it, he then recoils in anxious haste or struggles against adversity. A man should make rock bottom his abiding place, his nest.[4]

This rather Ghandian morality is too much for Leckie however.

Leckie as outsider, and in his erratic behaviour provides a useful illustration of Heppenstall's notion of the universal importance of the scapegoat in society, which he took from the psychologist D.W. Winnicott. The scapegoat is any individual whose behaviour or activity is outside the pale of social norms, and may therefore be censured by society, but is necessary to society to give it a clear feeling of the boundaries which the scapegoat transgresses and without which a society could not exist. The scapegoat is essentially innocent, carrying away the guilt and anxiety of the others. Heppenstall used this idea in *The Double Image* in dealing with the role of the priests in the novels of Bernanos, where he considered the possibility that 'all the key characters in fiction were scapegoats in one sense or another. Indeed I began to wonder whether the whole of our narrative and dramatic literature were not a concerted effort to find and employ scapegoats.'[5] Unfortunately, Heppenstall did not develop this idea further, and it is too big a topic to discuss here, but it does raise some interesting questions: are

---

1 Sat. 46: not in GI, where description of her is much less hyperbolic

2 Sat. 53: GI 66

3 They had been talking of Leckie's hallucination of the worm escaping from his mouth.

4 See IP 89/91

5 DI 30

literary characters scapegoats for the readers or for their authors or both? Did Heppenstall use Leckie (and later Atha, especially in *Two Moons*, where his own feelings of guilt were very strong) as scapegoats for his own anxieties? What, if any, is the relationship between this idea and the Aristotelian notion of catharsis, both of which seem to share the notion of vicariousness (the priests Heppenstall was discussing in relation to Bernanos are of course called 'vicars' in the Church of England). And, if true, where does this leave the writers who have disdained the 'novel of character', which is decried by many as obsolete, but which, according to Heppenstall's theory fulfils a vital social role?

A man tells Leckie that 'the past is man's worst enemy. I should like to abolish memory, particularly for you.'[1] While he is 'dead' the Guardian of the Threshold tells him that to lose one's memory, as Leckie tried to do, is to lose one's past, which is

> all that you have since become . . . your task is to face the future as you are. Your knowledge of the past is precious. You must accept it with gratitude and turn elsewhere. You must neither use the past as a means to shield you from the future with all its uncertainty. Nor must you strive to destroy the past in order that you may face the future without a burden, formless and impressionable as a column of water.[2]

This expresses the dilemma of existential concepts of the self: the individual is both in a sense determined by and in a sense free of past experience. The authentic individual must not seek to evade freedom and responsibility by using the past as a 'shield' – to deny the possibility of free choice – but cannot be completely protean either.[3] What then is the self which, as Jaspers put it, 'I am invited to become'? Heppenstall thought that the individual should not deny the past but come to terms with it and try to make it fully explicit.

> It seemed to me that a set of opinions was best not paraded as though it were a pure intellectual formation, that what one thought received meaning only in terms of its genesis. Thought should be, and should be seen to be, derived from, and expressive of, a body of personal experience, and the experience should be stated. In that sense, thought should be existential.[4]

---

1 Sat. 20: GI 25

2 Sat. 120: GI 144

3 In Heidegger's terms, *Dasein* must in conscience face its guilt, which is given by its *Geworfenheit*, and, with resolve (*Entschlossenheit*), balancing past and present in the move to the future.

4 IP 149

Only by understanding the workings and contents of one's memory can one understand the nature and extent of one's freedom. As Dunkel says:

> Memory is in one sense or another the clue to all things. It is the continuum, the ambience in which all our disjointed moments cohere into a whole. And it is certainly not, for instance, a specific faculty of the mind with which we go fishing into the past, angling for some incident or other which takes the bait or eludes it in the same apparently capricious way as ordinary fishes do. No, it is all pervading. It is the all-pervading activity of life, the principle of human existence, and if we begin to understand it we should be a great deal nearer than we are to knowledge of the world in which we live.[1]

Heppenstall wrote, as we saw, that the self can only be defined by its relationship to others. In *Saturnine* we see Leckie trying (largely unsuccessfully) to define himself not against others but against a self he does not understand and which seems to have no memory at all. In *The Connecting Door*[2] and *The Woodshed*,[3] the same narrator (i.e. Heppenstall himself), his name changed to Atha [the other?], seeks to define himself in relation to his own past experience (since other people are no more than shadows in either book) and, moreover, to recapture, Proust-like, his past life. Both novels juxtapose his 'present and past coexistence', though in two different ways. In *The Woodshed* the narrator revisits his childhood home and relives periods of his younger life; in *The Connecting Door*, the narrator literally encounters his past selves when he meets Harold - himself as a student (though the character was based on a friend of Heppenstall's) - and Atha, himself several years later.[4] The narrator does not give his own name, but he is clearly the same Harold Atha of *The Woodshed*. It is also clearly Heppenstall

---

1 BN 248: 179: 125: 132

2 London: Barrie & Rockliff 1962. Hereafter CD.

3 London: Barrie & Rockliff 1962. Reset and repr. Calder & Boyars 1968. Page numbers for both editions given. Hereafter referred to as W.

4 Heppenstall's ages on his own three visits to Strasbourg, where the novel is set (though this is not specified) were 20, 25 and 37.

himself; he refers, in the equally autobiographical *Two Moons*, to these two as 'a pair of highly autobiographical short novels'.[1] These three are in fact far more personal and informative about Heppenstall's life (despite the names being changed) than his ostensibly autobiographical works, and this raises the whole question of the relationship between the two forms. Heppenstall regarded writing novels as essentially writing about oneself, but also thought that a purely objective autobiography would be impossible: 'of course something personal must shine through all artifice, and I know I am really writing about (or expressing) myself. A difficult thing to do: we are all largely fictions, even to ourselves'[2] it seems that for Heppenstall, the difference between fiction and autobiography was purely an aesthetic one and not a matter of truth versus fabrication: all novels are personal, and not only all autobiographies but all lives are to some extent fabricated. He tried, in his novels, to close or at least bridge this gap, In *The Fourfold Tradition* he compares Proust and Jouhandeau and concludes that 'the achievements of both stand midway between autobiography and fiction'.[3]

The Connecting Door had its origin in a radio broadcast called 'Return Journey' which Heppenstall based on his own three visits to Strasbourg, and also in a radio portrait of Strasbourg which used stream of consciousness interior monologue, which he thought well suited to the medium of radio.[4]

> A literary cue for *The Connecting Door* had been provided in 1944 by Kierkegaard's *Repetition*. In that book, the narrator . . . on the one hand recounts the amorous and religious difficulties of an unnamed man, essentially Kierkegaard himself in his situation two years before, and, on the other hand, describes a return journey he had made shortly thereafter to Berlin in search of a 'repetition' which he equates with the 'recollection' of the Greeks and glosses in Latin as a *redintegratio in pristinum*, a search necessarily doomed to failure.[5]

The Woodshed also has a narrative present (which comes in between sections III and IV of *The Connecting Door*) covering four days (plus a Coda), but primarily concerned with the narrator's past, in this case the years from 1914 to 1927, the time of his childhood and early youth. When he wrote these novels, Heppenstall had 'become increasingly preoccupied by the past which moves forward constantly into a previous future so that the past recedes at every moment . . . It

[1] London: Allison & Busby, 1977. Hereafter referred to as TM

[2] Entry in *Contemporary Novelists*, ed. J. Vinson: London: (St James Press and New York: St. Martin's Press, 1976), 627

[3] o cit. 173

[4] IP p 213/4; PAPM 48

[5] IP 212

seems natural therefore to me to tell a past story within a present-tense narrative framework, which may be either interior monologue or the day-by-day notes of a man presumed writing.'[1] (*The Woodshed* uses the former method and *The Connecting Door* the latter). The interior monologue of *The Woodshed* takes place partly on a train, and 'in a train your consciousness streams like a cold',[2] but as Atha realises at the end of the novel, the stream is backwards-flowing, reaching into the past from the present. The stream of consciousness as normally practised is a necessary fabrication, since nobody can both write and be in the present at the same time.[3] There is another reason for using the present tense, and this is given by the nature of grammar:

> There . . . are too few tenses in our verbs. The pluperfect is difficult to sustain . . . while neither in English nor in French is there any yet further tense. From a narrative in the past tense, all retrospection must be in the pluperfect . . . A present tense narrative surface gives you easy retrospective perfect and, behind that, a pluperfect for occasional use.[4]

The Connecting Door also has flashbacks within the present-tense framework, which are also in the past tense. These loop back on themselves so that, for instance, the first section of chapter 3 ends with the sentence which begins the novel. To add to the embedded effect, the narrative present of both novels jumps forward a year in the final section so that what was regarded as present must now be regarded as past and moreover even this new narrative present has actually taken place thirteen years before the books were written, which to the present reader is twenty years in the past. All these effects add up to an ironic, distancing effect so that despite their present-tense framework, they seem a lot less personal and obsessive than the previous three. In *The Connecting Door* Atha is literally detached from his past selves and can view them with a laconic irony; in the case of Harold, indulgent and in the case of 'Atha' scornful. He tries always to remain emotionally detached: he describes his feelings on seeing evidence of Nazi atrocities: 'My reaction to all this was, of course coloured by a good deal of organic nausea'[5]; and he remarks that he is 'not much given to mysticism in summer'.[6] As in *The Lesser Infortune* he is trying to become the uninvolved recorder, though, unlike the *chosistes* he recognises the existence of emotion.

---

[1] IP 215

[2] W 17:13. Heppenstall makes the same point in *The Fourfold Tradition* 268

[3] Heppenstall makes this criticism of Dujardin in *The Fourfold Tradition* (143), but in general defends stream techniques and predicts their continued usefulness, and predicts that they will become quite usual (159).

[4] IP 215

[5] CD 108

[6] CD 52

Atha is thus unlike the Frobisher/Leckie of *Saturnine*, and is also unlike him in that he has given up the search for a pattern to life:

> Odd, how my Rhineland pilgrimages should at once thereafter involve me with my father again. But that is looking for coincidence and a pattern. There've only been two such pilgrimages, and this time there is no causal connection of a natural kind. The only conceivable link would be metaphysical.[1]

However, though he is not concerned with metaphysics he does still wonder about coincidences. His aunt and his father have strokes at around the same time: 'It is difficult to see mere coincidence in these two parallel calamities. There must, I feel, at least have been 'suggestion' a kind. It is all a bit eerie.'[2] Still, the feeling that things are 'a bit eerie' is not at all the same as believing in fate.

Atha is searching for an existentially authentic way of life. He recognises the inauthenticity of his father's life: 'Pleased absorption is a form of happiness'[3] and compares him to his vine in its 'thermostatically controlled, electrically heated greenhouse', which has for him 'a kind of symbolic identity'.[4] He contemplates suicide from the top of the minster dome, but is nevertheless afraid of falling: 'one's fate would have been taken out of one's hands. One would have been deprived of the last act of will'.[5] Atha remembers how he had previously searched for a (spurious) permanence: he compares 'not-yet-unconverted-Atha' to D.H. Lawrence, who contemplating the same (Strasbourg) Minster, 'thought it a disease of the spirit that men should wish to build so high and so permanently. He was, he says, himself always glad as a boy when his card-castles fell',[6] unlike his younger self who 'trembled with rage and frustration when his card-castles fell'.[7]

---

[1] W 23/4: 17
[2] W 35: 25
[3] W 30: 22
[4] W 30: 21
[5] CD 74
[6] CD 46
[7] CD 59

It is perhaps the death of his father (which occurs between sections III and IV of *The Connecting Door*, and is the basis of *The Woodshed*) which has finally freed him. While he is alive, Atha, though he identifies with him in many ways (for instance in his comparison of their scars), rejects him continually, though he later agonises over it: 'If I am dragged in chains before the Judgement Seat, it will be things like that rejection of my father which I shall have to answer for.'[1] His decisive rejection of his father comes when he has recently started at the grammar school, to which he has won a scholarship - no-one else in his family has ever had such a good education - and his airing of his knowledge leads to a disdainful reaction from his 'common-sense' father.[2] Not that it is only his family from whom he feels isolated by his intelligence: as a scholarship boy, he is rejected by other boys from his neighbourhood (and later, when they move to another area, by the boys at the grammar school there, who are mostly from a higher social class[3] as well as speaking with a different regional accent), and later he realises the inevitable isolation of the individual from all other people. He remains an outsider all his life, but it is this feeling of separateness which gives him the ability to write, for all narrative presupposes an irreconcilable difference between the experiences of the narrator and his audience: a community with exactly identical experiences can share a mythology but can ave no individually created literature.

The first realisation of the irreconcilability of this difference comes suddenly when, as a boy, he is rejected by two boys who had previously been his friends but had not gone to the grammar school. He later thinks: 'I am not dishonoured. I have done my best. A world ended. A world began. Humanity was diminished. Literature began. I can even think of the way down to Waterside Lane and the way I must now take as my Swann's Way and my Guermantes' Way in childhood'.

These two novels present opposed views of the past's relationship to the present self: to the narrator of *The Connecting Door* the past is external; his previous 'selves' are external to him and indeed are even created by him rather than vice versa:

> 'You remember? 'I said.
>
> 'You're not the only one who remembers!'
>
> 'All right', I said. 'Tell me, then. What were you doing . . . yesterday, for instance?'
>
> 'Yesterday? Why, I - I . . .

---

[1] W 28: 20

[2] W 144: 102

[3] This theme of the separation of the 'grammar school boy' both from his origins and from the class into which he was being thrust forms the basis of many 'angry' novels of the 'fifties. Heppenstall's experience was much earlier, and he felt that his generation would have had much to say to the 'Angries' if they had listened.

> 'You were doing nothing', I said, 'because I didn't think about you. In the past seventeen years, you've lived in occasional flickers, when I've had you in mind. You forget, or rather, you haven't quite realised, that without me you don't exist.'[1]

In *The Woodshed,* though present perceptions evoke past memories, they do not create them; the past self is 'I' just as the present self is. The child is father to the man; the past creates the present and the present recreates the past. It might seem that, in answer to the question of how free the individual is from his past experience in making present choices, the narrator of *The Connecting Door* would say that he was more free than the narrator of *Woodshed.* But even the former knows that 'nobody can leave himself behind',[2] even after apparently 'shedding all at once . . . our ties both to person and to place'.[3] On the other hand, at the end of *The Woodshed,* Atha does try to renounce the ties of memory as he leaves his home town for the last time. He thinks: 'And so I suppose I have finished with Hinderholme.[4] It won't matter. That is not the centre of my life'.[5] He knows that his roots were there but reconsiders the implications of this: 'Roots. Another dead metaphor. Men are not plants'.[6] And as he is leaving he feels nothing: no more memories are evoked by the industrial landscape. The train's 'scream is no anthropomorphic cry, no example of the pathetic fallacy. A train whistle is a whistle blown by steam . . . At present it is almost as though I were out on the open sea, glassily calm. If I again let down the deep trawl of memory,[7] I should bring up dabs and elvers by the ton. The catch would only be to throw back'.[8]

Nonetheless he is writing these novels thirteen years later with these memories still vivid, and it is the importance of memory which decisively separates these novels from the *nouveau romans* with which *The Connecting Door* was compared when it appeared.[9] Atha, far from being a *chosiste,* is like Proust, of whom Virginia Woolf said:

> The commonest object, such as the telephone, loses its simplicity, its solidity, and becomes part of life and transparent. The commonest

---

[1] CD 121

[2] CD 50

[3] ibid.

[4] Hinderholme is Huddersfield in Yorkshire, Heppenstall's actual birthplace in real life, and Carlin Beck is Guisborough.

[5] W 188: 132

[6] W 187: 132

[7] B.S. Johnson took this metaphor as the basis of his second novel, *Trawl.*

[8] W 189: 133

[9] Though they would bear comparison with, at least, Butor's *Passing Time,* and the use of the train journey in Butor's *Second Thoughts.*

> actions, such as going up in an elevator or eating cake, instead of being discharged automatically, rake up in their progress a whole series of thoughts, sensations, ideas, memories.[1]

There are, it is true, many passages in *The Connecting Door* which seem to show the influence of the *nouveau roman*, but influence is not really in question since, as we have seen, Heppenstall has been considered the father of the *nouveau roman*, and he points out[2] that parts of The *Lesser Infortune*, published in 1953 but written earlier, are every bit as *chosiste* as anything in Robbe-Grillet. Heppenstall certainly welcomed the *nouveau roman*, which had 'given me courage . . . had provided me with a moral example'[3] so that 'I had felt able without misgiving, to do what I had long wanted to do'[4] and admitted that Robbe-Grillet 'did boldly what I had been doing timidly'.[5] However, in his discussion of Robbe-Grillet in *The Fourfold Tradition* his welcome of the (then) new movement is quite guarded[6]: he admires the technical virtuosity and the conscious working on the novel form of Robbe-Grillet, but is disappointed that there is so little behind the technical display. And earlier in the same book, Heppenstall calls him 'highly doctrinaire', and dismisses his anti-humanism.[7]

Among the features of *The Connecting Door* which do recall Robbe-Grillet are the refusal to spell out exactly who the characters are; the long description of how he tries to determine the time while lying in bed; the many self-referring passages in which the notebook in which the novel itself is being written is mentioned (in the present-tense passages the novel reads like a diary or notebook) and the passages where he breaks off the present-tense narration to get up and walk around, as in this passage (which is itself a digression from the past-tense story he is supposed to be telling):

> This last was a bit of a dig, but my companion didn't rise. (Not satisfied with that sentence. Clearly, one doesn't 'rise' to a 'dig'. I suppose the sense also is clear, but perhaps this is my cue to look out over the street again. Nothing. No first-communion dresses or stretcher-cases. And go kiss Arlette behind the ear while discovering how far the *carré de porc* is

[1] 'Phases of Fiction', *Collected Essays* vol. II (London: Chatto, 1966), ??? This metaphor of transparency is also used by Nabokov in *Transparent Things*.

[2] IP 212

[3] IP 210

[4] ibid.

[5] *Contemporary Novelists*, o cit. 267

[6] p 265/271. He also discusses Sarraute, and Butor, whom he does not 'much like'.

[7] 191

> from being *au point*. That took longer than expected, because, despite the cooking instrument in her hand, she turned to me.)[1]

The Woodshed even contains a meditation on the method of its own composition:

> In a train your consciousness streams like a cold . . . If I had a secretary sitting opposite with a shorthand notebook, or a dictaphone, I could talk just like this.[2] They reckon about ten thousand words to the hour. In a journey of eight hours, you could finish a book. Change the names and you'd have a stream-of-consciousness novel. A man travelling somewhere for a purpose. What had led up to it, hopes and fears, retrospect and apprehension mingling, things noted as the landscape slid by. At the end, some kind of pay-off. The fears were groundless, the person was not there or had changed his mind, some accident took place, the person or place no longer existed. Had died perhaps.[3]

This is ironic however, since there is no pay-off, no climax (though his father does turn out to be dead), as Frobisher had explained in *Saturnine* there never is in real life. At the end of *The Connecting Door*, as he is about to discover who the person behind the door of the compartment is, Atha knows that 'I shall be granted no revelation about the long significance of my own life. No imaginative creation will be finished.'[4] And though the novel is finished, the ending is ambiguous; we do not find out who is behind the door, nor what difference it would make to Atha's view of his past life if we did.

The Connecting Door uses the conventions of the *nouveau roman* deliberately on occasion to subvert them. The most obvious case is in this passage:

> Let the harbour area be 551 *hectares*, with a water surface of 133 *hectares*, 18 grain warehouses and a coal-storing capacity of 600,000 tons. Let it. Let the Rhine question remain forever unanswered. Once our feet were on dry land, Hon. Bert and I ran for the first tram.[5]

Rather than imitating Robbe-Grillet's novels, what Heppenstall is doing is more like what Robbe-Grillet said was the province of the cinema. He said that the past

[1] CD 124

[2] cf. Robbe-Grillet's film *Trans Europe Express*, where he has a secretary on the train, and, again, Butor's *Second Thoughts*.

[3] W 17/18: 13

[4] CD 163

[5] CD 110

> has no reality beyond the moment it is invoked with sufficient force; and when it finally triumphs, it has merely become the present, as if it had never ceased to be so.
>
> No doubt the cinema is the pre-ordained means of expression for a story of this kind. The essential characteristic of the image is its presentness. . . . an imagining, if it is vivid enough, is always in the present. The memory 'sees again' the remote places, the future meetings, or even the episodes of the past we each mentally rearrange to suit our convenience are something like an interior film continually projected in our own minds as soon as we stop paying attention to what is happening around us.[1]

But the essential difference between Heppenstall and Robbe-Grillet is the former's warmth and humour – dry and laconic (and Northern) though this is. He called Robbe-Grillet 'doctrinaire' while admiring his stylistic boldness because he felt that this virtuoso technique was at the service of nothing, an empty formalism. Or worse, it was at the service of (in that it expressed) a dehumanised and dehumanising view of people. While he would perhaps have agreed that the modern world is dehumanising, he would not, as an artist, have connived with it. And this is true even of his next, most externalised novel. Here the concern is with other people rather than himself, and here the modern world seems an anachronism, but he is still concerned to explain – even if this is necessarily impossible to do fully – rather than merely to describe.

Until *The Shearers*,[2] all Heppenstall's novels had been written in the first person; and this was not accidental: 'All forms of printed fiction are artificial. The least unnatural are first-person narratives *in character*'.[3] In *The Double Image* he had commented on Sartre's criticism of Mauriac's passing from 'subjective' to 'objective' third person - in and out of characters' minds:

---

1 Introduction to *Last Year in Marienbad* (London: Calder, 1962; trans. R. Howard: repr. 1977), pp. 11/12

2 London: Hamish Hamilton, 1969. Hereafter referred to as Sh.

3 *The Fourfold Tradition* 249

at one moment he is inside his heroine's mind, thinking her thoughts and seeing with her eyes, and the next he is outside her, describing her and indeed passing judgement on her. I think Sartre makes a mistake in supposing that Mauriac alone displays this fundamentally dishonest use of the third person. It seems to me to be characteristic of the novel in general. It seems to me that the discomfort of this equivocation lies at the root of almost all modern experimentation in the novel form. Henry James and Virginia Woolf have largely done away with the objective 'he' or 'she' in one kind of novel-writing. I know of no novel in which at any rate the one character who functions as a quasi-narrator is without a subjective 'he' or 'she', though Conrad, Hemingway and Steinbeck have long passages in which they have managed to sustain a cinematographic objectivity. Indeed it seems to me likely that the wholly objective novel is impossible, and that the only completely unequivocal narrative form is that of a forthright first-person by which at least all the characters but one are clearly presented from the outside.[1]

Both *The Shearers* and the next novel *Two Moons*,[2] while not being first-person, juxtapose the intensely personal with the objective, but in both cases the omniscient, objective narrative is undermined and questioned by having a narrator who can 'see' all events all over the world simultaneously (it is suggested that this narrator might, given sufficiently powerful cameras, be recording them from the moon, but it is also made clear that the details are actually taken from the daily papers, so that when the narrator of *Two Moons* - who most of the time refers to himself in the third person[3] - cannot find a back copy of a newspaper for a particular day, the events of that day are not related). Heppenstall recorded the genesis of *Two Moons* in December 1974:

---

1 DI p 58/59

2 London: Allison & Busby, 1977. Hereafter referred to as TM.

3 On close consideration it can be seen that the third person passages refer to himself more than a year ago – rather like *The Connecting Door*; the exact nature of the time scheme is highly complex and not spelt out.

> I had worked desultorily and with little conviction at a sort of novel. This was almost nakedly autobiographical and documentary in content, placing my son's accident and much of its immediate aftermath in a context of the news of the day and in parallel with the death of a bellringer in the Buckinghamshire village in which M. and I had then stayed for the first time to be near Stoke Mandeville. To compensate for its lack of story and to mask the violence of feeling behind it, the narrative form was highly structured, the phases of the moon during two consecutive lunations being presented on facing pages of which precisely four were occupied by what was recorded for each day. The book had not been written consecutively The pages having all been numbered beforehand, I was able to fill them up in what order I chose.[1]

The first reviews appeared on May 22nd 1977, in *The Observer* and *The Sunday Times*.

> both are incredibly vicious. They are by Lorna Sage and Ronald Harwood, whoever they may be. Both devote their space to the way the book is laid out and hardly mention its content. Indeed, Harwood says nothing whatever about the content, but simply makes clever remarks about the form. To him, I am, though a distinguished man of letters, in this novel merely eccentric. To Sage, I am mad.[2]

In *The Shearers* there is a whole battery of narrative techniques, which itself questions the objectivity of any one technique: there are 'objective' third person, free indirect speech and indirect and direct streams of consciousness. The juxtaposition in both novels of the microcosmic and the macrocosmic[3] is not however an attempt at totality of representation; as the narrator of *Saturnine* said, any 'attempt at all-embracing consistency would be dishonest (and I believe that it is always so in life and that all novel-writing is dishonest in its degree)'.[4] The novels rather show just how partial all perception and knowledge are: even for the novelist who can go inside the heads of his characters, and even if technology should eventually 'present us with the omniscient eye we formerly attributed to God'[5] (and to the novelist). The omniscience of the author is further

---

1 ME p 144/145

2 ME 219

3 This is rather reminiscent of Dos Passos, as is the way of 'cutting' cinematically from one 'scene' to the next. The cinematic implication is emphasised by the fact that the narrator is considering making a film.

4 Sat. 93

5 TM 8

undermined by the lack of a resolution to the trial in *The Shearers*[1]; despite having access to some of the characters' thoughts we do not find out who, if anyone, committed the murders.[2]

The two novels also raise again the question of selection and relevance raised in *Saturnine*, much of the description of world events being (apparently) unrelated to the main narrative, and taken, seemingly at random, from the days' newspapers (*Two Moons* allocates three and a half pages to a day). The whole of *Two Moons* turns on the arbitrary juxtaposition of Adrian Tyler's accident and Atha's son's, along with more global catastrophes, and some of the narrated events seem to have no connection at all.

> So far as the author can judge, the story he is about to relate in bare outline has no close bearing on the general course of our narrative, while it is improbable that the reader would find its *péripéties* much more interesting than most of what he has already been and is yet to be told or reminded of.[3]

In *The Woodshed* Atha wonders what his fellow passengers will make of this notebook: 'They might think I was doing my accounts. In a way I am.'[4] All of Heppenstall's novels (with the exception of *The Shearers*) are attempts to account for, to explain and justify, his past life. *Two Moons*, though the most rigidly structured of his novels is also the most personal, even anguished. It is as if it is an attempt to exorcise the guilt he felt for his son's paralysis (the novels details are, except for the names, true of Heppenstall's own son) through objectifying it: 'autobiographical fact pretty well ceases to be that when it has been worked over several times. At any rate it is quite robbed of its autobiographical feeling.'[5] The striking difference between Heppenstall's autobiographical and fictional writings is how much more personal the latter seem; they certainly tell the reader far more about Heppenstall's life and feelings, once the names have been translated. In the autobiographical works his wife and family are hardly ever mentioned, and never by name. It seems that Heppenstall could not bring himself to write truthfully (and in some cases painfully) about himself unless he attributed his actions to others,[6] and had the formal constraints of the novel into which to channel the personal feeling. With *Two Moons* the formal constraints are the most severe he ever imposed (two parallel narratives,

[1] The novel was based on a real murder trial in France.
[2] cf. Robbe-Grillet's *The Voyeur*
[3] TM 139
[4] W 23: 17
[5] IP 314
[6] This relates again to the idea of the scapegoat in literature.

one on the left hand pages and one on the right, keeping exactly one month[1] apart - so that one narration finishes where the other one takes off - with three and a half pages to a day; the time scheme of past - a year previously - and present is highly complex, and the revelations are carefully controlled so that, for instance, the accident is not referred to in the second narration until it has happened in the first), and the story the most painful to tell. While he was wrestling with the formal problems he was less burdened by wrestling with his conscience; (not that he was in any real way responsible for the accident).

In *Two Moons* Atha has returned to the search for a meaning and pattern to life which had so occupied him in *Saturnine*. He considers again 'the possibility that traditional astrology may sometimes adumbrate a pattern where all at first had seemed meaningless',[2] and relate the seemingly unrelated, like the events in the novel. His search for a pattern leads him to dwell at length on the death of the young bell ringer Adrian Tyler whose death in a car crash the week before his son's accident seems just as pointless and tragic. 'The apparent meaninglessness of one calamity might, I felt, be illuminated by its coincidence with the other.'[3] Atha is asked to write a play on the subject of bell ringing, but this becomes the novel which is to be *Two Moons*.

> There was obvious symbolism in the fact that a young man's skilful practice of an old tradition had been ended by a lorry roaring along the road from spoilt Oxford to hideous Aylesbury. There was pattern in the interplay between the changes rung on bells and changes both in the *personnel* ringing and in the towers (their own strange usage) rung. The thing's coincidence in time with the worst that had ever happened in my small world would be far too much for half an hour on the small screen . . . That would require something more in the nature of a full-length feature film or a novel. The world of lorries and strikes and mixed populations and European unity would itself have to receive some representation.
>
> That Tuesday or Wednesday, I was already toying with the kind of narrative I am writing now, though I saw it perhaps as more cleverly schematic. I could, I felt, by the regular deployment of certain linguistic, syntactical and even typographical tricks, produce a narrative flow as distinctive as that of the best French exponents of the *nouveau roman*. An element I did not then consider introducing was that of the movement of the planets or that, simply, of the moon. Before I came to

[1] That is, one lunar month or, as the narrator calls it, one lunation.

[2] TM 82

[3] TN 107

> that, I had to despair of finding any meaningful pattern in what had happened.[1]

And in the end he does see that neither astrology nor any other system (he tried praying, but without much conviction) can pin down the randomness and contingency of life: 'I have quite enjoyed playing that old game. I am no nearer finding a meaningful pattern in the worst thing that ever happened in my life.'[2]

Not only can he find no pattern, he can attribute no blame for the tragedy. 'It was not clear what I could do. There was nobody at all evidently to blame.'[3]: 'Not even God could be blamed. He could not be blamed by me because I did not believe that he existed.'[4] Life is contingent and random and does not match the inevitability and regularity of the movements of the planets; despite the apparent inevitability of tragedy and suffering, as reflected in the newspaper reports and in statistics:

> the day's statistics could not yet be compiled. On the roads for instance, not all of the twenty were dead or the hundred seriously injured. Many of the thousand virginities had still to yield. An unspecified but smaller number of adults would yet consent and small boys be subjected for the first time to other practices.[5]

No amount of knowledge of statistics, the laws of probability or of astrology can, however, predict exactly who these victims will be. But humans have an innate sense of (or will to) order and pattern[6], which are reflected in *Two Moons* both by its formal structure and by the references to the patterns of bell ringing, which have a beautifully elegant logic far removed from the real world, and those of astrology.

But these are seen to be ultimately as false and empty as all the other rituals in which people seek to abrogate their personal responsibility: the trade unions in *Two Moons* ritually confront the management just as the barristers in *The Shearers* confront the judge, in the name of the law, which absolves them from the responsibility for the punishment of others, and as people ritually pray to

---

[1] TM 129 *The Woodshed, The Connecting Door* and *Saturnine* all also refer in different ways to their own composition.

[2] TM 188

[3] TM 104

[4] TM 106

[5] TM 78

[6] Worringer's argument, as we saw earlier, was that this will (*Kunstwollen*) expressed itself at time when man was least at home in the world; the twentieth century being one of these times.

God. In these novels, the many imperfections[1] and tragedies of human life are continually juxtaposed with the idea of perfection towards which people aspire, but which is not to be found in physical life. The most basic law governing human life (and the movement of the planets) is gravity. But paradoxically gravity, which literally holds the universe together and without which all life would be impossible also weighs us down spiritually as well as physically, clamping us to this imperfect world:

> Man's spiritual aspirations and woman's too, may be seen as an attempt to overcome or, as we say, transcend the downward pull, the sagging, the immobility. All aspiration is upward, it is lofty. The soul is without weight . . . Man's aspiration fails but he enshrines it in the Gothic arch, and his cathedrals soar.[2]

Man may temporarily rise above gravity and into space but 'in the end they will all fall, even the moon. Meanwhile, aeroplanes crash, tall buildings collapse, and the world's sleepers lie pinned to the earth.'[3] This is the simplistic view of Heppenstall's later years and it opposes the religious view, enshrined in the long quotes from Wesley in *The Shearers* that one day both the living and the dead will 'rise' to approach heaven to the scientific view that one day the 'heavens' will fall. This pessimism had surfaced earlier in *The Double Image* where Heppenstall had talked of the despair 'which a number of our contemporaries have shown to be an excellent medium'[4], and well suited to the modern world:

> I think we may confidently say that certain fissures have opened wider since the eighteenth century and that our world is more unstable in certain respects than any world of which we have comprehensive historical knowledge.[5]

However he did not seem to take this despair so seriously at that time; his earlier novels are sardonically humorous and he warned other novelists against taking themselves too seriously:

> The increasingly irksome characteristic of true novels or novels proper is their seriousness, their *trompe l'oeil* verisimilitude, their apparent preoccupation with human reality and truth although everyone knows

---

[1] Sh. 197/8 contains a catalogue of these.

[2] TM 198/9. The bell ringers of course occupy the 'soaring' church steeple; Gothic spires are also central to Worringer's argument.

[3] TM 199

[4] DI 44

[5] DI 65

> that a novel is in the first place a pack of lies, however much 'imaginative truth' it may be held in the last place to contain.[1]

Heppenstall's view of the world does not seem to have been as gloomy then as later: he was agnostic rather than pessimistic:

> such propositions as that the world is beautiful are not so much contrary to the truth as meaningless. They are pseudo-statements. It is like saying that women are beautiful. Some of them, of course, are, but then, on the other hand, some of them, and perhaps the majority are distinctly plain.[2]

In *Two Moons* the world has become a hostile-seeming place, as in *The Shearers* people are seen to be a lot less civilised than most people would allow. *Two Moons* is full of accidents, catastrophes natural and otherwise and there are a number of apparently motiveless suicides: Atha mentions the boy in the flat above, Henry de Montherlant (one of his most admired writers) and two other young novelists, to one of whom he was friend and mentor (this was actually B.S. Johnson, and the other novelist was Ann Quin, whom he knew slightly). There are even more, equally motiveless murders which become more horrific as the book progresses. But the world is not evil, it is merely oblivious; as Robbe-Grillet said, man looks at the world but the world does not look back, and this world is neither meaningless nor absurd (nor can it be called cruel), it is simply there.

The point of the juxtapositions of private, family tragedy with the larger tragedies as reported in the newspapers is this: what is the importance of one family's suffering (and this does not even involve a death) in *Two Moons* and one family's incest and possible murder in *The Shearers*, compared to the vicious and horrible violence committed every day, and what is the importance of these compared to the regular multiple deaths on the roads in aeroplanes and in natural disasters? And, further, what importance can even these have in a cosmic perspective, on the planets whose implacable notion is continually present in the novels?

---

[1] RR 91

[2] DI 61

Rayner Heppenstall left two versions in manuscript of a novel called *The Pier* at his death. This was due to be published in summer 1982 by Allison & Busby, but was not released until 1986. The same publisher in the same year also released *The Master Eccentric: The Journals of Rayner Heppenstall 1969-1981.*

The Pier is fundamentally a realistic novel and not obviously a Heppenstall work, except that the narrator is an elderly novelist called Atha, born in Yorkshire and now living by the sea in Kent who writes about French crime. Set in 1976-1978 it reads like the journal of the narrow domestic life of the narrator, who lives with his sister (unlike Heppenstall who lived with his wife). Nothing of any note happens to them until they start to have trouble with the next-door neighbours and Atha begins thinking of writing a novel set on a single day about a man who starts the day at the end of a pier, walks to his home, kills the neighbours and walks back to the end of the pier. At the end, he does in fact (or possibly in his imagination) buy a revolver in France with the intention of killing them. We do not see the murder scene, if there I fact is one. 'What has just happened was more unpleasant in several ways than I had expected. I shall try not to remember it. I am glad that it is all over.'[1]

Atha then switches to the future tense, describing how he and his sister are going to stay in France for a while.

> On the 24th we shall return to that town and to a house next door to the scene of a massacre which had interested newspaper readers for a few days and would do so again when the case came up for trial. The first thing I shall notice will be that the two cars still stand in the carport, where no doubt they will remain until court proceedings are over. both criminal and civil. At least one of the cars will be sold, perhaps both with the house. I shall be glad to see them gone. The house next door at the back will, meanwhile, be empty, blessedly empty, as it had been for the first ten months of our life there.
>
> As I flick open and put away my passport, I shall think again what a pity it is that passport control no longer date-stamps passports on either

[1] 188

> side of the Channel. It must make things so much more difficult for the police, who can neither alibi a man from his passport nor prove that he was abroad when he ought not to have been.[1]

Personal Afterword: I visited Mr. Heppenstall at his home in Deal in May 1981 while I was writing this chapter. He and his wife Margaret were exceptionally welcoming, helpful and encouraging to me. Mrs. Heppenstall looked at me quizzically and said 'have you read *all* my husband's books?' A few weeks previously he had had his first stroke and could not type his journal any longer; he could only write short notes. The last four entries in his journal read:

> 6 May
>
> Francis Booth came down from London[2]
>
> 7 May
>
> Hadn't slept. Rain in the evening.
>
> 8 May
>
> Hadn't slept. Rubbish collection a day late. Am very uncomfortable.
>
> 16 May
>
> 1.00 a.m. Thunderstorm

On May 17th he had another stroke and he died in hospital on May 23rd. He was a wonderful man as well as a wonderful writer and I feel very privileged to have met him.

[1] 191

[2] There is a footnote in ME which says 'An admirer of RH's work, particularly *The Woodshed*; he was writing a thesis on the modern novel.'

nicholas mosley[1]

3rd Baron Ravensdale, 7th Baronet of Ancoats, the son of Oswald Mosley and stepson of Diana Mitford, Mosley, born in 1923 seems an unlikely experimental novelist. His early novels had been conventional though internalised and highly wrought.[2] They seem to be organised on the premise that motives and emotions can be exhaustively described given a sufficient amount of words. Mosley was even then however wrestling with the problem of how to do this within the framework of the conventional novel, and was trying out a heightened, poetic style to try to capture characters' thoughts. He seems to realise that this was not working even in his first novel, where one of the characters says: 'I only write about myself from the outside. That is no good. I want to write about the world from the inside. I can't do that yet.'[3] Mosley did not find out how to do it until *Accident*, but some critics realised he was trying to do something different even then. One critic wrote of his first novel: 'It is written in at least half a dozen different styles, is badly written and is almost entirely lacking in characterisation',[4] which, given the state of the critical norms of novel-writing at that time must be taken to auger well.

Mosley's concern for the developing form of the novel is shown by the parodying of the critic in *The Rainbearers*, who criticises the modern novel:

> 'No, you see, there is no vitality any more, everyone is concerned with an analysis of death. Abstractions, abstractions' - he leered suggestively at

---

[1] This section was originally published as 'Impossible Accidents: Nicholas Mosley' in *The Review of Contemporary Fiction*, Summer 1982.

[2] *Spaces of the Dark*. London: Rupert Hart Davis, 1951; *The Rainbearers*. London: Weidenfeld and Nicholson, 1955; *Corruption*. London: Weidenfeld & Nicholson, 1957 and Boston: Little, Brown, 1958; *African Switchback*. London: Weidenfeld & Nicholson, 1958 ; *Meeting Place*. London: Weidenfeld & Nicholson, 1962. Trans. into French as *Aux Quatre Vents de Londres* by J. le Beguec, with preface by Henri Thomas. Paris: Gallimard, 1965

[3] *Spaces of the Dark* p. 193

[4] *Times Literary Supplement* review, 1951, p.65 (anonymous)

> the ceiling – 'They are no good you know, the art of literature is to know how to tell a good story, character and action, character and action' - he frowned at the solid earth beneath his feet - 'and that is what you don't get any more, not a trace of it anywhere. The business of the storyteller is to create characters, thus, large as life' - stretching his arms like an unbelievable fisherman - 'characters that stand, live, walk on their own two feet. Round characters, round like you and me' - he pointed to a girl at his feet who nodded sagely.
> 'But do you think people *are* round' Elisabeth said.[1]

Despite their evident concern for style and their striving for a means of expression, the first three novels are marred by sentimentality, and in his fourth novel, Mosley seems to have given up trying to penetrate the depths of his characters, and tries a completely new style. *The Meeting Place*'s narrative is carried solely by external, visual (that is as if described by 'a casual observer who knows nothing of the characters) description and dialogue. Its events are loosely connected scenes whose relevance is often not clear and the effect is disjointed, as if Mosley has decided that not only characters but also action are impossible to describe exhaustively. But the novel does not really work; its externality is not carried through into a full-blown *chosisme*, and the need to explain and understand is still present. Read in the light of Mosley's later novels it is tempting to see it as a kind of first draft for his next phase, especially the last section where the objectivity is abandoned in favour of a hallucinatory style which seems to point the way to *Accident*. Indeed, the notes Father Patterson makes for his sermon could almost be a manifesto for Mosley's future concerns:

> The fall of man into not evil but helplessness.
> A world which appears to have no meaning.
> The need to know the area within which meaning is experienced.
> When there is no meaning it is like a car out of gear: the engine moves but to no effect.
> When there is meaning this is experienced as movement in relation to the things outside it.
> What is the action that puts the car in gear?
> The need to know the point at which free will operates.[2]

---

[1] p. 13
[2] *Meeting Place,* p. 42

> 'Why is it', William said, 'that modern novels have to be so different, they can't just be stories of characters and action and society?'
>
> Charlie said, 'We know too much about characters and action and society.'
>
> William said, 'Then why write novels?'. . .
>
> Charlie said, 'This is the point, we can now write about people knowing.'[1]

Accident represented a break in Nicholas Mosley's work and one which could not have been fully predicted from his four previous novels. Mosley moved back inside one of his characters, not to explain him, but to show him to be inexplicable. Contrary to what Charlie said, we do not 'know too much about characters and action'. 'We understand only workings not meanings'. 'You never know a person; only what you put into them, their effects.'[2] In *Accident* the narrator, Jervis's thoughts bear little relation to his 'effects', and we presume that the other characters too have a life 'coursing underground. A river through caverns and gorges'.[3] The novel is rather like a Pinter play in which we have access to the thoughts of one of the characters, and it was entirely appropriate that Pinter should have written the screenplay for the film of *Accident*.[4]

Mosley had come to realise by now that there was no simple and unambiguous way to describe people, who are, by the standards of logic and ordinary language, paradoxical and self-contradictory, but had set out to try to find a way of expressing this:

---

[1] *Accident* (London: Hodder & Stoughton, 1965 and New York: Coward McCann, 1966; repr. London: New English Library, 1967; trans. into French, J. le Béguec and H. Thomas, Paris: Gallimard, 1968), p.72/3: 47. Hereafter referred to as Ac. followed by page numbers for both British editions. Like many of Mosley's novels, Accident has recently been republished by the Dalkey Archive Press.

[2] Ac. 17: 22

[3] Ac. 180: 116

[4] Published in Harold Pinter: *Five Screenplays* (London: Methuen, 1971). The 1967 film was directed by Joseph Losey and starred Dirk Bogarde

> I am obsessed . . . by trying to understand how human beings work. This makes novels important for me, since they are the best records of man's attempts to describe what a human being is. I always start by saying I'll write a straightforward story, but I can't . . . You see, one is concerned with the situation as it is and this must be reflected in the style. To describe how man works now without being two-dimensional you have to say two things at the same time - only through opposites can you say what man is.[1]

Jervis expresses a similar idea: 'We write in order to grasp it; to make a grab at the air. I wanted to say something about the world; about the meaning of it. Actions have not much to do with this. It is more of a feeling: this is what life is'.[2] For the novel writer the problem is that the more you come to know a person, the more difficult they are to describe.

> We describe best people who mean nothing to us - as a thing, an object. People we love we can't bring alive. Novels are usually about people we don't like, because we can portray them so clear and deathly.[3]

To describe a person is to fix and thus, paradoxically, to destroy their personality, which consists of contradiction and paradox.

To explain these contradictions to ourselves, let alone to others, words are inadequate. This is the paradox Stephen Jervis, as a philosopher faces: 'How accurate are words? I am a professional. Paradoxes.'[4] Even Jervis's philosophical views are not consistent; Anna reads her essay to him:

> An act of freedom breaking away from the limits of acceptance develops into commitment as well as rebellion, and it is this with which a person can identify himself. The statement 'I will' is at once a realisation that something exists within and yet there is something opposing it without.[5]

Jervis objects (he is an Oxford philosopher and Oxford philosophy has long been associated with positivist and linguistic philosophy):

> what is that, Sartre, Camus I suppose . . . The trouble is this is like poetry, private language, you can't analyse it. In what sense do you use

---

1 Interview with Timothy Wilson: *Guardian*, 29 June 1971, p.8

2 Ac. 192: 124

3 Ac. 42: 28

4 Ac. 186: 120

5 Ac. 48: 32

> the word freedom or rebellion or anything? The meaning is only in a state of mind, in which words are not doing much anyway.
>
> Anna said 'There's something in poetry'.
>
> I said 'Now less than ever. Your generation should see this who are so practical and unmythical . . . If I ask what are the ways you use the words 'I' or 'myself' you use other words about which I can ask the same questions. But this is the point of philosophy.[1]

But earlier he had himself told Anna that only art, not philosophy, could hope to answer the question of human identity, which rationality cannot grasp, to admit which is to question the whole basis of his occupation, which is his mental as well as physical security.

> A purely rational system is either faulty or sterile. It can go back to a position of certainty about existence, but from this point it has to introduce empiricism in order to describe what exists. About the self, for instance, it can say that something exists, because there is something that thinks it exists, but it can't say if this something has either substance or identity or continuity without appealing to experience . . . If you look into your own experience you find a succession of impressions of, for instance thinking, desiring, hoping, fearing, but you don't have a continued impression of a self that thinks or desires or hopes or fears. So the description of the self as an enduring entity is again impossible'.
>
> Anna said 'But surely people have been trying to find an answer. I mean writers and artists and so on,'
>
> I said 'Of course anyone can give his own answer. But you can't give an answer that would be generally acceptable.'
>
> Anna said 'Even a great writer?'
>
> I said 'It's true that art is the medium to offer answers, but these will of course be outside the scope of reason, which is all that can actually prove anything.'[2]

But even though Jervis realises that philosophy - at least his kind of philosophy - cannot answer the 'big questions' he still considers it important. Or so at least he tells himself:

> There is no more useful work than to illuminate old obscurities and contradictions, and by understanding them prevent more pathological

---

[1] Ac. 48/49: 32/33

[2] Ac. 29/30: 20

> confusions. For the rest - for what has to grow - this has to be found by the whole of life, and not particularly by intellectual discipline.[1]

Mosley, as we have seen, does not believe that the contradictions should or even can be removed; that this is reductionist and denies the irreducible complexity of existence. Even Jervis sees something of this: 'philosophy is more negative, a way of limiting personality. But so is all routine. What do we know about all this - in any form - we do not know.'[2]

Personality cannot be limited because it is so fragmented. No person can be exhaustively described because no one is simply one person: 'We are all fragments, disjointed.'[3] Jervis himself feels to be a different person when he is at home than the one he is in college. There is even a 'point on the road at which I move away from the person which I am in college and go into the person I am at home.'[4] The only way to avoid fragmentation is to fix one's own personality by sinking into a state of inauthenticity, of lack of self-questioning and responsibility. Jervis realises this, but also realises the difficulty of maintaining one's full complexity.

> This is what I think about, what I think is important. Either you turn into some sort of gutted thing, automaton, or you have to become involved with pain and birth again, the roots and all that nonsense. I keep on saying this. But I do feel this sort of crack-up, everything exploding, we're one person one moment and another the next; no continuity because no illusion.[5]

All Stephen's colleagues seem to have given up the struggle, become 'knowledgeable and deathly'[6], as does everyone over the age of forty: 'People become characters at forty. They stop. They don't feel anything.'[7] He is very attracted to this state himself, to becoming just 'that shadow against the wall'[8], at the same time as he is repelled by it (a typical Mosleian contradiction). 'There are oak pillars, fire, chair, bookcase. What I am making myself into. My surroundings.'[9] These surroundings and his work become him, delimit his

---

1 Ac. 14: 11
2 Ac. 15: 11
3 Ac. 111: 72
4 Ac. 18: 13
5 Ac. 145: 93
6 Ac. 29: 20. The idea of 'deathliness' will be of great importance in Mosley's later novel *Catastrophe Practice.*
7 Ac. 33: 23
8 Ac. 182: 118
9 Ac. 54: 36

personality. Like the other dons he is, in the full sense of the word, absorbed in his work: 'by now it has become something that you need; your personality. You are in a group, with dependence on the system. You stop asking what relevance all this has to anything else.'[1] And 'Oxford is conducive to all this'[2]; he feels that he and the other dons 'would be dug up here in another six hundred years. Or would remain permanently in a fresco. I had wanted some sort of destruction out of boredom with my work, my personality.'[3] Possibly due to the effect that Anna has on him, and possibly also due to his feelings for William, he begins to rebel against this 'deathly' safety: 'There were some dons who only cared about their work and nothing about their pupils: these touched no one. All caring was risky: you exposed yourself. It was better to be like this than the other.'[4] At the end, after the news that his child is alright, he determines to break out: 'I would run to the hospital past the ashes, the lava, the skeletons with their knees drawn up. I would say - I am alive.'[5] He has fully realised and accepted that life is full of contradictions; in his case that he can love Rosalind and at the same time Anna and William, and that the painful experiences of life are not to be avoided, but are the necessary conditions of happiness: 'how could you have life without this ache, this terror. How could you have joy? We were sitting around the table like masks, nothing behind us. Outside the world was roaring.'[6]

The question is: how does the authentic individual live? What is he to do with his free will? 'Now was the hardest time: man with his pretences, rationalisations gone: what is there to do, how is life possible.'[7] Stephen says that this 'is a story about free will'[8] and there is a clear reference to another story about free will: Dostoevsky's *Crime and Punishment*. 'To prove the independence of the will . . . You toss a penny: murder a pawnbroker. How else to prove the will?'[9] Stephen, at least for most of the book, needs proof of everything, even though he admits that free will is not something which can be rationally proved. And it is rationality which he clings to: 'It's reason at least that keeps the world going.'[10] This does not just mean that humans are rational, but that the universe itself can be rationally comprehended in a Cartesian sense, and that this comprehension is what sets man free:

---

[1] Ac. 28: 19
[2] Ac. 28: 19
[3] Ac. 190: 123
[4] Ac. 26: 18
[5] Ac. 191: 123
[6] Ac. 191: 123
[7] Ac. 181: 117
[8] Ac. 111: 71
[9] Ac. 96: 62
[10] Ac. 31: 21

> 'At least now we've got choice. Before it was just accident'.
>
> She said 'it can still be accident.'
>
> I said 'Your generation is obsessed by this. You think the world's going to blow up. That life has been unfair to you. I don't feel this. I feel that responsibility is better.'[1]

In the irrationalist philosophy which Anna seems to represent[2], where everything can be just accident, responsibility is problematic, just as it is in deterministic philosophies, to both of which rationalism is opposed. Jervis has a strong sense of responsibility amounting almost to a masochistic need to feel guilty, but at the same time (another Mosleian contradiction) he searches for a pattern behind the apparent randomness of events which will absolve him of this responsibility. To make this worse, he cannot, as a rationalist, admit the possibility of any metaphysical (not that rationality is necessarily opposed to metaphysics; just that Jervis's is) connection between events: 'One thing I must not, cannot believe; that the death of William had to do with the death of my baby. This was superstition. Just the ache, knowledge of it. Something.'[3]

The accident and the illness of his baby together strain this rationalisation to breaking point, and finally free him of it, and the novel itself is a refutation of the belief that all things have a rational explanation and an unambiguous and comprehensive description. There are many irresolvable ambiguities in the novel: it seems, for instance as if Anna, driving while drunk and without a licence, has caused the death of William and that Stephen and Charlie have conspired to hide Anna and tell the police she had not been in the car; after the inquest he says 'I am free now: only guilty.'[4] But things are not so simple. Stephen also says 'I had been all night at a party. I had driven off with a girl in a car. I had crashed.[5] I might even gain prestige through murder and adultery.'[6] The opening description of the aftermath of the crash and Stephen's later memory of it suggest that he may have been inside the car; he kicks the door open with his feet, possibly from the inside. But he also describes walking towards the crashed car and it may be that it is his need to feel guilt that lead him both to think of having been in the car, and (paradoxically) to be afraid of being accused of it; at the inquest he thinks 'I have been guilty of a crime I did not commit. . . . There was about to be a miscarriage of justice.'[7] Jervis often thinks of Anna standing on William's face to climb out of the car; if William was on the bottom of the car and the steering

---

1 Ac. 31: 21. Jeff Nuttall's *Bomb Culture* supports his view.

2 And which, as we shall see later, Mosley holds

3 Ac. 185: 119

4 Ac. 187: 121

5 Ac. 174: 112

6 Ac. 184: 119

7 Ac. 186: 120

wheel at the top, then it must have been Anna that had been driving. Or is he saying this to Charlie and himself to absolve himself, even to absolve William, whom he seems to have been closest to?

Like a good detective story the novel is seeded with clues but here there is no possibility of a - rational - solution. People's motives cannot be summarised neatly in the end as in the traditional detective story. It is also unclear whether Stephen has had an affair with Anna. The adultery he thinks about could have been that with the Provost's daughter Francesca, or even vicarious through William's and Charlie's relationships with her. There is even the suggestion that it could have been with William and that it is Anna of whom he is jealous, or at least that it is William that he really wants. He refers to himself and the Provost as two 'old homosexuals in a jigsaw'[1] and often mentions William in more tender terms than Anna. 'I wondered why I was not more sensible with William. Something unconscious: almost homosexual.'[2]

The other great ambiguity in the book is the identity of the narrator. There are many clues that it is Charlie, and that Stephen is his alter ego, his reflection. At one point Charlie seems literally to be Stephen's reflection: 'Upside down, above me, there was a face just like my own'.[3] William also seems to be an alter ego for Mosley; a 'fourth generation aristocrat. Living vicariously. Having learned it at Eton and Oxford.'[4] He also seems to be a reflection: 'I thought - Charlie and I would once have learned from William. By mirrors.'[5]. Charlie and Stephen often seem to merge: 'Charlie is my past. We walk one behind the other in a sort of patrol.'[6] Even the other characters notice the resemblance: 'Charlie is not my brother; but he is sometimes taken to be because we look alike.'[7]

Stephen seems to feel himself becoming absorbed into Charlie's personality, as if he himself did not exist: 'I find myself writing, speaking like Charlie'[8] 'I might always be writing of myself. Charlie might be writing this story.'[9] Stephen suggests that Charlie should 'write a novel about someone stammering,'[10] which is what Mosley later did in *Imago Bird*. Charlie even 'sometimes seems to be talking to himself; making up a story,'[11] and the book ends: 'Charlie is the writer: he will write this book.'[12] However, Charlie denies that all the others are

[1] Ac. 184: 119
[2] Ac. 26: 18
[3] Ac. 106: 68
[4] Ac. 47/48: 32
[5] Ac. 48: 32
[6] Ac. 139: 89
[7] Ac. 37: 25
[8] Ac. 45: 30
[9] Ac. 41: 31
[10] Ac. 74: 78
[11] Ac. 40: 27
[12] Ac. 192: 124

characters in his book and tells William that Stephen is making up a story to conceal his guilt.

> 'What story?' William said.
> Charlie said 'This story'.[1]

The ambiguities and open-endedness of Mosley's novels are not simply gratuitous; they are for him necessary for conveying his view of the world. Near the end of his next novel *Assassins*[2], when we are no nearer to an understanding of what 'really' happened to Mary, her father, Sir Simon Mann says:

> We may never know what really happened. People don't you know. We imagine we know what's at the back of things, what makes things happen, but we don't. Often, when we look too closely, there's just darkness and confusion.[3]

Things, that is, are just accidents. *Assassins*, like two of Mosley's other novels, *Natalie Natalia*[4] and *Imago Bird*[5] concern the difference between public and private life, and take place on the fringes of high-level politics. All three works are like inverted political thrillers in the sense that *Accident* is an inverted romantic thriller and, say, Tom Stoppard's *Rosencrantz and Guildenstern are Dead*[6] is an inverted *Hamlet*: that is, they take certain stories and conventions as being so deeply-rooted that they need not be stated but weave a pattern of variations around them without ever stating the theme. *Imago Bird* is also in

---

[1] Ac. 74: 48

[2] London: Hodder, 1966, repr. Penguin, 1969; New York: Coward McCann, 1967; trans. into French by Louise Servicen, Paris: Gallimard 1969. Hereafter referred to as As followed by page numbers for both British editions.

[3] As. 265: 252

[4] London: Hodder, 1971, repr. Penguin, 1975; New York: Coward McCann, 1972; trans. into French by Laure Casseau, Paris; Michel 1974. Hereafter referred to as NN followed by page numbers for both British editions.

[5] London: Secker, 1980. Hereafter referred to as IB.

[6] London: Faber, 1967

some ways a parody of a thriller, as is made clear near the beginning when the narrator Bert, the nephew of the Prime Minister, tells his psychiatrist about the gunshot in his father's study (which takes place behind locked doors as it might in a play; we never do find out the reason for it):

> 'What does it matter if a pistol goes off? They treat life like a detective story.'
>
> Dr. Anders said 'But the point of a detective story is to find out what happened.'
>
> I said 'But in fact it's just a man with a blank cartridge behind the stage.'[1]

Mosley's point here is that forms such as the detective story lead us to believe - wrongly - that the world is explicable in the same way as the story.

Like Rayner Heppenstall's last two novels, these three novels juxtapose the 'important' public life with the private. In *Assassins* Mann's dealings with the politically repressive Korin are contrasted to his relationship (such as it is) with his daughter, and the personal and individual terror she feels with the political terror of Korin's regime, and these are linked by her (possible) kidnapping. The conventional view is that politics is what matters, and Mann's aide Seymour says to Mary: 'Ultimately your father's work matters and you don't. That's the point.'[2] The point of these novels is, however, precisely the opposite.[3] Mary, like Bert, has been brought up on the fringes of political power,[4] and, like him, has trouble maintaining a sense of personal identity.

> I sometimes feel that I don't exist, that it is always other people working through me. I feel that there are other people outside and they have some sort of control, like knobs, and they can make me do what they want. I think there's some sort of conspiracy and everybody knows about it except me.[5]

Bert thinks the feeling of control is an illusion other people share, and that conspiracies are something they invent when this control does not seem to work.

---

1 IB 14

2 As. 173: 163

3 cf. Virginia Woolf's argument in 'Mr. Bennett and Mrs. Brown' op. cit.

4 As was Mosley: his father has been said to have been the only politician who could have been leader of either the Conservative or Labour party, and might well have become Prime Minister had he not joined the British Union of Fascists. His father's position during the war must have left him in a very isolated position and he certainly has a distaste for politics; see *Guardian* interview op. cit.

5 As. 73: 68

Anthony Greville in *Natalie Natalia* is a politician of whom we only see the personal side (rather like Jervis in *Accident*); we learn next to nothing of his mission to Ndoula and the intrigue surrounding it. However, it is the relationship between public and private, inner and outer, that both Mosley and Greville try to catch. As Greville says to the editor who wants him to write about his visit to Africa:

> I'll write your story. But it will be about what life is, instead of what it's supposed to be. From the inside, which is imaginary; and the outside, which is the same; and how they're joined together, which is different.[1]

Mosley's own jaded view of the efficacy of political action also surfaces in the book of 'lay theology' he wrote during his Christian period: *Experience and Religion.* There he says that politics is 'a game in which people plot, deceive, strike spurious attitudes, yet in which they are seriously working for the organisation of the world.'[2] But, says Mosley, the claims of idealists and 'single minded enthusiasts' have been proved disastrous[3]:

> By appalling trial and error it has been recognised that single-mindedness and devotion together with power are disastrous, that anything, even the cynicism of a political game, is better. But then, what matters are the game's conventions. The world is such that there are no absolutes in matters of power - no absolute good that is; and the best that can be hoped for and attempted is some balancing of forces, an arrangement whereby any too great concentration of power can be repudiated and cancelled, rather than the attempt to find some concentration and faith in it that will, finally, against all the evidence work . . . some state of affairs, society, in which scepticism and enthusiasm, mockery and admiration, all are

---

[1] NN 112: 90

[2] London: Hodder, 1965. Mosley's theology is of the type of liberal theology prevalent in the sixties, and associated in this country with John Robinson, though it does not seem to owe any direct debt to the German existentialist theology of the period. Hereafter referred to as ER. p. 120

[3] He does not mention his father, but the message is clear.

> recognised and play their part: a society which can never be thought to be achieved and balanced perfectly but which can be perpetually approximated to.[1]

This contrast between idealists and cynics occurs in all these novels too: the Young Trotskyites are contrasted both to Uncle Bill's pragmatism and Bert's political agnosticism and pessimism in *Imago Bird*; Simon Mann's amoral sense of expediency to the protestors against Korin in *Assassins* and Greville's indecisiveness against Ndoula's firm beliefs. In his book on Trotsky, Mosley similarly comments that direct political action in pursuit of some predetermined end will be doomed to failure, but that the struggle may in itself be valuable. (This is a later view from the period when Mosley has come to see history dialectically, and see that what seem in human terms to be great disasters may be historical necessities. This view will come up again later.) Mosley comments that the struggle for a worker's state,

> though Utopian, is nevertheless a necessity for mankind: [Trotsky] was a passionate fighter for the poor and underprivileged - which effort, though paradoxical (there always seems to be someone underprivileged at the cost of another's achievement) is also a vital and often effective necessity for mankind.[2]

Greville seems to share Mosley's distrust of direct political action. He sees politicians as 'deranged' people who 'imagine they are ordering the universe'.[3] He includes himself in this: 'I imagine I have some slight control'.[4] But he recognises this as a 'paranoiac delusion'; realistically he does not believe that

> by a social heave we can all get over the hill. People who imagine this have a sort of innocence, I think, like the deer that munch on these huge plains; they dream of a past or future heaven, where men in their cloth caps work on harps. And the predators get them.[5]Bert's upbringing on the side-lines of the political game has given him a strong sense of the unreality of it. He has no faith in anyone's ability to affect anything by political means: 'you can't change things just by putting one sort of organisation in place of another. You've got to free things in people's

---

[1] ER 121/2

[2] *The Assassination of Trotsky* (London: Joseph 1973; repr. Abacus 1972), p.17 (page numbers the same in both issues). Hereafter referred to as AT. Mosley also wrote the screenplay (unpublished) for the film of the same name.

[3] NN 11: 11

[4] NN 151: 121

[5] NN 204: 162

minds'.[1] Bert does not see the public sphere as having any separate existence apart from the lives of individuals. His uncle says to him: 'It's always been my conviction that things of a personal nature should be kept away from public life', and Bert thinks 'How can things of a personal nature be kept away from public life?'[2] Dr. Anders explains to Bert:

> You've had a glimpse of this sort of power: some of it's fantasy and some of it's not. I mean there are some areas power touches and some it doesn't. This has given you an exaggerated idea perhaps about the impossibility of organising things materially, except by some sort of casting of straws in the wind. . . . But I think you should realise that there are quite modest ways in which you can affect things for good or ill, quite practically; just by working at them; often, yes in quite negative ways , that is, by correcting this or that abuse.[3]

Which is what, she says, his uncle has tried to do. In contrast to this, Simon Mann, though he seems to lack Greville's self-doubt (but then we are not allowed access to his thoughts), thinks that it is precisely the little things over which we have no control:

> the unimportant things, how much we are dependent on the little things, at one of the meetings in Rome . . . when negotiations were going on which would decide the future of Europe . . . and it depended on a vote, a single vote, Panelli didn't turn up because his mistress had torn up his trousers.[4]

Here is the paradox: it is the unimportant things which matter most, the private determines the public, and must be the source of all values. Some of the time he seems to be unaware of this, or at least to ignore it in the name of expediency, either in his political dealings with Korin, or in his sexual ones within his secretary Connie, to whom he says

> 'There are many little things we have to do which we don't want.'
> 'Why?'
> 'For the sake of the greater.'

---

[1] IB 42. Mosley also says, in AT p. 71, 'political principles, if pursued truly, result in paradoxes that perhaps can only be held in a lively and complex way in the mind.

[2] IB 67/7

[3] IB 175

[4] As. 211: 222

'Then where's the truth?'[1]

However, he does admit that it is 'the small things, the irrelevant things, that alter history. Become symbols.'[2] And he realises that he cannot control these, and therefore cannot control anything:

> It's one of the fantasies of our time, the feeling of control. I don't think the old people had it. Tolstoy was right, you can't beat the Gods. It's the small things - the warp and the woof - that make up the pattern. And how much influence do we have over the small? Now that's a theme for a modern writer. The influence of the miniscule over the macrocosm.[3]

Indeed it is.

Greville seems also to feel powerless, and, indeed on the verge of breakdown, owing to his lack of faith in the efficacy of political action. Actually, his nervous state may be faked; he tells his friend that he is 'pretending to be having a sort of breakdown' but says: 'Actually, I am very well, but don't tell anyone.'[4] Greville hates himself for taking part in the cynical political game:

> I'm appalled by evil: I mean my own. I see everything as fantasy and duplicity. One tells no truth, knowing it can be the opposite: makes nothing better because worse can be useful. The more one knows, the more contempt there is.[5]

As a politician he knows that there is often no solution to a problem; there are moral tragedies, as with Ndoula: 'Ndoula's locked up, this is a great injustice, but is useful. He should be freed; but then there would be violence. This also could be useful.'[6] Sir Simon Mann does not seem to have any of Greville's qualms about political expediency in his dealings with Korin (who is a similar type of leader to Stalin, who of course appears in Mosley's book about real assassins - Trotsky's). He says 'I'm afraid in politics you don't have to like people or trust them, you have to know what is in their interest and of what they are afraid.'[7] Those around

---

1 As. 202: 214

2 As. 252: 265

3 As. 115: 121/2

4 NN 221: 175. Mosley mentions this in his later book *Catastrophe Practice* (London: Secker, 1979), p. 231, where he says that Greville 'made out that he was distraught deliberately in order to satisfy the needs of people around him: he had a delicate mission to perform and needed protection from simple demands and intrusions of others.'

5 NN 133/4: 108

6 NN 110: 88/9

7 As. 203: 214

him seem to think in similar ways: when Mary naively asks her bodyguard of Korin: 'Is he cruel?' the bodyguard replies 'I don't think that's the way to look at is Miss.'[1] For those who believe in the individual as the source of all moral values, such expediency cannot be right, but Sir Simon has a justification for dealing with people who you think are evil:

> This is not a matter of joining forces with the best available man to prevent aggression: this was in the old days: you used the lesser evil, the lesser man to fight the big. Times have changed. This is more important. Deeper. This is a joining of forces, to some extent, with one of the big men to help destroy what, formerly, the big man himself stood for. This is a more subtle battle than the old. It is more subtle by necessity now. The naïve and innocent think you can beat the devil by fighting him. You can't. You can beat the devil by using him. You can beat him by his not becoming a devil. By his becoming - split. Ordinary . . . The use of evil rather than the rejection of it. As before - for the purposes of good.[2]

As Mann is dictating this for a press statement there is no reason to assume that he means it, but the view of indirect action for remedying political wrongs rather than the direct approach of the 'single-minded enthusiast' does seem to square with Mosley's own view, and the idea of evil as a necessary part of good rather than something to be eliminated also comes out in *Experience and Religion*: 'What is required is a way of thinking which will take account of both the hope and the hopelessness, the good not in spite of but together with the evil.'[3] What we should aim for is the 'experience of goodness (if that is the word) apart from and beyond the polarity of evil and goodness.'[4] In this book, Mosley argues that good and evil are not absolutes and, in any case, man should not be concerned with ultimates and ends, these being the business of God not man, and unknowable, and must be the object of faith. Mosley's ethic is deontological: justification comes from the innate rightness of an action rather than its effects.

1 As. 176: 186
2 As. 87: 92
3 ER 18
4 ER 22

Moral rightness resides in 'the recognition of the freedom to choose not necessarily in the thing being chosen. The rightness is in the recognition and the holding to it, and the thing is done of itself.'[1] Knowledge of the rightness of actions comes not from judging them in relation to any desired end state: 'A man has to care about what he does here and now; this is his vital contact with an unknown and trusted end.'[2]

In *Natalie Natalia* good and evil are seen as opposites and absolute, but coexistent. This (paradoxical: Mosley has by now come to regard paradox as centrally important) antisyzygy of good and evil is summed up in the novel's long epigraph from Goethe, who refers to it as the 'Daemonic': 'something which was only manifested in contradictions, and therefore could not be grasped under one conception . . . only in the impossible did it seem to find pleasure, and the possible it seemed to thrust from itself with contempt': this element is not opposed to the moral order, 'yet crosses it, so that one may be regarded as the warp and the other the woof.'[3] Greville's mistress Natlia embodies this paradox. He calls her Natalia under her good, 'angelic' aspect and Natalie under her 'ravenous' aspect. This might be seen as a representation of the (male) idea of all women as 'bitch-goddesses' or 'whore-mothers', but Greville thinks everybody is equally contradictory, as he argues with his friend Tom:

> He said 'You've told me she wants everything in opposites'.
> I said 'So does everyone.'
> 'That produces chaos.'
> 'No. I think it demonstrates reality'. . .
> He said 'You're putting yourself outside human experience. The truth is single, not self-contradictory.'
> I said 'I don't believe that.'
> He said 'I know you don't.'[4]

These paradoxes and contradictions cannot ever be resolved by science:

> there's a predicament here not due to lack of knowledge but which seems to increase with the increase of it: an ambiguity at the heart, as in an atom. You can't pin-point what's going on in an atom not because you don't know enough but because of the nature of being human.[5]

---

1 ER 62
2 ER 132
3 NN 7: 7
4 NN 107/8: 87
5 NN 204: 162

It is the job of the artist, rather than the scientist to examine these contradictions (though not try to resolve them), and they are at the heart of all Mosley's later novels. They even surfaced in the earlier *Corruption*, where the narrator says: 'it seemed that the obscurity itself, the paradoxes and contradictions of it, were capable of arriving at an accuracy - a feeling for the whole - that choice and analysis could never hope for.'[1] Kate in this novel, like Natalia has 'a character as well as an appearance containing opposites that could ordinarily co-exist only in the age of story-books'.[2] Stories can, sometimes, contain these opposites but ordinary language cannot, and the failures of communication between people in Mosley's novels are attributable to this. People's thoughts and desires are often, if not always self-contradictory, but they cannot not put this into words. Bert, when talking to Dr. Anders often has at least two separate things he wants to say and ends up saying something entirely different. This is also complicated by the fact that he is always worried about what the psychoanalyst will make of his statements and always tries to say the thing he thinks will have the right effect (*Imago Bird* is thus, in part, a satire on psychoanalysis: Bert is always thinking in terms of "breasts and cunts and penises' - though only because he is undergoing psychoanalysis, which he associated with these things – but takes great care not to mention them). Bert's stammer in fact seems to be caused precisely by this impulse to say two contradictory things at once.

> Stammering, it seems to me, is often caused by a person's wanting to say two or more things at once; which, it also seems, is often the only way in which things can be made to sound true. But ordinary language is not suited to this: or at least, not without the struggle.[3]

Language is 'useless because it could only say one thing at a time: while what things are truly is always a network of connections.'[4]

---

[1] p. 6
[2] p. 129
[3] IB 5/6
[4] IB 56

Greville also finds language lacking: 'it is almost impossible to talk about this, because language has been mostly logical.'[1] 'All that I had to say remained secret. This was not an intention; it was to do with the nature of speaking. There was no structure for words to communicate what I knew.'[2] Greville, like Mosley, is seeking for a way to express paradoxes and contradictions: 'I wanted to find some way by which these paradoxes might be held: words being symbols; symbols meaning.'[3] It may be that words can never state these things, only allude to them, as a parable does: 'I'm trying to write a parable; which, one thinks, means something different from what it says. But it doesn't. What it says is inexplicable.'[4] That is trying to fix the meaning by translating it into some other form of words will get no nearer to the truth: words fix things and take away their essential life: 'The mechanisms of description are to do with what is pinned down. Perhaps I could get some style for all this. . . . I need a style that is saying two things at the same time.'[5]

Mosley analysed the inadequacy of language in *Experience and Religion*, where he showed how religious language and the language of art can express or imply things which discursive, logical language cannot. He also gives a justification of how own novel style, and the modern novel in general. Art, he says, used to deal in symbols because if

> man tried to put his experience of meaning into conceptual terms (his ordinary language) he came up against paradoxes and impossibilities that seemed due not to his own inadequacy but to that of language: but in the symbol, the thing fashioned and discovered on its own, these impossibilities disappeared. Art thus became the way of saying something that could be said in no better way; and was about the most important things in life.[6]

Then the advance of science seemed to hold out the possibility of revealing the whole - uncontradictory - truth about the world, replacing symbols in art with symbols in mathematics and logic, which do not contain opposite ideas. Art then retreated into solipsism, depicting the individual spirit which science could not penetrate (not that it needed to since it could deny the existence of such a thing). But then, recently, science has begun to discover that certain (mainly sub-atomic) features of the world are not describable in ordinary language, and that it is possible that the human mind literally cannot imagine the basic structure of

---

[1] NN 205:163

[2] NN 84: 68

[3] NN 31: 27

[4] NN 221: 175

[5] NN 214/5: 170

[6] ER 133/4

matter. There seem now to be 'phenomena only describable in two ways at once, a paradox'.[1] It has been discovered that at a certain level, observation affects the observed and both mass and velocity cannot be measured at the same time; scientific detachment and objectivity are seen to be only relative rather than absolute. Scientists realised that statements about the nature of the world were not

> statements about facts, realities of things, but were attempts to create models which would explain observations: they were themselves not directly to do with whatever the things might be but were to do with the way they worked - the things themselves remaining unknowable.[2]

Both art and science thus model the world rather than describe it; art the unique and particular and science the abstract and general.

Mosley's aim in this book is to show how religious language (and he uses religious in a very broad sense, so broad as almost to be meaningless: he describes Freud and Jung as the 'two great religious prophets of the age') can also contain these paradoxes of life, but because his definition of religious language is so inclusive, the argument becomes almost tautologous, religious language being just that which does contain them. Specifically, he compares the Old Testament to a work of art - indeed he says it is a work of art - in that it shows 'meanings, significance in a way that argument can never do'; it 'talks about the meaning of life on earth; what man is here for, what he is to do. In talking of this a work of art (the bible) just puts something (itself) before the reader and leaves him to make what he likes of it.'[3] The modern age, imbued but now betrayed by scientific language has lost the ability to recognise the efficacy of religious language. Worse, its artists have now lost the ability to express the paradoxical nature of reality, and modern man has nowhere to turn. Though it is true, says Mosley, that no serious modern artist falls for the fallacy of either naïve optimism or naïve pessimism, and artists have a more 'sophisticated view of chaos and evil'[4], they still cannot fully face up to the paradoxical nature of their enterprise. The view that the world is simply chaotic is too simple, and also encourages an apocalyptic quietism, where men feel they can do nothing about their situation.

> What modern works of art reflect as well as chaos is helplessness: man can either have a fling against his predicament (existentialists action painters, jazz musicians and so on) or he can stoically accept it (anti-

---

1 ER 139
2 ER 136/7
3 ER 51
4 ER 15

> novelists, abstract painters, again existentialists and so on). But whatever he does, he does not alter it.[1]

But

> if it is true that the world is chaotic and arbitrary then their position as writers, thinkers, artists and so on, is impossible which it is not. For any statement of profound meaning and impressiveness such as they produce in fact invalidates the impression that such a statement is mostly trying to make: however much it suggests that the world is chaotic, that is, its recognisable validity as a work of art (or process or thought) is evidence that the world is different. This is more than the difficulty of saying 'the truth is there is no truth'; it is a paradox of feeling and living too. Very few people do in fact live as if the world were meaningless; people certainly do not create as such.[2]

What is needed is a new type of language (which for Mosley at this stage will be a religious language, though he has since dropped this requirement; this idea will come up again in *Catastrophe Practice*), which will be able to express the co-existence of optimism and despair, good and evil, not as mutually exclusive but as mutually dependent.

> Because of its very complexity it will not be something argued, reasoned in a straight line as it were; but something of attempts, flashes, allusions - or a to-and-fro between a person and whatever he has to do and discover. What it will be saying will not be part of a comprehensive system but things-on-their-own, parables, paradoxes; the connections between which will have to be understood with difficulty, not justified.[3]

It will be 'something not single-faced but held between opposites; saying everything at once; a spark between poles',[4] which is how Mosley sees life itself.

---

[1] ER 14/15. This is in a way similar to Lukacs' criticism of Kafka who, according to Lukacs, portrayed alienation as universal and inescapable. The difference is that Lukacs saw alienation as a result of a specific historical and political situation, and thought that realism as a literary mode was necessary to describe the optimism necessary to overcome it. Mosley sees it as the result (partly at least) of language, which realism accepts as a given.

[2] ER 16

[3] ER 21

[4] ER 22

Bert thinks that this inability of language to reflect totality is the cause of much of the world's misery:

> is it any wonder that people don't make sense? How does anyone know what's going on. There are all these impressions coming in and of course we have to filter them, to make up stories, obsessions; or how would life be possible? To take in everything we'd be gods; or mad. But because people can't see this; can't see themselves making up stories; they have to imagine they make up the whole: and this makes them mad; or sad; because they're always disappointed. . . . Can you think of any work of European literature or of any other literature for that matter that's not to do with life being a disappointment? That's not trying to comfort people by saying how awful other people's lives are?[1] Well this doesn't mean that all writers are fools or liars. It means that they're doing with language what language lets them do: with the limitations it imposes. Language is to do with protection; it's part of the system that filters what's coming in; it's suited to saying what things are not rather than what they are . . . language is to do with parts, with stories that have a beginning and a middle and an end, and parts are properly sad, because they have limits. What is successful is to do with the whole.[2]

A language which took account of this would be 'a language not just of stories and obsessions and so a language to enable us to talk about this too; not just a filter but a way of looking at filters; to clean them even.'[3] (In *Experience and Religion* Mosley says that it is much easier and more usual to describe chaos and cruelty than joy and optimism, and Greville thinks that words are 'no use for happiness'.[4] There is certainly much emphasis on misery and cruelty in Mosley's novels: in *Spaces of the Dark* the central character has had to shoot his best friend in wartime and Mary in *The Rainbearers* has been cruelly tortured by the Germans who will not even shoot her to put her out of her misery; all her friend and her parents are killed, leaving her thinking that it's better to be dead than alive, as Greville also sometimes feels. In *Assassins* there is Korin's brutality and in *Natalie Natalia* the violence surrounding Ndoula. In *Impossible Object*,[5] too the

---

[1] Mosley makes exactly the same point, in almost exactly the same words, in 'Human Beings Desire Happiness' in *Lying Truths*, ed. R. Duncan Weston-Smith (Oxford: Pergamon, 1979), pp. 211-217

[2] IB 70/71

[3] IB 71

[4] NN 59: 49

[5] London: Hodder, 1968; repr. Penguin 1971. Hereafter referred to as IO. Page numbers for both editions given.

stories of live are counterpoised not just with the inevitable failures in communication but with images of the cruelty of the classical world.)

Bert tells Dr. Anders how people make up stories which simplify and explain complex and paradoxical events. They invent 'spies and secret service men' as people used to invent gods – to evade their responsibility.[1] People do not want power and the freedom and responsibility that goes with it, if politics were like sex, says Bert, everyone would want to be on the bottom. The stories they invent (like those of realist novelists perhaps) as well as the roles they act out not only simplify the complex, but give the impression of a determined chain of cause and effect, which again tends to deny human responsibility, and to deter people from trying to find out how things really work:

> that's what I hate about the grown-up world, they talk so fluently, whether they're telling stories or stories to cover up stories, they're still not trying to find out how things are. Language isn't suited to finding out this: language is for arguing, attacking, getting protection, getting responses. Stammering is perhaps a sign of trying to find out how things are: things are so complicated: there are so many of them: you can't get near them without a struggle.[2]

Bert, like Mosley, however, is sometimes accused of complicating things unnecessarily:

> One of the patterns that seemed to be emerging from my sessions with Dr. Anders was the way in which she claimed to have spotted in me a liking for turning things into mysteries; while I claimed that it was life itself that consisted of mysteries, which I tried to observe truly but which other people always seemed to be trying to turn into simple dramas that were false.[3]

---

1 IB 32/3

2 IB 13

3 IB 10

Life, as Mosley pointed out in *Experience and Religion*, may be mysterious but it is not completely chaotic and formless and neither is it completely determined. Greville, like Mosley, tries to resolve this paradox: 'we see everything in stories. These are constructions of our minds . . . But what are the patterns of construction'? These aren't random.'[1] What is the connection between our innate propensity to order the impressions we receive about the world (cf. Kantian categories, Levi-Straussian opposition and Chomskyan language capacity) and the way the world is really ordered?

> I want to find out something about how we understand rather than what. I mean - we receive impressions and construct patterns; the patterns are mechanisms of our minds that are there. But what are the mechanisms? We see life as comic or tragic; these patterns are primitive; they arise from our being half monkey and half god. About such a predicament there is something comic or tragic. But to see it only as this is also despairing, because tragedy and comedy are and not efforts to do anything about it.[2]

Greville envies the Africans who are not concerned with these things, or rather accept them without anguish: 'Here . . . life moves in a pattern which isn't looked at too closely but is not comic or tragic; people tread purposefully as if there were an old man dying upstairs. Only no one goes to look at him.'[3]

This concern with the order of things is not purely theoretical: Mosley is concerned with what people should do, how they should behave, and this depends on the effect that people's actions have on the world. This concern is present throughout Mosley's work, but he does not offer a solution, only a paradox: man can alter the world only by going along with it, but also by recognising what it is he is going along with: man has 'this freedom, perhaps his only; that this is his chance, in a world of laws, to change the world; that he is (can be) that which controls the laws (fits in with them) and that these are good.'[4] That these are indeed good can only be demonstrated by faith, not perhaps in a god - though with the experience of free will there has to be an idea of a God: without this there is only cause and effect'[5] – but in some telos, which is unknowable. In religious terms, a man must go along with the pattern of life, having trust in the rightness of it. In his biography of the monk Raymond Raynes, Mosley says: 'the point of any Christian life is not primarily to fulfil one's ambitions nor to become integrated (in the usual sense), but to allow oneself to

[1] NN 153: 122/3
[2] NN 202: 161
[3] NN 202: 161
[4] ER 143
[5] NN 293: 232

be used in whatever way God wishes.'[1] A year later, in *The Meeting Place*, Father Patterson, who has much in common with Raynes, writes in his notes:

> A point: theoretically of no magnitude; but without which magnitude has no meaning.
>
> If we try to influence magnitude directly, we fail. We have to work at the centre, by which the circumference is affected.
>
> Free will lies only at a single point.
>
> How in a position of no dimension can there be choice? . . .
>
> A point which has no dimension is that of God.
>
> Choice within this is first recognising that it exists; then in facing it; then in trusting in its efficacy.[2]

However, Father Patterson is contrasted with Jules, who replaces God with history, as Mosley himself was beginning to do at this period.

> 'man's got to surpass himself - think more, feel more. But he's got to go with history'. . . . Father Patterson said 'Where's history going?'
>
> 'There's an energy', Jules said. 'People don't know. They move blindly, without will. You have to feel it.[3]

Mosley was moving away from Christianity at this time (as were other people: the problem with the liberal and existential theology of this period was that it left very little to actually believe in). However, he seems to have maintained a belief in a necessary historical progression, but now instead of being 'pulled' by a (Christian or Hegelian) telos, it is 'pushed' by a (Marxian) dialectic. There is already some hint of this in *The Rainbearers*, where Richard tells Elisabeth that her negativeness may, paradoxically (and the dialectic does in many ways answer to Mosley's demand for a way to encompass paradox and the co-existence of opposites) may have positive results:

> I am too self-conscious . . . But you are not and so you destroy it, and through your capacity for destruction there is the chance of a positive return. That is the secret, the release, of all understanding. You are a person who is the symbol of the paradox, of creation through insistence on denial.[4]

---

1 *The Life of Raymond Raynes*. London: Faith Press, 1961; reissued by Hodder, 1963, p. 5

2 p. 3

3 pp. 82/3

4 p. 130

Also in *The Rainbearers* is the idea (presented by Mr. Gabriel) that even if the individual cannot change the process of history, he can at least stand back and observe it, and even defy it, futile though this is.

> the care of people who are closest to you, which goes on and on I know, but which will no more stop a universal death or your own than the arm flung across the face of a child in the path of an avalanche . . . I choose to make the deliberate and futile gesture of throwing my arm across the face of those I can to protect them: I do this knowing it is useless but at least is reality.[1]

The only other possible gesture is 'cocking a drunken snook at the world', with 'defiance and with luck obscenity, but which will do no harm to anyone, least of all to others.'[2] The place of man in the dialectic of history worries Greville, as it has worried many Marxists:

> I could not work this out. History was going in a certain direction. This was right, because it was the way history was going. But to be on the side of history some people, some time, had to be against it. Only like this could it go where it was going. But I was not concerned with this. I was concerned with what was right: which was, or was not, to do with the way in which history was going.[3]

The idea of history as dialectic also crops up in *Impossible Object*, where it is suggested that God's '*plan had been to make life so awful that man would at last become responsible; man had, after all, always worked in opposites.*'[4]

Later, this idea of freedom as the ability to stand back from the historical process and see it at work was exemplified for Mosley by Trotsky, who

> used dialectical in its profound sense of referring to the processes of change and of growth in life; of things being seen in their context not absolutely but relatively; of the play of opposites and contradictions of which an understanding is necessary for any true insight into nature. To understand this there is no place for cynicism; but perhaps for irony. A person has to be able to stand back from himself to perceive paradoxes; it is by doing this that he can best describe the processes of growth.[5]

---

1 p. 80
2 ibid.
3 NN 187/8
4 IO 33: 29
5 AT 15

But the individual cannot change the process, and this raises again the question of how a person should act, if even Stalin only 'did his job - according to the rhythm of history.'[1] Another figure caught up in a moment of great devastating historical change - this time the First World War - whose biography Mosley wrote was Julian Grenfell. Though Grenfell's participation in history might seem to be insignificant and passive compared to Trotsky, both, on Mosley's view, played their part. Mosley sees Grenfell as also, like Trotsky, having the ability to stand back from the events that seemed to be engulfing him, and over which he had no control (and if ever there was a great event which seems to have happened without being really controlled by any individuals, it is surely this war). Mosley says of Grenfell, who seemed to go almost willingly to his death, that he

> saw as a very young man some of the patterns that were driving his grandiose world to destruction; he tried to step aside - not just to rebel, but to form different attitudes within himself and towards society . . . In the event the values of the world in which he had been brought up defeated him: he accepted the war and even enjoyed it. He killed, and was soon killed himself. But there is the impression that he, more than the others, knew what he was doing. One of the insights he retained was that by standing back, a fate that could not be prevented need not seem desolating.[2]

It seems that all the individual can change is himself; how and in what direction are problematic since there are no knowable ends at which to direct oneself, and how, if at all, the change in the individual affects society and history are also mysterious: paradoxically the individual both can and cannot change history, and this paradox pervades Mosley's writing both during and after his Christian phase. Also, as we have seen, there is the possibility that it is in the small things that we have control, and that these are what affect the larger, and though Sir Simon Mann says that it is over the small things that we have no control, the 'we' could well be taken to mean politicians, which would mean that it is the politicians who in fact have the least control.[3] Certainly direct action is not the answer, and not simply because things 'work in opposites', but because the relationship between man and the outside world is so paradoxical and contradictory. On the one hand,

---

[1] AT 182

[2] *Julian Grenfell: His Life and the Times of his Death* (New York: Holt, Rinehart & Winston, 1976), p. 3. The idea of willingly embracing death recalls both Nietzsche's *amor fati* and Heidegger's being-towards-death, though Mosley does not discuss these ideas anywhere.

[3] This idea will be important later in Mosley's discussion of Nietzsche, where he is at pains to point out that, contrary to popular misapprehension, Nietzsche's idea of an élite is precisely not a political, power élite.

'man's role in all this is not just a passive one of analysing it or trying to control it as it were impersonally, but of having control over what he recognises himself as part of and committed to'.[1] On the other hand, 'the area of freedom . . . is in oneself, in the possibilities of understanding and changing oneself, not in the hope of changing another person, or not directly, at least.'[2] In *Spaces of the Dark* Paul says to Adam

> You want things outside yourself and so you think that everything is wrong and you fight to change it. And you fail. I only want something inside myself because I can't change the outside things, at least only in the small ways, where right and wrong don't matter.'[3]

The possibility that individuals can affect things not by what they do but by what they are is contained in the idea Bert has for his film. He envisages the audience having a set of buttons by means of which they can choose which direction they want the plot to take. But the buttons, unknown to the audience, will not be connected to anything. This will not worry the audience, who, if things do not turn out the way they wanted will simply thing that they were in the minority. But, by realising that they have a choice, and a free choice, people will be able to see themselves, to see what sorts of choices they do in fact make, and by this self-knowledge, have the ability to change themselves. This, paradoxical though it is, is Mosley's metaphor for the place of the individual in society.

> Writers have written about free will but not described it - not only its effects but its experience. Writers, in cutting themselves off, describe life as determined: or describe themselves alone, which is the same. Freedom, the experience of it, is the ability to move between the two. We live this, but can't describe it.[4]

It is this attempt to describe the relationship between the inner and the outer which is Mosley's continuing obsession; he attempts to do what Greville tells the editor he will do:

> I'll write your story. But it will be about what life is, instead of what it's supposed to be. From the inside, which is imaginary; and the outside, which is the same; and how they're joined together, which is different.[5]

---

1 ER 142
2 ER 44
3 p. 198
4 NN 214: 170
5 NN 112: 90

> There should be some style which would convey this - both a person reflecting and his actions . . . We see a moment or a pattern, not both: one cuts out the other. But if we do not know, perhaps from some third point, the moment and the pattern at once, then each seems meaningless. Because, on its own, each is an abstraction, not an experience. The experience is both. But our minds are not constructed for this: which is why perhaps we make myths . . . Writing a story is an effort at a view from a third point; it tries to see together reflection and action; to get the pattern in a moment and the moment as change. But this would be timeless; at the present because in comprehension. I wish I could write this.[1]

In *Impossible Object*, which follows *Assassins* and precedes *Natalie Natalia*, Mosley had tried to show 'a person reflecting and his actions'. The 'novel' is made up of interwoven short stories separated by surrealistic interludes,[2] but the connections between the stories are, in terms of realism, impossible, so that, for instance, the narrator can at one point meet himself. As we have seen, Mosley believes that people cannot be adequately described in what we consider 'realistic' ways, and he points out that realism as we think of it is only a historical phenomenon, and has not always held sway. 'The Egyptians had painted . . . with the legs and head sideways and the body straight to the front. You can only get the whole of a person by this sort of art, deception.'[3] Mosley might also have mentioned Byzantine art, which represents people as being different sizes according to their importance, not according to how tall they appear.[4] To Byzantine artists, these differences were objectively real

[1] NN 209: 165

[2] These interludes are italicised. Quotes from them will not be underlined but will be noted in the footnotes.

[3] IO 105: 91

[4] Worringer (opera cit.) argued that this 'empathic' tendency to copy nature was characteristic of ages where people felt that they could understand and control the world, but in times when people felt the world to be threatening and mysterious, art 'abstracted' an

and more important than the visual aspect of their subjects. Renaissance art restored the primacy of sight which had prevailed in Greek and Roman Art, along with the belief that people, as well as objects can be represented with complete objectivity given sufficient skill on the part of the artist.[1] This view was not challenged in any systematic way until the Cubists attempted to destroy single-point perspective: the 'truth' about an object, let alone a person, could not be contained in anyone of its visual aspects alone.

A similar presumption underlies the omniscient narrative in literature: if only a person could see everything, an exhaustive and objective account of every event could be given. Psychological novels extended this omniscience into the characters' thoughts (as Mosley's first three novels did), but an underlying principle was the same: a detached 'observer' (not just a visual one though) could, in principle, give a complete account of everything. Literature clung to this principle longer than the visual arts (it took it up later): 'Every other art was concerned with complexity. It was only literature that seemed infantile.'[2] That is, it tended to oversimplify, and the trouble with this is that it encourages people to prefer stories (as Bert said) to the complexity and uncertainty of life. Even the apparently great and penetrative literature oversimplifies, giving the (false) impression that we can understand life. 'We know about love; we have read Stendhal and Proust; as soon as we get one foot over the windowsill we want to be back at home reading.'[3]

Stories are, in fact, as traditionally understood, ways of dealing in elliptical ways with the paradoxes of real life, and it is only comparatively recently that literature has claimed to be able to describe life directly: 'life is impossible. Stories are symbols in which impossibilities are held.'[4] 'Stories are our only freedom'[5] as long as they are not taken as literally true. If stories are read literally, the nature of language prevents them from expressing the true nature of life, which is in terms of logic (and language, for Mosley, is tainted with logic) contradictory. Logic insists that a thing and its negation cannot both be true, and that a thing is either true or not; it excludes the middle. This is not characteristic of life, and Mosley uses the mad in the asylum at Turin as a symbol of this: Their

---

underlying order from the apparent chaos. The twentieth century was one of these; hence abstract art. Mosley's view is, of course, that the world is not describable by imitation.

[1] Hence Vasari's view of the progression from Cimabue to Michelangelo as a move towards the ultimate.

[2] IO 148: 128

[3] IO 116: 101

[4] IO 140: 121

[5] IO 149: 129

expressions are wholly violent or wholly passive; they have nothing to do with humanity which is paradox . . . Madness is in extremes like logic.'[1]

Human desires, as psychoanalysis shows, are usually, if not always, self-contradictory; the narrator in one of the stories feels that he 'both wanted her to stay so that we could make love and to go so that I would not be vulnerable.'[2] This should not be a problem as long as we can realise it and grasp it: Bert thinks of the story of the Zen master who says to his pupils that if they say he is holding a stick he will beat them with it and if they say he is not holding a stick he will also beat them with it; the pupils should take the stick from the master and beat him, and this is a metaphor for life.[3] Nietzsche, who will be so important in *Catastrophe Practice*, but who is mentioned in *Impossible Object* in terms mainly of madness and despair, tried to do this, but was defeated by it. 'He knew with sanity that you cannot be sane either with illusion or without it and so you go mad. And so he did.'[4] In the light of Mosley's later books, the point seems to be that only the *Übermensch* can truly grasp, or possibly transcend, these paradoxes, and Nietzsche was not an *Übermensch*.

The impossible nature of the book is (naturally) hard to describe. The central story, around which all the others seem to revolve, is' 'Public House' where the narrator describes a couple in love, married, but not to each other, who meet at lunchtimes in a pub where the narrator observes them. He mentions that he is thinking of writing a story about them 'I had already begun to think of them as characters in a story - both the one that they seemed to listen to like hidden music and the one that I was even then thinking of writing.'[5] (The story he is thinking of writing is both this one and, possibly, others in the book too.) Later in the story he meets the couple abroad where the man tells the narrator that he had written 'a story about the pub' (which, impossibly, is this story) and the narrator in turn says he had used the couple in a story about 'a journey up through Italy' (which is 'A Journey Into the Mind').[6]

> I said 'What was your story about the pub?' He said 'It was told by a man who had seen us that winter' . . . He said 'But you can't exist: Or you're myself. You see how this is impossible!'[7]

The narrator thinks

---

1 IO 129: 112
2 IO 137: 119
3 This also crops up in *Serpent* (London: Secker, 1981)
4 IO 55: 48. This is from an italicised section.
5 IO 88: 76
6 IO 104: 90
7 IO 104: 90

> I wrote the story about the man and the girl at their future meeting. But this became mixed with a story about myself, and had to be fitted into a larger context. I remembered how I had had the impression that I was a character involved in their story as well as they in mine; and none of us yet knew the endings.[1]

There is also the suggestion, as in *Accident*, that narrator and character are the same: 'he looked quite like me.' The characters are continually interwoven in this way, undermining the traditional absolute separation between observer and observed. All the stories concern the relationship between two people, with a previous lover or present spouse always present in their thoughts, but they are linked in such a way as to make an untangling into a series of 'realistic' stories impossible, since each character has memories, thoughts or attributes which occur in other stories but belong there to other characters. This gives a flickering effect, like an optical illusion or an Escher drawing (the covers of both *Imago Bird* and *Serpent* refer to Escher), which cannot be 'read' in any single way (and so is not comforting), and throws into relief the relationship(s), making them stand out like pictures in a pop-up book.

The relationships are not particularly happy ones: the point of some of them is that people say and do the opposite of what they intend and consequently fail to communicate. This is of course inevitable given Mosley's belief in the inability of language to express people's contradictory desires: 'Ultimately we make no contact; not with anyone, not with ourselves.'[2] Love and marriage involve a balancing of opposites which cannot be expressed in language, and which people therefore cannot discuss with each other, though they may simply have a mutual understanding of it: 'Ours is a good marriage because we can be together and yet separate like this; are not tied, which is the modern infancy. We are close by being apart. We are right to risk this, because there is no life without opposites.'[3] Not that this understanding is enough:

> We always worked in opposites. The only difference between us and other people, I thought, was that we recognised this and they did not.
>
> Not that this made life any easier . . . There is no solution: opposites are infinite.[4]

---

[1] IO 102: 88. This is similar in some ways to Emma Tennant's *Hotel de Dream* (London: Gollancz, 1976; repr. Penguin 1978), in which the characters in their dreams find themselves in the dreams of other characters.

[2] IO 98: 85

[3] IO 64: 56

[4] IO 137: 119

The story 'Intelligent People' concerns the failure of communication through the tendency to over-interpret what other say and do and to alter one's actions on the assumption that others will do the same (as Bert does with Dr. Anders). The 'intelligent' Mostyns can never really say what they want to each other; they really love and have sympathy with each other, but interpret the other's actions wrongly as signs of resentment and hostility. The Mostyns, who believe that there 'should be nothing outside man's intelligence and control',[1] have a purely abstract discussion about 'the different roles played in the psyche by intellect, feeling, intuition and sensation.'[2] Coming from Mosley, who is anti-positivist and anti-rationalist, and whose views on the efficacy of abstract discussion we have already seen, this is deeply ironic: these things, even more than the (apparently) concrete are quite beyond this type of discussion, and even for Mr. Mostyn there were 'some mornings when even physical objects seemed possessed, as if there could be some evil spirits.'[3]

The question of evil is not raised directly in *Impossible Object*, but arises in connection with the cruelty which recurs throughout the book, where the physical brutality of the ancient world and the middle ages is juxtaposed to the cruelty which is (paradoxically) an essential part of love. Mosley seems to be find people naturally cruel:

> *The crusades were a proper time in which to observe human nature - the pursuit of holiness for the sake of money, the use of torture for the sake of identity, a time of passionate care and commitment. Those who distributed pain were politicians; those who profited, saints. Either way, life was not easy; unless you died young, which was recommended.*[4]

This is linked to the question of the paradox of God's tolerance of cruelty and suffering as a precondition for love and redemption, but the answer here seems to be that suffering is a human rather than a divine need, necessary for self-definition; God being a justification to hide this need.

> *The baby crawls across no-man's land with its limbs shot off by the drug its mother took to keep it happy. It hopes that one day its mother will come to punish it, because then it will know who it is again. It looks out on a world in which slaves walk with their severed hands*

[1] IO 39: 35
[2] IO 43: 38
[3] IO 43: 38
[4] IO 79: 69

> *pierced and hung round their necks like identity discs. It is by pain that caring is demonstrated: we were taught this at Sunday School.*[1]

But the point is not whether what we were told at Sunday School is true or not, even supposing such a question were answerable (other than in the either/or way Mosley distrusts), but what to do about it; life is not an academic question, it must be lived rather than discussed. Like the Zen pupil we must grasp it, not wonder about it:

> 'How do you explain suffering children?'
> I said 'You don't. You do something about them.'[2]

Mosley's most dense and serious work up to 1980, *Catastrophe Practice*,[3] alludes, in 'three plays for not acting and a novel' to problems of life and fiction which are explicitly discussed in the plays' prefaces. One of the main themes is the opposition between 'liveliness' and 'deathliness', complexity and simplification, entelechy and entropy.

This opposition had cropped up previously in *Impossible Object* and in *Accident*, where Jervis had striven not to become 'knowledgeable and deathly' like the other dons. It also appears in *The Assassination of Trotsky*, where it is made clear that this is not a matter of those who refuse to take life against those who do not - Trotsky himself was responsible for many deaths - but

---

1 IO 80: 70

2 IO 142: 122

3 Catastrophe Theory, to which the title alludes, while not being very important in this book (it was added at the publisher's request) does illuminate some of Mosley's ideas. It is a branch of topology which provides a method of modelling states where two stable values are possible for the same input to a system, and jumps (catastrophes) between these states occur even when the changes in input are smooth. So what look like random 'accidents' May be explicable 'catastrophes', like Natalie's 'jumps', which 'like those within atoms, seemed without reason or location' (NN 23: 19). Jervis also notices how people move in jumps, and Kate in *Corruption* also seems to have two states between which she jumps (pp. 35 and 39). This can also explain how the small changes individuals can make can eventually have large, sudden effects (this occurs in *Meeting Place* (p. 181), *Rainbearers*, and *Assassins*)

> between forces which seemed to be battering men's minds with random and meaningless assault . . . and forces which, in spite of this natural tendency to entropy, were still fighting to keep going some order of mind and spirit. Of these Trotsky was the archetype.[1]

'The faith of his enemy was deathliness - the rigidity of violence and lies.'[2]

It is a paradox typical of those which interest Mosley that whereas evolution has produced biological forms of increasing complexity (of which consciousness is the most advanced so far), all biological systems, being dissipative (as are all mechanical systems subject to friction), tend, by the process of entropy to become less complex, and tend to a static rather than dynamic equilibrium. That is, they run down. Human consciousness, however, not being a closed system can try to increase its own complexity (by a Nietzschean or Schopenhaurian Will perhaps, though entropy contradicts Schopenhauer's idea of the ubiquity of Will) and thus transcend, or at least bypass the process of natural selection from random mutation. But, in humans too, there is the desire for simplification: 'We need someone to come along and shut us in small cages'[3] to protect us from the impossibility of life. (This idea also probably underlies Nietzsche's 'slave morality', Freud's Thanatos, Heidegger's *Das Man* and Sartre's *en-soi*.) This is reflected, for Mosley, in language with its base in logic, which by its nature can only express the simple and uncontradictory, and here Mosley's twin themes of the insufficiency of language and the need for continuously striving for self-transcendence are united.

One of the ways in which consciousness operates differently from simpler biological organisms is that it can learn by trial and error, and that, according to Karl Popper, whom Mosley discusses in the second preface, true scientific method actively seeks falsification (falsifiability being Popper's criterion for a truly scientific theory[4]) whereas simpler systems (including unscientific human ones) try to avoid error. Mosley quotes Popper's

> three distinct worlds - 1. the world of physical objects: 2. the world of states of consciousness: and 3. the world of objective contents of

---

1 AT 134

2 AT 136

3 IO 89/90: 77

4 As opposed to Marxism and psychoanalysis which are 'closed' systems and are not falsifiable since they can encompass seemingly falsifying evidence. Mosley does not discuss this side of Popper, nor does he point out that Popper's ideas are normative rather than descriptive, and are not accepted by many scientists in theory, and by very few in practice.

> thought - 'especially of scientific and poetic thought and works of art', this 'world 3' as Popper calls it is man's special accomplishment.[1]

In world 3, conflict does not involve killing (as in world 1) or intimidation (world 2) but 'impersonal argument'. In this world, selection could operate without violence.

Analogous to Popper's three worlds are Gregory Bateson's three types of learning, which Mosley also considers.[2] Learning I is purely behaviouristic, Learning II is 'an accomplishment of man, and depends on a man's ability to stand back from the processes of Learning I and see its patterns – and in this at least in some sense to be free of them.'[3] Learning III is 'rarely glimpsed by men, but perhaps is that which is necessary for survival . . . it is the chance for a man to see not just the patterns of his behaviour but also the patterns of his ability to see.'[4] This is the task Mosley set for the artist in *Natalie Natalia*, to 'see together reflection and action; to get the pattern in a moment and the moment as change.'[5] It also brings us back to the question of the paradoxical relationship between freedom and necessity, which has already been so important. It now seems that Mosley's earlier idea of this had been in terms of what Bateson calls Learning II, as it is in the first preface: 'If a man has the power to observe the controlling patterns of his mind it is here and not in the patterns that there is his freedom.'[6] However, Mosley sees here that this standing back is not enough, and must be transcended by the ability to stand back from the standing back, which (though he does not mention it here) is characteristic of Learning III. The (relatively) simple standing back seems now to Mosley to be the cause of the self-alienation which, more importantly than social alienation, is 'the predicament of modern man', caused by 'the split between what he knew, especially about himself, and his ability to come to terms with this knowing. It was this that brought him to lack of communication and despair; and to his cruel and futile rites to allay these.'[7] Modern art, no less than traditional forms, was comforting because it identified and therefore seemed to explain this split. The 'new human type' which Mosley sees evolving, can recognise this split as neither tragic nor absurd, like a Sartrean nothingness, but as a process to be assimilated. The new art must therefore, with the new human type in mind, not cease to make myths, but to

---

[1] CP 86

[2] Mosley does not mention, though he might well have done, Kierkegaard's 'aesthetic', 'ethical', and religious' stages, which may be an earlier expression of similar ideas, though in a different context, to Popper and Bateson's.

[3] CP 87

[4] ibid.

[5] NN 209: 165

[6] CP 18

[7] CP 17

make myths about the making of myths, symbols of symbols. As in Learning III, opposites can be seen from a 'higher point of view'[1] in which the necessary connection between, for instance, pain and its avoidance can be seen. The organism that can do this is well fitted for survival, but still runs the risk of being destroyed in the process of the more simple-minded struggles for survival of others.

But until and unless they are destroyed, consciousnesses are the 'fertile soil' in which the (random) 'seeds' of evolution may grow.[2] Man's environment, 'an environment not only, or even mainly, outside him; but of his heart, soul, mind',[3] may be controlled to give evolution the best chance. The highest freedom of the human type may be to choose its successor: or, by opting for despair rather than discomfort, deathliness rather than liveliness, the lack of one.[4]

In *Catastrophe Practice* Mosley's debt to Nietzsche is made explicit, and his individualism is spelled out. This is not just a matter of the defence of the individual against mass society[5] but a welcoming of some sort of 'new human type', not necessarily a Nietzschean *Übermensch*, but the self-transcendence of humanity. (Nietzsche thought this inevitable – and this secret spake life herself unto me. 'Behold' said she, 'I am that *which must ever surpass itself*'[6] – but Mosley sees it as a struggle which may well be lost.) This is a step forward in evolutionary terms, but in human terms may involve the tragic destruction of most if not all of humanity as we now see it.[7] Tragedy however is a human concept, and one which must be transcended in this movement. It may be that 'deathliness' will lead to the destruction of its adherents (perhaps literally through nuclear war, or because the more complex, evolving forms of consciousness are more adaptive). In *the Assassination of Trotsky*, Mosley had said that 'in life, at moments of birth and crisis, perhaps millions have to die for there to be a step of evolution forwards'[8], and in his earlier, Christian phase he had put the same feeling thus: 'For every growth of value, the seed has to die.'[9] Either from a Marxist, dialectical point of view, or from a Christian one, human life may be seen as forming part of some larger plan or pattern, and from an evolutionary perspective humanity has no claim to intrinsic worth: it is only in humanism that this possibility of the destruction of existing humanity is 'tragic'.

---

1 CP 88

2 CP 169

3 CP. 170

4 See pp. 233/4

5 As other existentialists have undertaken: for instance Kierkegaard's *The Present Age*, Jaspers' *Man in the Modern Age*, Marcel's *Man Against Mass Society*, Ortega's *Revolt of the Masses* and Berdyaev and Camus.

6 *Thus Spake Zarathustra*, ch. 34

7 This is also a favourite theme of Arthur C. Clarke

8 AT 128

9 *The Life of Raymond Raynes*, p. 286

But even here, the usual type of utilitarian humanism can be transcended by a higher humanism which recognises the true nature of human freedom in this ability to (potentially) choose its own successor,[1] having fully faced the nature and necessity of death and evolution. This idea is already present in *Natalie Natalia*:

> Waste. Things are born, come to fruition, die: in proliferation. This is necessity. A million seeds are blown; one lodges . . . We say each human being must be saved, yet step on bodies, use teargas against children. We chase each sperm to put it in a test tube; produce - impotence.
>
> What if we saw that in human generation as in any other there is waste - that bodies are driven to the fire where there is wailing. We might have dignity. But we can't say this; only know.[2]

Since evolution, like Popperian science works by trial and error, the rejected, the 'waste' is as valuable as the fruitful. And, if this new type can inhabit Popper's world 3 and encompass Bateson's Learning III then these atrocities Mosley hints at, committed as often as not in the name of freedom, would not exist. It may be, in fact that such atrocities will help to 'make life so awful that man would at last become responsible; man had, after all, always worked in opposites.'[3]

Greville had said that 'we can't say this', and Jason, who, it is hinted, is the author of *Catastrophe Practice* as Charlie is of *Accident*, and is the central character of *Serpent*, recognises that, apart from the difficulty of discussing these things, there is a strong taboo against them. Jason has written a film script (some of which is quoted in the novel) about the mass suicide of the Jewish Zealots at Masada in the face of inevitable defeat. The Jews were of course taken by Hitler to be the epitome of the Nietzschean slave morality (though whether Nietzsche himself actually thought this is debatable) and Jason's film attempts to question the common assumption that the Zealots' action was right. The script takes the viewpoint of Josephus, who went over to the Romans to avoid death and is normally considered the worst form of traitor. Jason knows that the film would be 'morally and politically objectionable' and would be considered 'fascist, elitist', but thinks that Josephus (like Nietzsche and Mosley) 'wanted to alter the way we see things.'[4]

The common view is that individuals should sacrifice themselves for the continuance of a society in which they believe (whereas in *Catastrophe Practice*

[1] Not merely in standing back as he had earlier suggested, or in rebellion in the style of Camus or Mr. Gabriel in *The Rainbearers*.

[2] NN 218: 173

[3] IO 33: 29

[4] *Serpent* (hereafter referred to as S.) p. 23

Mosley is considering the possibility of society sacrificing, or transcending itself for the sake of individuals in which it believes):

> It is true, is it not, that any society, if it is to hold together, has to have ideals which members of the society are ready to die for? What other sort of forces can hold a society together?
>
> And it is true, is it not, that if in such circumstances an individual chooses to live, then he will naturally be seen as a traitor by those who choose to die?
>
> All this is dependent, of course, on the belief that society is the unit that has to hold together.
>
> But then, if the members of a society are dead, what is it that holds together?
>
> If anything is to survive, is it not individuals that live?[1]

Jason thinks that 'as a symbol, Masada's dangerous if you care about society's survival.'[2] But, as Mosley has said, society may have to destroy itself in some way in order to transcend itself. Jason also considers this possibility: 'I don't know what an individual should do if a society seems set on destroying itself. Perhaps it should be allowed to. I mean perhaps it means destroy itself so that what it stands for can go on.'[3] (This is particularly a problem for a Jew like Josephus, who, believing himself to be part of a chosen race, must regard continuance of this race as a very high priority.) But now, partly because humanity has the physical means to literally destroy itself and partly because we now have the ability to see a better way, 'this is too dangerous. Something has to change, in the mind, if the world is to stay alive.'[4]

The individual who chooses liveliness/life must, like Nietzsche's *Übermensch*, do so in secret, but must also try to ensure the survival of his values, which may mean making them public, even if this brings odium and hatred on him, which is the most difficult thing; more difficult than dying, and this is partly Jason's defence of Josephus: 'it's not just a question of staying alive: it's a question of how to live with having done this.'[5] Most people would not be able to live with it, especially in secret, and Jason thinks that Josephus wrote his account of Masada in order to relieve himself of some of the burden of his private guilt.

Epstein, the producer, sees perhaps more clearly than Jason what is at issue;

---

[1] S. 22

[2] S. 62

[3] ibid.

[4] S. 62

[5] S. 24

> the most interesting thing was the struggle between people who wanted to be told what to do, who always had been told what to do, by gods or rulers or the unconscious or whatever; and those people who wanted to find out what they wanted to do themselves and do it.[1]

In this way, the Jews are the symbol as well as the embodiment of the slave morality.[2] But this slave morality tends always to dominate over the master morality (as opposed to the fascist version of it) because the majority always hold the former, which is easier. 'The people who wanted to obey, to be ready to die, always won. Perhaps they had to win - a church, an empire - for law and order.'[3] But now, this slavery, which may have been necessary at an earlier stage of consciousness, can be transcended, because now we have the ability to see the nature of it.

Mosley is, as he realises, on dangerous ground with these ideas, and in his championing of Nietzsche. However, he is at pains to point out that the fascist appropriation of Nietzsche (of which, of course, his father was a part) was based on a misreading (which is largely due to Nietzsche's sister, though Mosley does not discuss this). He does not specifically mention his father, but he does point out that the Übermensch's overcoming of himself does not involve overcoming or dominating others ('thus has Nietzsche been traduced'[4]), and he has 'nothing to do with power (except in so far as such a man has what might be called the power to overcome drives to power . . .)'[5], though 'his work was for a time taken up by power-politicians.'[6] Mosley's elitism, like Nietzsche's is based on a renunciation of political power and dominance; these things, or at least the obsession with them, being necessarily a hindrance to the ability to stand back and observe oneself, and therefore 'it is the conventionally powerful people who seem slavish.'[7]

Like certain post-structuralist philosophers, Mosley approves of Nietzsche's attempt to undermine conventional, discursive, logical language as being insufficient for his needs. Nietzsche's writing is 'elusive, allusive, poetic: it is a way of talking about truth by at the same time listening to, judging, what itself is

---

1 S. 38

2 For Epstein, that is. Jason (and Mosley) sees the Jews as, potentially at least, being able to stand back from, and thus transcend, both master and slave mentalities, as would befit a chosen race. People who did have this power of encompassing such contradictions might appear to others to be self-effacing and self-sacrificing (literally even) while in fact being transcendent *Übermenschen*. The problem for Jason is how this self-sacrificing can be compatible with continued survival, which is necessary for the Jews.

3 S. 39

4 CP 163

5 CP 164

6 ibid.

7 CP 165

saying: it is a way of defending itself against the comforts of dogma: it is a presentation by which people can, if they keep up in it, find their own truth.'[1] In a similar vein, Jacques Derrida has written that

> Nietzsche classifies as liberation (or freedom of thought) the movement by which one breaks away from language and grammar, which previously governed the philosophical order. In this very traditional fashion he comes to define the law of language or the signifier as an 'enslavement' from which we must extricate ourselves.[2]

He quotes Nietzsche:

> Logic is only slavery within the bounds of language. Language has within it, however, an illogical element, the metaphor. Its principal force brings about an identification of the nonidentification; it is thus an operation of the imagination. It is on this that the existence of concepts, forms etc. rests.[3]

Metaphor is central to Mosley's style, not simply as a grammatical trope but as representative of a mental process. For metaphor (at least on the interaction theory[4]) consists of the holding together of two incongruous or opposed thoughts or images, thus creating in this interaction a new, third meaning.[5] This process is how Shelley saw the growth of language from the time when it was 'vitally metaphorical'. In a 'scientific' age, the language becomes logical, and loses the capacity for holding together opposites, which, as we have seen, Mosley considers essential. He calls for a new use of language to encompass this.

In the past, religious and artistic language provided this, as Mosley has argued in *Experience and Religion*.

> the mind tends to be logical but the processes that inform it apparently are not. For the mind to be placated as it were - for experience to seem not too much at odds with that which comprehends it - there have to be glimpses of a unity in which such ambiguities can be held. This, traditionally, has been a function of art.[6]

---

1 CP 164

2 'The Supplement of Copula: Philosophy *Before* Linguistics', in *Textual Strategies*, ed. J.V. Harari (Methuen, 1980), p. 83

3 ibid.

4 as advanced by Max Black

5 This makes both oxymoron and simile sub-types of metaphor, and also makes possible a distinction between 'dead' and 'live' metaphors.

6 CP 13

Jason thinks that God gave men language to confuse them when there was a chance of them building the tower of Babel and becoming gods, and wonders 'what was the language that men had, when they were becoming equal to gods'[1]. The idea of a language spoken in Eden, a *lingua adamica*, is not new, and appears in the works of the mystic Jakob Böhme, who had a great influence on the Romantics. This was thought to have been a sensual, natural language which could directly apprehend experience and God, and which would be recovered at Christ's second coming.

Many modernists felt the need for a new language, but their metaphors for this tended to be in terms of purifying and emptying language to return it to a pristine state and strip it of all its acquired accretions. But this movement depends on a basic, nominalist, trust of language as a means of encapsulating and expressing feelings and ideas. Mosley does not share either this trust or a Wittgenstinian or positivist willingness to allow language to delimit experience. He believes that language can be made to allude to or suggest the truth, even though it cannot always express it directly. 'Liveliness can only be described in terms of what it is not: of what it comes up against: in life, in language.'[2] 'If this cannot be stated explicitly it can be grasped, let go, sought out again: as happens to anything that is loved; that wants, in what way it can, to perpetuate itself.'[3] Mosley's ideas about self-transcendence and the ability to observe the patterns of the mind can only be grasped in this way, as it necessitates the holding of opposite ideas and wishes.

> So - it might be possible to say to people publicly - For goodness sake, yes, destroy yourselves if you want to! - if this were said with love: this being the hope (the best hope) of preventing them. But this, certainly, needs a difficult sort of language. And some bright understanding. It would have to be seen - half seen - that one was talking about mind; but that this was of direct relevance (the most direct relevance) to the outside world; the outside world being available to patterns of mind; but not in the old bullying type of language; not even in the simple languages in which things are set out dead as on a platter; but in the circuits and secrets and lightning flashes that are the provinces and provenances of life.[4]

Mosley also sees the need for this new use of language to encompass both scientific and primitive modes of thought (and not, as he quotes Monod as

---

1 S. 30. George Steiner has already speculated on 'after Babel'
2 CP 232
3 CP 233
4 CP 171/2

suggesting, to transcend our genetically inbuilt need for ethical beliefs and taboos, but to find a way of incorporating and commenting on them.) A contender for this language may be psychoanalysis, or to put it another way, psychoanalysis may be a metalanguage for the language of dreams, which may arise precisely because of the insufficiency of ordinary language and its inability to express the illogical: 'such splits are vacuums that dreams rush in to fill'.[1] Of course Mosley does not think that these splits are tragic or absurd provided we can find a way of dealing with them. One way we try to deal with them is to tell stories, but as Bert in *Imago Bird* pointed out, stories, like language are necessarily incomplete and so are not suited to optimism and happiness.

> Language is to do with protection; it's part of the system that filters what's coming in; it's suited to saying what things are not rather than what they are; it deals with disappointments. Even if people do know about life being a successfully going concern they can't easily talk about this; it doesn't sound right; language is to do with parts, with stories that have a beginning and a middle and an end, and parts are properly sad, because they have limits. What is successful is to do with the whole.
>
> But what if people knew something about all this - I mean they do, but what if they tried to form some language about it - wouldn't the language they formed to try to describe how life might be a successfully going concern and thus about the whole, be a language not just of stories and obsessions but about our need to make up stories and obsessions and so a language to enable us to talk about this too; not just a filter but a way of looking at filters; to clean them even . . . Wouldn't it even be like psychoanalysis?[2]

And psychoanalysis is at the heart of *Imago Bird*.[3] It is not surprising that Mosley should be interested in psychoanalysis: both Freud and Jung were concerned in various ways with paradoxes and opposites. Jung said that the self is 'a union of opposites *par excellence*', combining the individual with the universal'[4] and that while modern science tried to reduce everything to logic, some primitive people,

---

[1] CP 160

[2] IB 71

[3] Imago was a term coined by Jung in 1911 to mean 'the image of a subjective functional complex' rather than the 'object itself' (*Collected Works* (London: Routledge, 1971), vol. 6, para. 812). Jung also suggested that literary characters may be imagos of the author's psyche (6, 813). Freud appropriated the word to mean, primarily, the idealised image of one's parents in childhood - which is how Mosley uses it in the epigraph. *Imago* was also the name of a journal formed in 1912 to deal with non-clinical applications of psychoanalysis.

[4] Jung, op. cit. 12, 22

and the ancient Chinese knew 'the paradoxicality and polarity of life'.[1] Jung considered the individual to be a mix of masculine and feminine and of extra- and introvert, but that to balance these correctly would require a 'higher consciousness' which is an 'altogether superhuman ideal. Still, it is a goal.'[2] Which is very much how Mosley sees it.

Freud's interest in 'antithetical ideas' went back to 1892, before his psychoanalytic stage[3] and his techniques for interpreting dreams depend on the assumption that dreams can ignore, or encompass, 'contraries and contradictions'[4], there being an 'intimate associative chain which links the idea of a thing with its opposite in our thoughts.'[5] Freud was later to be much impressed by Abel's book on ancient language which showed how ancient Egyptian often used one word for opposite concepts, or two words joined together which individually expressed opposed ideas but together carried only one of the ideas. Abel suggested that the reason for this was that concepts cannot be understood without some idea of their opposite or negation, and in a young language these needed to be explicit. As civilisation developed (for which, perhaps, Mosley's use of Babel is a metaphor) these contraries became implicit in both thought and language and with the rise of science and Aristotelian logic and taxonomy opposites came to be mutually exclusive rather than mutually dependent. But our minds still retain the older way of thinking even though they cannot adequately be expressed in our present language, and can only surface in dreams and (with difficulty nowadays) mysticism and art.[6]

The linguistic nature of Bert's problem (he is convinced that his stammer is caused by his continual attempt to say two or more things at once) suggests that Lacanian psychoanalysis might be relevant. His stammer could stand for his unsuccessful entry into the 'symbolic' realm, though, for Mosley this would perhaps be a good thing, since it is precisely the symbolic realm which is incapable of expressing Bert's contradictory thoughts. Jason in *Serpent* thinks about 'this symbolic world, in which we are trapped like patterns of thinking within brain cells'.[7] However, these references are not deliberate, and Mosley does not suggest, like Lacan, that the unconscious is 'structured like a language', since it is precisely the structure of language which is unsuited to the unconscious.

---

[1] Jung, 13, 7

[2] Jung, 7, 87

[3] Freud, *Collected Works* (London: Hogarth, 1957), vol. 1, pp. 121-7

[4] Freud, 4, 318. They also, like poetry use condensation and over-determination, etc.

[5] Freud, 5, 471

[6] The main article is at 11, 155-61; see also 4, 318, n. 3; 5, 661, n.; 15, 178/9; 15, 229-30; 23. 169

[7] S. 2

Along with the problematisation of language must go the problematisation of art forms, and Mosley follows Brecht, whom he discusses in the first preface in *Catastrophe Practice*,[1] in suggesting that the worst thing the artist can do is connive at the comforting effect which most art has (which is therefore an-aesthetic), and Mosley includes, as he had done in *Experience and Religion* those modern artists who comfort most by their lucid and self-denying protestations of despair and chaos:

> by their craft they presuppose the existence of order and meaning, yet their plays state nothing of that of which this order and meaning consist. The art of their productions, that is, belies their pretensions of meaninglessness. And this in fact seems to be a latter-day predicament: people can indeed be articulate about despair: what is difficult to be articulate about is the fact of their articulateness.[2]

Mosley, like Brecht, though in a different way both welcomes and tries to assist in the emergence of a 'new human type evolving'[3]. This 'scientific' man (who is perhaps in Mosley's view more post-scientific) is not only observer and observed (both of others and of himself), but reaches 'some further point of thinking' from which both these functions can be observed. Mosley seeks not to transcend myths, but to make man 'his own myth or totem' (the names of some of the characters in the plays are from myths, not just classical ones, but cultural myths too). This is one of the differences between Mosley and Brecht, but the main one is that Brecht saw the emergence of a new class, whose formation he tried to help Mosley's idea is of a new individual rather than a new community. The paradox for a socialist artist such as Brecht is that he feels that his art must be difficult because it must be radically new (unlike socialist realism, which is merely comforting) and must work dialectically, but this art thereby tends to become elitist and the province of the bourgeoisie, whom, to make things worse, it comforts and affirms in their superior understanding of despair and meaninglessness, which they do not, however, really accept. Mosley's work is also elitist in this sense, but this not a problem for him, since the new type he is aiming at is elitist in any case (though, again, precisely not part of any political or power élite). Only a few can be hoped to understand the message, but those few may be enough.

---

[1] Oddly, Mosley does not mention Pirandello, though the book might well have been called 'Six Characters in Search of . . .' something. Also Pirandelllo's concerns with fragmentation, the status of literary creation, the mistrust of words, the importance of masks and roles, and the relationship between acting and reality are close to Mosley's own.

[2] CP 14

[3] CP 16

Mosley does follow Brecht, however, in his problematisation of the nature of illusion in the theatre and the importance of roles. In *Imago Bird* Bert continues the meditation on these things begun in *Catastrophe Practice*. He sees the play (to which he continually compares the events in his uncle's house) as the public aspect of life, and the audience, in the dark but just discernible, the private: 'Might not actors in fact begin to glimpse their audience as if it were their unconscious?'[1] The public is the less real - 'they could come alive again, of course, after a pistol shot: to be ready for the next night's murder and self-mutilation'[2] – but is (in conventional plays) regulated and comforting: 'it is their job to, pretend, to cover up, to put something over. And by this they give comfort'.[3] Roles are comforting and people try continuously to find a suitable one:

> The people in the hall were already not interested in finding out what in fact had happened in the study: they were interested in discovering what sort of parts they should play in order to preserve, whatever had happened, some customary function and identity.[4]

They were trying to become a 'full crowd-scene; then we can jump up and down and shout things like Rhubarb, rhubarb; and not have to worry about meanings.'[5]

In *Serpent* Mosley uses the metaphor of Plato's cave, where the people sit watching the shadows on the walls, afraid or unaware of the sun. The novel too has been a reflection, instead of trying to catch the sunlight directly. "But if we know they're shadows, we know there's a sun'[6], and the novel and the individual should aim to come out of the cave, and out of their role-playing. As we have seen, very few individuals will have this courage: 'Human beings need miseries like snails need shells: to get out of the heat of the sun: to sit in a cave watching cinema screens showing

1 IB 4
2 IB 5
3 IB 7
4 ibid.
5 ibid.
6 S. 30

miseries: and so they get pleasure . . . If anyone wants to be out in the sun, out of the cave, they have got to be alone.'[1] In the light we may be able to see the patterns of life: 'Human beings should be aesthetic, but they are not. They are moral. They can't face: being morally superior to gods.'[2] And in these patterns are contained, not despair and chaos, but the things we have so much difficulty expressing, especially in modern art and literature, the things Mosley wants us to be able to see: love, joy, optimism, life.

> What I'm saying is, isn't it, that all the dramas, emotions of our ordinary lives, are of little interest except in so far as we observe them, connect them, try to understand them, in order to make something quite different from them -
> - To worry about them is cancer: to see the shape in them is life.[3]

---

[1] S. 69

[2] S. 70. The movement from the moral to the aesthetic is exactly opposite to Kierkegaard's move from the aesthetic to the ethical.

[3] S. 139

christine brooke-rose

Christine [Frances Evelyn] Brooke-Rose (1923 – 2012)[1] was born in Geneva to an English father and a Swiss-American mother and grew up speaking English, French and German. She went to school in Folkestone in Kent, England and during the Second World War she worked in the intelligence section at Bletchley Park, where all the intercepted German messages were decoded. After the war she attended Somerville College, Oxford before attending University College, London, where she wrote a doctoral thesis on mediaeval French and English philology, completed in 1954, of which she said 'I made a detailed comparative study for a monumental and quite unpublishable thesis, which need not concern us here'[2] in *A Grammar of Metaphor,* 1958, an academic and highly technical work creating a typology of metaphor written before her interest in the emerging literature of structuralism and the *nouveau roman.* She was regularly reviewing books for the *Times Literary Supplement* from 1956 and by 1958 she was already reviewing Beckett for John Lehmann's *The London Magazine*, and had a sympathetic view of the 'anti-novel'.

> It seems necessary to the development of the novel or play that every now and then anti-novels or anti-plays should be written, which for various purposes turn the form inside out, hold it up, perhaps, to ridicule, and give it a thorough beating, or at least an airing. These are often considered to lie outside the history of the novel proper, and yet they are indispensable to our knowledge of the form: *Don Quixote*, Furetière's *Le Roman Bourgeois*, *Tristram Shandy*, Hoffmann's *Kater Murr, Epitaph of a Small Winner* by Machado de Assis, Gide's *Les Faux Monnayeurs*, Irzykowski's *Paluba*, Thornton Wilder's *The Skin of Our Teeth*. And now we have Beckett. Even if I have missed out some names,

[1] Professor Brooke-Rose died on March 21st 2012, while I was revising this section. The photograph is from the cover of *Out*.

[2] p. 2

> the tradition makes a sparse alignment compared with the vast body of 'straight' novelists whose main concern is to tell a story about persons recognizable as human beings in recognizable situations.[1]

Brooke-Rose had already published her first novel at this point: *The Languages of Love*, 1957. This was followed by *The Sycamore Tree*, 1959; *The Dear Deceit*, 1960 and *The Middlemen: A Satire*, 1961. Although these are all relatively conventional, *The Dear Deceit* has already begun to question the nature of narrative by telling the story in reverse. Then, in 1964, she began a sequence of far more experimental novels: *Out*, 1964; *Such*, 1966; *Between*, 1968 and *Thru*, 1975,[2] in between which came a book of short stories: *Go When You See the Green Man Walking,* 1970. In her later novel/autobiography *Remake* she describes how, in the early 1960s, after a serious illness, when she loses a kidney she has a

> literary turning point, after illness and meditation, in a more experimental, less popular direction, as if near-death had let the near-past die and strained backwards to early poetry and forwards towards renewal, inviting, inventing the future in a deep anxiety. Slowly Tess [her alter ego in the novel] writes a completely different novel, and two more, all three quite different from the swift first four and from each other, told over and over about barking up wrong trees, though the first two win prizes, But then the time is unpropitious, even to the great: when Tess had asked the head of Faber and Faber, at a party in the late

---

[1] 'Samuel Beckett and the Anti-Novel'. *The London Magazine*, December 1958, volume 5 no. 12, p. 38

[2] These four novels were subsequently collected in the single volume *Omnibus*, 1987. Brooke-Rose's later novels include: *Amalgamemnon* 1984; *Xorandor*, 1986; *Verbivore*, 1990; *Textermination*, 1991; *Next*, 1998; *Remake*, 1996 – two autobiographical novels: *Subscript*, 1999 and *Life, End of*, 2006. Her other later works include: *Stories, Theories, and Things*, 1991 – a book of literary theory and *Invisible Author: Last Essays*, 2002. Later works about Brooke-Rose include: *Christine Brooke-Rose and Contemporary Fiction*, 1994 by Sarah Birch and *Utterly other discourse: the texts of Christine Brooke-Rose*, 1995 by Ellen J. Friedman and Richard Martin; Word-*worlds : language, identity and reality in the work of Christine Brooke-Rose* by: Michela Canepari-Labib. Oxford University Press, 2002.

> fifties, why the firm did not publish Beckett's novels as well as the successful plays the answer was: wouldn't touch those with a barge-pole.[1]

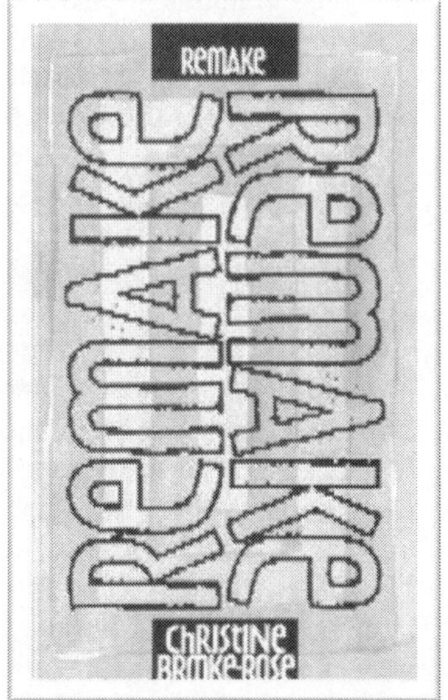

Before the publication of *Between*, Brooke-Rose had published a translation of Alain Robbe-Grillet's *In the Labyrinth,* 1959, and so was by now immersed in the *nouveau roman.* In 1969 she took up a position at the University of Paris VIII at Vincennes, first as lecturer in European Literature, then as professor, a post she kept until 1988. While there she wrote two works on Ezra Pound: *A ZBC of Ezra Pound*, 1971 and *A Structural Analysis of Pound's Usura Canto,* 1976. Her interest in Pound, particularly his use of parallel languages in a text, had already been very obvious in *Between*, whose narrator is a bilingual translator living in a babel-like world of multiple countries and languages. In 1981 she published *A Rhetoric of the Unreal: Studies in narrative and structure, especially of the fantastic*,[2] a very academic, post-structuralist work, consisting mainly of articles previously published in various academic journals from the late 1970s. The book is a survey of the academic literature on structuralism and postmodernism, especially as it relates to fantastic literature. She draws heavily on Todorov and Barthes and to some extent on Kristeva, Derrida and Lacan. There is also a long section on *The Turn of the Screw*, and one on Robbe-Grillet.

> It is true that the novel seems to have lagged some fifty years behind the other arts, which all underwent their equivalent crises early in the century; lagged behind, even, other language forms such as poetry and drama. But changes in the novel had been occurring elsewhere. . . The resistance was great, in France but especially in England, where traditionalist critics and realistic novelists organised strong campaigns, which they no doubt feel they have won.[3]

---

[1] London: Carcanet, 1996, pp. 162/163

[2] Cambridge University Press, 1981;

[3] p. 311

Possibly they had: at about this time, the cut-off for my survey of experimental novels, most novelists did turn away from experimentation (though not Brooke-Rose herself). In this work, as in her others, Brooke-Rose is concerned almost entirely with French *nouveaux romanciers* and American, mostly fabulist novelists; she does not consider or even mention any British novelists. Even in her section on 'the new science fiction' she specifically says: 'with a few exceptions, two of which I shall examine here, there has been little or no formal regeneration'[1]; she concentrates on Vonnegut and McElroy, and passes over the *New Worlds* phenomenon and the British New Wave (examined in a later chapter of this book) completely. From her position as a bilingual academic working in France at the time of the rise of French post-structuralism her perspective is perhaps not surprising: French academics all completely ignored what was happening in Britain. She is however very approving of the fabulist tradition in the American novel which she compares favourably to the French.

> The turning away from realistic representation has taken the way of the fantastic, the absurd, the carnivalesque (Barth, Vonnegut, Barthelme, Brautigan, and others), with corresponding formal mutations. Certainly the French experiments seem very dry to many Anglo-American readers. I do not know myself where the novel will go.[2]

Christine Brooke-Rose herself decided where the novel should go and took it there herself, arguably leaning more towards the French than American model, though she cannot really be compared to any other novelist of either nationality. Commenting on living in France, she compares the lack of a serious press in Britain to the situation in France, which is rather like 'walking round a national exhibition, entering one fantastic and beautiful structure after another, the Lévi-Strauss Palace, the Derrida Daedalus, the Lacan Labyrinth, the Kristeva Construct, the Barthes Pavilion, the Planetarium showing the Sollers System.' However, she says :

---

[1] p. 256

[2] p. 338

> I find it very difficult now to read most of the novels and what passes for criticism here – and I do try – it quite simply seems to be written in a new meaningless language. And this is not so, oddly in America.
>
> For my exile is a double exile. I am not only living in France but teaching American literature – pace Pound, one has to call it something, if only for syllabus purposes.
>
> And American literature, both poetry and fiction, has a vigorous relevance to all this, which I do not find, on the whole, in England.[1]

In some ways it is misleading to consider her a British novelist, but she wrote in English and continued to publish in England and I have therefore claimed her for the British tradition, especially since she is one of the few novelists who kept on writing experimental novels after the early 1980s, sticking to her guns both in terms of theory and practice. 'For all I know the technique I derived from Robbe-Grillet was a mere fashion and we've long been plunged back in certainties and intervening authors. But all attempts to change the conventions of fiction are interesting.'[2] Brooke-Rose is also important as a woman experimental writer; although the experimental novelists I have considered in this book split roughly half and half into male and female (through no conscious effort on my part; possibly British experimental writers were more gender-balanced than American or French), Brooke-Rose and others have considered it harder for female novelists in general and female experimental novelists in particular. She says that it is 'not only more difficult for a woman *experimental* writer' to be accepted than for a 'woman writer . . . but also peculiarly more difficult for a *woman* experimental writer to be accepted than for a male experimental writer.'

> Perhaps one of the safest ways of dismissing a woman experimental writer is to stick a label on her, if possible that of a male group that is getting (or better still) used to get all the attention. Fluttering around a

[1] 'Viewpoint, Time Literary Supplement, June 1 1973
[2] Introduction to Brigid Brophy's *In Transit*, 2002, published by Dalkey Archive press, 2006

> canon. The implication is clear: a woman writer must either use traditional forms or, if she dare experiment, she must be imitating an already old model. Indeed, the only two advantages of 'movements' are (1) for the writers, to promote themselves (hence they are usually men), and (2) for the critics, to serve as useful boxes to put authors into. But women are rarely considered seriously as part of a movement when it is 'in vogue', and then they are damned with the label when it no longer is, when they can safely be considered as minor elements of it.[1]

Brooke-Rose herself though resists labels, as she herself realises. 'I have a knack of somehow escaping most would-be canonic networks and labels:

> I have been called '*nouveau roman* in English' and '*nouveau nouveau*', I have been called Postmodern, I have been called Experimental, I have been included in the SF Encyclopaedia, I automatically come under Women Writers (British, Contemporary), I sometimes interest the Feminists, but I am fairly regularly omitted from the 'canonic' surveys (chapters, articles, books) that come under those or indeed other labels. On the whole I regard this as a good sign.'[2]

She does however seem to accept for herself the label 'experimental', even if it must stay in quotation marks: in 'Illiterations', a discussion of the issue of experimentalism for women writers she says: 'To be an 'experimental' writer is one thing. To write about the situation of women 'experimental' writers is quite another. This will not be a discussion of specific writers, least of all myself'.[3] However, in her discussion she does not name any of the writers I have claimed as experimental in this study, all her examples being from an older generation, with only Nathalie Sarraute being anywhere close to her own age.

And although she has been embraced by feminist critics and in some ways been one herself, she refuses to be dogmatic.

> Clearly the silencing of women critics and writers and especially of women experimental writers, is true, is constant, and is done by ignoring them, or, more often than might be supposed, by stealing from them without acknowledgement. I have experienced both myself and simply put up with it. Nevertheless I have always been deeply suspicious of movements and labels which create blind obsessions. A writer, man

---

1 'Things' in *Stories, Theories and Things*. Cambridge University Press, 2009. p. 262

2 'Theories as Stories' in *Stories, Theories and Things*, p. 4

3 'Illiterations' in *Stories, Theories and Things*, p. 250

> or woman, is essentially alone and will be 'good' or 'bad' independently of sex or origin.[1]

Christine Brooke-Rose certainly had her own voice; in her late work about growing old, *Life, End Of,* 2006 she has a discussion with the reader on voice in the narrative and the role of the author: she discusses Narrative Mode and Speech Mode; she says that historically all novels started off in narrative then later moved towards speech mode.

> By the twentieth century this is all highly developed, a healthy mixture of narrative and speech mode. But many try to get away from this distant yet omniscient and interfering author. . . by the mid-century many try to use the forbidden present tense for the narrative sentence, bringing in immediacy but losing distance, falling back into speech mode, using pronouns that go with it, especially the first person. . . when what is needed is the present tense, but without the first person. Dropping subjectivity but retaining immediacy and distance. Difficult. But it produces the rare impersonal present tense of our literary criticism, among others, and ultimately derives from science.
>
> Is that what you learnt? Or taught?
>
> A few authors succeed in renewing the tired narrative sentence in this way, with the present tense and no 'I', but it hasn't really caught on for the novel. It creates characters who must be constructed by the reader entirely out of what they see hear feel think or say, that is, without any help from the author. Whether anyone cares to exploit it further is another question altogether.
>
> So, who speaks?
>
> Yes, sorry. You have to understand that the author writes every sentence in the book, whether representing a landscape or words from a character.
>
> That's obvious.

[1] 'Theories of Stories' in *Stories, Theories and Things,* pp. 225/226

Not always. And not to everyone.[1]

Go When You See the Green Man Walking, 1970 collected a number of Christine Brooke-Rose's stories, some of which had been published before. They are mostly quite traditoinal and some are ghost stories, two of which had already appeared in ghost story anthologies, and some are about the nature of identity and existence.'George and the Seraph' is about The Point of no Return; a metaphor perhaps for death. The narrator is the seraph, lighter than an angel, who acts as a mirror for those who approach the point. 'On Terms' has a narrator whom we presume to be dead, and has committed suicide, though she seems to have chosen to stay as a ghost so that she can watch the world change, especially to see the man with whom she had been 'on terms' but who had betrayed her.

> Nobody knows that my body lies there in my bed in the locked flat in the big city, its atoms all bombarded by those of the barbiturates and slowly undergoing the chemical reaction into compost that will feed no earth no worms no mulching vegetation, only the small room all windows closed. I die alone because I live alone.[2]

But

> It is because I am acting out a fantasy that I can wear the semblance of my temporal body and move about as if I existed, which of course I do. Anyone with enough love or hate exists even when out of mind or dead. . . Existence is not a temporal state but an energy which does not stop merely for lack of flesh although in many dead people this energy does degrade itself for lack of love so that it shrinks like a degenerate star into less than a pinpoint weighing many tons.[3]

'Medium Loser and Small Winner' is a more experimental story; the (preumably male) narrator and an imaginary female meet a man at a party. The narrator says

---

[1] p. 68
[2] p. 18
[3] p. 19

he can imagine the man's life just by looking at him and describes a version of his life.

> - Do you always invent stories about people you don't know?
> - Sometimes. Some people aren't worth inventing stories about.
> - And do they come true?
> - As true as a straight isotrope.
> - And how straight is a straight isotrope?
> Her eyes sized me up, measured me as a heavy industrialist in the back of Christopher who talks to Felix fully aware of shifting polygons. Her hand holding the glass is white and elegant with long nails varnished silver pink. Since it doesn't exist she says with sudden intensity that promised much in bed, I imagine it can be taken as straight or as unstraight as you wish to make it, and the verbs rouse my masculine prerogative to a sudden steady now, nothing deserves a rush of preference. So you play games with words. Dangerous games.
> - No, I don't like games. I always lose them. But then, I tend to lose things.
> - Things?
> - Oh, boring things, like the sex-war and all that, if it exists. By saying it now, you see, I've lost it already.[1]

The title story concers a woman rather like the narrator of *Between*: a woman traveller in a strange place who takes comfort from the familiarity of everyday objects; in this case her clothes and the way they feel.

> GO WHEN YOU SEE THE
> GREEN MAN WALKING
>
> Says a woman's voice.
> The woman has guessed her language, here in the strange city at the traffic lights. Has guessed her nationality from what, her blonde hair no there are blonde women in this country also and hairdressers. From her clothes then driving clothes crumpled cotton shirt and skirt and canvas shoes that had stepped forward too fast drawn by a lull in traffic, before the green man had appeared.[2]
>
> The red man stands his legs apart. He is extraordinarily squat and thick with hos short rectangular legs. And luminous.
> She waits.

---

[1] pp. 136/137
[2] p. 180

> No car glides by along either street.
> The green man walks, equally luminous with equally rectangular legs ending in square green shoes. And yet less squat and thick because he walks.
> She goes.
> She passes the bookshop without a glance. The silk of the blouse caresses her breasts the silk lining of the skirt her thighs and buttocks as she walks the light long earrings swing from clips that softly bite her lobes. The supple leather of her expensive shoes firmly hugs her heels and toes, leaving the instep bare. The heels knock loudly on the pavement for it to open up.
> The red man stands, rectangular legs apart.
> She waits. The streets are empty.
> The green man walks light an dairy.
> She goes.[1]

Traffic signals are a kind of universal semiotic language, though in the woman's country 'they have discs only, green amber red'[2] All that is necessary in a strange environment is to understand and follow 'the code'. 'One could walk miles and miles obeying the code.' The green man is the 'safe man,' unlike the threatening red man.

> The man lurches out of a doorway. She steps aside. He steps in front of her, legs apart, barring her way. She steps into the street. He does the same. He is squat and thick. She steps back on to the pavement. He follows. He has red hair, a crackling forest fire, he sways, flays out his arms, utters words that gong her body with brutal tenderness all over from the breasts still and high under the silk down to the pubic hair that touches the silk lining as the warm air from the pavement floats up her thighs kissing the open lips like violins. His arms come down in a swift movement to his green corduroy trousers unless blue sea-blue in the sea-blue light unzipped to a white flash of foam that roaring breaks as the sea opens to reveal a coral reef around a huge white peak. It has a pinkish tip like snow in sunset but it can't be snow under the suddenly silent sea in this blue light and it moves, due to the sea water perhaps it swims and two white creatures swim down and surround it or a white octopus and grip it moving up and down with deep quiet grunts. She contemplates the vision and it makes animal noises that paw her body with brutal tenderness as she stands in a tranced stillness smiling kindly

[1] p. 187
[2] p. 180

> waiting for the red-haired man to switch off and turn into the green man walking.[1]

But at the end, by 'following the code' she gets back to the safety of her hotel room.

In *The Dear Deceit* Christine Brooke-Rose had reversed time by telling the story backwards; in *Out*, she reverses conventional racism. After a mysterious incident, known as 'the displacement', all 'Colourless' (i.e. white) people are potentially subject to 'the malady'. They are unemployable, forced to live in 'settlements' and are treated as untouchables by the dark-skinned upper class. The narrator and central character has no real character at all; he hides his previous occupation, saying he has previously been a gardener, fortune teller or joiner (though he later describes himself as having been a 'humanist').

We presume this is because the educated, intellectual Colourless people have been persecuted, perhaps killed, but this is never made clear. In this world of reverse racism, the unemployed Colourless men are given 'unemployment pills' that they must collect every day from the Labour Exchange. The native inhabitants of the place (described only as Afro-Eurasia, as opposed to the foreign territory of Sino-America) such as the main character, Mrs Mgulu are only described as being Asswati – 'her smooth Asswati face' – or, like her maid, Bahuko. Though the society is profoundly racist, the upper class deny it in exactly the same terms that white Europeans use in our society: 'I mean I'm not one for prejudice in these matters. One of my best friends was a Uessayan of Ukay extraction'[2]

> We have no prejudice that's an article of faith. But there is an irrational fear of the Colourless that lingers on, it's understandable, in some cases, even justifiable, with the malady still about, well, it makes them unreliable.[3]

---

[1] pp. 189/190
[2] p. 37
[3] p. 49

Resettlement Camp No: 49 **File No:** AS/239457/Z

Ex-nationality: Ukayan

Ex-occupation: humanist

Re-training: fitter

Observations:

DISCHARGED

Labour Exchange No: 174 **Card No:** 3BL/4963/81

Ex-nationality: Ukayan

Ex-occupation: Ph.D.

Re-trained as: odd jobman

Employment history: unsatisfactory, see D.P.I.

CONFIDENTIAL

State Hospital No: 897 Southern Region

File No: PSY/L8I5325 NOT TO BE HANDLED BY PATIENT

Ex-occupation: ~~psychopath~~ gardener

Present occupation: unemployed

Present address: Settlement No 4512(c)

Local doctor: none, see letter from Mrs. D. Mgulu

Seen by: Dr Fu Teng

Recommendation: Psychos copy

Observations: Biogram attached

This 'unreliability' makes the Colourless undesirable as workers: 'the Ukayans have long had a bad reputation as workers, you know'[1] Despite this, there is no official segregation, and the society prides itself on its (non-existent) tolerance just like many Western societies do. Sometimes this world seems like the exact inverse of South Africa:

> But we don't have segregation here, we're a multi-racial society, exalting all colours to the detriment of none, don't you know your slogans?[2]

Also in an ironic inversion of white-on-black racism, Colourless women can be objects of sexual desire.

> Her legs are thin and very white, which, in a black man's world, has more than adulterous appeal, the tender, incestuous appeal of love within minorities.[3]

The 'malady' that has afflicted the Colourless is never explained but its onset is described by the narrator:

> That is how the malady begins. The onset is insidious, well advanced before diagnosis. Anaemia, progressive emaciation, fatigue, tachycardia, dyspnoea, and a striking enlargement of the abdomen due to splenomegaly and heptomegaly. But the spleen remains smooth and firm on palpation and retains its characteristic notch. The black fingers tap the flaccid white flesh, the wrist emerging dark from the white sleeve of the doctor's coat. The imagination increases in size progressively and usually painlessly until it fills most of the abdomen. Enlargement of the lymphatic glands may occur in the later stages of the disease, with a general deterioration to a fatal termination.[4]

This listing of technical terms is typical of the book's methods: biochemical and technical data may fill a whole paragraph. This passage also typically questions the narrator's sense of reality. Is the malady in the mind? In the narrator's mind? The reality of the novel is constantly questioned in a number of ways. Mrs Mgulu tells the narrator that his wife Lilly is ill (with the malady?) and the doctor is doing all he can.

---

[1] p. 36
[2] p. 123
[3] p. 28
[4] p. 64

> But Dr. Lukulwe is only a psychoscopist, a charlatan, he will make her worse, he will make her suffer with his machine, please get a real doctor.
> - Real? What is real? His eyelids are the right colour.
> - Please let her die in peace without self-knowledge that is false, built up by instruments and the minds behind the instruments.
> - Oh but it bears a close resemblance to the real thing.[1]

It is never clear what is real, as all we see is through the eyes of this completely unreliable narrator. Sometimes he even seems like the alter ego of Mrs Mgulu:

> I am there. Wholly and fully, my presence burns up your psychic energy as the road burns through the thin soles of your shoes. I shall always be with you, talking to you and sharing your observation of phenomena, until you die, because that is the way you want it, and I am your dark reality.[2]

The narrator implies continually that his/one's own perception creates reality:

> At the beginning it was sufficient. It was at times and within certain limits sufficient to imagine a movement for the movement to occur, although it was easier in the negative.[3]

> Sometimes it is sufficient to imagine an episode for the episode to occur, and that is the terrifying thing, though not necessarily in that precise form. The first failure is the beginning of the first lesson. Learning presupposes great holes in knowledge.[4]

The whole narration may be a fantasy of the narrator, though he admits that some of his fantasies 'can be ruled out of order by the Silent Speaker.'[5] 'You are talking to yourself. This dialogue did not necessarily occur.'[6]

> - Look, since you're inventing this dialogue you ought to give something to the other chap to say.
> - But I must get those facts in.
> - He won't let you, he exists too, you know.[7]

---

[1] p. 166
[2] p. 159
[3] p. 172
[4] p. 173
[5] p. 65
[6] p. 15
[7] p. 17

In contrast to the narrator's 'mobile eye' is a static, objective viewpoint: 'The pale eye that doesn't move is fixed on the shelf of can-recipes, but the mobile eye stares towards the reflected moon in the darkness beyond the window.'[1] There are constant references to this objective viewpoint, contrasting with the subjectivity of the narrative. Watching a fly on his knee, the narrator reflects:

> A microscope might perhaps reveal animal ecstasy in its innumerable eyes, but only to the human mind behind the microscope, and besides, the fetching and rigging up of a microscope, if one were available, would interrupt the flies.[2]

As with Heisenberg's Uncertainty Principle, measurement affects the thing measured and humans will always add their own viewpoint to any supposedly scientific, objective measurement. Emotions can be measured, but there is no objectivity.

> A psychoscope might perhaps reveal the expression to be one of pleasure in beauty, rather than self-love. The scene might occur for that matter, in quite a different form.[3]
>
> A stethoscope might perhaps reveal that her heart beat faster on seeing him appear round the East corner of the house.[4]

There is very little emotion of any kind in *Out*. Human interaction is minimal and the Colourless characters have no character, no attributes, and only have names like Mrs Ned.

> - Two flies are making love on my knee.
> - Flies don't make love. They have sexual intercourse.
> - On the contrary.
> - You mean they make love but don't have sexual intercourse?
> - I mean it's human beings who have sexual intercourse but don't make love.
>
> Very witty. But you are talking to yourself. This dialogue will not necessarily occur.[5]

---

[1] p. 85
[2] p. 9
[3] p. 24
[4] p. 67
[5] p. 10

In fact, the only description of sexual interaction in the novel does bear out the narrator's bleak view:

> Sexual Intercourse takes place on the kitchen chair. It is satisfactory. The woman is on top, carrying out the necessary motions, smelling of sweat, chopped-up onions and washing-up water.[1]

As might be expected, the novel has no resolution, and at the end we are left only with the narrator's (or author's) voice, musing again on uncertainty, on the impossibility of objectivity, of measurement, of distance.

> That is how it all began. There is a secret but it is not a story. It is not possible to witness the beginning, the first ticking of the metronome, because all you are entitled to assume is that it would have been as now described if it had been seen by minds with the kind of perception man has evolved only quite recently. Those that cannot grow with it must die.[2]

In the final paragraph, there is a description of a fire bursting forth, disintegrating the 'human element' into the 'huge consciousness of light'.

> We are merely marking time and time is nothing, nothing. A moment of agony, of burning flesh, an aspect of the human element disintegrating to ash, and you are dead. But that's another story.

And Brooke-Rose's next novel, *Such*, is indeed a story about death and resurrection.

---

[1] p. 67
[2] p. 196

At the start of the *Such* (1966) the narrator, who has no name at this stage, and is, or believes himself to be dead, meets a 'girl-spy' who is carrying five 'planets' on her 'left spiral arm'. She has no name but he calls her Something and she calls him Someone. The planets are called after early blues tunes: Gut Bucket; Potato Head; Tin Roof; Dippermouth and Really the Blues. They go into orbit around the world Someone has created in his (dead/dying/ unconscious) world. He remembers

> moving through space, forwards but back at the same time, as if I consisted of anti-matter for ever cancelled out. . . as if in our words and gestures, acts and attitudes we effected some sort of parallel penetration into whatever had originated them, their primeval atom, say, with built-in unstableness[1]

Something seems to be perhaps the narrator's alter ego; his female, dark, principle, even a version of his wife. They have a 'marital quarrel':

> The atoms of our will-powers collide in the pressurised hum, and a long drawn battle ensues. Bombarded atoms whirl round each other, emitting particles of pain, withdraw, get reinforced with fresh electrons, begin again.[2]

The strange names of the five 'planets', in some way the narrator's children with the 'girl-spy' Something, are never explained but names are in any case questioned in the novel. We think that by giving names to things we gain power over them, can control them, but this is an illusion. 'We give names to sicknesses, but we don't heal, merely create new dependencies.'[3] In giving names to things and people we trap them in a story, pin them down and close off possibilities of interpretation. Tin Roof says to the narrator: 'We all remain. You can't get rid of us merely by giving us names and sending us into oblivion.'[4]

---

[1] p. 107/8

[2] p. 17

[3] p. 145. Susan Sontag's *Illness as Metaphor*, 1978 takes this argument to book-length.

[4] p. 133

Such revisits several of the themes of *Out*; again we are in a private world created by the narrator. We also have references to quantum uncertainty, where people are seen as particles, destroyed and recreated in each moment, questioning the whole notion of continuity and causality.

> You try to live without causality, pretending that each moment has its own separateness, that anyone might come and go in that one moment like an electron.[1]

But, if there is no causality, how can we live our lives? And how can storytellers construct stories? Talking to his daughter, Elizabeth, the narrator tells her not to leave him alone in order to see her doctor, who does not deserve her attention.

> - Larry, everyone deserves the attention of definiteness
> - Even if they prefer the uncertainty principle?
> - They only pretend to prefer it. While they have to. You used to say that. Someone would come along and find a unified theory that would do away with indeterminate interpretations, you'd say, and revert to causality. I thought perhaps you might.
> - I thought so too. In psychic terms at least. But I didn't. In the meantime we do the best we can, some of us preferring to pretend causality exists, and others, others preferring its absence. But you can never know with absolute certainty that what looks like the same particle, with the same identity –
> - Yes but for practical purposes you have to, Larry, in the chemistry of people. Otherwise how can you live?
> - You can't. Not really. You pretend to. To save the appearances.[2]

As in *Out*, the narrator of *Such* compares the indeterminacy of quantum phenomena with the predictability and order we expect of life. Seen from a distance or en-masse, people can be seen to behave according to certain patterns that we have come to accept but, like atoms, when examined closely enough, this determinacy breaks down.

> The moment you try to find out its condition the very process of investigation must disturb it. So with people. compared to mass ideas and mass people.[3]

---

[1] p. 43
[2] p. 191
[3] p. 167

Also as in *Out*, Brooke-Rose points out that the act of observing, or measuring changes the thing that is being observed, and that this is true of people as well as objects. Narratives, like life, must be complex, like quanta and, in trying to describe reality objectively, from a position of disinterestedness, are bound to fail as the act of telling a story must change the story. And also, as in *Out,* people are described as complexes of waves and particles. Laurence says his eyes 'see people in the map-like shapes of their radiating coronas, inner meridians, latitudes and spirals.'[1]
His wife Brenda, though, prefers order and simplicity; she needs to live according to a programme, even if the programme makes no sense.

- Brenda –
- Won't it wait, Larry?
- I've remembered something[2]
- What?
- Something . . . of the narrative, the location.
- Oh, go away Larry, can't you see we must finish this programme?
- What programme?
- Track, eight four two one. Sync shot. Block Prime Pulse Mesh.[3]

Brenda also prefers simplicity in men. She seems to have been having an affair with what the narrator calls a one-stance man, who 'sits behind his telephones and trays, inventing his own indispensability with red zigzags, curves, black bars of varying heights, regiments of rectangles'[4], the opposite of the complex, electron-like dead/alive narrator. She prefers more simplicity: 'sometimes I wish I had married a simpler man, more imaginatively illiterate, I mean, who couldn't read me'[5]. However, the narrator says 'I didn't choose the way, I wanted only opaqueness, nothingness. I didn't order these complexities, these secret laws and their priggish mystifications.'[6]

Also a believer in complexity is the character of the narrator's friend, the scientist Professor Head [*sic*], a mathematician, and a believer in doubt over certainty. 'Nurturing doubt needs much more care than nurturing the spiritual life, he says.'[7] Professor Head's assistant Tim contrasts science to poetry:

---

[1] p. 70
[2] Probably a reference to Something, the name he gave to the character from his memories of death
[3] p. 130/131
[4] p. 121
[5] p. 122
[6] p. 46
[7] p. 71

> I suppose pure scientists tend to get frightened of words, because they don't use them. I believe that poets also get frightened of them, for the opposite reason. But it all comes to the same thing in the end. We all have to face the same facts.[1]

Except, of course, we know that there are no objective facts, at least in Christine Brooke-Rose's novels. In a similar vein, Professor Head says of mathematics:

> You start with nothing, treat it as something[2] and in no time at all you have infinity or thereabouts. Storytellers do the same I believe.
> - Yes, but I have no story to tell.
> - You will, you will. In the last sentence.[3]

As is to be expected, the last sentence of the novel – 'the unfinished unfinishable story of Dippermouth, Gut Bucket Blues, my sweet Potato Head, Tin Roof, Really, Something and me' does not bring any conclusion to the story, not even an ending, only an end.

> Once upon a time, in 1968, there appeared a novel called *Between*, by Christine Brooke-Rose, hereafter in this metastory or story-matter referred to as the author, author of *Out, Such*, and earlier novels. *Between* deals with (?), explores (?), represents (?), plays around with (?), makes variations on (?), expresses (?), communicates (?), is about (?), generates (?), has great fun with the theme / complex experience / story / of bilingualism. The I / central consciousness / non-narrating narrative voice / is a simultaneous interpreter who travels constantly from congress to conference and whose mind is a whirl of topics and jargons and foreign languages / whose mind is a whirl of worldviews, interpretations, stories, models, paradigms, theories, languages. Note that in this metastory the simultaneous interpreter has no sex.[4]

[1] p. 105
[2] Another reference to the character of Something?
[3] p. 71
[4] 'Theories as stories', op. cit., p. 6

In the novel *Between,* 1968 we are again in a private world, seen only through the eyes of a narrator, but this time the world seems relatively real and substantial. It is the world of a simultaneous translator from French to German, travelling constantly and existing in a world of planes, airports, hotels and conferences. This time the narrator seems to be female (*pace* Brooke-Rose's statement above) and may relate more directly to Brooke-Rose herself, who had a Swiss mother. Brooke-Rose had recently translated Robbe-Grillet and was soon to publish two books on Ezra Pound's *Cantos*, which of course also inhabit a world of multiple simultaneous languages, though far less concrete a world than the narrator of *Between*. Later she specifically mentioned her debt to Robbe-Grillet.

> Alain Robbe-Grillet is the only writer in the Fifties who explored the present tense, quite paradoxically, not just for Speech-Form situations but *as* a Narrative Sentence (in which no-one speaks, events narrate themselves'), a sort of 'scientific' present tense, thus restoring, contradictorily and only apparently, its authority.
>
> Moreover, in his early novels, notably in *La Jalousie* (1957) and *Dans le Labyrinth* (1959), literally 'no-one speaks', there is no first person, only a poised description of all that is being seen, heard, supposed, and we have to construct the character out of that. Of course this is a constraint, a limitation, but it gives other freedoms. I myself was profoundly influenced by this technique from *Out* and *Such* (1964, 1966) to *Between*, and developed it later in all sorts of ways[1]

Despite Brooke-Rose's complaints about reviewers, at least one review of Between was very positive.

> Impressively, unsentimentally, Miss Brooke-Rose sets aaside the familiar opposition between the word-spinner and the full human being. Her central figure brings no solutions, but we may begin to wonder

[1] Introduction to Brigid Brophy's *In Transit*, 2002, published by Dalkey Archive press, 2006

> whose language reveals emotional poverty – the narrator's? The others'? Ours?
>
> The glittering surface of the novel – free-running association, superb multilingual forgings, pompous reported talk, word-play – suggests a comic extravaganza ("exploiting language to the full and in a very funny way", says the blurb). In fact, while the comedy is very much there, it is firmly controlled by a self-derisive and vulnerable consciousness.[1]

Whereas in the previous two novels there had been much questioning of the possibility of objectivity and continuity and a basis in the Uncertainty Principle, in *Between* the world seems very objective and there is a strong temporal flow, even though every hotel, airport and plane is alike. The style is much more *chosiste* in the Robbe-Grillet sense; here, as Robbe-Grillet said 'we look at the world but the world does not look back.' The objectivity here is given by the constant listing of the multiple languages written on the labels of everyday objects found in the hotel rooms and conference centres in which she spends nearly all her time (she seems to have no home of her own; she is always 'between' locations and languages): bottled water; shaving equipment; toiletries etc. Only the language that appears first on the items lets her know what country she is in.

> Služi za brisanje. Za skidanje šminke. Für Rasierklingen. Zum Abschminken. Pour le rasoir. Pour le démaquillage. For the razor. To remove your make-up.[2]

These labels and instructions are regularly repeated, like litanies of comfort, reminders of reality in a world of waking up in strange places and needing some reminder of what country she is in. 'Sometimes a chambermaid serves Frühstück or Micul Dejun in camera. Or a smooth floor-steward in white unless a waking call with a collazione down below in a black plastic bar.'[3] In this novel, unlike the previous two, *things* have a definite reality.

> Sometimes German comes first then French then English or vice versa in endless permutations with the language of the country always at the head however such as ΣΑΡΙΖΑ ΑΡΙΣΤΟΝ ΕΠΙΤΡΑΠΕΖΙΟΝ ΙΑΜΑΤΚΟΝ ΥΔΩΡ hardly worth the effort on account of SARIZA Table Water natural-curative Eau de Table naturelle-curative. Analyse de l'eau de SARIZA (en milligr par litre) Silice, Acide Sulfurique, Chaux, Résistivité

---

[1] 'Loded Language', *Times Literary Supplement,* October 31, 1968

[2] p. 16

[3] p. 25/26

> électrique en Ohms Radioactivité (unités Mache) to the TOYAΔETTA with care not to enter AVΔPΩN by mistake when the door bears no skirted figurine or high-heeled shoe in the imprecision of a mere smattering acquired among the Cinzano Jerez-Quina Liquor Beirao Ouzo St. Raphael what will you have my dear in low square black armchairs the bar lit up like a reredos.[1]

As a translator, the narrator's job is simply to translate other people's ideas, not to interpret them. She is not employed to be interested in the ideas of themselves: 'We merely translate other people's ideas not to mention platitudes, si-mul-ta-né-ment. No one requires us to have any of our own. We live between ideas'.[2] However, 'one has to understand immediately because the thing understood slips away together with the need to understand.'[3] So she has to understand the ideas only as long as it takes to translate them. She attends

> conventions conferences congresses in castles palaces public buildings university halls where no communication of course occurs. Ever? You exaggerate. Something gets across.[4]

The languages are not a barrier to communication, as they are translated, but there are barriers between individuals, symbolised by the borders she constantly has to cross. 'In der Luft gibts keine Grenzen. . . Ah, but airports have frontiers.'[5] And at every border she is asked if she has anything to declare; metaphorically she has nothing to declare.

> Have you anything to declare such as love desire ambition or a glimpse that in this air-conditioning and other circumstantial emptiness freedom has its sudden attractions as the body floats in willing suspension of responsibility to anyone, stretching interminably between the enormous wings towards the distant brain behind the orange curtain and beyond, no doubt, the little door.[6]
>
> Please declare if you have any love loyalty lust intellect belief of any kind or even simple enthusiasm for which you must pay duty to the Customs and Excise.[7]

---

[1] pp. 21/22
[2] p. 19
[3] p. 41
[4] p. 27
[5] p. 14
[6] p. 28
[7] p. 50

This distancing between people is symbolised in the Turkish hairdresser, where 'The man talks to the mirrored reflection of the lady and the lady talks to the mirrored reflection of the man. Seen from the profile they do not proffer anger dissatisfaction and polite attempt to please each other at all but only at the mirror.'[1]

Brooke-Rose clearly means us to regard this space between languages, cultures and territories as a metaphor for modern life: 'We live in an age of transition, haven't you heard?'[2] Not that this is necessarily a bad thing. Perhaps there is a Chomskyan deep structure that all languages share:

> As if languages loved each other behind their own façades, despite alles man denkt darüber davon dazu. As is words fraternised silently beneath the syntax, finding each other funny and delicious in a Misch-Masch of tender fornication, inside the bombed out hallowed structures and the rigid steel glass modern edifices of the brain.[3]

Certainly Brooke-Rose herself loves the words of many languages that inhabit her brain, and enjoys playing games with them. 'E allora the languages fraternise in a frenzy of fornication'[4]. She clearly, though not necessarily approvingly, refers to Saussure and her language games seem definitely to be influenced by Barthes, Derrida and others, despite her parodying of them; elsewhere she said 'George Steiner once told me that my books weren't novels but language-games; the context was so friendly I still don't know whether this was simple categorizing, or praise, or dismissal'.[5] She specifically questions the need for or even the possibility of meaning for writers. Attending a conference on literature and semantics the narrator asks

> What has the writer to do with Semantics? I ask myself that question. I even went so far as to look up the word sémantique in the dictionary and found it meant: SIG-NI-FI-CA-TION. La science de la sig-ni-fi-ca-tion. But what has literature to do with science? With analysis of meaning until the meaning vanishes under the academic weight of analysis? Rien! Ou, pour aider les interprètes, nikts, notting, nada, niente. Vous voyez! Il n'y a aucune difficulté le langage speaks for itself.[6]

---

[1] p. 72
[2] p. 71
[3] p. 53
[4] p. 148
[5] 'Theories as Stories', op. cit., p. 5
[6] p. 85

Elsewhere, Brooke-Rose seems to abandon the narrator temporarily and dives into an analysis of 'the central Saussurean dichotomy of Langue et Parole'[1]. Sometimes it seems that she would like to free her mind of these multiple languages to find a meaning-free space for contemplation. Entering a mosque, she finds the Islamic calligraphy, which even she seems not to be able to translate, more conducive to inner peace than Christian churches.

> And the huge white columns covered with dark calligraphy so much easier to worship than plaster images because totally devoid of any sense proper or improper, at least to the neutralised transmitter in the brain except in a particular context of perfect proportion between matter and space, presence and absence that signifies nothing at all, no love, no lust, no ambition, no disappointment, no personal messages in any code to any god of love or power or anger, revenge humiliation eternal torment repentance absolution or even death. . . . The stones contain the temple, cavern, sepulchre which contains one alleinstehende Frau sitting cross-legged on a prayer rug.[2]

Like the life of the 'alonestanding' narrator, the novel has no apparent point, no structure, no development throughout or resolution at the end. However, she is not unhappy in her endless journeying to nowhere and finds her comfort in the lists and labels that surround her, where words do seem to have objective meanings, or at least refer to definite external objects, unlike the languages of ideas and feelings.

> And if you look up the word happiness in the dictionary you will find that the apparent definition contains words which themselves need defining and so on ad infinitum which makes one very merry Il n'y a jamais de sens propre au dictionnaire, the proper sense living only in an expressive and particular context like menus for example where the sound does not disintegrate into one inert element and a confusional sliding from active to passive, from swallower to swallowed which we find in all the myths of depth descent and feminity.[3]
>
> The moving finger writes and having writ scrubs out the diagram. Tous les signifies du portrait sont faux but even altogether cannot succeed in naming the falsehood, although they point to it in a hermeneutic gap chock full of the parenthetic fallacy whereby the falsehood is long

[1] p. 167
[2] p. 171
[3] p. 173

> desired but evaded by way of the evasive mouth and its paradismal trick of articulation.[1]

Whereas *Between* is clearly influenced by Christine Brooke-Rose's exposure to the nouveau roman as well as by Ezra Pound, structuralism and post-structuralism, *Thru* (1975), which came seven years after *Between,* seems to relate more to Anglo-American concrete poetry than French philosophy. Abandoning conventional narrative even more thoroughly than before – though it does have named characters – as well as sense and readability, *Thru* is a typographical extravaganza that questions the very idea of the novel. Between about 1966 and 1969 there was an outpouring of books, pamphlets and exhibitions of concrete, or visual poetry in England, led particularly by the Benedictine monk Dom Sylvester Houédard (dsh), John Furnival and Ian Hamilton Finlay; *Thru* seems to belong to this tradition far more than the European traditions Brooke-Rose is most associated with, though inevitably one thinks of Apollinaire, Marinetti and e.e. cummings, not to mention Hölderlin's *Fragments*. If language and meaning were tested in *Between*, they are tested to destruction in *Thru*.

> *Thru* was conceived in 1970 but for obstetrico-typographical reasons did not appear until 1975. This was the only novel in which two selves, actual author and theoretical critic, came together. It was [author-comment] a novel about the theory of the novel, that is, a narrative about narrativity, a fiction about fictionality, a text about intertextuality and [*hors-texte* analepsis] it took four summers to get 'right'. The author had enormous fun with it and was duly rapped on the typographic knuckles for it – typographic because by the time it came out it all seemed pretty external to him. She had stuck her neck out and his neck knew what it would get. [Conclusion in proleptic analepsis: the external harm this book did to her reputation as incomprehensible and pretentious was lasting and profound. He was dismissed and had a long *traversée du desert*.] It was, at that point [author-comment], her best

[1] p. 112

and most daring book in the self-reflexive genre. Concluding moral: this chapter is a metaphoric metapardigmatic model metastory of my relationship to theory.[1]

Through the driving-mirror four eyes stare back
two of them in their proper place
Now right on
Q ask us

to de V elop foot on gas
how m(any how) eyes?

four two
of them correct

on either side ▽ of the
nose the other

two ⚠ O danger
slow down

eXact replicas

nearer the hairline further up the brow but dimmed as in a glass
tarnished by the close-cropped mat of hair they peer through

The mat of hair is khaki, growing a bit too low on the brow
the nose too big.

Who speaks?

le rétro viseur (some languages
more visible than others)

1

[1] 'Theories as Stories ' op. cit., p. 8

never the lesS
this is noT
nO
(My)
the hYsTeRy of The
Eye
becAuse I would noT SeE thY cRuel Nails
boaRish fAngs
pluck ouT hIs
pooR old (E Xtract) (Cruel
Cruel nAils) uPon These eyEs of
tHine
I'll set (C RuEl fanGs)
my foOt PooR old eyes
These eyEs hIs eYes
pooR old eyes
beAm Mote
Cruel fanGs
Eyes cRuel fAngs
boArish
beaM
Moat
Etc
alreaDy (all read eye)
naIls
Nails
upon These
eyes of tHine I'll
sEt
the re Mote sTone
Wide Eyes wEt?
pArch Ment waX
arXi stOne Trace
dRy
papYrus
eye 'S

6

writing – for the foot men who say
O in the mountain break fast tonguetables (thou shalt

eat thy prisoner) for a feted calf

```
                    b
            t           o
          a         o
                        u   d
        f n h     a d t
← a g r i d i r o n y o r g u y a s t r i c →
        r   n i   t   m   r
                            e
        e     n   i   b   i
              d           l
```

so poor Midas and other goldicondeologists prisoners of

well-planned desires for their own excrement obscurely alimenting them while nevertheless consuming them up regardless.

So more
or
less
literally

It has all been dreamt up by the trait-or markster of the comment, the tale-bearer as eiron-monger hatching against his homo-logos a plot from fear of trans fer ring a handful of
silver
displaced
condensed
metonymised
such a
man
would not
fight
the eagle in the

15

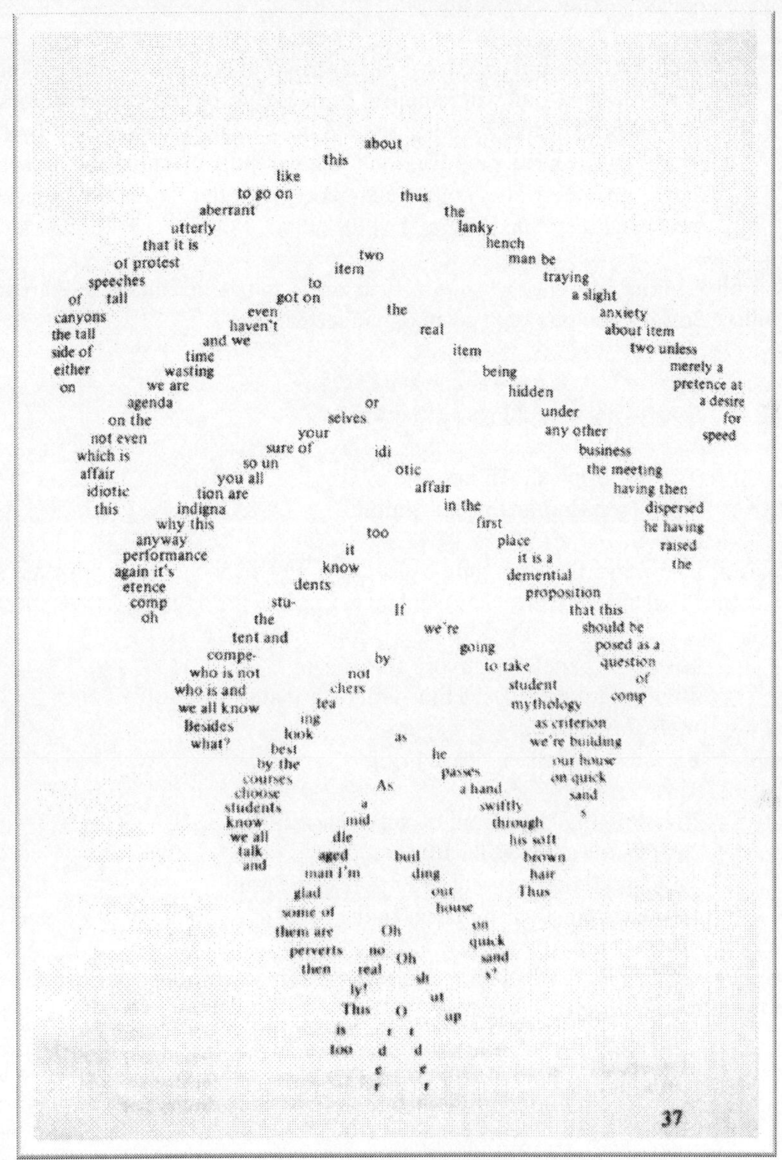

about
this
like
to go on thus
aberrant the
utterly lanky
that it is hench
of protest two man be
item
speeches traying
to
of tall a slight
got on
even the
canyons anxiety
haven't
real about item
the tall
and we
two unless
side of item
time
merely a
either
wasting being
on we are pretence at
hidden
agenda or a desire
under
on the selves for
any other
your
not even speed
sure of
business
which is idi
so un
the meeting
affair otic
you all
having then
idiotic affair
tion are
in the
this indigna dispersed
why this first
he having
too
anyway place
raised
it
performance
it is a
the
know
again it's
demential
dents
etence
proposition
comp
stu-
If that this
oh the
we're should be
tent and
going posed as a
compe- by
to take question
who is not not
of
student
who is and chers
comp
tea
mythology
we all know
ing as criterion
Besides
look
as
what? we're building
best
he
our house
by the
passes
courses on quick
As
a hand
choose sand
a
students swiftly
s
know mid
through
we all die
his soft
talk aged buil
brown
and man I'm ding
hair
glad our Thus
house
some of
on
them are Oh
quick
perverts no
Oh sand
then real sh
s?
ly!
ut
This O up
is r r
too d d
e e
r r

37

On page 1 (see illustration) the novel asks: 'Who speaks?' This is not immediately obvious. Later it becomes apparent that there is a voice speaking: a male character in a university department called Armel, and there are other characters that are named but not described.

> Not that I need to describe him, descriptions capture so little and people are becoming more stereotyped. I am becoming more stereotyped. You are becoming shall I conjugate? But no, you are the exception to all the stereotypes or are you? Have you not carefully invented the person you have become? Not of course a stereotype, rather a unique unrepeatable model with cropped hair and a blue guitar.[1]

The blue guitar is mentioned more than once and is of course a reference to Wallace Stevens' famous 1937 poem on modernism:

> They said 'You have a blue guitar
> You do not play things as they are.'
>
> The man replied, 'Things as they are
> Are changed upon the blue guitar.'

Larissa, who plays the blue guitar also 'does not play things as they are'. She sometimes occupies a world between languages, like the one in *Between* itself.

> No vale la pena el llanto or l'amore é un
> altalena or love is just a four-letter word and
> more; love is a bore, a soap op
> era a telephone that doesn't ring
>
> In many languages from Lucan to Lacan
> she fills the air as well with
> syntagmatic silence – from Phaedrus to Freud
> Homer to Husserl and Locke to the Li Ki[2]

So perhaps *Thru* is trying to represent things as they are in an age when the voice of the author/authority has broken down.

> Once upon a time laid out in rectangles which you enter as into a room saying once upon a time the author had supreme authority surrounded

---

[1] p. 26
[2] p. 16

> with floating faces some bent some gazing into diasynchrony or scrutinizing the chain of phonic signifiers with listening eyes.[1]

This once upon a time, was the time of 'mythic discourse, in which the relationship between emitter and receptor is univocal.' as 'the community assumes both roles, emitting and receiving a discourse it addresses to itself. Indeed the community is the discourse, existing by, through and for its myth, not before or after.'[2] Now that the community of the myth has broken down in the twentieth century, we can no longer accept the omniscient narrator.

> Omni scient qui mal y pensent.
> Ooooh.
> My! That's a terrible pun.
> Not when you think about it. I can do more.
> So I noticed in your work.
> Nomnipotent O miniomnipresent narrator with his interdiscoplenary comment hominivorous or deivo
> rous consuming his patrimony.
> (   )
> Omni rident![3]

But as readers we do still try to create narrative and characters from the smallest clues, as we see faces in clouds; just as we are starting to identify Armel and his 'love' Larissa, we find that their names are near-anagrams of each other:

> ARMEL SANTORES
> LARISSA TOREN
>
> Yes! It figures. So that's why she said about Armel finding his ME in her and she not finding her I. Why, the names are anagrams. Except for ME in hers and I in his. Am I going mad? Help! I should have stuck to pronouns as in late twentieth century texts which refuse biographies since a name must have a civic status. In the pluperfect. Or a camouflashback pluperfect. That's the rule. Written up there. In the grammar of narrative.[4]

Anagrams are the perfect form of word game to distance texts from any external 'reality' and concentrate the reader on the words themselves, drained of any signification by being deconstructed into their component letters and

---

[1] p. 27
[2] p. 28
[3] p. 29
[4] p. 69

reconstructed as different words. As a lecturer in literature in Paris, Brooke-Rose would no doubt have been well acquainted with the OULIPO group (*Ouvroir de Litérature Potentialle*), founded by Raymond Queneau in 1960 and including, from 1967, experimental novelist and poet Georges Perec, who used rule-based language games to determine the forms of literary works.[1]

Being set in a university, the characters quote and discuss structuralist and post-structuralist ideas and authors – Kristeva and Propp are mentioned.

> You said women don't want a name from a man in the twentieth century.
>
> Oh for fictional purposes yes.
>
> Ah. I mean, so nothing has changed then, in the twentieth century?
>
> That's the whole point, you see, out of the zero where the author is situated, both excluded and included, the third person is generated, pure signifier of the subject's experience. Later this third person acquires a proper name, figure of this paradox, one out of zero, name out of anonymity, visualisation of the fantasy into a signifier that can be looked at, seen. You should read Kristeva, that's what she said. Though we mustn't forget that in the grammar of narrative the proper name coincides with the agent.[2]

Unlike many of the French Deconstructionists though, Brooke-Rose never takes herself or the novel too seriously. Like the previous three novels, *Thru* plays language games for fun and pleasure, always witty, ironic and self-deprecating.

> The moving finger with its dumb designation maintains the truth (of the falsehood) in a pregnant plenitude the piercing of which) with the punishing finger in its final position), both liberating and catastrophic, must bring about the end of the discourse, and the character (finger or pistol) is never more than a passage of the enigma with which you dip us all in the eternal debate with the sphinx that has stamped the whole of occidental paradismatics. Therefore the truth (of the falsehood) must be evaded at all cost until the death of the discourse.
>
> Or at any rate, it needs adjusting.[3]

---

[1] Their first publication, number 1 of the series *Bibliotheque Oulipienne*, was Perec's *Ulcérations*, a sequence of 'isogrammatic' poems, published in 1974, just before the publication of *Thru*. Perec had already published *La Disparition*, 1969), a 300-page novel written without the letter 'e' and *Les Revenentes*, 1972) in which 'e' is the only vowel.

[2] p. 69

[3] p. 114

alexander trocchi

Although he is still largely ignored by the staider organs of literary reference, as he was in his lifetime by most of the establishment of the day, Alexander Trocchi remains one of the most interesting, if controversial, writers of his time, still much read, and not only in the Scotland of his birth, where he is widely admired by younger writers. He is the British equivalent of the American beats, but the tradition to which he belongs is really more that of the 'damned' French writers, from Baudelaire and Rimbaud to Céline and Genet. One could almost also mention Cocteau, who was responsible for introducing him to heroin, the cause of his eventual downfall and death. It was responsible for his short career as a novelist: after the Fifties he could only concentrate on shorter work, such as articles, stories, translations handed in a few pages at a time and, of course, poetry.[1]

Alexander Trocchi (1925-1984) was born in Glasgow, Scotland, to an Italian father and a Scottish mother. He attended Glasgow University but was called up in 1943[2] and joined the navy, only returning to complete his degree after the end of the war; he finally finished it in 1950. Later, after travelling around Europe on a grant he moved to Paris, where he edited the avant-garde magazine *Merlin*, an early publisher of Beckett[3] and Henry Miller and a supporter of Jean-Paul Sartre. Trocchi led a group of expatriate collaborators on *Merlin* – Beckett called them the '*Merlin* juveniles' - including Richard Seaver, who later edited *Evergreen*

[1] John Calder. Preface to Trocchi's *Man At Leisure*. London: Calder, 1972

[2] For a detailed chronology of Trocchi's life see *A Life in Pieces : reflections on Alexander Trocchi,* ed. Allan Campbell and Tim Niel, Edinburgh: Rebel, 1997

[3] Beckett's *Watt* was first published, in 1953, by an imprint called 'Collection Merlin', which was managed by Maurice Girodias.

Review[1], the English poet Christopher Logue[2], the American George Plimpton, who co-founded *The Paris Review* in 1953 with Peter Matthiessen and Harold Humes, and South African poet Patrick Bowles. Merlin's second editorial said: 'MERLIN is for any innovation in creative writing which renders creative writing more expressive.'[3] A later editorial expanded on this:

> The aim of this review is to print new writing, contemporary writing: not simply the work of younger or less well-known writers, but of those whose achievements, refusing inherited complacencies, are distinguished by an effort to push beyond the tradition which, we consider, is dead, or is dying and which, in any case, is paralyzing our letters – our writers and their readers as well.'[4]

In the early 1950s Trocchi met Maurice Girodias (1919-1990), owner of the Olympia Press[5], founded in 1953 which published many works that could not be published in America or Great Britain, including the first English editions of *Lolita, The Ginger Man*, Genet's *Thief's Journal* and *Our Lady of the Flowers*, as well as de Sade, Anaïs Nin, Burroughs' *Naked Lunch* (having been introduced to Burroughs by Allen Ginsberg) and Beckett's *Watt* and *Molloy*.[6] John Calder explained Trocchi's relationship to the French publisher:

> Girodias had noticed a group of English-speaking expatriates[7] who frequented the cheaper cafés of the Boulevard St. Germain and discovered that they were all literary hopefuls, some of them putting out

[1] Founded in 1957 by Barney Rosset, whose Grove Press was roughly an American equivalent to John Calder's publishing house; the first issue of *Evergreen Review* carried an article by Jean-Paul Sartre and the second 'San Francisco Scene' issue concentrated on the Beat writers. Burroughs' *Naked Lunch* and Genet's *Our Lady of the Flowers* were excerpted in later issues, as well as work by Hubert Selby, Frank O'Hara and other writers whom mainstream publishers shunned.

[2] Like Trocchi, Logue wrote pornography for Maurice Girodias, including the novel *Lust*, 1959, under the pseudonym Count Palmiro Vicarion, published by the Olympia Press's Ophelia imprint.

[3] vol. 1 no. 2, Autumn 1952

[4] vol. 2 no. 4 Spring/Summer 1955

[5] See John de St. Jorre, *The Good Ship Venus: The Erotic Voyage of Maurice Girodias and the Olympia Press*. London: Faber, 2009. The Olympia Press is still in existence as of 2012 and still publishes Trocchi's works under his own name.

[6] Girodias also had the Ophelia Press, as John Calder said 'for straight pornography, and Olympia for erotic works with some literary quality. The latter appeared in a distinctive green cover 'Traveller's Companion' [paperback] series, and sometimes hardcover as well.' Op. cit. p. 97

[7] Girodias called them 'Les Merlinois'

> a magazine called Merlin. The guiding spirit was Alexander Trocchi, a Scot of Italian parentage on his father's side, a former brilliant student of Philosophy at Glasgow University, who had received a special grant to travel and write, and was now living impecuniously in Paris, extremely ambitious and convinced that his chance to forge a big literary career for himself would come. That chance, up to a point, came when Girodias, in return for subsidising Merlin, commissioned the young hopefuls to write pornographic novels for him, some of which became erotic classics of their kind and a few others major modern literary works. Trocchi was the most prolific as well as the leader of the group and churned out a series of sado-masochistic fictions under a number of pen-names, which included Francis [*sic*] Lengel and Carmencita de la Lunas.[1]

Trocchi wrote the pornographic novels, which Girodias called d.b.'s (dirty books) under the *noms de plume* Frances Lengel , whom he called 'my alter ego in the early 'fifties' and Carmencita de las Lunas. It was under the former pseudonym that he wrote the first version of *Young Adam* in 1954, later rewritten and issued under the name Alexander Trocchi. Girodias describes Trocchi in those days:

> The erratic pope of that pagan church was Alex Trocchi, of Italo-Scottish extraction, Alex of the somber, fiery brow – who turned himself into a literary lady of little virtue by the name of Frances Lengel and wrote a novel called *Helen and Desire* which was to become the model of a new brand of erotic writing.[2]

> When Alexander Trocchi arrived in Paris he was an eager young Scotsman with a brilliant academic future; he was so misinformed of worldly things that he went to live near the Gare de l'Est – the city's most neutral and forbidding district.
>
> It took him one year to discover the Left Bank and to understand why he had come to Paris. When, at last, he moved to Saint-Germain-des-Près, he was immediately transformed; he shed his subdued provincial manner to become the big bad literary wolf of his time and day.
>
> Alex was always busy cultivating extreme attitudes, extravagant styles and wild dreams with great gusto and appetite. Sometimes he misunderstood his appetite for ambition, and launched into great

[1] Calder, op. cit., p. 98. See also Christopher Sawyer-Lauc. *The Continual Pilgrimage: American Writers in Paris, 1944-1960*. London: Bloomsbury, 1992

[2] Introduction to *The Olympia Reader*. New York: Grove, 1965, p. 18

projects, very few of which succeeded because there were too many other interests and too many girls around.

But Alex had a certain amount of electricity buzzing around his shaggy brow, and he naturally became the center of a very active literary group which formed around his short-lived magazine, *Merlin*.[1]

In 1957 Trocchi moved to America, where he worked on a barge in New York City, the setting for *Cain's Book*, 1961, before moving to California. While in Paris Trocchi had been a founder member of the Situationist International and when he was jailed in New York for drug taking in 1960, the Fourth Conference of The Situationist International delegated a group of intellectuals associated with the movement to circulate a petition for his release.[2]

FOR SEVERAL MONTHS, the British writer Alexander Trocchi has been kept in prison in New York.

He is the former director of the revue *Merlin*, and now he participates in experimental art research in collaboration with artists from several countries, who were regrouped on 28 September [1960] in London in the Institute of Contemporary Arts (17 Dover Street). On that occasion, they unanimously expressed in public their solidarity with Alexander Trocchi, and their absolute certainty in the value of his comportment.

Alexander Trocchi, whose case is due to be tried in October, is — in effect — accused of having experimented with drugs.

Quite apart from any attitude on the use of drugs and its repression on the scale of society, we recall that it is notorious that a very great many doctors, psychologists and also artists have studied the effects of drugs without anyone thinking of imprisoning them. The poet Henri Michaux has hardly been spoken of in recent years on the successive publication of his books announced everywhere as written under the influence of mescalin.

Indeed, we consider that the British intellectuals and artists should be the first to join with us in denouncing this menacing lack of culture on the part of the American police, and to demand the liberation and immediate repatriation of Alexander Trocchi.

Since it is generally recognized that the work of a scientist or an artist implies certain small rights, even in the USA, the main question is to bear witness to the fact that Alexander Trocchi is effectively an artist

[1] Afterword to excerpt from *Young Adam* in *The Olympia Reader*, p. 472

[2] Guy Debord, Trocchi's friend and author of *The Society of the Spectacle*, another friend and collaborator the Danish artist Asger Jorn and Jacqueline de Jong, later (May 1962 – December 1967) editor of the Situationist Times.

of the first order. This could be basely contested *for the sole reason that he is a new type of artist;* pioneer of a new culture and a new comportment (the question of drugs being in his own eyes minor and negligible).

All the artists and intellectuals who knew Alexander Trocchi in Paris or London ought to bear witness without fail to his authentic artistic status, to enable the authorities in Great Britain to take the necessary steps in the USA in favour of a British subject. Those who would refuse to do this now will be judged guilty themselves when the judgment of the history of ideas will no longer allow one to question the importance of the artistic innovation of which Trocchi has been to a great extent responsible.

We ask everyone of good faith whom this appeal reaches, to sign it, and make it known as widely as possible.[1]

In the early 1960s Trocchi moved to London, where he stayed for most of the rest of his life. Jeff Nuttall remembers:

> Trocchi arrived in Britain in 1963[2] from the United States, accompanied by his wife [Lyn] and child. At Edinburgh he was joined by Burroughs for the International Writers Conference organized by John Calder. At the conference Burroughs gave the first public demonstration of his cutup technique. Together he and Trocchi moved down to London[3]

His addiction prevented him from writing any more novels even though he lived for another 20 years. He occasionally did translations for John Calder and wrote occasional poetry, some of which John Calder published as *Man of Leisure* in 1972, the year Trocchi's second wife Lyn died, though he had to break into Trocchi's flat to get the manuscript. Trocchi was heavily involved with the underground scene in London, based around Better Books in Charing Cross Road from where he ran the sigma project with Jeff Nuttall and others.[4] And because drugs were one of the important topics of the day, he was often interviewed on

---

[1] Dated 7 October 1960

[2] *A Life in Pieces* dates this as 1961, and the conference Nuttall mentions was held in 1962, so Nuttall's recollection may be wrong.

[3] *Bomb Culture*, p. 181. According to Calder this was 1962 not 1963. At the 1962 conference The Future of the Novel Burroughs referred to Trocchi: 'In my writing I am acting as a map maker, an explorer of psychic areas, to use the phrase of Mr Alexander Trocchi, a cosmonaut of inner space, and I see no point in exploring areas that have been thoroughly surveyed.'

[4] See *Bomb Culture*.

radio and television, taken by the media as a British representative of the beat generation. Jeff Nuttall again:

> Through that summer of 1964 we turned our possibilities over between us like enigmatic stones. Alex and Lyn moved back together. Lyn had kicked her habit successfully. Their flat was a three-room place near Westbourne Grove. The discarded cars rusted away in the street. . . Alex rigged up his study like an office. People passing through London dropped in, Jack Michelin, Gregory Corso, Bob Creeley, Ian Sommerville. Posters went up on the walls, statements of policy, plans of action.[1]

His flat also became a meeting place for various international underground artists, and he was master of ceremonies at the International Poetry Incarnation, or Wholly Communion, a poetry event attended by over 4,000 people at the Albert Hall in London on the 11th June 1965.

Nuttall said 'Alex Trocchi once told me he first took heroin for the sense of inviolability it gave him.'[2]

> The mind under heroin evades perception as it does ordinarily; one is aware only of contents. But that whole way of posing the question, of dividing the mind from what it's aware of, is fruitless. Nor is it that the objects of perception are intrusive in an electric way as they are under mescalin or lysergic acid, nor that things strike one with more intensity or a more enchanted or detailed way as I have sometimes experienced under marijuana; it is that the perceiving turns inward, the eyelids droop, the blood is aware of itself, a slow phosphorescence in all the fabric of flesh and nerve and bone; it is that the organism has a sense of being intact and unbrittle, and above all, *inviolable*. For the attitude born of this sense of inviolability some Americans have used the word 'cool'.[3]

This inward-turning certainly describes Anna Kavan's writing, though she never felt inviolable. Trocchi was clearly not inviolable for very long, and produced almost nothing from the mid-sixties to his death, but his high reputation today is probably sustained by his being one of the coolest writers of all time.

---

[1] *Bomb Culture,* p. 221

[2] *Bomb Culture,* p. 133

[3] *Cain's Book,* p. 8

POETS OF THE WORLD / POETS OF OUR TIME

Royal Albert Hall - Friday June 11th 6.30-11.00pm

Poets to date:

Allen Ginsberg
Gregory Corso
Lawrence Ferlinghetti
Alex Trocchi
Michael Horovitz
Pete Brown
Anselm Hollo
Pablo Fernandez
John Esam
Dan Richter
Barbara Rubin
Simon Vinkenoog
Ernst Jandl

and many more to come

READINGS, IMPROVISATIONS, SYMPOSIUM AND

FINAL POETS COMMUNIQUE

at neo popular prices!

COME COME COME

TICKETS now available at The Royal Albert Hall
and Better Books 5/- and 10/-

Like many of his Merlin colleagues, Trocchi wrote dirty books to order for Maurice Girodias' Olympia Press. Girodias describes the process:

> I usually printed five thousand copies of each book, and paid a flat fee for the manuscript which, though modest, formed the substance of many an expatriate budget. My publishing technique was simple in the extreme, at least in the first years: when I had completely run out of money I wrote blurbs for imaginary books, invented sonorous titles and funny pen names (Marcus van Heller, Akbar del Piombo, Miles Underwood, Carmencita de las Lunas, etc.) and then printed a list which was sent out to our clientele of booklovers, tempting them with such titles as *White Thighs, The Chariot of Flesh, The Sexual Life of Robinson Crusoe, With Open Mouth*, etc. They immediately responded with orders and money, thanks to which we were able to eat, drink, write and print. I could again advance money to my authors, and they hastened to turn in manuscripts which more or less fitted my descriptions.
>
> The d.b.'s (short for "dirty books") were published in the green paperback volumes that constitute The Travellers Companion Series, side by side with more respectable items. The confusion was deliberate, as it made it easy to sell the higher class of literature: the d.b.'s fans were as fascinated by the ugly plain green covers as the addict by the white powder, however deceptive both may prove to be.
>
> Writing d.b.'s was generally considered a useful professional exercise, as well as a necessary participation in the common fight against the Square World – an act of duty. . . The colourful banner of pornography was as good as any other to rally the rebels: the more ludicrous the form of the revolt, the better it was, as the revolt was primarily against ordinary logic, and ordinary good taste, and restraint and current morals.[1]

Trocchi's first pseudonymous pornographic work, and Girodias' first commissioned d.b. was *Helen and Desire*, written under the (female) name Frances Lengel and published by Olympia in 1954[2] along with its sequel *The Carnal Days of Helen Seferis,* though it must have been written earlier as Trocchi later said it had taken him a long time to be able to write the sequel[3].

[1] Introduction to *The Olympia Reader,* p. 19 - 23

[2] First published as no. 2 in Olympia's Atlantic Library series, it was reissued in 1962 as *Desire and Helen* (to avoid the censors) as no. 29 in Olympia's green paperback Traveller's Companion Series.

[3] Introduction to *School for Wives*. North Hollywood: Brandon, 1967

He was the first of Olympia's all-out literary stallions; his novel. *Helen and Desire*, published under the pen name of Frances Lengel, became a model of the kind. It was the first of a series of Frances Lengel productions, all of them very robust and funny parodies of pornography; and some, as *Young Adam*, of excellent quality.

Although all his books had the honor of being banned by the French authorities, *Helen and Desire* was saved from total annihilation by being reprinted under a different title: *Desire and Helen*. The French police never found out; perhaps now they will.[1]

Helen and Desire is a first-person narrative purporting to be by a masochistic woman who is put through a series of sexual acts.

> The desire for the new pain which would bring the terrible pleasure into my body made me feel weak, tensionless, dragged downwards from the roots, like a flag drooping in a windless atmosphere. Once again I felt his fingers examining the orifice, then, gently, he pulled my sweating buttocks apart and laid his smoothness on the puckered indentation . . . I realised that I was now pinioned hopelessly before his lust. There was no way of escape. Indeed I wanted to escape and give myself at the same time.'[2]

Although there is no question that the book is entirely pornographic in intent, the quality of the writing is far higher than it needs to be for this purpose alone. There is also a strong existentialist strain running through it – it was after all written in Paris in the early 1950s, where existentialism was a dominant force, and Trocchi's *Merlin* had published Sartre – and if it had actually been written by a woman it might now almost be considered a feminist work celebrating female sexual liberation.

---

[1] Maurice Girodias: afterword to excerpt from *Young Adam* in Olympia Reader, p. 472

[2] p. 99

> Once again I have experienced the terrible joy of annihilation, the deliverance of my whole being to the mystery of sensual union, and this time with a male whom I would not recognise in daylight.[1]

> I am Narcissus. I look into the water and find myself beautiful, indeed the only beauty. The comings and goings of my lovers are merely the gentle showers which nurture the plant. And the plant is myself, living on and on with a slow stirring motion through nights and days and nights and days of voluptuousness[2]

The sequel, *The Carnal Desires of Helen Seferis*[3] is completely different: it is detective story told by the male narrator Anthony Harvest, who is looking for Helen in an Arab country, where she has been kidnapped. Although it has sex scenes it is not pure pornography and is more of a pastiche of early detective stories set in exotic locations, or a John Buchan novel. However, as in many experimental novels, and in Trocchi's *Thongs*, the main part of the text purports to be a found manuscript; Trocchi was already a virtuoso writer using a whole range of techniques.

The blurb for a later edition of another Frances Lengel novel, *White Thighs*, describes it breathlessly:

> Anna of the white thighs. He loved her totally, selflessly. He killed for her - first his foster father, then her husband. And when he could not become her slave, he made her his slave, and enslaved himself to the white thighs of the monstrous Kirstin. Revolting yet compelling, a book that plumbs the darkest depths of human nature.

However, though it is clearly intended as pornography – as one of Girodias' specially commissioned 'dirty books' - it was published

[1] p. 26

[2] p. 190

[3] Paris: Olympia, 1954, republished San Diego: Greenleaf, 1967 and North Hollywood: Brandon, 1967

by Olympia Press as a Traveller's Companion issue, not by Ophelia; this meant, as John Calder said, that Girodias considered it had literary merit. Certainly Trocchi, even more so than in *Helen and Desire,* is intending to write a serious novel and it begins like a heavy French existentialist work; readers looking for titillation from the outset may not have appreciated it, though like other Frances Lengel novels it was later published as 'by Alexander Trocchi' in titillating covers. Like the narrators of *Young Adam* and *Cain's Book*, the narrator here has an explicitly Old Testament name.

> My name is Saul. There is nothing in my history, or my family's history that would justify the name, which is a significantly biblical one. In all these years I have been able to discover no shred of reason for the appellation. So be it, I am not one to look for reasons. I prefer the lightning thrust of intuition. The name is like any other and it appears on my birth certificate.
>
> From the beginning I was a kind of stranger. What is that? Ha! Baudelaire came near to expressing it:
>
> 'Your friends?'
>
> 'You use a word that I have never to this day been able to understand.'
>
> 'Your country?'
>
> 'I know not on what latitude it lies.'
>
> 'Well then, what do you love, extraordinary stranger?'
>
> 'I love the clouds . . . passing clouds . . . over yonder . . . the wondrous clouds.'
>
> There is no fact that does not appear to me to be at bottom absurd.[1]

As a boy Saul has fallen in love with Ukrainian immigrant Anna, 10 years older than him. She introduces him to corporal punishment when he is young and he becomes obsessed with her. Later, discovering that his uncle has been having sex with her, he kills the uncle. He goes to university in England but 10 years later he has still not found a woman to love or found any pleasure in 'normal' sex, and

---

[1] Olympia 2004 edition, p. 3

returns to his family home, where he meets Anna again. However, she now seems too submissive and he takes up with the monstrous Kirstin, who keeps girls in a dungeon to be whipped and demands his obeisance, 'deriving more pleasure from my utter abasement than I had ever drawn from abasing another.'[1]

> Here, at last, was the risk that I was looking for; the intensity, the obscenity, the criminality to which I could bring the willing consent of my own body and soul. The vision of Anna paled before the image of Kirstin. The one wished nothing more than to be a victim; the other would dare to victimize. What hellish green fires must have burned within Kirstin to turn her into the woman-beast I had seen in action![2]

His lust for Kirstin is inseparable from his disgust for her; along his journey through adolescence he had been with a prostitute who had originally brought out his fascination with the grotesque. This passage could almost be by Jeff Nuttall:

> Her thighs were fat and the color of damp chalk, wounded where the split sex, almost unhaired, splayed open like a mass of pale calf's liver. Her belly hung down over it in a rounded fold, as abrasive as rough sandpaper where the hairs had been shaved. Crabs probably.[3]

But she is too 'utilitarian' for his needs: 'She had no notion of sacrifice, no acquaintance with the sacred. I was, at that moment, confronted by a big, stupid cow submitting dutifully to a veterinary examination!' He kicks her into unconsciousness. 'Now that she was no longer conscious, no longer free to display her vulgarity, she was beautiful. The heaps of pink and white flesh had a warm life of their own.'[4] At the end of the novel, Kirstin and Saul recruit new girls to their household, including Ursula, a member of the Plymouth Brethren, to whom Saul eventually submits.

> I thought I gleaned a shadow of a smile on her face. It was not a smile of simple pleasure, but one that seemed to hold the secreted knowledge of evil. I was surely going insane, for Ursula had no knowledge of evil, but was virgin soil, untainted, pure. . . I was committing sacrilege, worshipping a new god. She clamped my head between her flawlessly white thighs, the tender flesh of them burning my cheeks, my ears, suffocating me and cutting off all sound. It was then, as I swirled in the

---

[1] p. 92

[2] p. 88

[3] p. 39

[4] p. 41

> thick eddy of her release, that I gleaned the future: I would have to prove my devotion to her; there would have to be a sacrifice.[1]

The Olympia dirty book *School for Sin*[2] tells the story of two Irish farm girls, Peggy and Doreen, from a community so religious and conservative that even being seen walking out with a boy means a girl would have to marry him. They make their way via Dublin and the Isle of Man to the yacht of the criminal mastermind Mr Alexopoulos, who trains girls in his floating academy to seduce men so that they can attract rich husbands and lover and repay the debt they have unwittingly incurred by unwillingly taking his course. He threatens them with dire consequences if they do not repay him.

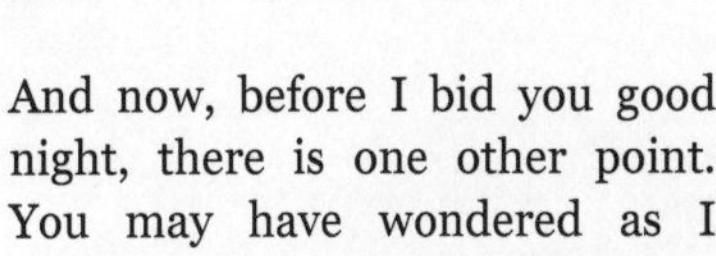

> And now, before I bid you good night, there is one other point. You may have wondered as I spoke how I can be sure that you will honor your debt to me. Of course, I cannot be sure, but I hope for your sake as well as mine that you will. The world is a small place to a man with an organization like mine. I have many agents, and I should be extremely sorry to have to advise them that you have failed in your commitment. Do you take my meaning?[3]

Although the two women have very healthy sex drives they are not, unusually in a Trocchi/Lengel novel, addicted to pain and submission. They have not asked to be inducted into Alexopoulos' school and in the early days of their initiation they are drugged to keep them submissive.

> She was sure of one thing only, that her present condition had something to do with the injections they gave her periodically. Already, she was beginning to live for them. Each time she felt the needle prick the taut skin of her left buttock she was moved to moan for joy. Each

---

[1] p. 126

[2] Paris: Olympia, 1956. No. 20 in the Traveller's Companion series, republished as *The School for Wives*. North Hollywood: Brandon, 1967

[3] Olympia 2004 edition, p. 113

> time she felt it slide out again from between the willing muscles, she felt herself carried away above everything, as though some huge, tender lover dragged her skywards. And there, risen, floating in the ether, she watched her lover approach, like a hesitant fly, pitter-patter, pitter-patter, across the floor towards the bed on which she lay, naked and smelling of scent, sometimes with feathers decorating her voluptuous moon-yellow-hips, or her nipples painted gold, of black, or red, her ankles feathered or clamped in chains of gold, or silver, or iron, the moss of her mount oiled and combed. She waited for him as a spider would, her long limbs the web, the strands of her black hair on the pillows, her teeth at her groin, waiting.[1]

This certainly reads like the genuine writing of an addict. Also unusually for a Lengel or Trocchi novel it has a happy ending: it turns out that Doreen's lover at the Alexopoulos academy was an undercover policeman, who returns to her and saves the women from the villain.

[1] p. 74

Trocchi also wrote a d.b. for Girodias under the name Carmencita de las Lunas,[1] who was the 'author' and heroine of *Thongs*, published by Olympia in 1956. A sado-masochist novel about a woman from Glasgow who becomes the greatest 'painmaster' in the world; it was suppressed in 1956 and prosecuted in 1958. Like *White Thighs*, *Thong*s starts out as if it is going to be a 'literary' work before turning into straight pornography; possibly this was in the hope that the censors would only read the first few pages, or perhaps Trocchi just wanted to establish his literary skill. The novel starts like *The Carnal Days of Helen Seferis* with the first chapter purporting to be by an editor who has found a secret manuscript: 'if it had not been for a chance find of mine in a Madrid bookshop . . . the amazing story of this woman's violent and passionate life might have been buried with her bleeding corpse.'[2] The book he finds is the journal of a Glasgow girl named Gertrude Gault, who becomes the Carmencita to whom the work is attributed. Her journal starts in the grim Gorbals district of Glasgow, Scotland[3], in 1916 where the men all fight with knives for survival and supremacy and where her father, the 'Razor King' is the leader of the pack. Although the poverty and violence are not minimised, this life is mythologised in a way rather reminiscent of the 1953 Marlon Brando film *The Wild Ones*, James Dean's *Rebel Without a Cause* of 1955 and the slightly later *West Side Story*, first produced in 1957, though with more menacing violence than any of these. It is also reminiscent of the London and Paris of Orwell's down and outs, 1933; the Paris of Céline's *Mort à Credit,* 1936; the Brest of Genet's Querelle, 1953; the Amsterdam of Camus' *La Chute*, 1956 and of course the New York of Burroughs' *Junky*, 1953. Possibly Trocchi is staking Glasgow's claim as the setting of great works of literature.

The editor's introduction blames Gertrude's fate on her upbringing, Trocchi perhaps feeling that this provided a justification for another novel about a woman who is a willing victim of men: 'Perhaps only such a brutal tribe of men could have produced a woman with such an infinite longing to me a victim.'[4] The story opens with a flashback to Gertrude's brother Johnnie's fight with her father.

---

[1] Paris: Olympia, 1956. No 25 in the Traveller's Companion series

[2] Olympia 2004 edition, p. 3

[3] Though Trocchi himself was from Glasgow he was not from this underclass.

[4] p. 5

> Now, less than ten yards apart, neither man moved. From the windows on the fourth story above the street, because of the dark clothing of the men and because of what they held in their hands – the one, razors, the other a long black belt – the slow approach had appeared almost beetle-like. The impression was accentuated by the minute tremor in the posture of the younger man and by the slight swaying motion of the other as he advanced. When the latter came to a halt, the whole street seemed to halt with him, to freeze to immobility, the crowd paralysed by its own acute lust for violence, strung taut as a man is at the instant before he is involved utterly in love or dying, the protagonists seized in the religious certainty of their commitment[1]

Johnnie Stark was a real person, known as 'Razor King' in interwar Glasgow, and was famously novelised in *No Mean City,* 1935, by Alexander MacArthur and H. Kingsley Long, from whom Trocchi no doubt drew his inspiration. Some of the earlier novel's passages are quite similar to the above:

> within an hour all Gorbals was buzzing with news of the coming fight. The respectable element was delighted to feel that the tension in the air had lessened and that the coming trouble – however big it might be – would be settled on the Green, which meant that peaceable folk could keep away from it if they chose. The gangsters and their girls were equally pleased, for there was no thrill quite like the matching of champion against champion, and they knew, from experience, that when the big fight was settled, there would be ample opportunity for general war.[2]

The men in Gertrude's life have no redeeming features. She moves from the Glasgow slum world of her father to the upper-class world of sadists and masochists. 'For my father, fucking was rape. He was a wolf and he liked nice fat fear-ridden bitches for his lust. White thighs.'[3] And for the women there is no escape.

> There would be no more dancing for her now. Not until my father got tired of her anyway, and by that time she would probably be pregnant. And that would be the end of her. She would settle down with some man or other in a slum flat. She would become one of the hairy, gaunt,

---

[1] pp. 14/15

[2] *No Mean City: A story of the Glasgow slums*. London: Longmans, Green & Co., 1935. p. 148

[3] *Thongs*, p. 20

> hatless women in shawls. My mother was one of those women. I suppose everyone thought I was going to be one too.[1]

After Gertrude becomes Carmencita and quickly rise up the organisation devoted to pain that she joins there is little of literary merit until the end: she has chosen to be crucified: 'You will die naked, nailed to a cross, near the Holy Seat. You will die for us, and affirm your own great passion, and your agony will be a light for us who are condemned to live on.'[2] As she lies in her room waiting the writing changes and her internal monologue takes on a fevered, existentialist tone.

> I see my dead father and the women sprawling in the slums, white putty colored flesh quivering, animals, their big thighs stung into heat and hot fear by his rampant prick. And I lie alone and everything has receded into the familiar sound of my own breathing. I am left only with my awareness of it. And then, gradually, I come into another world, a close and confederate consciousness of my own softness and the sound of my breathing and nothing more, and there is nothing to which I am related. And now I come to know that it is my body which is soft, the thighs, my little belly, set and smooth as a watch glass on a fine watch, and that it is I and not my body which is aware. And now I am conscious of existing without at the same time being conscious of myself as existing alone and in relation to instants in time and points in space which hold themselves off from me and which escape me, for I have not the power to draw them back to myself out of my memory. And the room comes back with its dark corners, the open window, night sounds, and now I know myself to be wide awake and alone.[3]

---

[1] p. 34
[2] p. 96
[3] pp. 103/104

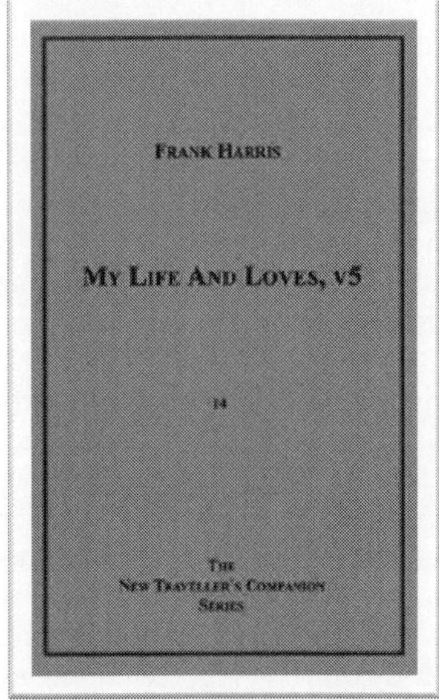

Trocchi's virtuosity and speed were exploited in a fraud perpetrated by Girodias: he had founded Olympia after the failure of his Obelisk Press, which owned the rights to the four volumes of Frank Harris's *My Life and Loves* but was bought by Girodias' rival Hachette. In 1958 Girodias bought, for 1 million francs, the manuscript to a fifth volume from his widow Madame Nellie Harris via the agent Monsieur Adolph but the so-called manuscript turned out to be just fragments plus a few articles. Girodias, who had suspected this might be the case, commissioned Trocchi to produce a 'fifth volume' from the spare parts.

> Alex was madly excited by the idea of it. We rehearsed a few Harris idiosyncrasies: Never to write: she said in a dialogue, but always: *she cried*, etc.
>
> When the brand new fifth volume was delivered about ten sleepless days and nights later, tingling with sex and fun, I felt that Frank Harris himself would have been proud of it. I have always held that versatility is one essential ingredient of literary genius, and Alex had administered the proof, in lightning fashion, that he was able to do just anything with perfect grace and power. Even the odd twenty per cent of real Harris derived from Monsieur Adolph's time-stained papers appeared rejuvenated in that new context.[1]

Girodias did not feel in the least guilty about the fraud: 'Harris himself was a self-confessed fraud and nobody of sane mind has ever taken those memoirs of his seriously'.[2] Later, however, the trick was revealed and the fifth volume was subsequently republished as an 'irreverent treatment' by Trocchi. The book starts with a long italicised preface railing against censorship; 'Harris' then says:

> *In some previous parts of 'My Life' I have said that I would later write about sexuality as understood in India, China and Japan: a good many*

---

[1] Girodias' introduction to the Olympia Press Travellers Companion no. 10 *Frank Harris: My Life and Loves (fifth volume).* Paris: Olympia, 1958, reprinted as *The Fifth Volume of Frank Harris's My Life and Loves: An Irreverent Treatment by Alexander Trocchi.* London: The New English Library, 1966

[2] ibid

> *friends have written to me asking why I did not keep this promise. I hope to make ample amends in this volume.*[1]

'Harris' says that the east is more sensual than the West and more comfortable with sex and nudity; he mentions that the Japanese bathe every day in public and 'sexualise everything'. Trocchi mixes, as would Harris, pornography with geopolitical interludes considering the history and future of the world; Harris's sexual encounters with mostly very young women have the same status in his recollections as the origins of the first World War, poverty and social change across Asia and Africa and the actresses Ellen Terry and Sarah Bernhardt. He travels across India, where he has sex in Bombay with young girls and describes lesbianism and the use of sex toys. He then visits Burma where we get a digression on rebirth, followed by Shanghai where he enters an opium den. 'Frankly I was very disappointed. I achieved neither the desired physical effect nor that intense state of clear vision attained by Coleridge on the eve on which he wrote Khubla Khan.' The opium does not even help his sexual experiences.

Having published *Cain's Book* in 1960, and having moved to London, Trocchi's involvement in the underground scene produced no further serious literary works; the few pieces of writing that survive are from the sigma project, an amorphous and chaotic underground project that produced some pamphlets and THE MOVING TIMES, a poster-sized, single-sided magazine with stories by Trocchi (a very disappointing, disjointed piece) and Burroughs, and sections of a manifesto.

> sigma[2] . . . was Alex Trocchi's name for the cultural tendency to progressive alienation and for his own ideas. It was a term he applied to both praxis and process of the whole movement. It was also a bid to convert a stage in social evolution into an international spiderweb with himself at the centre. Since then it has become evident that the movement is linear rather than concentric, that there are no power figures, and that there is no centre for such a figure to occupy.[3]

The heading of MOVING TIMES says: general editor: A. Trocchi; associate editor: J. Nuttall. Jeff Nuttall quotes at length from these manifestos in *Bomb Culture*. 'I woke up one morning at this time, early summer 1964, to find a loosely packed parcel thrown on my bed, thrown by my wife with a certain amount of resignation. It contained two typescripts from Alexander Trocchi – *The Invisible*

---

[1] p. 12

[2] Trocchi always spelt it with a lower case first letter.

[3] *Bomb Culture*, p. 181

Insurrection of a Million Minds[1] and *Sigma, a Tactical Blueprint.*'[2] Among the points in the MOVING TIMES manifestos is: 'We must reject the conventional fiction of "unchanging human nature". There is in fact no such permanence anywhere. There is only *becoming.*' Trocchi also outlines a 'spontaneous university', to be housed in a country house, 'mill, abbey, church or castle' close to London and 'preferably on a river bank' where sigma could 'foment a kind of cultural "jam session". . . It should be large enough for a pilot group (astronauts of inner space) to situate itself, orgasm and genius, and their tools and dream-machines and amazing apparatus and appurtenances.' Nuttall replied 'by return, saying simply, 'What do you want me to do?"[3]

In *Tactical Blueprint* Trocchi describes the aims behind sigma:

> In looking for a word to designate a possible international association of men who are concerned individually and in concert to articulate an effective strategy and tactics for this cultural revolution (cf. *The Invisible Insurrection*), it was thought necessary to find one which provoked no obvious responses. We chose the word 'sigma.' Commonly used in mathematical practice to designate all, the sum, the whole, it seemed to fit very well with our notion that all men must eventually be included.
>
> It is not simply a question of founding yet another publishing house, not another art gallery, nor another theater group, and of sending it on its high-minded way amongst the mammon-engines of its destruction. Such a firm (I am thinking in terms of the West for the moment), if it were successful in sustaining itself within the traditional cultural complex, would 'do much good,' no doubt. But it is not the publishing industry alone that is in our view out of joint (and has no survival potential); to think almost exclusively in terms of publishing is to think in terms of yesterday's abstractions. A softer bit and more resilient harness won't keep the old nag out of the knackery. Of course sigma will publish. When we have something to publish. And we shall do it effectively, forgetting no technique evolved in yesterday's publishing. (Or we may find it convenient to have this or that published by a traditional publisher.) But it is art too in which we are interested. With the leisure of tomorrow in mind, it is all the grids of expression we are concerned to seize.

---

[1] Originally published in French as 'Technique du Coupe du Monde' in *Internationale Situationniste* #8, January 1963.

[2] *Bomb Culture*, p. 156. Both texts were published in *New Saltire* #8, London, 1963 and *City Lights Journal* #2, San Francisco, 1964 and reprinted in Andrew Murray Scott ed. *Invisible Insurrection of a Million Minds: A Trocchi Reader*. Edinburgh: Polygon, 1991.

[3] p. 159

Trocchi's description in *Tactical Blueprint* of how sigma should operate is a rather naïve, utopian view of a future where art has escaped commerce and international artistic groups will co-operate across borders.

> **sigma as international cultural engineering cooperative:**
> (a) *The international pipeline:*
> When sigma-centres exist near the capitals of many countries, associate artists and scientists traveling abroad will be able to avail themselves of all the facilities of the local centre. They may choose simply to reside there or they may wish to participate. If the visitor is a celebrity, it would probably be to his advantage to do any 'interview' work (audio or visual) in the sigma-centre where 'angle' and editing can be his own. Sigma will then handle negotiations with local radio and television. The imaginative cultivation of this international pipeline would be a real contribution to international understanding.
> (b) *Cultural promotion:*
> This field is too vast to be treated fully here. It includes all the interesting cultural projects, conferences, international newspaper, publishing ventures, film and television projects, etc., which have been and will be suggested by associates during conferences. Many of these ideas, realized efficiently, would make a great deal of money. All this work would contribute to the sigma image.
> (c) *General cultural agents:*
> Some of the associates, especially the younger ones who are not previously committed elsewhere, will be glad to be handled by sigma. Obviously, we shall be in a position to recognize new talent long before the more conventional agencies, and, as our primary aim will not be to make money, we shall be able to cultivate a young talent, guarding the young person's integrity.
> (d) *General cultural consultants:*
> The enormous pool of talent at our disposal places us in an incomparable position vis-a-vis providing expert counsel on cultural matters. We can advise on everything cultural, from producing a play to building a picture collection. A propos the latter, one of our proposed services is to offer an insurance policy to a buyer against the depreciation in value of any work or art recommended by sigma. It may frequently be advisable, economically or otherwise, for sigma to encourage some established company to undertake this or that cultural project: that is to say, sigma will not necessarily wait passively to be consulted. (Obviously, ideas ripe for commercial exploitation cannot be made public in this context.)

In *Revolutionary Proposal* Trocchi is even more utopian (he quotes approvingly the utopian American Black Mountain College, an experiment even he acknowledges to have failed), taking ideas from his Situationist friend Guy Debord and proposing to use them to overturn the 'gulf between art and life'.

> Art anaesthetizes the living; we witness a situation in which life is continually devitalized by art, a situation sensationally and venally misrepresented to inspire each individual to respond in a stoic and passive way, to bring to whatever acts a banal and automatic consent. For the average man, dispirited, restless, with no power of concentration, a work of art to be noticed at all must compete at the level of spectacle.

The Situationist International (SI) was at first not completely hostile to Trocchi's 'proposals':

> Our project has taken shape at the *same time* as the modern tendencies toward integration. There is thus not only a direct opposition between them but also an air of resemblance, since the two sides are really contemporaneous. We have not paid enough attention to this aspect, even recently. Thus, it is not impossible to interpret Alexander Trocchi's proposals in issue #8 of this journal as having some affinity – despite their obviously completely contrary spirit – with those poor attempts at a 'psychodramatic' salvaging of decomposed art expressed for example by the ridiculous 'Workshop of Free Expression' in Paris last May. But the point we have arrived at clarifies both our project and, inversely, the project of integration. All really modern nonrevolutionary ventures must now be recognized and treated as our number-one enemy. They are going to reinforce all existing controls.[1]

After publication of these pieces however the SI disavowed Trocchi:

> Upon the appearance in London in fall 1964 of the first publications of the 'Project Sigma' initiated by Alexander Trocchi, it was mutually agreed that the SI could not involve itself in such a loose cultural venture, in spite of our interest in establishing contact with the more radical individuals who may be drawn to it, notably in the United States and England. It is therefore no longer as a member of the SI that our

[1] Situationist International, 1964

> friend Alexander Trocchi has since developed an activity of which we fully approve of several aspects.[1]

Part of the manifesto in *Revolutionary Proposal* reprinted in THE MOVING TIMES, co-edited by Jeff Nuttall says:

> the cultural revolt must seize the grids of expression and the power-house of the mind. Intelligence must become self-conscious, realise its own power, and, on a global scale, transcending functions that are no longer appropriate, dare to exercise it. History will not overthrow national governments; it will outflank them. The cultural revolt is the necessary underpinning, the passionate sub-structure of a new order of things

This sounds like the work of a very immature student. It shows how far the virtuosity of the mature, cynical, junky, porn-writing Trocchi had been destroyed by his addiction. Earlier, like Anna Kavan, the heroin had sharpened his writing and, like Burroughs, given him a subject to write about but, unlike Kavan, Burroughs or Jack Kerouac, who all produced a number of novels, his powers were destroyed by it long before his life was. Alternatively, perhaps writing those pornographic novels blunted his need to write long fiction or perhaps he genuinely believed, as he said in *Tactical Blueprint*, that conventional fiction was dead.

> That is what we mean when we say that 'literature is dead'; not that some people won't write (indeed, perhaps all people will), or even write a novel (although we feel this category has about outlived its usefulness), but the writing of anything in terms of capitalist economy, as an economic act, with reference to economic limits, it is not, in our view, interesting. It is business.

But in the end, perhaps even the heroin could not give him quite the inviolability he needed, especially after the death of his second wife Lyn in 1972: 'The individual is powerless. It is inevitable. And the artist has a profound sense of his own impotence. He is frustrated, even confounded.'

---

[1] *Internationale Situationniste* #10

Man at Leisure, published in 1972, contains poems written over a period of years, though none are dated so it is impossible to tell their chronology or where Trocchi was geographically of psychologically when they were written. John Calder says in the Preface:

> it was only by obtaining unauthorized entry to his flat and desk drawers that I got hold of the manuscript. The book had been contracted, but Trocchi kept on avoiding delivery on various pretexts. As a result I had to edit poems that the author had little looked at, and in some cases had to revise and finish them. Otherwise they would never have been published or perhaps would have been sold to another publisher, because Alex, always in desperate need of money, had no scruples about selling the same manuscript to as many different publishers as would sign contracts.

None of the poems is especially distinguished or distinctive and the collection would be of very little interest if it were not by Trocchi; even knowing that it is, it adds little to our knowledge or appreciation of his other work. 'Tabula Rasa' is of some interest for what it might say about Trocchi's state of mind:

Tabula Rasa

To begin with: a *tabula rasa*
enter 'I'
in sigmal, or metacategroical
posture
green is garden peas
& the leaves of trees,
the living stalk of youth
exudes a green juice
stains thigh
lean loin
white abdomen
a map of molecules, of i
chor
or
(for) to seep
deep dam
of ham-
merer Thor!
A second song of Maldoror?

To begin with
Continue with:
a *tabula rasa*

And another poem which seems to highlight Trocchi's feelings, especially with regard to his statements about heroin giving him a sense of inviolability, is 'Fear'.

Fear

Where you have fear
you will have rot,
& rats of fear will run.

So
Build a broad stages
with many burrows off
into which the rats of fear may run.

William Burroughs said, rather kindly, of *Man at Leisure:*

> The poems in this book are reminiscent of John Donne and the metaphysical poets, and I had already described Alex as a modern metaphysical poet before I came across his poem to John Donne. Alex writes about spirit, flesh and death and the vision that comes through the flesh... 'Somewhere between Nice and Monte Carlo and must depart soon in beds, fields, cinemas or pigsties centuries of rock laugh white teeth at death in a brown land children play dirty in marketplaces crunching sugar skulls cats laugh their pointed teeth from the wet streets a boy's cry over the city'.
> 'My personal Ides,' he said.
> Wrote at night red ink on cheap paper
> 'I wonder when a woman will walk naked to me?'
> Chalk marks on a wall in a black cave
> Ob scene
> Ab sent
> Shut the lavatory door and lock it like he was hot see?
> The Milky Way whips my sperm to the sky starship text book
> for today warm blood snake thrust pure salt visibility excellent
> on what fantastic world in the desert distances are not far not a
> whisper of a tent plague above the city and the weapons of war
> are perished. Fuck. Good luck.[1]

[1] William Burroughs, 'Alex Trocchi Cosmonaut of Inner Space', Introduction to *Man at Leisure*

Young Adam may be considered Trocchi's first 'proper' novel[1]. First published under the name Frances Lengel by Olympia in 1954, it contained several graphic sex scenes, but was by no means purely pornographic and is a form of murder mystery, where the mystery is not who did it but if. Nevertheless, the amount of sex it contains would have prevented *Young Adam* being published anywhere but Paris and the 1954 edition's back cover says 'not to be introduced into the U.K. or U.S.A.' After the *Lady Chatterley* case in England in 1960, Trocchi revised it for republication under his own name in 1961[2], deleting all the sex scenes except one which is key to the motivations of the central character.

The first American issue of *Young Adam* was called *The Outsiders*, published after *Cain's Book* in 1961; it contained the rewritten novel and four short stories, presumably to bulk out the newly-shortened novel. The blurb implies it is a new work: 'Alexander Trocchi, author of the highly praised CAIN'S BOOK, has written a remarkable new work . . . perceptive, honest, full of beauty – and pain.'

Rather like Robbe-Grillet's *Le Voyeur*, 1955, who may also be a murderer, the narrator of *Young Adam* has an affectless, distanced tone; he, and the novel experience a discontinuity of time and place.

> there existed between the mirror and myself the same distance, the same break in continuity, which I have always felt to exist between acts which I committed yesterday and my present consciousness of them.. . . I do not ask now whether I am the 'I' which looked or the image which was seen, the man who acted or the man who thought about the act. For I know now that it is the structure of language itself which lacks continuity. The problem comes into being as soon as I use the word 'I'. There is no contradiction in things, only in objects, that is, in the words we invent to refer to things. It is the word 'I' which is arbitrary and

[1] It was made into a film in 2003 with Ewan McGregor and Tilda Swinton

[2] New York: William Heinemann, 1961; in paperback, London: New English Library, 1966; London: John Calder, 1983,

> which contains within itself its own inadequacy and its own contradiction.[1]

Although the novel is set firmly in and around Trocchi's Glasgow, there is very little sense of place. The narrator, Jo (we never learn his last name as he uses a pseudonym, and we do not even learn his first name until a long way through the novel), like the narrator of *Cain's Book* and Trocchi himself, works on a barge; one morning he discovers the semi-naked body of a young woman. The first part of the novel contains scenes of his life, and sex life, with what becomes a series of women, all related in an unemotional, uncommitted prose, and interspersed with details and press cuttings, of the murder. Although he is now with a woman called Ella, he thinks back to his time with Cathie. In the first, Frances Lengel version there is a lot of physical sex, never accompanied by any hint of love or romance. Trocchi is at this point moving from the author of pornography-to-order to the serious avant-garde novelist; his writing about sex is better than that of the great majority of novelists, and almost all experimental novelists. Writing about sex in experimental novels usually ranges from the grossly physical sounds, smells and c-words of Jeff Nuttall to the poetic, high-flown and euphemistic. Trocchi is explicit and physical, direct and earthy; far more convincing than D.H. Lawrence, whose lawsuit had paved the way for him.

> Soon my palms moved upwards away from her flesh and I was caressing it with my fingertips. Her whole body reacted to it, the buttocks tightening and straining to rise from the towelled sand in which they were embedded, her mound purposeful beneath the wafer of nylon which was wet at my groping fingertips.
>
> The bottom part of her bathing costume peeled off the sultry white flesh of her lower abdomen like the bark off a supple switch, and suddenly the short hairs were there, windblown and rising from her damp skin in a minute commotion as the constricting nylon was pulled away. Without further delay I pulled the costume down over her willing thighs and calves and twisted it of her feet.
>
> Her eyes were still closed. Her body was entirely bare now except for the brassiere. Gently, I insinuated my hands under her shoulder blades and unhooked it. Her breasts caved slightly to their natural set and the firm purplish teats were exposed, stranded with spiderwebs of sweat which ran up over her breasts towards her armpits. She made no effort to resist as I exposed myself and laid my sex in the groove between the hotly bunched flesh of her thighs. A moment later, our lips came together, and I felt myself sucked inwards. She groaned. We rolled over

[1] Frances Lengel edition, p. 10

> under the shade of the rocks. That was my first experience of Cathie. We were together a long time.[1]

Perhaps unfortunately, most of these scenes were taken out of the 1961, mainstream version. Part two of the novel opens with 'go back to the beginning' and restarts the story. The narrator now says the corpse was Cathie and he killed her.

> I wanted to talk about Ella, about how she suddenly came to me, like a brainwave, almost. For that reason I said nothing about Cathie, at least I didn't show where she fitted into the picture. She was there all the time of course, but you didn't know it. She was the corpse.
>
> I nearly said *my* corpse. But a corpse, strictly speaking, doesn't belong to anybody, and although I could have laid some claim to a stake in her body, I like to think that I have no claim, not even a murderer's, on her body.
>
> I killed Cathie. There is no point denying it since no one would believe me.[2]

He turns out to be an unreliable narrator, and we can never be sure whether he did kill Cathie, whether it was an accident – as it seems to be in some of his various versions of the event - or whether he actually had nothing to do with it, and is simply making up these scenes. 'Or was it an accident? I suppose it was. It never occurred to me to kill her. I was merely walking away. She tried to hold me back.'[3] It seems Cathie had also been holding him back metaphorically, in the sense of wanting commitment and children. 'Cathie's thighs were smooth, under oil some of the most beautiful thighs I have ever seen. But they represented a prison. She wanted children. That meant that I had to find a job, to make a home. Cathie always agreed that this was unfair on me.'[4] 'If I had allowed her, she would have spun a chrysalis of respectability into which my desires, castrated, perhaps defunct, would in a few years have been absorbed.'[5]

The extreme coincidence of his having found the body is never addressed or resolved and someone else, a plumber called Goon, is arrested and tried for the murder. Goon is found guilty though the narrator tells us nothing of the trial, why Goon was arrested and what the evidence is against him or why, even if, he knew Cathie. Throughout parts two and three of the book, Jo continues his affairs with women, taking very little interest in the trial and never feeling he should confess

---

[1] p. 45
[2] p. 85
[3] p. 94
[4] p. 137
[5] p. 142

his own guilt and save Goon. He posts a letter to the judge saying the plumber Goon is innocent but not naming himself, and not offering any new evidence.

In a flashback to Cathie he tells the story of how, one day, he made custard for her and when she would not eat it he beat and then raped her, in the only sex scene to survive into the 1961 version Although Cathie is by no means the submissive, masochistic Helen Seferis, it is not clear how hard she resists: she 'was never able to bring her resistance to the surface. It rose and melted into the gentle chubbing motion of her loins against mine, and soon I was able to release her arms without fear that she would renew her attempts to resist.'[1]

The last of the series of girlfriends is Jacqueline, who agrees to go away with him before Goon is sentenced. He confesses to her at the same spot Cathie fell in, but tells her he will never confess, even if Goon is hanged. The novel ends on cliff-hanger; after confessing he asks her: 'Are you still decided? I said. You will still come tonight? I craned forward to look into her eyes. On her answer, on perhaps her mere tone of voice, her life depended.'[2]

The stories included in the first American edition of *Young Adam*, issued as *The Outsiders* and published separately in Britain by John Calder in *New Writers 3*, 1965 are not dated and are not specifically set in any location though they are obviously taking place in a big city like New York; however, whenever currency is mentioned it is always British.

The first story, 'A Being of Distances', bears out the explicit reference to Camus in the book's title. 'He found himself not part of and therefore driven to reject the world into which he had been born.'[3] In 'The Holy Man', the inhabitants of a seedy apartment block come and go, but are all grotesques: 'Among others were the keys of the hunchback, the dwarf too old for the circus, of the strong man too weak to break chains, and of one of the blind men who, crossing a boulevard, got accidentally run over by a bus.'[4] In 'Peter Pierce' the narrator is a petty criminal and fugitive who never leaves the apartment; his only contact with

[1] p. 141
[2] p. 190
[3] p. 122
[4] p. 132

the outside world is through the blind ragman, literally living on the detritus of society. The final story 'A Meeting' turns this on its head by being set in a small office where the employees are always together, crammed into a hot stuffy space but, in true existentialist style, have no real human contact with each other.

> I always find it difficult to get back to the narrative. It is as though I might have chosen any of a thousand narratives. And, as for the one I chose, it has changed since yesterday. I have eaten, drunk, made love, turned on – hashish and heroin – since then. I think of the judge who had a bad breakfast and hanged the lout.[1]

Trocchi's most well-known and most celebrated novel, *Cain's Book*, was also his last - if it can be considered a novel at all; it has no narrative in the conventional sense. When he wrote it, at the end of the 1950s Trocchi had moved from New York, where the book is set, to the West Coast, where the beat novelists and poets were living, and it does share something in common with Kerouac's *On the Road*, published 1957 and Burroughs' *Junkie*, 1953, though Trocchi's writing is entirely distinctive. Burroughs himself was a fan:

> I remember reading *Cain's Book* for the first time: the barge the dropper the heroin you can feel it or see it. He has been there and brought it back. Many writers when they start to write withdraw from the source of their writing, but Alex has not done this and if his life may have taken time from his work it gives back a rare vitality.[2]

Cain's Book mainly consists of the thoughts of a drug addict who, like Trocchi works on a barge but spends most of his time and energy looking for his next fix. Seized by police in Sheffield, England, *Cain's Book* became the subject of a court case, defended by John Calder, who lost the case (according to Calder, because of Trocchi's trenchant testimony) and the appeal, leading to a new precedent in English law that a description of drug-taking could be considered obscene and

[1] Calder edition, p. 30
[2] 'Alex Trocchi Cosmonaut of Inner Space', Introduction to *Man at Leisure*

banned under the Obscene Publications Act. Trocchi's view on censorship and the author's responsibility had already been spelt out in the novel:

> *Cain's Book*. When all is said and done, 'my readers' don't exist, only numberless strange individuals, each grinding me in his own mill, for whose purpose I can't be responsible. No book was ever responsible. (Sophocles didn't fuck anyone's mother.) The feeling that this attitude requires defence in the modern world obsesses me.[1]

This is one of a number of metafictional/self-referential passages in the novel; the narrator continually refers to his narration. The subject of *Cain's Book* is the writing of *Cain's Book*. 'For a long time now I have felt that writing which is not ostensibly self-conscious is in a vital way inauthentic for our time.'[2] In addition to challenging conventional fiction by its self-awareness, the text is also disorganised and seemingly random.

There is no story to tell.

> I AM unfortunately not concerned with the events which led up to this or that. If I were, my task would be simpler. Details would take their meaning from their relation to the end and could be expanded or contracted, chosen or rejected, in terms of how they contributed to it. In all this, there is no it, and there is no startling fact or sensational event to which the mass of detail in which I find myself from day to day wallowing can be related. Thus I must go on from day to day accumulating, blindly following this or that train of thought, each in itself possessed of no more implication than a flower or a spring breeze or a molehill or a falling star or the cackle of geese. No beginning, no middle, and no end. This is the impasse which a serious man must enter and from which only the simple-minded can retreat. Perhaps there is no harm in telling a few stories, dropping a few turds along the way, but they can only be tidbits to hook the unsuspecting as I coax them into the endless tundra which is all there is to be explored.[3]

There are times, he says, when his thinking is 'entirely frivolous, when, in barely connected sentences and unresolved paragraphs, I shit idiocy and wisdom, turd by turd, thinking impressionistically, aware of no valid final order to impose.'[4]

---

[1] p. 31
[2] p. 45
[3] p. 113
[4] p. 54

The text of *Cain's Book* was in fact made up of fragments written at different times and in different places.

> The grey table in front of me strewn with papers, inventories from the past, from Paris, from London, from Barcelona, notes neatly typed, notes deleted, affirmations, denials, sudden terrifying contradictions, a mass of evidence that I had been in abeyance, far out, unable to act, for a long time.
>
> I wrote for example: 'If I write: it is important to keep writing, it is to keep me writing. It is as through I find myself on a new planet, without a map, and having everything to learn. I have unlearned. I have become a stranger.'[1]

The title of the book had been decided much earlier: '*Cain's Book*: that was the title I chose years ago in Paris for my work in progress, in regress, my little voyage in the art of digression.'[2] As *Young Adam* refers to the first man (though there is no other reference to Adam within the text) Cain, his son, the first murderer - 'Third profligate, the first poet-adventurer'[3] - seems to be an existential metaphor for the image we have of ourselves: Trocchi, like Cain, destroys what is around him in an act of defiance that leads to a necessary renewal of the old. 'I always felt it was strange that the butcher Abel should be preferred to the agriculturist Cain.'[4]

> The past is to be treated with respect but from time to time it should be affronted, raped. It should never be allowed to petrify. A man will find out who he is. Cain, Abel. And then he will make the image of himself coherent in itself, but only in so far as it is prudent will he allow it to be contradictory to the external world. A man is contradicted by the external world when, for example, he is hanged.[5]

So, one cannot go too far away from the norms of a society which has the power to remove its enemies for ever. Like Camus' outsider, Trocchi is a rebel not a revolutionary, a stranger to society, concerned only for his own salvation (in the form of the next fix). The role of the artist is to destroy the old, but only within the existing framework.

The most important thing for an addict is always the next fix, and therefore the money to buy it. For the women in *Cain's Book*, this often means prostitution,

---

[1] p. 88
[2] p. 179
[3] p. 178
[4] p. 139
[5] p. 30

and for the men a chance to get a fix from their earnings. 'In itself heroin doesn't lead to prostitution. But for many women it does make tolerable the nightly outrage inflicted on them by what are for the most part spiritually thwarted men.'[1] There are portraits of several women in the book, one or a composite of which may be Trocchi's wife Lyn, who was in this position herself. The narrator says: 'I couldn't have anything to do with a woman who didn't know she was a whore.'[2] Like the narrator of *Young Adam*, he is terrified of being imprisoned by a woman, and one way to ensure this is to only have relationships with women who can never be exclusive. Fay is one of these: 'Past forty, and with her blue look, Fay finds it difficult to interest a John . . . Dracula's idea of a good lay.'[3] She becomes in the narrator's eyes almost a mythical figure.

> Fay, owning nothing but the clothes on her back and ridden by her terrible craving, is more than anyone the grey ghost of the district; she can always cop, and she has burned everyone. She invokes horror, disgust, indignation, a nameless fear. She is the soul's scavenger, the unexpected guest, a kind of underworld Florence Nightingale always abroad with her spike and her little bag of heroin. She is beyond truth and falsity.[4]

Trocchi clearly saw himself as the cool, junky outsider-artist but the junky took control of the artist within him and prevented him from any further assaults on the art of the past. Like other outsiders he was incorporated into the mainstream, as he knew he would be: 'anti-literature is rendered innocuous by granting it a place in conventional histories of literature. The Shakespearian industry has little to do with Shakespeare.'[5] *Cain's Book* has some passages that seem to indicate that he knew it would be his last – perhaps only - major work, and the only novel written originally under his own name; he may have intended it to contain everything he had to give. Like 'damned' writers such as Lautréamont and Rimbaud, who gave up writing too early, he did not leave much behind but what he did leave put him in the pantheon.

> The past is always a lie, clung to by an odour of ancestors. It is important from the beginning to treat such things lightly. As the ghosts rise upwards over the grave wall, I recoffin them neatly, and bury them.

[1] p. 121
[2] p. 120
[3] p. 27
[4] p. 28
[5] p. 45

It is, I suppose, my last will and testament, although in so far as I have choice in the matter I shall not be dying for a long time. (One can only cultivate oneself as one awaits the issue.)

If eternity were available beyond death, if I could be as certain of it as I at this moment am sure of the fix I have only to move my hand to obtain. I should in effect have achieved it already, for I should be already beyond the pitiless onslaught of time, beyond the constant disintegration of the present, beyond all the problematic struts and viaducts with which prudence seeks to bridge the chasm of anxiety, with the ability to say, avoiding unseemly haste: 'I'll die tomorrow,' without bothering to intend it, or not intend it, as bravely as the fabled gladiators of Ancient Rome. It is because it is not so available (- I beg of you, Abel, refrain from flaunting your faith at me) that I have to suffer the infinite degeneration of objective time . . . a past that was never past, was, is always present; a recent past and a past present both distinct from the present prospect of the past degenerating already into a future prospect which will never be . . . suffer that, be prey to anxiety, nostalgia, hope. . .[1]

[1] p. 184. Elisions in the original

alan burns

Alan Burns[1] was born in London in 1929 and attended The Merchant Taylors' School. He served in the British Army from 1949 to 1951 and then became a barrister in 1956. He worked at the London School of Economics and later as a legal executive for Beaverbrook Newspapers from 1959 to 1962. Having published his first novel, *Buster*, in 1961, he moved away from the law and into the academic world. He was awarded Arts Council grants in 1967 and 1969 and bursaries in 1969 and 1973 and was a Henfield fellow at the University of East Anglia in Norwich, England in 1971. He also won the C. Day Lewis fellowship in 1973 and the Bush Foundation Arts fellowship in 1984. In 1975 he moved abroad to become a tutor in creative writing at the Western Australian Institute of Technology, returning to England to take up a writing fellowship from the Arts Council at the City Literary Institute in London in 1976. In 1977 Burns moved to America where he became professor of English, at the University of Minnesota, Minneapolis, where he stayed until 1991, when he returned to England and a creative writing post at Lancaster University. Burns' wife, the artist Carol Burns, published the short novel *Infatuation* in Calder & Boyars' *New Writers 6*, 1967 (the same edition also included Penelope Shuttle's first short novel *An Excusable Vengeance*) and *The Narcissist*, Calder & Boyars, 1967.

Burns published eight novels between 1961 and 1986[2] and his play *Palach*, directed by Charles Marowitz was produced at the Open Space Theatre and published by Penguin. In addition to his fiction, he also wrote *To Deprave and*

---

[1] For several articles on Burns, see *The Review of Contemporary Fiction*, Dalkey Archive Press, 8 Jan 1997. See also *A Conversation with Alan Burns* by David W. Madden on the Dalkey Archive website.

[2] *Buster*, published in *New Writers One,* London, Calder, 1961; republished in New York by Red Dust, 1972; *Europe after the Rain.* London, Calder, 1965; New York, Day, 1970; *Celebrations,* London, Calder and Boyars, 1967; *Babel,* London, Calder and Boyars, 1969; New York, Day, 1970; *Dreamerika! A Surrealist Fantasy,* London, Calder and Boyars, 1972; *The Angry Brigade: A Documentary Novel,* London, Allison and Busby, 1973; *The Day Daddy Died.* London, Allison and Busby, 1981 and *Revolutions of the Night,* London, Allison and Busby, 1986[2].

Corrupt: Pornography, Its Causes, Its Forms, Its Effects, 1972 and co-edited *The Imagination on Trial: British and American Writers Discuss their Working Methods*, Alison & Busby, 1981.

Burns described his working methods in 'Essay', introducing his short story *Wonderland* in the 1975 collection *Beyond the Words: Eleven Writers in Search of a New Fiction*.[1] He says that he had been struggling to describe scenes in words that were not 'literary and a bit absurd'; one day he saw a photograph of a couple kissing which reminded him of his parents.

> It recalled the relationship between my mother and father and between them and me, which I had tried to define but had been defeated by its complexity. I solved the problem simply, by describing the photograph, the image. This was the key to my being able to write my first book, *Buster*. Using my memory intensely, I found I could review my life in pictures and describe them in sequence. At the same time I discovered I could lie.[2]

In *Buster*, Burns describes how the boy types the word 'onion' and then looks for the word most remote from it; he comes up with the word 'man'. Putting these two remote words together - onion man – creates a phrase which we can imbue with meaning: an onion seller or onion eater perhaps[3]. This led Burns to consider 'the question of connection and flirting with the notion of disconnection.' From then on Burns 'continued to see how far apart I could make succeeding images and yet connect them by ingenious or devious or extravagant or so-called surrealist means.'

The idea of disconnection fascinated Burns 'partly from an immature wish to shock, to go to an extreme, make a break, an iconoclastic need to disrupt or cock a snook at the body of traditional literature.' He also considered writing as a way of setting himself puzzles, which he needed constantly to make things more difficult: 'the further I pushed the thing the more striking it became.' These literary disconnections expressed his own 'social estrangement, my distance from others, with the dual sense of superiority and yearning for closeness.'

> My parents were separated by my mother's death. My elder brother and I were separated by his early death. The consuming nature of this experience showed itself not only in the disconnected form but also in the content of my work.[4]

---

[1] ed. Giles Gordon, Hutchinson, 1975

[2] p. 64

[3] *Buster*, p. 77

[4] p. 65

The intellectual satisfaction of playing with metaphors and connections/disconnections was balanced by a 'political rejection of bourgeois art as a self-indulgence irrelevant to the struggle for social justice' and Burns' works are all, to some extent, about power relationships in fragmented societies.

A true pioneer and one of the most serious and respected writers in the experimental vein, Alan Burns and his wife Carol knew, admired and were admired by B.S. Johnson and Ann Quin, both of whom committed suicide. Unlike them, and despite his sense of disconnection and 'disgust with myself', Burns carried on and even went on to teach creative writing, no doubt inspiring many students, but his own body of work is relatively small considering his occupation: six novels between 1961 and 1973 but then a gap until 1981 and another until 1986. His novels are all short – he said of *Dreamerika*: 'I was having a problem, as ever, in making it bulky enough to sell as a novel'[1] – and intense; each one uses a different technique but each is complete and satisfying in its own individual way.

Alan Burns' first published work was the short novel *Buster*, included in Calder & Boyars' *New Writers 1*, 1961[2]. Quite conventional in style, it is a *roman à clef*, the telescoped early-life story of Dan Graveson [*sic*], a boy of great promise whose life is diverted by national service and never really recovers. Three years older than B. S. Johnson, Burns was of the generation that were too young to fight in World War II but were evacuated as children from the city to the country and then as young adults had to serve in the army. Johnson edited two books of memoirs of these two experiences: *The Evacuees*, 1969 and *All Bull: The National Servicemen, 1973*. Burns' entry in *All Bull* tells, in the first person, his brother Peter's story rather than his own.

> I tell his story rather than my own for two reasons: my novel *Buster* covered the ground so effectively (for me) that I am now unable to disentangle fact from fiction; and Peter's story is better than mine.[3]

---

[1] David Madden: '*A Conversation with Alan Burns*' op. cit.

[2] Also included were works by Dino Buzzati and Monique Lang

[3] p. 81

In the course of the novel, Burns' real-life tragedies: the deaths of his father and brother appear, fictionalised. 'The dirty words in our home are dead wife and dead son. Never mentioned. Not a picture, not a word.'[1] So *Buster* is avowedly, at least partly, autobiographical. The reason for the title is never entirely obvious, but the novel is prefaced by the following list of definitions:

> Buster:
>
> A small new loaf or large bun
> A thing of superior size or astounding nature
> A burglar
> A spree
> A dashing fellow
> A Southerly gale with sand or dust
> A piece of bread and butter
> A very successful day
> Hollow, utterly, low
> To fall or be thrown
>
> (Dictionaries).

Like *Portnoy's Complaint*, *Buster* has an early masturbation scene, though far less explicit: 'That night he wrapped the sheets round it, then a mountain of blankets, then the eiderdown tucked in, Small pig hot inside. Then wet.'[2]

Dan is a very promising student at school but during his school-leaving exam, the prose in his essay on Dr Johnson turns rather avant-garde, unlike the narrator's tone.

> Johnson was god. And typical of his age. Era of Goodsense worship, sameness the ultimate ideal, piggery and prudery rife, nonsense wisdom, pomposity prestige.
>
> So the Nightmareman Must – mountain of conventional revulsion, foul- mannered filth loving big boar beast – of course he Must be part of every mantelpiece. A great lumping tasteless Victorian grandfather clock, stumpgomping on top of and right through the pretty coffee cups and sniki simplicities. How he bounds!

Like Alan Burns himself, Dan has a brother Bryan who is also in the army but, being brighter, Dan gets a commission as an officer. This causes friction between them. Their mother remarks on how smart and well Dan looks. Bryan replies: 'Killing must be good for you' though Dan has not yet killed anyone. Dan is told

---

[1] p. 128
[2] p. 63

to resign his commission after he becomes an activist – his commanding officer calls it 'sheer pacifism' - and some of Burns' socially-conscious and anti-war themes come out in the book. 'Then tell me, who profits from the war? Korea? China? The answer may show who started it.'[1]

After leaving the army, Dan takes law exams – as Burns did – but fails. He decides to form a branch of the Peace With China Committee.

> For ten days he knocked on doors, asked Beekeepers, Octogenarians, Pacifists, Conservatives, Folkdancers, Scouts, Labour and Communist Party members, Rose-Growers, train-spotters, curates, trade unionists, stamp-collectors, youth leaders to Stop McArthur, Prevent International Conflagration and keep their hands off China.[2]

Dan goes into a decline: 'Unshaved and unwashed because a spider stayed circling shrivelling still crawling round the wash-basin, he lay on the hard bed, looking at the nude on the wall, the blackblistered cold fireplace, the gas ring squatting on the lino.'[3]

The meaninglessness of post-war existence weighs on him as it does on Burns himself. Unable to get a job because his 'heart's not in it', he asks 'what's the point of it all?' but his father says: 'The posing of that question is a luxury you can no longer afford. You can start worrying about philosophy when you are in a steady job.'[4] In the job centre 'Bums in lines queued for jobs and thirty bob doled out by clerks from behind heavy wire.' He finds himself in the Manual Labour queue, unable to get jobs even Charles Bukowski would fit into.

> Multilith operator, Adrema embosser, accounts clerk, upholsterer, Burroughs P 600 operator, invoice checker, delivery man, marine engineer, Capstan lathe operator, warehouseman, stove enameller, reinforced concrete engineer, window dresser, pig man. He was none of these. He wasn't even a Hairdresser's Assistant.[5]

Homeless, he sleeps in a park and wanders around post-Blitz London, which looks to him like a precursor of the post-apocalyptic landscape of *Europe After the Rain*.

> Raw Noise. Tens of thousands of wheels on roads. Heaps of persons, hives of them, pouring from and into buildings, crowding up steps from

[1] p. 99
[2] p. 121
[3] p. 125
[4] p. 132
[5] p. 136

> underground, crouching in cars, stopping up the street gaping at gadgets in windows, getting pinched elbowed killed drunk dazed, reading evening papers, obeying policemen, selling (and buying) fruit. He bored through them to Holborn and the dead City where the daytime moneymagnet was switched off and it was empty. . . Blitz sites. He was walking with conscious leverage from leg to leg. His legs weighed impossibly heavy. He came to a thudding hellplace, gleams of fires, men swung shovels, the ground shook, it was between mountains.[1]

Dan ends as he starts, powerless in the house of his father, and the novel ends with its first sentence: 'They stood over him.'[2]

[1] p. 137/138
[2] p. 140

I've stumbled on the side of twelve misty mountains
I've walked and I've crawled on six crooked highways
I've stepped in the middle of seven sad forests
I've been out in front of a dozen dead oceans
I've been ten thousand miles in the mouth of a graveyard
And it's a hard, it's a hard, it's a hard, and it's a hard
It's a hard rain's a-gonna fall.

Bob Dylan, 1962

When evil-doing comes like falling rain, nobody calls out stop!

Bertolt Brecht

The affectless, burnt-out tone of the nameless narrator in *Europe After the Rain* is, on the face of it a counter-instance to my thesis of British internalised experimental novels. However, J. G. Ballard, whose post-apocalyptic novels *The Drowned World*, 1962, and *The Drought*, 1965 present worlds similar to that in Burns' novel, asserted that the destroyed worlds of this type of novel reflect the shattered internal world of the writer.

> As an author who has produced a substantial number of cataclysmic stories, I take for granted that the planet the writer destroys with such

> tireless ingenuity is in fact an image of the writer himself. But are these deluges and droughts, whirlwinds and glaciations no more than over-extended metaphors of some kind of suicidal self-hate? . . . On the contrary, I believe that the catastrophe story, whoever may tell it, represents a constructive and positive act by the imagination rather than a negative one, an attempt to confront a patently meaningless universe by challenging it at its own game.[1]

Elsewhere, Ballard said:

> The dream worlds invented by the writer of fantasy are external equivalents of the inner world of the psyche . . . This zone I think of as 'inner space', the internal landscape of today that is a transmuted image of the past, and one of the most fruitful areas for the imaginative writer. It is particularly rich in visual symbols, and I feel that this type of speculative fantasy plays a role very similar to that of surrealism in the graphic arts. The painters Chirico, Dali and Max Ernst, among others, are in a sense the iconographers of inner space.[2]

Ballard's *The Crystal World,* 1966, and his story collection *The Atrocity Exhibition,* 1970, like *Europe After the Rain,* have details of Max Ernst paintings as their covers[3], and the *The Drowned World* also features Ernst's jungle landscapes.

> Over the mantelpiece was a huge painting by the early 20th-century Surrealist, Delvaux, in which ashen-faced women danced naked to the waist with dandified skeletons in tuxedos against a spectral bone-like landscape. On another wall one of Max Ernst's self-devouring phantasmagoric jungles screamed silently to itself, like the sump of some insane unconscious.[4]

The title of Burns' novel is in fact taken from the Max Ernst work of the same name[5] painted between 1940 and 1942 as Europe was being destroyed from the

---

[1] J. G. Ballard, 'Cataclysms and Dooms', in *The Visual Encyclopaedia of Science Fiction,* 1977.

[2] J. G. Ballard, 'Time, Memory and Inner Space', in *The Woman Journalist,* 1963. Already quoted in the Anna Kavan section

[3] As does James Blish's science fiction/religious novel *A Case of Conscience,* 1958

[4] J. G. Ballard, *The Drowned World,* 1962, p. 29

[5] Now in the Sumner Collection, Hartford

air, which is reproduced on the cover and inside of the book[1] and shows a ruined, organic landscape with what may be two human (or post-human) figures. The American publication did not feature the Ernst paining, presumably for copyright reasons.

The title may also be a reference to Bob Dylan's *Hard Rain*, written during the Cuban Missile Crisis of 1962, thirteen days in which it looked entirely possible that the whole world would be destroyed. This even had a huge impact on writers and artists: Jeff Nuttall called his 1968 memoir of the time *Bomb Culture*. And in Buster, Bryan had said 'since that bomb I've felt that I had leprosy, like bits of me were dropping off'.[2]

After the events of 1962, post-apocalyptic novels became quite common: in addition to Ballard's work, Christine Brooke-Rose's *Out* of 1964, though in a completely different narrative manner to Burns, shows a world in which the order of society has been reversed after an unnamed catastrophe; apart from Ballard's works, Anna Kavan's *Ice*, 1967, Christopher Priest's *Indoctrinaire*, 1970, *Fugue for a Darkening Island,* 1972 and *Inverted World*, 1974 are all in this category, as are Brian Aldiss's *Hothouse*, 1962, *Greybeard*, 1964, and the experimental *Barefoot in the Head*, 1969[3]. Burns said that he found the visual analogue of the landscape he had in mind, as well as in the Ernst painting, in a 1946 book by a journalist about his time in post-war Poland.[4]

> I put the book by the side of my typewriter. Then I 'looked' at the page. I looked yet didn't look. I did that thing painters often do, which is to screw up their eyes so only bits and pieces percolate through. I typed, forgetting what I was about, that I was writing a novel, blocking out . . .

---

[1] Only the UK edition; the U.S. edition, published by John Day in 1970, has a different cover, possibly for copyright reasons.

[2] *Buster*, p. 89

[3] Aldiss's *Report on Probability A*, written in 1962, could not find a publisher until 1967 when it was printed in Michael Moorcock's *New Words 171* and became a key work in British New Wave Science Fiction.

[4] Which possibly explains why the book calls to mind Jerzy Kosinkski's shattering *The Painted Bird.*

> as much of the rational mind as I could. I picked out images, not always the most startling, not worrying about connections, just batting away for a week or two. Of course the result derived partly from a conscious decision: I spotted the book and saw how to use it . . . And of course the raw material was transformed, re-worked through a number of drafts. I also use Burroughs's cut-up technique which I insist I invented because I used it before I'd heard of Burroughs.[1]

Europe in the Rain appears to be set in a time of revolution, after a cataclysmic war when the survivors struggle to survive but have formed a resistance. The narrator speaks in a cold, clipped and tone that forms strong rhythmic patterns.

> We walked fast in a strong cold wind, among loose stuff lying about. A viaduct led to the destroyed bridge, we ran down stone steps to the street, whole steps were missing, the gaps protected by wire. Single walls crashed. Music sounded from a church, people with dogs waited at the entrance, the stairway was packed with a stationary crowd of listeners. Two new trolley buses were being tested. I counted thirty wooden huts. Girls stood in a circle singing a patriotic song.[2]

No-one in the novel is named, and names do not seem to be permanently attached to people; a boy the narrator meets 'wasn't sure of his name, it had been signed away to someone else.'[3] Burns explained that he could not 'find the 'right' names . . . something connected with Kafka's 'Joseph K'.[4] The narrator is accompanying a girl whom he seems to be protecting, but who turns out to be the daughter of the brutal resistance leader. It is never made clear who the narrator is, why he seems to be able to meet at high levels with the armies on both sides, or what his role is – though in the interview Burns says he is an assassin and his role is deliberately ambiguous.[5] His cold, clipped narration makes him seem like the moving eye of a camera, dispassionately and with a complete lack of involvement noting everything but feeling nothing.

---

[1] Interviewed by Charles Sugnet in The Imagination on Trial, ed. Alan Burns & Charles Sugnet, Alison & Busby, 1981, p. 166

[2] p. 8

[3] p. 11

[4] Madden interview, op. cit.

[5] Burns says: 'The narrator's uncertain role and status is vital in maintaining the novel's precariousness and ambiguity. Give him a job, and the novel becomes more reportage—everything would have been watertight, rational, the reader would demand it. But I have made a contract with the reader that allows me the freedom to slip in and out of the rational. That has to be established from the start and iterated and reiterated (implicitly, by conduct) consistently throughout.'

As in the post-Blitz London of *Buster*, there are shortages of everything and there is a black market. 'Everyone did a little buying and selling. Loot. Though there was little left.'[1] 'People disappear, no one knows where they go'[2] and there are many children in the orphanage, where 'each floor is isolated to prevent the spread of infection.'[3] In the compound he visits, the people have nothing, 'no flowers, no books, no work but mental death. The faces were happy. The lack of hope brought calm.'[4] This strange calmness also affects the narrator; meeting a woman who tells him about the terrible treatment of prisoners he says: 'It was not that I was indifferent, I was not, but I was calm, I had no part of her trembling, there seemed no place for me. I felt that I did not care for the means by which this woman's mind had been broken'[5]. The calm even turns to an appalling sense of complicity in the brutal actions of the troops. 'They had held up a car and robbed the passengers, the driver had been taken out and shot. And I had discovered the fun in such business.'[6]

The troops regard the resistance as 'bandits' and 'gangsters' who 'must be shot down', this characterisation reflects many civil conflicts and resistance movements that had been taking place around the world at about the time Burns was writing: the Malayan National Liberation Army fought the British from 1948 to 1960; the Mau Mau rebellion in Kenya took place in the mid-1950s; the Algerian Revolution against the French ran from 1954 to 1962 and in Vietnam the Vietcong had been formed in 1960 and the first American missions against them were in 1962.

In all these cases, indigenous nationalist rebellions had been brutally put down by occupying forces (though all eventually drove those forces out) who also regarded the insurgents as gangsters and bandits. This 'us and them' mentality also brings to mind the famous Asch experiments, published from the early to mid-1950s, where student volunteers were randomly assigned to be 'guards' and 'prisoners' and rapidly came to identify with the worst aspects of their assigned roles.

But also in these cases, as in *Europe After the Rain*, the occupying troops were themselves treated badly by their commanders and their savage behaviour was engendered by a mixture of neglect and fear, brilliantly portrayed in Coppola's *film Apocalypse Now*, 1979, which was based on Joseph Conrad's *The Heart of Darkness*. Burns describes a similar situation.

---

[1] p. 9
[2] p. 20
[3] p. 10
[4] p. 24
[5] p. 27
[6] p. 28

> I waited for the long train carrying soldiers from one part of the country to another, men without boots, with no food, crowds waited for the train, they had to make sure of their places. I slept on the platform with a block of wood for a pillow. I could not sleep. The others slept and could not wake, and when they woke they shouted or wept. Because they could hate, apathy in death was easy. Indifferent, they celebrated hysterically, which intensified their indifference.[1]

The girl he accompanies throughout the narrative seems at first to be some kind of saviour, perhaps like the girl in Fritz Lang's *Metropolis*.

> For years she had led an abnormal life. She had been intensively trained. This had lowered her capacity to concentrate. She had formed habits of thought. Here was a powerful and unknown force. Her structure had been completely destroyed, in blood and burning. The structure of this girl was a new and unknown factor in history. It would be known only in the future. It would be something quite different from what her teachers had intended.[2]

Towards the end of the novel she has joined her father and is working with his group as one of them. 'I could not protest or protect as she scuffled past, hollow, narrow, unknown. She had shaved her head, she was dry earth, burnt grass, blackened wire, torn and scrubbed, she worked on uneven ground, crawled, moved, marched, portrayed the work, a show of work.'[3] The girl, rather than the narrator is the actual centre of the novel. In the end, she becomes like a despised prophet, without honour in her own community.

> She had been years in the grave. I remembered her long curls but now they were faded. She could not live again. But she found friends. Two middle-aged ladies began to take an interest in her. They took her out for walks with them. It became an unnatural thing. She fell in love with them. Then she sent them flowers, and they were returned burnt, and with them, her note torn in pieces. With her memories of the dead she caused bitter suffering, she had no friends, in the night she cried terribly. She offended many people. She told them too plainly what she saw.[4]

Perhaps a metaphor for the novelist himself?

---

[1] p. 82
[2] p. 13
[3] p. 96
[4] p. 120

> *Celebrations* grew from a mosaic of fragments written with no concern for ultimate plot connections. Delaying until the last minute any notion of what the book was about, I gradually assembled a series of heavy public rituals: marriages, funerals, wakes, steadily growing grander until they tipped over into absurdity. I got away from the bare, staccato style of war and found a full, baroque form to suit the content.[1]

In his third published novel, *Celebrations*, 1967, Alan Burns uses an 'I do not seek I find' cut-up method to create striking and surreal metaphors: 'the mouth hidden behind obscure houses,' 'the end of the life was the sound of yellow,' and 'he talked like a sickness'. Burns says he 'literally 'found' (having carefully set up the conditions in which I could peer at and then find) those separate images: 'mouth,' 'houses' 'obscure' . . . and found a way to hurl them together.'[2]

The novel is set in a world where the 'factory' is all-consuming. It is reminiscent both of Fritz Lang's film *Metropolis* and Yevgeny Zamyatin's novel *We*, a precursor to *1984*, written around Zamyatin's experience of organised labour in the shipyards of Newcastle, England. *We* was written in 1921 in Russian but first published in New York in an English translation in 1924. The inhabitants of the glass-walled, panopticon-like One State in *We* have no names or individual freedom. The whole state is designed to maximise production, along the lines of the 'scientific management' first advocated by F.W. Taylor in 1910 and famously adopted by Henry Ford. The flat tone of the narration in *Celebrations* brings to mind Charles Sheeler's cool, unpopulated Precisionist paintings of Henry Ford's River Rouge plant, done in 1927, the same year as *Metropolis,* and the similar, dehumanised industrial landscapes of Louis Lozowick and Charles Demuth. Like River Rouge, in *Celebrations* 'the first factory was built by the river where the vessels came from the north.'[3]

---

[1] 'Essay' op. cit. p. 66

[2] Madden interview, op. cit.

[3] p. 39

The principal character at the beginning of the novel, Williams, is a rather Henry Ford figure, the inventor and owner of the factory. He has a son and heir, Michael as Joh Frederson in *Metropolis* had Freder and Henry Ford had Edsel. Although Williams seems a paternalistic and concerned boss, the conditions of the workers are as bad as those in *Metropolis*.

> They were harnessed to their work, they experienced a more intense loathing for the factory than for any other point on earth. . . The unskilled workers were transferred from place to place like units of meat.[1]

The workers leave the factory with glee whenever they can but they leave 'knowing that at any time they could be picked up precisely and securely, removed back to their place of work and anchored there so they could not move.' As in *We*, the workers in *Celebrations* do not use names. 'No name was understood. To mention a name was to cause uneasy smiles.'[2] It is not just the factory that is under scientific management: the whole social system is run on similar lines.

> The inquest was to be conducted by one of those institutions under managerial control and meticulous supervision staffed exclusively by lawyers. The two judges resembled each other and all lawyers resembled them, they were pressed alike, without charm, no love on their faces which showed two black curves on the head, imitation eyebrows, a nose and lips, apparently a face, which could be studied, the neck of each different when examined closely.[3]

Williams seems to have no wife living and when his other son dies, we assume another reference by Burns to his brother's and mother's deaths. Williams takes his widowed daughter-in-law Jacqueline as his secretary, she then marries Michael and eventually becomes the central character in the novel. She has no love for the factory and its organisation. 'The arcade was crowded with meaningless machines. Jacqueline said if she had her way she would break up and destroy all machines.'[4]

---

[1] p. 32. Possibly 'units of meat' is a reference to Upton Sinclair's *The Jungle*, 1906, one of the first industrial novels that exposed the appalling working conditions in the meatpacking industry in Chicago.

[2] p. 22

[3] p. 22. Burns himself, of course, had been a lawyer.

[4] pp. 47/48

The timescale in the novel, as in *Buster,* is telescoped and Williams soon grows old and loses control of his creation.

> The old man became a memory, a name without distinction. He gained a reputation for being unhappy, he made his friends unhappy, apart from that he was unknown. . . For a long time Williams could not find his way along the constellation of unknown corridors, he seemed stationary, wandered around, played with matches, he felt his way as an automobile drives down a street of closed windows.[1]

Williams had been a more imaginative person then Michael, who has now taken over the running of the factory. 'The son dominated by fact, the father by his primitive spirit, the one dominated by intelligence but of greater importance were Williams' habits and character, his enjoyment of life against Michael's wasting energy.'[2] Williams is unable to cope with his loss of power and faculty, and 'on his seventieth birthday he found a way out.'[3] With him gone, Michael increases output even further.

> The speed-up in the assembly room was under way. No fewer than seventeen workmen had 'died of heart attack' recorded by a woman doctor who missed the signs of suffocation, she failed to turn the body over, it needed imagination.

After Michael has 'collapsed in a London street'[4], Jacqueline leaves the factory to go to the mountains. She 'had been offered lots of love affairs but forty years old, she did not believe in friendship, a man might make her leave her flat and she would not like that.'[5]

> On account of allergy she had lost track for two years, she had friends who died, 'you don't see many people in the dark'. She was contented religiously, able to follow the big dogs, sex was her husband in the ground, that side of things was going to fall from the sky when she had mapped it out, but the good life lived a long time and married somebody else.[6]

---

[1] p. 72
[2] pp. 84/85
[3] p. 95
[4] p. 112
[5] p. 114
[6] p. 115

At the end she meets a parachutist who does indeed fall from the sky and the novel ends with her looking out of her window, alone.

In the interview about *Europe After the Rain*, Burns said he had used, not the cut-up techniques of Burroughs, but a folding technique. This is not so obvious in the earlier novels but seems to be the central organising principle of *Babel,* 1969. Far more radical than his earlier work, it completely subverts the idea of a novel. It was written in 1967 and 1968, the central period of Jeff Nuttall's *Bomb Culture*:

> High days and holidays, it was a time to be alive! Events of Paris, and 'things happening' in London too. The great antiwar (I always think it's wrong to say anti-Vietnam) demo outside the US embassy (there with my wife, met B. S. Johnson and others)[1].

Burns used press cuttings to form the basis of the book, folding them 'to join the subject from one sentence to the object from another with the verb hovering uncertainly between.' Burns' own example of this is 'Heavy bombers again pounded the open rock garden, the valley area, especially the primulas.'[2] This relates to the rhetorical technique known as syllepsis or zeugma, and can create a hallucinatory metaphor, joining two dissimilar ideas (as Burns did with the example onion-man) to create a surrealistic montage effect: bombers pound but so does the sea.

Babel is written in short sections, usually two or three to a page, some of which could almost be self-contained, twisted versions of the very short, surreal stories of Daniil Kharms, Robert Walser, or the palm-of-the-hand stories of Yasunari Kawabata[3].

> THE PHOTOGRAPHER LOVED THE PRINCESS well enough to make a perspicacious move: he tied one hand firmly under her chin, to alleviate feelings of guilt. 'Taking off her clothes is a moral dilemma, isn't it?'

---

1 Madden interview, op. cit.

2 'Essay' op. cit., p. 66

3 Or what is now called flash fiction.

> Now she is setting off for St Petersburg, and setting up business in such places as Monte Carlo and Nice, where it turned out, the shops were not quite good enough.[1]
>
> TWO THINGS MADE HER FAMOUS: never having been seen dancing, and never having set foot in America. She compressed within her time with easy grace. When news reached her of her past, being one day read in the papers, she never contradicted any story. She appeared to make her life consistent with her past. Being in the company of men from her home town, she lived in a hotel room with a man older than herself. Though she married the Dutchman, her preference was for the beautiful days of her life with her soldier husband.[2]

Other, even shorter sections are like aphorisms, sometimes bringing to mind Kafka's *Zürau Aphorisms*.

> MOST PEOPLE WILL CLAIM TO BE PEOPLE, USUALLY.[3]
>
> CAN WE SALVAGE ANYTHING? Is there anything to be saved?[4]
>
> A GOOD PLUMBER IS A THEORIST WHO KNOWS PRECISELY WHAT IS HAPPENING.[5]

Some, however, are too absurdist even to be read as aphorisms.

> WE ARE OFFERING CATS TO EVERYONE TO RELIEVE TENSION, a little bit of button is homosexual and happy, happiness is a very good product, the law should be nationalised now and then, pancakes at breakfast remind people of the underground, start the day with urine distilled from tea, it will save you from the liberal arts.[6]

The book's cover says it contains over two hundred characters and, although over two hundred names are mentioned in the book, and all are listed at the end of the book, they are not characters in any normal, novelistic sense, just names from press cuttings. However, some characters do recur so that we can start to build up some kind of picture of them, though Burns does his best to subvert this process. One 'character' who recurs is the bishop: 'THE BEAUTIFUL BISHOP WAS ONE OF THE

---

[1] p. 25
[2] p. 70
[3] p. 18
[4] p. 20
[5] p. 55
[6] p. 10/11

FIRST PEOPLE TO CRAM THREE SECRETARIES INTO ONE DAY, he showed me two himself, he had one every hour on the half-hour.'[1]

The link between characters and their names – first raised in *Europe After the Rain*, crops up again:

> A PERSON IS HIS NAME. When he needed a new name he turned however indirectly towards his bread and wine. When he had been reinforced by his family name, the remote midway name, when asked his name, he had heard the slight danger sound of the high accordion. Now Jesus was taking chances. He needed the radio link with revelation.[2]

Jesus recurs several times, though religion is portrayed in a very ambivalent way. 'Christians have manifest faults, but their aggressive approach, their ruthlessness, transmits profits from far afield.'[3] Another theme to recur is Burns' concern with war; this passage could almost be from *Europe After the Rain:* 'THE NEED TO KILL WITHOUT EXPRESSION. What have you to say about war? He said today it is a necessity, though here the country unhappily is often sub-human.'[4] Burns' related theme of social justice also makes several appearances.

> ECONOMIC OBSCENITY WAS SUPPORTED BY THE PEOPLE, the aim was a few dollars' worth of inflation. The police were certain to win, the army occupied the streets in total silence and steadiness, the minority died of cold.[5]

The title *Babe*l does not refer to the difficulty of communication between different languages, as does Christine Brooke-Rose's *Between*; however, Burns does begin in this book to use non-standard typography, as she was to do in *Thru* in 1975 and he would do in his next novel, *Dreamerika!*

---

[1] p. 17
[2] p. 149
[3] p. 149
[4] p. 52
[5] p. 19

everything grows from war nightmare
x vx x v v
second I extend my hands again
mickey mouse
minnie mouse
two sweeps of steel

see time h
what I see time o
a young time r
xxxxxxxxxxxxx time r
mister time o
r
------------------ h
scrutiny time o
----------------- r
last swoop of love time r
no matter how filthy or ugly her time was o
I should have a visored cap r
AB in this place I smelled resin
ME
the
shot
which
skinny
shot
cold here[1]

[1] p. 46

In another break from his previous styles, Alan Burns' *Deamerika! A Surrealist Fantasy*, 1972, mixes a twisted version of the history of the Kennedy family (though their surname is never mentioned) with what seem to be unrelated newspaper headlines, printed very large on the page. *Babel* had destroyed all the conventions of the novel, indeed of prose writing in general. The lack of any narrative or characterisation begs the question: why keep reading if nothing is going to happen? With collections of poetry, short stories or Rimbaudian prose poems we accept the lack of structure and narrative, the lack of connection between the individual pieces but presented with what we believe is going to be a novel we expect some signposts, some markers to show us the way, and Burns' previous novels have at least these[1].

Burns himself saw this: '*Babel* had gone to unrepeatable extremes in the fragmentation of narrative, now I latched on to the story of the Kennedys whose characters and activities gave the reader reference points to help him through a sea of disparate images'.[2]

> I seized on the idea of referring to, using as a basis, some story line universally known—much like the Roman and Greek gods—part of the common language, common reference points, myth. I thought of Robin Hood, Bible stories, all sorts, and finally hit on the Kennedys as perfect to do the job I needed them to do.[3]

The story of the Kennedys, as a powerful myth, can be subverted without losing the audience, especially if the retelling produces truths that go beyond, or even contradict the facts. '

> I played hell with the documented facts, made crazy distortions of the alleged truth, in order to get some humour out of it, and also raise questions about the nature of documentary realism.[4] Screwing up the

[1] However, as of 2012, *Babel* is the only one of Alan Burns' books in print.

[2] 'Essay' op. cit. p. 67

[3] Madden interview op. cit.

[4] In his next novel, *The Angry Brigade*, Burns would go in the opposite direction, in a 'documentary novel'.

story made some very undocumentary truths emerge. Like when old Joe Kennedy buys the United States for 17 billion dollars.[1]

Capitalist

The rise of the capitalist:
was born in

Joe revived his financial operations, he had nerve. He wanted to sell New York to Florida, and the Archbishop was eager. 'I could make a hundred million dollars.' Joe went to the heart, he re-built Manhattan which had fallen, he grew richer than himself. (He bought some properties in the names of his sons, as some observers realised.)

'The newspapers say I'm worth five hundred million dollars. Why, if I had that kind of . . .

With his fortunes in his hands he moved in and out, he created values brilliantly. When cash was short he bought St. Patrick's Cathedral for$200,000 and sold the parcel for shopping centres. He broke the bank. He bought Boston for his children. He spread his name all over.

OUTRAGEOUS

No landlord made more than Joe. Some tenants remained when he sold a slum for $250,000, which meant that the slum was worth less than its share of taxes. Then he succeeded in Chicago with a deal that made him owner of the city. It had cost $30,000,000 in 1945 but was no longer required. He offered to buy America for seventeen billion dollars and received assurances that the government would move out as their leases expired.

[1] 'Essay', op. cit.

In *Dreamerika!* John F. (Jack) Kennedy is the first US president to be promoted and elected in the full glare of the media. Where Richard Nixon, his (narrowly) unsuccessful opponent, looked shifty, swarthy and sweaty on TV, with a permanent 5 o'clock shadow, Kennedy looked like a media god.

> Jack looked magnificent in the Pacific where people live in colour, and they found Jack's flesh fascinating in Los Angeles. But the other guy's film took place in a grey telescope, Dick was told he was out of touch, was attacked by a heart attack, and somehow fell down.
>
> # really good news
>
> The electrifying sense of collective reputation, it is this that is dazzling, that is why Jack's victory is fantastic. His revolution is rapid innovation. The public appreciates public relations, the democratic republic has gone into show business. The new President shares this mass experience.
>
> ## **Our winning streak.**[1]

This passage of course relates to Guy Debord's highly influential 1967 work *The Society of the Spectacle*, first translated into English in 1970. Debord, a founder of the Situationist International, whose influence peaked with the 1968 revolts in Paris and elsewhere, proposed that authentic social relationships had been replaced by the 'spectacle'. Kennedy was the first president of the spectacle, and the visual style of *Dreamerika!* makes it one of the first novels of the spectacle.

> The spectacle is able to subject human beings to itself because the economy has already totally subjugated them. It is nothing other than

[1] p. 20, previous page p. 11

> the economy developing for itself. It is at once a faithful reflection of the production of things and a distorting objectification of the producers.[1]

Another, similar novel of the spectacle is J. M. G. Le Clézio's slightly later *Les Géants*, 1973, published in England as *The Giants* in 1975, which also uses press cuttings and non-standard typography to try to represent the spectacle. For Le Clézio, the power of words has been taken over by the Masters to reclaim them the people must shake off traditional language.

> Those who speak with words alone are not free. Those who only read words in books remain prisoners.
>
> Speak: but from the far side of language, too, from the side of those who create it. Each word needs to be turned inside out like a glove, and emptied of its substance. Each speech should wrench itself from the ground like an aeroplane and smash through the surrounding walls. Up till now you have been slaves. You have been given words to obey, words to enslave, words to write slavish poems and slavish philosophy. It is time to arm words. Arm them and hurl them against the walls. Perhaps they will even reach the other side.[2]

> The Masters speak. The language of the Masters streaks across the world, with all its rapid, practical, terrifying words. It is not a language like the others. It is a language that never hesitates, never stutters. Its words are constantly in action, always at work. One can neither see or hear these words, for they travel so fast that one has no time to become aware of them.[3]

> Words are the sentimental weaknesses of mankind. The Masters have no words. They have figures, impulses, lightning flashes, explosions, circuits, card-indexes.[4]

Like *The Giants, Dreamerika!* attempts to use the techniques of the Masters (and the Kennedys were certainly among the Masters) against them, as far as possible within the confines of a novel, not as a mirror to reflect them but as a Brechtian hammer to beat them with. In both cases, the paradox remains: how can a book confront the Masters if those who only read words in books remain prisoners?

---

[1] Paragraph 16. The aphoristic style of *Society of the Spectacle* is somewhat reminiscent of the style of Burns' *Babel*.

[2] J. M. G. Le Clézio, *The Giants*, Hutchinson, 1975. Le Clézio won the Nobel Prize for Literature in 2008.

[3] ibid p. 155

[4] ibid p. 163

Still, within the confines of the novel's possibilities, Burns does try to take apart the Kennedy myth in surreal prose, with sections for Bobby, Teddy and Jackie, while still remaining sympathetic to them as individuals, rather than Masters. There is a particularly vivid description of Kennedy's assassination:

'NOW TAKE CARE THIS TIME'

The motorcade approached, the unarmed guest entered, the convertible people crouching, the coat-collars turned up. Eight shots shouted, he was caught, hit, the unheard order came.

window

He had been frightened by a man in a window. The sound of cheers as he fell. He stood up instantly. He seemed to need the masses, he was making love, remember his good laugh, he did not want the narrow place.

JESUS, DID YOU SEE THAT

The convertible was long, three men stood on the trunk. A goat on the hood of the car screaming 'Dee! Dee!. The body shook, the man was hurt. The battered man in the back of the car surrounded by strangers, knees moving towards him, the heart stopped.

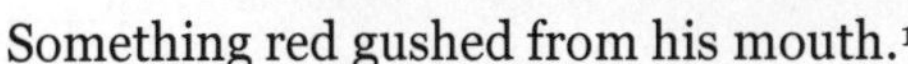

Something red gushed from his mouth.[1]

[1] p. 31

After Jack's death, Lee Harvey Oswald and Jack Ruby become the focus of the story, which is then taken over by Bobby.

> The politicians were impressed by this new purity and simplicity. They could use him, but when they pleaded with him, he faced them fighting: 'You need me? Hell with you.' 'AMERIKA calls you.' OK. OK. But I bring bad luck. You still want me?' Yes, we need you, won't you come back?' 'All right.' (With heavy heart.) Sold. OK. OK. He bawled.[1]

DO YOU GET ON WELL WITH PEOPLE?

He learned the way. It was true. He would be President. One immense day . . . .

Are you big enough?

He slammed his hand. The victim trained hard. The results of his work appeared. He did things his way. He continued for four and a half years. He worked for the years that followed.

4½

Here's the built-in quality, the lasting good looks, the strength, the style of the best

He found his audience. He spoke to AMERIKA!

He saw them waving, their vehement gestures escorted him home. Politics were his work. Finish it. I can't. Why? The future is not for me, I will be stopped on the way. Get on with it. Get out there! On Monday he would be President. What? You heard me. The boyish face demanded. 'What's this crap?' He snapped.

shout to get noticed.

He grabbed a microphone, he broadcast to AMERIKA! He

---

[1] p. 68, next page p. 69

After Bobby's assassination, Teddy's drowning of Mary in the river is given an extended and sympathetic airing.

Why is it easier to swim in the sea than in fresh water?

Teddy had swum three miles in either direction. Now he rested half-way, at a safe place. He pulled himself up, he had got there, that was good. By swimming across so many miles of water, Teddy surprised even himself. He had never expected to see land again. But there he was:

KEEPING COOL

IN STICKY SITUATIONS

He went straight to his hotel, to minimise the chances of running prematurely into the arms of the police.

[1]

---

[1] p. 94

After a section on Jackie, the novel moves on to Bobby's rebellious son Joe and the counterculture, ending with what may be a fast-forward into a far future, or a comment on the ruined landscape of the present.

> When they lost control of their world there was confusion
> in the area. They began to record the glories of the past.
> This ancient people once had power. They founded the city.
> city. They chose the site.
> The site has not been found. Its history is lost. It was
> probably laid waste. Its position was presumably fairly central. We cannot be sure.
>
> Sounds of wheels. The routes are haunted. Where are relics found? (Whose names mean little.) Under dust. They
> have not been found. Only ruins remain. Emptiness. Snakes. Silence under light.[1]

[1] p. 134/135

> After *Dreamerika!* I gave up writing from the subconscious, making a mosaic of found pieces. I had written four books that way and the fun had gone out of it. But I was unable to sit at a typewriter and make up a story without raw material to work on. I was grounded in a method by which I found patterns and connections in a mass of indiscriminate stuff. I could no longer use journalistic material so I had to find something else. I hit on the idea of using a cassette recorder to record many hours of natural speech. I transcribed the cassettes and use the resulting material as previously I had used press-cuttings. I made a collage of voices. I carried over from *Dreamerika* the use of a well-known story and a set of characters to create a framework and points of reference. The result was *The Angry Brigade*. Again I set out to free myself from my obsessions and again I was trapped. Same pattern: powerful State, youthful sacrifice. Like *Palach*, the book was about physical action as opposed to mere discussion. From *Babel* came the anarchist ideology and its concept of the state.[1]

The *Angry Brigade*, 1973, is tautologically subtitled *A Documentary Novel*; to paraphrase Gertrude Stein, a novel can either be a novel or it can be a documentary, it can't be both. At the same time B. S. Johnson was making documentaries for film and television, and editing anthologies of recollections[2] but even Johnson did not call any of them novels. *The Angry Brigade* challenges, as did *Babel,* how far the concept of a novel can be stretched. If we accept Burns at his word that the words are in fact from tape recordings and not written or rewritten by him; if his job was simply to organise the words into sections and give structure to the whole, how is this different from the editor's job that Johnson was doing? But perhaps we should not take Burns' *Documentary Novel*

---

[1] 'Essay', op. cit., p. 68

[2] *The Evacuees*, 1968; *All Bull: The National Servicemen*, 1973; *You Always Remember the First Time,* 1975.

at face value. In a 1981 interview he said that, because nobody really knew who the Angry Brigade were, he felt free to invent them.

> I purported to have discovered them and the book contained what seemed to be a series of tape-recorded interviews with them. Needless to say it was fiction and those 'interviews' were mainly conducted with my friends on topics quite other than those discussed by the characters in the book.[1]

In a much later interview he was asked if the whole thing was a product of his imagination. 'While most of the material came from 'friends,' I did talk to one or two genuine extreme anarcho-left guys and groups, and used those tapes more directly, though much cutting and shaping was still needed.' But in both interviews he also says that he was trying to write in a more demotic and less high-art style, in response to Heinrich Böll's Nobel acceptance speech.

> It was about the need for novels especially to make—to be designed to make—a political impact—this in rather high falutin' terms—writers' political responsibility, etc.—and that the self-indulgent elitist 'art' novel was intolerable. This hit home, and I resolved to write in a plain, accessible style, literally a 'conversational' style, via the tape recorder. The recorder was a godsend to me. I cut out the cut-up and found this other way of creating the 'ocean of raw material' I have always needed, so that I could 'find' the good stuff among the debris—to mix my metaphors. I also discovered the wonderful music and subtlety of people's speech, and there was a bit of politics in that also. (I also found out what an exhausting method it was, with hundreds (?) of hours transcribing tapes, editing and rewriting them.)[2]

So, we cannot say how much of the text is Burns' words, how much just 'cutting and shaping'; how much Burns is editor and how much author. Obviously the breakdown of authority, including the authority of the author, was a feature of this time of Bomb Culture. Many young middle-class people ceased to identify with the police and the establishment: cases like the prison sentences handed out to the Rolling Stones following drug convictions in 1967 - when William Rees-Mogg famously asked 'who breaks a butterfly on a wheel?' – and to the Oz magazine obscenity trial defendants in 1971 led to an alienation of youth, accelerated the rise of the counterculture and led to the formation of groups like the Angry Brigade in the UK, the Red Army Faction in Germany, the Red

---

[1] Sugnet interview, op. cit., p. 164

[2] Madden interview, op. cit.

Brigades in Italy and the Japanese Red Army, all operating around the late 1960s to mid-1970s.

The characters in *The Angry Brigade* are from this alienated middle-class, caught between the values of their upbringing and the assumptions of the counterculture. While they are living in a Church of England hostel, where men and women are segregated, they are in trouble for having their own keys cut so they can come in late. One of the leading characters in the novel, Dave, says; 'It was rather ironic because we'd come in at one in the morning after we'd been to a concert of classical music. We all got very indignant, saying we'd only been out to enjoy a bit of culture.'[1] This is a culture clash that could sum up the whole period: the establishment (landladies, the Church of England) are automatically suspicious of all young people which just feeds their resentment and leads them to rebel.

One of the implicit oppositions in the text, which perhaps had ramifications for the issue of the experimental novel is between rebel, in the sense of Camus and revolutionary, in the sense of Trotsky. Barry says Dave is an 'incredible person: a young poet, revolutionary, street theatrist, cultural and political activist.'[2] Barry himself however, as a rebel but not a revolutionary; knows what he is opposed to but not what he wants to replace it. He does not even have an image of how he wants himself to be, let alone how he wants the world to be. 'I'm put down because I don't have an image. I'm not a successful illustrator and I'm not a successful graphic designer, I'm not a successful writer, I've no desire to be. I'm just nowhere.'[3] Dave identifies most, not with revolutionary politicians but with Kafka, Orwell, Reich and Jung.

> Kafka was more important because more real. Kafka was a person very much on his own, as I suppose I was, cut off from each side, cut off because I wanted it and because I couldn't help it, cut off from what my parents were going through and from what my friends were going through. Kafka didn't put anything new into my head, he confirmed what I'd always known.[4]

The sense of alienation from one's parents, especially among working class boys in the post-war period, was often caused by the grammar school experience, where the sons of factory workers were taught Latin and Greek and pulled apart from their culture and background. These isolated individuals found and identified with similarly isolated friends in the counterculture movement and found a new culture of their own. 'The Movement became . . . an individual

[1] p. 13
[2] p. 8
[3] p. 9
[4] p. 14

personality becoming more collective.'[1] The tension between the individual and the collective became the defining dynamic of opposition groups like The Angry Brigade. Ivor, born working class and Jewish feels the tension acutely.

> But I was dissatisfied with hippy individualism (I use the word with caution), their sensationalism, their view that experience was what mattered, their basic lack of thought: that you didn't have to think about the real nature of the world you lived in. I always had one foot in the underground and one foot in the straight left. I got involved with a group of people who were doing cultural guerrilla stuff on a small scale. They were going round defacing posters rather brilliantly by reprinting parts of the poster very sophisticatedly, then sticking new bits on top so that the poster had a completely different message.[2]

These are hardly revolutionary activities; the group at first 'tried to stay legal but from the start we were prepared to become an underground organisation'.[3] Like experimental novelists staying within the novel form but subverting it? But the individual's power is limited compared to the collective's. 'Suddenly: the realisation that you could do things. You were just one person but you could actually do things with other people, you could be effective, change things, make a difference.'[4] Later the group moves closer to violence. The had identified with the Yippies, a largely non-violent culturally anarchist group based in Chicago in the 1960s, but soon moved closer to the Black Panthers and the IRA, who were committed to violent direct action, and, especially in the case of the IRA, had a specific end in mind as opposed to the vague aims of the counterculture.

In the group's first major direct action – a 'Demonstration/Sit-in/Confrontation' against the Ministry of Housing for which the core group recruit a large number of followers – was explicitly non-violent though Ivor took a replica hand grenade. 'It was the first piece of direct action I had taken part in and it had a very strong effect on me. It had an effect on them too, of course, they looked pretty frightened.'[5]

As a result of this activity Barry and Dave are sentenced to jail, Dave for seven years. After Barry's release he tries to escalate into violent action but Suzanne disagrees in a confrontation that sums up the whole liberal dilemma.

> Ivor said my objection to the use of explosives was that they caused pain. He said morality was based on the avoidance of pain and he didn't

---

[1] p. 15
[2] p. 20
[3] p. 33
[4] p. 39
[5] p. 96

> accept that. The typical liberal attitude to any painful situation was immediately to try and end it . . .
>
> Barry said: 'Blowing up something *will* change the system. Better one person dead than millions existing the way they are now.' I asked: 'Is the regime so bad that we have to kill people to get rid of it?' . . . We're talking about death, the death of people's potential, the death of people's freedom[1]

Barry later says he understands 'Ivor saying killing, especially killing civilians, is easily dramatic, powerfully dramatic. I don't care what people say, it gets things done.'[2] However, the unintended consequence of their violent actions is more repression. 'The papers caught on to it and they said, Hey, wild revolutionaries throwing bombs all over the place. . . Then they passed new laws to make the country more repressive than ever.'[3]

As if going even further towards satisfying Heinrich Böll's criterion for social activism in novels, *The Day Daddy Died*, 1981 is a slice of raw social realism, or even naturalism. It seems to be connected to the earlier novels only in that it seems to be based on taped interviews, and the style of the writing feels as if it is based on actual speech. In line with this, the story does not have the structure of a novel but, like *Buster*, simply tells the story of one person, Norah, starting on the day her daddy died at the beginning of World War II, again like *Buster*, and ending somewhere close to the present time.

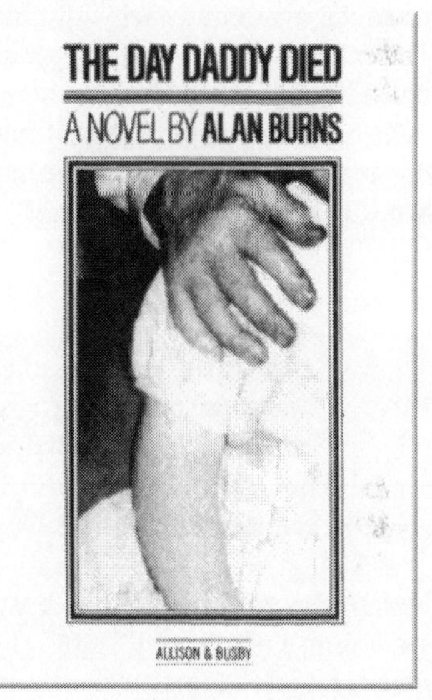

> The book is composed of a number of strands. The first I call the 'Norah' strand. It revolves round a woman I knew some years ago in London, a remarkable woman, about fifty when I knew her, blonde hair, wonderful skin, blue eyes, a working-class woman, very tough indeed, five children by five fathers. I spent hours talking to her. . . Of course the men in her life were successive manifestations of the father she's searching for, without

[1] p. 155
[2] p. 163
[3] p. 164

> making too heavy psychological weather of it; and the second story was about an older man and a younger girl. I could marry those two strands.[1]

Norah has a hard life, though no doubt a conservative, Mary Whitehouse viewpoint would say this is her fault. She becomes pregnant early in the story, and continues to do so, ending with five children by different men. An interesting parallel is with Jeremy Sandford's BBC television play *Cathy Come Home*, directed by Ken Loach and shown in 1966, and his 1971 follow-up, *Edna, the Inebriate Woman*. The former had a huge audience and raised the issue of homelessness, leading to the formation of the charity Crisis.

Like *Buster*, the timescale seems telescoped, compressing almost the whole of Norah's life into just over 100 pages. Unlike Burns' earlier novels we have very specific places and times; the world of *The Day Daddy Died* is definitely the world around us. Norah's life, like Cathy's, never benefits from the post-war economic and social optimism; whenever she begins to settle she becomes pregnant again and each child makes it harder for her to keep a job and a home. The men she meets and makes love to are not evil, or even particularly feckless, but never seem able to help her, and the social security system always seems to fight back. The establishment have no sympathy and no systems to help. In the divorce court, after she has been unfaithful to her husband, who was away in the army, the judge enters the court.

> He began to drone. Thinner rigid speech was used, deeper sound was used when needed. Norah shrank more and more. People massed against the unspeakable person. Lawyers made her fall. Trap was neat. Made prisoner, tied tight. . . The dark doors opened over her head. She blew her nose. Lost time, loose teeth, trotting hands, bad night. Then her eyes blew up and hoped to die. She stood up, shouted, jumped, crimson tears in her eyes, turning round and clapping.[2]

Norah tries to start her own business but fails for lack of money. 'She could not see a future of any kind.'[3] And then her children are taken away. 'The family was found, huddled together on the street, and the N.S.P.C.C[4]. was called. They came in a car and took away the three youngest, Eugene, David and James. That was terrible. That was the end. Until then they had stayed as one.'[5] As with *Cathy Come Home*, the details of poverty are telling: a few pounds can make the

---

[1] Sugnet interview, op. cit., p. 165

[2] p. 36/37

[3] p. 59

[4] National Society for the Prevention of Cruelty to Children.

[5] p. 66

difference between having a home and being homeless, between having children and having children taken away.

> For herself, Eugene, David and James, Norah was getting seven pounds and one shilling a week. After rent and fuel she had less than five pounds to live on, in 1964. Terry was still in jail so he could not help. For Norah to feed her kids was almost impossible, but others were worse off. one woman had six children, she kept a big pan of porridge on the stove and fed them all on that. They lived on porridge. By pooling her money with Elaine, Norah could make stews, from neck of lamb and things like that.[1]

To make things even worse, her eldest son, confined in a home, kills himself. 'Once he'd preconceived it and arranged it and he knew the time and how it would be, he felt tremendously peaceful because it didn't matter.'[2] However, the story ends on a relatively optimistic note. Norah's fifth and last child, Joanne, turns out to be highly intelligent and gets a scholarship to a good school and two of her other sons get good jobs, finally allowing her to buy her own house.

Burns said that there were two stories that made up *The Day Daddy Died*: Norah's story and a separate story of a younger woman's relationship with an older man. Burns merges them together, if not entirely successfully, giving Norah a strange relationship with the mysterious Dr Peck, who, unknown to her has had Terry on drugs, from which he never recovers, fathers one of her children, and claims to be able to talk to her dead father, from whose death she dates her downward slide (hence, presumably, the novel's title). The doctor convinces her that her father, the biggest influence on her life, can communicate with her. Considering an abortion, she takes pills to try to end one of her pregnancies.

> Then she heard the tapping. It was daddy saying no. For nights she had not been sleeping, she had heard this tapping and left her light on all night. It had happened four or five nights in a row. She was frightened by the tapping though it could have been the heating or a water tap. Now she knew her father had been tapping in her room.[3]

A key feature of *The Day Daddy Died* is the eighteen photo-collages by British multi-media artist Ian Breakwell.[4] The collages are not illustrations of the text,

---

[1] p. 98

[2] p. 120

[3] p. 48

[4] 1943–2005. Breakwell worked with the Artists Placement Group, which put artists into government institutions; Breakwell himself worked in secure mental institutions. See Ian *Breakwell's Diary 1964-1985,* Pluto, 1986, later adapted for television.

nor are they integrated into the text as in the books of Jeff Nuttall or Ann Quin's *Tripticks*. If anything, they are more reminiscent of the collaboration between B. S. Johnson and the photographer Julia Trevelyan Oman on *Street Children*, 1964 and even *Let Us Now Praise Famous Men*, 1941, James Agee and Walker Evans' collaboration on southern poverty in the U.S. Both the above are, *like The Day Daddy Died*, works of social realism, though not socialist realism; they do not expose a situation but do not propose a better alternative, as do some illustrated works of the 1930s, like the woodcut novels of Lynd Ward or the illustrated revolutionary works of Hugo Gellert or William Siegel.[1]

> Ian refuses, quite properly, to call them illustrations. The collages don't give another version of what is already in the text; it isn't Little Nell in an etching. He has constructed a narrative that runs parallel. I don't know if his work acts as an undercurrent or an overcurrent, because pictures make such a tremendous impact, words have some difficulty in standing up to them.[2]

Burns explained his working method with Breakwell:

> I felt from the start there was no point in simply 'illustrating,' I wanted—and yes, this hooks up with your comments on 'host of voices'—another voice. Ian seemed the right choice just because of his range of interests, literary and visual. I sent him early drafts of the novel, and he responded with early ideas for his collages. It was a neat additional interaction between his work and mine, that the text and the pictures together formed a collage, also the text and the pictures themselves were collages—a collage of collages.[3]

---

[1] see Francis Booth, *Comrades in Art*, 2012.

[2] Sugnet interview, op. cit., p. 166

[3] Madden interview, op. cit. In form the collages are reminiscent of earlier German works such as those of the Berlin Dada Group: John Heartfield; Hannah Höch; Kurt Schwitters (published in the UK by Stefan Themerson's Gabberbochus Press) and Raoul Hausmann, as well as the collages of the Russian Alexandr Rodchenko. Max Ernst himself, Burn's sometime inspiration, also made photomontages.

Burns' last novel, *Revolutions of the Night*, published in 1986[1], to some extent revisits the themes of his first: again we have a family with a mother who dies at the beginning (like Burns' own family)[2], as *The Day Daddy Died* had begun with the death of the father, though this time there are a son and a daughter rather than two sons, and this time we back in a realist/surrealist narrative in line with the Max Ernst painting, which, like *Europe After the Rain*, gives the book both its cover image and its title[3]. The first of a series of surreal images occurs right at the beginning of the novel.

> A watchtower had been constructed in a clearing in the forest, a trellis of scaffolding sixty feet high. A series of steel stairways led up to a viewing platform surmounted by a tall mast At the top of the mast was a weathervane.
>
> On that day the high platform was occupied by two people. A man in a wide-brimmed hat stood back and surveyed the forest. A young woman leaned over the guard rail and looked across at the next tower[4]

When asked to explain these two figures, Burns said:

> Those figures atop the tower are who they are. Where did they come from? From one of the hundreds of pictures, paintings, photographs I collected and assembled and from which grew the novel. I wanted to use the Ernst (cover/title) image early on, but not start with it—boring merely to repeat what the reader has just seen. Also needed to 'place' the three figures from Ernst, and did so by placing them in a landscape suggested by another Ernst picture with a tower and a forest clearing. The three on the tower echoed the three on the ground. The two groups

[1] I have extended my arbitrary cut-off date of 1980 so as to include all of Burns' novels.

[2] The novel might almost be called *The Day Mummy Died*.

[3] Pietà or Revolution by Night (Pietà ou La révolution la nuit, 1923, now in the Tate Gallery, London

[4] p. 9

> were connected by the young woman on the tower being Harry's sister, revealed in the penultimate line on page 10.[1]

This opening passage brings to mind Bob Dylan again: both the surreal imagery of *All Along the Watchtower*, released in 1967, which refers to the *Book of Isaiah*, and the line 'You don't need a weatherman to know which way the wind blows' from *Subterranean Homesick Blues*, released in 1965, which refers to the Weather Underground, a rough American equivalent of the Angry Brigade.

The narrative quickly introduces the family: the father Max [*sic*], 'the father of the family: his brick backbone, his strained back'[2], who feels his 'life had been water'[3]; his mistress Martha, who 'had money and two double chins'[4]; son Harry, 'cold as a soldier'[5] and daughter Hazel: 'Nude to her soul, like a Siamese cat, she spent hours brushing her hair and manicuring her slender fingers.'[6] Max and Martha make surreal love.

> When she showed him her way of loving, he fell against a table. Then he heard her giggle as he cuddled her, slipping hot milk under her skin. With the table lamp back on the table, the pillows plumped at the foot of the bed, her small eyes curled when he licked between her toes. Her head bent back, her legs lifted, as he pushed her on to pillows slippery with semen. His table legs were added to the fire, his worn-out stumps crackled with pain. Eggs in hand, eating her dinner, her mouth ached from being muzzled.[7]

Some of the passages seem like descriptions of surrealist paintings; this could describe a Magritte (and in fact the cover illustration's central figure does look as if he is from a Magritte painting): 'Two men were transferring brainpans from the tables to wickerwork baskets brought for the purpose. All wore homburg hats, town coats, sombre suits, clean white shirts, decorous cravats.'[8] And at one point, the reference to a painting becomes post-impressionist rather than surrealist: 'In the formal gardens, glimpsed through the tall hall windows, gentlemen in morning dress escorted ladies carrying parasols' is an exact description of Georges Seurat's *A Sunday Afternoon on the Island of La Grande Jatte.*

---

[1] Madden interview, op. cit.

[2] p. 31

[3] p. 15

[4] p. 16

[5] p. 15

[6] p. 37

[7] p 18

[8] p. 121

Harry becomes the main character and with his girlfriend Louise and Hazel's boyfriend Bob go to the coast after a highly surreal party.

> Harry picked up and smashed his sister's chair. He snapped its legs across his knee. . . Bob was preening his feathers. His famous eagle headdress now reached down to his waist. . .Most of the time, Martha had been upstairs with Pierre. She chose this moment to crash through to the refectory below. . . For a while, Bob had felt outdone. Now he charged in as an elephant, with a body made from a barrel, a lampshade hooked on the end of its trunk.[1]

After their trip the two couples become involved in a demonstration that they know nothing about; unlike in *The Angry Brigade*, this demonstration does not seem political. 'Here the crowds had gathered. Their banners bore crosses, doves, stars.'[2] Harry finds himself in the middle of a police charge and is arrested; a woman standing close to Hazel is shot by the police. Inside Harry's prison things become even more surreal.

> The warder outside their cell had the head of a lion. Each hour on the hour, he used his massive head as a door-knocker, with the big brass ring in his mouth. He held a club in one hand, a net in the other. From his belt hung a hoop of keys. The hoop was attached by a chain to a statue of the Virgin Mary bolted to the wall beside the door. At change of shift he was uncoupled and replaced.[3]

Harry, Hazel and Louise go south 'to be ready for the revolution when it comes'[4] and are involved in what seems to be a bombing.

> Crouched at the end of the path was a man in shock. Harry used his boot on a tall figure behind the hedge. A trooper with a machine-gun sprayed the sky. A hail of slugs caught the man. . . A red holdall had been left by the front door. It contained an alarm clock and a stick of dynamite. They both went off at half past eight.[5]

On the run, they catch 'the last train out of the country'; Hazel is assassinated, possibly by detectives in bowler hats, as worn by the central character in the Ernst painting; also as in the painting, all had 'the same features, the same neat

---

[1] p. 70
[2] p. 80
[3] p. 104
[4] p. 128
[5] p. 130

haircuts and suits, the same pensive look, the same sad, dutiful expression. They could have been brothers. The victim's features suggested that she, too, was a member of the same family.'[1] At the end of Burns' last novel, Harry ends in a landscape that could be from his first full-length novel, *Europe After the Rain*.

> The ruined town was like a continent after the flood. Masses of masonry and metal towered over rivers of bones and boulders, the trunks of trees, broken pipes and pylons, drains, poles, pillars. ladders, scaffolding, monumental gravestones, rusted machinery, worn-out engines, the rotting skins of animals and shreds of cloth, the skull of a buffalo, the skull of a horse, a siege of herons, a clamour of rooks, statues of princes mounted or on foot, an abandoned gantry, skeletal remains of old canoes, antlers, bedsteads, rafters, flowering heaps of rotten fruit, collections of corsets, an avalanche of carcasses, burning docks, a fairground, a forest, a quarry, an open cast mine, an ocean bed, a lone pinnacle of bone.[2]

[1] p. 159
[2] p. 162

eva figes

In an earlier chapter we saw how Nicholas Mosley envisaged both the evolution of a new human type, and the possibility of a new use of language. Feminists might reply to this that the new human type could be female, or, at least, that the new human values might be those now considered feminine, and that women may develop a new use of language, since existing languages are all imbued with the dominance of male values and not suited to women's expression and communication of their real feelings, which are thus partially hidden even from each other. Arguing this point, the French psychoanalyst Luce Irigaray criticises the logical basis of language, as Mosley does, though from a different perspective:

> Can female sexuality articulate itself, even minimally, within an Aristotelian type of logic? No. Within this logic, which dominates our most everyday statements - while speaking, at this moment, we are still observing its rules, female sexuality cannot articulate itself, except precisely as an 'undertone', a 'lack' in discourse. But why would this situation be unchanging? Why can one not transcend that logic? To speak outside it?[1]

Feminine language for Irigaray, as with Mosley's new use of language, would not be reducible to one meaning; there will not even be a 'superimposed hierarchy of meaning' for 'at each moment there is always for women 'at least two' meanings, without one being able to decide which meaning prevails'.[2]

This irreducible ambiguity of a feminine language would seem to work in favour of women writers becoming more experimental in their approach to the novel, or becoming poets. The reason more women have become novelists

---

[1] 'Women's Exile: Interview with Luce Irigaray', *Ideology and Consciousness* no. 1 May 1977, p. 64

[2] ibid. p. 65

according to Virginia Woolf, is that it is a younger, more malleable form than poetry (which, indeed, is as old as literature) and one which women have a chance of moulding to their own needs. However, even in the novel, a woman has the problem, according to Woolf, that 'the first thing she would find, setting pen to paper, was that there was no common sentence ready for her use.'[1] For Woolf, however, the novel should not become completely feminine, since too much femininity, like too much masculinity, spoiled any literary creation,[2] and nor should women consciously write from any sense of grievance.[3] Dorothy Richardson, on the other hand, deliberately saw herself as 'attempting to produce a feminine equivalent of the current masculine realism'[4], but also without any conscious feminine message.

Eva Figes, 1932-2012[5] is perhaps better known as the author of *Patriarchal Attitudes*, a work of feminism, than for her several novels and criticism, and indeed has complained that "I have written only one rational polemic whilst I am the author of six highly irrational and emotional novels'[6], yet she is often dismissed as merely a feminist. However, there is no explicit feminism in any of her novels, and, if anything makes her a 'feminine' writer, it is the ambiguity and duality, which is contained in her plots, as well as her sensitive and evocative use of language, rather than any polemicising.

Nevertheless, her novels are often concerned with women's lives and experience, which are uniformly meaningless and hard, but which they are unable to express, even to each other. The picture she paints in the novels is bleak and resigned, where *Patriarchal Attitudes*[7] looks to a radically different future. Whereas *Patriarchal Attitudes* portrays women's inability to escape from the trap of marriage and childbirth as

---

1 *A Room of One's Own* (London: Hogarth, 1929, repr. Panther 1977), p. 73. the same point is made in 'Women and Fiction', *Collected Essays* op. cit.

2 Femininity was not for Woolf necessarily the same as female.

3 *Room* op. cit. p. 99 and 'Women and Fiction', *Collected Essays* op. cit. p. 145

4 Quoted by John Rosenberg in his *Dorothy Richardson: The Genius They Forgot* (London: Duckworth, 1973), p. 84

5 Eva Figes died on August 28th 2012, six months after Christine Brooke-Rose.

6 Letter to *Times Literary Supplement* 12 Nov 1976, p. 1426

7 London: Faber, 1970, repr. Virago, 1978

something social to be altered, the result of long political and social repression, in the novels it always seems to be existential and inescapable.

The difference between the feminine and the masculine, or at least, the roles assigned to men and women are presented clearly in Eva Figes' first novel, *Equinox.*[1] Martin Winter, husband of Liz, is a scientist, and a logical thinker, exemplifying the Aristotelian type of thought we have seen Irigaray rejected for feminine expression: Liz says to him: 'You're always so logical - doesn't anything strike you as mysterious?'[2] His ways seem to Liz to be too simple:

> It's all right for you: you've got your job, one experiment logically leads to another, you don't have to make anything out of thin air, all you have to do is to uncover things that are already there and the things that are there are endless.[3]

Their respective attitudes to chess encapsulate their differences: 'his eye took in the problem from every angle, the idiocy of chance and luck ruled out, the variables assessed. It was her sort of game too: she liked the board with its grained wood and the ancient shape of the pieces.'[4]

In fact, Figes has said that the Winters represent the two sides of her own personality: 'the husband was not my husband really, though he had certain characteristics of my husband; he was me. I split myself into several bits: the husband was German-Jewish like me, and the woman herself was another aspect of me.'[5] Virginia Woolf, as we have seen, and Ann Quin, as we will see, also showed the co-existence of masculine and feminine in everyone.

Liz cannot accept either her mother's religious attitude or her husband's deterministic one, but feels that every life is unique and irreducible:

---

1 London: Secker & Warburg, 1966. Hereafter referred to as Eq. followed by page number.

2 Eq. 9

3 Eq. 10

4 Eq. 119

5 Interview in Burns & Sugnet op. cit. p. 34 (recorded several years before publication).

> we keep trying to plan and replan into the future, plan everything as though it were a well-organised fugue or a game of chess. Birth, marriage and death, all pre-ordained and made in heaven and leading into each other on Aristotelian principles . . . It can't be like that and if it were you would die prematurely of boredom. If it were like that there would be no sense in it either, simply the extension and repetition of absurdity. Every pattern grows out of itself: every life is a prime number.[1]

However, in Figes' other novels, life *is* 'like that'; rather than people's lives being prime numbers, they are seen as repetitions of each other, and as absurd and with 'no sense'. The traps which women fall into repeat themselves exactly for generation after generation, and the women, even though they know this, cannot warn each other or alter the cycle. In *Days*[2] , the lives of mother, daughter and grandmother are inextricably linked and doomed (the word is appropriate) to repeat each other; indeed it is sometimes impossible to tell whether the interior monologue is the mother's memories or the daughter's present thoughts, or both.

> My mother who is now an elderly woman, fell down yesterday . . . I knew it would happen, just as I already know how it will end . . . my mother's mother had a fall. Similar. That was a long time ago. A day, a number of days before now . . .
>
> But the fact that the two accidents are similar is merely an unfortunate coincidence.
>
> No. Not an accident. Not coincidental. I know what the x-rays will show, just as you know.[3]

'I knew. I had seen it happen before. And so, in fact, had she.'[4] There is the suggestion in *Days* that there is an atemporal fourth dimension in which these accidents are the same, and so escape from their repetition is impossible.

---

[1] Eq. 124

[2] London: Faber, 1974. Hereafter referred to as Da. The novel was much later made into a play and staged by the BBC in 1981.

[3] Da. 74

[4] Da. 103

In *Waking*[1] this inevitability is shown again as a woman's life is portrayed in seven short interior monologues at points in her life ranging from childhood to old age, or, alternatively, seven different women's lives are presented; it is never clear which. An implication of this is that women all share common experiences, and the worst aspects of these are inescapable. Though the women in Figes' novels cannot communicate these experiences to each other, even from mother to daughter, they sometimes feel a solidarity that goes beyond mere verbal expression: 'Suddenly we were the same age. She laughed. Comradely: girls together'[2]. However, Liz Winter, unlike the daughter in *Days*, feels estranged from her mother, and feels that she ought to have been able to communicate a sense of the misery and pointlessness of life, thereby giving her a chance to avoid it:

> if you had told me a long time ago, not necessarily in words either, not facts but the pain and pleasure and punishment which go to make up those facts, then you could have set me free, and kept yourself alive at the same time, because an umbilical cord runs both ways.[3]

The woman (or women) in *Waking* clearly sees the inevitability and cyclic nature of a woman's life:

> My life is clearly marked out now. When the child is fifteen I shall be forty. When she is a woman of twenty-five I will be fifty, the age of my mother. I worked it out in the hospital ward a few hours after she was born. Nil, twenty-five, fifty, in a recurring pattern . . . Once it had occurred to me it was as though the time was already spent in advance, everything I am reduced to numbers.[4]

---

[1] London: Hamish Hamilton, 1981. Hereafter referred to as Wa.

[2] Da. 55

[3] Eq. 128

[4] Wa. 40

In *Days*, the way women pass on the cycles of their lives is represented by the chair in the mother's hospital bedroom, which she waits for her daughter to occupy:

> I have studied the chair so long it has begun to resemble some sort of monument, a statue. A stiffened lap figure in a perpetual sitting posture, arms deprived of hands, extensions of wood which are able to accept but not touch, not hold, not grasp. The eternal figure with brave shoulders but no head. Mother, woman, as man has carved her out of wood or stone.[1]

The chair, the stone statue, represent the role of womanhood which men have created over the years, and from which women cannot escape, becoming always like their mothers. The daughter in *Days* does eventually occupy the chair, and the young woman in *Waking* sees that she will soon be as her mother is now: 'I have hardly begun to live, but soon I will be old'[2];

> I am changing, I know that. I will continue to change, and some day I will be old, a woman like my mother. Except that I do not want to turn into somebody like her, that is why I write it down, to remind myself how it was, how it is now, everything so intense.[3]

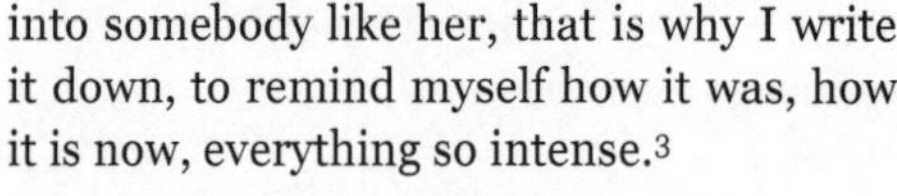

At this age, she compares herself with a chrysalis, and her clothes as the husk from which she emerges at night, but she knows that, far from turning into a butterfly, the time of her bright colours is now and that things will only become more drab and constricting; she will never be able to fly away. Not that this recurrence and inevitability affect only women: Stefan Konek in *Konek Landing*[4] also feels a sense of it: 'clearly, I have been witness on more, many occasions'[5]; 'having come round having once more realized that I had come round in a curve was that more

[1] Da. 42

[2] Wa. 24

[3] Wa. 28. She does in fact come to resemble her mother: pp. 62; 65

[4] London: Faber, 1969. Hereafter referred to as KL

[5] KL 125

should have appeared round full circle'.[1]

In both *Days* and *Waking* there is the implication that, in the state of semi-consciousness preceding full awakening there is at least a temporary relief from the trap of repetition and the straitjacket of socially imposed roles:

> Exist, followed by I. The knot of nerve ends looking out from the bedclothes. After that it does not take long to come back. Previous days come back to mind and modify me. Continuing to exist, I conclude: I still exist.[2]

In *Waking* too the woman says: 'In a sense I am born each morning'[3] (hence the ambiguity as to whether there is more than one woman, as all the sections portray women in this state of awakening, before their role takes over and they do not have to conform to imposed identities which differentiate them). This freedom is thoroughly enjoyed by the woman in *Waking*, the more so for being so temporary, but the woman in *Days* feels apprehensive about the loss of identity which, though constraining, is also her self-definition:

> That is when the trouble starts, after dark. Once the day has been terminated and I am delivered back to the womb of the dark, lying alone with my thoughts. Then the data so carefully sorted and arranged to make sense becomes jumbled again. I do not know where I am, or who. The walls, so carefully constructed to protect me, fade away, leaving me exposed, disoriented in incalculable dimensions of darkness.[4]

Liz Winter eventually finds her 'equinox', a balance of darkness and light, of solitude and relationship, freedom and constraint, which no subsequent Figes character discovers, and the others remain in their 'domestic martyrdom ', except for the short period of awakening. Also in this short period of solitude, they can feel free from the guilt which seems to be part of a woman's condition, however little deserved. The adolescent girl in *Waking* feels that: 'Nothing I do is right, nothing can, nothing could ever be enough.'[5] Liz Winter is seen and sees herself as 'wilful' for having a mind of her own, and the mother in *Days* is continually trying to be 'obedient' and no trouble to anyone: 'I was always good as a child. Obedient. I always disliked making an exhibition of myself, openly showing anger, rage, or hurt feelings. Now it has become easy: there is nothing

---

[1] KL 128

[2] Da. 9. *Winter Journey* (London: Faber, 1967; hereafter referred to as WJ) also begins with Janus awakening.

[3] Wa. 76

[4] Da. 8

[5] Wa. 21

left to hide.'[1]; 'When sister comes round I shall smile, and somehow show how anxious I am to co-operate.'[2]

In all Figes' work, the inevitability of life is set against the inevitability of nature, and its cyclic nature, which is reflected, as we have seen, in the cyclic nature of experience. Most of the novels are based on or at least refer to the cycles of nature: the titles of *Days* and *Equinox*; Liz Winter's name, the seven sections of *Waking* (the seven days of a week as well as the seven ages of man/woman); the single day of *Winter Journey;* Janus's name and his interest in clocks, and the twelve months of *Equinox* all keep the inevitability of nature continually in view. In *Winter Journey* and *Waking* the metaphor of life as a succession of seasons is made the most explicit: the winter journey is obviously death, as it is in the Schubert song-cycle which inspired it[3], and the woman in *Waking* describes her middle years as her 'summer': 'Now it is high summer, and if it has come late, it has come.'[4]; 'My body is awake after its long winter. It sings, it blossoms . . . It has come at last, the summer of my life.'[5]

But she knows that, in life as in nature, autumn and winter must follow summer: 'The summer will fade to the chill mists of autumn, after which come the dark nights, snow and death'[6]. This is the same for all life forms, but only humans are aware of it, and try to find some meaning and purpose in it:

> Flies carry germs, death on their feet, but I bear it no ill will. It was, after all, custom made for a purpose . . . It goes through life, single-mindedly fulfilling that purpose. I only wish I could do the same, but I have no idea what that purpose is, for which I might have been born. If there is one.[7]

---

1 Da. 18
2 Da. 25
3 See the interview with Figes in Burns and Sugnet op. cit.
4 Wa. 48/9
5 Wa. 51
6 Wa. 55
7 Da. 25

Even though they know it to be futile, people strive to avoid the inevitable movement of the seasons of their lives, and it is the gap between their feelings of free will and choice, which is given by rationality, and the dependence on a mortal body, which alienates humans permanently from nature: 'I do not like it, but no doubt it is a necessary part of the cycle. I am a tool of evolution, though it feels wrong.'[1]

> life which is consciousness should not become aware, realize itself from the outside, living organisms are a blind circuit, once realize that and the circuit is broken, what is the point, none, so that paralysis must follow, contemplate the mathematical proof of eternity in an age when it comes too late to mean anything, matter that has no meaning, that is only itself.[2]

The juxtaposition of inevitability and apparent freedom is felt most strongly by women, who have more awareness of cycles; not only menstrual ones, but daily and hourly ones, 'coping with each thing as it comes, within the narrow confines of each day'.[3] However, this alienation from nature does also affect men too, as Janus Stobbs's feelings show:

> Everything running into everything else and distinct, wildly illogical logic . . . so completely vulnerable and yet still there. Only I, you, stand in the middle and know not which way to turn, open-ended, look, stop, consider destruction. Steal the eggs, shoot the pheasant, frighten the squirrel out of his tiny wits. I am master here and I'll show you. Only I, you, stand empty-handed in the centre, pick things up and drop them . . . Only I have to listen to the spirit walking, confess in church on Sunday, I have sinned, only I have to choose, wanting nothing, walk through the snow in thin boots, wanting only to hibernate. Only I am shut out.[4]

But humans, unlike animals, cannot hibernate, and wake to a new life in the Spring. Human life, despite Janus's name, does not begin again where it ends – he knows that January is a month of 'palpably false beginnings'. 'When the leaves fall they fall, and the sun fades. Nothing comes back, not really. It isn't the same.'[5] Figes' use of cycles seems thus to refer to the sort of recurrence that Yeats and

---

[1] Wa. 73
[2] 'Bedsitter' in *Signature Anthology* (London: Calder & Boyars, 1875), p. 37
[3] Wa. 43
[4] WJ 97
[5] WJ 10

Joyce used, and even more to Eliot's *The Waste Land*[1] and its use of Frazer's account of the vegetation myths and ceremonies, which are also mentioned by Northrop Frye as being characteristic of the tragic mode; its opposite - spring and rebirth – being associated with comedy.[2] Also, this gap between rationality and physicality, as well as forming the basis for tragedy is precisely Camus' absurd. The sense of tragedy and absurdity is continually underlined by Figes' stress on the new beginnings which nature seems to provide for plant life and trees and grass and so on:

> Half a year from now, green planes, surfaces liable to shimmer when the wind blows, will appear in an orderly profusion cunningly designed to catch the maximum of falling, slanting summer light, energy sucked as greedily from the air as deep roots probing and branching underground. Everybody absorbing such nourishment as can be found in his immediate surroundings, trying to keep a firm foothold in the world, a grasp on his reality. Structured, an imprint that somehow functions, which is why the imprint continues, blindly struggling towards the sources of light.[3]

The tree outside the woman's hospital room in *Days* is often in her thoughts and she compares it to an old man, but one that will revive:

> Outside the old man's arm is getting misty, the outline dimmed and now lost in the dusk. I hope it will break out into leaf one day. I hope so. I should like to think so. A leaf, seen against the sun, is a webbed hand. The whole forest is a pattern of webbed hands, praying to the summer light.[4]

In *Nelly's Version*, Nelly has a similar feeling about nature's ability to start again: 'Why should trees be allowed a fresh start year after year, when human beings only have one springtime?'[5], and thinks of the new blouse she has bought in an attempt to give herself a new appearance: 'in no way is it comparable to the flowering fruit trees'.[6] *Nelly's Version* is in fact about a woman trying precisely to escape this cycle and make a new start though of course she never succeeds.

---

[1] Though here, winter is kind because it brings forgetfulness, and spring cruel, where in Figes the opposite is true.

[2] *The Anatomy of Criticism* (Princeton U.P., 1957, repr. 1971), p. 36

[3] WJ 123

[4] Da. 78

[5] London: Secker & Warburg, 1977, p. 134. hereafter referred to as NV

[6] NV 135

In *Konek Landing*, alone of all Figes' books, is, briefly, a pointer to overcoming this alienation from nature: Koenigson's father tells him that, instead of struggling against nature's inevitability, we should accept and come to terms with it.[1] Nature

> holds a message for all who still have ears to hear, those who are not at war with the world. What is beauty but law, and man has his essential being within that framework. We struggle and strive to no purpose.[2]

But Nature

> is all part of a purpose not understood but lived through, in accord with some infinite wisdom. So man, if he would only hear, the murmurings of these gracious woods, our heritage, a peace that comes from knowing that both man and his world are good.[3]

However, Koenigson says, 'that wood and surrounding land became an army practice range during the war, barbed wire ran through the undergrowth'[4]; so man, abusing both himself and nature, is 'at war with the world', and no chance to find peace with it.

None of Figes' characters can find a resigned attitude to life; partly because of the false expectations they have, leading them to see their lives as a lack. In *Equinox*, for instance, Liz's life is implicitly compared to the order and happiness of romantic fiction[5], where marriage is always the desired end. The reality of marriage is very different from the romantic image, and Figes not only shows this in the novels, but he describes it in *Patriarchal Attitudes*, where, as in *Equinox*, it is shown to be a trap which is 'endless, sprung from generation to generation'.[6] Not only is there no romance in any of Figes' marriages, there is a deep distrust and lack of communication between the sexes: the daughter in *Days* is wary of all men, having learnt from her father's example:

---

1 Cf Nicholas Mosley on the acceptance of inevitability, especially his comment on Julian Grenfell (p. 135)

2 KL 157/8

3 KL 158. This is ironical on Figes' part: Koenigson's was intended to satirise 'the pompous Teutonic type who loved walking in the woods etc. and then became thoroughly militaristic. The relationship between Koenigson and his father is based on that of Kafka and his dad.' (letter received from Eva Figes, 20th April 1982)

4 KL 158

5 Eq. 22/4

6 Eq. 16

> he was only a man after all, like other men, sympathetic certainly, kind as no one else I had wanted to confide in, but whom, in the last analysis, could one really trust? . . . It weighed like a lead ball, what I was keeping from him. I could feel it in my chest, expanding against my ribs. I wanted to trust him, I needed to. But he was also no doubt like my father, being a man, imponderable, mysterious. There was something about the breed I had not reckoned with till now.[1]

In *Waking* the girl sees the frustration and futility of her parents' marriage, and as an older woman she herself feels no real contact with her husband: 'his body is a hard cliff. The waves of my misery beat hopelessly into that rock, to fall back on itself. Nothing is allowed to crack his composure.'[2]

Nelly Dean, who almost escapes from the traps of marriage and identity, also finds her husband (when he catches up with her) unfeeling and unsympathetic; he thinks that people are easy to understand and seems to have no conception of their complexity or their needs. He certainly has no real feeling for Nelly, whom he uses merely for his own sexual gratification, having no thought either for her feelings or for her sexual satisfaction. Like all the men in Figes' novels, Paul Beard in *B.*[3] is completely unable to understand women. He is a great misogynist, and his name is intended to refer to Bluebeard: writing of *Jane Eyre*, Figes has said 'the story has obvious parallels with that of Bluebeard. Men destroy their wives, both because of the nature of their sexuality because of their economic advantages'[4], and Beard, in his remote house, like Bluebeard in his castle and Rochester at Thornfield Hall, does seem to destroy his wives, though unintentionally, since, like Beethoven, to whom the B. also refers, he is too absorbed in his work to take any notice of people. (His son's running away from the house is a reference to Beethoven's nephew's similar act.) However, Beard's misogyny and feelings of superior emotional strength are belied by his emotional collapse and his inability to come to terms with reality.

---

[1] Da. 61/2

[2] Wa. 34

[3] London: Faber 1972

[4] *Sex and Subterfuge: Women Writers to 1850* (London: Macmillan, 1982), p.133

Janus Stobbs also failed to understand his wife while she was alive, or to comprehend her frustration and misery:

> You've no feelings or you'd make me feel. What was she on about? What did she expect? Should have given her the flat of my hand like my mother would say, then she'd have felt something all right. But it was never like that. If I'd known what she meant: I tried hard enough . . . Men, she'd say in her rock bottom voice, all you can do is kill each other and then come home and give us more kids to fill the gap. Women.[1]

The trap of marriage makes women prisoners (though the adolescent girl in *Waking* feels a prisoner before she even thinks about marriage), both physically and emotionally: Liz Winter becomes a prisoner of her jealousy: 'my own feelings have become a trap, instead of a springboard like they used to be once.'[2] But she cannot escape either this 'Victorian' attitude or the institution of marriage. Even if she does escape long enough to have an affair with John, she knows that he too will 'take possession, like Martin took possession and you'll be a puppet again, on a string'[3], though she is ambivalent about the security that comes from this manipulation as opposed to the emptiness of freedom. When Martin tells her that she should be more free and live her own life, she replies: 'I wonder if I knew what it was. Only what is a life? If I had a life I'd be living it, don't you see?'[4] Similarly the mother in *Days* feels to have no life of her own: 'I have never had my own life to lead. It has always belonged to other people.'[5] Liz used to be a writer, which gave her a sense of independent existence she has now lost, and a sense of purpose she cannot now recapture:

> I'm not equipped for anything, except apparently for having babies that don't live. I can use words, I know, but you have to use words for something, you can't spin them about in a vacuum to make pretty patterns. And I'm in a vacuum, I don't have a life, apart from being your wife.[6]

Although her own baby died, she does not envy Frances, who has children, and therefore something to live for, but because of this, 'never seems to have time to

---

1 WJ 25
2 Eq. 56
3 Eq. 147
4 Eq. 10
5 Da. 80
6 Eq. 11

live'[1]. The paradox is that if she has freedom her life seems pointless, but finding a point to life would destroy the freedom to live it.

The only purpose she can see to her life is to have babies, and this seems to completely override her mental, rational life, as nature, as we have seen, ultimately overrides thought by its ability to destroy it. So Liz feels that, for all her creative powers as a writer, her procreative will take over, and she is merely a receptacle, however much she may feel like a complete person: 'Two days after the baby came and died her breasts became full and painful. She lay in bed knowing for the first time that her whole body was designed just for the purpose of procreation . . . I am a pod, bust open'[2]. This is exactly the feeling Paul Beard's wife Martha has about childbirth: "It's as though a huge hand came down and took hold of your body and squeezed the life out of it. I was just a pod, nothing more. As far as this force was concerned, it didn't matter whether I lived or not, after I had fulfilled my function.'[3] And again, the woman in *Waking* feels the incompatibility between her intellectual self and her childbearing function: she also feels like

> a pod, an envelope. To be torn up, used. Not the person I was so proud to be, so carefully cherished, nurtured through the growing years, a unique structure defined by high walls of emotion, shelves of intellect stacked with a whole armoury of definitions, constructs, the lofty roofbeam hung with colourful ideals, their fine silk stirring with each wind that blew.[4]

During childbirth 'the whole structure had come tumbling down'[5], and left her feeling empty and betrayed.

But if this childbearing function creates these feelings of helplessness, its removal would not restore a sense of free will, but would merely destroy any sense of purpose at all: 'Imagine how it must have been for her, having it all removed, her function. Nub. Kernel. Nothing now but a husk, for throwing away.'[6] Either way, the women cannot win.

---

1 Eq. 14
2 Eq. 29
3 *B.* 100
4 Wa. 30
5 ibid.
6 Da. 32/3

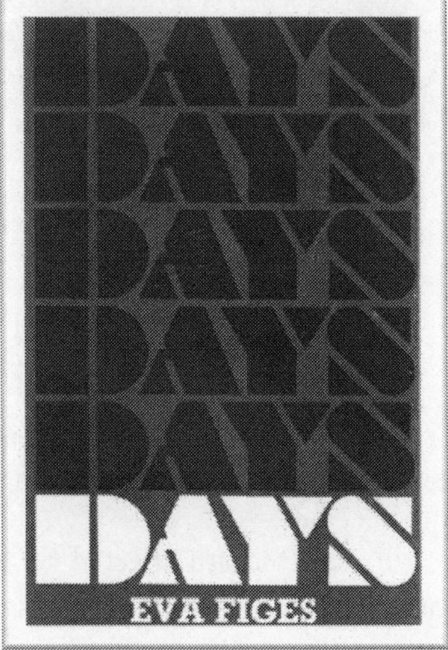

To give some sense of purpose to otherwise meaningless lives, Figes' women tend to lose themselves in housework – 'domestic martyrdom'. For the mother of the girl in *Waking* there could 'never be enough furniture to dust, silver to polish, or unnecessary chores to propitiate her rage'[1], and the daughter in *Days* similarly has to keep the house in order while her mother is in hospital, because 'neglect undermined the purpose of her whole life'[2]. But this is how her mother had also thought of her grandmother, and the cycle repeats itself: 'I dared not question how much was really necessary. It would have been like questioning her right to exist.'[3] As the women grow older they can lose themselves in pointless domesticity but when young they can still question this, and the mother in *Days* can still remember her own search for meaning and purpose and can imagine her daughter going through similar searching, to as little purpose:

> When I look at the chair I suddenly realise that the hours have dragged, heavily. It has all been a waste of time . . . Somewhere out there is a young girl, making her way through the day, looking for an explanation. By the time she comes here, probably towards the end of the day, she will not have found one. She will arrive baffled, confused, knowing that what she does know cannot be told. It is too much for the human mind to grasp. It certainly cannot be tolerated by the sick and ageing woman she will have to confront.
>
> She will try to avoid speaking the truth.
>
> Instead she will offer comfort, lies and evasions, knowing that eventually she must come to grips with the truth, the hard facts.[4]

Even though the mother knows her life has been pointless, she still hopes her death will provide some meaning:

---

1 Wa. 31
2 Da. 35
3 Da. 54
4 Da. 32

> There is, I now realise, nothing to wait for. Except, perhaps, a conclusion. Which will complete the pattern, like a jigsaw puzzle. Everything will fall into place, and I shall realize how much time I wasted, struggling to make things fit, looking at things from the wrong angle.[1]

The woman in *Waking* at this age has not yet become so resigned to the futility of her rapidly passing life:

> I want to push it into the background, the accumulation of failure, loss, nothing has turned out as I intended it should, when I was so sure I knew how, and why, and now the structures are falling down anyhow, the pain in my side, nobody to turn to, the world full of dying.[2]

Men too are affected by the sense of pointlessness, as they also are by cycles and repetition: Konek sees how humans are all joined in a 'progression' which goes inexorably on regardless of any individual, and which itself has no point or justification. Humans always have to seek a justification, however, and in this are worse off than butterflies:

> death not known but flown to, accepted utterly, being built in like life not known but flown through, integrated totally, cog within metaphorical cog, wheels within wheels each fitting into each other so that all can turn and the whole be none the wiser, not knowing the self as self from the outside the idiot progression having no senses tuned or turned for anything but the progression which when it comes to an end has so little sense of end . . . the whole progression need never have occurred at all.[3]

Death is one thing that men and women have in common, and it occurs as a theme throughout the novels. Whatever the individual's circumstances or action, death is inevitable: '*All faces wear the same hard masks, holes for predator's vision, does it matter just what shape the disease that finally kills us takes?*'[4] For Janus Stobbs, his winter journey, like that of the traveller in Schubert's *Winterreise*, must lead to death whichever road he takes: 'every path leads to the goal . . . / every stream reaches the sea / and every sorrow its grave'[5]. Figes uses

---

1 Da. 91

2 Wa. 68

3 KL 78

4 KL 79

5 From 'Irrlicht' by Wilhelm Müller, number nine in the Schubert *Winterreise* settings. My translation.

this winter landscape to throw things more sharply into focus, and emphasise people's solitude, as she made clear in *Equinox* where Liz, thinking about Christmas presents, thinks:

> Schubert's *Winterreise* for father. If I could paint I would paint only in the winter. When there is little you notice it more: the small touches of green against miles of brown earth, the intellectual interest of naked trees, brown-black against subtle grey-white skies.[1]

Like Schubert's wanderer, Stobbs feels the need to keep going while realising that his journey is bound to lead to death, and at the same time desires rest: 'I wander without end / restless and seeking rest / I see a signpost standing / imperturbably before my eyes / I must travel a road /along which nobody has yet returned.'[2] As the *Wanderlust* of the Romantics encapsulated this contradictory desire for continual movement and for death, so are Stobbs's desires contradictory. On the one hand, he feels that to keep moving is to keep alive - 'If you could keep moving for ever you could keep alive for ever, it stands to reason'[3] - but on the other, he knows the journey ends in death, and sometimes seems to wish this: at his wife's graveside he thinks: 'don't look down don't ever look down for the fear of falling and the wish to'.[4]

The other winter journey referred to in the novel is Scott's to the Antarctic. Scott was travelling to get nowhere or at least to nowhere better: 'To turn out day after day to the same trial over ice which is a little better, sometimes a little worse'[5]. The pole Scott is aiming for can be seen to represent death, from which, since all roads lead to it, every direction is the same: 'all directions are the same direction, stand on the south pole and look north, turn round and look north again. Man and beast are there none.'[6] Scott's journey is a metaphor for all human efforts and endeavours, which are all as futile and aimless. 'Once we have reached the pole there are other things, the frosty silence of the Milky Way, the North Star overhead, each direction the same direction'[7]. Like the mother in *Days*, Stobbs realises this futility as he grows older, and as she cannot pass the knowledge to her daughter, neither can Stobbs to his son:

---

1 Eq. 68. This well describes the rationale behind Figes' minimalism, and links her to Beckett, whose *Malone Dies* is in some ways similar to WJ (as is Eliot's *Gerontion*, though the inspiration was not these but Faulkner's *The Sound and the Fury* with its use of defective perception).

2 Müller, 'Der Wegweiser', Schubert's setting number 20.

3 WJ 15

4 WJ 41/2

5 WJ 63

6 WJ 117

7 WJ 116/7

> my son. He does not know and there is no way of warning him, that the sun will go out and a man must journey. Is it possible not to? To stay put in the sun? If he dies before his time, maybe. Otherwise the time will come: the black hole in the ice, the cold that burns, strange shadowless light. Even if you stay put in the afternoon sun there comes a point. And then only one direction remains.[1]

If men and women cannot help their sons and daughters, no-one can help anyone, and we are all alone, as Scott's companion Oates realised as he walked out alone in the snow to die: 'We cannot help each other, each has enough on his own. I am just going outside and I may be some time.'[2] All Figes' characters are ultimately alone, as Liz Winter tries to explain to her husband: 'I've been on my own since I was eight, and I know. We are all alone, all of the time, and the sooner you find that out the sooner you can start taking what you can find where you can find it.'[3]

Eva Figes has been interested in the difference between the identity and the self, the persona and the person, ever since, as a German Jewish child in England during the war, she found she was not considered like other people, but was seen as an alien, both because of her nationality and because of her religion. She had been discovering herself at her small English school when she was told by another child that she did not believe in God, since she was Jewish:

> Now it seemed that I did not know myself at all, or at least that the world had a label for me which I did not understand, which flatly contradicted everything I knew about myself. How was this possible? Was it like a secret

[1] WJ 65/6

[2] WJ 63

[3] Eq. 155

> disease, something under the skin, in my blood, which I did not know about? . . . The puzzle of identity remained at the back of my mind. I suppose it has been there all my life.[1]

Figes' women try to find an identity in various ways, often, as we have seen, by losing, or trying to lose, themselves in 'domestic martyrdom'. Even this is no guarantee of a stable and comforting sense of identity however:

> I can see the pattern of my day spread out. It is tied to the walls of this house, to the floors and windows, to objects such as milk bottles and saucepans, blankets, spoons and small shoes which need to be buckled regularly I do not know who I am amongst all this.[2]

They have a role, or various roles, but seem to find it impossible to identify completely with them, or to find an identity outside of them.

Stefan Konek also has various identities imposed upon him by different people: he is given a false name as a child; old Nelly seems to see him as her great-nephew; the landlady uses him as a substitute for her husband; Jan sees him as the helpless innocent he used to be, and the two children living rough see him as their protector. Nelly, in *Nelly's Version*, however, seems to have made the break from the roles of wife and mother by (or so it seems from the first notebook) losing her memory and hence her past and all it entails. Reading a book in the library she notes how

> the author describes human logic as a net of meridians and parallels thrown across the universe to make it captive. The more I thought about these lines, the more convinced I became that this insight had something to do with my own condition at present. I had escaped the net, just as, the author points out, the sun and stars had not conformed to the pattern established by man.[3]

This pattern is established not only by man for woman's identity, but by humans as a whole for the whole of reality: perception 'imposes a grid on reality'[4], as Figes has said that novelists do, and we cannot get outside of this grid, even though Nelly seems to do so temporarily. That for Figes memory and identity are linked and the only means of escape from the grid of identity is by escape from memory is established in *Equinox*:

---

1 *Little Eden: a Child at War* (London: Faber, 1978), p.74

2 Wa. 39

3 NV 118. These references in NV are to Donne.

4 Figes' note to 'On Stage', in *Beyond the Words* ed. Giles Gordon (London: Hutchinson, 1975), p. 113

> I am nothing, cold, clear and empty. I can't remember feeling quite like this before, pulled in no direction, impelled by nothing outside or inside to do anything. Not involved. Invalid. I'm a stranger to my own life, none of it means anything to me. I might have lost my memory (but I remember, the way I remember that Napoleon went to Waterloo in 1815) or walked into the wrong house by mistake. And maybe stayed there until it was too late to extricate myself.[1]

This is almost exactly Nelly's situation (and, according to the second notebook, she may not really have lost her memory any more than Liz Winter: the important point is that memory and identity feel to both women to be interlinked).

Nelly does not consciously think of having escaped from the domestic martyrdom of her previous identity (she could not, since, if she could remember it she would be trapped by it), but she does reflect on the way that most women drift from the dreams and promise of their youth into the futility of their maturity (as the women in *Waking* and *Days* do): 'Is this what we dreamed about from the start, or did we just allow ourselves to be carried along on the conveyor belt, until it was too late and we found ourselves trapped? Did we even struggle, protest?'[2] And we are given the ageing spinster Miss Wyckham, trapped completely in her futile life, who says (with unintended irony): 'But we mustn't think it has all been wasted, must we? We must remember the good times, mustn't we?'[3] No-one in a Figes novel ever has any good times.

Nelly's Version is about what is left when the socially imposed system of roles is removed – what, if anything is behind the mask. Nelly, without her past, is 'alone with myself, a stranger'[4], a 'walking blank, a node of nothingness'[1], who

---

[1] Eq. 116. This equation between loss of memory and loss of identity also informs Martin Amis's *Other People* (London: Cape, 1981) and Peter Marshall's *Ancient and Modern* (London: Hutchinson, 1970).

[2] NV 203

[3] NV 40

[4] NV 10

'lacked definition'[2]. As with Liz Winter, if she has some freedom, she has no direction or purpose for it, and so she waits in her hotel for someone to tell her, not merely what to do, but who to be. Initially she is worried about her lack of definition more because of what other people will think of her than for her own sake; she is at first quite content to wait. She invents a husband for herself and 'ceased to be questionable the moment I stopped being just myself, by myself.'[3] Nelly seems to see the flowing river as a metaphor for the self which exists, formless and ever-changing, behind the identity. Could it, she wonders,

> be right to name a river which was liquid in continuous motion, and could not really be called the same river for two minutes together . . . The pattern repeated itself again and again, but it was different water, not the same at all. Could it be said that the woman who walked through that porch on the left bank some time before lunch this morning was the same woman who had come out just now?[4]

All the people Nelly meets, however, seem to think everyone should have a fixed identity: her husband says 'where would any of us be without a past?'[5] And Miss Wyckham, who keeps all her old photographs, says to her: 'If you don't keep a hold on these things, how do you know who you are?'[6] The woman in the hotel also thinks people should know 'their place': in the old days, she says,

> 'children knew their place. Everybody did. One knew who one was.'
>
> 'Really?' I asked, and nodded warmly: 'That must have been nice. I wish I did.'
>
> 'There you are. That's just it. Nobody does nowadays. It can only end badly . . . All this so-called freedom. I don't hold with it. What's the good of being left to think for yourself if you don't know who you are . . . And you don't know who you are until you've been told. Nobody does. If people are left to decide for themselves it just wastes a lot of time and messes things up.'[7]

The woman's idea of the incompatibility of freedom and a sense of self seems to sum up the paradox Figes is presenting. Although she has been widely classed as a feminist writer, it is clear that she does not accept that women can simply throw

---

1 NV 17
2 NV 25
3 NV 10
4 NV 28
5 NV 145
6 NV 43
7 NV 75

off their imposed identities and become 'themselves', since it is not at all clear what those selves would be apart from the roles imposed on them.

Figes has explicitly tackled this problem in her feminist book *Patriarchal Attitudes*, and even here, though she is arguing that women's roles are not based on 'natural' properties of people, but are invented, she sees that they are not contrary to nature either, since nature does not provide us with an identity:

> what is a 'natural' man or woman? One is forced to answer that there is no such thing, unless one concludes that, since man is a social animal, his 'natural' condition is to be artificially conditioned, with variations in time and place. For centuries the word 'nature' has been used to bolster prejudices or to express, not reality, but a state of affairs that the user would wish to see.[1]

Women's identities are seen in Figes' books not only in terms of roles and masks, but also as an image in a mirror, an image created by men, and not a true image but a distorted one. Women therefore are not identical with their identity, and are necessarily split within themselves as they try to fit their self to its image: 'Woman, presented with an image in a mirror, has danced to that image in a hypnotic trance. And because she thought the image was herself, it became just that.'[2] But the image never did become completely the person, and a rigid image must of necessity split, since the most compliant reality can hardly fit it absolutely.'[3] The mirror is traditionally often used as a symbol of women's vanity, which is blamed for man's fall from Grace (into self-knowledge, self-consciousness, which looking in the mirror gives), and Milton's Eve's first action is to look at her own reflection. But Figes turns the tables and shows that the reflection a woman sees is created by men, and leads not to self-knowledge but to self-deception and self-estrangement.

Nelly (who may be schizophrenic, judging by the second notebook) feels separate from her own mirror image:

> Someone was in the room with me. I swung round sharply and said out loud: 'who are you, how did you get in?' and found myself staring into a long mirror. She stared back at me, this middle-aged woman, standing near the foot of the double bed with the wardrobe behind her. Neither of us moved. She looked as startled as I felt, just as aghast. The porter must

---

[1] op. cit. p. 14

[2] *Patriarchal Attitudes* p. 16. The connection between the mirror age and identity occurs in much modern women's writing - Isaak Dinesen for instance. Virginia Woolf reverses it in *A Room of One's Own* and says
that women reflect men's image, magnified to twice real size, back to them.

[3] ibid. p. 18

> have made a mistake and put me in the wrong room. I turned round to apologize and the room was empty. The figment of my imagination, this visual error, had vanished as suddenly as it had appeared.[1]

The image she sees is of a woman thoroughly trapped in a subservient role: 'I got the impression she was the kind of woman who had always relied on other people to make her decisions for her . . . I suspected that she had all her life known what she did not want, but had not dared to voice her objections for lack of an alternative.'[2] This is just the mirror image that Figes described in *Patriarchal Attitudes*, and of which Nelly is the 'true self'.

The girl in *Waking* also sees her mirror image as something apart from her self:

> Who are you? I whisper, and the solemn eyes stare back without a word. Sometimes I have felt their strange power turned on others, adults, those in authority. Now I turn it on men. I do not know why I, or rather she, since I do not feel completely one and the same person on such occasions, should do this, or want to.[3]

As she grows older, the self-division becomes wider, and she feels that her 'real' self is dead, while her 'mind disowns the body in which it is trapped.'[4]

> Nothing will bring back the person I used to be, who smiled at herself in the glass . . . What happened to her? I do not know, only that she slipped away one night, is now dead, will not come back, that I am doomed to drag about this other body who fills me with disgust, whom I do not like, nobody could. Eyes in the street . . . glance past or look straight through me as though I did not exist, that was when I first knew something had happened, that the person I had always been was dead, that nothing I did or could do would bring her back.[5]

Only in her 'summer'[6] does she look in the mirror and identify with (feel identical with, see her identity in) her image, her body, and even there she seems to feel some separation between her self and her body, as if they were identical but not the same, like twins.

---

[1] NV 13
[2] NV 169
[3] Wa. 26
[4] Wa. 71
[5] Wa. 70
[6] Wa. section 4

As well as the metaphor of the identity as mirror image, Figes makes much use of the comparison between social role and stage role. Liz Winter 'can't say no to anything behind footlights'[1], and Martin and Mrs. Reading are described as acting in a pantomime.[2] In *Days* the daughter, confronting her father with his adultery, consciously adopts a ready-made, theatrical role: 'I tried to control my voice, sustain this level of icy sarcasm. I was conscious of putting on an act. In a film I had seen a wife confront her husband with his adultery in this manner, using just this tone.'[3] The daughter is not only imitating a film role (and a cliché at that) but is usurping her mother's role as the injured party.

In *Tragedy and Social Evolution*[4], which is an account of the social functions of tragedy, Figes points out that, not only were women's stage roles written by men[5] but they were even acted by men until quite recently, who, in their performances emphasised the 'feminine' aspects of the character.[6] Women's stage roles have traditionally emphasised one or other of the two extreme versions of women's character (as imagined by men): the witch/whore/harridan, and the saint/angel[7]/virgin[8]. Cordelia as opposed to Goneril and Regan in *King Lear* illustrates the two types. Men have created an image of woman on the stage just as in life, where the 'types of women that our society has produced in the past, the roles they have played or failed to play, sprang from the dictates and expectations of men. Women have been largely man-made.'[9] Virginia Woolf pointed out that in literature written by men women were rarely friends: they were only seen in their relations to men. In Figes' work, the women are not seen in relationship to men as in the dramas she analyses, but neither are they seen in any real relationship with each other. Although they are destined to repeat the same cycles, Figes' women can never communicate this to each other.

---

[1] Eq. 34

[2] Eq. 69/70

[3] Da. 116

[4] London: John Calder, 1976

[5] Figes agrees with Woolf and George Eliot that the novel is the only art form young enough not to be imbued with male values and prejudices. See *Patriarchal Attitudes* p.19

[6] This is still true of, for instance, Japanese Noh drama

[7] cf. Virginia Woolf's Angel of the House

[8] Figes excepts Ibsen and Euripedes from all of this

[9] *Patriarchal Attitudes* p. 15

The themes of identity as role and of inescapable repetition in life come together in 'On Stage', a short story/play (the first two acts are described and the third is presented as a script), where a young actress looks to the theatre to provide her with a ready-made role/identity:

> do you think play-acting is the answer? I mean to find an identity? . . . I thought: if I have to get up there, in front of all those people, knowing I was being watched, having to remember my lines, I mean, you know, already written for me, makeup on my face, so that I looked like somebody. I thought, it would give some purpose to my life, a direction. I would have an identity, even if it was ready-made.[1]

Her male companion 'hadn't thought about it', but for the woman the stage brings a 'new dimension. That's what theatre means to me. Because outside, everything is so meaningless.'[2] In 'On Stage' the young couple find on the stage an old woman, who has started the play much younger, and came on the stage literally looking for a role to play, as the young couple do later (they are expecting to be auditioned for a part in a play, only they do not know, as we do, that they are in one already, as we all are in the sense of always playing roles). The older woman, and the man she earlier had with her, find themselves stuck on the stage and spend their lives there, just as, it is apparent, the younger couple will do, in a cyclic repetition typical of Figes. The older woman, Nelly, makes the best of her role, 'though, like all Figes' older women, she is not sure what the point of it is, and resorts to a striving for a spurious order and meaning:

> Nelly, once so sure about her future role, is now no longer sure of her own identity, and the past seems like a dream. But, being a lover of consistency, she believes in going on as they have begun. Life must be tidy, a well-made play, or one can be accused of having wasted it. She also considers it important to keep up appearances.[3]

---

1 in *Beyond the Words*, op. cit. p. 117
2 ibid. p. 126
3 ibid. pp. 115/6

The Nelly of *Nelly's Version* also sees herself as an actor looking for a part. She tries out various roles for the want of any 'direction' or script to go by: signing in at her hotel she thinks

> I admired my own coolness: I had seen it done in so many films and now I was doing it myself. Really, it was quite easy. I watched myself standing at the foot of the stairs and admired my own poise, the way I stood there, relaxed and confident, quite unafraid of scrutinising eyes. The porter arrived to show me to my room and I followed him up the carpeted staircase, noting my own progress with approval.[1]

Nelly not only realises that her role is not her identity, unlike most people, but can even watch her performance with detachment: 'it was the performance of my dreams, every line came pat.'[2] She does not perform quite so well when the police inspector arrives and she decides 'to act it out . . . the bystanders turned into an audience . . . one really needs a prepared script for this sort of thing'[3]. In the absence of a script or any knowledge of the 'plot'; 'I had totally miscalculated in my performance, got lost, and ended up by overacting in somebody else's story.'[4]

She does not know whose story she is in, but seems to see all the people she meets as characters also: looking at the old woman in the restaurant she decides 'there was something theatrical about her'[5], and the waiter seemed to be in a 'supporting role'.[6] At first she seems quite happy with the character she has been given to play: 'Whatever I was or might once have been, I certainly did not seem to be boring. In fact, I decided, it looked as though I would be good company.'[7] But she soon comes to resent the woman she sees in the mirror, and describes her as a 'certain character who is unfit to be written into any scenario I would wish to take part in or even pay to watch on an idle Saturday afternoon'[8], and she feels she is 'trapped by my unfortunate resemblance to a pathetic creature for whom I feel no affinity, only pity.'[9]

Despite her initial decision to wait until someone tells her what her role is to be, when her son and husband turn up, she resents their intrusion, and seems to prefer even her directionless freedom to the role they try to impose on her. She

[1] NV 9
[2] NV 10
[3] NV 61
[4] NV 63
[5] NV 22
[6] NV 24
[7] NV 11
[8] NV 15
[9] NV 186

says to her son: 'you really cannot expect me to try and fit in with your image, stop being me, and play some role you have assigned to me in your mind'[1]. She feels that 'since David's mother had appeared on the scene, my time was no longer really my own, and I no longer felt the sense of freedom I had known, however briefly, before David introduced her'[2]. Though, like Liz Winter, she does not know what to do with her freedom, she prefers it to the role of wife and mother she so nearly escaped, when she felt that 'one could, if necessary, go back to act one scene one'[3]. She realises, even early on, that however 'much I might dislike this appalling, this awful old woman, however distasteful I found her, it was becoming clear that I was not going to get rid of her so easily, if ever. I was stuck with her.'[4]

Nelly and her mirror image are 'stuck with each other now, like two inseparable sisters. One timid, the other hard and rebellious.'[5] Figes' men do not seem to have such split identities and mirror images as the women, but both Stefan Konek and Paul Beard seem to have *alter egos*. Konek says that Koenigson had 'begun to talk to me occasionally, much as a voice coming out of my own head. In the confined narrow spaces of a ship out at sea it is not usual for anybody to plan solitude, for the two of us to talk undisturbed occurs without warning.'[6] The two of them talk only when he has found solitude.

---

1 NV 161
2 NV 171, (David is her son.)
3 NV 14
4 NV 13
5 NV 169
6 KL 139

B. is a novel about the relationship between a writer and his creations.[1] Paul Beard is writing a novel about B., who may or may not be 'real', and *B.* may or may not be the novel he is writing. However, it is just as reasonable to see B. as the author of the novel and Beard as his creation; they represent two entirely different types of writer who both envy each other to some extent, and might invent a character of the other type to vicariously represent them: Beard is the commercially successful novelist writing books the public want to read, while B. is the stereotype of the Bohemian, inspired poet, living in squalor (as Beard later comes to do). Beard says:

> My books have earned me a comfortable living. But my own dogged and conscientious craftsmanship, my perhaps rather boring dedication to a work routine, do not bear comparison to the rare immediacy of his work, which was unique and irreplaceable.

Although he consciously detests the squalor of B.'s life, while drunk he fells his ordered life dissolving into something like it: 'I seemed to be acquiring a remarkable resemblance to my own character, B., although this was the side of his character I least wished to emulate.'

At the party where Beard first 'became aware of' B. (not 'met' him), Beard remembers: 'I felt split, a frequent occurrence on these occasions, acting myself conscientiously and. at the same time standing outside my own skin, watching myself act with some disapproval'[2] This could have been the time when Beard invented the persona of B. to be the Hyde to his Jekyll, and later he becomes more and more like B. in his squalor while B.'s identity becomes less and less independent: 'There are times when I cannot even remember why I wanted to write a book about B., whose existence is becoming increasingly doubtful.'[3]

It is, however, just as easy to read the book as though B. did 'exist', but only in the sense that any fictional characters do: Beard says, after B.'s death, because

---

[1] *B.* 31. This is rather reminiscent of Mosley's *Accident*, and the novel also resembles in some ways Bernard Malamud's *The Tenants* (London: Methuen , 1972) and Christopher Priest's *The Affirmation* (London: Faber, 1981)

[2] *B.* 31

[3] *B.* 105

he is dead I now have a duty to make him exist on the page, use my memory'[1]. Beard, near the beginning of the book at least, seems to be able to tell between 'real' and 'imaginary' characters, and says that Judith (his second wife) is 'my wife and not a character in of my own novels'[2], but his sense of the distinction between 'life' and fiction is often blurred, since he has removed himself from life, Flaubert-like, so that he can write, and thereby lost a grip on the reality he is trying to recreate: 'The figures of B. and Martha seem remote and hopelessly two-dimensional, little more than fictitious characters.'[3] To Beard, his fictional characters are more real than the people around him, whom he cannot understand or penetrate: 'although I have known my wife for two years and lived with her, that does not mean I could possibly really know her'[4]; and yet this was someone I had married, unhesitatingly, when I would never have presumed to use her as a character in a book, knowing her, as I did, so little.'[5] A review of *B.* at the time said: 'The novel insists upon a danger in the making of fiction; the fear of being eclipsed, forced out of reality by imaginary people, and the need to make fiction is characterized by a particular temperament.'[6]

The real point of *B.* seems to be the nature of the relationship between reality and imagination: Beard is invented by Figes; B. is (possibly) invented by him, and so on. Literary characters do have a reality in our minds, indeed, as Beard perceives, they may seem more real to us than actual people. Art, in fact, causes things to exist which did not exist before, or so Beard seems to imply when he reads from Plato: 'Any action which is the cause of a thing emerging from non-existence into existence might be called poetry.'[7] Beard compares the image in his mind after switching off a light to the image created by fiction: 'an after-image on the retina. How real was it, any more than the picture I would carry in my head for years and then transpose to the page, as I am doing now?'[8] He seems to see his literary creation as analogous to actual creation, and has to battle mentally to construct, and keep standing, the cottage: 'In spite of all disturbances yesterday, the cottage now stands . . . And although my mind holds the walls upright against immediate collapse I know just how tenuous the entire edifice is.'[9] Later in the book, as his reality starts to fade, he lives more and more in the edifice he has

[1] *B.* 31
[2] *B.* 58
[3] *B.* 56
[4] *B.* 58
[5] *B.* 62
[6] 'Imaginary invasions' *Times Literary Supplement, March 31* 1972
[7] *B.* 96
[8] *B.* 48
[9] *B.* 26

created: 'all I could do now was hold on, rely on words, I had built up a structure from inside my head.'[1]

This mental structure, difficult though it is, is easier than real life: writing is 'an escape from my real problems, an attempt to play God on paper, create order out of chaos because real life is always beyond my control.'[2]

> when it comes to it you are not much good at coping with reality. What is the good of this profession if it does not help me now? Instead I relegate anything really unpleasant, death or disaster, to a fantasy world where I idiotically think I am able to control it.[3]

Like all Figes' characters, Beard cannot control his own life, nor see any meaning to it, though he at least, like Liz Winter in her earlier life, can create order and meaning in his writing. But it is perhaps natural in all people to try to find order and meaning, as Liz says to Martin:

> 'Perhaps we expect too much, think life ought to be like art.'
> 'It's man's privilege to expect too much. That's why he didn't remain like the apes.'[4]

It may be that it is indeed art which leads people to see life as

> so unfinished and incomplete. We use art as a yardstick because it's full and rounded - but life isn't, bits lean nowhere in particular, there's a yawning gap somewhere in the middle, as for the beginning and end, they're there all right, as birth and death, but they're both more or less arbitrary and accidental.[5]

Not only art, but language itself creates the feeling that life itself should have a meaning:

> Meaning grows out of the word itself, unfolds like a seed and sprouts in all directions, bearing strange-tasting fruit. And we feed on it, hungry for meaning or just new flavours. Mankind is a breed of small monkeys swinging through a gigantic tropical forest grown out of the seeds of their own words. They never see the sky, the foliage is so dense and high. But then who wants to see the sky? Perhaps they actually grew the

---

1 *B.* 135
2 *B.* 56
3 *B.* 79
4 Eq. 117
5 Eq. 65

> forest of words to hide the horrible empty sky, vacant and grey and always the same.[1]

Like Liz, Paul Beard is concerned with the nature of the world: 'As a boy I was fascinated by structures . . . I thought, if I could only study the snowflake, catch its shape before it melted in my palm, somehow I would hold the secret of the universe.'[2] As he grows older, Beard realises that the world does not consist of neat patterns like snowflakes, or even like the movements of the stars, which he watches, but still feels that, through language and his writing, he can capture and understand reality:

> now I confine myself to human relationships, the way isolated experiences connect and form patterns . . . language does not melt quite as fast as a snowflake in the palm of your gloved hand, this was the only hold I could have on the world, apart from this I had to be satisfied, living with shadows, mostly in the dark.[3]

But, as we have seen, far from understanding human relationships, he hardly see others as people at all, just material for his work, into which he pulls them and destroys them: he is like

> a spider under some blind compulsion to go on spinning a thread of language from its own body, to fashion it into a wondrous web, then sit in the centre unable to communicate at all. They all become victims, those close to me.[4]

Nelly too thinks that writing can give order and meaning to life, and she decides to write down her experiences to form them into a pattern (though of course they do not form any pattern at all; writing only imposes order on life by falsifying it to some extent):

> I have now decided to impose some kind of narrative coherence on my life, or what is left of it. There must be some sense to it somewhere. Meanwhile it is passing, and I cannot get a grasp on it. 1 can find no meaning in it. The whole thing slips through my fingers like water or sand.[5]

---

[1] Eq. 92
[2] *B.* 92
[3] *B.* 125
[4] *B.* 89
[5] NV 186

She does in fact realise that to give any semblance of order to her life she must distort it, but still does it because the alternative is to have no meaning at all: 'I can never be sure to what extent I am falsifying. Everybody should have a story which is coherent, with a certain consistency. If I cannot vouch for its total accuracy, it does relieve my boredom and help to pass the time.'[1] Nelly's record of events is simply her 'version' of events, and has no unique claim to objectivity.[2]

Figes herself realises that in all writing a 'grid' is imposed on reality, and she tries to impose a different one, no more right or wrong, but simply one which questions existing ideas about reality and the recording of it. 'The artist provides messages about the nature of reality which, if he is successful, become internalized by one or more generation and becomes accepted as reality itself'[3]. The truths which come to be accepted tend to be those which are comforting and reassuring, such as that life has a meaning and a pattern. The mother in *Days* realises this as she tries from her bed to judge whether the window is square by swinging an imaginary ruler, but she knows she cannot be sure it 'does not change to fit on the journey. Hands have a habit of doing this too . . . They move towards the desired conclusion. Regardless of reality.'[4]

But Figes is not concerned about presenting the 'desired conclusion', or indeed any conclusion. She wants to leave us with a sense of irreducible ambiguity, to pose questions rather than answer them.

> Fiction, like all art, consists in making statements. Once a statement is repeated several times over people begin to forget that a statement is being made and really begin to believe that what they are being given is the whole and absolute truth. Most people prefer this, because it is so reassuring. But I do not wish people to be reassured in this way.[5]

'Good writers are concerned with truth, and truth compels the writer to tell it how it is, not how he or she would like it to be.'[6] Figes wants to present a vision of life, and particularly of women's 'wasted and tormented lives'[7], and not to entertain and reassure: 'I am less concerned now with creating beautiful artefacts and more with the problem of going on, of survival, of grasping where I am and coming to terms with it.'[8]

---

1 NV 187

2 *Wuthering Heights*, which is also partly narrated by Nelly Dean, could also be called Nelly's version, though this is not pursued in NV.

3 Note to 'On Stage' op. cit. p. 115

4 Da. 19

5 Note op. cit. pp. 114/5

6 *Sex and Subterfuge* op. cit. p. 56

7 Wa. 21

8 Note op. cit. p. 115

Although her vision of life is bleak and pessimistic in her novels, (as opposed to *Patriarchal Attitudes*, where she showed how the futility of women's lives is, at least partly, the result of male dominance as old as civilisation, but nevertheless changeable if women could learn enough about it), Figes sees her work as 'highly subversive, painful, disturbing, but ultimately constructive.'[1] For, as Kierkegaard said, the greatest misery is not to know that one is in a state of misery, and to feel pain, frustration and anger are at least signs of life: 'You believe in thinking for yourself, in being honest, and that's important . . . If you can feel pain you're alive all right. The people who are dead are the ones who don't know what's happening to them.'[2]

In a thought which would sum up Figes' work, Beard, rationalising his reasons for returning to the house where he spent his childhood, says:

> I am drawn to this house not only by a wish to recapture the past, a sense of loss which is, I suppose, a recurring theme in my writing, but by a wish to confirm isolation in physical surroundings. My wounds are the only way I now have of knowing I continue to exist.[3]

---

1 ibid.
2 Eq. 145
3 *B.* 107

b.s. johnson

The best-known and most vocal of the experimental novelists of the period was B. S. (Bryan Stanley William) Johnson, 1933-1973. He was born in Hammersmith, West London and, apart from his evacuation during the war, lived in London all his life.[1] After leaving school he worked as a bank clerk and then as an accounts clerk before taking a part-time pre-university course at Birkbeck College, London in 1955, after which he went to Kings College, London to read English. He was poetry editor of *Transatlantic Review* and in addition to his seven novels he published poetry[2], short stories[3] and edited several anthologies.[4] He also wrote and directed several film and television scripts, including the most well-known, the television programme *Fat Man on a Beach*[5].

Unlike most of the other authors of the time, he consciously labelled his work 'experimental', was a constant polemicist for the new in his own and others' writing and wrote a highly tendentious piece on his views on literature in the

---

[1] For a very full biography, see Jonathon Coe, *Like a Fiery Elephant: The Story of B. S. Johnson*, 2004. See also the Rayner Heppenstall chapter in this book for Heppenstall's personal views on Johnson's life, work and death, and the Ann Quin section for John Calder's comments on her and Johnson's deaths. For readings of Johnson's work, see Philip Tew, *B. S. Johnson: A Critical Reading, 2001;* Nicholas Tredell, *Fighting Fictions: The Novels of B.S. Johnson;* the collection of essays *Re-Reading B.S. Johnson*, ed. Philip Tew and Glen White, 2007; James Adona, *Graffiti and Late Modernism in B. S. Johnson's "Christie Malry's Own Double-Entry."*, 2011, and (in French) Vanessa Guignery, *Ceci n'est pas une fiction: Les romans vrais de B.S. Johnson,* 2009. Many details are also available at bsjohnson.org, the website of the B. S. Johnson Society and bsjohnson.info.

[2] *Poems*, 1964; *Poems 2*, 1972

[3] *Statement Against* Corpses (with Zulfikar Ghose), 1964 and *Aren't You Rather young to be Writing Your Memoirs?,* 1973

[4] *The Evacuees,* 1968; *All Bull: The National Servicemen,* 1973; *You Always Remember the First Time,* 1975

[5] Part of the script was reprinted posthumously in Giles Gordon's *Beyond the Words: Eleven writers in search of a new fiction*. The film can be viewed on YouTube.

introduction to his short story collection *Aren't You Rather Young to be Writing Your Memoirs?*

> Literary forms do become exhausted, clapped out as well. . . That is what seems to have happened to the nineteenth century narrative novel, too, by the outbreak of the First World War. No matter how good the writers are who now attempt it, it cannot be made to work for our time, and the writing of it is anachronistic, invalid, irrelevant, and perverse.[1]

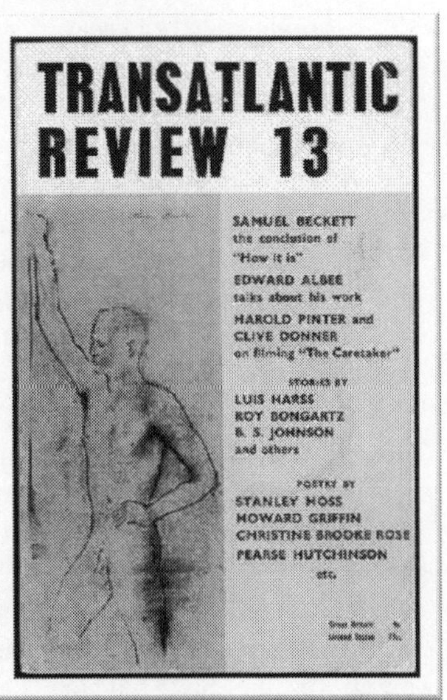

Johnson insisted: 'Telling stories really is telling lies. . . I am not interested in telling lies in my own novels.' For Johnson the term 'novel' is not synonymous with the term 'fiction', which itself is the opposite of 'truth'. All Johnson's works are to some extent autobiographical; not, to him, autobiographies, but novels. Advocating a new approach to the novel, Johnson compares it to other art forms, where the '*avant garde* of even ten years ago is now accepted in music and painting, is the establishment in the arts in some cases.'[2]

> The novelist cannot legitimately or successfully embody present-day reality in exhausted forms. If he is serious, he will be making a statement which attempts to change

[1] p. 14

[2] Anaïs Nin in *The Novel of the Future* said similarly: ' People accepted abstract painting in their homes and studied the abstractions of science, but in the jet age read novels which corresponded to the horse and buggy.' However, *pace* Johnson, the avant garde in music was no more accepted by the public than in literature; even though the elitist musical establishment embraced serial music, the public never accepted it. However, unlike in the literary life of this country but like that of France an establishment was formed at BBC under William Glock, who was controller from 1959 to 1972; contemporary, atonal music was privileged over traditional music, to the exclusion of tonal music, and the majority of the audience. See Leo Black, *BBC Music in the Glock Era and After: A Memoir,* 2010; A. M. Garnham, *Hans Keller and the BBC: The Musical Conscience of British Broadcasting 1959-1979, 2003* and, for the previous era, Jennifer Doctor, *The BBC and Ultra-Modern Music, 1922-1936: Shaping a Nation's Taste,* 2003.

> society towards a condition he conceives to be better, and he will be making at least implicitly a statement of faith in the evolution of the form in which he is working. Both these aspects of making are radical; this is inescapable unless he chooses escapism. Present-day reality is changing rapidly; it always has done, but for each generation it appears to be speeding up. Novelists must evolve (by inventing, borrowing, stealing or cobbling from other media) forms which will more or less satisfactorily contain an ever-changing reality, their own reality and not Dickens' reality or Hardy's reality or even James Joyce's reality.
>
> Present-day reality is markedly different from say nineteenth-century reality. Then it was possible to believe in pattern and eternity, but today what characterises our reality is the probability that chaos is the most likely explanation; while at the same time recognising that even to seek an explanation represents a denial of chaos.[1]

However, despite, or more likely because of his persistent championing of experimentalism and the and sarcasm about traditional novelists, there was a view expressed by many of his reviewers, no doubt feeling bated by Johnson's combativeness, that underneath the stylistic innovations there was an old-fashioned storyteller trying to get out and, worse, that the innovations stifled rather than revealed the stories and Johnson's gifted prose style. The reviewers wanted to like him but felt he was deliberately masking his talent, as if deliberately to spite them. A.S. Byatt commented on Johnson's 'holes, serifs, columnar and shuffled printed surfaces. Through and athwart them we glimpse a plain, good, unfussy, derivative realist prose that can somehow only come about by declaring that *that* was not what it meant to be, not what it meant at all.[2] About *Albert Angelo* a reviewer said:

> The reader is aware all the time of the novel as it might have been written in conventional form. Mr. Johnson builds up admirably his sense of place, his schoolmaster's feelings of frustration and his unbearable loneliness. He parodies amusingly and can write movingly.

[1] *Memoirs*, pp. 16/17

. 'People in Paper Houses' in *The Contemporary English Novel*, Stratford-Upon-Avon Studies 18, ed. Malcolm Bradbury and David Palmer. London: Arnold, 1979, p. 30

> His experimental techniques, instead of enhancing these qualities, seem to detract from them by intruding his own acute self-consciousness. There is a danger, which his defensive passages emphasise, that this sort of writing, far from making for greater honesty, sets up the author as an additional barrier between the reader and the book's subject.[1]

And in a review of *Trawl*:

> B.S. Johnson sees himself as an avant-garde novelist and at first sight *Trawl* – format, epigraph, opening page – looks as though its claim on our attention might be originality. The appearance is misleading: Mr. Johnson's sensibility is thoroughly traditional and the technical method turns out to be a simplification of that used by Joyce in the Stephen Dedalus chapters of *Ulysses*. None of it presents any difficulty to the common reader, but it provokes a good deal of irritation at the sight of misused talent. . . Mr. Johnson's real talent is for the traditional novel of character and narrative. His dallyings with experiment are irritating because they produce arbitrary gaps in what is elsewhere a coherent story. Most unjustifiable of all is his insistent echoing of the rhythms of Beckett, to whom he gestures self-consciously by naming the trawler's wireless operator Molloy. In Beckett the pedantic enumeration of trivialities is an index of desperation about the status of perceptions: but Mr. Johnson's narrator is no Watt and his mimicry merely leads to an unintended facetiousness and a feeling of the consciously literary which obscures the true nature which is elsewhere given him, convincingly and even movingly, by his creator'[2]

Perhaps not surprisingly, *The Unfortunates,* consisting of short, bound sections in a box and designed to be read in random order found a great resistance among reviewers, while drawing the same accusation of disguised naturalism. One seemed to accept William Burroughs but not Johnson: 'Cut-ups are all very well, but B.S. Jonson's new "experimental" novel is more like a carve-up, discreetly doctored naturalism in a brazen avant-garde wrapping.'[3] And about the novelist's interventions in the text of *Chrisitie Malry* another reviewer said:

> Mr. Johnson's best defence of his minimalist techniques might lie rather in the writing of better novels, in this form or another form, than in such slyly self-excusing interventions. As so often with this gifted, ingenious, amusing – and frustrating – writer's work, the better novel does, indeed

[1] Unsigned review 'Author as Obstacle' *Times Literary Supplement*, (TLS) August 6 1964
[2] Douglas Hewitt 'The Shallow End', TLS, November 10 1966
[3] Unsigned review 'Shake Well Before Use' TLS, February 20, 1969

> seem to lie somewhere just round a corner which he continually refuses to turn. . . In the last analysis, the tribute one pays to Mr. Johnson, who has yet again obscured his abilities in gauze of fictitious devices, is that one finishes his novel wanting more of everything in it that even remotely begins to *extend* him. Unhappily, at least while he is set on his present course, it is likely to be the last tribute he actually wants. [1]

Similarly a review published a few days before Johnson's death said:

> B.S. Johnson continues to tantalize his readers with the prospect of a novelist who commands very many of the old-fashioned virtues and yet resolutely strives to cast them out of his writings. Naturally they keep turning up, much against his conscious will; a considerable storyteller's skill, a talent for creating characters who tend to live beyond his control, an ability to write sustained and vigorous prose, a robust an inventive humour. It is all very inconvenient because Mr. Johnson would not have it this way. He is against narrative, against fictions of all kinds, against novels which require effort to appreciate, and balefully serious about his conception of the way his medium should develop.[2]

On top of this relentless negativity in the press were accusations, sometimes justified, that his innovations were not in fact original, and were borrowed from

[1] Unsigned review 'Please be Brief", *Times Literary Supplement,* February 9 1973
[2] Unsigned review 'Against Nature', *Times Literary Supplement,* November 9 1973

earlier writers. It is true that definite influences and precursors can be traced for most of his novels: it has been suggested[1] that Günter Grass's *Tin Drum*, 1959 is a direct influence on *Travelling People* in addition to its obvious, and acknowledged debt to Sterne; *House Mother Normal* seems to take its grid technique directly from Philip Toynbee's *Tea with Mrs. Goodman*, 1947 (see Goodman's illustration of this in his section in the Fellow Travellers chapter in this book); *Trawl* is very Beckett-like, as was pointed out by the reviewer above; *Christie Malry* is like Fowles' *The Collector*, 1963 in subject; *The Unfortunates* may have been influenced by French novelist Marc Saporta's *Composition No. 1*, 1962– also a novel of unbound pages in a box, with instructions to shuffle them like a pack of cards[2]. Jeff Nuttall implied that the idea for *Albert Angelo* was taken from his *Mr Watkins Got Drunk and had to be Carried Home*, 1964, an idea he himself had got from William Burroughs.[3] Sadly, the exception to all this is his last novel, the posthumously published *See the Old Lady Decently*, the first of a projected trilogy. This is an original and deeply felt novel, which may have pointed the way in which he would have gone if he had lived. Sadly he did not live and took his own life in November 1973, soon after Ann Quin.

---

1 By Ronald Hayman in *The Novel Today: 1967-1975* (Harlow: Longman, 1976), p. 6

2 First published in English in Richard Howard's translation. New York: Simon & Schuster, 1963. Saporta's instructions are:

> The reader is requested to shuffle these pages like a deck of cards; to cut, if he likes, with his left hand, as at a fortuneteller's. The order the pages then assume will orient X's fate... the number of possible compositions is infinite.

3 'Keith, John, Bob, Lois, me and Nick Watkins provided accounts and Nick set it as a subject at the school where he was teaching, so provided some marvellous copy a good long time before Brian [*sic*] Johnson used the same technique in *Albert Angelo*. The result, sieved and shuffled, was *Mr. Watkins*.' See *Bomb Culture* (London: McGibbon and Kee, 1968), p. 150. However, even if Johnson was influenced by Nuttall's technique of using his school children's misspelt writing in the text it could not have been a 'good long time' before, as *Albert Angelo* was also published in 1964.

The 1964 text for *Street Children* by Johnson accompanies photographs of London children playing in the street by Julia Trevelyan Oman (1930 – 1973), mainly remembered as a set designer for film and theatre. In a way it is reminiscent of *Let Us Now Praise Famous Men*, 1936, where James Agee's text mythologises the poverty captured by Walker Evans' photographs. The images are printed in a very grainy black and white, and so look older than their 1964 publication date; they might almost be wartime photographs. But although they give no hint of the 'swinging sixties', and seem to come from a different and much older world, they do reflect a community that was being rapidly lost at that time, as slum clearances were destroying old housing and replacing it with high-rise tower blocks. However, the way the children look at the camera is always ambivalent and Johnson's text eschews nostalgia and brings out the threatening and threatened aspect of the children's response to the camera in a rather existentialist tone.

> *They don't have to tell me about this human condition: I'm in it. They don't have to tell me what life's about, because I know already, and it's about hardness. Hardness and being on my own, quite on my own. You understand that much right from the beginning, from the first time the pavement comes up and hits you, from the first time you look round for someone you expected to be there and they aren't. Oh, I know you can get close to people, but that's not the same. In the end you're just on your own.*
>
> *But that's not the point. The point is that you have to go on living in it, life, and not only just put up with it, either, but let it see that it doesn't matter to you. That you're going to go on living however many times things come up and knock you flat, however many people aren't there when you expected them to be.*
>
> *So they don't have to tell me about it: I'm in it, right in it. You just have to go on.*[1]

This Beckettian passage, especially the last sentence, which is reminiscent of the end of the *Unnameable*,[2] is set opposite a picture of a young boy looking fierce, with fists clenched, which is also on the front cover. The text is laid out in a

[1] no page numbers
[2] first published in English in 1958.

variety of typefaces and styles, and sometimes approaches an early form of concrete poetry.

diffident *restless*
nervous *distrustful* *anxious*
timorous *faltering*

hesitant suspicious perturbed concerned
unconfident disquieted uneasy apprehensive
dismayed

alarmed
dreading intimidated
chilled threatened beset
scared

afraid frightened harrowed
despondent unmanned

aghast appalled panicstricken

horrified

terrified

petrified

Although Johnson is interpreting the pictures in his own way, possibly reflecting his own childhood, the existential terror of some of the text sometimes goes beyond mere interpretation, giving the pictures another dimension and telling another kind of story altogether to the cosy reminiscences usually expected to accompany images of the children of this time; solidarity not solitude is the normal reading.

> . . . don't want to have to stay with lady again while she goes to buy a baby . . . don't want a baby . . . lady . . . I don't want to have to stay with a lady again while she goes . . .

The 1964 collection *Statement Against Corpses* contains nine short stories by Johnson and five by his close friend and collaborator Zulfikar Ghose; two of Johnson's stories reappear in *Aren't You Rather Young to be Writing your Memoirs?* The book is prefaced by a statement of intent, combative and provocative as all Johnson's early statements of intent were:

> These short stories have been written in the knowledge that the form is in decline, but in the belief that this is due to no fault inherent in the form.
>
> The short story deserves, but seldom receives, the same precise attention to language as that given normally only to a poem.
>
> This book represents a joint attempt, through demonstration of the form's wide technical range, to draw attention to a literary form which is quite undeservedly neglected.
>
> B. S. JOHNSON
> ZULFIKAR GHOSE

All the stories are noticeably London-centred. 'Clean Living is the Real Safeguard' is about evacuees, like Johnson himself, and the subjects of his anthology of that name; 'Perhaps It's These Hormones' about a pop star who is already *passé* only two years after hitting stardom and 'Statement' is a monologue, or one side of a conversation; a statement to the police by a young man in a car accident.

> Since we were cut off from our environment, our home back-ground that is, we thought we ought to take our places in a higher one, just like we thought our education had fitted us for. So Terry and me knock around with the middle-class women we find at college, and he gets married to this Janine from Chichester. . . Anyway, this business of not fitting in anywhere is what Terry and me spend nearly the whole of tonight talking about. You see I'm a teacher now, I teach these kids at a Sec Mod, and I feel about this. Of course they don't accept me as one of

> themselves, as I was, once. I'm just to them a representative of authority, just as you bastards are.[1]

> I know you don't believe I went to college. But I'm a London boy, mate. I'm talking like this to you because you *din't* go to university. See? I can put the right accent on for the right people. That's what it does for you, a college education. Makes you so's you can talk to everybody but be accepted by nobody.[2]

Like Johnson, the narrator is separated from his roots: Grammar Schools tore that generation away from the working-class families they grew up in and made it difficult to communicate with their parents; he is also just out of being a teenager; too young to be considered fully adult but too old to connect with the school children he teaches. He has suddenly become part of the system of authority he resents.

'Broad Thoughts from a Home' and 'Never Heard it Called That Before' are reprinted in *Memoirs*. In 'Sheela-Na-Gig', a Londoner in Wales sees in an old church the mythical figure of the title: 'narrow face, huge eyes, thin lips, skeletal ribs, legs haunched high and wide, stick-like arms outside and under the thighs for the hands to hold open an enormously exaggerated vulva.'[3] The terrifying female deity symbolises death and procreation, the twin aspects of life, in the same figure, inextricably linked as they are. He later picks up a hitchhiker who turns out to be her embodiment. Finally in Johnson's section of the book, 'Only the Stones' is about Henry, who doesn't believe in God; he almost literally throws rocks at God in his frustration with life. 'If there is a fucking God, then He's going to have a fucking lot of explaining to do when I fucking meet Him, I can fucking tell you that.'[4]

---

[1] p. 44. This scenario returns in *Albert Angelo*.

[2] p. 41

[3] p. 95

[4] p. 108

Named after the game of Consequences, in which one person tells part of a story and passes it on to the next person[1], *London Consequences* was commissioned by the Festivals of London 1972 and edited by Margaret Drabble and B. S. Johnson, who invited eighteen London-based novelists to contribute a chapter each, including, from this study Alan Burns, Eva Figes, Rayner Heppenstall, Stefan Themerson, Paul Ableman and Julian Mitchell.

> The editors, who wrote the first and last chapters together, gave the other novelists a very brief outline of the two main characters and apportioned a fixed period in one day for each to write about them; the typescript then circulated consecutively, each writer reading all that his predecessors had written.'[2]

> 'The idea for this novel came up in a committee meeting of the Literary Panel of the Greater London Arts Association. We were discussing ways of involving writers in the 1972 Festivals of London, and a communal novel seemed a possible method of doing this. . . . everybody promised to write his or her chapter in five days, and pass on the accumulating manuscript. Nobody was late and nobody dropped out.'[3]

One of the novelists invited, Rayner Heppenstall recalls a meeting at Margaret Drabble's house on April 2nd 1972 to discuss it. By April 11th he had the details.

> The action of the composite novel is to take place on yesterday's date. each of us being allocated either the wife or the husband for an hour and a half. I have the wife in the afternoon. I shall receive three-fifths of the novel from Piers Paul Read on June 7th and on the 12th will pass it on to

---

[1] The French Surrealists played a similar game with figure drawings called *Le Corps Exquis,* and the practice goes back at least as far as the medieval Japanese poetry tradition of *renga.*

[2] Back cover

[3] Editors' Note

> a coloured novelist, Wilson Harris. This sequence will be convenient, in that we live within walking distance of each other.[1]

The first chapter sets up a domestic breakfast on Easter Saturday 1971, with political journalist Anthony Sheridan and his wife Judith, with children Harriet, Charlotte and Aaron. They had planned to spend the day together but he is called in to work by his boss, Twomey; he does not know why. The novel ends with chapter 20, on the afternoon of the same day with the couple back at home. The novel winds through many unlikely events in the course of the day, with each novelist determined to put her/his own twist into the narrative, and at the end the two editors write a satirical summary as if spoken by the two characters, who know they are characters in a novel.

> 'I've never had a worse day in my life.' He said.
> 'Neither have I,' said she.
> 'All those novellers at us, one after another.'
> 'I've never been through so many hands in one day.'
> 'I'm absolutely knackered.'[2]

> 'I know it's impossible.' Said the interviewer for all tele-cultural occasions, 'but what would you do if you were invited to write a novel together?
> Twenty voices answered in Babel of incomprehensibility: realists and experimentalists, cynics and idealists, obscurantists and populists, men and women, young and unyoung, poor and poorer, all talked and none listened.'[3]

The book included a competition with a £100 prize for any reader who could identify all the novelists correctly; there was an entry form to be torn out from the back of the book. It does not seem to be recorded if anyone claimed the prize but it seems unlikely that anyone could identify all of them from such short sections. I personally could only identify one for certain: Chapter 18.

> "Actually, I must confess that the only thing I still remember of my studies is that last sentence, you know, the sacred Number 7. At my time it was the craze of all undergraduate parties!" '
> 'What was the Number 7?' the White Poodle asked.

---

[1] *The Master Eccentric: The Journals of Rayner Heppenstall*. London: Allison and Busby, 1986

[2] p. 149

[3] p. 150

> '*Whereof one cannot speak, thereof one must be silent,*' said the Black Poodle.
> 'Oh,' said the White Poodle.
> '"What is that number 7?" asked the detective. But they were completely ignoring him by now.[1]

Only Stefan Themerson could turn a domestic story about a marriage into a philosophical disquisition concerning a detective and two talking poodles who bark 'Wwow, Wwow'.

The collection *Aren't You Rather Young to be Writing Your Memoirs?* was published in 1973 after all Johnson's other books except the posthumous *See the Old Lady Decently*, though several of what Johnson prefers to call 'pieces of prose (you will understand my avoidance of the term *short story*)'[2] had previously appeared elsewhere, going back as far as 1960. Johnson took the opportunity, as we have already seen, to write a manifesto in the form of an introduction setting out his ideas on experimental writing and describing his approach to each of his works individually.

In the title story the narrator is fishing with his wife; he meets some young men with shotguns whom he presumes to be poachers. However, he does not presume too much, nor give the reader any resolution of the story, even after the gunshots are heard.

> But you can provide your own surmises or even your own ending, as you are inclined. For that matter, I have conveniently left enough obscure or even unknown for you to suggest your own beginning; and your own middle as well, if you reject mine. But I know you love a story with gunplay in it.
>
> I am concerned only to tell you what appears to me to

---

[1] p. 138
[2] p. 30

have been the truth, as it happened to me. as it
appears to have happened to me. Why me?
That, I may honestly reply, is a good question.
Have I not interested you enough to make you want to
read this far? Have there not been one or two wry
moments, the occasional uncommon word?
Why do you want me to tidy up life, to
explain? Do you want me to explain?
Do you ask of your bookmaker that he
explain? Madame, I am a professional![1]

'Never Heard it Called That Before' is a rather Shandean 'dissertation' on the origin of the name of the famous Balls Pond Road London, often sniggered at by schoolchildren – Johnson sniggers too; 'A Few Selected Sentences' is just that: a collection of apparently random sentences and paragraphs with no discernible connection or narrative form; 'Instructions for the Use of Women; or Here, You've Been Done!' is a short and explicit description of an uncomfortable sexual encounter with a young woman, whose name changes every time she is mentioned:

I shall call her Winnie, or
Rachel, or Stella, or any other name that reasonably
preserves her gender, as the mood takes me, or rather as
whatever comes to mind at the time a proper name
seems to make the rhythm of the sentence a little less of
a failure. And I shall make unthrifting use of the feminine
personal pronouns. But, whichever, no burden of
universality is to be laid upon the appellative; or on
anything else, either.

I wonder is anyone still reading?[2]

Johnson admits that 'the unsatisfactoriness of the relationship is being reflected or refracted in what it would be a joke to call the narrative. A suicidal point: make it as unsatisfactory as possible for the reader in order to convey more nearly the point of unsatisfactoriness.'[3] In view of the hostile reviews noted above and Johnson's actual suicide, this is an arresting statement. The story ends, as the second half of the title indicates with an apparently unrelated, crude and very old

---

[1] p. 41
[2] p. 83
[3] p. 88

dirty joke. 'Broad Thoughts from a Home' is told entirely in the form of headings and descriptions, highly reminiscent of the beginning of Flann O'Brien's *At Swim-Two-Birds*, 1939. The beginning description is very like those from Henry Henry's description of himself in *Travelling People*, the descriptions of the characters in *House Mother Normal* and some passages in Ann Quin's *Tripticks:*

> *Description of Robert:*
>
> Height: 6' 8"
> Weight: 14 st. 10 lbs.
> Eyes: honeybrown
> Complexion: pallid
> Hair: Fair, riotous
> Features: mobile
> Collarband: 15
> Disposition: agitated
> Bearing: all over the place
> Age: twenty-two years
> Sex: unimportant
> Spectacles: worn, horn
> Teeth: irregular
> Apparel: eccentric only in colour
> Overall impression: long
>
> *Nature of statement*: exploratory-aggressive.
> Samuel said: Crap.
> *Description of Samuel*: large
> *Description of description*: pithier
> *Nature of reply*: somewhat obscene.[1]

The piece ends with a choice of three endings: the Religious, the Mundane and the Impossible. 'These Count as Fictions' is about a man who regularly visits a brothel, told in a self-consciously old-fashioned, polite tone; the final piece, 'Everyone Knows Somebody Who's Dead' is a story about the narrator's relationship with a friend over a period of several years, but told with the explicit instructions of the *XLCR Mechanical Plot-Finding Formula*, which had been put under the door of the narrator of the previous story. It, and the book, end: 'There, I have fully satisfied the XLCR rules, I think. Popular acclaim must surely follow.'[2] But of course it wouldn't.

---

[1] p. 93
[2] p. 140

In the *Prelude* to his first novel, *Travelling People*, Johnson is already aggressively (and arrogantly - though the arrogance is presumably intended to be ironic) attacking the conventional novel. 'After comparatively little consideration, I decided that one style for one novel was a convention that I resented most strongly.'[1] He goes on to say that he intends to keep the devices of the novel constantly visible. The reader's 'suspension of disbelief . . . was not to be attempted'

> I should be determined not to lead my reader into believing that he was doing anything but reading a novel, having noted with abhorrence the shabby chicanery practised on their readers by many novelists, particularly of the popular class.[2]

The obvious debt to Sterne is made explicit early on when the central figure (he cannot exactly be called the narrator) Henry Henry refers to his 'parents' Shandean fixation with economy in nomenclature.'[3] He also refers to 'my greatly beloved Rabelais' and lists, *a propos* of nothing, the library of one of the characters:

> Which reminds me to tell you that Maurie has a great collection of feelthy books down here – including a first edition of Cleland's *Fanny Hill, or the Memoirs of a Woman of Pleasure*, which must have set him back a bit. All in a bookcase in one of the public rooms, too, Harris, Pretonius, Apuleius, Catullus, a Swedish *Lady C*, war crimes books (with Gory Atrocities), the *Decameron*, *Moll Flanders*, *The Monk*, Huysmans in French, Casanova in Italian, Boswell's *London Journal*, a biography of de Sade, the lot, in fact. And more than a dozen other things, mainly in Olympia Press editions. Oh, and a splendid crushed Morocco *Kharma Sutra*.[4]

---

[1] p. 11, reprinted in the introduction to *Memoirs*

[2] p. 12

[3] p. 21

[4] pp. 60/61. One wonders if the Olympia editions in this 'ideal' library would have included any of Alexander Trocchi's pseudonymous pornography.

The comments of the reviewers noted above to the effect that Johnson's novels all had a realist novel at their heart is certainly true here: the story is linear with characters and plot, which remain even when the narrative changes from first person to a variety of interludes, lists and film script. Johnson himself later called it a 'disaster' and refused to let it be reprinted. There are passages which are thinly-disguised autobiography; in at least one he vents his frustration with the university education that he undertook later in life; feelings probably shared by many mature students.[1]

> I left a safe job in insurance to go to college with a genuine, if unfashionable, thirst for knowledge, in all humility, expecting to have to work hard to keep up with the bright brains who had come straight from grammar school or public school. It took only a few weeks to see that practically all of these were not serious about intellectual work; what came as a greater disillusionment, and not long afterwards, was to find that the majority of the staff were not either! I found no difficulty in working to the 'satisfaction' of most of these apathetic tutors: I remember the first week I waffled instead of doing a genuine essay and received a better mark! And the other students were nothing to keep up with: the girls colourless, with names like Thelma and Muriel, and the men usually either unbelievably immature or dogmatically, self-assertively wrong.[2]

Although this is told in character it does seem to reflect Johnson's combination of fragility and arrogance which put so many people off him.[3] Johnson as author does try to keep his distance from Henry as narrator, intervening in the narrative several times: 'Henry was unable to find words to describe the events of the night of Saturday, August 24th; I am under no such difficulty, however, and feel it no less than a duty to record what happened.'[4] However, the details he does give of Henry's background – half way through the novel, in one of the regular Interruptions he says: 'It seems to me that the point has been reached, if not passed, when I ought to make a serious attempt to provide my hero, Henry

[1] In one of several parallels between Johnson's life and my own (which do not include literary talent) I was a mature student, attended Birkbeck college among other universities and lived near the Angel in North London.

[2] p. 125

[3] See the Rayner Heppenstall section in this book for his initial dislike of but eventual close friendship with Johnson.

[4] p. 159

Henry, with a background, a childhood and a youth'[1] – are very much those of Johnson's own life.

The most (in)famous feature of *Travelling People* is undoubtedly the use of greyed-out pages interspersed in the middle of the fragmented stream-of-consciousness, indicated by text spread out on the pages, of Maurie while he is having a heart attack, culminating in a completely black page as he dies. It is a brave technique but raises the question as to whether a dying or 'mad' person's consciousness can be rendered in words at all; comparisons with Beckett are inevitable as well as with Eva Figes (especially *Konek Landing; Days; Waking*), Rosalind Belben (*The Limit*), Ann Quin (*The Unmapped Country*), Paul Ableman (*I Hear Voices)* and Christine Brooke-Rose's returned-from-the-dead narrator in *Such*, among others. It also questions to what extent the novel can be stretched to describe the indescribable. A reviewer of Christine Brooke-Rose's *Thru*, mentioning *Tristram Shandy*'s non-textual effects said:

> The material for the patterning is too often of the visual "concrete" sort for which the printed page always offers meagre and imprecise opportunities. . . The means of producing a rich or controlled visual experience are simply not available to an author using the ordinary process of printing and publishing a text.[2]

These restrictions apply also to Johnson, though much of *Travelling People* is laid out as a film script. Johnson later began the introduction to *Memoirs* with:

> It is a fact of crucial significance in the history of the novel in this century that James Joyce opened the first cinema in Dublin in 1909. Joyce saw very early on that film must usurp some of the prerogatives which until then had belonged almost exclusively to the novelist. Film could tell a story more direct in less time, and with more concrete detail than a novel[3]

Johnson himself did take to film-making (Eva Figes' *Days*, for example, though apparently unfilmable became a film) and one wonders why Johnson persisted with the novel form for so long.

---

[1] p. 143

[2] Michael Mason 'Textual Tensions' Times Literary Supplement, July 11 1975

[3] p. 11

Albert Angelo, 1964 again uses a variety of techniques to tell the story of a short period in the life of an architect *manqué* (a term he hates) who is forced to work as a schoolteacher to make a living, as Johnson himself did. Throughout the text is woven a hymn or love song to the Islington area of North London (which he had covered before in his shaggy dog story about the Balls Pond Road in *Memoirs*. In fact his last name seems simply to be Angel (the name given to the centre of Islington) with a 'o' on the end. The narrator lives on Percy Circus, an oddly-named and oddly-shaped circular street, lovingly described in detail – 'it stands most of the way up a hill, sideways, leaning upright against the slope like a practised seaman'[1] - and walks the surrounding areas with an affection that Johnson (who lived in London all his life) obviously and genuinely feels.

> You decide to walk home slowly, up the City Road, towards the Angel. City Arms; St. Mark's Hospital for Fistula &c,; Mona Lisa Cafe Restaurant; vast anonymous factory block shouldering Georgian first-ratings mainly used for light industries; Albion House with two lovely bow-fronts spoilt by nursery stickers inside the windows and two comically sentimental plaster dogs guarding the steps.
>
> Sale Closing Down. Aspenville wallpaper. Claremont Mission. Overgrown gardens this side. Claremont Square. The bank again, yellow, saffron, green. Across Amwell Street, down Great Percy Street, to the Circus.[2]

The problem with these and the many other descriptions of walking around this area is what if anything do they mean to the reader who is not familiar with it? Johnson can obviously see these walks clearly but does not describe them in enough detail for the reader to imagine. Again, one wonders whether Johnson should have been making a film or photo-essay as he did in *Street Children*.

The above passage was in the second person; the narrative switches between first, second and third but, unlike in Giles Gordon's *Girl with Red Hair* or George

---

[1] p. 13
[2] pp. 40/41

Macbeth's *The Transformation* the effect is not unsettling, as we know by now who 'you' is: it is the 'he' that is Albert. In these other two novels the question of 'your' identity is never resolved and this gives a worrying strangeness which Johnson misses. And again, in the several pages devoted to the calling out of names in the class register Johnson misses the menace and black humour of Giles Cooper's 1958 radio play *Unman, Wittering and Zigo,* also about a new teacher trying to control a rebellious class (though Cooper's children are far more threatening than Johnson's).

They don't like that. Means they'll have to work.

And you can do it without talking!

How I hate this perpetual nagging. Ninety percent of teaching is nagging. Someone won't have a pencil

- Mr. Albert, I need a new roughbook.

Thick, virginal, sensuous pile of new books. A small pleasure.

Here.

Now, has everyone got a pencil? Or something to . . . with which to write?

Amazing. Now what to say next, no respite?

Put the heading 'Geology' just as I'm spelling it on the board.

Now, different sorts of stone have different ages, and I'm going to start with the oldest. The earth was once a ball of flame, its surface a mass of material so hot that we can hardly imagine it. The sun is like this today, and the centre of the earth is, too. The heat was so great that it melted. . .

- 'Ow does 'e know about the sun and the middle of the earth? 'As 'e bin there?

True, how do I bloody well know? Might have been a ball of shit for all I know, a ball of stinking shit. So? You don't have to believe in anything to teach it?

The lessons, rendered like this in two columns again look as though Johnson were writing a film script with internal monologue alongside. Johnson as Albert clearly hates teaching as much as he loves London buildings. The children have an ambivalent relationship to him too; a series of 'essays' they have been asked to write about their teacher are printed in the book; these were apparently genuine, or at least based on genuine responses (as were Jeff Nuttall's in *Mr Watkins*).

What I think of mr Albert

> I think mr Albert is a good teacher sometimes what I like about him is he gives a lot of work sometimes he gets to big for his boots he jumps on kids for nothing. Someday good old mr Albert will come a cross someone his own Size who will splatter him to bits and pieces he gives us good lessons sometimes I feel like swearing at him but still he's a good English teacher. There's on thing wrong with him he needs a haricut. And one thing more he reckons his self to much he gose round the class punching us for nothing and on Friday night I am going to break his Stick. And I next term he better not go round the class hiting us for nothing like he dos'e NOW for his sake.[1]

Immediately after this Johnson turns philosophical: 'Part of the trouble, he thought, was that he lived and loved to live in an area of absolute architectural rightness, which inhibited his own originality, and resulted in him being – OH, FUCK ALL THIS LYING!' This ends the section titled 'Development' – the others have been called 'Prologue' and 'Exposition', again relating the work to a musical work or an old philosophical treatise. Perhaps Johnson is telling us that the children are not lying, that their bad spelling and grammar, their raw thoughts, are nearer the truth than anything a novelist can tell us. The next section, 'Disintegration' starts he same way:

> - fuck all this lying look what im really trying to write about is writing not all this stuff about architecture trying to say something about writing about my writing in my hero though what a useless appellation my first character then im trying to say something about me through him albert an architect when whats the point in covering up covering up covering over pretending i can say anything through him that is anything that I would be interested in saying
>
> - so an almighty aposiopesis

[1] pp. 162/163

- Im trying to say something not tell a story telling stories is telling lies and I want to tell the truth about me about my experience and my truth to reality about sitting here writing looking out across Claremont Square trying to say something about the writing and nothing being an answer to the loneliness to the lack of loving

- look then I'm

- again for what is writing if not truth my truthtelling truth to experience to my experience and if I start falsifying in telling stories then I move away from the truth of my truth which is not good oh certainly not good by any manner of

- so it's nothing[1]

As well as echoes of Gertrude Stein this writing invites comparisons with Samuel Beckett, whom Johnson has hubristically and dangerously quoted at length at the beginning of the book[2]. Compared at one extreme to Beckett's transcendental prose in the quoted extract from *The Unnameable* and at the other to Jeff Nuttall's light-hearted and hilarious cut-ups in *Mr Watkins,* Johnson in all his earnestness and combativeness appears to be neither as great a writer as the former nor as funny and entertaining as the latter. Then as if to inflame reviewers and readers even further he goes on:

- And another of my aims is didactic: the novel must be a vehicle for conveying truth, and to this end every device and technique of the printer's art should be at the command of the writer: hence the future-seeking holes, for instance, as much to draw attention to the possibilities as to make my point about death and poetry.

- A page is an area on which I may place any signs I consider to communicate most nearly what I have to convey: therefore I employ, within the pocket of my publisher and the patience of my printer, typographical techniques beyond the arbitrary and constricting limits of the conventional novel. To dismiss such techniques as gimmicks, or to refuse to take them seriously, is to crassly miss the point.[3]

But readers and reviewers do not always want didacticism and never want to be accused of being crass, especially when the holes Johnson had cut in the pages

---

[1] pp. 167/168

[2] Johnson and Beckett were friends for some time.

[3] pp. 175/176

were not actually future-seeking but revealed an apparently unrelated story about Christopher Marlowe, very much in the past. And in fact in this novel Johnson does not make use much of his right to place signs anywhere on the page, as he had done before and would do again. Nothing he does typographically (for that matter, nothing Christine Brooke-Rose, Rosalind Belben and even Stefan Themerson do) is more experimental than Mallarmé's *Un Coup de Dés,* 1897 (Even back then Mallarmé had said in the preface that there was no novelty in it except in the 'spacing of the reading'[1]), or even *as* experimental as Apollinaire's *Calligrammes*, 1918 or the poems of Marinetti and Tzara, not to mention the contemporaneous British concrete poetry of dsh, John Furnival et al. Perhaps the reviewers were only upset when the 'experiments' happened in novels rather than poetry.

Finally, it is not clear what the 'truth' Johnson wants to tell us actually is: is it just about the loneliness of a writer who loves London and is forced to teach ungrateful children? If so, that story is beautifully told, as the above reviewer admitted, and without the didacticism reviewers would no doubt have appreciated it for the simple and touching story it, at its heart, really is. And Flann O'Brien had already summed up Johnson's position far more wryly and succinctly in his epigraph to *At Swim-Two-Birds*, which could also be an epigraph to any of Johnson's works: 'All the characters represented in this book, including the first person singular, are entirely fictitious and bear no relation to any person living or dead.' Johnson however could not see a bull without waving a red rag at it, and he saw bulls everywhere. [2]

---

[1] 'le tout sans nouveauté qu'un espacement de la lecture'.

[2] Rayner Heppenstall recorded how he was at first put off by Johnson's bluster but came to be a close friend; see the Heppenstall section in this book.

As if to make peace however, Johnson's next novel *Trawl,* 1966 uses no typographical eccentricities and no changes of narration. It does still recall Beckett, not least because one of its characters is called Molloy, and also Trocchi's *Cain's Book* and the original version of *Young Adam*, not only because the narrator is on a trawler but because of the affectless, dispassionate sex scenes. However, the very negative attitude of the reviewer quoted above can only have come from past provocations – imagined or otherwise, as there is nothing experimental about the narrative, which just presents the unstructured memories of the narrator – whose memories are almost exactly matched with Johnson's own life – trying to reconcile himself with his past, which at the end of the book he does. Johnson was not being the least didactic or provocative, just telling a touching story in affecting prose; with any other author one might be tempted to say, telling the truth. The trawler is used metaphorically in two ways: the motion of the waves and the CRAANGK! of the boat are used to drive the rhythm of the prose, and the narrator is trawling his memories as the ship trawls the ocean. 'The rhythms of the language of Trawl attempted to parallel those of the sea, while much use was made of the trawl itself as a metaphor for the way the subconscious mind may appear to work.'[1] Rayner Heppenstall claimed that Johnson took the metaphor from his novel *The Woodshed*:

> At present it is almost as though I were out on the open sea, glassily calm. If I again let down the deep trawl of memory, I should bring up dabs and elvers by the ton. The catch would only be to throw back'.[2]

Trawl is a good illustration of Johnson's – and Heppenstall's – distinction between 'fiction' and 'the novel': truth and fiction are the opposites but a novel is not necessarily fiction and can be 'true'. '*Trawl* is all interior monologue, a representation of the inside of my mind but at one stage removed'.[3] The novel opens with:

---

1 *Memoirs,* p. 23

2 *The Woodshed*, p. 189. Johnson had earlier sent Heppenstall a copy of *Travelling People* for his approval and the two later became close friends.

3 *Memoirs,* p. 23

> I · · always with I · · one starts from · ·
> one and I share the same character · · are one ·
> · · · one always starts with I · · one · · ·
> · · alone · · · · · · · · sole · · · ·
> · · · · · · · · · single · · · · · · · ·
> · · I[1]

Some of the memories are beautifully invoked, and it is hard to see how any reviewer could become apoplectic at haunting sections such as this:

> They told me cats were put to sleep to doctor them. I knew something of what doctoring meant. For nights after that I was afraid to go to sleep. I kept awake for as long as possible in case they doctored me after I had been put to sleep. Peter was the cat we had then. I remember Peter. They told me they bought him not long after they were married. So Peter was older than I was. I was there on my own when he died, poor Peter. I must have been thirteen or fourteen, then. The war was over, I know. I was back home after being evacuated. Peter was skinny by then. Feeling his bones through the skin was not pleasant. But we all loved him still. Peter was a country cat. His hair, long black and white hair, became matted under his tummy. Perhaps it was our fault, that it was matted. We should have combed and brushed him more often. And he smelt and messed a lot, as he grew older. But I loved him. I was glad I was the one who was with him when he died. I had come home from school one afternoon. I was always in before they were. They worked up in town.[2]

Similarly evocative is the long list of music he was listening to: just a list but a list of synesthetic pleasures evoking a time in his past more efficiently than any number of pages of 'fine writing' could. At one point though he stops himself:

> · · This is woolly, indeterminate · · · · · ·
> I must try to analyse more, not just go over things,

[1] p. 7
[2] p. 33

> over and over things, the past, glorying in, almost, rather than analysing, now the hurt is past, over, enjoying the sex, vicariously, too much on sex, perhaps, no, it is important, so little else seems really relevant, though there were of course long periods without girls, or with useless girls. · · · ·
> Time? I ought to get up. Time?[1]

And, eventually, the time he has spent at sea, confined with his memories, does seem to have exercised the past – for the narrator if not for the author.

> Full of pity for the boy I was, recalling the girls my women were. Yes, yes, all these loves and wished-for loves. I need never think of you again, have exorcised you, I need never worry about what you did or what I should have done: have distanced you in mind as well as time: you will never enter my thoughts again in the same way, only by accident, by association with the impersonal: I am glad to be rid of you.[2]
>
> I am only what I am now · · · · · · I am not what I have been · · · · · · It is as if I am free to be what I may be · · · · · · I am not what I shall be · · · · · · I am what I am now.
>
> And things do slowly become better, the vision does come, as I see it, slowly: only have patience with the slowness, more and more belong with the movement forward, which is the only movement away from my own isolation, if only it can be borne, the slowness of the advance · · · · · ·[3]

---

[1] p. 129
[2] p. 180
[3] p. 181

As if writing *Trawl* had indeed been cathartic, and he had now cleared out his memory-chest, Johnson's next novel was a return to experimental form. Whereas in *Trawl* the memories are presented in apparently random fashion, in *The Unfortunates,* 1969 they are printed in individual, numbered sections of different lengths and presented in a box to be read genuinely randomly, except for the first and last sections which are titled as such. Johnson had been sent to report on a football match in Nottingham and had remembered the death from cancer of a friend who had lived there.

> The main technical problem with *The Unfortunates* was the randomness of the material. That is, the memories of Tony and the routine football reporting, the past and the present, interwove in a completely random manner, without chronology. This is the way the mind works, my mind anyway[1]

Whereas *Trawl* had the narrator combing through all his memories, *The Unfortunates* is only concerned with the memories of his friendship with Tony; nevertheless they are painful memories, looked at from beyond the point of Tony's death. 'It is difficult to think of these things without terror, the pity is easy to feel, easy to contain, but so useless.' In some of the memory-fragments the narrator is in the same situation as Albert Angelo and the younger Johnson; Tony comes to stay with him in his London flat so he can work on his thesis on Samuel Johnson (one of B.S. Johnson's heroes) at the British Museum:

> He used to catch a bus, a 73, at least, I told him that one, I don't know if he took my advice, to go to the BM. Perhaps I was home first in the afternoons, from school, exhausted, it was a very tough school I was at that term, on supply, they had a policy then of putting the worst children in the worst school buildings, and the problems I had to face were insurmountable, for me, I was not able to manage, I was not interested in managing, I chose to teach for the money, ha, though I enjoyed the kids, not the other teachers, no, their attitudes.

[1] *Memoirs*, p. 25

> Remember meeting him the first time he came to my flat, Tony, I had come home at lunchtime from school, met him in the street, like a stranger, for a moment, both agreed we had just combined to act out an authentic alienation-effect, we thought. That must have been summer. In the evenings we would talk, discuss, drink, go out for a drink, for dinner at least once at an Italian café near the Angel, I would show him Kings Cross, as I knew it, the desperate pubs, and he would be interested in a very academic way, incorruptible, or something.

On another visit he and Tony have had a discussion about the nature of literary criticism: 'To Tony, the criticism of literature was a study, a pursuit, a discipline of itself: to me, I told him, the only use of criticism was if it helped people to write better books.' As we know, for Johnson almost all book reviewers and critics in this sense failed, not only him but the whole of contemporary literature, though there is no didacticism or aggression in this book. Tony may have been the only person he could have these discussions with; possibly his only constant friend. He is contrasted with Wendy, who appears in other sections; she seems to have been a great passion but has 'betrayed' him and he realises he only ever knew her externally.

> Wendy standing after dropping her dressing-gown, washing those breasts with a casualness inconsistent with the way they affected me. the way her pubic hair parted between her thighs, was not random, followed as the thighs, the cleft directed it, into a shape I could love, could recognize, could now know as one more part of her revealed to me, could observe, being recently spent, what I had really hoped for, that sort of broadening, accession of knowledge about her, what the King James version translators meant by knowing a woman, I suppose, very neatly, perhaps, my coming away with her, in wanting to be away with her for a weekend as distinct from the limited observations of our comings together at home, at our homes, at college.   But that all seems exterior now, only knowing from the outside.

He has never really known Wendy, as he has perhaps never really known anyone. Tony and his wife June have helped him to get over this memory of betrayal, which has lasted for years: 'and it did me a lot of good, helped me to understand that it was the loss I wanted, the self-suffering, not her'. But Tony's death reminds him that he had written a poem for Wendy on the day she betrayed him. 'I even now forget what it was she betrayed me over, some other man, yes, but I have dealt with that, I do not have to think of that any more, it is past, why does Tony's death and this city throw them up at me again?' Despite the random nature of the sections, it is impossible for the reader not to piece together a chronology of Tony's illness and death, which affect the narrator badly.

> It was obvious to me that even if he was still there the following week, he would be less able to talk, at the rate he was deteriorating, disintegrating, so the last thing I said to him, all I had to give him, alone with him, with my coat on, about to go, the car waiting outside to run us to the station, staring down at him, facing those eyes, he staring back all the time now, it must have been a great effort for him, yes, and I said, it was all I had, what else could I do, I said, I'll get it all down, mate.   It'll be very little, he said, after a while, slowly, those eyes. That's all anyone has done, very little, I said.

Only one of the sections covers the football match which has evoked the memories of Tony.

> City seemed to believe that comma   surviving this comma   that they could survive anything comma and gradually came out of defence full point   Furse comma after an idiosyncratically hyphen executed run Furse comma after an idiosyncratically hyphen executed run by Stevens comma   brought a fine save from Edson comma and in the twenty hyphen seventh minute   had the ball in the United net   only to be ruled offside full point

The section titled 'Last' ends

> The difficulty is to understand without generalization, to see each piece of received truth, or generalization, as true only if it is true for me, solipsism again, I come back to it again, and for no other reason.   In general, generalization is to lie, to tell lies
>
> Not how he died, not what he died of, even less why he died, are of concern, to me, only the fact that he did die, he is dead, is important: the loss to me, to us

Like *Trawl, The Unfortunates* was obviously cathartic for Johnson as well as being novel [*sic*] in construction. Obviously he could have used the same material and arranged it randomly himself to be printed conventionally: *Trawl*'s recollections are not in chronological order and it is possible, even inevitable, that a reader will construct a timescale around the memories and most readers will simply take the sections in the order they first come out of the box, without shuffling them. Unlike the unreliable narrators in Heppenstall, Figes, Quin, Ableman and others, Johnson's narrator is coherent and honest – brutally so. But *The Unfortunates* certainly does work as a reading experience and its format is not gratuitous or extreme. Reviewers complained that inside all Johnson's works was a naturalistic story trying to get out and here, as in *Trawl* it does.

House Mother Normal is an altogether less personal but equally experimental novel. It does not start with 'I' but with a structure almost identical to Philip Toynbee's *Tea With Mrs. Goodman*, 1947. Toynbee drew a diagram at the beginning of his book to explain the process[1], where Johnson leaves it for the reader to figure out, but he does explain in *Memoirs* the composition process, which is that each chapter is the internal monologue of one person in the home and that all the monologues take place at the same time and same speed, so that each chapter has the same number of pages, which are numbered 1 – 21; many pages are almost or even entirely blank to keep them in step. The speakers are in various stages of dementia and the text, using a similar technique to the heart attack sequence in *Travelling People* uses fragmented and widely spaced words to try to map these fragmented minds so that many of the pages resemble concrete poetry.

> What I wanted to do was
> to take an evening in an old people's home, and see a single set of events through the eyes of not less than eight old people. Due to the various deformities and deficiencies of the inmates, these events would seem to be progressively 'abnormal' to the reader. At the end, there would be the viewpoint of the House Mother, an

---

[1] Illustrated in the Philip Toynbee section in the Fellow Travellers chapter of this book.

> apparently 'normal' person, and the events themselves would then be seen to be so bizarre that everything that had come before would seem 'normal' by comparison. The idea was to say something about the things we call 'normal' and 'abnormal' and the technical difficulty was to make the same thing interesting nine times over[1]

Each person is introduced at the beginning of their chapter by a description of the strength of their faculties, which includes a 'CQ' count; the House Mother explains that this is the number of correct answers out of 10 to simple questions like where are you and what day is it to gauge senile dementia. The first few characters have a score of ten but this drops to zero for the final character. Each one also has age and pathology; even those that are mentally competent have physical difficulties: 'contractures; incipient hallux valgus; osteo-arthritis; suspected late paraphrenia; among others.' At the start, the House Mother invites the reader to 'join our Social Evening' at which we will 'find our friends dining, first, and later singing, working, playing, travelling, competing, discussing, and finally being entertained.' All the page 5s have the inmates singing a song that starts, with heavy irony: '*The joys of life continue strong / Throughout old age, however long*'. Obviously as the book progresses and the inmates' CQ count drops they become less aware of the singing. By Ron Lamson's section half way through the book page 5 has become:

Oh, the song, must make
some effort
she must
see me singing
of life continue strong
Throughout old age, however long
If only we can cheerful
stay, And every day.
not what we'll
What matters most that we're free
joys of life continue strong
Throughout old age, however long.

Important to do
stay alive

---

[1] pp. 26/27

No matter if *future's*

knows best, and brings good cheer AAA!
the pain shoots again
again

Page 14 similarly has a game of pass the parcel which is opened by Ron, who has a CQ of 8.

It's my turn, that old woman's cheating *Pass it on!*
No need to chuck it at me! It's stopped,
it's me, I can get it undone, I'll win, what is it?
SHIT! It's a parcel of shit! Is that
what I've won? Is that all? Stinking shit!
shit shit shit shit shit shit shit shit shit shit shit
shit shit shit shit shit shit shit shit shit shit shit

shit!

Further through the book, by the time we get to George Hedbury, CQ count 2, things on page 14 become more fragmented:

when I get better

Package
for me pass, parc

what?

And by the time we get to Rosetta Stanton, with a CQ of zero page 14 becomes:

amongst those left

gwron

atodiad

ifanc

However, by the next page Rosetta suddenly has some clarity and the entertainment becomes more poignant:

> I am
> terrible, Ivy
>
> Now I can every
> word you say I am a prisoner in my
> self. It is terrible. The movement agonises me.
>
> Let me out, or I shall die.

When we get to the House Mother's chapter we have been told to expect that she is normal, but we also know that Johnson was being ironic all along so we are not too surprised to learn on her page 14 that she herself had wrapped up the parcel with shit from her dog Ralphie.

> How disgusting! you must be saying to yourself,
> friend, and I cannot but agree. But think a bit
> harder, friend: why do I disgust them?
> I disgust them in order that they may not be
> disgusted with themselves.

And if the reader is not disgusted enough we now find out from the House Mother what has been happening on page 20:

Here, Ralphie! up on the table
with Mummy! That's it, you know what to do with
your long probing red Borzoi tongue, don't you Ralphie!
Lovely!
oooooh!
that's it!
Oh, Ralphie! Faster! we're getting near the
end of the page, Ralphie! oooooh! oh!
iiiiiihl! oooooh! nearly! YES!

Whereas in *Albert Angelo* Johnson's po-faced seriousness contrasted unfavourably with Jeff Nuttall's playfulness, here the situation is reversed: Johnson is hilariously entertaining and obviously enjoying himself enormously compared to Philip Toynbee's high-minded portentousness in *Tea With Mrs. Goodman*; this makes *House Mother Normal* a completely successful experiment. However, even here Johnson cannot resist a Shandean intervention in the voice of the House Mother right at the end:

> And here you see, friend, I am about to step outside the convention, the framework of twenty-one pages per person. Thus you see I too am the puppet or concoction of a writer (you always knew there was a writer behind it all? Ah, there's no fooling you readers!), a writer who has me at present standing in the post-orgasmic nude but who still expects me to be his words without embarrassment or personal comfort. So you see this is from his skull. It is a diagram of certain aspects of the inside of his skull!
> What a laugh!

Indeed it is. Johnson seems to me to be at his best here, relaxed despite, or more likely because of the technical challenge, looking more towards Sterne and Joyce than Beckett and perhaps most of all to Flann O'Brien, whose famous phrase from *At Swim-Two-Birds* would fit well at this point in the book, and at many points in most of Johnson's books: 'Shanahan at this point inserted a brown tobacco finger in the texture of the story and in this manner caused a lacuna in the palimpsest.'

Christie Malry's Own Double Entry also refers to its own status as a novel throughout the text: 'Christie was the only mourner, economy as to relatives (as to so many other things) being one of the virtues of this novel.'[1]

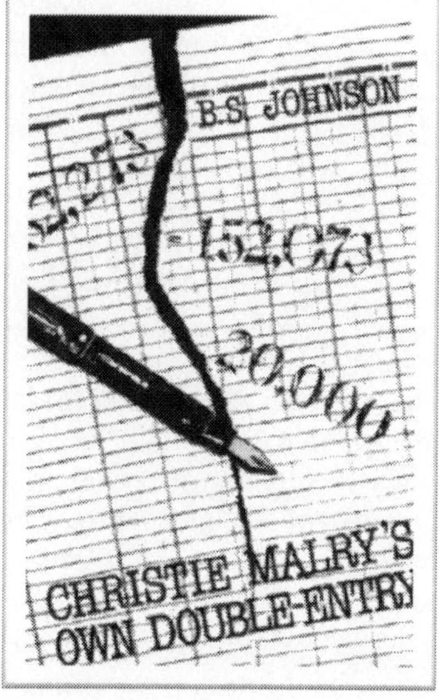

> 'Haven't I heard that story before?' said Christie.
>
> 'I don't know said Headlam, crying into his beer, 'I don't know, how could I? But since I seem to be the comic relief in this novel . . .'
>
> 'It needs it,' said Christie.[2]

And towards the end Johnson as novelist causes a lacuna in his own palimpsest by addressing his central character directly:

> 'Christie.' I warned him, 'it does not seem me possible to take this novel much further. I'm sorry.'
>
> 'Don't be sorry,' said Christie, in a kindly manner, 'don't be sorry. We don't equate length with importance, do we? And who wants long novels anyway? Why spend your time for a month reading a thousand-page novel when you can have a comparable aesthetic experience in the theatre or cinema in only one evening? The writing of a long novel is in itself an anachronistic act: it was relevant only to a society and a set of social conditions which no longer exist.'[3]

The novel is indeed very short according to the novelist/narrator's own reckoning:

> A total of just over twenty thousand people died of cyanide poisoning that morning. This was the first figure that came to hand as it is roughly the number of words of which the novel consists so far.

---

[1] p. 33
[2] p. 103
[3] p. 165

CHRISTIE MALRY in account with THEM

FINAL

		DR AGGRAVATION					CR RECOMPENSE		
Aug	1	Balance brought forward	325,765	36	Aug	3	Overordered carbon paper	00	31
Aug	7	Beetle in curry	4	00	Aug	7	Call to Public Health Department	0	75
					Aug	7	Stromboli bomb hoax	1	20
					Aug	13	Balance written off as Bad Debt	352,392	
			352,394	53				352,394	53

ACCOUNT CLOSED

One of the main differences noted already in the introduction to this book between American experimental novels on the one hand and British and French experimental novels on the other is length: the American fabulists, trying to write the Great American Novel (originally the title of William Carlos Williams' very short 1923 work) did equate length with seriousness: John Barth's *The Sot-Weed Factor* was 800 pages and *Giles Goat-Boy* over 700; William Gaddis' *The Recognitions* over 950 and *JR* over 700; Thomas Pynchon's *Gravity's Rainbow* over 900 and *V* 500. British experimental novels tend to be, in Johnson's phrase, nasty brutalist and short.

The conceit of Johnson's novel is that Christie has had a Great Idea: he has devised a system where he will repay the slights life gives him – the aggravations or debits caused by society, or 'them'– with compensations or credits. He is not very good at this as every account he produces has him massively in debit, despite poisoning as many people as there are words in his novel. He is a loner, working in a dead-end job, as Johnson had done and taking little comfort in the camaraderie and banter of the firms he works in.

> Christie warmed and warmed to Headlam the more he came to know him. Indeed, such was the conjunction of sympathies that Christie was tempted to reveal his Great Idea to Headlam and enlist his help in carrying it towards its inevitable fruition. But his principles stayed him: *I am a cell of one!* In that way he could not be betrayed, in that way he was responsible for and to no one but himself. It was the only way; it had been proven to be the only way.[1]

Christie's mother has died at the start of the novel, as Johnson's did around the same time, but he does not miss her too much. He thinks about death and the immorality of killing but decides that the callousness of society excuses him: he cannot 'possibly kill as many as they do.'

> Of course the death of those near to one is distressing: of course the death of a mother makes one think she was indispensable. But if she really was indispensable, then you yourself die. Otherwise she was not indispensable. And in any case, society does not, they do not share any concern for your mother, what she meant to you. It would not be society if it did.[2]

Christie has a girlfriend – the Shrike - with whom he shares a close and mutually satisfying relationship. It is also sexually satisfying, and Johnson makes explicit the sexual *double entendre* in the title:

---

[1] p. 100
[2] p. 116

> Christie was considering the application of Double-Entry to sexual pleasure. He had, he soon realised, only one instrument with which to make entries: conversely, the Shrike had, in common with most women, at least three points at which entry was possible. Christie permutated the possibilities in his mind, and then mentioned them to the Shrike. To her credit, she did not treat him as someone in whom the beast had gained the upper hand. Two she would have but the third was her own, she maintained stoutly, inviolate.[1]

But Christie remains a loner, like his creator, despite his many chances of a relationship. At the end, the novelist determines to kill him off and goes to see his character. 'At least your Great Idea prevented you from becoming bored to death with life,' I told Christie when I paid what he must have seen as my last visit to him.'[2]

> Christie appeared weaker, closing his eyes and breathing through his mouth rather than his nose. Then he suddenly rallied:
>
> 'Amongst those left are you'[3] he said accusingly.
>
> 'So far,' I said.
>
> 'Will the Shrike go on?' he asked.
>
> 'I don't know. I've grown very fond of her. Perhaps another time,' I answered as honestly as I could.
>
> 'I hope she does go on,'[4] said Christie.
>
> A pause.
>
> 'And I'm very fond of you, too, by now, Christie,' I told him.[5]

---

[1] p. 58

[2] p. 178

[3] Now, reader, as Johnson might have said, you know where I got the title for this book.

[4] The ending of Beckett's *The Unnameable,* from which Johnson had quoted in *Trawl* is:

> You must go on.
>
> I can't go on.
>
> I'll go on.

[5] p. 179

See the Old Lady Decently was Johnson's last novel, completed before his death but published posthumously. It shows a mature Johnson, still thoroughly experimental but not didactic or argumentative; mellowed, married with children he obviously loves, celebrating the life, rather than bemoaning the death of his mother, who had recently died and the decline of his country and its empire. It is warm, nostalgic and melancholy but it is hard to believe that its author killed himself very soon after it was completed. We learn from Michael Bakewell's introduction that it was planned to be the first of a *Matrix Trilogy*. The other volumes were to have been be *Buried Although,* which would take up the story at Johnson's birth in 1933, where its predecessor left off, and go on until the end of the Second World War. The final volume, *Amongst Those Left Are You* would concentrate on his mother's death in 1971. The three titles would then read across to form *See the Old Lady Decently Buried Although Amongst Those Left Are You*. The old lady refers to his mother but also to the British empire and the English language. 'Our task is to see that the old lady gets a decent burial. Our task is to see that the language gets a decent burial.'[1] To add to the loss of his mother, Johnson had only weeks before his own death learnt about Ann Quin's suicide; he may have felt that he himself was amongst those left.[2] However, given the tender passages where his children interrupt the writer and the novel, it is hard to believe that he could leave them amongst those left.

> During the above my daughter came up to my room,
> practising her writing before going to bed. BOOTS and
> SNOW are the words she likes best, at the moment.
> Then she went down for her supper. Afterwards she
> came up and gave me a delicious café Liègois, or rather

[1] Quoted by Michael Bakewell in the introduction, p. 14

[2] Johnson rang Rayner Heppenstall on September 1st 1973 to tell him of Ann Quin's suicide. By November Johnson was also dead; On November 16th Heppenstall recorded: 'It is not much over two months since Ann Quin committed suicide. Ann was beautiful, though highly neurotic. It has crossed my mind to wonder whether there was any love affair between them. I conclude that it is unlikely. On the other hand, I feel quite sure that Ann's suicide continued to affect Bryan, from whom I first heard of it.'

> the remains of one. Mummy had the cream, she informed. Spaghetti for lunch, green peppers, café Liègois, whatever became of England? Now she is drawing round her hand, one at a time, with my red pens, one after the other. Do you like this? She is fluttering the paper at my elbow, demanding attention. I give it to her, telling her to put it where I can find an envelope for it in the morning, Suddenly she leaves the room, not saying *Night Night*, and the loss
> is noticeable. I call her, she does not return.
> The loss is [1]

And again, here he specifically relates his affection for his daughter to that for his mother, though since all the sections regarding his mother take place before his birth take place before his birth she is always Emily, a young girl and not yet a mother. So his affection in the novel is for the young girl who would become his mother and the young girl who is his daughter and perhaps will eventually become a mother herself – an aspect of *The Great Mother* - in the process of regeneration the novel celebrates:

> Where were we? I did actually break off at a full stop above, at Emily's knowledge of swearwords, by the way, though it must look like a contrivance. And so must this, since that little girl with something of my mother in her face has just brought me a roll baked by her mother, bread that could not be fresher, with butter melting, through it, brown and yellow-golden, interrupted me where I write in isolation at the top of the house, such sweet interposition!
>
> I shall eat now, the manuscript stained on purpose with the melting butter.
>
> What a pity it is not possible for you all to read the ms!
>
> Where was I again?[2]

This extremely tender metaphor of a manuscript deliberately stained by the melting butter of his daughter's offering does not seem as though it could have come from a man about to commit suicide, especially as the writer in him is not

[1] pp. 56/57
[2] pp. 27/28

even annoyed at the 'sweet' interruption However, with hindsight there is at least one passage where Johnson does seem to have given up the fight. He has been to 'the AGM of a society of which I am a member. It was on a subject which is very important to me. This novel trilogy is also very important to me.' He does not tell us what the society is but his motion has been defeated and he wonders whether the digression and the drain of energy from his writing is worth the effort. 'Does it matter? Does anything matter? The thing is that all seems very similar. Nothing seems capable of being new, I feel as old as the whole of history, knowing everything that mankind can. Except the details.'[1] So Johnson in the novel tries to reconstruct the details.

There are several kinds of section, all headed with a code, which is explained by Bakewell in the introduction but not in the novel itself. There are poems, including a concrete poem on the word and shape of 'breast', sections headed GB, which are fragmented versions of guide books or tours of Great Britain – the mother country, and BB sections about Broader Britain and the decline of empire. There are also sections headed in apparently random letters (a key is given in the introduction, but does not add anything). There are also descriptions of photographs Johnson found, letters to Emily from her father in the army and two from the army telling her mother of his death. The letters from Johnson's grandfather to his mother show the same tenderness he shows for his daughter.

LETTER FIVE

My Dear little Daughter
just a line from your dear Daddy hoping you are all
quite well as it leaves me quite well I had some of pinks
jam for tea and I feel in the pink (now then I can just
see you are going to laugh) well my little Darling I hope
you will have a good time at bushy Park and don't forget
to look after phil which I know you will I hope it will be
nice weather for you I wish I was with you never mind
my pet I will take you all somewhere when I come
home so I think I will close now with heaps of love
from your loving Daddy

p. Lambird

xxxxxxxx keep this letter
xxxxxx and I will give
xxxxxx you a penny
for it

[1] p. 76

Obviously she did keep it but we do not know whether he lived to give her the penny.

There are also sections headed O (representing the Great Round) concerning 'birth, death and regeneration', which are direct quotes from Neumann's *The Great Mother* and short, savage sections headed H about Field Marshall Lord Haig. Many of the sections tell the history of his mother, from her childhood to Johnson's own birth, including a long section imagining his conception, gestation and birth, with which the novel ends. About his mother's early life he does not have enough information to tell a story so he invents a kitchen where he imagines she worked and a monstrous chef called Virrels; these sections are headed V.

> Virrels the chef was a terrible man, a horny man, one of the kind one is glad to have known. Virrels was certainly to be known, to be remembered! Even apart from his weskit.
>
> 'Chop, you cunts!' Virrels would bellow across the elm bench tops at the vegetable preparers. 'What do you think this is, a kindergarten for pencil sharpeners? Chop! Chop! Chop![1]

This is how Johnson imagines his young mother being initiated into the wider world. The result of all these different sections is a collage of disparate elements all linked by the themes of the death of motherhood and regeneration. The collage undoubtedly works and if the trilogy had been completed it would have been a work of great significance. The introduction quotes Johnson:

> Something for everybody! If you do not like this part, or that part, or the other, then skip ahead or back to a part you did enjoy. It is no part of my intention to provide a continuous narrative, no, that you can get from television at the turn of a switch, who can compete with that? No, the purpose is to reflect with humility the reality of the chaos, what life really seems to be like.

This does indeed have a humility and wit lacking in Johnson's earlier diatribes which so much upset the reviewers, but it was now probably too late to win them back, even if he had lived to write more.

---

[1] p. 28

GB3

The green was quite filled with, all in their Sunday,
and when their arrived a band struck up 'God save the' and
the people cheered. The sad 'I shall always
love little for this.' When she took up her in
the Palace, it was used as an ornamental dairy.
She would go and see the butter.[1]

Towards the end is a section imagining the night of, but not actually describing the act of his conception; the scene starts as if it is going to imagine the actual act but goes into a digression, ending, in true Shandean fashion:

- Sir! to the point!
- The point! Where is your point?
- You still haven't come to the point!

Sirs and Madam, that is the point.[2]

The journey of the sperm is then described after an ironic dated section (the first number is the year, the second number his mother's age).

33 (25)

Two strong men came to power this January; all would be well. Roosevelt won an election, Hitler was made Chancellor.

h

Out they all set, then, on this exciting journey, full of vigour and overwhelmingly inspired by their sense of purpose, dedicated to one object only. Between thirty million and five hundred million of them, if one is to believe the educated guesses.[1]

---

[1] p. 38
[2] p. 125

And then: 'Early the following week, however, what does Me do but insinuate itself into the cosy inner lining of the womb! Follow that!'[2] The growth of the Johnson-foetus is then described at length until the mother (now called Emma) is 'in both labour and Queen Charlotte's Annexe.'[3] The novel ,and Johnson's literary output ends – far too soon but perhaps fittingly:

> Me was big, waxing on such nourishment and with
> little exercise all that time.
>
> **r³**
>
> Here
> she said
> I love you
>
> **0²**
>
> They gave her no drugs, just a whiff of chloroform
> towards the latter stages.
>
> Which were over by about half past one in the morning.
>
> So: it began with the Great Round, and everything had
> to follow:
>
> from them
> from Em
> from
> embryo
> to embryan
> from Em,
> Me

---

[1] p. 129
[2] p. 130
[3] I am sure Johnson would want me to tell you, Sir or Madam, both that this literary trope is called either a syllepsis or a zeugma, and that my own wife was born in Queen Charlotte's, whose location Johnson describes at length.

jeff nuttall

Jeff Nuttall, 1933 – 2004[1]: painter, poet, sculptor, illustrator, performance artist, collaborator, critic, essayist, social historian, biographer, actor, teacher, collaborator, jazz cornet player – is not normally thought of as a novelist. Born in Lancashire he studied painting at Corsham, started *The People Show* and was a leading figure in the performance art movement, which he documented in two books[2]. Nuttall presented the *Artist at Work* series on London Weekend television and was a school teacher before becoming a lecturer in art at Leeds and Liverpool universities. He was most well-known for *Bomb Culture*[3], which documented the underground movement in 1960s Britain, of which he was a key part and also wrote another work of social history, *Common Factors, Vulgar Factions*[4], about Northern working class life, as well as two biographies[5]. He also contributed short, autobiographical pieces to B. S Johnson's two anthologies *All Bull: The National Servicemen*[6] and *You Always Remember the First Time*[7].

Although much of his poetry[8] is relatively conventional, at least in layout and style, many of his prose works are unclassifiable, combining drawings, hand lettering, cut-ups and type. However, some of his works are presented as novels and two as 'novelettes'. The cover of *Snipe's Spinster* even presents him as a saviour of the novel form.

[1] Two memorials volumes to Nuttall were published after his death: *Jeff Nuttall: A Celebration*. London: Arc, 2004; *Jeff Nuttall's Wake on Paper*. ed. Michael Horowitz, London: New Departures #33, 2004

[2] *Performance Art: vol. 1, Memoirs* and *vol. 2, Scripts*. London: Calder, 1979

[3] *Bomb Culture*. London: McGibbon & Kee, 1968

[4] London: Routledge, 1977

[5] *King Twist: A Portrait of Frank Randle*. London: Routledge, 1978; *The Bald Soprano: Portrait of Lol Coxhill*. London:, Art Data, 1989

[6] London: Quartet, 1973

[7] London: Quartet, 1975

[8] Illustration from the cover of Objects, 1976; see Bibliography for full list. Just before he died Nuttall completed a selection of his poems: *Selected Poems*. Cambridge: Salt, 2003

> We feel this is an important book, not only for the clear picture it gives us of the time in which we are living, but for the possibilities it opens for the novel. With most of our priests dead and the languages of science having long ago become obscure, hieroglyphic; with our political *essayistes* seeing their subjects as characters in a masque; and with languages under perpetual fire. . . we are left with a handful of novelists preoccupied with purifying their own means and materials, and whose best work is a commentary on their times. Jeff Nuttall has pushed this situation toward one of its most interesting ends, and in doing so, with so many around predicting its early demise, has given the novel a whole new voice to work with[1].

Nuttall knew and collaborated with most of the writers and artists in the British underground, as well as many Americans. He was widely respected by all of them. William Burroughs wrote of him:

> Jeff Nuttall is one of the few writers today who actually handles his medium. He moves pieces of it from here to there using the repetition techniques of recurring themes in music. His structures are essentially musical as is his prose[2]

As T. S. Eliot said of *Nigthtwood,* Nuttall's works will be most appreciated by readers used to reading poetry: even at its most realistic, Nuttall's prose is surreal and heightened. It has some similarities to Burroughs' cut-ups but is more controlled, more 'really written' in Eliot's sense. However, Nuttall's prose is like that of William Burroughs, Henry Miller and Alexander Trocchi in its revelling in grotesqueness and obscenity as a deliberate device. Nuttall made it clear in *Bomb Culture* that this was always his intention. Writing about *My Own Mag: a Super-Absorbant [sic] Periodical,* an experimental journal that was Nuttall's first use of the cheap and easily-available medium of duplicated (mimeographed) texts in 1963, he said:

> My intention was to make a paper exhibition in words, pages, spaces, holes, edges, and images which drew people in and forced a violent involvement with the unalterable facts. The message was: if you want to exist you must accept the flesh and the moment. Here they are.
>
> The magazine, even those first three pages, used nausea and flagrant scatology as a violent means of presentation. I wanted to make the fundamental condition of living unavoidable by nausea. You can't pretend it's not there if you're throwing up as a result. My hope was that

[1] Elisions in original
[2] Introduction to *Pig*

> a pessimistic acceptance of life would counteract the optimistic refusal of unpleasantness, the deathwish, the bomb.[1]

Nuttall at this time had only read Burroughs in magazine extracts 'and misunderstood them' but Burroughs contributed collaged pieces to twenty one issues of *My Own Mag* between 1964, when he was in Tangier, and 1966. According to Nuttall, Burroughs was aiming at 'the dissolution of language, the dissolution of definition, the dissolution of individual identity and the formation of a harmonious mind telepathically informing all bodies in an interminable life out of time.' Burroughs was trying to create a new society; Nuttall was trying to lay bare the old one in as uncomfortable a way as possible and force people to confront the obscenity of reality.

> The similarity to my own imagery showed me that we were in the same place but Burroughs was travelling in the opposite direction. It took some time to realise this. Beyond acceptance, my direction was towards the aesthetic of obscenity. Clearly what is called beautiful is merely what was called ugly previously. It was time to step up the pace. Circumstances left us with unrelieved obscenity. So, I thought, let us take that obscenity and make beautiful things with it, as Picasso had with bombed people, as blues saxophonists did with all the anal-erotic grunts and squeals of sexual discord. But let's first (and this, I thought, was my common ground with Burroughs) let's show people where they stand in such a way as to force them to acknowledge the unalterable elements in their condition. Let's force people to accept life and live it.
>
> But the obscenity of *The Naked Lunch*, far from being a device for contriving the acceptance of life, was intended as a device for obliterating life as it had ever been known.[2]

Most of Nuttall's prose writing contains scenes of sex, presented in all its most graphic, raw, physical reality, and without any romance or romanticism, but never simply realistically. All his writing is poetic, his prose is prose poetry, and might even be called lyrical if it were not for the fact that the grossness and horror of sex, death, defecation and decay are always present. Asked to write about his first experience of sex for B.S. Johnson's anthology *You Always Remember the First Time*, he admits to difficulty in describing it in 'objective' prose.

> People who are familiar with my poetry, performance scripts and short novels will recognise the images, personages and settings that spring

[1] pp. 141/142

[2] *Bomb Culture*, P. 142

> straight from that original situation into my work. I write poetry about it all so naturally, and have done so frequently, that it's something of a discipline to write it down with the prosaic objectivity a book like this seems to demand.[1]

He goes on to describe early sexual encounters with one particular young girl – a subject that will recur in *Pig* and *Snipe's Spinster* - and subsequently with a group of boys who threaten him with the police, which have informed all his subsequent writings: fear of the police, who are 'After my knackers', the erotic power of 'clean cool stone in old churches', and that 'sex, for people, is not the simple animal process middle-class liberals would like it to be.'

> For even though I have deliberately gone about scouring all sexual guilt and repression out of my own system and everybody else's and even though I found out they were lying when I was ten years old, there is something old and deep in me that still believes them, without which I doubt if I would ever have written a line of poetry.[2]

Like B.S. Johnson, who was exactly the same age, and the slightly older Alan Burns (who wrote about it in *Buster*), Nuttall had to serve in the army even though the war had ended. In Johnson's anthology *All Bull: The National Servicemen* he describes how the experience formed him, as a man and as an artist.

> The army changed me immeasurably. I got to know the urban working-class intimately by being forced to live with them. They shattered my middle-class fastidiousness and the intolerance that goes with it. I became capable of extreme callousness.
>
> I acquired a will-power and with it the knowledge that there is very little a determined man cannot do, the belief that there is nothing a determined man cannot do. I learned that energy and ability will stretch much further than idleness and fear normally allow it to.
>
> Most of all, best of all, I learned that life is a desperate, terrible, magnificent joke.[3]

Nuttall rarely commented on his own work, but in the introduction to *The House Party* he described how the heightened activity of the 1960s of *Bomb Culture* had led to the negativity and emptiness of 1970s art and how he was trying to build in

---

1 op. cit. p. 113
2 op. cit. p. 117
3 p. 24

his art, not reduce it to Laing's 'No Thing'. In this introduction he gives as good a statement of his aesthetic as he ever would.

> In this building, myself and my comparatively unremarkable sexual predicaments are not so much a field of study or a point of argument, more bricks and mortar, construction materials, fuel. "The House Party" follows,
>
> after my enormous determination to arrive at some point of literary structure as multi-levelled and self-perpetuating as "Finnegan's [*sic*] Wake" – which, as I wrote ten years ago, stands with Picasso's "Guernica" and Schoenberg's "Moses and Aaron" [*sic*] as a monument past which subsequent innovators have failed to go;
>
> after my preoccupation with the interplay between auto-suggestive images and formal accident;
>
> after my wish to create a literary adventure-labyrinth as dense and interpenetrative as a Pollock or a Shepp ensemble.
>
> My work has always been preoccupied with the visionary potential of sexual hysteria. Certain poems in "Songs Sacred and Secular" are clear statements of a determination to find beauty and transcendence (not to mention art, and form, a new language, and humour) in the areas of experience from which one most readily recoils – particularly those of bodily nausea and sexual pain (not the sadistic kind – the moral kind).[1]

[1] no pagination

> In 1968 Granada Publishing Company commissioned, published and richly sponsored a book by me called *Bomb Culture*. I wrote it because I wanted to distance myself from the underground on a number of scores, because I wanted to make it clear publicly that there were aspects of the underground I wanted none of – particularly marihuana and rock-and-roll. I also wrote it because the opportunity was there to write it. I had no idea that I was stepping so far into the enemy camp. The iconoclast had come home, shown himself articulate, rational, prepared, in fact, to talk things over sensibly. The embrace was flattering, remunerative and smothering. Rave reviews followed by television appearances, followed by new commissions and a tide of invitations to speak about socio-cultural problems at Universities. Sociologists beamed in my direction and so did the British Council – briefly.[1]

The most well-known, best-selling and longest of Nuttall's works is partly a reflection on and history of modernism, and partly a series of personal reminiscences about the underground art scenes in America and Britain in the 1950s and 60s. It is an essential source for anyone interested in the arts of the underground at that time, to be read alongside the two volumes of Nuttall's *Performance Art*.

> To a certain extent the Underground happened everywhere spontaneously. It wass imply what you did in the H-bomb world if you were, by nature, creative and concerned for humanity as a whole. Not concerned just for self and friends or for any corny abstract humanity thrown up by church, charity or politician, but concerned for the business of being human in whatever happened to be the conditions surrounding humanity, convinced that the business of being human and

[1] *Performance Art: Memoirs,* p. 143

> the continuation of that business is intrinsically, not relatively important, possessed by a sense of warm and sensuous well-being in one's membership of everybody else.[1]

One of the books biggest figures is William Burroughs, a source of ideas and inspiration for Nuttall and his circle. In an idea he will come back to in *Man, Not Man*, he says: 'Dissolve language, said Burroughs, and opposites drift into harmonious unity. Man has been cheated of oneness.'[2] But although Nuttall is very approving of Burroughs, Ginsberg and other American writers, he calls at the end of *Bomb Culture* for British culture to go its own way.

> It is surely time we turned away from the Americans, a nation of agoraphobic neurotics whose only native excellence lies in the skill and grace of their movement (the benefit of which the world has felt) who are, in any case, in an irrecoverable state of civic rot, and called upon the native European sense of classic form and rational serenity.[3]

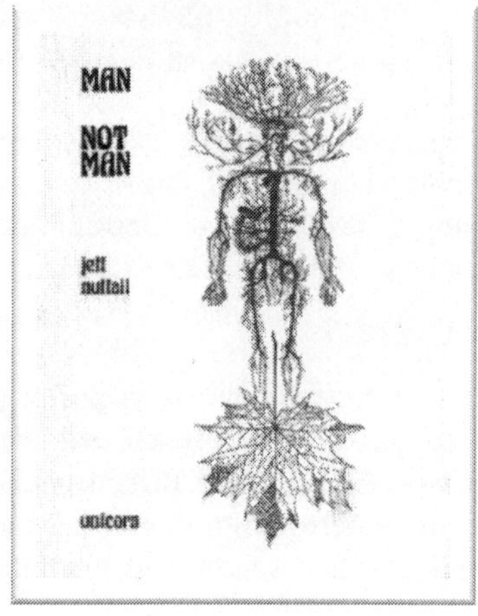

Man Not Man, 1975 is a polemical, philosophical work; part poetry, part confessional, containing anecdotes, stories and arguments, sometimes all at once. Following on from *Bomb Culture* Nuttall muses on the failure of the revolution that had promised so much in the 1960s. 'In '68 the revolution failed. The revolution I mean is the one that sprang directly out of poetic vision. I think it failed because its links were faulty. The link between spiritual awareness (the original usage of the word "psychedelic") and dialectical materialism.'[4] It is man's very humanity that prevents him from experiencing the joy of direct, unmediated experience.

> Self-awareness has divided man off from everything else in existence. In terms of his passivity, separated by unique ability to regard himself in terms of his activity, separated by inability to follow the simple patterns

---

[1] p. 160

[2] p. 143

[3] p. 244

[4] p. 3

> of nature, man is condemned to make his own decisions. As long as he is in the state of being human he is denied the warmth and vitality of direct, organic natural life.[1]

Nuttall argues that a literature of liberation can, at its best, help man close the gap between himself and the divine.

> The perpetual expansion of human limitation reaches its highest peak at its most logical extreme, the urge to appropriate the Godhead, the urge not to dissolve oneself in eternity, in nature, but to appropriate eternity, nature, to conquer death, to control the entire cosmos, to become God. The most capable prophets of this point of view are, in the past, de Sade, Nietzsche, Apollinaire, Breton, and currently Leary, McClure and Trocchi.[2]

Clearly situating himself in this tradition, Nuttall's works are mostly attempts to regain this direct connection with nature, partly by gross, Rabelaisian celebrations of bodily functions.

> When I lie with my ear nuzzled against the working muscles of a passionate woman's belly, the churning, the relentless natural engine, the squirtings and red-drain garglings of shit and mucous, blood and body acids all along the labyrinth within her, when I hear the hungry-puppy-sucking of her cunt, the little suckings of air as her vagina contracts or the muted horn of her fart, when I smell the smudged sunset of her stench, the whole experience is sharpened beyond ecstasy to panic by the fear of not getting to the pot in time.[3]

---

[1] p. 10
[2] pp. 18/19
[3] p. 10

Performance Art, in two volumes: *Memoirs* and *Scripts*, which appeared ten years after *Bomb Culture*, details Nuttall's time as a performance artist with The People Show and other groups; he makes it clear that it is autobiography and not social history, perhaps to distance it from the earlier book, and its focus is mostly personal not philosophical, local not general. Nevertheless it is, with Adrian Henri's *Environments and Happenings*[1], the best record we have of that ephemeral art form and its period. He describes the beginnings of the 'happening, later the event, still later the performance piece', as it 'lunged out of painting, sculpture and music as these media merged in their concern for the found object.' Nuttall is concerned, in his work with other people, to strip away all their instincts to *interpret* existing scripts and instead to create in the moment, using found objects. Actors, writers and artists look for the symbolic in their work, for words and actions to resonate outside themselves; he wants to destroy this, as Themerson had tried to with Semantic Poetry. 'What the found object never is is a symbol. The broken rifle, the mailed fist, the lover's rose, are not found objects. They are pieces of language with clear legible meaning; something else.'

> I had an urgent fascination for pushing language as near abstraction as possible without joining the ranks of the concrete poets and the pure sound manipulators. I was interested in the fact that absurdity in language doesn't just make people laugh, it also strips language of sense and leaves the bare bones of syntax showing; reveals linguistic structures by paring away the clouding of emotive communication. Far from the chaos which the prosaic mind takes it to be, Dada is the way to a very lucid constructivism.[2]

---

[1] London: Thames & Hudson, 1974
[2] p. 132

Another non-fictional work is *The Anatomy of My Father's Corpse,* a short pamphlet containing reflections on seeing his father's body in the coffin. His fond memories seem to want to express themselves in poetry, but he resists this.

> A determination ot to write this down in verse, this subject that lends itself so readily to poetry, that seems so extensive and ambiguous in its nature that it constitutes the very prototype of poetry from the observation of which the practise of poetry primarily sprang; but to put this in prose that the wonder of it might not be that flexing copper irony of pain felt before the Channel sea at dusk when the sea itself was clouded with metal-browns from mud and clamorous hurricane clouds massed over the land of the North reflected.[1]

[1] not paginated

An early typewritten and cheaply-printed work is *Mr. Watkins Got Drunk and had to be Carried Home.* Subtitled 'A partypiece cut-up by Jeff Nuttall from an idea by William Burroughs', *Mr. Watkins* was written in 1964 and published in 1968. It was published by Writers Forum, typewritten and printed on orange and green paper. Nuttall said: 'I put *Mr Watkins* together wrongly, treated the idea like a wild way of making a word object. That was okay but Burroughs meant the project as dissolution of time.' However, he says it is a 'fair record of Writers' Forum'[1], which, as he says was mainly run by his friend, sound poet Bob Cobbing. He said of its genesis:

> The people I invited to write their accounts and come to the party were from Writers' Forum and Group H. They seemed handy and literate. Keith, John, Bob, Lois, me and Nick Watkins provided accounts and Nick set it as a subject at the school where he was teaching, so provided some marvellous copy a good long time before Brian [*sic*] Johnson used the same technique in *Albert Angelo.* The result, sieved and shuffled, was *Mr. Watkins.* I ran off a handful of copies and distributed them around WF.[2]

The text is a collage of recordings made at a party for Writers Forum poets by pupils at the school Nuttall taught at, interspersed with texts by the pupils themselves. Nuttall gives his role as 'scissorman' rather than author.

> GUESTS as opposite wrote their own forecasts of what would happen PLUS accounts in advance from pupils of Ravenscroft School A TAPE RECORDER recorded or did not record the proceedings the creative CUTUPRY was done by Jeff Nuttall

Some of the pupils' writing is hilarious, intentionally or otherwise.

> There is going to be a party on Saturday at a house in Sailsbury. Jeff Mutton as having it, my idea of a beatnik party Will be lots of men with beards and glasses like Mr. Watkins ladies with long hair and lots of beatniks.[3]

---

[1] From 1965 Writers Forum published a long series of radical poetry pamphlets; in 1973 a 100th celebration volume was issued.

[2] *Bomb Culture*, p. 148

[3] p. 2

The recordings of the party scenes proceed as the guests get drunk and more philosophical. Three of the participants are Bob Cobbing described by Nuttall as 'painter, poet, art commando', John Rowan, 'poet, progressive Tory' and Keith Musgrove, with whom Nuttall collaborated on an early work[1].

> JR: The tape recorder isn't working.
> JN: Yes it is - the nightingale has reversed all the equinoxes This is removal day at least this is half removal daynot arf it isn't the day of judgement Lois is of course a biblical naaman so is john rowan berries aucuparia last poems of jeff Just take a huge bite out of everyone we like pomes de terre and enhance I don't like potatoes in their jackets Ionesco Unesco Tesco Fires gone out Electricity's off and on
> BC: Cocteau is overrated
> JR: Jean Cocteau is dead. De mortus nil nisi mortuum and all that[2]

After an incomprehensible poetry reading and some Nuttall-esque scatology, the work ends:

> KM: Death
> Death
> Death
> Death
> Death
> Death
> Death
> BC: (through window) Ferlinghetti is overrated.
> KM: (Dies.)
> JM: Oh well, let's see what we've got on the tape. Oh, it wasn't on after all (shoots himself with an old teacup lying handy and collapses into an old bath lying handy.) Ave et vale!

---

[1] *The Limbless Virtuoso*, London: Writers Forum, 1963
[2] p. 3

There were about ten people at Slisbury Road, they was MR & Mrs Rowan and MR & Mrs[1] cobbing, later on in the party after we had some eats we had some records and one or two got a bit drunk it was held by Jeff Nuttall and his wife.
at Saulisbury Road at 7pm at Jeff Nuttall House
The first to arrive was John Rowan who had a beard and Mrs Neil Rowan ho did not and the rest followed afterwards they hada few records and sandwiches Mr Watkins who had a beard and smashed some plates. He had some drings mind you and so did a few overs. Mr Watkins got drunk and had to be carried home.[2]

---

[1] Jennifer Pike
[2] pp. 45/36

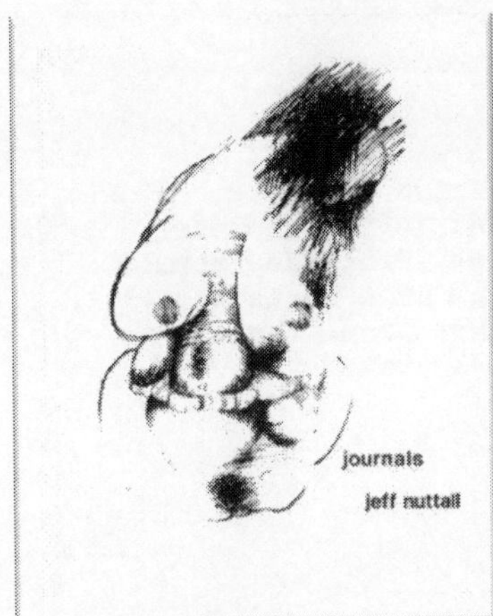

Jeff Nuttall produced several relatively conventional, or at least, conventionally-presented books that are easy to classify as volumes of poetry, mostly in what he called his 'lyric impressionist vein'[1]. The only exception is *Journals*, which is a series of short, illustrated, dated, impressionist pieces that may be classified as prose or prose-poetry (not that Nuttall was interested in classification; he said 'an art form defined is an art form half way to castration'[2]). It might be suggested that if Nuttall's poetry is impressionist, his prose is expressionist, though this is obviously a dangerous generalisation. His prose fiction is roughly split into two types. There are several conventionally-printed books, not illustrated except on the front cover, that might be classed as novels (though none is more than novella-length), and a number of short prose works. Some of these short works are plain text and others combine typewritten text, hand-lettering (sometimes barely legible), illustrations and cut-up news articles. The illustrated works are impossible to describe and do not have a linear story, so I have just included two pages from each to try to give an impression of them.

[1] *Performance Art: Memoirs*, p. 132
[2] p. cit., p. 24

Come Back Sweet Prince: a Novelette

15.18 hrs.: Entered the crucifixion clearing. Appeared to be completely deserted. Proceeded across clearing in a northwesterly direction. The sun is intensely hot.

15.20 hrs.: Silence becoming curiously oppressive. There is a sense of someone walking immediately behind me but this is absurd.

15.22 hrs.: The significance of the flayed dog is suddenly clear to me. I wish Christine had not been involved.

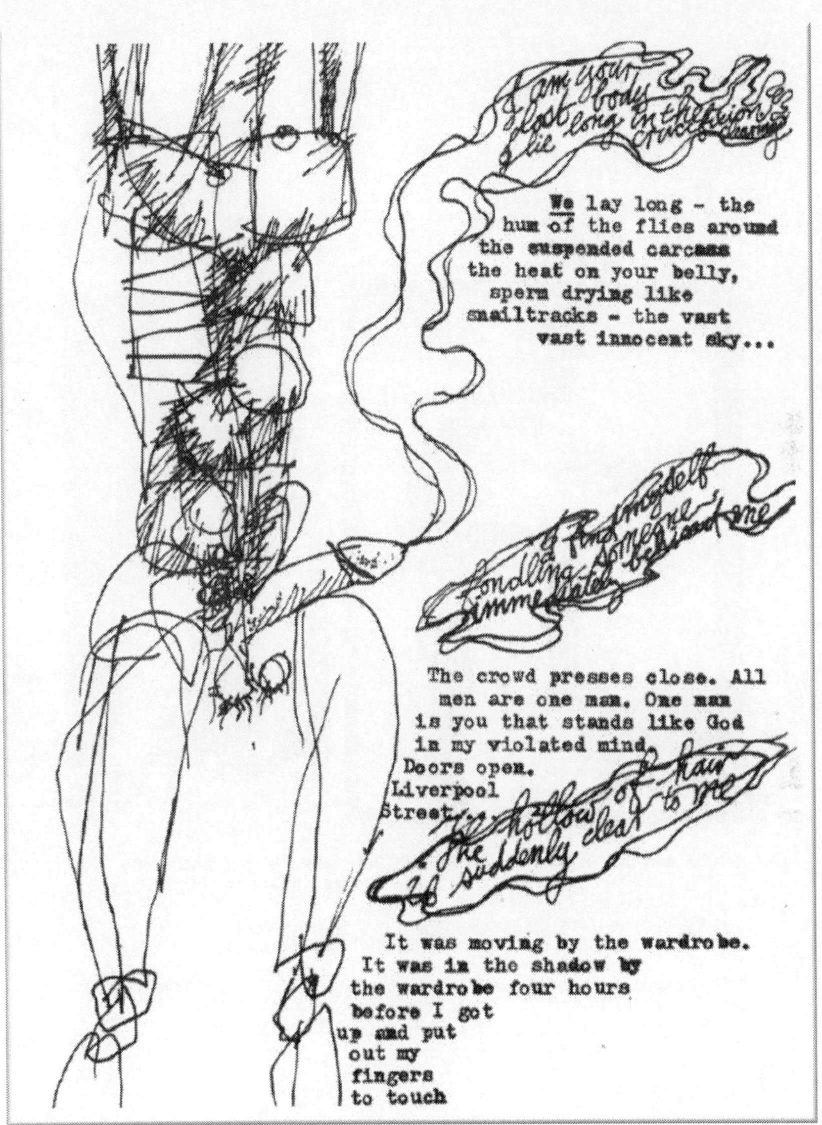
I am your
lost body
lie long in the
We lay long - the
hum of the flies around
the suspended carcass
the heat on your belly,
sperm drying like
snailtracks - the vast
vast innocent sky...
fondling
someone
immediately
The crowd presses close. All
men are one man. One man
is you that stands like God
in my violated mind.
Doors open.
Liverpool
Street...
the hollow of hair
suddenly clear to me
It was moving by the wardrobe.
It was in the shadow by
the wardrobe four hours
before I got
up and put
out my
fingers
to touch

Oscar Christ and the Immaculate Conception: Another Novelette

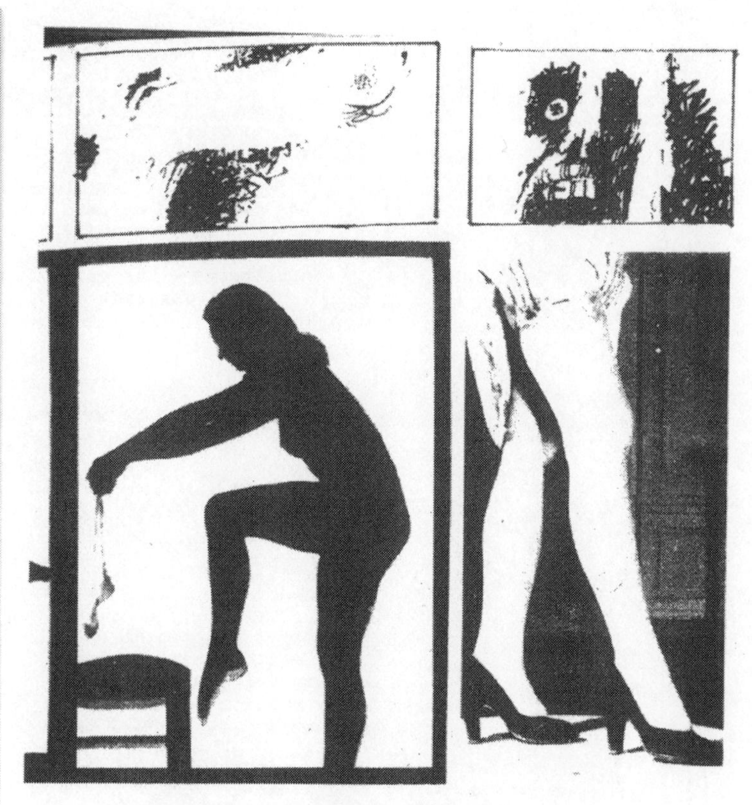

"I am the emissary of Christ" he said. "I am the
winged messenger. I come to pump his leaden
love into your starvation."
Mother, the flame stammered out of his webbed crotch.
Mother, the seed of Christ ripped through my tender
bouquet.
I writhed on the floor nine hours mother, and halfway
through the ninth hour of labour the greasy
hands of Europe dragged from my corpse the
new Messiah.

our legs in their cheap black-market
nylons that his triumph
trickled down, unless we
we caught it first, like
tears, on stolen Red Cross
cottonwool.
Our man brought home
no food. He brought home

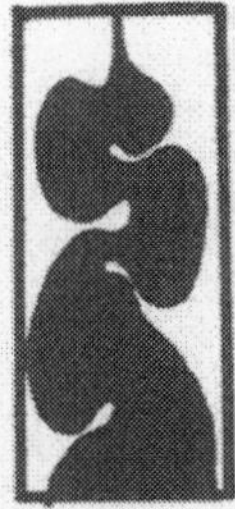

swazzle-stukas

hengink hup apove

his razorbeak cheescutter.

only sickness, malcontent and
surly passion. Lying on us
in his millions, trick after
trick, night after night.
That night I woke and said
"What's your name, Oscar?"
"Christ" he said.
"My love" I sang into his
shrouded loins "You're dead
as any other Jew. Take me
with you."

The Foxes' Lair

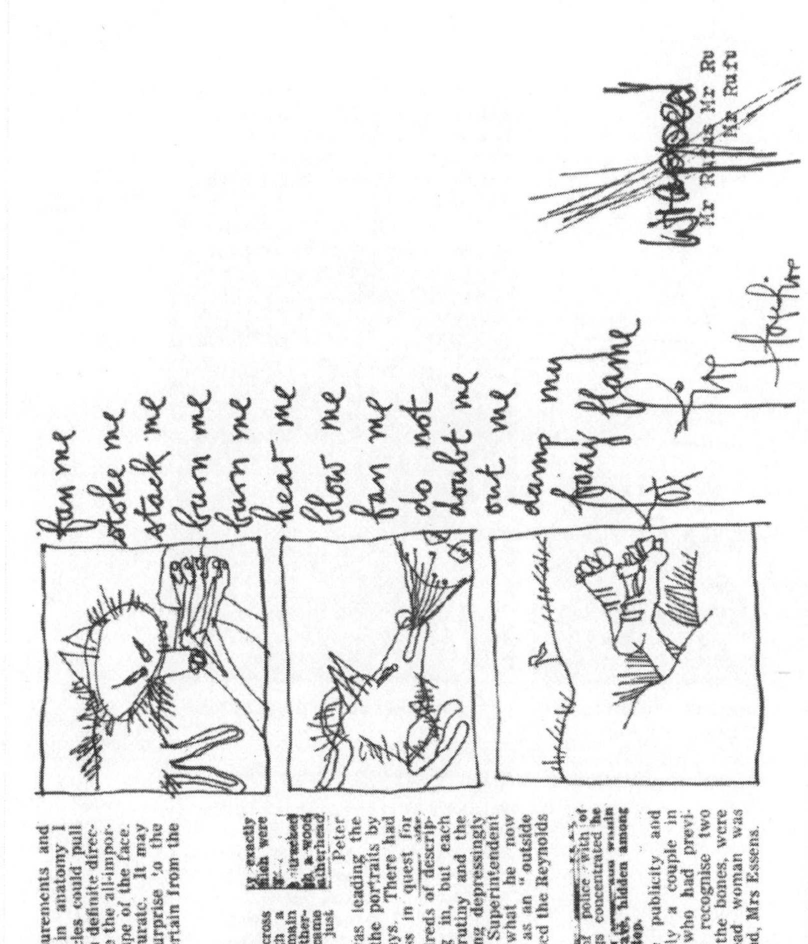

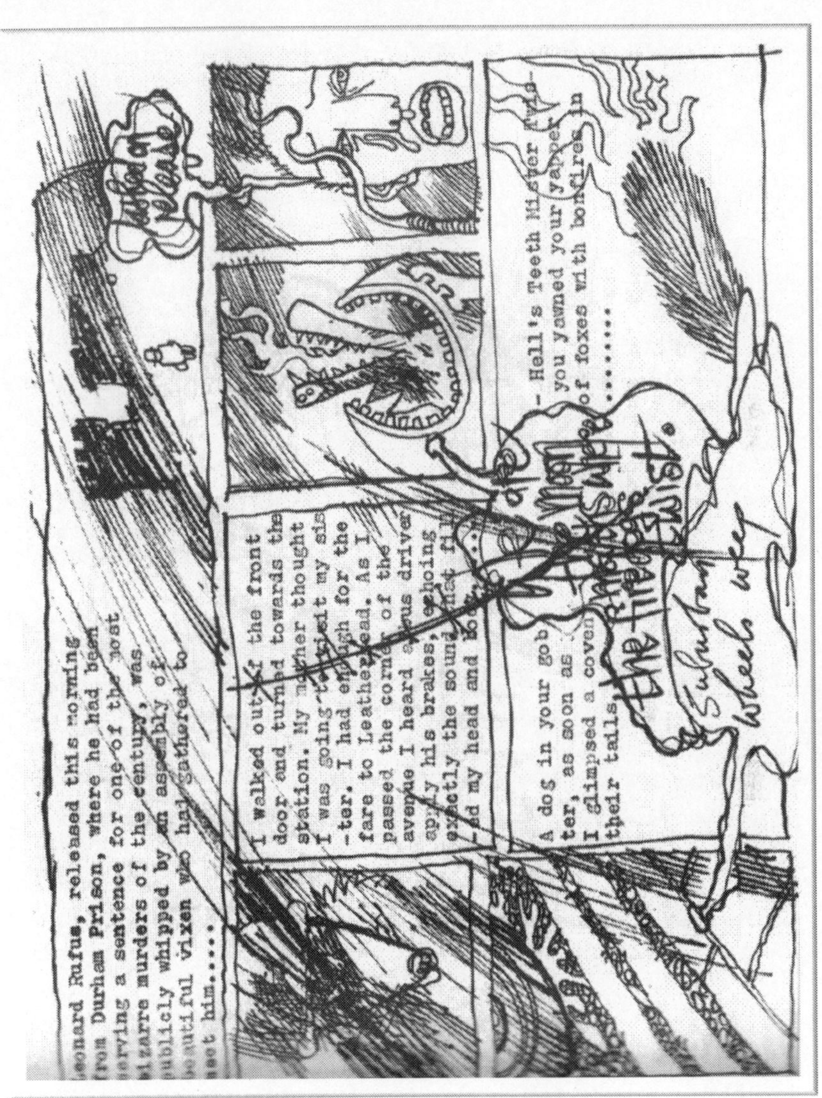
eonard Rufus, released this morning
rom Durham Prison, where he had been
erving a sentence for one of the most
izarre murders of the century, was
ublicly whipped by an assembly of
eautiful vixen who had gathered to
eet him.....
I walked out of the front
door and turned towards the
station. My mother thought
I was going to visit my sis
-ter. I had enough for the
fare to Leatherhead. As I
passed the corner of the
avenue I heard a bus driver
apply his brakes, echoing
exactly the sound
-ed my head and
A dog in your gob
ter, as soon as
I glimpsed a coven
their tails
- Hell's Teeth Mister Fox-
you yawned your yapper
of foxes with bonfires in
....

Krak

She touched it lightly pryingly, peering through a mist of condensation into the dressing-table mirror. The calamine lotion dried across the delicate bruises her index fingers had left He sat on the edge of the bed nursing the wrist that still ached from her pelvis's insistent plunging, feeling some fear in the face of her immeasurable orgasmic deeps. A parsimonious legislator within demanded that all such oceanic creatures, housing such cyclones, should be controlled in the interest of the general good order of things.

Her passion burst through her normal frigidity with the force of the menstrual gushing which usually followed it, so that, when "The Curse" had fallen, her pain came as an extension of her previous passion, a cruel reprisal for the way in which she had betrayed her forbearan born in a kind of [illegible] ecstasy. There was something perverse about the way she

t here," I hissed.
st a touch," she whimpered.

Stopped at the bottom of the stairs.
My hand was fussing into my pyjamas. "I'm not
coming back," she shouted.

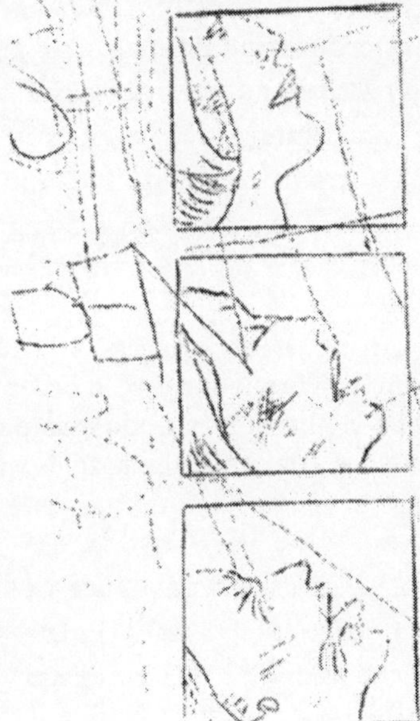

Stretch 'em in your hand.
Pull them across your face.
The harshness of the nylon, the
auntie's kiss of old-fashioned
silk.
Smells of the body, smells of
a mess in a drawer - the whiff
of the things that are stolen
away from little boys, corners
of living where no man can go.
Backs of the cupboards in
red-curtained rooms. Items of
merchandise wrapped in brown
paper, whispers and giggles
that stop sharp on coming back
to the party, subjects dropped
on the threshold of the powder
room and left there - shed
stockings, dropped skins,
sheaths discarded, the soles of
the rumours yellowed and stained.
Bury your nosein a whisp of
laughter, taste the musk of a

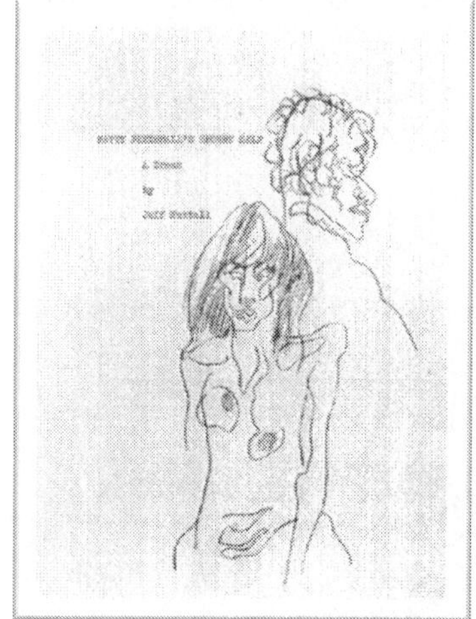

Fatty Feedemall's Secret Self , an unillustrated, typewritten pamphlet is about a man who has no 'contingency' in his memory, who lives parallel lives, one of which may be a dream.

> Awaking in the chamber, amazed at his familiarity to that image of himself that lay in the bed, amazed at the presence in his head of the address 92, Lugborough St., wondering at the strangeness of this very familiarity as he had once wondered on seeing a strange face in a café, not knowing why it was familiar or why he suddenly knew the name of this man who had no contingency in his memory.
>
> That sense that he had, in dreaming, caught himself out in a second life which he had, all along, been living, parallel with the first.[1]

Dreaming of a crash in a van he has been driving, he experiences a 'weary reluctance to get out and lift. Return to the warm moist cunt of sleep, in order to wake in his own bed.' He is not sure whether he is 'the sleeper in the bumping vehicle or the loving husband in the honey-chamber.' He meets the harpies who inhabit his dream world.

> Along the lower stave lines of a voluptuous sequence of sevenths a gaggle of emaciated noblewomen climb, their stilettos hooked on the ladder, the wires cutting across the shallow curves of their upper arms.

A harpy tells him, 'while her gaggle of friends sang like a saxophone section in ecstasy': before he wakes out of 'that wanked out body in which you dwell, consider this secret other self of yours as a fiction. Never doubt the strength of a good yarn well spun, lovely.' There is a long biography of Fatty, who is clearly Nuttall himself, and who is 'tart, aware, sharp, and completely mediocre.' until he becomes Fatty Feedemall, 'the lovable fuckup we all embrace.' He wakes up

[1] no page numbers

beside his wife but dreams of a life in a Brighton boarding house, 'that never-lived day.' He has an affair with Rosamond but she herself turns into the harpy. The questions are raised: are all women harpies; do all men have a Fatty Feedemall inside, and should they try to become him? The work ends:

> Rosamond Drew was a scrawny duchess dangling from the lamp bracket in her dusky nylon gauzes. Cackling a chorus with a flock of syphilitic sisters.
>
> "Well, it wasn't a bad idea, was it; my bumbling loverbee, to write a new life, turn over a dead leaf. come into your - other skin . . . We maidens of the grave are your righteous guardians. Back to the garden and the passing moment while we climb back on to the death-stave to whistle the living awake. No other love. No greater love. Give us a kiss, fuckdust."

The Case of Isabel and the Bleeding Foetus, 1968, was the first-published of Nuttall's full-length (all around 25-40,000 words) prose works, not illustrated apart from the cover and conventionally printed in hardback book rather than pamphlet form. The prose is poetic in the sense that it is not linear, does not tell a conventional story, but is neither the inner, dreamlike, nocturnal prose of Kavan, Shuttle, Figes and some of Heppenstall or Belben nor the cut-up/stream of consciousness writing of Burroughs, Trocchi and some of Alan Burns. Nuttall fits more easily into the English tradition of Fielding/Sterne/ Fanny Hill, though his scatological, deliberately excessive writing is closer to Rabelais; Nuttall himself was a Gargantua figure. The novel alternates different sections: diary entries, dated 1966, poems, interview tapes and transcriptions of interrogations. There are recurring characters, but they merge into each other: Henry and Joan; Henry and Charles the Interrogator; Gary and the Immovable. 'It has occurred to Gary and I that a plane of consciousness has been reached whereby separate identities have become fluid and are, in fact, merging together.'[1] Vera Lynn appears as Vera Lung and with many other surnames; we also have the Phallic Ghost and the mysterious Isabel, whose identity we never discover. The foetus of the title is not fully explained either, but is associated with the Phallic Ghost.

> The place visited by a moment and the moment is the Phallic Ghost who brings with his song his strange inevitable partner (can be found in ditches – the ditch behind the pavilion separating sportsfield from secret back-gardens of gaunt stockbroker's Tudor villas – can be found (if we look) crumpled in that darkest corner of the changing room – is in the crotch of the tree we climb through to get back onto the road – always is, when found, a crumpled weeping foetus with an egghead of blood and a fleshknot of a face from whose screwed-up cuntformation eyes the tears of blood splash big and black – stain his messed trouserfront – and his tiny gibbon hands move fingers like the fronds of seaplants before his face and the whole of his tiny strained aborted flesh swells rubicund rich purple with the guilt and anger visited on him (*who is the self I know*) by the tall ghost – the ghastly quiver that screams songs rendering the very earth itself into demon energy with head of live bone that sings that's always singing THIS: I am the death and the orgasm and nothing exists that is not there by the grace of me – that you and any independent man must always be a crying thing – a wrinkled purple fruit dropped early – painful and your pain, all all your wrinkled purple pain will not affect my stance, my quiver song, my ghastly electricity – look look at the evening colours – how they sing.[2]

Much of the text consists of transcriptions of 'Interior Interrogation Tapes', between the Interrogator, who is trying to find the identities of Isabel and the Phallic Ghost, and Immovable – the Immovables live in the Interior Area.

> Interrogator: You say this Phallic Ghost of which you speak is constituted not only of bone, but also of precious metal and thirdly of feathers.
>
> Immovable: I wing the feathered bone in the sun.
>
> Interrogator: You imply a dichotomy between the sun and the ghost who are, as you say, locked in collusive oral intercourse.
>
> Immovable: Scream songs up the stabstab. Blade for my deathly love.

---

[1] pp. 39/40

[2] p. 12

Interrogator: But now the Ghost takes on qualities previously the prerogative of the sun.
Immovable: I bled myself to gold and the Phallic Ghost entered me.[1]

The Immovable, who may or may not be intended to bring to mind Beckett's Unnameable, seems to identify himself with the Moors Murderer Ian Brady, who also occurs in *The Patriarchs*, or at least seems to have absorbed Brady's guilt.

Immovable: Isabel is an arch of pale bone in Cannon's Park Pavilion. Isabel brings gentle hand. They *will* soothe sores for me and Brady. Smooth wind power – no, no other peace or soothing –
Interrogator: Ah! As I suspected! And what *exactly* do you know about Cannon's Park Sports Club Pavilion? I knew we'd find someone or something there that could give information.
Immovable: What do you find that could know?
Interrogator: Now listen, you little swine – Who is Isabel? What is the significance of Isabel and where can I find her?
Immovable: Spread thighs bowstrung with your stretch pants
Thighs arch bone beneath the grimed stone arches
- Tunnel of Hungerford Lane
- You, spatterlacing cobbles, legs wide –
- Wiry spraddle, sprung like a mad cat,
- Jet lemon gems fine as a cat's slash –[2]

As the interrogation continues, Vera's voice begins to break in and the Immovable starts to address Ian Brady: 'I held my secret rite as a secret and kept it as a secret, didn't carry out the grace-note with the saw-edge razor'. Brady's 'disgrace is disinterred while we tend ours as a secret . . . all we can do now is wither in the ditch and weep and weep black scum of guilt, moor mist making spidergems on our quivering shoulders.'[3] So his guilt may or may not be real but either way he needs grace, and at the end we are told: 'The name of Isabel is grace. . .'[4]

---

[1] p. 25
[2] pp. 38/39
[3] p. 60
[4] p. 61

Pig, published in 1969 by Fulcrum, mainly a poetry publisher, has an introduction by William Burroughs, who says Nuttall's 'structures are essentially musical as is his prose.' This is especially true in this novel, which has several kinds of narrative, all highly evocative of a certain Northern English working class life. The opening paragraph sets the tone.

> At the back of the house (trodden-in plaster on hall lino 20s jazz-modern geometric pattern in browns) was the suds yard (soap slime on the grate grid) – decent brick and flags and nurtured bunch-grass growing from grit all smelling bland and carbolic of soap, those kind foetal slimes, smell of a fat mam's hands – Pears Soap ovals of her loosely cradled breasts as she stoops to cat-lick your cheeks with spit on a hanky for where is the archetypal moother mooTHER!! haunting me with bellows bloomers – fond ballooning caricature of airborne motherhood[1]

There are three sections: The Rain; The Train and The Coast. The middle section seems at first to be unconnected to the first, but turns out to be a flashback, giving one of three versions of what may have happened on a train between George Gland – the pig of the title – and a young girl. In the first and third sections George is 'the old man', a disgusting figure described by Mike, the main character and sometime narrator of these sections, who later refers to him as Uncle George.

> I sat with the old man the whole four hours of a sunday afternoon and for the whole of those four hours we hated one another and for the whole of those four hours there was no talk. We sat beside the stained dinner plates and the empty light-ale bottles and by four o'clock I was in a jade ecstasy of nausea at the occasional glimpses of his soiled and flaccid penis – sleeping, fingered fish – when his greatcoat fell apart in the course of his dozing. I sat bilious with hatred, the corners of the room swimming into oceans of Down Your Way radio sounds, some disgusting fragments of shredded Dimbleby-foreskin flapping listlessly

---

[1] p. 9

> among the spiderfairies, and I noticed the tide-marks of dysentery unwashed from the old man's knotty thighs[1]

Mike is visited by the police looking for the mysterious Hector Jurgens, but it may have only been a dream: they threaten his wife Sue, but she says they can't hurt her in a dream. Sue seems also to have been seduced by the old man, in a section closer to *Ulysses* that to Burroughs: 'for how can I tell poor Mickey that the old man took me with trembling hand feeble in its excitement and led me out into the – I'll take care of you, me flower. Come and cop a look at this, me little blossom' with him 'pleading me to pass the benediction on his filth and on his act that fixed us with a clotted stare of one thumbnail paring of iris under the drooped lid'[2].

In the middle section, a younger George is on a train when a young girl and her dog come to sit in the same compartment.

> Little girl got on, saw them in the corridor – goodbye Mum. Mum dark against the evening sky and he could remember goodnight kisses – scent of goodnight kiss called scent not perfume.
>
> Little girl slid open the door, lower lip up under her teeth for the effort.
>
> Glances crossed like parrying knives a moment – hers serious, attentive, unsentimental, recorded him, touselled hair, pink cheek, grey pinstripe suit, flowertie, fat wrists. Her case on the rack, her dog – near spaniel – on the corner seat. She sat in the middle seat, read Bunty and her thighs were very smooth – no hair or pores yet visible.[3]

George follows her into the toilet on the train (or, according to a later version of the story, fantasises about it). The harming of children is something of a metaphor for inexcusable guilt for Nuttall; in other works he refers to child-murderers Brady and Hindley. In a cinematic scene, featuring Elvira Death, who may be his death-wish, the action is replayed from another angle.

> A pig-like man in a crumpled pinstripe suit and a flowertie was sitting in a railway

---

[1] p. 19

[2] p. 14

[3] p. 32

> compartment: Close-up of George Pig looking at something furtively. . .
> "Old friends, small world Georgieboy," said Elvira Death, winding her gesture round the drillpig paradestick.
> "I am not in that railway carriage," said George, confirming his presence by denial.
> "I am on the left-hand side of the page."[1]

Later on we get a second version of the incident on the train. As the girl goes to the toilet, the 'thought of the functional unveiling there to take place further inflamed the man's admittedly infantile sexuality. He did however restrain himself from following her.' In this version, all he does is to construct 'an elaborate fantasy in order to sublimate his desires.'[2] The third version of the incident comes in another cinematic episode.

> The screen showed a railway compartment. A schoolgirl, accompanied by her dog, was sitting opposite a florid man.
>
> Schoolgirl: (*to dog*) Sit quietly Flossie! Sorry, she's awfully fretful
> Man: Hm? Mmmm.
> Schoolgirl: She's on heat.
> Man: Er – really?
> Schoolgirl: I think it's awfully exciting when that sort of thing happens. Don't you?
> Man: Exciting? Well – heavens – yes I suppose – er, yes.
> Schoolgirl: I suppose it's exciting because – well – it's all nature really. It's all like us.
> Man: S'pose it is really.
> *Schoolgirl suddenly flopped her legs apart and lay sprawled, ostensibly in a tomboyish pose. Her thumb crept up to her mouth. She spoke around the thumb.*[3]

The Lolita-ish girl appears to be trying to seduce George, though this may be only his fantasy and we think it is the 'real' version because it is presented as the script of a film we can 'see'. '*Close-ups showed mischief giving way to a certain glistening dreaminess in the girl's face.*' She says to George: 'Shall I show you how to play with Flossie?' He grabs her to try to '*cover her thighs. She gripped his hand in her thighs and locked it there, crossing her ankles in their white*

---

[1] pp. 41/42
[2] p. 79
[3] pp. 88/89

socks.'[1] Whichever version of the story is the 'truth', if any, George seems to have been kept in some kind of institution as a result of it for a long time, emerging as the old man of the first and third sections. In the home, George descends to the gross physicality so prevalent in Nuttall's characters: we have seen in *Man Not Man* that the 'fear of not getting to the pot in time' informs al his writing. Talking to the doctor George says:

> You will have noticed my disturbance is marked by my growing obsession with human anatomy, particularly those parts related to sex and defecation. You will see that my whole sphere of thought is a long-playing educational record on the subject of How To Scour Out Your Potty Training With A Whirling Douche. You will have noticed the needle is stuck in a repeating groove.[2]

Evidence, if it were needed, that George Gland is to some extent Nuttall's alter ego. At the end, the girl reappears at the edge of the sea, possibly in ghostly form: 'a dim smudge dimmer than the timid curls of surf'[3]. As in *Snipe's Spinster* and *The Gold Hole*, the novel ends with a gun. As the old man looks up from the child, he tells Mike they should both confess. 'Fly away to the lands of total freedom.'

> Mike didn't move. He tried to force himself to look at the child but he couldn't – just looked ahead at the grey old man grinning in the grey landscape and watched the whole picture getting watery and blurred. It was into this grey blur that his hand rose almost automatically, hovered there clenched around the gun while he tried to will his eyes to focus. He heard the old man's voice "Now 'oo the fuckin 'ell do you reckon you're kid –" and he noticed it had stopped and the echoing explosion had stopped and the watery mess which was all he could see had blossomed crimson in the grey.
>
> He stood there, hoping the tears would clear. He felt small hands clinging climbing his trouserleg. He turned and made his way to dry land, dragging the child like a trap clamped to his ankle. His wife was waiting – face, eyes, her breasts were luminous with morning rain. . . . . .[4]

---

[1] p. 89
[2] p. 58
[3] p. 93
[4] pp. 95/96

The 1975 novel *Snipe's Spinster* was published by Calder & Boyars, who had also published Burroughs and Hubert Selby as well as much of the European avant garde and in Britain Ann Quin, Penelope Shuttle and the early Alan Burns. It is somewhere between a philosophical novel and a social history; a fictional follow-up to *Bomb Culture*. It is a meditation on and elegy for the 1960s and the 'failure of invention in the arts.'[1], describing the seriousness and pessimism of the early 1970s as compared to the heady atmosphere of *Bomb Culture*. Nuttall also described this in the introduction to *The House Party*, also published in 1975.

> The early seventies saw a wind-down of a period of incredibly dense change and development in art. If things are at a halt it's because the way of mounting complexity leads to the meditative vacuum. Kaprow leads to Beuys. Pollock leads to Reinhardt or back to Malevitch. Parker leads to the long simple notes of Rollins. White on white. Black on black, white sound, the world falling away to reveal Laing's No Thing. I'm a naive optimist. Rather than sit in meditative prayer with my mind blown as clear as Leary's I attempt to continue to build.[2]

Snipe's Spinster is set in a specific location and time – Edinburgh in 1971 – and the narrator, Snipe, is a jazz musician who is planning to shoot 'the Man', a mysterious figure representing power and authority.

> "We're going to hit the Man."
> "Right. Why we gonna hit the Man?"
> "Because of Vietnam and the South American mines and the Chicago trial and the bomb and napalm and poison gas and the smog and the money and the pigs."
> And why else we gonna hit the Man?"
> "Why else Crane?"

---

[1] p. 30. This was later explored more deeply for the visual arts in Nuttall's *Art and the Degradation of Awareness*.

[2] no pagination

> "Because we know that history ain't nothin'. That Vietnam ain't nothin'. That the world is but a glass bubble man. That the Man is no more than a tick of the second hand of a cheap clock baby. That it don't *matter* baby, so we gonna do it for *kicks*. An' we can do that man, because we connected. We got the motherfuckin' power."[1]

Snipe believes, however that since the 1960s power has moved from the people to the authorities, though none of his contacts seems to realise. Symbolically, perhaps, the first sentence of the novel is 'I got my haircut in 1971.' 'Energy was handed over to the electronic suppliers, to the government authorities, to the impresarios and the studio technicians. Power was lost. The original bid to take over the media was reversed,'[2]

In addition to the fictional characters, who are mostly representative types rather than rounded characters, the narrator names and quotes from many figures in popular and underground culture; there is a section of notes at the end as in a scholarly book. Snipe is more bourgeois and fussy than he wants to be; he has an internal 'spinster' whose prissiness he resents but cannot escape. 'I don't like my spinster. She is a bore and a virgin. She never learns not to goad me into ambitious moral decisions. She is the best person I have in that tribe my skull contains and I hate her for it.'[3] His American friend Crane, who represents the stoned hippy, reports a mutual friend saying of Snipe 'you're a bourgeois motherfucker an' you fuck with a mess of middle class intellectuals, an' you is a fake an' a phony an' he don't want nuthin' to do with ya.'[4]

Since Nuttall is speaking through a narrator, unlike in *Bomb Culture*, it is not clear whether this is his view of himself, also a jazz musician. It is also not clear whose side he takes on the issue of folk music's purism versus the new urban electrification of music, symbolised by the electric Blues of Chicago and highlighted by Bob Dylan's 1966 tour, where his electric guitar prompted cries of Judas. The people he calls he calls the Peacenicks, in their thirst for knowledge, had let the moment of possibility pass them by, lost in their theoretical fog and surrounded by a sea of apathy.

> Peacenicks in those days wanted to know. It is no accident that the rendezvous of the Underground were not pubs, clubs or discotheques, but bookshops. Better Books in London. Peace Eye in New York. Giat Froget's in Paris. City Lights in San Francisco. The Paperback in Edinburgh. They read continuously, not just the journals of folk and jazz, not just one another's poetry. They read Marx and Engels and

[1] pp. 24/25
[2] pp. 27/28
[3] p. 12
[4] p. 13

> Russell and Fromm and Thoreau. They read Hegel and Sartre and Heidegger and Shaw and Nietzsche. They read Kerouac and Ginsberg and Corso and Ferlinghetti. They read Steinbeck and Dos Passos and Thomas Wolfe and Nathaniel West. They read Osborne and Lessing and Colin Wilson and Adrian Mitchell and Christopher Logue. They read Teilhard de Chardin and Thomas Aquinas and the *I Ching*. They read *The Guardian, The New Statesman, The Observer, The Sunday Times, The Times, Time* and *Life, The Daily Worker, The Daily Mirror* and *Mad Magazine*. They read Blake and Burroughs and Beckett and Rimbaud and Joyce. And they saw about them a vast drift of people so ignorant and consequently so bored with their empty lives they walked willingly and eagerly towards the big bang and the big numbness, lubricating their slippery progress with the usual rationalisations about the facts of international power and the spirit of Dunkirk.[1]

As the peaceful movement for people's power has failed, groups like the Angry Brigade, as featured in Alan Burns' novel of the same name, have used violence to take the place of peaceful protest. One of the violent characters is the disfigured Jack: 'harbouring the irony that his ruthless intelligence casts over his own miserable situation, he sees the world properly, through a vast panoramic window of pain; and thus he approaches his politics properly by throwing everything he can at the window in an attempt to break it.'[2] Jack, younger than Snipe, sneers at his idealism. 'you're such a fucking kid Snipe. All you older faces are kids, Kidcats. Oh never mind. I mean you still think, you still think, you're going to make people into that shining ideal that never was. I mean, it's a joke and young people can see it's a joke and they're right.'[3] Snipe's main connection with younger people is his underage girlfriend, Lindy, a 'hard-headed young Scot, all savagery and dry irony'[4], with whom he has sex in abandoned cars. 'She slides along the seat of the cab until she can breathe and mouth and salivate along my prick' while Snipe is thinking of Rimbaud, Verlaine and Baudelaire. Compared to her, Snipe is deeply bourgeois, as their different descriptions of her mother show.

> "Ma mither's thirty six and she's seven bairns and varicose veins and a nasty cough. The peak of her life is Bingo, and a black eye, roughly twice a year, is the peak of passion she draws from me father. An' she's a lively woman still, fine bones and fond of a fuck. . ."
>
> "Your mother, my archangel of the twilight, is worn down by seven kids and no money. The back of your father's hand doesn't help. But she

---

[1] pp. 18/19
[2] p. 83
[3] p. 85
[4] p. 28

is sustained by the depth of her relationships – intertwining psychic roots. Your mother might be pathetic but she's dignified with it. She's decent."

"Decent? She'd sleep with anybody."

"But one man she shags continuously."

"The man that pays the bills and breaks her nose."

"Your father. The father. The man isn't the pivot finally. The pivot is you and your siblings."

"What in the fuck's a sibling?"[1]

In the end, it is not clear whether Snipe is in fact going to shoot the Man. He falters but then picks up the gun again as the story ends. But his spinster has already pointed out to him that the Man is really no different from him. With 'eyes the colour of a washingday sky' she tells him:

> The Man is somebody's father, uncle, son, husband. He is two arms and legs, balls and fallible brain like you, Snipe. Like you. All he ever did in Vietnam is what *his* spinster told him to do. He is going to look at you as he dies. He is going to suffer pain. The political chaos following his death may be worse than the dictatorship he maintains and the butchery he precipitates. But we, we have decided haven't we? I have my stern carbolic finger right up your arse.[2]

---

[1] pp. 69/70

[2] p. 96

In his introduction to *The House Party*, 1975, Nuttall had stated a very grand ambition to be in the same league as *Finnegans Wake*, Guernica and Moses und Aron: 'multi-levelled and self-perpetuating', a 'monument past which subsequent innovators have failed to go.' Unlike his other longer prose works it is illustrated and uses non-standard typography. It subverts not just the novel in general but the country-house novel in particular. Like Tom Phillips' *A Humument*, 1973, it is a form of treatment and a parody of the Victorian novel of manners. There is a large cast of characters but, as with Alan Burns' *Babe*l, they do not join together to form a plot, and the book is structured more like a cut-up, with characters and dialogue switching rapidly and seemingly at random. There are four main characters do recur: Sir John; Henry, George and Isabel – who may or may not be the Isabel of grace from *The Case of Isabel and the Bleeding Foetus*. Although the text does not seem to have any meaning beyond itself, is not, as Nuttall says elsewhere, a symbol of something else, the introduction says that the last few paragraphs state 'fairly clearly' the 'burden' of the novel: 'It is, I suppose, a perverse and aggressive for of pantheism, the worshipful adherence to a painful situation in the belief that such a situation is likely to be more illuminatory and fulfilling, than the mere pursuit of happiness.' This, however is not so clear; the novel ends with Henry meditating:

> should I save my face and reap my resolutions, should I get up off my back and cry the positive love I play with in promises, then I forfeit possibly my greatest privilege in my short drop from birth to death, which is to eat the black refuse and scream into the hollow chasm that is the only thing to which I truly progress, the only thing that's left desirable beyond the grave, or back there in the motherlove, the fond enclosure beyond the funky antechamber, the great waste cackle, the gaunt stench of God.[1]

[1] no pagination

But the woman rose, retrieved her enormous hat from where it rested on the shrubberies, and walked across the lawn with her loose-shanked stride. He and George carried Sir John and Julia indoors. They undressed them with difficulty. Julia was extremely beautiful, the night of her striking up from her thighs across her shallow abdomen, the dew of the previous night in swathes bathing her laving her salvation slave.

COCKATITCHICK

Do not respond to this patronising whimsy. I don't have to be every fucker's fat clown, least of all yours, you incestuous little prick teaser. "Well said, old man," muttered George and vanished again, leaving a dull after-image of his white tie and shirt front. "Ruth has great need of you," Edna had said.

Five pints of Guinness in the evening.

"Them wor all mines ower theer," said Tom Barret, looking like a puff from the coal-dust in his eyelashes. "Fuckin' cowboy-oiles all owert' 'illside." Drunk enough for numbness....

HENRY JUMBO IS CAPTURED BY THE GREEN NOSE PEOPLE. HOW CAN HE ESCAPE? KIND WIDOW PUGGY-WUGGY WILL DRAG HIM OUT BY THE KNACKERS

HOUSEWIFE Jean Adams sniffed suspiciously at her daughter's new toy, Lulu the golden-haired rag doll.

SHAGGY BLOSSOMS
IN THE FLOWERBEDS

WITLESS ON AN
EMBROIDERED
BUS

A CARDBOARD
CROWN IN AN
EMPTY ROAD

The 1975 work T*he Patriarchs: An Early Summer Landscape* alternates two types of narrative: reports on readings at the 'Airebridge' festival by the poet 'Jack Roberts' and dated, daily reports from ward 5, Bradford Royal Infirmary.[1] Some of the pages are illustrated by line drawings.

> The poet Jack Roberts has dominated the narrow world of English letters for at least fifteen years As it happens this is little credit to him. English letters during these fifteen years has been in the hands of a talentless and unadventurous group of poets who see to it that most good writing doesn't get published.[2]

Nuttall is presumably referring to the poets of The Movement[3], whose concerns with taste, economy and moderation were anathema to him. 'Here in this island of spurious gentility, Roberts articulates the animus, bitterly and inevitably famished to his very bones for want of gentleness.' Roberts reads his verse to the festival audience: 'Spectral gigantified nursery picture. Protozoic childhood oozing through sleep's prehistory. The archetype. The rock turned beard, the step scree of the father's hand.' Although this is clearly parody, Nuttall's prose in the alternate, hospital sections echoes it and might almost be by Ted Hughes. 'A godgiven sheepsbladder filled to capacity with sunlight like weedpollen strains at its moorings from the blackstone building's blunt west wall. The hausers creak.' The character Rose, whom the narrator (presumably Nuttall himself) had described as a 'rat' in a 'recent poem' but could also be a 'night animal; field mouse; shrew; lemur', is his antagonist in a series of arguments about the nature

---

[1] According to a note in *Jeff Nuttall: A Celebration*, Roberts was based on Ted Hughes, a fellow Northerner, whom Nuttall appreciated as a poet but disliked as a media celebrity; Airebridge is Ilkley and the hospital scenes describe the time when Nuttall had a serious operation, made worse because he woke up in the middle of it.

[2] no page numbers

[3] See Robert Conquest, ed. *New Lines: An Anthology*. London: McMillan, 1956; Robert Conquest, ed. *New Lines II: An Anthology*. London: McMillan, 1963; Blake Morrison. *The Movement: English Poetry and Fiction of the 1950s*. Oxford University Press, 1980

of language and communication. The narrator fails to understand her need for both love and isolation.

> "Isolation", I said, "is surely impossible. It's not that I don't comprehend it. I comprehend it very well and I know that in terms of the human personality it doesn't exist."
>
> It does, it does", she said bloodily . . . "Evil", she once said, "You don't understand evil, its purity – its isolate integrity." Drove me then away, turning her self-awareness in her carrion breast as a ceremony of evil's purity.

Evil enters the narrative through mention of real-life 'Moors Murderers' Brady and Hindley, and in the mention of local folk stories of the abuse of orphan children used as labour in the early Industrial Revolution, which began in the area of Yorkshire where the story is set; the antithesis of Hughes' romanticising of the Yorkshire landscape.

> Hairy-backed shepherds with bleak blue eyes and sceptical mouths . . . dragged their ailing children on a hempen halter the way they were to drag pack-mules bent under wool, recalcitrant wives bent under the knuckle, the way the valley millworkers were to carry unwanted children and lay them along the crags four thousand years later: victims and sacrifices being dragged bluntly, impassively over the rocks over the heather to be tipped through the strata of spring leaves, through the mustard-yellow peppering of the foliage, into the rock throat down which the water roars at dambank.

As well as the natures of evil and isolation, Nuttall and Rose argue about the ability of language to communicate thought and emotion. He says:

> "Those who continue to relate their understanding to language end in despair. They make the media into their content. All you can ever do with language is describe understanding."
>
> "Despair", she bit out as though defending children. "Despair is beautiful. Where have all your majestic convictions gone? Where's your fucking pride? . . . The whole purpose of art is to divert the natural course of things. You do that. To bend the state of things you're born to is to achieve eroticism. You're thinking about fucking happiness."

At the end of the book Nuttall, presumably, wakes up after the operation which has saved his life[1].

> And suddenly no drift to death, the ocean not at the mother's vagina warmly lapping me home, but a drop, when the throat catheter drops from my mouth by accident and I am wrenched from my detached, dreamed picture of my open funk, of prised out rib, wedge-parted bones like the bone lips of some secretly contained reptile . . . trajectory complete. Dark warmth the root of noonday ecstasy. The face of death the edge of pain and thus the very name of living.

The short novella *What Happened to Jackson* was published in 1978 though the manuscript is dated 1972. Unusually the cover is illustrated by someone else and the text is not illustrated except for four, apparently gratuitous close up photographs by Nuttall of a woman's pubic hair at the beginning. The back cover describes it as a 'bizarre and disturbing crime story by the author of Bomb Culture', though it is not obvious what the crime is, or what did in fact happen to Jackson. In some ways it is closer than any of Nuttall's other books to the French, *nouveau roman* style of a Robbe-Grillet, with a colder, more direct, less expressionist prose than is usual. It starts:

> Things open, ready to be entered. Things offering themselves for the adventure and the exploration of others to such an extent that they break their own separate gestalt, become not an integrated monolith, become a spread environment.[2]

However, the prose varies between the poetic and the demotic; from:

> I can never really introduce the honeyed things, the trans-personal sun that gleams through her irritative membranes, or the light that gleams through her like the Pole Star at the end of everybody's intra-personal tunnel, this warming that penetration and making of it not a dagger

[1] Or possibly during it.

[2] no pagination

> sunk in the oblivious but an adventuring in the willing wilderness of someone else. Disarming light, soothing the more venomous attributes of alienation which still she nurtures as her right if not her condition.

to this, in relation to Jackson's visit to a prostitute:

> he shouted into the kitchen of his flat "ere 'e is then. The next fuckin' customer. 'Ow many d'ye do in a day, then eh? ''Ow many fivers d'you gerrunder yer mattress in a day?"
>
> "Oh shut yer fuckin' yap," said the woman with bleached hair. The man looked down over the bannisters. "Come on up, Mr fuckin' Jackson. It's all 'ere fuckin' waitin' for yer."

What little we know for sure is that Jackson has a girlfriend, Rose, to whom he will not commit and who may have slept with his colleague Bullock. Jackson goes away by himself and meets the strange and possibly dangerous old man Beeching, whom Bullock warns him against. It is not clear how Bullock knows Beeching, and why he and Jackson met. At the end of the story, Jackson is knifed (unlike several of Nuttall's novels, which end with a gun) by the 'man with the labyrinthine pores'

> "You posh cunt, you big posh bastard. You think you can come in 'ere, with yer posh clothes and yer big fuckin' car –"
>
> The man with the labyrinthine pores set about the attack using the knife like a hand axe. He swung it about Jackson's head from left to right. with big deliberate movements of his whole arm.
>
> There was blood and there were footsteps on the stairs. There was a bustle of bodies come hurriedly into the room out of the cold street.
>
> "Not a chance," said Beeching, "no chance at all. Complete disaster area, what?"
>
> "Jack, my love," said Rose, near to him. "I'm sorry. I'm so sorry."
>
> Jackson closed.

The Gold Hole, 1978 was, unusually, published by a relatively mainstream publisher – Quartet – with a cover designed by someone else. It starts with a reproduction of a newspaper article from 1967 about the murder of a ten year old girl and mixes narratives about the murders, the couple Jaz and Sam, who is suspected of the murders by Sergeant Phillips and who has lyrical sections addressed to his mother, and the mysterious man with the red hair. The writing ranges from the almost-realistic to the highly poetic. In the first section it seems as though Sam's mother has deserted him when he was young.

> *The child was discovered by the welfare authorities just before dawn. The mother is thought to have deserted him there three or four days previously. There were bruises and some breakages of skin on the flesh around the mouth. The toilet had been out of order for some time . . .*
>
> *Shy eyes / morning puddles of wonder. Imagine, said the smirking judge, the assembled slaughtered children of Auschwitz, Buchenwald, Hiroshima and Hanoi, nailed in the choirstalls howling out their requiem teething-pain – the teeth, the small rats' teeth and insect-saws in baby bellies – cut to the rolled-up sugar cotton of a May morning.*[1]

Sam (who, as we later find out, is speaking in this section) has a dialogue with his mother.

> 'Lonely robe / your great dark dream / *the dark I left you with Mother Butcher Mrs Ribbentrop Mrs Himmler Wetnurse pumping the*

[1] p. 1

uric acid from her withered tit, mothermilk filtered through blackshirts.

Self-sovereignty / wine and love / *gold in the blood, you panned it Mother, like a prospector crouched over the trickle from a country hillside pisshouse, passing the yellow of it through his tilting pan and letting it disappear back to earth.'*[1]

The next section has letters to and from Sam and Jaz, after they have separated. The letters are never sent. Jaz's letter contains a harrowing reference to an abortion, which may have been the cause of their break-up.

> It was a nasty place, Sam, a grave. It's made of ashes, Sam, ashes and flint.
>
> It was at the dying of the day. All the colours were going. I held her in my hands, her tiny hard round head in my hands. I can't stand completeness, Sam. It was at the dying of the day.
>
> It left a hole, Sam. The gap it left was sore. The gap it left was round and sore, Sam. I was hungry all the time.
>
> Why had other women such a plenitude? Why had other women such riches? I watched them, watched the little beams of light playing over the crags of ash.[2]

Sam is having a sexual relationship with another woman, Terry and is being watched by the police. They have found a poem – possibly the poem Sam had sent to Jaz – inserted into the dead body of the latest child to be murdered. While they are having sex, Sergeant Phillips enters the room unannounced.

> *The man with the newspaper was sitting reading it.* THIRD BODY FOUND. POLICE INTENSIFY HUNT FOR KILLER. He seemed embarrassed. He stood up and faced the mantelpiece, stuttering, blustering 'Er – perhaps I shouldn't have – Well – Well, my name is Phillips. Scotland Yard. Grateful if you'd tell me when you're – er – presentable. . .'
>
> 'Fucking fuzz,' she said. 'Get in everywhere'.[3]

Sam is also having sex with Susan, in one of the many sex scenes in the book; he is perhaps using casual sex as a way to forget his guilt over the abortion.

---

[1] p. 2
[2] p. 23
[3] p. 46

> Thighs parted to his nose, to his ship's prow nose, and he sailed down the slimy flood of lanes to the land of final flood marshy wellsprings tampon for the deluge of tiny whimpering embryonic experience, glad swim with eternal star and floating splendour down the sun and moon, to the land of sun.[1]

In the section titled 'Arrival' it seems to be the aborted foetus that is speaking, the second foetus in Nuttall's works, after *The Case of Isabel and the Bleeding Foetus*. It may be speaking either to Sam in his sense of guilt, or to Jaz.

> *You have the sense that an orgasm has been stolen from you. It has, of course. I've got it. That's how it was in the beginning for me. When the being reached climax, I, quite a long way away, started to be.*
>
> *How small I was. How pink I was. Nothing more than something you might dig up in the garden.*
>
> *You might, of course, actually dig me up in the garden one day, things being what they are. The situation is not without its irony. Feeling like a shrimp or a snail is, no doubt, the way to get treated like one.*
>
> *I got bigger. I got bones.*[2]

Sam may also be guilty of the murders of the children – in perhaps yet another reference to the Moors Murderers Myra Hindley and Ian Brady. Sergeant Phillips interrogates Sam about the poem found on the murdered child, which he shows to Sam.

> Handwritten blots and rain. Must get the weather in hand.
>
> It as crumpled by now and had it been handwritten ink would have run into the stains, the blots and weather-edges of rain. There was mud on it and there was blood on it. 'Yes,' he said. 'It's my poem.'
>
> 'Your copy of your poem?'
>
> 'My copy of my poem.'
>
> 'Wouldn't you like to look more closely?'
>
> 'No, I don't want to look at all. It's my copy of my poem.'
>
> 'Top copy?'
>
> 'Tip-top, Mr Phillips.'
>
> 'There were no other copies?'
>
> 'There were two carbons.'
>
> 'But this isn't a carbon.'

[1] p. 61
[2] p. 77

'No.'[1]

Sam struggles to find an alibi, and we don't know if he did it or not. At this point, the mysterious man with dyed red hair starts to appear, apparently following Sam and later appearing in some of the several sex scenes that comprise most of the books' last sections. 'The man with the pain of his dyed red closed his invisible face, vacuum snapped on a crimson wince that was never locked and knotted into a silent map of stress.'[2] The novel ends with another shooting; Sam and Jaz are back together and have just had sex when Sergeant Phillips knocks at the door.

> 'I think – recognize this' said Phillips. He held out a crumpled sheet. As he handed it to Jaz he looked over her shoulder and met Sam's eye.
>
> 'Read it,' said Sam. 'Read it. The sergeant wants to hear it.' Jaz read:
> 'You don't know who you messed up,
> You and the fester doctors.
> You locked us in a slimy hole.
> What prize dropped from the bandit's mouth
> By your sensible welfare pence?
> What was the blood group of the gold the hole spilled? How
> Shall we sleep or make love
> Now that there's someone watching?'
>
> She smiled and then laughed lightly. Sam had come close up behind her. He took the pistol from behind his back and shot Phillips and the constable.[3]

---

[1] p. 65
[2] p. 84
[3] p. 100

Muscle, 1982, like *Snipe's Spinster*, is part story – in this case at least semi-autobiographical – and part social history. Like *Snipe* it is a lament for the failed revolution and lost idealism of the 1960s as described in *Bomb Culture* and like *Snipe* it is set in a very specific location – West Yorkshire, where Nuttall himself lived and worked. Unlike *Snipe* however *Muscle* presents positive trends in society: anti-racism and feminism. The narrator, Terry Bunn, a Nuttall-like figure, is a stand-up comedian in working class, racist Northern clubs; 'a half-pickled club comic with a liver like an anchovy.'[1] His girlfriend is Araminta: 'With the size of a sparrow she has the presence of a King Cobra.'[2]

> Araminta was crucified on the sexual liberation of the sixties. Militant transgression whipped her up into its gaudy carnival float and threw her around like a beach ball. The multicoloured retinue, hipsters hugging their advertised crotches, fucking and blinding across the arenas of the era, burned up child-paramours like Araminta with the brisk enthusiasm of a Jet engine eating oil.[3]

Terry is led towards feminism and away from his unconscious sexism by the women around Araminta; one says to him: 'There might have been a revolution by now if the whole thing hadn't been rotten with sexists tilting the scene so that they could exploit the real revolutionaries.'[4] Terry explains in his narration how the dominant male view of sexuality is wrong. 'The penis is not a muscle. . . A vagina is a muscle. A vagina is a powerful organisation of muscles like a fist or jaw. . . The penis stabs blind, betting on its own blood'.[5] He works this idea into his stand-up act, but the routine does not go down well with the audience in the club.

> "Cunt, y'see," I say. "All there is lads. And we've been fooled all these years. Not really a hole. Nothing you could drown in. Nothing you could suffocate in although you might get strangled. No teeth no pack-

[1] p. 8
[2] p. 11
[3] p. 22
[4] p. 27
[5] p. 41

> drill, see warrimean? Better way of kissing, that's all. Better way of cuddling up to the world, that's the number. Treat it right you don't need an E type, nor a Barclaycard. Get to know it, you don't need a friend. Dinosaurs lads, that's us. I'd say we got our brains in our tails but that's flattery. Spend a lifetime out in the alley pullin' yer wire and punchin' Paks. Waste a lifetime watchin' the other lad's length and gaugin' the Bristols. All wrong."

Having been the definitive chronicler of the 1960s British artistic underground, Jeff Nuttall lived to see a massive change in attitudes to race and gender equality. But he also lived to see the marketization and corporatization of art and its taming into the quiet pet of a polite society rather than the rabid dog he made it into. He chronicled all this in *Art and the Degradation of Awareness*, 2001, like *Bomb Culture* thirty years on, a passionate personal and social autobiography/ critique of the times he lived through and personally influenced.

JEFF
NUTTALL
A CILIBRATION

JEFF NUTTALL'S
WAKE ON PAPER

ann quin

Ann Quin (1936 - 1973) occupied a peculiar position in relation to the literary scene; a close friend of Robert Creeley[1], Henry Williamson, Alan Burns, and known to Henry Miller, B.S. Johnson, Rayner Heppenstall[2] and others, she still always remained a marginal figure, even after she had won the D. H. Lawrence award[3], a Harkness Commonwealth Fellowship[4] and an Arts Council £1,000 award[5]; she visited America and Mexico as part of her various awards. Quin had left her Brighton Catholic girls' school with only one GCE – in English, having failed English Literature – and a 'death wish and a sense of sin. Also a great lust to find out, experience what evil really was.'[6] She had been writing stories since she was seven; she 'lived in a dream world and created dreams out of everyday situations until nothing ever seemed what it appeared to be.' Deciding that writing was too solitary a life she tried to keep a job in the theatre and later tried to find work as an actor, but failed at both; she 'fell in love with poverty-stricken painters, who needed feeding as much as I did, so that never lasted long.' She found various secretarial jobs and mostly continued in this work except for one summer when she escaped London office life to work in a hotel in Cornwall. But being a waitress 'was not unlike going on stage' and she fled back to London.

> I arrived at the railway station in utter terror of being discovered, made to return to the hotel. I reached home speechless, dizzy, unable to bear the slightest noise. I lay in bed for days, weeks, unable to face the sun. If I

---

1 He wrote about her (though did not mention her by name) in *Mabel: A Story and Other Prose* (London: Boyars, 1976), pp. 119-122

2 He wrote about her in *Two Moons* (op. cit.)

3 In 1965

4 From 1965-1967. John Calder, who had published *Berg*, *Three* and *Passages*, suggests that the much older author Henry Williamson, with whom she was having an affair, helped her get these awards. *Pursuit: The Uncensored Memoirs of John Calder*. London: Calder Publications, 2001, p. 272.

5 In 1969

6 'Leaving School – XI': *London Magazine*. July, 1966, p. 63

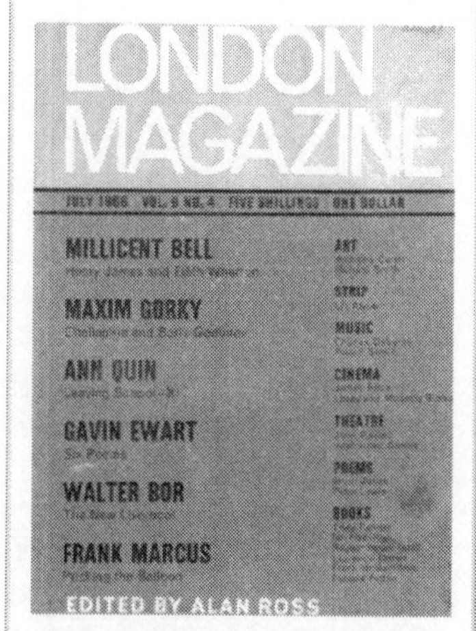

> went out into the garden I dug holes and lay in them weeping. I woke up in the middle of the night screaming, convinced my tears were rivers of blood, that my insides were being eaten away by an earwig that had crawled into my ear. I went to see a psychiatrist, going more from curiosity, and spent a few hours entertaining the horrified lady. I decided to climb back out of madness, the loneliness of going over the edge was worse than the absurdity of coping with day to day living.[1]

She suffered repeatedly from mental instability: after spending all her Arts Council award in one spree, she had a mental breakdown in Stockholm, where her fancy had taken her, and spent some time in a psychiatric hospital in London. According to John Calder:

> after returning from America, where the Harkness grant had taken her, she had written little else, but had spent much time with American hippies, was drinking too much and had experimented with a number of drugs. [Henry] Williamson[2] by now had lost patience with her. I managed to get her an Arts Council grant of £2,000 but they ignored my suggestion that it should be doled out over a year. She cashed her cheque into liquid currency, went to the airport, took a plane to Dublin and spent some time in Ireland. . . she returned to Britain, took the next 'plane that was leaving, which landed her in Amsterdam and no more was heard from her until, in mid-winter, she was rescued, half-frozen from a snow-drift in Stockholm! After lengthy hospitalisation there, she was returned to Britain, but her mental condition was precarious and she had to take daily doses of Lithium to regulate her body and mind. This made creative writing impossible. She took a job as a secretary, seemed better, but was obviously unhappy. I spent an evening at her flat with other friends of hers and could see that she was now a manic-depressive and just moving into a manic phase. She was also trying to reduce the Lithium in order to start writing again. Shortly afterwards she went down to Brighton to stay with

[1] 'Leaving School', p. 68

[2] Calder said Quin 'met the elderly, distinguished and eccentrically fascist-admiring author, Henry Williamson in a Chelsea pub and started an affair with him, an obvious father-replacement.' p. 272

> her mother. A fisherman saw her on the beach at twilight, taking off her clothes and entering the water. Her body was found, a week later, washed up further down the coast. It was a waste of a great talent and helped blight my intention to form a group of writers, including Ann, into a school like the *nouveau roman* in France and the *Gruppe 47* in Germany.'[1]

Calder says the Arts Council should be held at least partially responsible for the suicides of Quin and B. S. Johnson for 'doing things in the way that was bureaucratically easiest for them. Most of the time they subsidised holidays and drinking bouts, not time to write.' Rayner Heppenstall, who had introduced Quin to B.S. Johnson, confirms the relationship with Williamson.

> Henry Williamson, a talkative and engaging old man of remarkable vitality, had fallen heavily for Ann and did a great deal for her, arranging, for instance, an American tour for which she was not yet ready, intellectually or temperamentally.[2]

In 1972, with four novels published, she decided that she needed to further her formal education (she had left her convent school at 16), and enrolled on a liberal studies course at Hillcroft adult education college preparatory to applying to read English at university. Reports of her mental state at this time vary: the principal of the college[3] and the reports of her tutors[4] suggest that she was quiet, stable and good humoured (they had no idea of her history of mental illness, about which she lied on her application form). She returned to her mother's home in Brighton at weekends. It may be that the routine and discipline of the college were beneficial, but she may also have found the attitude of the tutors humiliating, since they seem not to have appreciated her importance as a novelist, and to have treated her like any other student; her marks were only ever average.[5]

Whatever the effect of the college, in September 1973, less than a month before she was due to take up a place at the University of East Anglia, she walked out into the sea at Brighton, and was not seen again until her body was washed up the next day. At the inquest[6] her mental instability, and the possibility of a

---

1 Calder op. cit., pp. 272/273

2 *The Master Eccentric: The Journals of Rayner Heppenstall*. London: Alison and Busby, 1986

3 In conversation with me.

4 Her reports were still held on file at Hillcroft in 1981 when I visited.

5 Her principal said, in a note to a tutor: 'I still can't work up such enthusiasm for her novels', and her English tutor once commented that an essay 'began with a lot of pretentious waffle about divided souls reflecting the universal schism, which I think she found in some introduction or other. If she can grow out of this kind of party chat she should do well enough. Borderline.'

6 Report in *Brighton Evening Argus*, Friday, Sept. 14, 1973

broken romance were mentioned, but in the absence of any real evidence, the coroner recorded an open verdict, an event astonishingly predicted in her second novel, *Three*,[1] where a young girl is found drowned, and the people who are left try, unsuccessfully, to discover whether she committed suicide. It may have been that she felt that her writing career was over (she hinted at this in an interview[2]) or perhaps that she no longer felt she could express herself adequately in her writing.

All her novels are highly personal and, with the alteration of some details and the addition of some fantasy, autobiographical. The same themes tend to recur: her mother (*Berg*[3], 'Motherlogue'[4]); her father, who left them when she was a girl - her parents never married but she took her father's name - (*Berg*, *Three*, 'Every Cripple Has His Own Way of Walking'[5]; the last mentions him by his correct names); her brother who died ('Motherlogue', *Passages*[6]), and the importance of the number three, which occurs in all the novels.

When Quin died she was working on a novel[7] about a woman in a psychiatric hospital which, though quite conventional in narrative style was a return to a more personal novel, for the woman is undoubtedly Quin herself. It seems as if she could only portray reality in a hallucinatory style, but to describe her own hallucinatory reality she had to adopt a straightforward style. Also, the book seems to have been meant as a condemnation of psychiatric hospitals, and for this purpose she may have felt that directness was an advantage. None of the novels she completed was directly about her own illness, and it may have been her inability to describe this that led to her feeling of not been able to say anything genuine any more in her writing, which seems to have been about the only way she could communicate adequately with the outside world.

---

1 London: Calder & Boyars, 1966; N.Y. Scribner 1968

2 John Hall: 'Landscape With Three-Cornered Dances': *Guardian* Apr. 29 1972

3 London: Calder & Boyars, 1964; Quarter 1967; N.Y. Scribner 1966

4 *Transatlantic Review*, Summer 1969, pp.101-105; reprinted in, Philip Stevick, ed. *Anti-Story: An Anthology of Experimental Fiction*. New York: Simon & Schuster, 1971

5 *Nova*; Dec. 1966 pp.125-135

6 London: Calder & Boyars, 1969

7 *The Unmapped Country*, in Giles Gordon, ed. *Beyond the Words* (London, Hutchinson, 1975), p. 251-275

Quin published very few stories but they appeared in a wide range of journals: from an avant garde Marxist magazine in Mexico, through literary journals *London Magazine* and *Transatlantic Review* (where B. S. Johnson was poetry editor) to the British fashion and style magazine *Nova* ('a new kind of magazine for a new kind of woman') which published 'Every Cripple has his Own Way of Walking', a story of a young girl who lives with her grandmother and great-aunt in a big house near the sea; 'The house was old. They were older'. This is a typical Quin threesome with a strong autobiographical feel.

> The house full of newspapers. Paper bags within paper bags. Letters. Photographs. Pieces of brocade. Satin. Ribbons. Lockets. Hair. Broken spectacles. Medicine bottles. Empty. Foreign coins. Trunks. Cases. Cake. Biscuit tins. And mice. The child never knew whether it was the mice or one of her aunts wheezing in the long nights.[1]

Grandma owns everything because unlike Aunt Molly she was previously married, though only because her late husband had proposed to the wrong sister.

> They lived as best. The three. In the worst. Through thick and thin. They lived their roles. Respected. Detested. Each other's virtues. Little vices. Whims. And waited for the day the child's father would pay a visit. That day would surely be tomorrow. If not tomorrow then the next day. When Nicholas Montague. Monty to them all. Would tread the path. Into the house. Receive their love. And tell them of his travels. Successes. Though Aunt Molly would look past him. As is she recognised in his shadow some remembered dream.

Without the father the house carries on in its inevitable routine as the girl watches. 'The days grew into each and out of each night. With the habits. Dreams,

[1] *Nova*, December 1966, pp. 125/126

Tales of days gone by.'[1] The girl, effectively alone in the big, creaky house fantasises, is in a way very reminiscent of Anna Kavan:

> The Goose Girl. The Snow Queen. Cinderella. Each of these she was. She saw her aunts as grown ancient but with a wave of the magic wand they would change into beautiful queens with quick queenly steps. She felt sure her father would have this wand. Transform the old castle on the hill. The old ladies. Herself. Into a magical world where they would all live happily ever after.

As in Kavan's fictional/autobiographical reminiscences the house has its own character; it is in fact a character in the story of a lonely child with distant and/or absent parents.

> Tomorrow came as yesterday. And the next day. With the wind. Rain. The child stayed in the house. Listened to what the wind told to the walls. And then again to what the walls told. Showed. What was shown when a door flew open. When closed. At times the house had secrets the child found were not revealed to her. When the place wrapped itself up. As if wounded.[2]

She tells her dolls 'tales of the magician they would see tomorrow' with his magic wand, ready to transform her lonely, repetitive existence into a magical world. One day the father does finally come (possibly brought by a woman), but of course he has no magic and does not even stay overnight. The girl is too shy at first to come out from hiding but listens to him play the piano and take money from the women to 'tide him over'. It seems he is a professional piano player and has concert the next day; he has only come because he is playing nearby. He says that he is having piano in the house collected – his only link to the place apart from the three women – and leaves without saying goodbye to his daughter.

> The child turned over and listened. Listened until the walls. Doors. Breathed in quietness. In the dark. She gave her secret to the house.'[3]

---

[1] p. 126
[2] p. 129
[3] p. 135

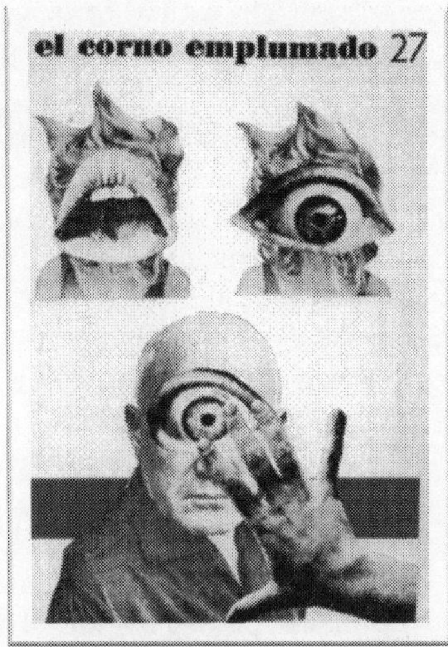

One of Quin's two published Mexican stories, 'Never Trust a Man who Bathes with his Fingernails' was published while she was still in Mexico, in July 1968 by the avant garde bilingual Mexican Marxist art and poetry review *El Corno Emplumado,* which was distributed across Latin America and the U.S. The story is again of a threesome – one of Quin's regular motifs – a man just called 'the husband', who is 'the husband of one of the women, lover of the other'[1]; 'the wife' and 'the woman': 'Not sure of her sense of place, the placing of where she might sit, walk, sleep between husband and wife. Wife. Husband.' They are living in a remote cabin with a motorcycle-riding drifter called 'the man' who works for them as a handyman; 'a small man. Half Cherokee. His silences were those of the Indian.' The husband, a writer, is jealous and suspicious of the outsider, though the *ménage à trois* are themselves outsiders already and the woman is an outsider to the couple, having sex with the husband while the wife is out.

> The wife quick, with a quicker
> laughter than the other, who laughed slowly in
> the spaces of the wife's laughter. The silence
> coming from the room above them, she later
> entered, when the wife went shopping. A
> quickness then between them on his studio
> couch, listening for the car rattling over
> the bridge, and all the while below them the
> lower sound of nails slowly driven into the wood,
> the man's whistling louder. The louder noises
> of the wife returning, putting things in
> cupboards, banging of dishes, as they straightened
> their clothes, the couch cover. He lifted up
> the door for her to clutch her way down into
> the kitchen, into the bathroom where she powdered
> over the heightened colour of her face.

[1] p. 8

The man went on hammering, hummed, bent
into his work. The typewriter a jerky rhythm above. [1]

Both the man's hammering of nails and the husband's hammering of the typewriter keys are the sounds of men working, but perhaps the husband's suspicion of the man is partly caused by his work being physical and more 'real', making him a threat to the husband's power over the two women. The wife suggests all four of them go to a local rock pool and bathe naked; the husband is negative and resentful but agrees reluctantly. When they are all bathing naked the husband compares his penis with that of the man.

He smiled, smiled at his largeness, at the smaller,
almost childish, hairless body of the other man,
the other side of the pool, who started scratching
the grime off his body, digging this out from his
nails, picking out the dirt slowly, carefully.
'He certainly makes use of the people he works
for – and just look now what he's doing – never
trust a man who...'[2]

The husband looks down at the other man, an intellectual sneering at a darker-skinned, smaller man. 'Ha, you think his silences are profound or something – he's dumb – hasn't a thought in his head – he just drifts'. As they leave the pool the husband puts in a parting shot: 'Well I didn't think much of this hot spring pool – I mean I though at least it would be larger'[3]. And finally the woman, the outsider in the marriage, brings herself into the circle by defining the group to include her but exclude him: 'maybe the next time just the three of us will come.'

---

[1] p. 10
[2] p. 14
[3] p. 16

Another Mexican story is the short but searingly intense 'Eyes that Watch Behind the Wind, published posthumously in Calder & Boyars' *Signature Anthology* in 1975, alongside works by Beckett, Ionesco, Elspeth Davie, Eva Figes and others. It possible she did not want it to be published during her lifetime because it was too personal. It describes part of a journey through Mexico by a woman and her boyfriend. The relationship between the couple is compared to that of the distant, snow-covered mountains: 'they had passed the cone shaped volcano Popocatepetl contemplating Ixtaccihuatl, the White Woman.'

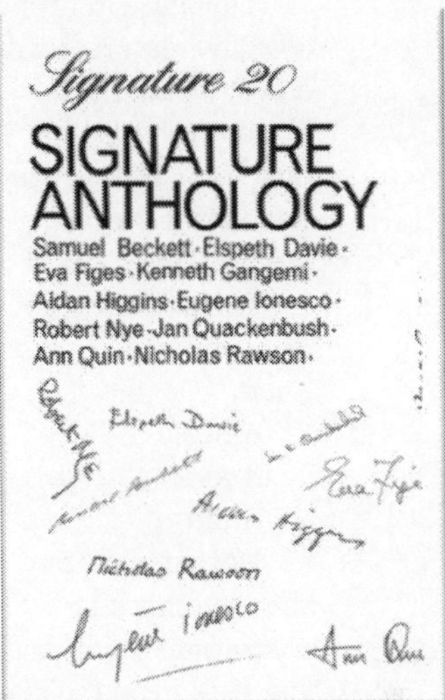

> Ixtaccihuatl
> Popocatepetl watching
> watching behind the wind eruptions under skin. Under eyes. Of those who wore slick nest city suits, who stepped heavily along the hot concrete. She was glad to leave that.
> Glad not to be furtively looked at by those dark shells.
> Eyes not her own.[1]

The woman implicitly compares her own situation to the 'sleeping princess' Ixtaccihuatl, wooed by Popocatepetl. When he failed to win her, he turned her to stone, and then himself too, so that he might contemplate him forever.'[2] (Being turned to stone, untouchable and serene, was Anna Kavan's key metaphor for her ideal state.) 'But not a waiting between life and death. Arrows and stones. Rather a sitting still on some high rock facing the mesas. So still she would seem a statue.

She has always been an outsider, a *gringo*, in this strange country - 'Confronted by her own strangeness, helplessness in the face of their defeat, their resigned acceptance of life conquered by death' – and she is also becoming estranged from the man, their relationship as distant as that between two mountains. Their relationship, at least from her point of view, is based on power and pain, symbolised by the bullfight.

> The two facing each other. It was physical. Sensual almost. Yes, she could understand his fascination with a sensual kind of violence. Seeing it there in his face, watching intently every move mad and bull made.

[1] pp. 134/135
[2] p. 147

> The pulse in his neck moved
> a small creature, ready to jump out, seize her own neck that arched back down, where she felt the ache. The ache at times of wanting this violence in him to break out. Devour her. Hurt me hurt me hurt me. But not in this way. Not in the heavy silence of them both facing each other, weapons concealed. The final turning away, not even in anger, but resentment.
> The challenge not met.
> At such time she almost wanted the frenzied shouts of an audience: *Anda* – Go on
> *Anda*
> *Anda*
> *Anda*
> Not this rejection.
> She couldn't take it. Nor the verbal attacks. When words became only accusations slung at each other. If no words, then it was a sword-thrust that goes in on the bias so that the point of the sword comes out through the skin of the bull's flank.[1]

He is, in one sense the bull; she resents 'the way he tossed his head, stomped off', but in another sense the picador, wounding her in her pride; she wanting to be wounded physically but not mentally, not by words. Her masochism even extends to thoughts of rape; in the blazing heat she fantasises about going into the jungle alone. 'Give herself to some Indian, Without words. Be ravished. Even raped. Then killed. A quick death from a *machete*.'[2] During the period of the story the rainy season is about to begin and the intense heat is unbearable, making everyone mad. When the rain finally arrives, it is explicitly equated to sexual release.

> The rain started. Soon heavy rain like tidal waves on the roofs. She took him in her mouth. He moved gently, then faster.
> Rain above. Below.
> Soon rushing down her throat. Filling her. Filling the area she had so nearly reached.
> So it was in moments.[3]

Just before this, there has been a scene involving the ocean, which calls to her: in hindsight it seems chillingly to prefigure her own death by drowning.

---

[1] p. 141
[2] p. 147
[3] p. 148

> She threw her body, no longer her own body it seemed, but just a body hurled out of the ground, into the mountains of water, she hurled out of the ground, into the mountains of water, she bent her head under, rose up, bent again, and struggled out. Further out to higher and higher mountains. Away from the beach, where she knew he waited, watching, not quite knowing. Unsure again
>
> And if she returned?
>
> If she chose not to, but moved out into the ocean until perhaps the area she had so nearly reached could be touched upon.[1]

The title of 'Motherlogue' is presumably a contraction of 'mother' and 'monologue', though it may also allude to 'motherload'. This 6-page text, published in 1971 in an American anthology of experimental writing[2] appears to be one side of a phone conversation between a mother and her daughter, who may be Quin's mother and herself; we cannot know how close it is to any actual conversations but it seems very one-sided and the mother is rather distant to the daughter, which seems to have been how Quin felt. The daughter seems to have recently been in America, as Quin had, and the mother and father appear to be separated, again as Quin's were. The 'conversation' seems to be taking place on the birthday of a dead relative, which may relate to the death of Quin's brother.

> Oh hello darling how lovely to hear you thank you for calling on this day yes I know I know one shouldn't but still we share this don't we dear his death of course it's really his birthday Well how are things anything happening it's been cold here are you warm enough in that flat I told you how cold it would get the snow's coming through my kitchen window no no it's all right now I've stuffed newspaper in it mmmmmm is it well I haven't been out today are you using the electric blanket I gave you because if not you could bring it back next time you come all it needs is a longer lead I'm sure Richard

[1] pp. 142/143

[2] Philip Stevick, ed. *Anti-Story: An Anthology of Experimental Fiction*. New York: Simon & Schuster, 1971

> can fix that has he done it yet   I see well if you aren't using it I may as well have it back[1]

Richard seems to be the daughter's married boyfriend, of whom the mother does not approve. Part of the monologue concerns Christmas: first the mother says she is going off by herself but later she assumes her daughter will be with her. There is no resolution to the story, and nothing happens except a portrait is painted of a distant and domineering mother and a restless and unsettled daughter: a touching but sad portrait.

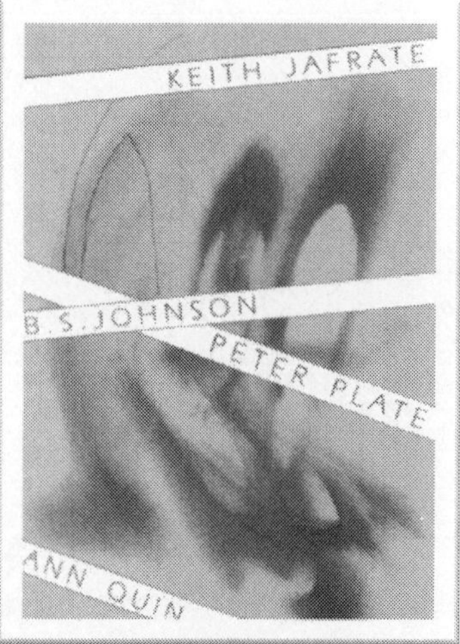

Even more formless is the unfinished story 'Ghostworm', published long after her death by small British magazine *Tak Tak Tak* in 1993. As well as being unfinished it may well also be unedited and not how Quin intended it to appear – if she intended it to appear at all. More like a Rimbaudian prose poem than any of her other works; it has no apparent structure or plot and the narration switches between 'I' and 'she'. However it is possible to make out just an outline of a typically Quin threesome where the narrator has been having an affair with a married man who is now dead; she has his ashes. Some of the sections may be remembered or imagined conversations between them. 'I'll take the ashes to his wife tomorrow. Idiot. No not again – go away. Get off my back. You're obsessed. I'm not you were I am.' The woman may be intending to leave the country. 'Tomorrow or in two, three days I will cross that border, the papers are ready.' Despite its dissimilarity in style to any of her other work, it is certainly clear that this is written by Quin and written about herself.

> Do you still fantasise about killing your father? Chop him up into little pieces – yes why not I'm playing at sanity anyway. Ah you think you're mad – never. Neither sane or insane – the thin edge I tread and I want to go over. And end up like me – yes perhaps that's what you want EXPERIENCE in caps period. To live beyond myself. Such a craving. Ashes into ashes.[2]

---

[1] Stevick p. 127

[2] p. 72

> Death of the Father would deprive literature of many of its pleasures. If there is no longer a Father, why tell stories? Doesn't every narrative lead back to Oedipus? Isn't storytelling always a way of searching for one's origin, speaking one's conflict with the Law, entering into the dialectic of tenderness and hatred? Today we dismiss Oedipus and narrative at one and the same time: we no longer love, we no longer fear, we no longer narrate. As fiction, Oedipus was at least good for something: to make good novels, to tell good stories.[1]

Ann Quin's first published (third written[2]) novel, *Berg*[3] was widely praised and compared to Beckett, Nathalie Sarraute and Graham Greene, though her early influences were from an earlier age: Chekhov, Lawrence, Hardy, and in particular 'Dostoievsky and Virginia Woolf - '*Crime and Punishment* and Virginia Woolf's *The Waves* made me aware of the possibilities of writing'.[4] - and Camus. There are also parallels with Robbe-Grillet's first two novels, in the way that *The Erasers* and *The Voyeur* subvert the traditional detective novel, and *The Erasers*, like *Berg* has often been seen as an Oedipus story. As in *The Voyeur*, the central character is not a detective trying to discover the identity of the murderer, but the putative murderer trying to find out if a murder has been committed, thus undermining and merging the detective/criminal relationship. There are many ironic references to detective stories: 'then perhaps the mystery would be solved'[5]; 'this was the very clue he had been hoping for'[6];'the plot is undoubtedly

---

[1] Roland Barthes: *The Pleasure of the Text*

[2] In 'Leaving School' she describes her first two novels, which were completed and sent off to publishers but never accepted for publication.

[3] London: Calder & Boyars, 1964 and New York: Scribners, 1966. repr. London: Quartet (with Afterword by Dulan Barber), 1977. Trans. into French by Anne-Marie Soulac. Paris: Gallimard, 1967. Trans. into German by Elisabeth Fleitscher. Insel, 1966

[4] ibid.

[5] Berg p. 111 (page numbers refer to both British editions)

[6] p. 115

thickening.'[1] The point of this subversion of the genre may be to deny that in life, as in the detective story, there are no clear motives, no unambiguous explanations, and no happy endings.

Berg's first publisher John Calder said it was

> very different from the run of British fiction. Set in Brighton during the off-season, the seedy atmosphere is beautifully described and three characters, Berg, a young protagonist, his father (really a portrait of the author's father) and his mistress weave around each other in a situation where sex and violence are always present. It ends in murder and the body of the older man is washed up by the tide, prescient of what, in a short time, would happen to the author herself. But basically she was writing about her love-hate relationship to her own father, on whom she had an obvious fixation.[2]

The character Berg and the Raskolnikov of *Crime and Punishment* do, as Quin suggested, seem to have much in common, and one passage particularly seems to recall the earlier book: after Berg thinks he has killed his father, he feels guilty but tries to convince himself that he has transcended the ordinary morality, and ordinary people:

> A parasite living on an action I alone dared committing, how can they possibly convict, or even accuse one who's faced reality, not only in myself, but the whole world, that world which had been rejected, denounced, leaving a space they hardly dared interpreting, let alone sentence. Surely I've served imprisonment long enough, this, now is my birth right, the after-birth is theirs to cope with, along with the rest of the country's cosy mice in their cages of respectability.[3]

Berg wants a life of direct, unmediated action; 'a man of action conquering all'[4], to raise him above the common crowd:

> weren't most people aware of their inferior position, situation, role in life, didn't they all sooner or later assume a negative attitude, the other side of the grave - two feet in one hand out? This time it means a leap, if I pursue the idea, lay it out before me for much longer it could so easily collapse. It means of course supreme action.[5]

---

[1] p. 117

[2] op. cit., p. 272

[3] p. 81

[4] p. 23

[5] p. 31

But he is plagued by doubt and indecision and, like Hamlet, continually sinks into reflection. At first he seems to be deliberately prolonging his action, which is 'like a love affair . . . the preliminaries must be prolonged; flirt a little with the opportunities'[1], but it soon becomes clear that he is far from the detached manipulator he wants to be. His reflections often build up to a climax, only to lapse into indecision and procrastination:

> If I could only make things bow down before the majesty of complete omnipotence, draw a halo round desires. Why does power escape as soon as touched? Is it all that necessary to have minions down the line carrying out orders to succeed and shed responsibility by denying oneself the extreme point of action? ACTION! Even now he was dragging on the skin that covered the growth; I must tear apart, bring it into sight, why hesitate any more? . . . a slight mistake over the margin either way, so easy to make a mess of things. One small slip, something overlooked . . . Strategy definitely is needed, thought before action.[2]

Despite his belief that 'the supreme action is to dispose of the mind, bring reality into something vital, felt, seen even smelt'[3], he can never manage this immediate contact with reality, the 'moment caught between two moods, that space within, separated from life, as well as death, when the sun is faced without blinking, when eternity lies here inside; no division whatever'[4]. Instead of being an existential, or even a Greek hero (as he at one point sees himself), he is only 'a Pirandello hero in search of a scene that might project him from the shadow screen on to which he felt he had allowed himself to be thrown'.[5]

Although he tries to obliterate desire, Berg seems to have two, contradictory desires: to belong, especially to the masculine world, and to be free of all attachments. He has always felt an outsider - 'have I ever been inside?' - and effeminate: he was 'just a common cissy'[6] with 'ringlets up to the age of five'[7]; a 'sticky, sickly child who longed to be accepted with the others, by those who were healthy, tough, swaggered'[8]. He feels the need to measure up to his father, worthless though he is, and become a 'real' man; he remembers his mother saying 'there you see that's your father, you'll have to do a lot to overcome him

---

[1] p.12

[2] p. 33

[3] p. 23

[4] p. 23

[5] p. 48

[6] p. 10

[7] p. 46

[8] p. 11

Aly, before I die'.[1] His father's brutality is contrasted with Berg's effeminacy: 'that sadistic curl of the old man's mouth, of course that's what she Judith, perhaps even Edith enjoyed, the brute force in him.'[2] He tries literally to overcome his father to prove that he is not a 'coward to the end'[3], and when he thinks that he has killed him, he feels, not simply a member of a masculine society, but 'unique . . . no longer the understudy but the central character, as it were in a play of his own making'[4]

This uniqueness is the aim which he consciously pursues, but never attains (note that in the last quote he still sees himself as a character in a play, even if it is his own). He tells himself: 'I don't belong to anyone, therefore attachment means betrayal, self-banishment, renounce self-continuity, self-transcendence, the ego only there to give significance'[5]. But at the end, he is as weak and submissive as ever, having failed to carry out his act of freedom.

Berg's ostensible motive for the attempted murder of his father - revenge - is soon seen through, even by him: 'of course it's ridiculous to think the whole thing is simply a vehicle for revenge, or even resentment - hardly can be called personal, not now.'[6] The killing is obviously primarily, if not totally, a symbolic act, and a symbolic substitute will do. The budgerigar seems to symbolise his father (Judith says that 'when Nathy's not around it never sings, not a single note'[7]), as the cat seems to symbolise Judith, and its death seems to satisfy him for a time. 'He picked the cover off, the budgerigar lay on its side, a yellow puffed up mound of dry feathers, and brown slits for eyes. He put the cover back, this was adequate enough'[8]. He has not killed the bird himself (perhaps Judith has, or perhaps it simply cannot live without Nathy, who has left), but he enjoys killing it symbolically by dropping it subsequently down the fire escape, which also annoys his father. Alternatively, the dummy is a perfect symbolic substitute: 'I could mutilate an effigy of him, squeeze into a pulp, and then from this shapeless mass a beautiful god-like form might rise up.'[9] The form would presumably be Berg himself, in his new guise as the existential hero who has equalled the power of gods over life, death and morality. Despite having not killed anyone, Berg still feels guilty:

---

[1] p. 46
[2] p. 140
[3] p. 46
[4] p. 77
[5] p. 32
[6] p. 38
[7] p. 18
[8] p. 60
[9] p. 53

> do you plead guilty? Yes. Guilty of all the things the human condition brings; guilty of being too committed; guilty of defending myself; of defrauding others; guilty of love; loving too much or not enough; guilty of parochial actions, of universal wish-fulfilments; of conscious martyrdom; of unconscious masochism. Idle hours, fingers that meddle.[1]

Guilt would not be a feature of the true existential hero; Berg, like so many others in life and literature, falls victim to it and lapses into symbolic and imaginary evil. In *The Rebel*, to which *Berg* seems to owe much, Camus speaks of de Sade, the 'prophet of liberation through evil', who, like Berg's father, was killed in effigy: 'At last he reigns supreme, master and God. But at the moment of his greatest victory, the dream vanishes. The Unique turns back towards the prisoner whose unbounded imagination gave birth to him and they become one . . . he . . . only killed in his imagination. Prometheus ends his days as Onan'[2].

Berg realises 'how much easier it would be to carry out orders from a hierarchy'[3] than to take absolute personal responsibility and by the end of the book has come to accept this completely: 'you can't expect to be a god and switch .life on and off like an electric light. No, it's far simpler, you just allow it to drift on, if lucky enough, you drift with it. But I refuse to be swept out or even in-shore; I shall remain in mid-ocean'[4]; in a sea of mediocrity.

Towards the end of the book it becomes obvious that it is his mother from whom Berg needs to be free and not his father; earlier on he seems to be motivated by love for her and revenge for her sake, but gradually her continual carping and nagging in his memory become insufferable; she is the one who is holding him back from a fully independent life if anyone is, and her remembered remarks like 'you have your own life to lead, and I'll not stand in your way'[5] come increasingly to seem ironic. At the same time the hatred for his father never materialises; if anything he seems to feel almost affectionate towards the old man, and in the two scenes where he might be expected to show the most revulsion - when his father is vomiting on his bedclothes, and when Berg is scrubbing his back in the bath and looking at his pimples - he seems to feel nothing in particular.

The real cause of revulsion for Berg seems to be women, whom he also seems to find threatening: he remembers as a child at school suffering 'the laceration of

---

[1] p. 56. Berg's only premeditated act of violence is his killing of Judith's cat, and he never feels any guilt about that. The suffocating burden of guilt Berg feels may well reflect Quin's own convent school education.

[2] trans. A. Bower: (Harmondsworth: Penguin, 1971), p. 41

[3] p. 57

[4] p. 133

[5] p. 7

Miss Hill's vagina'[1]; he refers to Judith's 'battle dress'[2] and is transfixed by her pearl necklace, 'a few of the beads chipped - decaying teeth against three circles of her neck, above these her scarlet mouth, that yawned and yawned wider, nearer' as she 'prowled round him'[3], a 'cat at any minute about to claw his eyes out'[4] (we have already seen how the cat Sebastian is often identified with Judith and the budgie - its prey - with his father), 'a whore, a bitch-goddess'[5] who would 'only eat you whole, drain everything out of you within a week'[6].

There is a lot in *Berg* to suggest that it should be considered as a dream, and a Freudian dream at that: the Oedipal structure - a man trying to kill his father and sleep with his father's 'wife' - is obvious, and there are elements in the story which do not fit a realist interpretation. The fact that Berg thinks he has killed his father when he has only strangled a dummy, and his father's inability to tell that the 'woman' he is seducing is a man in woman's clothes, along with his failure to recognise Greb as a reversal of his own name, do not of themselves make much sense; they would not be out of place in a comedy of errors, and nor would they in a dream. Judith's similarity in name to his mother Edith, and her status as his father's lover, together with the fact that she is, presumably, about the age Berg's mother would have been when his Oedipus complex was formed, suggest that Berg has, in Freudian terms, an unresolved Oedipus complex. Freud suggests that 'the boy wants to be in the father's place because he wants to put him out of the way'[7] (and Berg does end the book literally in his father's 'place' - his room and his ex-lover's bed), but points out that the child also has affection for his father and 'finds relief from the conflict arising out of this double-sided, this ambivalent emotional attitude towards the father by displacing his hostile and fearful feelings onto a *substitute* for his father'[8], as Berg does. Also, the idea of Judith as reminding Berg of his mother when he was a child accords with Freud's view that 'in being in love with one's own mother one is never concerned with her as she is but with the youthful mnemic image carried over from one's childhood'[9].

An unresolved Oedipus complex would also explain Berg's feelings of guilt; Freud said that the Oedipus complex was the 'source of mankind's guilt in general'[10]. 'Whether one has killed one's father or has abstained from doing so is not really the decisive thing. One is bound to feel guilty in either case'[11]. Freud

---

[1] p. 4
[2] p. 60
[3] p. 83
[4] p. 95
[5] p. 95
[6] p. 125
[7] Freud: Dostoevsky and Parricide' in Wellek ed. *Dostoevsky* (Prentice-Hall, 1962), p. 103
[8] Freud: *Totem and Taboo* (London: Routledge, 1950), p. 129
[9] Freud: *Collected Works,* op. cit., vol. 6, p. 178
[10] Freud: *Collected Works;* 14: 332
[11] Freud: ibid; 21: 132

saw the fear of castration as integral to the Oedipus complex, and Berg thinks about this too, in connection with his masturbation (for which, Freud said, castration is the feared punishment): 'Two years of castration, the silent masturbation in lavatories'[1]. Berg seems to want as well as fear the punishment, and thinks of his 'longing to be castrated'[2]. In Freudian analysis, the threat of castration is seen to come from the father, but, as we have seen, it is women whom Berg finds threatening. Judith's name links her to the story in the Apocrypha (where, moreover, she has an ancestor named Nathaniel; Berg's father's name) of Judith cutting off the head of her seducer Holofernes, and decapitation is linked by Freud to castration[3], as is the cutting off of all the hair in dreams[4], and this ties in with Berg's (otherwise unexplained) profession of seller of hair restorer, which mends 'Delilah's damage' as his slogan says (Delilah, like Judith, being a symbol for the castrating aspect of woman); 'Buy Berg's and be a man' runs another slogan.

Judith's middle name is Helen, the perfect beauty of antiquity (who was nevertheless responsible for the deaths of a large number of men) so that the name Judith Helen matches the oxymoron 'bitch-goddess' which Berg has applied to her. Also recalling Freudian dream-symbolism is Judith's cat Sebastian, named perhaps after the saint who was martyred by arrows - phallic symbols for Freud. Judith's room too seems to be described with Freud in mind (the room can be a symbol for the womb, to which we all desire to return), with its purple velvet and leather, to which Berg's room is only an 'antechamber' (i.e. a stage on the return to the womb, Judith being a substitute for his mother). Berg only reaches the room (permanently) by breaking down the partition, which is so often referred to, and which may stand for the incest taboo.

The other piece of overtly Freudian symbolism is the sea imagery; the sea for Freud represents women and entering the sea represents intercourse. It is in the sea that the tramp dies (and the tramps seem connected to his 'dark', homosexual feelings), and after he has passed out in the sea thinking he is going to die, he returns (i.e. is reborn?) and makes love for the first time with Judith, his homosexual desires having been left in the sea with the tramp. His thoughts make the connection between sea and sex explicit:

> Oh Aly make it last, he never could you know, well not more than - oh you are gorgeous, so big, so beautiful there, oh it does feel good to be with you Aly, do you love me, say you love me a little Aly won't you?

---

1 p. 45

2 p. 4

3 Freud: *The Interpretation of Dreams* (Harmondsworth: Penguin, 1976), p. 485

4 ibid.

> Like entering the sea. The sea alone. Alone by the sea. By the sea. Alone. By yourself. Oh it's nice when you do that, do it again, oh it's lovely. Nathy [*sic*], oh Nathy my darling.[1]

Berg has here completely taken his father's place, as Judith calls him Nathy.

However, if this is a dream, it was dreamed by Ann Quin who was a woman, and the scene where Berg is dressed in Judith's clothes (i.e. his/her mother substitute's) and is being seduced by his/her father could represent the female equivalent of the Oedipus complex: Freud said that 'I was able to recognise in this phantasy of being seduced by the father the typical expression of the Oedipus complex in women'[2]. This might however relate to Quin's professed bisexuality: one female homosexual patient of Freud's 'changed into a man and took her mother in place of her father as the object of her love . . . Since there was little to be done with the real mother, there arose from this transformation of feeling the search for a substitute mother to whom she could become passionately attached'[3].

As well as Freud, *Berg* seems to relate in some ways to Jung, whom Quin had also read[4]. Jung also laid great stress on the incest prohibition, 'which created the self-conscious individual, who formerly had been thoughtlessly one with the tribe, and in this way alone did the idea of individual, and final death become possible . . . The mother's defence against the incest appears to the son as a malicious act, which delivers him over to the fear of death'[5]. 'The mother then appears as the supreme goal, and on the other hand as the most frightful danger - the 'Terrible Mother'.'[6] This attitude seems to capture Berg's feelings for his mother-substitute Judith, by whom, as we have seen, he is repelled, but to whom he is also drawn. Jung also shows that for Quin to have written *Berg* from a male viewpoint need not be a problem: 'The fact that the seeker is masculine and the sought-for of feminine sex is not so astonishing, because the chief object of the unconscious transference is the mother . . . The daughter takes the male attitude towards the mother'[7].

But perhaps the most striking application of Jung's ideas to Quin's work is his idea of the number four as the number of wholeness, and three as the number of incompleteness; all Quin's novels are permeated by the number three, as are mosty of her stories; *Berg* contains three characters in the action and one present

---

1 pp. 145/6

2 Freud: *Collected Works*: 22: 120

3 Freud: 18: 158

4 According to her application form for Hillcroft.

5 Jung: *The Psychology of the Unconscious* (London, 1933), p. 167

6 Jung: 'Symbols of Transformation', in *Collected Works*, op. cit. 5: 236

7 Jung: *The Psychology of the Unconscious*, p. 188

in memory, which is how one Jungian has described the dreams of certain neurotic patients:

> In dreams, especially at one stage of analysis, there is sometimes something enigmatic about a fourth person by comparison with a trio; he or she sometimes manages to be remarkably conspicuous by his or her absence.[1]

One final way in which Jungian ideas may relate to *Berg* is the view of one Jungian that the creative artist 'like the hero of myth, stands in conflict with the world of the fathers, i.e. the dominant values'[2], since in the creative individual the 'archetypal fantasy world' cannot be repressed to fit in with these values; in 'the creative individual, regardless of biographical details, reductive analysis will almost invariably discover mother-fixation and parricide.'[3] In this way, I think *Berg* can be seen as a metaphor for the writer's need to destroy or transcend the hegemony of the dominant values, literary and moral. The artist is, on this view, a rebel, and that is how Quin's admired Camus sees the novelist: 'The novel is born simultaneously with the spirit of rebellion and expresses, on the aesthetic plane, the same ambition.'[4]

Ann Quin

"CONTROVERSIAL"

is the word that has attached itself to **Ann Quin**, whose second novel THREE (25s.) has been greeted with high praise ("The most naturally delicately gifted novelist of her generation"—Robert Nye, *Scotsman*. "There is no doubt about Ann Quin"—*Daily Telegraph*), respectful, unenthusiastic admiration ("even if it is only partially successful, it is worth any number of unambitious 'achievements'"—*Sunday Times*) to positive hostility. One of our most important British discoveries, we have no doubt that this highly original, poetic revelation of a young girl's involved relationship with a married couple is one of the most original and significant books of recent years, completely contemporary in feeling and a worthy successor to BERG (25s.), her brilliant first novel which was compared to Graham Greene, Beckett and Sarraute. An important German author **Reinhard Lettau** makes his debut here with OBSTACLES (27s. 6d.), a volume of short prose, which gives an astonishing range of insights into modern preoccupations. One of the most admired of current German writers, Lettau is a *must* for those who wish to keep up with the principal directions of modern literature, the most individual new voice since Peter Weiss.

---

1 Victor White, *Soul and Psyche* (London: Collins, 1960), p. 96

2 Erich Neumann, 'Creative Man and Transformation', in his *Art and the Creative Unconscious* (London: Routledge, 1959), p. 185

3 ibid.

4 Camus: *The Rebel*, op. cit., p. 224

In *Three*,[1] as in *Berg* we have a triangular relationship, but this time more closely matching Ann Quin's stated fantasy of herself and another couple.[2] The details the girl, S, leaves behind also match Quin's own life in many ways: a girl who went to a convent school, whose father left her and her mother when she was young to become a touring musician[3], who has been seeing psychiatrists and who - possibly - takes her own life by drowning. The book never makes it clear exactly what happened to S, and this exactly reflects the open verdict recorded on Quin's own death. In the book, as with Quin herself, we are left with fragmentary and confused evidence with which to try, and inevitably to fail, to piece together what has happened. One of the points that emerges from the book is the impossibility of pinning down either individuals' motivations or events into any simple and unambiguous pattern. As for the likelihood of anything written seven years before her death being related to it, the book may even answer that. Leon says to Ruth: 'Most suicides do it on the spur of the moment anyway without much thought. That's a fallacy Leon if ever there was there are some people who write notes saying they've been contemplating it for forty years.'[4]

I said earlier that *Berg* was in some ways an inversion of the detective story, but *Three* is both closer to the genre and more subversive of it; undermining even more the detective story's certainties and resolutions. Ruth, Leon and the reader all try to reconstruct events from S's tapes and journals, but no 'reading' of the situation such as a detective would produce is possible, and we know little more about S at the end of the book than we did at the beginning. The book is, however, seeded with clues, some of them red herrings: what are the black marks

---

[1] London: Calder & Boyars, 1966 and New York: Scribners, 1968. Trans. into French as *Trio* by Lola Tranec. Paris: Gallimard, 1970. Trans. into German as *Drei* by Marie Bosse-Sporleder. Insel, 1967

[2] See Hall, op. cit. Marion Boyars, who was close to Quin, thought the couple represented Alan and Carol Burns, to whom *Tripticks* is dedicated and which may also owe something to Burns' *Dreamerika!*

[3] This detail about her father also crops up in *Berg*, 'Every Cripple Has His Own Way of Walking', and 'Leaving School'; this last also refers to the fantasy, reflected in *Three*, of being her father's lover.

[4] p. 116

in Leon's diary; why does Ruth burn the photographs and who are they of; did Leon bite the cat's ear; what will Leon put on the tape and Ruth in the journal? All these things, plus the narrator's suppression of vital information such as S's suicide note make Ruth's 'not a word not a clue' obviously ironic. (Also, Leon's preoccupation with orchids brings to mind Rex Stout's Nero Wolfe, another house-bound detective who keeps contact with the outside world to an absolute minimum.)

S has disappeared before the book begins and we assume that her body has been found together with a suicide note, the contents of which, however, are never revealed. Later Leon reads that the 'unclothed body of an unidentified young woman, with stab wounds in back and abdomen was found yesterday by a lake near the Sugarloaf Mountain. A blood-stained angler's knife and hammer were also found.'[1] On checking back, we see that Leon's diary entry had merely said: 'Boat found capsized. Coat identified. Also note in pocket - looks like suicide'[2], so that it may not have been the body that was found in the first place but only the coat, or it may be that Leon knew about the knife and hammer, but said nothing about them. Either way Leon looks like a suspect for S's murder, and this is given added weight when we are told how Leon had been watching her secretly as she rowed on the lake. But then on the last line of the book, which is part of S's journal, we read: 'The boat is ready, as planned. And all that's necessary now is a note'[3] Three pages previously we had also had: 'Perhaps the idea evolved on just such an evening - but to write down would almost be like performing the action itself. Yes it is best to let it nurture'[4]. So, instead of the book ending in a revelation, it ends with a further twist: we know there was a plan, but not what it was, and the possibilities of suicide, murder by Leon (with the knife and hammer; we are never told if the body had been assaulted before drowning), or suicide with Leon's connivance are all equally possible.

Apart from the mystery of S's death there are others: why for instance did S stay with them? 'What did she want of us Leon what was she after I really don't understand'[5]; 'What did she want of us, need from him, myself? We shall probably never know.'[6] S makes frequent references to her manipulation of the couple but does not say (does not know?) to what end. 'Mantis-like I hang over many desultory designs, toy with subterfuges.'[7] 'My hands are instruments of torture . . . a feeler once an appetising victim found, hovers, then pulls quickly to

---

[1] p. 131
[2] p. 41
[3] p. 143
[4] p. 139
[5] p. 116
[6] p. 125
[7] p. 56. The image of the mantis – females of which eat the male after mating – also occurs in *Passages* and *Tripticks*.

the nest'[1]. Her manipulations do not seem to work, however, and she soon loses this predatory pride: 'Three months now of living with two people and not any nearer - nearer. Tactics flounder before even begun. There seems no answer. And yet . . .'[2] Then she herself seems to feel the victim: 'When I arrived back the house was in darkness. I felt more than a mere trespasser as I opened the door, made for my room. But what is there to take, other than what they have set out as decoys to distract from the main objective. After all I have become the victim now, and from that there is no turning back.'[3]

Seducing either or both of them may well be part of her plan; she certainly seems to have some kind of affair with him. Ruth does not seem to have suspected this until after S's death, and even then she takes the black marks in Leon's diary to be the times she and not S had sex with him, even though they do not accord with her memory: 'Why on this day and that I don't remember'. Ruth searches the diary and S's tapes to try to find clues, but the tapes are ambiguous as to whether S is merely fantasising or recording facts. There are clues (to the reader but not to Ruth) that these are more than fantasy, but there is 'nothing definite to go by. No substantial evidence as it were.'[4]

S's desires and motives, like Berg's, are not to be summarised neatly, though, again like Berg, there seem to be two, contradictory impulses: on the one hand to disrupt Ruth and Leon's mindless domestic routine, and on the other hand to become one of their family; the child they never had. Leon recognises this ambivalence: 'there was a need in her for security yet at the same time she rebelled background convent family everything contributed.'[5] S records hating the dinner party where everyone is 'immediately concerned in being doing what is expected of them'[6], and wants to 'see their cotton wool faces, zipper mouths expand shrivel, contract. To throw their salt-cellar out of the window, drill through their sound-proofed walls'[7]. But at the same time she is drawn to their 'bourgeois stronghold. So often scorned before, but soon understood, almost succumbed to: an ambiguous luxury'[8]. Still, she fights the temptation to conform and records her 'attempts at censoring any desire to think what should be felt. This the most difficult. So conditioned are the reflexes they become part of a mausoleum, when emotions outweigh surrounding matter a figure monstrous in

---

[1] p. 58
[2] p. 75
[3] p. 135
[4] p. 124
[5] p. 117
[6] p. 57
[7] p. 63
[8] p. 61

shape chiselled from soft substances'[1]. Sometimes the effort is too much and she longs to give herself over to a life she knows to be false:

> I remember at the convent love was imagining what lay behind Christ's loin cloth. This is no less imagining. But a situation I long to wade in right up to the very limits of imagination if possible . . . for the time being I ask of nothing else but to be, live as they live.[2]

S seems to suffer from the lack of any identity of her own, possibly resulting from her abortion, though she never really discusses this, and thus needs to define herself in relation to Ruth and Lean. She seems to feel that of herself she does not really exist: 'I become almost a shadow. The kind that extends up the wall, across the ceiling, dwindles gradually into other larger shadows. In my room. Theirs.'[3]; 'How to begin to find a shape - to begin to begin again - turning the inside out: find one memory that will lie married beside another for delight? Seems beyond attainment.'[4] Mountains seem to be used in *Three* as a symbol for identity and climbing mountains represents facing oneself, while the lake in the mountains stands for the inner peace, the resolution of ambivalences and the stability of identity. S reaches this state, presumably, in death in a lake in the mountains.[5] Connected with this and apparently opposing it are images of fragmented moons; the moon may represent woman, so that the problem of fragmented identity may be primarily a female one. Alternatively, the shattering of the moon could represent either her pregnancy (which interrupts the monthly cycle) or her abortion. Near the end of the book Leon tells Ruth he wants to go back to the mountains where he was interned during the war (= recapture his youth?) and Ruth asks 'what's wrong with these mountains and the ones we always meant to climb'[6], implying that he should face life as it is, with her, and not try to live in the past. S is certainly drawn to the mountains, though for her it seems that any mountains (identity) are better than none.

> Mountain peaks
> cut off
> by clouds. The one that will be climbed soon
> soon.[7]

---

[1] p. 56
[2] p. 62
[3] p. 62
[4] p. 56
[5] There is similar imagery in the story 'Eyes that Watch Behind the Wind', op. cit.
[6] p. 8
[7] p. 106

The problem is that

> Mountains
> appear. Move forward. When one is static.
> retreat when approached.[1]

S, it seems, can only reach the lake in the mountains through her own death. Closely related to the question of identity is role playing: Quin said of herself that she 'longed for roles that would suit my various moods and for an immediate audience'[2], and both here and in *Passages* are frequent references to roles, masks and facades. Ruth, Leon and S perform mimes in the empty swimming pool, which, if the lake represents the whole self, may stand for the empty of protean self. Interestingly, Ruth, who seems to have little or no personality or original thought is the least willing to playact; perhaps what little self she has is at least her own. S, on the other hand, is good at mimes: 'look at her movements Ruth how she entered into every part. Yes I guess she had that ability'[3]. She had apparently always wanted to go on stage, as Quin did as well as her father, who is in this respect like S's father. 'You want to go on the stage well why not. Why not in the blood I suppose'[4], inherited from her father. There are also many things in the book which are not what they seem, and where surfaces mislead: the dancing girls in the night club turn out to be men; and just before this is revealed Ruth touches an artificial flower; Ruth has had plastic surgery to her face, which is thus a kind of permanent mask (and hence the burning of the photographs, which were of her before the operation). S seems often to feel all surface: 'my own reflection a carved face in the middle of a stone wall'[5].

S also recognises, and perhaps forces Ruth and Leon to recognise, that perhaps there is nothing behind the facades of individuals' roles, or at least that everyone is always acting some role: she feels more close to Ruth when Leon is not there, as if 'R plays a role when he is with us. Except I wonder if it is not a certain role she plays with me, when we are on our own'[6]. Leon realises this ubiquity of role playing when analysing himself: even during the war when he felt most alive he was 'yet another person another role . . . Even in that cell solitary confinement when time became meaningless even there I had the part to play out . . . Soon one believes that is oneself and the change settles into corners.'[7] People, says S, are

---

[1] p. 24. See also pp. 27; 104; 110; ;39
[2] 'Leaving School', op. cit., p. 64
[3] p. 84
[4] p. 30
[5] p. 60
[6] p. 142
[7] p. 122

Interpreters in isolation
Chameleons in company.
Shapes
construct their own fancies.[1]

If S had been hoping that the couple would have strong personalities against which she could define herself, she is disappointed. Of the two, Leon seems to be the less vacuous, and at least has a past. (He also makes sculptures, though Ruth prefers his father's statues: 'at least they are whole and one can see what they are'[2]. Not only are Leon's figures less whole than his father's to start with, and smaller in scale – his father seems to have an outsize personality which his sculptures match – but Ruth finds them broken after S's disappearance, pointing to his fragmented personality.) During the war, Leon had been politically active and had been interned for his views; 'it was something while it lasted very real at least meaningful at the time though probably meaningless now yet it's the full measure of what I am.'[3] He is now an art historian, sterile emotionally, politically and, presumably, physically, since he and Ruth have no children. The only thing he can breed are his orchids, that symbol of decadent aestheticism, and seems to have spent his whole life, part from the brief spell of internment, in isolation and non-involvement:

> In childhood having no playmates, his stepmother wouldn't allow, so books became his sole companions. In regal state he played, dreamed alone. Relationships hardly comprehended for a long time no place in the world he had created.[4]

His lack of feelings is indicated by his diary, which is just 'headaches, appointments, library dinner and lunch engagements'[5], and which makes a striking contrast to the expressiveness of S's journal. The entries days around S's disappearance show an appalling coldness:

October 15th	Clear day. Sun at last. S hasn't returned.
October 16th	Rain again. Still no sign of S. Informed police.
October 18th	Boat found capsized. Chat identified. Also note in pocket - looks like suicide.

---

1 p. 21
2 p. 9
3 p. 7
4 p. 61
5 p. 65

October 19th	Two hours questioning by police sergeant. River and coastline dragged.
October 20th	R in bed all day. Translation completed.
October 21st	Dinner with the Blakeleys. A good hock.
October 22nd	Orchids making good progress especially Barbatum.

S is said to be good at restoring dolls[1], and this is perhaps what she is doing to Leon, restoring him not to life, but to a semblance of it. She certainly seems to seems to set him questioning himself: 'That I've been in a trance no doubt. Confronted by an existence I can no longer believe in'[2].

Both Ruth and Leon seem to indulge in self-examination after S's death, but, unable to communicate directly with each other, they confide in, in Ruth's case a diary and in Leon's case a tape. Before S's death, she seems to have been content in an empty way, indulging in all the latest trends and fads (see the list on p. 26). On their honeymoon, Ruth just wanted to lie on the beach while Leon wanted to visit the galleries and museums - though she paints still [*sic*] lifes herself - and recently her outlet has been her autoeroticism[3]; indeed she is quite sensual when Leon is not around. But when she begins to suspect Leon's infidelity with S, she sees that it was not mere physical unfaithfulness, but that he and S also communicated mentally. She begins to feel an 'appalling separation, a certain loss of identity . . . here was someone who shared something with him I failed to find?'[4]

Left alone together, Ruth and Leon are merely '[s]hadow players . . . indifferent to each other's interpretations on revolving stages, swinging them perhaps together, or out into space'[5]. 'Each held a corner of the room, cigarette smoke formed a screen between them'[6]. They have separate rooms in their town flat, and separate beds in their seaside cottage (aptly named Grey House), and their fragmentation as a couple matches S's fragmentation within herself. The sterility of their relationship is indicated by the contrast between the 'order' of their enclosed world at the cottage and the threatening 'chaos' of the outside world (this at least is how Leon sees it), where the people are "like beasts'[7]. Grey House, a mock [*sic*] Georgian building, faces

---

[1] p. 9
[2] p. 120
[3] See pp. 12/13 (which is intercut with very sensual descriptions of Leon and his orchids), 15, 76.
[4] p. 124
[5] p. 56
[6] p. 50
[7] p. 9

> an empty stretch of coastline, which belongs to them up to a certain breakwater. Beyond are the bottles, cartons, orange peel, banana skins, sanitary towels, stockings, contraceptives, gloves, boots, spare parts of prams, cars, bicycles, tins, mattresses, dolls, occasionally a chair that needs just upholstering.[1]

All the evidence of life, in fact. The outside world, always threatening, does in fact intrude one day while they are miming , and the statues (Leon's father's) with which their domain is 'inhabited' apparently come to life[2]; but, apart from some minor injuries to Leon, it leaves their lives untouched.

Though S does not completely change their lives, she has shown them that there is more to life than they have been used to, and, potentially, more to themselves than they have recognised, though her presence seems to have been needed to make them come alive: 'Her eyes at times as though she knew what I felt, was in fact the spinner of my dreams . . . I somehow envied her life, that sense of freedom she so obviously had, when everything seemed possible.'[3] But everything is not possible; S tries to face her life and fails, and solves the problem the only way she can, leaving us with the question: which is better, a life of continual struggle and inevitable defeat or a life of apathy and inauthenticity, without thoughts or goals? For Ruth and Leon, who live the latter life, there are now only 'the nights of self-pity, wishing in a way he would leave. That I could go, but the effort. Effort. And we remain'[4]. 'The possibility of what might have been sinks away. Into what is left.'[5] We all remain, faced with the existential dilemma. Ann Quin's answer is given in her own death, if it was not already clear; and as B.S. Johnson, whose answer was the same as hers, put it: amongst those left are you.

---

[1] p. 54. This threatening image of the detritus of everyday life is also important in *Passages*.

[2] pp. 104. 136/7. This is a case, as in *Berg*, of an element that is incompatible with realism: apparently the people have been standing, dressed as statues, since the previous day and no-one has noticed.

[3] p. 125

[4] p. 125

[5] p. 115

Passages, like *Three*, contains more than one type of narrative, one of them being a journal, and three characters, one of whom does not appear but whose absence dominates the book. Again the different narratives alternate, though this time there are only two types, and the journal sections are annotated, recalling two other narratives about journeys both literal and metaphorical through strange lands: Malcolm Lowry's 'Across the Panama'[1], and that story's inspiration, *The Rime of the Ancient Mariner*. Lowry's story is also similar to *Passages* in that its annotations combines quotations (in Lowry's case, from the *Ancient Mariner*) and extracts from a book about the country in which the journey is set[2] with the narrator's thoughts, which refer obliquely to the journal entries.

The narrative sections of *Passages* themselves are unusual in many ways: sometimes a paragraph will end without punctuation and the next will begin in the middle of a sentence. For example:

> She . . . watched the flight of many birds move into various designs over the sea. Specks against the horizon. Confused there, perhaps by a stronger wind they spread out. Specks
>
> on blotting paper trailed across. Doodles he made while on the telephone.[3]

> Always he was there. The blonde hairs, the slender
>
> shadows of almond trees . . .[4]

---

[1] From the collection *Hear Us O. Lord From Heaven Thy Dwelling Place* (London: Cape, 1962). Other works which make use of annotations or glosses include Stefan Themerson's *Special Branch*; Jeff Nuttall's *The House Party*; Henri Michaux's *Infinite Turbulence* and de Montherlant's *The Boys*.

[2] The quotes in *Passages* are, taken from Jane Harrison's *Prolegomena to the Study of Greek Religion* (Cambridge 1903; repr. Meridian 1959). *Passages* may however not be set in Greece, as its reviewers assumed, but in Lowry' s Central America or Mexico, which Quin knew.

[3] p. 63

[4] p. 67

Although it is characteristic of many modern novels to 'cut' cinematically from one scene to another, and some novels even do it in mid-sentence like this[1], Quin's technique is not based on any logical, causal or temporal connection, but on connections made in the narrator's mind; they are metaphoric rather than metonymic like typical narrative[2] and thus undermine the idea of cause and effect on which narrative is based. Also, the relative lack of connectives like 'then' and 'next' carry this to the level of syntax, and this, together with the relative lack of verbs in Quin's sentences, conveys a mere succession of impressions without any obvious connection, where past and present, experience and fantasy, are indistinguishable. This also serves to undermine the belief in the power of the individual to act on events, since with Quin's syntax there is often no easily discernible subject or object; the characters are neither, or both, agents and victims.[3] Furthermore, though the ability to mix past and future, fact and fantasy, has often been exploited by the cinema, only written narrative can, as Quin does by suppressing the use of names, merge several possible characters (or even, as I shall argue later, possibly split one character) into a simple 'she' and 'he', who may or may not be only two people, and the same people throughout the book.[4]

The journal sections ensure, by referring to some of the same events as the narrative, that some idea of chronology and who the characters are can be maintained, but, since diaries are normally intended to be meaningful only to their authors, they are as opaque as the narrative sections. The annotations sometimes clarify but usually mystify: they are sometimes cryptic thoughts relating loosely to the main entries[5]; sometimes extracts from the Talmud, and mainly direct (though sometimes abbreviated) quotes from Harrison. They usually seem to bear no direct relationship to the main text[6], though often the references to threatening female figures - the Sphinx, the Sirens and Medusa (which recall the threatening images of Judith in *Berg* and the recurring image of the mantis) - are echoed in the main entries, It is possible to discern some overall, broad meaning for many of the extracts, though not to find a single 'reading' of them. The journal's author (hereafter referred to as 'he' or 'him') notes: 'Decision

---

1 Some of Claude Simon's for instance.

2 See David Lodge: *Modes of Modern Writing*. London: Arnold, 1977 for a discussion of this dichotomy in modern literature.

3 John Sturrock has made very similar comments on Claude Simon in *The French New Novel* (Oxford U.P. , 1969), pp. 56 and 101/2

4 This opacity was what Susan Sontag argued was the proper function of the contemporary novel in 'Against Interpretation', op. cit.

5 It is not usually possible to say whether the entry was made before the note – though some were: for instance the top of p. 45 – but the annotations are not always, as the blurb claims, 'those thoughts which provoked the entries'.

6 According to Quin's publisher, Marion Boyars, she lined up the annotations precisely and asked for them to be printed exactly.

between madness and security is imminent'[1], and this seems to recall (besides the predicament of S in *Three*) the frequent references in the Harrison extracts to the Dionysian 'divine madness'[2], as opposed to the Apollonian idea of order, which Harrison treats at great length. Reference is also made to the 'Orphic doctrine of eternal punishment': this and the references to the symbolic use of wheels in Greek temples seems to be related to the endless nature of the quest the couple are engaged in, though it is surprising that Quin, with her love of Camus, should not have mentioned Sisyphus in this context.[3]

There are, however, some more direct references, such as that between the Arab sacrifice[4] and his implied homosexual encounter with the guard, to the story of Antigone[5], who was also trying to bury her brother, though the woman in *Passages* (hereafter referred to as 'she' or 'her') seems to be trying to do this metaphorically rather than literally; she is perhaps seeking to bury his memory in her mind. The annotations also refer to ancient beliefs and superstitions which the people in the modern civilisation cling to as consolation in their hard existence. They 'still have their rituals their God(s) their traditions. They have a cause they'll willingly die for'[6] They both seem willing to become involved in this way of thinking: they both refer to his 'High Priest look', and she says: 'If there's such a thing as reincarnation I see you as a kind of Priest, somewhere in the time B. C.'

To add to the opaque effect of the novel, not only is the book split into two, representing (possibly) masculine and feminine, but the characters also seem divided in themselves, referring to themselves in both the first and third persons[7]. This is also used to create uncertainty as to who is writing at any point: 'Movement of not seeing her, perhaps dust blinded. I thought I heard his voice from another compartment. She stood in the doorway. He didn't look up.'[8] Here it seems that each sentence is written by a different character, though it is impossible to be sure. In the same way, 'In the next room I pictured her smile'[9]

---

1 p. 32

2 See especially the Lycurgus quote on p. 30

3 It is also interesting, though presumably coincidence, that the references to Orpheus's 'bleeding head singing always' are the same as those used by Ihab Hassan as a metaphor for the literature of 'silence' in his book *The Dismemberment of Orpheus*. (New York: O.U.P. , 1971)

4 p. 46

5 p. 34. Quin also notes in 'Leaving School' how she herself felt like Antigone when her half-brother died.

6 p. 35

7 This is not simply reported speech or *Erlebte Rede* since the first person passages are almost entirely narrative, not thoughts or speech.

8 p. 8

9 p. 6

comes from a section of the book which seems to be narrated by her, as does the following, which seems to be describing things she could not have seen:

> He unfolded from his stunted position and took out the ear plugs, their small roundness in his arm pits for softening. Shaped to his ears. The shape of these she came back to. Hello had a good rest? I think his eyes were open. He didn't reply in the darkness.[1]

It is even possible that there is in fact only one person in the story, with masculine and feminine aspects; Quin thought, like Virginia Woolf, that everyone had both aspects[2]. There are passages where two people do seem to be talking, but in each case either the man could be a stranger or the conversation could be imaginary or remembered, and there is at least one case where they both use almost exactly the same words to describe an incident where there do not seem to have been two people present: 'She stumbled over cripples in alleys, passage ways . . . The thought of knives thrown at her back.'[3]; 'I left and stumbled over cripples in passage ways, alleys. The thought of knives thrown at my back'[4]. Another thing which supports the notion of the book containing only one split character, male or female is the way they attribute the same words to each other: 'Perhaps they think we are spies, he said laughing.'[5]; 'She feels we are being watched. 'Perhaps they think we are spies".[6]

This way of looking at the book is the only one in which it is not an 'impossible' story, like Mosley's *Impossible Object*, or Robbe-Grillet's *The House of Assignation*, but still leaves the problem of whether the narrator is really him, who stays in his 'cave' while she goes out into the world, or her, where he is an invention of hers to compensate for the loss of her brother. In this latter way, the search for the brother could be a metaphor for her search for wholeness; that is, the integration but differentiation of the masculine and feminine aspects. Certainly he seems sometimes to feel merely an aspect of her: 'What can I do - continue to be a metaphor for her despair?'[7]; 'She now used him to perform her own tragedy for herself'[8]; Am I truer to her than to myself perhaps?'[9]; 'do you

---

[1] p. 9
[2] See Hall, op. cit.
[3] p. 12
[4] p. 51
[5] p. 10
[6] p. 45
[7] p. 107
[8] p. 91
[9] p. 35

think I'm mad - have I killed someone - is there someone dead - I feel I'm your brother'[1].

If the two do represent masculine and feminine aspects, it is not clear what their respective characteristics are. On the one hand, there are references to the physical attitude of women as compared to the mental attitudes of men: 'And the women wait, bound up by their physical approach to things, no illusions, no ideals, wanting to be slaves, knowing no other role, accepting death as the order of things.'[2] She seems sometimes to live in a world of pure physical sensation:

> Water heavy with smoke, heat, a bitter taste. Hardness of the glass, she saw herself in. Buzz buzz buzzing of a mosquito round a candle. Wax formed green rivers. Frozen . . . Wall of mirrors. Circles of water, trees, faces edged off by shifting light. He rubbed an oblong stone. A fig opened slowly. Lips thin. Eyes narrowed on the deeper textures. Moments flashed, yellow, blue, orange. Sky so blue startles the eyes.[3]

In contrast, he is 'preoccupied with concerns she would call indulgent, metaphysical, calculating.'[4] But on the other hand, she is the one who lives on memories, while he seems to have no memory at all (he does not seem to remember having been to the country before): 'What annoyed him most was her use of memory'[5]; ' How is consistency ever possible I have no sense at all who I was yesterday, he said'[6]. She is also said to live 'with/from her passions'[7], while he says 'I try to kill my passions. To find a kind a kind of balance would be more natural'[8]. In the last paragraph of the book we can discern another facet of their difference:

> So let us begin another journey. Change the setting. Everything is changing, the country, the climate. There is no compromise now. No country we can return to. She still has her obsession to follow through and her fantasies to live out. For myself there is less of an argument. I am for the moment committed to this moment. This train. The distance behind and ahead. And the sea that soon perhaps we will cross.[9]

---

[1] p. 66
[2] p. 35
[3] p. 6
[4] p. 40
[5] p. 97
[6] p. 68
[7] p. 41
[8] p. 43
[9] p. 112

It seems from this that he (the masculine aspect) lives syntagmatically, diachronically, metonymically, while she (the feminine) lives paradigmatically, synchronically, metaphorically. (This makes Quin's narratives 'feminine' in these terms, since, as I said earlier, they are based more on metaphoric than on metonymic progressions, on the paradigmatic rather than on the syntagmatic.)

The emphasis on split selves seems to recall R.D. Laing, and especially his *The Divided Self*,[1] a book Quin knew and admired[2]. Certainly, some of Laing's concepts throw light on aspects of *Passages*, some of which seems to relate so closely to Laing's book that it may have been written with Laing in mind. Like Laing's patients, the characters in *Passages* have problems with their (lack of) identity, and there are many references to anonymity and lack of individuality: 'Rooms we take the shape of . . . Number amongst numbers'[3]; 'many have died in this country - many have been buried unidentified'[4]; the interpreter says that theirs is 'a case of mistaken identity'[5]. There is even doubt as to whether they exist at all: 'We climbed the bank, slipped in ruts, mule tracks, but made no tracks of our own'[6]. Alternatively, one of them, as I have suggested, may be merely an aspect of the other, and even the brother may not ever have existed: 'A museum I remember where I came across his signature that perhaps wasn't there at all'[7], and she is not even sure that the photograph she has is of him.

'She finds a metaphor for her condition without defining it'[8], and perhaps the journey through a hostile landscape in search of a male character is her undefined metaphor for life[9]; the life of a schizophrenic. This possibility is strikingly illustrated by a quote given by Laing from 'Joan', a, cured schizophrenic:

> Meeting you made me feel like a traveller who's been lost in a land where no one speaks his language. Worst of all, the traveller doesn't even know where he should be going. He feels completely lost and helpless and alone. Then, suddenly, he meets a stranger who can speak English. Even if the stranger doesn't know the way to go, it feels so much better to be able to share the problem with someone, to have him understand how badly you feel.[10]

---

1 Tavistock, 1959; repr. Penguin, 1965
2 According to her application form to Hillcroft College.
3 p. 9
4 p. 19
5 p. 11
6 p. 19
7 p. 6
8 p. 91
9 Alan Burns' *Europe After the Rain* (London: Calder 1965) concerns a similar search through a hostile landscape; though in this case for a girl.
10 Laing, op. cit., p. 165

In *The Divided Self*, Laing uses the term 'false-self system' to describe the alternative persona the schizophrenic adopts, and notes how one patient referred to this false self as 'he' or 'she', regarding it as external, and even of different sex.[1] In *Passages*, there are various ways in which false selves could be operating: either he or she could be the false self of the other, or there could be two people, both with false selves, which they refer to in the third person. She not only refers to herself in the third person, but to see herself as if from a distance: 'I remained in an upright position, and saw her body unfold from the folds of her dress'[2]; 'Laughter. Afterwards recognised as my own'[3]. In a similar way, Laing's Joan reports the feeling of looking down at herself from the ceiling.[4]

When he says that she lives 'with such frenzied intensity', she replies that there is nothing else to do - I would be eaten up by reality', and this is what Laing describes as the fear of 'implosion'[5], one of the forms of what he calls 'ontological insecurity', where the individual feels the 'world as liable at any moment to crash in and obliterate all identity'.

Also in accord with Laing's ideas on schizophrenia are the references, as in *Three*, to roles and masks: 'My face a mask. Body later attached.'[6] She can, according to his diary, be a 'Mature Woman', 'Femme Fatale', 'Mystic', or Country Girl at Heart', and in each case 'the illusion is the most real thing for her'[7]. She can also be the (schizophrenic?) 'Separated Woman'[8], which she often seems to be, as in the whipping scene at the party which she describes:

> what did I see, for when that scene reappears it merges with a dream, fallen back into slowly, connected yet not connected in parts. So what I saw then was as much a voyeur's sense, And since has become heightened. Succession of images, controlled by choice. I chose then to remain outside. Later I entered, allowed other entries. In that room a series of pictures thrown on the walls, ceiling, floor, some upside down. Only afterwards could I see things.[9]

It is impossible to tell from this whether she was merely watching all the time and there was another woman there whose place she took in her mind, whether three

---

1 Laing p. 198
2 p. 10
3 p. 6
4 Laing p. 166
5 Laing p. 45
6 p. 62
7 p. 43
8 p. 40
9 p. 24

of them took part, or whether she and he alone were there and she splits herself into two roles; and his description of the scene[1] does not clarify things.

A further possible reference to Laing is the use of the Medusa legend: he seems to see, like Berg, women as threatening, but here, unlike Berg's castration anxiety (if this is what it is), the reference may be to what Laing refers to as the fear of 'petrification', another manifestation of ontological insecurity. Laing uses the term to refer to the fear of becoming an inanimate object for other people, to forestall which the individual tends to treat others as objects, as she and he both do with their other lovers (though this is counterproductive, since one cannot be seen by an inanimate object). Laing actually mentions the Medusa legend as being an early expression of this.[2]

The temporal discontinuity of the narrative, and her apparent inability to distinguish between past, present, memory and fantasy would also, according to Laing, be an expected part of schizophrenia. She seems to live her life pursued by 'memories/visions making the moment a catalyst . . . plagued by dreams as if they were carved on me, on a sheet of metal'[3]; 'in that describing at times I lose track as in relating a dream'[4]. Laing's descriptions seem to match this well:

> A further factor is the discontinuity in the temporal self. When there is uncertainty of identity in time there is a tendency to rely on spatial means of identifying oneself. Perhaps this goes some way to account for the frequently pre-eminent importance to the person of being seen.[5]

> In so far as reflective awareness was absent, 'memory', for which reflective awareness would seem to be prerequisite, was very patchy. All her life seemed to be contemporaneous. The absence of a total experience of her being as a whole meant that she lacked the unified experience on which to base a clear idea of the 'boundary' of her being.[6]

If both characters are schizophrenic, she seems to be more successful than him in coping with the world; he seems to be constantly on the brink of insanity. The problem in considering him is that in the narrative sections 'he' seems to refer to at least three different people: the keeper of the diary, the brother, and at least one other lover, so that only in the journal can we be sure there is only one person, though we can use the events referred to in the journal to check whether he is the 'he' referred to in the narrative sections dealing with the same events.

1 pp. 57/60. This is also referred to on pp. 76 and 110.
2 Laing p. 96
3 p. 33
4 p. 62
5 Laing p. 109
6 Laing p. 197

There is still however doubt as to his role in the story, and his motives and desires. At times, especially early in the book, he seems to be terrified of arrest, but later he claims to have had her followed (which she seems to confirm) and to have pictures of the island (which assumes almost the symbolic importance of Virginia Woolf's lighthouse, and seems to have a similar function in the story) taken from a helicopter. Perhaps he is some sort of undercover secret agent, possibly for the Israelis, since he is said to be Jewish[1]. No such speculations are really justified by the text, but, looked at in another way, *Passages* can be seen as fragments from several possible novels, from which the novel we have is a selection of 'passages' (this would explain the 'impossible' nature of the story), and one of these could well be a spy story: they are arrested and interrogated, and seem obsessively secretive.

His Jewishness may partly explain his feelings of estrangement and being 'in exile'[2], 'completely lost in this country'[3], and to give him 'a meaning for being persecuted'[4]. 'He often sees himself as the scapegoat'[5], though, like Berg, his guilt is presumably imaginary or vicarious, but nonetheless pervasive, and he makes frequent references to it in his journal. His sense of separation seems to be deeper than the racial however: 'What have I in, common with the Jews? I have hardly anything in common with myself'[6]. Despite his recognition of this self-division, and his continual self-analysis (especially in his 'Notebook of a Depressive'[7], where he seems to be thinking in Freudian Oedipal imagery), he seems to get worse as the book progresses. Earlier on he has been able to cope: 'I look in all the corners and don't find myself. However within these limits there's space to live, and therefore the possibility to exploit them to a despicable degree'[8]. Later on things seem to get worse:

The mind goes out to meet itself

> A maniac in the cave I lie alone and look at the edges of the world.[9]
>
> I am on the verge of discovering my own demoniac possibilities and because of this I am conscious that I am not alone within myself.

---

[1] p. 89 refers to his 'middle-class Jewish upbringing'.
[2] p. 108
[3] p. 31
[4] p. 38
[5] p. 62
[6] p. 29
[7] p. 142
[8] p. 30
[9] p. 86

> The question then: who is it that inhabits me?[1]
>
> There must be time enough for preparation and for destruction, for the scheming, for reconstruction. A kind of dream made to order. To arrive finally at a unit with contradictory attributes never moulded or fused together, but clearly differentiated.[2]

Like Berg and S, he wants a 'dream made to order', and, as in dreams, expresses contradictory desires. But in reality, contradictory desires cannot all be satisfied, and he does not succeed in his plan, whatever it is. His dream is 'a unit' where the 'contradictory attributes' can be held together (as Mosley wants of language), among them, presumably, the masculine and feminine, which as we have seen, Quin thought should co-exist in everyone. He does not succeed in moulding them, that is in becoming her as well as him, and joining the two halves of his split self, and it seems likely that Quin, who surely recognised her own feelings in Laing's books and tried to set them out in *Passages* and the other novels, never managed to resolve her own split.

---

[1] p. 111
[2] P. 111

Ann Quin's least personal novel, and the one which does not fit into the tendency for internalised writing which Quin otherwise exemplifies, is *Tripticks*[1], which reflects her experiences in America. Here, in a rhythmic, driving, 'pop' style, she tried 'to write about America, about it being a dream'[2].The novel is a satire on American society, containing elements of Kerouac, Pynchon, and Barthelme, and uses cut-ups and fold-ins along the lines of Burroughs and Alan Burns, though the narrative tone of *Tripticks* is perhaps closer to the earlier Burroughs of the 1st person *Junky*, 1952 and the 3rd person *Queer*, 1952/53.[3] Burroughs and Jack Kerouac, like Quin had also been to Mexico and incorporated it into their writing: Burroughs wrote 'Mexico City Return' there and Kerouac lived with him while writing *Mexico City Blues*. Quin said she thought 'in terms of cartoons, each frame changing'[4], and the novel is illustrated by cartoons in a suitable style to emphasise this. In fact, the beginning of the novel looks remarkably like one of Jeff Nuttall's novelettes, especially *Come Back Sweet Prince*, 1968, though as far as I know there is no evidence that she was aware of Nuttall's work. The drawings themselves[5] appear mostly as thumbnails at the bottom of some of the pages and are mainly based on American hard boiled comic strip heroes of the 1930s to 1959s, like Rip Kirby, Steve Roper and Secret Agent X-9, which was written at one point by Dashiell Hammett, as well as some apparently based on S&M magazines.

The novel is mostly in the 1st person; the narrator himself, with his three ex-wives mainly speaks like a hard-boiled hero from a Hammett or James M. Cain story, or from *Black Mask* magazine – whose covers the illustrations resemble - though placed in a psychedelic, late 1960s environment and with a more existential self-awareness. He can also seem like a rootless, shiftless, travelling character from Bukowski, John Fante or Alexander Trocchi. He lists his personality traits:

[1] London: Calder & Boyars, 1972. It would, however, fit in with my overall argument if books about America were always externalised.

[2] John Hall, op. cit.

[3] She denied this influence (Hall, op. cit.), though Burns was a friend.

[4] *Tripticks* p. 44

[5] The illustrator, Carol Annand, also produced book covers in a similar pop style[5] and contributed images of God as a business tycoon in glasses to the *Oxford Illustrated Old Testament*, 1968.

I have many names. Many faces. At the moment my No. 1 X-wife and her schoolboy gigolo are following a particularity of flesh attired in a grey suit and button-down Brooks Brothers shirt. Time checked 14.04 hours Central Standard Time. 73 degrees outside. Area 158,693 square miles, of which 1,890 square miles are water. Natural endowments are included in 20 million acres of public reservations.

7

smart, well-educated	Lack of respect for authority
ambitious	lack of spiritual and moral fibre
deep concern for social problems	lack of responsibility
good values, character	lack of dialogue with elders
independent thinker	values ill-defined
poised personality	lack of good study habits
vocal, will speak up	lack of love for fellow men
mature, prepared for life	lack of self-respect
versatile, able	too impetuous
intellectually curious	too introspective
well-groomed	too introspective
care about community[1]	nothing missing

These are obviously not Ann Quin's own traits, and this is not in any way an autobiographical novel. And although the narrator mentions Greek myth – 'your family adventures may not match those of ancient Greece, but you're equipped to make history and why shouldn't you be'[2] – this is a long way from the introspection and classical reference of *Passages*. This is very definitely an 'American' novel in a way that very few British experimental novels were, with the exception of Burns' *Babel* and *Dreamerika!*[3], and it is significant that *Tripticks* is dedicated to Alan and Carol Burns. Jeff Nuttall knew, was admired and influenced by William Burroughs, but even his novels are firmly rooted in England, and a specific part of England at that. The narrator here uses Americanisms freely; his hard-boiled description of himself also includes:

> In my sophomore year I was considered a clean-cut boy, born of a sturdy woman whose mother once killed 45 Indians with a broom handle. Weaned on moonshine liquor when I was three years old. He can walk like an ox, run like a fox, swim like an eel and make love like a mad bull.

[1] p. 16

[2] p. 8

[3] And, like them, it also brings to mind J M.G. Le Clézio's *Les Géants*.

This makes him sound more like the cartoon-strip heroes listed above, or like Parker, the laconic, amoral anti-hero of Richard Stark's novels.[1] He notes how his women

> would be lying on the bed waiting for a he-man
> body strength powered with
> 520 muscles
> 18½ inch big arms powerful to land a knock-out blow
> fast
> 52 inch Heroic chest housing tireless lungs for
> endurance in work, sports, and women
> a broadmuscle packed back
> wonder-wide super man shoulders tapering to a slim
> punch-proof waist
> big muscular forearms
> a steel grip
> legs with marathon endurance. I was at their beck and
> call.[2]

The writing in *Tripticks* contains many lists like the above, designed, no doubt to subvert and break up the linear narrative of the traditional hard-boiled detective story, which is often alluded to:

> Perhaps she had finally killed him.
> At first I felt out of it, caught up among the fuzz all turned on at the start of a murder enquiry. But on studying the tooth marks on the body I felt I might be of some use. The marks, were, after all, plain enough to identify the person who had done the biting.

Despite the many references to the pulp fiction and comics of the 1930s and 1940s, *Tripticks* is set firmly at the very end of the 1960s as it is becoming the 1970s (the period described with such disappointment by Jeff Nuttall in *Snipe's Spinster*). The narrator's girlfriend, who later becomes his third wife and with whom he lives in *a ménage à trois* with his second ex-wife is the typical hippy – she says things like 'don't bug my trip' - and appears in several drug scenes that

---

[1] Richard Stark was one of the many pseudonyms of Donald E. Westlake. Parker was adapted into a film character, becoming Walker in *Point Blank*, 1967 and the Englishman Carter in *Get Carter*, 1971.

[2] pp. 62/63

seem to have been strongly influenced by LSD or mescaline. Drugs seem to be everywhere, mostly supplied by the mysterious Nightripper[1].

> I had the feeling that other than the potions Nightripper had handed out he had also passed around something else. The scene resembled a Bosch vision of hell. Some of the women were staring, some were screaming, and some said the walls were moving. These days if one escapes being hijacked in an airplane, mugged in the street, or sniped at by a man gone berserk, one apparently still runs the risk of getting accidentally zonked by the hors d'oeuvres at a friendly neighbourhood cocktail party. As soon as I thought this I began hallucinating, and ultimately freaked out, overturning the altar, calling Nightripper my motherfucking father.[2]

In the middle of the novel there is a selection of letters to the narrator from his first ex-wife, mother, his girlfriend, who signs herself 'your favourite Karate Kitten'[3], or FKK; and strange communications from Nightripper: 'Explain Sodom and reveal thyself. The Mysterium is babbling beyond comprehension'[4]. Both his first ex-wife and FKK begin to criticise him, and as the letters go on they become more scornful of him. His ex-wife says he is now 'both fawning and snotty at the same time. Instead of energy you have an irritating and clumsy effrontery, a puerile brashness, a sweaty freneticism.'[5] His girlfriend agrees: 'I didn't find your letter all that inspiring – pleasant enough but the energy level was almost zero', and calls him a 'Shakespearian clown who has read Reich'.[6] Towards the end of the novel, the narrator does indeed lose energy and focus, becomes more existential and inward, possibly as a result of the drugs.

> I woke up in a cold sweat. What was real, what wasn't? All merged into an immense interior region. Somehow, somewhere there ought to be unusual flood-light illumination. My mind was a crucible containing a constantly burning fire. A row of musical stalactites

---

[1] The Night Tripper was the sobriquet of Dr John, whose 1968 album *Gris Gris* was a landmark in psychedelic music

[2] p. 62

[3] p. 97; note the British English spelling

[4] p. 96

[5] p. 108

[6] pp. 114/115

> surrounding. Electrically charged. The night. Days were nights. Dreams were reality. Reality seen through a rear-view mirror. No sense of time.

This seems closer to the sound of Ann Quin's voice (or, indeed, Anna Kavan's), and the novel ends with the narrator as a solitary outsider living on an Indian reservation, a loner looking for order, unable to live in the world and dreaming of leaving it, as Anna Kavan recently had.

> How unlike those iron stairs of the subway: the turnstile a symbol of authority, a meter of the capitalist system, a regulator of human movement, a metal-petalled flower of law and order. And like hell I was part of that system, that turned men into well-fed and well-cared for pigs only interested in consumption and excretion. But secretly bearing the image of death-devoted Tristan - a modern day existential hero who is haunted by a world he can neither leave nor take.[1]

[1] p. 189

It seems from a fragment of Quin's uncompleted last novel[1], which seems to have been a record of her time in a psychiatric hospital, that she always remained separated both from herself and from the world. She tried in all her works to express this, but perhaps never felt she had succeeded, or that in expressing these feelings she could not as she had hoped exorcise them. In *The Unmapped Country*, Sandra reports on her interview with a psychiatrist in the journal she keeps, and this could be an epigraph for all her work:

> I see the whole situation as an outsider looking on. I have not felt myself as the individual in the situation. I only see myself, what, looking as though at another person . . . I have to sort of, what, struggle around to try and find something that describes it all and the terminology used. I make no guarantee of its accuracy.[2]

Like the stories in Anna Kavan's *Asylum Piece,* Ken Kesey's *One Flew Over the Cuckoo's Nest,* 1962, and Peter Weiss's *Marat/Sade,* 1963[3], the inmates of the institution all live in their own private world and the medical staff have no real idea of how to help them, nor any particularly strong desire to do so. The narrator, Sandra's only real form of communication is with her journal, in which she writes notes and dialogues. She is alone and isolated in this enclosed world; having gone to a school staffed by nuns, she is now in another form of enclosed order, though one without God. Fellow-inmate Thomas is writing a book pointedly called *God's Joke* and Sandra herself paints the face of God as a Blakean figure who 'laughed, belched, snored and picked His nose'[4] but did not come to save her. In this physical and metaphorical closed world, where she has lost the sense of how long she has been there, and does not know when or even if

---

[1] printed posthumously in Giles Gordon, ed. *Beyond the Words: Eleven Writers in Search of a New Fiction.* London: Hutchinson, 1975

[2] p. 259

[3] *The Persecution and Assassination of Jean-Paul Marat as Performed by the Inmates of the Asylum of Charenton Under the Direction of the Marquis de Sade;* first performed in Britain, in English, in 1964

[4] p. 260

she will be released, she wonders if anyone in the outside world is still really there. 'Out there another world; were they still waiting? No, they had gone'[1]. The ending of the fragment we have of this novel gives no clues as to what direction it might have taken, or whether this is its beginning. Taken as a self-contained short story, however, its ending has a satisfying finality, and might act as a summary of all her work.

> Soon there was just the sound of the clock, and breathing, wheezing, dream murmurs, and bodies turning over. The long night stretched out. Wind rattled the windows, and snow mixed with hail pounded like small fists against glass. In the middle of the dormitory, a nurse read or slept under a lamp. Sandra stared at this light until it spun from its orbit and approached. Right at the very beginning – but there was no beginning. Vague notes for a basis of shape. The first section interrupted by the last. No continuous movement. A starting point somewhere. Chords superimposed on chords. The pendulum swung back.[2]

ANN QUIN

Ann Quin, one of our most unusual novelists, died in August at the age of 37. Her first novel **Berg** (£1.25 and 75p paperback) was a milestone in modern English writing, one of the best novels of the sixties to escape from naturalism, the best Brighton novel since Brighton Rock. Her second book **Three** (£1.25 and 75p paperback) was highly praised and in its oblique record of a girl who disappears, prophetic of her own death by drowning. **Passages** (£1.25 and 75p paperback), more experimental and poetic, moved into a new sphere of higher prose. Her latest **Tripticks** (£2.25) fuses Jazz improvisations and the techniques of the comic strip . This fine and tragic writer should now be collected by all who care for important writing.

New books from Calder & Boyars this summer include Tonesco's **Macbett** translated by Donald Watson (£2.75 and 95p paperback), Wolfgang Bauer's unusual Austrian plays **All Change** (£2.60) and the film edition of Anthony Shaffer's **Sleuth** (£1.95 and 85p paperback). Ivan Illich's important book **Tools for Conviviality** (£2.25) will be published later in the month.

CALDER & BOYARS 18 Brewer Street

[1] p. 252
[2] p. 274

penelope shuttle

Penelope Shuttle was born in West London in 1947. She began to write seriously at the age of fourteen and finished her first novel when she was seventeen. Her early novella *An Excusable Vengeance* was published by the prestigious Calder & Boyars in the collection *New Writers VI*, 1967[1]; they then published the first of her four full-length novels, *All the Usual Hours of Sleeping* in 1969, when she was only 21 and had only previously published one volume of poetry with a small press. After this she received a grant from the Arts Council of Great Britain which enabled her to give up her part time secretarial job and move to Cornwall and write full time. In 1972 she won another Arts Council grant and an E.C. Gregory Award for poetry. Calder & Boyars (later Marion Boyars) obviously believed in her as they also published her next three solo novels: *Wailing Monkey Embracing a Tree*, 1973, *Rainsplitter in the Zodiac Garden*, 1977 and *The Mirror of the Giant*, 1980.

During this time she had also published several volumes of poetry with small presses[2] and in 1980 published her first full-length volume of poetry, *The Orchard Upstairs* with the equally prestigious Oxford University Press.

---

[1] The same issue also contained a novelette by Carol Burns; Calder & Boyars also published Ann Quin and Alan Burns.

[2] Including: *Nostalgia Neurosis*. St. Albert's Press 1968; *Jesusa*. Granite, 1971; *Branch; A Poem*. Sceptre, 1971; *Jesusa*. Granite, 1971; *Moon Meal*. Sceptre, 1973; *Midwinter Mandala*. Headland, 1973; *The Dream,* Sceptre. 1974; *The Songbook of the Snow*. Janus, 1974; *Photographs of Persephone*. Quarto, 1974; *Autumn Piano and Other Poems*. Rondo, 1974; *The Songbook of the Snow, and Other Poems*. Janus Press, 1974; *Four American Sketches*. Sceptre, 1976; *Period*. Word Press, 1976; *The Orchard Upstairs*. Oxford University Press, 1980; *Prognostica*. Martin Booth, 1980; *Child-Stealer*. Oxford University Press, 1983; *The Lion from Rio*. Oxford University Press, 1986; *Adventures with my Horse*. Oxford University Press, 1988; *Taxing the Rain*. Oxford University Press, 1992; *Building a City for Jamie*. Oxford University Press, 1996; *Selected Poems, 1980-1986*. Oxford University Press, 1998; *A Leaf out of his Book*. Carcanet, 1999; *Redgrove's Wife*. Bloodaxe, 2006; *Sandgrain and Hourglass*. Bloodaxe, 2010; *Unsent: New & Selected Poems. 1980-2012*, Bloodaxe, 2012

In 1975 her play *The Girl Who Lost Her Glove* was broadcast on BBC Radio Three. Robert Nye said of her: 'it becomes difficult to escape the conclusion that no new English novelist since the late Ann Quin has started out with more promise, or already accomplished so much.'

Shuttle also published two novels jointly-authored with her husband, the poet Peter Redgrove, whom she met in 1969: *The Terrors of Dr Treviles: A Romance*, 1974 and *Glass Cottage, A Nautical Romance*, 1976. The two also published a joint volume of poetry: *The Hermaphrodite Album*, 1973 and *The Wise Wound: Myths, Realities, and Meanings of Menstruation,* 1978, an attempt to break the taboo that has surrounded this difficult subject since at least Leviticus.[1] The relationship with Peter Redgrove was obviously of huge importance to Shuttle's life and work; after his death in 2003 she published a collection of poems title *Redgrove's Wife*, Bloodaxe, 2006. As Redgrove's name was placed first on the title pages the joint novels are discussed in the separate section on Redgrove in the 'Fellow Travellers' chapter of this book. Their collaborations, covering poetry, the novel and women's bodies were practically unique and it is hard to think of any parallels, let alone any successful ones. The epigraph to *The Hermaphrodite Album*, from Goethe, is, fittingly: 'My work is that of a composite being, which happens to be signed.'

Shuttle's novels merge poetic language with the novel form unlike virtually anyone else before or since. This was a problem for many reviewers at the time, especially as the writing contains many strange metaphors and obscure words which hardly serve to move the plot of the novel along, and the novels do have plots. One is reminded of Eliot's comment on Djuna Barnes's *Nightwood* that it needs to be read twice as the second experience will be very different to the first. But this begs the question: do we want to read novels twice? And can we read them like poetry: paradigmatically rather than syntagmatically, or can we even combine both modes of reading, as with Mallarmé's or Rimbaud's prose poems? Can we suspend time as we appreciate the beauty of the writing while being carried forward by the plot? Eliot said that *Nightwood* would be best appreciated by readers of poetry, though he was not advocating poetic language and was

[1] Redgrove and Shuttle subsequently published another book on the same subject: *Alchemy for Women: Personal Transformation Through Dreams and the Female Cycle*, 2005

quick to point out: 'I do not mean that Miss Barnes's style is "poetic prose". But I do mean that most contemporary novels are not really "written".'[1] Rayner Heppenstall, a prose stylist diametrically opposed to Shuttle and an admirer of French *chosisme*, said in a review of Philippe Sollers' *Le Parc*:

> The blurb (written, one would guess, by the author) describes it as a *poème romanesque*, as opposed to a *roman poétique*. That sounds fine. It means that we do not get a lot of purple, metaphor-laden, incantatory prose (Mr. Durrell's Alexandrian fours are, one supposes, poetic novels). It should mean that the book finds other ways of making its final effect than those of steady and-then and-then, that it organizes itself otherwise.[2]

Anaïs Nin's[3] *The Novel of the Future*, first published in America in 1968, and in the UK in 1972, addresses the question of the 'poetic novel', which Nin herself wrote, and in which she strongly advocated Anna Kavan; it also seems very relevant to Shuttle's work.

> As a prose poet becoming fascinated with a rich source of images, I concentrated on describing the dream world, perhaps tempted by the difficulties involved. Obviously the physical world is easier to describe. The first misunderstanding about my work which arose and has continued to the present was that I was writing dreamlike and unreal stories.
>
> My emphasis was on the relation between dream and reality, their interdependence.[4]

Nin says that 'poetic symbols are today more than ever necessary in writing novels, not because they are poetic, or mysterious, but because they alone are capable of dealing with the relativity of truth about character.'[5] B. S. Johnson would probably not have approved (he died in the same year as the publication of Shuttle's second novel). For him, poetry was for 'the short, economical lyric, the intense emotional statement, depth rather than scale'. In contrast 'the novel may not only survive but evolve to greater achievements by concentrating on those things it can still do best: the precise use of language, exploitation of the

---

[1] Introduction to Djuna Barnes, *Nightwood*. New York: Harcourt, Brace & Co., 1937

[2] 'The Pursuit of a New Novel', Times Literary Supplement, February 9, 1962

[3] Nin's first published study was *D. H. Lawrence An unprofessional study*, Paris, E. W. Titus, 1932

[4] Macmillan, 1968, p. 5

[5] p. 11

technological fact of the book, the exploitation of thought.'[1] Except for the last of these, Shuttle, pursuing her own unique vision, goes completely against Johnson's ethos. However, in her sympathetic and sisterly review (titled 'Blood sisters') of *Rainsplitter in the Zodiac Garden* Victoria Glendinning said the opposite of Eliot, that it 'must be read fast, with concentration and sympathy; if one does not cooperate, it disintegrates into a barrage of fragmented images.'

> It is not entertainment; and it is not poetry, although Penelope Shuttle has an established reputation as a poet and takes a poet's licence with language. Rather it is an invitation to trace the mythology of a mind that has left the scheduled tracks and timetables . . . Penelope Shuttle is an uncompromising explorer, digging away in the moist rabbit-hole of the subconscious, hoping we can follow her. If she used her insights to illuminate the upper world she would win a wider readership, but that's a different matter.[2]

A rather less kind (anonymous) review, of *Wailing Monkey Embracing a Tree,* titled 'Strictly for the bards', said of it:

> Blurring the distinctions between poetry and prose, Penelope Shuttle's nervous and exciting talent still deals too strongly in arcana. There are many beautiful, fresh and turbulent passages in her new "novel", but her frequent examples of bardic overflow may be nothing more than the contemporary version of the pastel rhapsodizing once associated with the *poème en prose*. Whether this is a sign of excessive strain in her methods, or a sign of placing too heroic a faith in exotica dragged out of the subconscious (or the Thesaurus), it is probably too early to tell.
>
> Often the reader's imagination is likely to be shocked without being convinced. But images and phrases do not entirely suffocate the story, while the uncommon poetic speech in which the narrator and the conjugal protagonists themselves present their meditative perceptions and reveries has the effect of mythologizing that familiar theme in contemporary fiction, a stale marriage. . . . Working within its ardent and exacting mode, Miss Shuttle's linguistic concentration inevitably produces the feeling that the story she tells is more important for the poetry it elicits than for its social strangeness and significance. Yet she is dealing with common unhappiness, with trapped feminity and trapped masculinity, with breakdowns and hysteria. Such an emphasis is, in

[1] Introduction to *Aren't You Rather Young to be Writing Your Memoirs?*, 1973

[2] Times Literary Supplement January 28, 1977

> fiction as much as much a contrivance as any other, the promulgation of a poetic view of life an insult to the ordinary.[1]

Of all the novelists in this study, Shuttle's dreamlike prose relates most closely to that of Anna Kavan, though Kavan was perhaps not so much a prose poet in Anaïs Nin's sense. Apart from Shuttle, the only other novelists I can think of who were combining poetry and the novel, in diametrically opposed styles both to each other and to Penelope Shuttle, are Philip Toynbee, whose *Pantaloon* series of verse novels[2] Johnson would also not have liked ('You would agree it would be perversely anachronistic to write a long narrative poem today?'[3]) and Jeff Nuttall, poet and performance artist, some of whose books combine a very different kind of poetry with the novel form. But Shuttle is her own woman; she is not influenced by or comparable with any earlier or contemporary writers.

Penelope Shuttle was a poet before, during and after her time as a novelist, though her first full-length solo collection with a major publisher was *The Orchard Upstairs*, published in 1980 Some of the poems had been published in magazines considerably earlier – one is dedicated 'i.m. B.S. Johnson', who died in 1973. A proper study of her poetry, let alone a discussion of how her poetry and poetic prose interact would be well beyond the scope of this book but a brief look at the poems may help to explicate the novels to some extent. Perhaps surprisingly the language of the novels is more difficult and dense than that of the poems; the novels use far more obscure words and are in many ways harder to 'read'. Also surprisingly the novels seem less personal than the poems which, though never confessional in the mode of, say Anne Sexton – there is nothing in Shuttle's work like 'In Celebration of My

[1] *Times Literary Supplement*, February 15, 1974
[2] *Pantaloon or the Valediction*, 1961; *Two Brothers: the fifth day of the Valediction of Pantaloon*, 1964; *A Learned City: the sixth day of the valediction of Pantaloon*, 1966; *Views from a Lake: the seventh day of the Valediction of Pantaloon*, 1968
[3] B. S. Johnson ibid.

Uterus' or 'Menstruation at Forty', both published in 1969 – nevertheless do obviously refer to herself. She certainly seems to be the 'dancer stuck between the moon and the earth'[1] and, like Sylvia Plath[2], uses both the moon and blood as recurring symbols: 'Around the moon, / my dreams cluster, not moths'[3]

That new moon waiting for me
to step out into twilight
is no desolate island:

Not that little moon
around which the minnow-blue sky flows,
no.

Nor is that new moon
made of snow

That moon has the strength of a million spines.
It is this moon alone which stays awake all night.[4]

Perhaps the most explicitly personal in *Orchard* is the poem 'Period.'

Waterfall (of legendary bone)
blood manuscripts
A seed of melancholy, a blind red lizard
belonging to me

Night bird of red
and a morning handled roughly
Fatigue, deity of darkness

I ache without eggs
My belly is an extinct door
The red pinnacles hurt
The brink of my forehead is cold
                    blue accents are there

Bleak trees on a slanting bank

---

1 'The Dancer' in *The Orchard Upstairs,* p. 2

2 Plath's 'Thalidomide' for instance has 'Oh half moon' and 'blood-caul of absences'. Shuttle and Redgrove quoted Plath in a letter printed at the end of this chapter.

3 'The Orchard Upstairs', p. 49

4 'Four American Sketches', p. 26

I shiver because of my scarlet cargo

Wan language I speak unwillingly

The reprimands twine, prolonging the dark

Go away, this is too much moon,
soaking my underclothes,
hodding my day with weariness[1]

Like Anna Kavan, Shuttle also has imagery of glass and snow, bringing to mind Kavan's fragile glass-girls.

Dress me in glass!
Shoes, sleeves, all . . .
Let me move with great care,
interned in glass garments,
until I become glass,
cool and irreversible change,
glass eyebrow,
fingernail, clitoris . . .
Bone, blood and breath: all glass.
Until I am a devotee of glass,
reflecting all its famishings.[2]

---

[1] p. 37
[2] 'Glass-Maker', pp. 12/13

In Penelope Shuttle's first prose publication, the 70 page novella *An Excusable Vengeance* an unnamed couple in an unnamed country meet several times through the seasons in separate scenes, and are both attracted to and afraid of each other. They seem to have had a previous relationship and he has apparently betrayed her. The season of the year is like a third character in the story; the sun is a constant presence and metaphor, unlike the moon symbolism so prominent in the later novels.

> The sun showed its bones fully in the early evening, stretching the all-encroaching and entirely despotic power it bore to send it through the universe of the house shaking down with anger on her. The silence pushed at the ceiling, the melancholy barrier to the sky. One sound broke the spell. All day she waited for this conversation and now it has meant little. Only the possibility of seeing one another has come from it; no speaking of love such as they were sure would come, such as they wished to come, has been sent from either one to the other. The room is darker, darker than it is in the outside darkness.[1]

The house where the woman lives also becomes a character in the story. While the sun is shining it seems the couple can bear to be apart from each other but in winter they need to be together. However, neither seems able to commit to the other, in his case because of his betrayal of her.

> When the house was saturated with intense heat it had seemed impossible to bear but now she longs again for that sense of fear with which she could form a distinct and elongated enemy. The hissing effigy of the sun had been a strange but understandable force in her existence. This coldness, the great empty unemotional and penurious atmosphere

[1] p. 108

> emphasizes a sense of alarm and terror more terrible than the mere fear of surroundings, of living things, of loving things.[1]

Later he 'remains in the house and by his presence throws back the aspect of morbidity that otherwise the house would inspire.'[2]

Visiting a funfair they go into a hall of mirrors, where they 'gaze curiously at each new aspect of themselves. Their real personages vanish. The first sights lend them a cause for laughter which alleviates the tension as the grotesque and the absurd that mingle into mutations of their true selves can be laughed at without fear.'[3]

It seems that 'the sin he has committed is a sin against himself and against her memory; but more than this it is a sin against the land, against his own creation. It is this sin and loss of innocence that he howls for and the sobs comfort him as if the tree were her body.'[4] The sin is apparently dendrophilia.[5] 'From her he must hide the maladjustment of rain-drowned happenings and never reveal to her the tortured limits of his darkened imagination.'[6]

The first section of the story was titled 'A Vision of Sun'; in the second, 'The Temperature of Fear', the season and the story both turn colder. (The section has an epigraph by Thomas Chatterton, 'the marvellous boy', who died at the age of 17, Shuttle's age when she wrote the story.) While it is still summer, he appears to have committed to her completely but the mirror symbolism returns as a premonition.

> His love becomes a white winter day in the calendar of summer, a purity of necessity, a clarity of suffocation. He does not comprehend the confinings of love or the dangers of their containment. Instead he blends the day together with his love. The air is permeated with promises he cannot yet keep. She sees him with the eyes that she has kept hidden all week. His face reflects the future for her and that the mirror is shattered neither of them can see.[7]

Later, possibly realising his secret, she runs away. 'In spite of the obligato [*sic*] of blood that covers her eyes she sees, in the truth of recovery from her fall, all that

---

[1] p. 144
[2] p. 155
[3] p. 112
[4] p. 117
[5] Eliciting a perhaps unfortunate thought of the comic novel '*A Melon for Ecstasy*, 1971 by John Fortune and John Wells, which is also about a dendrophile.
[6] p. 125
[7] p. 130

has been forbidden to achieve and all that has been shut away from her.'[1] As winter ends the house again seems to turn on them.

> Winter was a type of shelter to them: they are losing that entirely. Whilst the house strove against the battering wings of the chilled air there was no occasion for it to turn on them. But in the lapse of winter the house has also negotiated and gained more tenacity with which to manipulate a clash with her and once winter has vanished it can again begin to control its boundaries.[2]

At the very end of the story the couple have sex on the beach but he 'cannot refund trees from his heart. Her cold flesh feels like bark on him, her fingers like leaves.' Violently he 'thuds into her the whole of the fears and hatreds that he has been carrying with him all the days of winter beneath a mirror of snow. He cleaves her apart as enjoyment and revulsion struggle for first place in him.' The revulsion wins.

> Her eyes open for a half-cried moment as her hands writhe out to halt him. His mouth distends long and volcanic and he presses harder to squeeze all the emotion out of him until there is no love in him. The pressure flies up; she sags greasily between his knees. Her fingers are pieces of death.[3]

Finally, as her body washes out to sea, he finds 'a cleanliness and acceptance' in the sand. 'Only by returning to the sand does he find it and lose trees. . . He burrows down more implacably into the jamming rock-mist to breathe steadfastly and constantly as, alternately, he sacredly jerks and buries himself. Soon he does not move at all.'[4]

---

[1] p. 138
[2] p. 157
[3] p. 165
[4] p. 168

Shuttle's first full-length novel *All the Usual Hours of Sleeping*, 1969 is a large and dense work, full of rich, poetic imagery but at its heart is a love story involving four people: the lawyer Tomas who is currently in a relationship with Herma[1], who was introduced to him by his former partner, Rachel and Rachel's new partner, Daniel. Rachel has left Tomas to travel abroad and has met Daniel but is not committed to him. Herma has had a baby which has died shortly after its birth. Rachel returns to Tomas and tries to win him back, despite the presence of the almost irrelevant Daniel. It turns out that Rachel is Herma's older sister – the 'secret' they keep for most of the novel. Herma eventually kills herself and Tomas and Rachel are together again.

It is the use of language taken well beyond its normal descriptive function rather than any formal experimentation that makes this novel stand out. As an example from the first page, where Tomas and Rachel have met again:

> The distance between them, although composed of only a few feet, is, in another sense, made up of intangible areas as impassable as the hyperborean fall of avalanche. A regiment of months holds them rigidly there and has no intention of letting them go free just yet. Sun moves. Sun flees. The faience of sunlight slide gradually down the walls until the lavender disapproval of dusk encloses the man and woman. The weight and drought of this dimness binds them further to the room.[2]

This is wonderfully evocative of mood but at the same time may seem frustrating as a description of a literal scene. Some of the metaphors and images are deliberately jarring: her knuckles are 'the shade of obsidian', the 'fidelity of the pluperfect shadows thwarts him.'[3] 'They stand amongst shadows of Castilian gold

---

[1] It may be relevant that Shuttle and Redgrove's 1973 joint collection was called The *Hermaphrodite Album;* the word hermaphrodite comes from Hermaphroditus, the son of Hermes and Aphrodite who was united with the nymph Salmacis, combining male and female in one body. However, there is nothing in Herma's character or behaviour to further this idea.

[2] p. 9

[3] p. 10

down-pouring, like deer hunted away on the necessary air.'[1] Spicy rain falls to the shingled lawn and the broken circles of moonlight. . . It makes a lagoon of flowers: evening rain has the smoothness of angels. . . Rachel's Lucerne heart is cruel.'[2] The limits of this rich style of writing are revealed in two areas: writing about sex, which is rare in this book, and reported speech.

> He throws some cushions on the floor for them to squat there, semi-nude flimsy ruined inhabitants of a precarious world. They rub their bodies sensuously together, fumigating the flesh, suffusing, stuffy air clapping hands over their outstretched mouths. Her breasts make a figure of eight. His sticky balls are two old crabs.[3]

There is an inevitable bathos where the grossly physical facts of sexual encounters meet the language of myth, or where obscure, slightly comical words are used to describe sexual passion. 'Her cascading body awaits the impetus, feeling him shuddering like a spillikin and she arches herself for the happy entry'[4] The reported speech hovers between the allusiveness of the prose and the everyday ordinariness of actual speech and sometimes jars bathetically. 'Threat stands out like a basilisk. Chiaroscuro. Herma hits out at Rachel. O you bitch.'[5] However, the writing is mostly very beautiful and evocative. 'The music produces its wasted chords without revelation, without affection: the stony warbling of a caryatid.'[6] 'Innocent moonmoodlight whitewashes the darkness. They walk up flights of steps, kindred stones, clinging to one another.'[7] Although the characters seem as solid and real as characters in a conventional novel, their identity does seem to exist fully only in relation to each other. Having left Tomas and her home country, Rachel is a

> celluloid figure marking time in a passive syncopation. When she glances sideways at her reflection in the shop windows she tries to see the face of her great grandmother there. But her poise is tainted. Immediately after she left Tomas, she made sure of fastening a tight intellectual crupper around all of her recollections.[8]

---

[1] p. 117
[2] p. 176
[3] p. 41
[4] p. 57
[5] p. 176
[6] p. 54
[7] p. 55
[8] p. 20. A crupper is a strap to fasten a horse's saddle and is representative of the obscure words Shuttle obviously loves to use.

Like Rosalind Belben's women, her 'liberty suffocates itself with her loneliness.'[1] She has left Tomas to find herself:

> to achieve the identity I wanted and still want, I had to break away from everything else. I had to do it. I'm not like Herma, I want more than the simple truth, a pat explanation. I want the whole picture. I want what lies behind the whole picture.[2]

Rachel can never seem to find her real self, and perhaps needs Tomas to complete her identity. She has to travel constantly, both literally and figuratively, to be constantly in motion.

> Rachel, the watcher in the doorway, is the motionless figure who will never find a field a road a sea upon which the sole of her foot might rest. Her very stillness sums up the difficulty she has in being simply her own self, the plain object: it gives away her inability to represent her nature openly for all observers to deprecate or adore. Each individual has its own rosebeds and high walls: its atlas and its economy. She does not understand this.[3]

Herma seems at times only to exist as a pawn in the game between Tomas and Rachel with no will or power of her own. 'The Pawn moves only straight forward (except in the act of capturing). However, it is permitted to go two steps when first played.'[4] In a long internal monologue she thinks bout recapturing herself. 'I wish I could have another chance. I wish I could recreate my old childish fears. I wish I still feared shadows and drunks singing in the street. Instead of myself.'[5] She regrets the loss of her childhood and the loss of her own child. 'I didn't want to be left behind with this emptiness I can never satisfy. Why does it seem that I am watching myself vanish into thin air?'[6] After her death, Rachel says 'she had an internal existence she was trying to hold on to: yet which she simultaneously questioned and repressed. I think we all strained her beyond the point where she could control this inner world.'[7] Whereas Rachel and Tomas seem unable to live without each other, Herma could have remained her own person. Tomas compares the gentle Herma to the more assertive and manipulative Rachel.

---

[1] p. 42
[2] p. 91
[3] p. 199
[4] p. 74
[5] p. 105
[6] pp. 105/6
[7] p. 237

> O Rachel, I'm confused, I'm tired, I can't say goodbye to you, jezebel, virago Boadicea. Madonna my own. This little Herma, the young, the stupid, just a girl, what's she to us? With her, picnics. With you, banquets. God. Some laws. I call for them. A pillar of fire. To lead me out of the wilderness. No. I forgot. There is nothing here. Nothing visible. nothing empirical. Rain smelling of joss. Again running. Running. The two women in their lily-white beds. Walls, a corridor, and their lewd libretto separate them.[1]

In Tomas's relationship with Herma, the subject of faith and religion have come up; with Rachel he had had a very practical, empirical relationship. Their discussion raises the issue of how they and the novel balance the eternal with the diurnal: what, if any, are the universal implications of the story. 'Tomas why are you asking me about the way a universe works when surely the problem is just between the two of us?'[2]

Tomas is only seen and only seen to exist thorough his relationships with the two women. As a lawyer he is surrounded by the mundane, among which Herma tries to maintain her faith.

> Embezzlements, evidence, liability, statements, Limitations, persons in debt, persons taken and given in adultery. He ticks them off on a list. The wind and rain descend the scale, a ponderous cello. She fidgets. Hang on to it, she thinks, this invisible faith.[3]

Rachel warns Tomas: 'Herma's taking you in a strange direction, towards everything you hate: altars, hymns, visions'.[4] Daniel is a 'poverty stricken character' compared to Tomas, and Rachel is never committed to him. 'She needs Daniel as a prop, to help her regain her balance.'[5] He tells her 'I've no ties except you, my name is interchangeable with a dozen others where work is concerned. . . and my private life is not worth the question'.[6] He is a 'man without qualities'[7]: 'there's no duty in my life, I've always believed in keeping myself free from everything, because if I participated, the process of time, of setting myself free from a certain prison would be much too painful.'[8] At the end of the novel Herma kills herself in a vivid and powerful passage.

---

[1] pp. 82/83
[2] p. 33
[3] p. 40
[4] p. 134
[5] p. 116
[6] p. 60
[7] A reference to Robert Musil's elliptical novel?
[8] p. 61

> She leans forward. She stands at the edge of a long hidden long retrained desire. Her hands bless. And no more. O outlaw. She falls and feels the real and sharp and broken glass rip and gash her: a yoke of glass tears her mouth with no lips to remonstrate. She falls forward into the hedges of snow. The air meets her, the stony ground rushes up at her, cold waters of death flow from a broken dam: she falls on to a shore of salt and ice and her body is carried out to sea, She sustains fatal injuries. She lies there supreme and sacerdotal. She has warded off perfection. She has entered an ultimate clime. a region where the hunter and the hunted are extinct.[1]

Unquestionably Shuttle's novels are hard to read: the prose is very dense and filled with arcana, strange words and obscure and baffling metaphors. But the language is also unquestionably sumptuous, like a vast, overwhelming banquet of rich and rare delicacies: beautiful to look at and to sample but perhaps too much to digest in one sitting. On taking Eliot's advice and rereading the novels one is tempted to open pages at random and read a selection of passages as with a poetry collection. As if aware of this, Shuttle's second, much shorter novel is split into short, titled sections like a set of linked prose poems and the dust jacket tells us that the sections are 'intended to read as images and not as chapters.' However, the cover says that this is a novel not a collection of poems, and it does indeed have characters and a linear plot, as do all her novels.

[1] p. 234

Wailing Monkey Embracing a Tree, 1973 (the cover informs us that this is the Chinese name of a sexual position, though it is not otherwise mentioned in the novel), dedicated 'For Peter', gained a number of reviews in the serious press, some hostile, some more positive. 'Penelope Shuttle writes the kind of prose that gives poetry a bad name. To read *Wailing Monkey Embracing a Tree* is like eating a meal of which every course is smothered in clotted cream.'[1]

> It could be that Miss Shuttle has become the prisoner of her own verbal inspiration, so that the language is telling her what to do. It could be that I have not yet perceived the relation between the rhythm and the story. This is not a book which gives you all it has on one reading. On the contrary, it is *designed to be reread*—a lot is made to depend upon memories of linguistic echoes, cadences that came once like this a while before, now changed from the major to the minor, or vice versa.[2]

Indeed, on rereading, some of the writing is evocative and very beautiful. 'In their house by the sea they exist with all the bright useless energy of a circus.'[3] 'I swallow the preceding year. Now it has gone. I take a sip of blood, a bite of jellied bone.'[4] 'Moonlight leans against sea, a membrane of metal and bone.'[5] However, sometimes there is the same bathos as in the previous novel. On the same page as the wonderful phrase 'the day is a wildness of swans and shadows' we have 'her hand, the hand of a britannia strokes her buttocks.'[6]

As we have seen *Wailing Monkey* has short, titled sections rather than chapters, which may be read independently, as one would read a collection of poems. As if to encourage this way of looking at it, the text is flushed left as if it were poetry, not justified as a normal novel would be (and her others are). The narrative does move forward but barely and slowly and so each section is to some

---

[1] John Mellors, in *London Magazine,* June/July, 1974

[2] Robert Nye, *Books and Bookmen,* November, 1974.

[3] p. 10

[4] p. 16, in the section titled SHEWBREAD DREAM

[5] p. 52

[6] p. 25

extent self-contained. The paradigmatic is raised to or above the level of the syntagmatic. The titles of the sections (like the title of the book) bear no obvious relation to what is contained in them and some sections appear like interludes, prose poems unrelated to the narrative. Here is the whole of one of the sections:

> THE GODDESS SEKMET
> Deities catch sphinx moths and eat ghosts. A javanese puppet takes refuge behind a mirror. Someone hidden in her own darkness signals to the army. A worshipping world hunts for ivory shells and weeps over its last child. A watcher in the hall is declaring names silently. The controller of the houses of the Red Crown remembers a running girl with a long cloak. The time between January and March is an avoided zone. The day the snow melts, Elinda is sitting in a fireless room, a woman of rank, on her lap a closed book inscribed Elegiae. After sleeping, we swam, she thinks.[1]

Elinda[2] is the centre of the book; the narrative switches between third-person and her first person thoughts. She is married to Luke, whom she does not love and who does not love her. 'Elinda and Luke are both substitutes. Both are seeking supine consolation upon a randomly chosen breast.'[3] Elinda wants to leave so that she can return to her former lover Matthew, which she does at the end of the book. Most of the novel is scenes from Elinda and Luke's aimless and unsatisfying life by the sea in the 'strangeness of a dying world'.[4] Like Rachel in *All the Usual hours of Sleeping*, Elinda has no unambiguous and well-defined sense of her identity. 'There is the Zouave[5] woman she pretends to be, there is the Salome creature she longs to become, and lastly, the aimless girl she is. She lives her life in instalments.'[6] And the format of the book reflects this. Also like Rachel, she has no faith in religion or anything else. 'She touches the little gold crucifix strung around her neck but is not apprenticed to any master.'[7] However, unlike Rachel, she wants her freedom, even if it comes with loneliness. 'I am not free, she declares. Now the silence is infected. He breaks into it by laughing

---

[1] p. 72
[2] The name, Like Herma, sounds like a character in Greek mythology and is in fact a Greek name as well as the character in an Estonian folk tale.
[3] p. 8
[4] p. 8
[5] The Zouave were Algerian soldiers in the French army, exotically dressed and renowned for their bravery.
[6] p. 8; a possible reference to Prufrock's 'I have measured out my life with coffee spoons'?
[7] p. 8

dispraisingly. Free, he sneers, thinking of knucklebones, who is free, Elinda? No one is free. Free!'[1]

Unlike Herma, Elinda cannot contemplate killing herself to be free from disappointment:

> both the facile chorus and the oratorio fail her. A painless death is what I want, thinks Elinda on this Caucasian morning. But I cannot end my life with a stilted suicide. No, I must go on presiding over myself like a mechanical muse nourished on acid. I used to think: one day I'll awaken, smoothed out by rhythmical sunlight and say, look, I'm complete now, I can close a door on everything ugly and move freely with an elemental grandeur. But now I know such a day will not arrive.[2]

Elinda is the feminine to Luke's masculine, the yin to his yang, the moon to his sun. 'Both sun and moon are visible in the early sky. The sun is violent. But the moon is pale and legendary, a weakling, the result of genetic experiments.'[3] Luke cannot express himself as well as Elinda – 'he discovers that he must approach the parapet of language but he does not know how'[4] - and is reduced to crude insults, as Tomas had insulted Rachel in *All the Usual Hours of Sleeping*: 'bitch, cow, vixen, tigress.'[5] 'Enraged by the sublimated smile on her face, 'he knocks her unconscious and rapes her. He is hardly aware of the birth of violence, thinking only, I will not be subservient to any newt of a woman.'[6]

Although the couple are distant from each other they do have sex and the issue arises again of 'poetic' writing about sex: 'she tears at her concubine's hair, she utters postponed threats. Her husband catches hold of her. Now the lovers are grasping flesh and their bizarre bodies melt together, the avatarick heartland slowly infiltrated by genitalia.'[7] Sex in fact is the only thing that binds them in any way. 'It is the toxin between our copulations that denies us acceptance of deaths. Crippled yet hand in hand, Luke and I are approaching an unapproachable glebe.'[8]

As Elinda thinks of Matthew, so Luke remembers his first wife Hagar.[9]

---

[1] p. 11
[2] p. 17
[3] p. 9
[4] p. 27
[5] p. 45
[6] p. 56
[7] p. 16
[8] p. 34
[9] Shuttle herself was a second wife: Peter Redgrove was previously married to the sculptor Barbara Sherlock.

> And you still see her, don't you? Even if she were secluded in the menstrual hut, you would crouch in the doorway. wouldn't you? Her psittacine anger condemns his voyages. Yes, he admits to this ichneumon night, yes. I still see her.[1]

Luke had left Hagar because of her infidelity and Elinda says that she 'hoards anger instead of bracelets.' 'Hagar is the sort of woman who'd really eat up your soul and then want more and not ask prettily.'[2]

After she eventually leaves Luke, Elinda does try to kill herself, despite her former denial that she ever will. 'Eaten up by her humiliation, she lies on the floor, one wrist bleeding endurance from a self-inflicted wound.'[3] But the attempt was half-hearted. 'I wanted a cleverly contrived death! But I was not brave enough. I had too great a fear of that unmuscled decent. I could not die. I could not bear to see the true faces in the dark.'[4] Now she is free but alone. 'Having no name, I envy the snail's mantle. My younger sisters write to tell me they envy my freedom. They don't know that I have lost my bigeminal self to find this liberty.'[5] She is not meant to be alone, her true self she now knows is 'bigeminal'.

> Matthew comes back to her but despite her aloneness she rejects him. You are reeking of more pain for me. Matthew. He places his hand upon her orphrey sex. No! My soldered heart hurts me, she cries. You are not allowed my breasts, Matthew. . . I myself am on a journey now. I've often thought of your body, especially your hands and the recapitulations of your sperm. My longing for you turned my life into a ruined temple. It was so hard for me, being alone, but I've survived it, yes, and taught myself how to be healed.'[6]

At the end. Elinda is both alone and with Matthew. 'No one can punish me, she crows, no one. I am the ring leader. I am the lady in the chair. She lifts her arms and unfastens her crucifix. It weighs nothing in her hand.'[7]

---

[1] p. 59
[2] p. 61
[3] p. 76
[4] p. 77
[5] p. 98
[6] pp. 110/111
[7] pp. 127/8

Rainsplitter in the Zodiac Garden, 1978, Shuttle's third full-length novel, has a different tone to the previous two: the prose is bleaker, harder and more direct. Again there are two women, one strong and central, the other weaker and more peripheral. And again the narration moves between third and first person, though this time we also occasionally get the first person narrative of the principal male character, Micah – an Old Testament character compared to the New Testament names Matthew and Luke we have had previously. The story and the prose have a mythic quality and seem to exist in an ahistorical or trans-historical continuum of time and place, but is then sometimes brought into the present by cars and telephones. The sections, each an independent scene, are numbered not named and can again be read as prose poems, especially as the narrative is apparently not linear.

> I am at the edge of time, I am at the centre of the playing place, I am the pupal chamber growing. I watch them. They stand at gateways, they shelter in tithebarns and stables and ruined tin mines. They take passage by water, they wait in the field's stubble corner. Now I've lost sight of them. I go followingly over rockstrewn land, my boundary is that ash tree. Time is arranged like the fingers of a hand, its skeleton is lost at the bottom of a lake, is strong as a bird standing on a rock out to sea, natal as death, a louse on a human head, lives on a borderline between two habitats on the edge of a wood.[1]

The central character is Faustina[2], whose fear of pregnancy and childbirth is the central theme of the novel. As the novel is not temporally linear, in some of the

---

[1] p. 13

[2] The name may relate to the Faust of the Faust Book and its many retellings; it was a common name in the later Roman Empire – Marcus Aurelius' wife and daughter were both called Faustina – and there are two saints named Faustina, the later of whom founded the Divine Mercy mission in Poland. Elizabeth Bishop had a poem 'Faustina, or Rock Roses' in her 1955 collection *A Cold Spring*; here Faustina's 'sinister kind face / presents a cruel black / coincident conundrum.' Emma Tennant later wrote a novel called *Faustine* and

scenes she is pregnant and in others afraid of becoming pregnant. Micah, who has been involved in a war, sometimes confines her to the house and dominates her until she finally finds a way to break free. Faustina has a friend, Anna, with whom she has a close, sometimes sexual relationship; she introduces Anna to her brother Stefan, who eventually marries him. Faustina feels physically and emotionally distant from her origins and her unrealised self.

> I was born in a village in another country. That village was situated midway between Cape Disappointment and Cape Flattery, allegorical names, given to the headlands because of the sea and its wrecks. But I was brought here, to keep on crying like an impersonatrix. The people are strange here. They deny the divinity of Christ. Every church is in a state of dilapidation. Priests are figures of fun.[1]

Faustina is frightened of Micah and distant from him. 'An analysis of the relationship? Is this my task? I must understand. Is he orphic? Or bestial? He is too far away from me now. All his words are made of silence. Crucial silence.'[2] He is a grim presence to her rather than a person to whom she can relate. 'For me he has no names. Poverty of me. In our bed he wrecks me, enters me, knows me: but I know nothing. Night. Forlorn departure of beneficiaries. Gates of my blood are locked.'[3] Faustina is not just afraid of pregnancy, she feels fated not to give birth:

> the weatherworn eye of the storm sees me. It watches me murder my father. It knows I am neither ghost nor dove. It says holy women do not breed. It reminds me that I am alone and nameless in a strange land waiting for a great storm.[4]

As a 'holy woman' (in the sense, perhaps, that all women's bodies are holy) she 'cannot tell him that she knows the bone behind the uterus is called the holy bone, the os crucis. Curse of myrrh. My wooden wedding dress contains me, like water. I see the priapic hand pointing the way to an everlasting flight of stairs, spiral upon spiral'.[5] She cannot even tell her mother that

---

Shuttle elsewhere uses what may be a feminine version of a male name in the poetry collection *Jesusa*.

[1] pp. 48/49

[2] p. 8

[3] p. 9

[4] p. 14

[5] p. 34

> the effigy of a womb terrifies me and that my bones terrify me and that I dread the time of telling the amberina secret, the nights he visits me, the month when the blood will not come, the day when my body will kill me by a glance of its eye. I cannot get free, the handwritten clocks never freeze. Lost in the fog forest, I add the mystic numbers together. There are flaws in the wind. I see winding-sheets of candles.[1]

In some of the sections it seems she already is pregnant. 'The clues returned, carriers of thorn, and I knew I was pregnant because now the taste of sea was in my mouth. The unborn howls and I bend my body to avoid the evil of the coming day'[2]. Anna tries to show her that the pregnancy gives her power over Micah. 'You hold his child a prisoner. Think of it, Faustina: in his house of secondhand furniture, you, for the first time, possess your own wealth.'[3] But Faustina thinks of getting rid of the unborn child. 'The removal of the foetus is a simple matter. I reach into my womb with a chisel. I find the blood and bribe the ghost to rise up out of the grave.'[4] But she does not go through with it.

> No, I did not try to kill the unborn child, it was the bad air I breathed when I was near the marshes, it made me sick, I did not reach into my body with a cat's cry, I did not. . . The child sleeps, a thousand years old. I watch him, my unwanted son.[5]

'I remember the birth of my son. Woman of wineskin, I drag moons down. I don't know anyone who can save me from the long driftless days of my repentance.'[6]

Faustina is rightly afraid of the violent Micah, who hits her and accuses her of witchcraft as he forces himself on her. 'His penis strained upwards to terrorism. He promises himself that tonight he will couple with her again, even if he must behave like a thief.'[7] Later he does appear to rape her, but she is too frightened to resist. 'He devours my kimono heart. He grunts. My half-learning pleases him Did I cry out? No, I am afraid of giving any trouble. What else did I feel? No, I have lost my memory.'[8] She fears sex with him also because of the possibility of pregnancy, which he would welcome. 'He criticises my cold womb. He wants to plant death in my body.'[9] However, sometimes she seems to welcome

---

[1] p. 47
[2] p. 91
[3] p. 119
[4] p. 145
[5] p. 167. Elision in original
[6] p. 178
[7] p. 26
[8] p. 28
[9] p. 131

sex with him, especially at her brother's funeral. 'When I was naked my voice disappeared. He turned me round and touched my buttocks. He moved his hand between my legs. Then I didn't want to wait.'[1]

As in the previous novels, the women are represented by moon symbolism. Faustina tells Micah that men have landed on the moon, walked upon it.[2]. 'What am I? Mindmooncandle. I am watertight inside a dozen wombs.'[3] There is related symbolism of white/moon versus darkness/blood[4]: 'you will recite to him your prayer of whiteness, the death colour: describing moon, snow, white skin of the youngest canephore[5], white words of an old song, unlit candles, chalk hearts.'[6] In line with this ancient moon symbolism relating to the power of the feminine, Faustina sometimes appears like a pagan priestess or shaman.

> Anna brings her an offering of salt water in a heavy quartz dish. She places it in Faustina's hands. With the utterance of a word that sounds like the caw of a bird, Faustina pours the water upon the earth. She wears a robe of bison hide painted with figures of the spider and images of the whirlwind. She takes Anna's hand and leads her into the cave of children's games. Soon: the interception of a churching. Soon: the inswathement of a moon.[7]

Faustina and Anna 'try to read the ancient deity language' but Micah will not let her go to church. Why won't he let me have even a small piece of the Host? Does he think the feet of my christ will crush him like an ant?'[8] Her relationship with Anna is far closer than that with Micah. They meet 'in a garden at night beyond the voices of rock.' 'They have swerved from the path of the night and formed their own allegiance. Their hesitation belongs to this hour, within the zone of the cave. Faustina spreads the rug on the ground.' Then 'Faustina demonstrates the use of her tongue and attacks Anna's cunt. Anna yields but her skull is full of razors.'[9]

Faustina tries to end Anna's relationship with her brother Stefan: 'you're a weakling, Anna. Stefan will tear your skin off with his hardships.' But Anna has

---

[1] p. 90

[2] This was in 1969

[3] p. 37. The neologism mindmooncandle, like moonmoodlight in the previous novel is to me reminiscent of Paul Celan.

[4] *The Wise Wound*, about menstruation, was published the year after this novel.

[5] Canephores are the women with baskets on their heads in Greek festivals and the stone caryatids supporting beams in Greek temples.

[6] p. 35

[7] p. 41. As in the previous novels, the identification of woman with Greek priestesses and prophets brings to mind the novels and post-Imagist poetry of H.D.

[8] p. 45

[9] p. 42/43

chosen Stefan over her, male over female, sun over moon. She 'kisses Faustina, she says, the days and nights of our bodies have finished, I must find another year or lose my memory, please Faustina, understand, I want to know the language and customs of a man.'[1] Anna eventually deserts Faustina: 'I cannot reach my translatress. . . I am finished with Anna because her ash-white mouth has become servile towards Micah.'[2]

Faustina is raped by a 'holocaustal young man', who has seen her with Anna, watched at a distance by Micah. 'Whoredom, the man says. In your dark empty houses. In the whitethroat forests I have seen you and the other woman.'[3] After Faustina leaves Micah, her brothers try to return her.

> She kneels, she lies on the ground, this is her termination, dark pours in through the holes in her head, her hair is going to be sold, her mouth swaddles the night with great mechanical cries, she shrieks, matrix-hurt. Her brothers listen. But they belong to the future. Star-roots of the sky bur. Moon zigzgas. Her storm brothers drag her to her feet, the elder of the two holds the candle. She shouts: I am nippleless. And I am afraid of him. Stefan says, whether you have blood smeared on your forehead or agonies in your uterus when we hand you over to him is of no importance. We know about pain and it is of no importance. We cannot be free of ice. We cannot save you from a cold climate.[4]

As men, they cannot share her 'uninhabited world'. 'So what remained of the features of her soul? Burns, blindness and death.'[5] And it later seems that Faustina is not her real name at all, just what Micah calls her. 'He calls me Faustina, a name to kill weeds growing among grain, a name legendary as war-butchery on the sea coast.'[6] 'Why do you call me by that name? You know my old name. Call me by my old name.'[7] She does not say what her old name was but she identifies with Jesusa, the female christ and the title of her 1971 poetry collection in the penultimate section of the novel.

> I walk along the road, thinking, if Lammas overtakes me, if the grail castle imprisons me, I am lost to fear. If a man speaks to me, if I guess the moon's true age, if I wear a dress of six different colours, if I gnaw at

---

[1] p. 111
[2] p. 50
[3] p. 67
[4] p. 56/57
[5] p. 59
[6] p. 150
[7] p. 166

> my veil, I am lost. If I tell you what I saw hovering over the seaway, then I am lost and the taboo of Jesusa will find me.[1]

In the very last section, she remembers seeing a girl walking alone along a country lane with a haversack and a baby in a sling and, finally free, escapes to become that image.

Shuttle's fourth and last full-length novel *The Mirror of the Giant*, 1980 is subtitled 'A Ghost Story'; this has two meanings: Theron is haunted by the ghost of his dead wife Vellet – literally, as Vellet is a character in the novel – and his current wife Beth is metaphorically haunted by her former female lover Ash, whom she has not seen for five years. Another major character in the book is the giant at Cerne Abbas, whom Vellet consults and on whose gigantic carved penis she has formerly copulated with two men while still alive. The cover of the book tells us that 'the man with the knobbled club [who is illustrated on the back cover] represents Nodions, the hunting and fertility god of the Durotriges, the Celtic tribe which inhabited Dorset.' Again we have the merging of Beth's and Ash's first person and third person narratives but this novel is far more directly narrated than Shuttle's previous works; despite the fact that one of the characters is dead is a more conventional novel altogether. It is less of a poetic novel than its predecessors and more a fantasy in the mould of Angela Carter and Emma Tennant. In his review Andrew Motion says that is is a novel of two very different halves:

> her opening chapters abound in sentences of excessively wrought luxuriance. . . while her closing ones adopt a tone of more tightly disciplined naturalism.
>
> This is partly explained by her decision to cultivate purple patches when emphasizing elements of mystery and surprise – since these necessarily diminish as the action unfolds, what has been called her "Shuttle-music" inevitably becomes simpler. But it is also due to the fact

[1] p. 180/181

> that she seems to begin writing a different kind of novel half-way through. Where she starts by concentrating her imagination on images and metaphors, she concludes by fixing her mind on the ideas they sought to enact or illustrate. The end product, as a result is seriously flawed.[1]

Note Motion's rather masculine criterion of 'tightly disciplined naturalism'.

Vellet – the 'beast-girl' - has drowned while her husband watched and did nothing; unable to find peace she has come back to haunt him.

> He cursed her, the ghost of veins. He remembered how she drowned, like a wooden doll denying he possessed any part of her. Her husband, the darkest possible bugger, stands in the shadows and does not dive in the river to rescue her. He hears her cries but does not want to rescue her.[2]

Most of the time it is only Theron who can see Vellet. 'So is there a dead woman? thinks Beth. Or does Theron wallow in some dream? Some nightmare he wants to put on me? Breathe your uncanniness on me, Vellet.'[3] Vellet comes to Theron mainly at night and he often has sex with her.

> She was silent, she was reconstructing signals for his flesh. But she felt no pleasure. There was no sensation in her cunt, ever. Dead. To him it felt warm, because she intended him to feel a warmth, but to her it was like clay, her dead sex, cold and unamplified.[4]

But when Beth witnesses this she can only see Theron masturbating. 'Vellet is invisible at the moment, but Beth smells the foul gas of her presence in the room. Theron gives a final moan and the spurt flies up in the air, a white arc, and he sags down in the chair, eyes closed, satisfied.'[5] Beth and Theron never have sex and her fantasies are mainly memories of Ash. 'Blood's given language could map our hearts, if we met now. The masks of twilight crowd around me, whispering Ash, Ash.'[6] As Faustina had Anna in the previous novel, so does Beth have Ash. Vellet asks the giant to help her – she wants to be released from her life-in-death.

---

[1] 'Overblown Apparatus'. *Times Literary Supplement,* February 1, 1980

[2] p. 50

[3] p. 57

[4] p. 49

[5] p. 71

[6] p. 37

'I suppose I am too wicked to be helped?'

'No. But it is not my business to help.'

'What is your business, Giant?'

'To remember the thinness of my own self. To understand my blindness'. This is the voice of the earth itself now and turning to dust. Vellet does not understand and dances across a red planet and back again to the edge of the giant.[1]

Beth herself also talks to the giant about how to free Theron from Vellet's presence. He tell her Theron will be free when Vellet is free but that he himself is 'a prisoner of this hill. . . All darkness is here for me to consume with my white vigilance. I am the guardian of ghosts'.[2] The giant gives Beth a vision of Vellet's orgy with two men to show her wickedness when she was alive. Later on in the novel we find out that when she was fifteen Vellet had been the mistress and model of a local artist. The giant tells Beth she must 'grip the thorny veils that bind Vellet, grip them and tear them off' in order to free her. 'Remember, Beth, in the giant's mirror, all broken creatures can be healed.'[3]

As Beth talks about her troubles with a friend from the village, she begins to confront and conquer Vellet's ghost. 'We must not be trapped, we must read the runes of these apparent ghosts. What are they trying to tell us?'[4] 'Why should I listen to the ghost, try to help the ghost?'[5] The giant shows Beth, in his mirror, the way to release. She sees his vision of six women: Eve, Sarah, Tamar, Rhahab, Ruth and Bathsheba.

Whose blood stains the altar cloth?
Bathsheba says, not mine.
Tamar says, not mine, not mine.
Ruth laughs and says not mine, not mine, mimicking exasperation.

---

[1] p. 47
[2] p. 59
[3] p. 117
[4] p. 119
[5] p. 120

> Sarah shouts, not mine
>
> Eve is silent and her five companions watch her. It is mine, she says, the blood is mine.
>
> The six women swing round rapidly and stare out of the mirror towards Beth. They all wear the same face now. Beth recognises the face. It is the face of Ash, repeated six times, weaving back into the mirror'[1]

Ash returns to Beth; as they make love Ash says 'I am piecing you together'[2] and Beth feels she herself has 'taken on the shape of a giantess.'[3] Beth thinks: 'We are adding the finishing touches to ourselves. . . We are almost complete.'[4]

> In that mirror long ago I saw the fountain of my life. As I stared I wanted to sleep but I was not allowed to sleep. The fountain swayed and began to flow over me, silver water and red blood, moonlight and seeds, and in the water I saw the face of Ash. . . I saw her, the fountain of my life. My companion.[5]

Now that Beth has found happiness, the ghost of Vellet is freed.

> Ah Beth, I am dissolving in this witnessed reflected love. . . The pangs of my ghosthood are erased . . . and I open out into a hemisphere of water and light, blood and warmth and oh, how easy it is, how easy, how simple at last, the freedom, I am lifted from my prison'

And Vellet 'fades, wafting into this misty exhalation'. [6]

---

[1] p. 142
[2] p. 145
[3] p. 144
[4] p. 149
[5] p. 151
[6] p. 159

Penelope Shuttle's symbiotic and synergistic relationship with Peter Redgrove extended from the verse collection *The Hermaphrodite Album*, 1973 to collaborations on two novels: *The Terrors of Dr Treviles*, 1974 and *The Glass Cottage: A Nautical Romance,* 1976. The former is a mostly conventional novel, though concerned with witchcraft and the supernatural power of the imagination but *The Glass Cottage* is far more experimental. It is on one level a murder mystery but is also a philosophical and psychological examination, often containing surrealistic and hallucinatory imagery, mostly of black and white against the red of blood. Although Shuttle's credit is 'with Penelope Shuttle' - '*with*' not '*and*' – her influence seems clear both in the poetic nature of the novel-writing and in the recurrence of the emphases on blood and the cycles of the moon and tides.

> I wonder whether women travelling by ship
> synchronize their cycles so that all menstruate
> together? Then it would be a great moonship,
> with towering sides. Nightly, it is a ship of fools.[1]

The narration switches forms, and the location, which is mainly on board a ship, also moves around but the central character is again an impressionistic portrait of Redgrove. 'I had been invited to lecture in this remote university almost on the Canadian border;'[2] Redgrove himself had been a guest speaker at Buffalo University in upstate New York, and the narrator, like Redgrove, has passed through the 'coloured grades' of judo. Like Silas-Jonas in Redgrove's *In the Country of the Skin*[3], the narrator here is split into a mirror of himself.

> One by one the portholes went out,
> and the library reappeared in the lake. He was
> at the library table, and the books in that
> reflected library were as much good to him as

[1] p. 1
[2] p. 16
[3] See the Peter Redgrove section in the Fellow Travellers chapter of this book.

> their originals, for when he glanced at one before him on the table, preparatory to closing it up and putting it away, he found that he could not understand the type. He took his pocket-mirror out of his briefcase: the book was printed in mirror-writing. So was that book, and this: he had read about this condition: the nerve-pathways to the hemispheres of the brain reversed spontaneously, or as a result of prolonged emotional stress, and the person afflicted became his mirror-self, his own doppelganger.[1]

The dual aspect of personality is also compared to the planet Venus: 'Hesperus, star of the evening . . . Lucifer, star of the morning. Both are the same planet, Venus; depending on whether you look at it with the light of the rising sun, so its nature changes.'[2] For Redgrove/narrator, as both a therapist and the subject of 'therapy' himself, successful therapy can 'unlock hidden memories, not just individual memories going back to before birth, waiting for . . . the spiral passage down into the womb'; they can be

> earlier still, but these were more difficult. memories of animal life, or fantasies of them, of running like a horse, or gliding like a snake among the feet of wise persons who conversed beyond the grave. And once upon a time in this timeless land where past and future seemed mixed and all knowledge and experience seemed possible, in this place the memories of which, the psychologist began to see, were what living men called the Unconscious, a dead person spoke through a patient's mouth. The patient spoke as a young woman who was to be a poet in the future, and die by her own hand. She spoke of the future as though it were the past. She wandered unhappily through the only objects and events she could remember, predicting her miserable life as a prodigy, and her poetry.

The psychologist writes down the poet's verses and many years later reads of a woman poet who has killed herself; her verses are the same as he had written

[1] p. 71
[2] p. 202

down from 'his patient wandering through the unborn state, the Bardo, before that unhappy young woman had been born.'[1]

The Glass Cottage provoked quite a row in the letters columns of the *Times Literary Supplement*, where the academic Gay Clifford accused it of being 'a modern piece of anti-feminism.' In between the two letters opposite Shuttle and Redgrove (their letter is signed in that order) had indignantly replied:

> Ms. Clifford should not say that in *The Glass Cottage* we are not controlling the associations of sex with violence, rape, etc, when the book *says* that the reason for these abuses is a fear and neglect of the woman's experience. . . This is what the book is *about* and it is argued in an extended passage at the heart of the novel. It is quite obvious to most people who have read this passage that we are *against* the old "equation between murder and making love." One aspect of this equation is an old cultural saw expressive of the taboo we refer to: if you make love at the period you are said to be doing so in the blood of your unconceived child. This is one of the ancient prohibitions that has severely restricted feminine experience – and does so to this day in many cultural groups.[2]

The debate over who is the more feminist is well beyond the scope of this book, not to mention my own competence but it does seem extreme to call the authors of *The Wise Wound* and *The Hermaphrodite Album* anti-feminist; their collaborations were certainly, and triumphantly anti-male domination of literary discourse; something worth celebrating however one may evaluate their achievements.

---

[1] p. 169
[2] November 12 1976

Sir,—We are grateful to your reviewer and yourself for the interested notice of our novel *The Glass Cottage* (September 24), but terribly upset that she calls it a "modern piece of anti-feminism". This is all the more so since we are feminists and have just written the first feminist book on menstruation: *The Wise Wound*, to be published by Gollancz next year.

We are afraid that Gay Clifford may have been brainwashed by underhand and very subtle anti-feminists, whose masterpiece has been to call "the destiny of menstruation" a "curse". The truth is that a feminine sexual peak, as Kinsey, Sherfey and many others have shown long since, accompanies the period—so in what sense is it a "curse", the pro or anti-feminist's?

Our *The Glass Cottage* is about a murder, which is like The Jesus-Murder in that many people feel guilty about it without being able to decide whether they have actually been involved in it or not. The murder we write about in our novel is The Goddess-Murder, of which any woman deprived by convention or taboo of her natural abilities of menstruation is a victim. We suppose that a religion could be based on a goddess who sheds her blood in sacrifice from which life arises, and our book partly satirizes attitudes which are dismissive of this possibility. So we are decidedly non-antifeminist. As Sylvia Plath says: "The blood jet is poetry,/ There is no stopping it."

PENELOPE SHUTTLE.
PETER REDGROVE.

Cornwall.

Sir,—Impatience with the relentlessly *ad feminam* style of argument used by Penelope Shuttle and Peter Redgrove (Letters, November 12) inspires some baffled questions:

(1) What is a "privileged position" for sexual experience?

(2) Do lecturers, at Warwick or anywhere, occupy such a position?

(3) Do lecturers not as a matter of course "talk to their working-class students" or for that matter to people quite unconnected with universities?

However the debate (if it is that) began not with the social mores of dons, or the sociology of menstruation, but with the politics of fiction; and given that the authors insist that social influences powerfully control people's response to their own bodies, it is odd that they will not allow that such influences also operate on the reading of novels. Far from paying the compliment of withdrawing from my former position, I repeat it by quoting the "printed review":

> some criticisms are to the point: to demur at the fact that the murdered woman has had more reality and power dead than alive, or at the equations sex/murder cunt/wound, is not to resist myth but a modern piece of anti-feminism pretending to be a myth.

Equations made metaphorically in a book are scarcely the same thing as the book in its entirety. The authors, however, are determined to merge parts with whole. They assert that "the book *says*" something, and then quote in support the words of one character, speaking as a spirit, in one scene not without comic irony.

It seems unlucky that writers who are so alert to myth should offer themselves as the ordained interpreters of myth: myth is, almost by definition, so culturally flexible that it resists exclusive meanings by encompassing antitypes. It would also be a pity if readers who resist the notion that writers are absolute authorities on feminine experience should be deflected from reading what is (repeat) an imaginative, funny, and formally very inventive novel.

GAY CLIFFORD.

Department of English and Comparative Literary Studies, University of Warwick.

rosalind belben

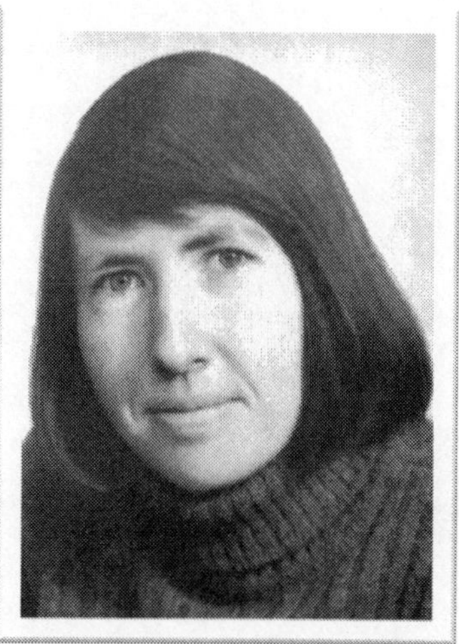

Rosalind Belben was born in Dorset, England, in 1941. Her first novel, *Bogies,* 1972 was published by New Authors Ltd, a non-profit 'experiment' of the publisher Hutchinson, which was started in 1957 as 'an attempt to reconcile the difficulties and frustrations of the new writer with something to say, with the harsh economic climate as it is today.'[1] Although New Authors Ltd did not generally publish any experimental work, it might be interesting to speculate as to whether such an unconventional first 'novel' (*Bogies* is in fact composed of two, apparently unconnected stories) would have found a conventional publisher. The intention of New Authors Ltd was that writers' second books would be published by the main Hutchinson imprint, as was Belben's second novel, *Reuben Little Hero*, 1973, though it was released as a 'Midway Original' – a format half way between paperback and hardback – presumably to reduce cost. After this relatively conventional novel, Belben published *The Limit*, 1974, a more experimental novel altogether, and then, after a rather longer gap, *Dreaming of Dead People* was published by Harvester in 1979[2].

Belben's novels, like much of Eva Figes' work, and to some extent Anna Kavan and Ann Quin's, concern women's sense of identity, or the lack of it (two of the narrators, in the *Somewhere Else* section of *Bogies* and *Dreaming of Dead People*, do not know or do not give their names); their solitude even within a relationship; their sexual desires and the terrors of ageing. Apart from *Reuben, Little Hero* they are all told from a woman's perspective – though not explicitly a feminist one – and apart from Ilario in *The Limit*, there are no sympathetic male characters in her work.

---

[1] *Bogies*, p. 205

[2] Belben's subsequent and relatively conventional novels include: *Is Beauty Good* (1989); *Choosing Spectacles* (1995); *Hound Music* (2001); *Our Horses in Egypt* (2007), which won the James Tait Black Memorial Prize. *Dreaming of Dead People* was reissued in 1989 by Serpent's Tail in their Masks series.

Bogies, subtitled *Two Stories,* consists of two separate sections: a novella-length piece called *Somewhere Else*, and a shorter piece called *Flight*. In *Somewhere Else*, an English female narrator appears to be in a prison in what later turns out to be an African country, being interrogated by an American man. She does not appear to know why she is there, how she got there or where she is.

> I am
> I am in prison
> No, I am not in prison
> I am not in A prison
> I am imprisoned.
>
> These weeks of interrogation make me think in staccato sentences. Repetitive. That is all you can do. Repeat. Say after me. Repeat. What I know.
>
> 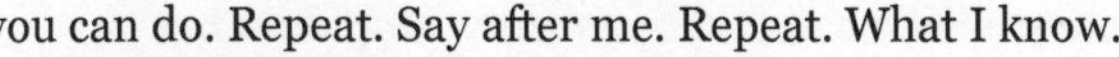
>
> Can I make up what I don't know?
> Should I?
> What I don't know is what they want to know. They would find me out.
> I can't remember what I do know.[1]

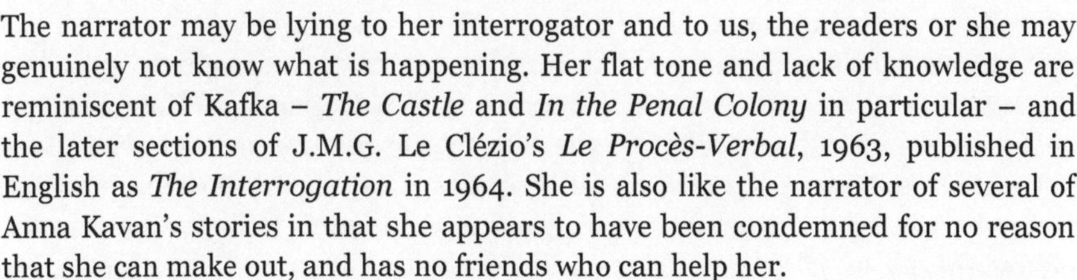

The narrator may be lying to her interrogator and to us, the readers or she may genuinely not know what is happening. Her flat tone and lack of knowledge are reminiscent of Kafka – *The Castle* and *In the Penal Colony* in particular – and the later sections of J.M.G. Le Clézio's *Le Procès-Verbal*, 1963, published in English as *The Interrogation* in 1964. She is also like the narrator of several of Anna Kavan's stories in that she appears to have been condemned for no reason that she can make out, and has no friends who can help her.

She (the narrator has no name) lives in a hot, filthy cell with no fellow-prisoners and no view to the outside world; all she sees is her cell and her only human contacts are her guards, the mysterious Al and the interrogator McKinley. She, and therefore we, does not know who McKinley works for or what information he is trying to elicit from her.

[1] p. 1

> If I look out of the window there is
> to the front a wall;
> to the left a wall;
> to the right, a wall.
> The wall is made of concrete
> I should think
> It is very hot[1].

While she is there, they are trying to make her learn a language. Although the interrogator speaks English, he is trying to make her speak a language she cannot identify. Like the narrator in Christine Brooke-Rose's *Between*, she inhabits a state between places, languages and memories. And like her the narrator of *Somewhere Else* uses flat, factual descriptions of her surroundings to give some kind of objective reality to a life without roots.

> You might imagine I would sleep a great deal.
> I don't.
> The bed is not the problem.
> It is my brain. It goes on and on like perpetual motion with the distant intensity of a bad dream. I cannot stop thinking.
> I am occupied chiefly with
> where I am.
> I dislike the feeling of being in limbo.

She insists to her interrogator that she is English (he keeps insisting she is Jewish) and she does seem to have some memories of a middle-class English childhood. Sometimes she writes to 'Dear Mummy', though not 'Dear Daddy', who, she says works in the City of London, as 'Daddy will be busy'.[2]

In the constant, repetitive interrogations, McKinley constantly asks her about her meetings with a man called Pierre in New Orleans and Hamburg and about her time in Moscow. She does have memories of these events but she does not seem to remember the reasons for them or see any significance in them. She remembers being abducted in Copenhagen but then seems to have no memories of how she got to her present location. It may be that Pierre has been spying for the Chinese but at all times we only know what the narrator both remembers and admits to, so we cannot be sure.

After a while, the narrator realises there is another prisoner in a cell above her, who wails constantly.

---

[1] p. 3
[2] p. 28

> I wonder if it is a man or a woman. Why is it wailing? Or do I wail too? I shouldn't think I do.
> It doesn't sound tortured or
> anything.
> It sounds sad.
> Sad
> like
> me.
> I wish it didn't get dark for so long at night. Darkness has no sound here.
> Even the wailing stops like a light being switched off.
> Is there only the wailer here with me?
> Prisoners.
> It's no use wailing, is it? I don't wail.
> I am BRAVE.[1]

In part two of *Somewhere Else*, the narrator appears to have been moved to a completely different prison. Her last memory is of McKinley with a syringe and instead of being in unbearable heat she is now somewhere so cold that her 'whole body aches with it.'

> I know I have been moved. I was not here before because I cannot say I have ever seen anything like this so it is quite impossible that the other place was in
> a dream
> or I should have some recollection of where I was before I started dreaming.
> You see.
> No one but me sees it.[2]

She now has a new male contact in this all-female prison, who turns out to be the British Consul. He appears to be convinced she has been in this place all along and has not been moved. Now she in a large, noisy prison with many other prisoners in cells arranged like 'egg boxes'. Here her perception of reality has changed; perhaps she really has been here all along?

> Unlike, shall I call it X, where I was
> before,
> there is no unreality, no feeling of
> limbo.

---

[1] p. 49
[2] p. 64

> Everything here is solidly grounded on fact.
> Facts.
> 'We have all the facts,' he says.
> In a way, being able to compare it with X, my mind is clearer, my mind has something to work on which is
> tangible, if you like.[1]

It seems that now she has been sentenced for something; she doesn't know for what or when, but the Consul tells her there is no possibility of an exchange of prisoners, which leads us to believe she has been sentenced as a spy. The Consul has brought her books from her mother and even more importantly, he calls her by a name, though not her own:

> 'I'm so sorry Krissie,' he says. 'We really are doing our best to get you out of this beastly hole. I'm so, so sorry.'
> Now who in the world is Krissie?
> Certainly not me.
> All the old suspicion rises in me like a bucket being filled. I stare at him.
> The women have closed in on me, which I have not noticed, being absorbed in the moment of contact.
> It is over. I am alone again.[2]

She reads Krissie's letters from her mother, even though they are not written to her and shortly afterwards the 'real' Krissie is put into her cell. Krissie ignores her, as do the guards. 'They do not leave her alone. I am a forgotten onlooker.'[3] She soon comes to resent Krissie's presence in 'her' cell and wishes she were alone again. Eventually Krissie does speak to her, though she does not tell Krissie about the Consul or discuss anything much. 'we discuss little but talk a lot.'[4] They play 'I spy' and free-association word games; they use words but the words have no depth or meaning. Although the narrator has abandoned hope, and the need for human contact, Krissie has not.

> I am defeated
> beaten
> subdued entirely.
> Without hope.
> Krissie hopes. She

---

[1] p. 65
[2] p. 73/74
[3] p. 80
[4] p. 82

prays.
And she is keen
on me.
She tries to grip me around the waist and lay her head in my lap. She tries to
feel me, to
kiss me, to
make love.[1]

After trying to poison herself at the end of part two, in part three she seems to be back in the original prison in the hot country, which turns out to be in Liberia. She has another new interrogator, a man of Armenian extraction, called Karakashian. But now, even though she seems to be in the same cell, it is decorated with chairs, cushions and pictures. Karakashian is nice to her, unlike McKinley, whose notes he has and whom he calls an American fool.

'Why did I go to the other
place?' I ask. I must ask.
You may forget about that now. You have been handed back. They won't have you again.'[2]

But, even though Karakashian is nice to her and lets her have toiletries, magazines and other unimaginable luxuries, he still continues to interrogate her along the same lines as before and still does not explain why she is there or what they want of her. He also appears to come close to questioning her reality, her existence.

'You know,' says Karakashian, 'you have no depth. You are a cardboard person. You have no memory, no joy, no
passion.'
'Perhaps I did have those things before I was brought here.'
'I don't think so.' He tilts his head to look at me in speculation.
'No ambition.'
'Must one have ambition?'
'Certainly. It is a driving force. But you, you believe in nothing. no God, no work, not even in fate. You are simply blown in the wind. Very sad.'[3]

---

[1] p. 83
[2] p. 89
[3] p. 100

Other prisoners appear in the formerly empty prison and she is allowed to talk to them, even to go out of her cell; Karakashian tells her: 'This is not a punishment'[1] and even talks of her release. She opens up and starts to talk about her time with Pierre, though we still never really know what, if any, her part in the spying operation, if that is what it was, had been. Karakashian eventually not only lets her out but takes her to stay at his house on the beach, even though she is not allowed out onto the beach itself. She is amazed to see the sea.

> Reality is something you walk on. Inside, even the ground was a strange territory of the mind. Now, I am
> muddled.[2]

Even though he calls her 'my love' she has her own room and he does not make any advances, but continues to interrogate her about Pierre, her time in Moscow and about her 'involvement' in whatever the operation was. She continues to either not remember or to not say. Months pass like this until one day, without explanation, he takes her to the airport, telling her she is 'free' and not to come back.

In the short part four, she is in London and sees Pierre in Trafalgar Square. Al from the African prison is following him and Karakashian is behind her. He implies that she has led them to Pierre but she appears not to realise. The story ends:

> He looks at me sympathetically.
> My breath is drawn in thumps and jerks as if I have been running in panic from something which frightens me and yet I am so numb I cannot speak,
> But I am not crying.
> Oh no.
> It is quite a dry
> anguish.
> 'Now', says Karakashian 'shall we go to Paris, and live there together?'
> Happily
> ever
> after.[3]

Moving back to London, has she reconnected with her family and former life? Has she betrayed Pierre accidentally, deliberately or subconsciously? And is the

---

[1] p. 104
[2] p. 112
[3] p. 133

betrayal the key to her happiness? Had she remembered all along and chosen not to betray him, or did she really not remember? If she had been loyal to Pierre, how can she now live happily ever after with his nemesis Karakashian? None of these questions is answered.

The second part of *Bogies* is the story *Flight*. It is apparently unrelated to the previous story and is completely different in form. Here, instead of a possibly unreliable 1st person narrator, we have a conventional, omniscient 3rd person narrator who can convey the characters' thoughts. We also have names – the central character is 'that strange, solitary, the spinster Miss Thomassina Dark' - and an exact location: Bradford on Avon.[1] However, all is not as it seems, as Thomassina appears to have delusions, or hallucinations. Walking her dog Ham, she sees a dead body, which is described in almost forensic detail from Thomassina's point of view.

> It was a woman, a young girl, or a student. It was white like a dead fish, it was long hair like Ophelia, it was dressed, it was not dressed. There were little things caught in the hair. It was a red jersey. It was trousers. But it looked naked. The river had the red jersey, the water-coloured trousers. The body was only half there. The other half was under. It was washed in. To a little bay worn out between two tree roots. Some of the body lay on the soft mud which sloped down deep into the water, under the river.[2]

Despite the vividness of this description it appears later that there may in fact have been no body. She reports it to the police but they seem to have no knowledge of it. And a neighbour brings back the dog lead she had left by the river without mentioning any dead body.

Thomassina lives a very solitary life, has no relationships with her neighbours and no friends. She lives alone and has a regulated life, but is not lonely.

> Preparations for bed are an agreeable ritual. She likes bed. The night-time. The reading before going to sleep. The dreams. Vividly she dreams and remembers, dream after dream, night after night, hardly a nasty one ever, never a keeping awake, a terror, a fright. Bed is not a loneliness, because there is no one about to make her feel lonely.[3]

Until one night she wakes up to find an intruder in her room, who turns out to be Nancy, the daughter of her next door neighbours. Nancy claims to be a regular

---

[1] In Wiltshire, England, the county next to Dorset, where Belben was born.

[2] p. 138

[3] p. 144

burglar, and to have hypnotised Ham; she says she can hypnotise dogs and this is how she carries out her burglaries. Thomassina soon begins talking to and confiding in 19-year old Nancy, who is 'not pretty, but she is effortlessly dramatic. Long blue-black hair dangles down her bony back and round her pallid un-made-up sombre – she never smiles, withdrawn, possessed by abstract thought, seemingly.'[1] Nancy promises not to steal any of Thomassina's effects but she does, returning them only after Thomassina (who confesses to Nancy that her former nickname was Dodo) has a confrontation with Nancy's parents. Other than that, Dodo's life continues as normal, punctuated by an unpleasant visit from her unpleasant sister-in-law and another visit from Nancy until, two days after the 'discovery' of the body, she suddenly decides to leave and simply drives away.

> It was low tide, and when she dared to look, she saw the swirling treachery below, and far away down the estuary, the grey hump of a lonely island in the haze.
>
> She was afraid on the bridge, but she knew she would never return this way again. She had escaped. She was running away. Into the setting sun. For ever.[2]

But she has not escaped, she is only in a nearby town. And, prosaically driving to get meat for Ham she sees the man who had brought back her dog's lead and, while she is looking at him drives into the back of a lorry killing both herself and Ham, who 'is not left to live on without her.'[3]

---

[1] p. 145
[2] p. 201
[3] p. 203

In Rosalind Belben's second published novel, *Reuben Little Hero*, 1973 we have a fundamentally conventional novel about a rather smug couple who have moved to the Dorset countryside to live in harmony with nature and who have a diabetic son, Reuben. The story is of Reuben's and particularly his mother Polly's struggle with his illness, and the strain on the marriage of Polly and Mike caused by the diabetes and by Lionel, Mike's disgusting father, who lives with them. The novel has an omniscient narrator and is firmly grounded in an external reality.

However, sometimes the writing becomes heightened, particularly when describing sex, or especially Reuben's sexual thoughts.

> she lay down on top of him smothering him with her body so that no portion was left sticking out not a finger a toe a hair of his head; she spread like a soft downy quilt something like a squishy rubber dinghy not fully inflated, smelling of honey and treacle and eau de Cologne, floating upon him a powerful spectacle of white flesh and spongy unreality, unreal but he could feel her acutely. Just as he could feel his cock grow in her hands, swelling out of his child's fist, stuck up towards his face like the Giant's at Cerne[1] only bigger, reaching up to his tummy, growing, heavy. . . Even then it wasn't big enough to stuff Nina so he doubled up and crawled inside her big red tunnel, walking in his bare feet over the bloody pulp which sank and heaved, which threw him at each step against the wet roof[2]

Reuben's mother is also 'haunted by her dreams', most of which feed her guilt at Reuben's illness and seem to involve her putting Reuben and her friends' children in danger.

---

[1] The Cerne Abbas Giant is a huge and ancient figure carved into the hillside in Dorset with an enormous, erect penis and also features in Penelope Shuttle's *The Mirror of the Giant*.

[2] p. 28

> It was difficult to stop dreaming, and when she lay awake at night she looked back on what she had done with horror, everything wrong, trying to cure him, or herself, whichever it was.[1]

Polly herself has no sexual fantasies and her lack of interest in sex drives Mike to a passionless sexual encounter with neighbour Millie.

> Lying back there on the pink candlewick counterpane like an idiot, helpless, looking up at his erection and the absurdly high ceiling, Mike so casual and unconcerned and direct.[2]

> he was thrusting this new first-time strangeness like a lump of wood it was foreign, unreal, unbelonging, into her, lying over her so near.[3]

This lack of passion with women is strongly contrasted with his memory of his first sexual encounter at school with Francis, which floods back as he is about to have sex with a man he has just picked up in a bar.

> remembering the flood of stunningly new adventurous gratitude with which his mouth swallowed Francis, who seemed to be in every part of him at once, smothering him . . . touching him, gently leading him on, the soft dry sweet-smelling skin of the penis between his lips, his teeth holding gently not to bite, touching with his tongue, moving past it down down burying his face in Francis licking around his testicles feeling them fall onto his cheek until he reached a clutch of tiny wrinkles hot smell of
>
> and oh the sheer relief of that exquisite tightness, and he thought of Polly long ago who didn't like it, said it made her want to pee; he put spit on his cock and pushed – in deep, crudely tantalised, after all these years of sloshing around in a woman, the beauty[4]

Reuben has his fantasies too, of sex and of violence towards animals, which he also commits in real life. In his dream he has tied up a chicken in the barn.

> He pulled with his eyes shut, pulled blind. And her leg split from the hip in one ghastly gory wrench, innards tumbling out like the intestines of a dead jackdaw he had recently disembowelled from curiosity and for a test of courage with his knife.

---

[1] p. 175

[2] p. 74

[3] p. 75

[4] p. 136

Reuben later does actually plunge a knife into the leg of his pony Plum, one of his few real friends. He has had to learn to combat the abuse, bullying and threats he gets at school because of his illness with violence, the only thing the bullies respect. He surprises even his school friends with the casual way he pulls the legs off flies and spiders.

The country idyll the couple had hoped for turns out to be grotesque and Polly's unhappiness with her life and her guilt for Reuben's illness cause her to try to commit suicide in a desperate, almost comic manner.

> she was on her own entirely at the end of a long spiral, the spiral was made of black iron steps full of squiggly holes but she bloody well wasn't going to walk up again, or perhaps she didn't know what she was doing perhaps she did quite deliberately know she
>
> undid the syringe (two hundred and one injections later) pulled the piston right back, tangled herself in her nightie, had to strip; standing there naked in the bathroom she took a grab of her bottom, merrily thinking how much more there was of her than him (not him, no one, better off without her), smiled at the cold air on her asshole as she took this great slab of fat bottom, the needle like a dagger held aloft and zoomed into her soundlessly up to the hilt totally without pain or feeling.
>
> and then
>
> laughing away to herself grimly silent as she pushed the grey plastic plunger shot 1ml of good clean air into myself and waited to die
>
> you're always on your own really in this world
>
> instead of regretting it she saw it suddenly as a right
>
> to be claimed[1]

[1] p. 186/187

Rosalind Belben's third published novel, *The Limit,* 1974, is dedicated to Giles Gordon, who was an editor at Hutchinson as his 1974 experimental novel *Girl With Red Hair* is dedicated to her.[1] This short novel intersperses different narrative perspective under repeated chapter headings such as *The Passage of a Soul at Death into Another Body* and *The Carrying of a Person to Another Place or Sphere of Existence.* Even within chapters the narrative shifts from third person to the voice of the Italian Ilario and his 20-years older wife Anna. Anna has her own chapters titled *The State of Time of Being a Child*, where she recalls her childhood, but for most of the novel she is old, ill and dying.

> The woman stirs: I sit at my bedside watching. Because I cannot, there is no way in, to enter, her, she is cut off, not with me, I not with her, I imagine it is myself. It is the nearest, that I can in memory and mind do for her. That woman is my wife.
>
> He sat: perfectly still, as if in a trance. But see, his eyelids move up and down, he is blinking, a tiny flexing in his hand. His hands are streaked like a seal's back, he is holding the dry hair. They are together in the lap.[2]

As in *Bogies*, the female narrator seems to have lost not only her memory but her whole sense of who she is. 'She is pondering: who am I? what is my name? this man will speak my name for me, he knows who I am, he knows.'[3]

Despite the age difference and Anna's decaying body, Ilario still loves his wife and has only tender thoughts of her, though we hardly ever get her thoughts on him. As in *Reuben, Little Hero*, sex is important but unsatisfying, and the writing about sex is intense and unflinching. When she marries him, Anna is a 40-year old virgin and cannot encompass sexual penetration. Like Polly in *Reuben*, Anna dislikes sex, though in her case it is because of the pain it causes her; however unlike Mike in *Reuben,* Ilario is not unfaithful to her, and despite

[1] Both are also dedicated to Tony Whittome, editor at Hutchinson

[2] p. 9

[3] p. 14

Anna's disgust, tries other ways to find sexual release with her. 'Ilario, you are hurting my *hand*. The polite Italian catches sperm in his handkerchief. Mortifying his wife.'[1] Nevertheless, she seems to have a morbid fascination with sex: 'she pleaded, hurt me.'[2] At times, the narratives of the couple merge far more than their bodies ever do.

> Anna, the wife that I have, strains my cock like a corkscrew, she arches her back, pleading. There is something I want, Ilario must give me, I must give him, must give us, must give myself, must give. It is me, in me, between us, not him, his: his fault. Let it be now. It is not.
>
> And la fica weeps without ceasing, endlessly, of my own dearest, there's no limit to these tears from the womb, the moment never comes, oh she is so bitter to taste, sour in my mouth, on my tongue. Or, vinegar to wash the anguish, and in my hands a sponge of perpetual sorrow.
>
> Acid of our marriage, strange, symbolic, a mortification. The wormwood, shadow, deadly belladonna, gall. Her cunt streaming: caressing ourselves we are stung: kissing, I poison him.[3]

The layers of symbolism attached to the vagina foreshadow in some ways Penelope Shuttle and Peter Redgrove's 1978 *The Wise Wound*, a study of the taboo subject of menstruation, a topic that so horrified the authors of *Leviticus* and other male-centred religious works. The vinegar and sponge seem like a reference to Jesus on the cross, as does the gall: 'They gave him vinegar to drink mingled with gall'.[4] Wormwood [Artemisia absinthium, named after the hunter-goddess Artemis] is of course an epithet for bitterness going back to at least the Old Testament and is mentioned as a falling star in the *Book of Revelation*: 'the name of the star is called Wormwood: and a third of the waters became bitter; and many people had died of the waters, because they were made bitter.'[5] The implication of wormwood as a metaphor, especially in the Old Testament, is of something *too* bitter to taste; something whose eventual value is not worth the bitterness involved in achieving it. Wormwood has also been associated with witchcraft, as has belladonna, the other poisonous plant the narrator (it is not clear who is speaking these words) thinks of.

Despite Anna's disgust at Ilario's sexual appetite, he is not equally disgusted by her decaying body. In fact Anna never seems to love Ilario as totally as he loves her; he has not become part of her being as she has his.

---

[1] p. 19

[2] p. 30

[3] p. 57

[4] *Matthew* 27:34, King James Version

[5] *Revelations* 8:11, King James Version

> My husband Ilario is part of memory. The meaning of I is left to me. No one has helped me, no one has changed me, I believe in nothing but myself. Nor shall our love transcend death. At my expiry I *will* cease.[1]

In the sections titled *The State of Time of Being a Child*, Anna clearly remembers her normal, upper or middle class childhood mainly through memories of death (perhaps we are meant to understand these sections as her inner thoughts as she is dying). She thinks about her father's suicide when she was 11, the deaths of her cats and dogs and the day when she joins a fox hunt and is 'blooded':

> the Master [of the hunt] shakes me by the hand tips up my chin as if to kiss me and dabs my cheeks with a bleeding stump. Oh tears of anguish, exhaustion. Anna clutched her prize possession, it dripped down her breeches. A very great honour: a little girl.[2]

Ilario also has sections devoted to his life as a sea captain, titled *A Change Brought About by the Sea.* This could almost be a subtitle for B.S. Johnson's *Trawl*, which it brings to mind. In one passage, he and Anna almost drown in a hurricane, described with the absolute objectivity of the captain's log in stark contrast to the internal and subjective tone of the rest of the book. '2300hrs 0102, 0200hrs 1007, 0400hrs 1002. 0500hrs 997. Or 5mbs in 60 minutes. Falling, still falling.'[3]

Anna does die and Ilario goes to see her corpse on page 54, so we have no doubt about the outcome; where B. S. Johnson cut holes in the pages of *Albert Angelo* to show what was to come, Belben uses the device of different types of chapter containing narratives moving at different paces.

At the very end of the novel Belben uses the device of blank sections of page to indicate a stop. On the penultimate page he sees her die. 'The woman, whom the man loved, longs to die: but I do not know what I cannot imagine. Her last clear idea.'[4] Then, at the bottom of the last page: 'It is finished, it is not finished, the moment never comes, this bitter taste in my mouth can be the only end.'[5] So in the last reference to her we have the idea of bitterness again: in life she tasted bitter and in death she leaves him with nothing but this bitter taste.

---

[1] p. 37
[2] p. 111
[3] p. 94
[4] p. 123
[5] p. 124

Here, in Rosalind Belben's fourth novel, *Dreaming of Dead People,* published in 1979 we have a female narrator, a 'spinster' like Thomassina Dark in the *Flights* section of *Bogies* but in this case one who has travelled widely and experienced the world. As in *The Limit* each chapter has a different kind of narration, though all are first person. Also as in *The Limit*, the narrator has a strong sense of her childhood and, unlike the narrator in *Somewhere Else,* she has a strong sense of her own identity and the places she is and has been in. There is a strong autobiographical feeling about the novel, reinforced by the narrator's statement that she was born two months before Virginia Woolf died and that she lives in Dorset, England. Belben herself was in fact born in the year of Virginia Woolf's death, 1941, in Dorset.

If the novel is, at least partially autobiographical then it has an uncommon bravery: Belben describes herself at the age of thirty-six as 'a shrivelled person, I have sucked myself dry; I am a figure of fun; an object for curiosity; an old maid; or I shall be, old; don't suppose I don't mind. I do mind.'[1] The narrator, having in the first chapter described a very pleasant return to the Veneto region of Italy, gives us in the next chapter, titled *The Act of Darkness,* some very graphic descriptions of female masturbation. This extreme confessional style is in some ways reminiscent of Anne Sexton, in poems like 'The Ballad of the Lonely Masturbator' and 'In Celebration of My Uterus' (both from the collection *Love Poems*, 1969) though, despite their deliberately shocking titles Sexton's poems are nowhere near as explicit. One might also think of Molly Bloom's monologue in *Ulysses*, but this was written by a man with a man's fantasies and one might remember that *Portnoy's Complaint* was banned in 1972 for its detailed description of a young man's masturbation.

Having told us that she has not 'fucked for ten years. . . the whole of the middle of my life'[2] and comparing herself to other 'withered spinsters' like Virginia Woolf, she tells us how much she misses sex.

> I have woken sopping and swollen, with a devil to suppress between my legs, and dismay. To the splatter of summer rain.

---

[1] p. 7
[2] p. 24

> I have woken with my cunt crying out, lips throbbing and puckering, and an empty thumb print pressed into the back of my ear.[1]

She then tells us that she had never experienced an orgasm, or even really knew what one would feel like, until she discovers how to use an electric toothbrush. Calling herself 'medically frigid', she feels 'threatened by women in the tube: feminine, neatly painted and scented women, who would cry out at the moment of orgasm, that literary cliché which leaps from the page of every book as if to insult and torment me'[2].

> I have very little feeling in my clitoris – that dreary word again; in my oyster, my mussel; hence the expressions 'the world's your oyster', and 'the oyster of your eye'; almost none; and it is diminutive, heavily hooded. It may be a question of nerve-ends. It is, mine, a useless organ; my feeling is all inside, or at the mouth of my cunt. I cannot come *by hand* for my life.[3]

The orgasm she gets from the electric toothbrush, which object is described in minute and objective detail, is a catharsis for her and the toothbrush becomes her constant, possibly only, companion. She says wryly of it: 'I use an ordinary toothbrush for cleaning my teeth. Not from squeamishness. Not at all. To preserve the batteries.'[4] There follow pages of unflinching descriptions of her subsequent, constant masturbation, no doubt deliberately hard to read for both male and female readers. But although she is now sexually satisfied, she is still emotionally empty. 'I would much, much rather fuck. But I need to come. And never the twain shall meet.'[5] She still feels the need of male companionship, and of sex with a man, even though she knows this will not satisfy her and she has already exploded the myth of the vaginal orgasm.

> I am attuned emotionally to the explosiveness of sex, of male sex. I love that, to be whipped up, and to whip up, quickly.
>
> I mind, I mind dreadfully; of course I do.[6]

We know that she has had a long-term relationship with a man in the past, and that after this she had a period of promiscuity in Venice. We also know that she became close to an Italian ship's captain (like Ilario in *The Limit*) and then visits

---

[1] p. 26
[2] p. 37
[3] p. 39
[4] p. 40
[5] p. 45
[6] p. 45

Africa (as does the imprisoned woman in *Bogies*) but now seems, at the age of thirty six, to have given up hopes of returning to such a life. She realises she will never give herself to another person: 'I am not so generous I can give myself, my body, to the imagination of other people, unless the tune is called by me.'[1] And, indeed the first chapter is now sees as a nostalgic reunion with Venice.

> In dreams and fantasies I want cocks in my mouth. In Italy the slang expression *una madonna*, of all things, describes the act of cock-loving in the mouth. I have always liked it. A taste: where words are failing me, are they not? But who the hell am I talking to anyway?[2]

Who indeed?

In the next chapter, *Cuckoo*, there is a complete change of tone and subject. It is about Robin Hood, a mythical figure but described in the chapter as a historical person. The narration is interspersed by apparently unrelated mediaeval songs and hymns, though one song has verses that begin 'I have a gentil cock', which certainly seems to relate to the preceding chapter. The narrator seems to have an affinity for him: he has been ostracised from society and is 'civilly dead' , a 'non-person. . . Therein a metaphor of myself.'[3] The chapter is partially about the ability of the narrator (who now does not talk about herself) to get inside the mind of another person, and one from a very different era at that.

> But can I project my consciousness, and obtain a result which is remotely close to the truth? I not only have to shed modern man, I have to regain another life, another landscape, quite another sensibility; with certain awareness stopped, like earths; and others – new, exposures – open. Why should I wish to?[4]

It is not clear why Belben or her narrator would wish to leave the first person, or why choose Robin Hood. In this chapter he is not at all the good character of myth, though he does resist (unsuccessfully) the sexual advances of a married woman (not Maid Marian of the myth).

---

[1] p. 33
[2] p. 46
[3] p. 49
[4] p. 50

Whenne mine eynen misteth
And mine eren sisseth
And my nose coldeth
And my tunge foldeth
And my rude slaketh
And mine lippes blaketh
And my mouth grenneth
And my spotel renneth
And myn her riseth
And myne herte griseth
And mine handen bivieth
And mine feet stivieth –
Al to late, al to late
Whenne the bere is at the gate!

Thenne I shal flit
From bedde to flore
From flore to here
From here to bere
From bere to pit
And the pit fordit
Thenne lith myn hous uppe myn nese:
Of al this world ne give ich a pese!

R
o
b
i
n

l
e
n
d

to me thy bow

Alas, the silver bells were censers, the cockleshells monks and prelates, the pretty maids nuns. It was but a dig at the garden of Catholic Mary.

I interpret illusions.

At Torcello, it is God, the Christ-child, who carries salvation, in the form of a scroll, symbolising the word. Or nobody carries salvation. I perceived a medieval, sacred pun. MARIA, PORTA SALUTIS, MARIS ASTRUM, sea star, salvation's door; by her Son, sets free those whom Eve had made sinful.* Her single trembling tear speaks quicker than the word of God.

The silence of winter. The owl and the hoar-frost. Breath suspended like disbelief in the air. The trees slumber so deeply during the night he feels they may be dying. He sees the faces of his imaginary friends drop and glide away. His hands shake. He has chilblains. His arrows fall short, or fly wide, too high, too low, or break. The arrow shafts snap. They shiver with their heads in the brittle grass. Whistling in the wind, derisively. They are lost. He can do nothing. He can do nothing right. It

*FORMULA VIRTUTIS MARIS ASTRUM · PORTA SALUTIS PROLE MARIA LEVAT · QUAS CONIUNGE SUBDIDIT EVA

In the next chapter, *Owl*, the tone changes again, becoming more meditative, and blurring the narrator's identity.

> Is disguise the deception of self, or of others, or of both; of some yet not others; selective; of the characters in the play, not the audience; has one forced oneself to believe in one's own disguise?[1]

She mainly describes her childhood love for animals and the cruelty of nature. She had a dog as a child whose loyalty and closeness to her has never been matched by any relationship she has had – or believes she ever will have – as an adult. However, the dog, like several of Belben's characters, is not given a name. Her middle-class, rural, English childhood seems to have been very much like Anna's in *The Limit*, where cruelty is also a feature.

In this chapter the narrative of her memories starts to break apart and dissolve into fragmented, distorted and repeated prayers, like collages; 'stuttering, incantatory'.

> Lighten our darkness we beseech thee O lord; lighten our darkness; we beseech thee; O lord, that in . . . our darkness; lighten we beseech thee darkness we beseech thee lighten our darkness . . . darkness. Shadows of the night. Put to flight. Fleeing shadows this long night which is not a night but a life. Or part of a life.[2]

Near the end of this chapter is a sentence almost identical to one at the end of *The Limit*: '*How can I imagine what I do not know*.'[3]

The final chapter of *Dreaming of Dead People*, the narrator (whom we now see to be called Lavinia) is reminiscing and dreaming (hence, perhaps, the title) about her childhood; she mainly remembers her mother and her dog and her nanny; like Anna in *The Limit* she has a nanny called Nannie. She also fantasises about how she would bring up her own daughter if she had one: in the town not the countryside she still loves. 'I wanted a daughter, which is odd, seeing I have softness for boys. I have wanted – God forgive me – to perpetuate myself.'[4]

Her dreams only make her seem more alone: 'Is one ever excluded from one's own dreams, excused from taking part? I might like that.'[5] But her own dreams remain unfulfilled sexual fantasies.

---

[1] p. 75

[2] p. 93; elisions in the original.

[3] p. 95

[4] p. 110

[5] p. 142

> I dream of mucus running from my cunt in a stream, flowing across the floor and out under the front door.
>
> I have temptation dreams, with the strength to pull explicitly; I saw my neighbour, next to whom I have lived for five placid years, with a huge erection; come on, I said; and he did; we did[1].

Like all Belben's narrators, she is fundamentally alone, though unlike the others, she is free and understands who she is.

> I do long to say 'we' not 'I'. But at least I can't remember ever wanting to be anyone other than myself; a deep blood-red root of confidence. It has been no problem, identity; leant heavily upon, it was there; accessible. That's luck.[2]

She is *Frei aber Einsam*. 'I have fuel enough in me to blaze alone.'[3]

[1] p. 142
[2] p. 145
[3] p. 146

fellow travellers

In this section I want to look at some writers who could not be called experimental novelists but, in some of their work, interrogated the novel form and produced at least one experimental novel in a body of other kinds of work.

From the early 1960s to the mid-1970s there was a focus on the future of the novel and experimental writing in conferences, symposia and anthologies like Giles Gordon's *Factions*, Emma Tennant's *Bananas* anthology, Calder's *Signature* and *New Writers* series, Margaret Drabble and B. S. Johnson's *London Consequences* and his three collections of reminiscences by various writers; all provided opportunities to showcase new writing.

During the mid-1970s, several publishers asked writers and academics to edit collections of essays and interviews with writers talking about their methods: Giles Gordon's, *Beyond the Words: Eleven Writers in Search of a New Fiction*, 1975; Bernard Bergonzi's *Innovations*, 1975; Malcolm Bradbury's, *The Novel Today: Contemporary Writers on Modern Fiction*, 1975; John Atkins', *Six Novelists Look At Society*, 1977; Alan Burns' and Charles Sugnet's, *The Imagination on Trial: British and American Writers Discuss Their Working Methods*. London, 1981; and in America such collections as Joe David Bellamy's, *The New Fiction*: *Interviews with Innovative American Writers*, 1975. Publishers like Peter Owen and John Calder, who had published Beckett, Burroughs and the *nouveaux romanciers*, along with their equivalent

in France, Maurice Girodias of the Olympia Press and the American Barney Rosset of Grove Press, took a personal interest in and encouraged emerging and experimental writers, while companies like Allison & Busby, Faber and Faber and Hutchinson New Authors Ltd were open to interesting new work.

Radical presses like Writers Forum and Gaberbocchus published the otherwise-unpublishable and found space in bookshops like Better Books in London's Charing Cross Road and the Paperback Shop in Edinburgh, which became meeting places and outlets for underground writers[1]. Several small literary magazines were devoted to the encouragement of new writing. The relative conservatism of Cyril Connolly's *Horizon*, 1940-1949, where Anna Kavan published stories and wrote book reviews, *Encounter*, founded in 1953 by Stephen Spender, and *The London Magazine*, which had originally been founded in 1732 but was revived in 1954 under John Lehmann, gave way by the end of the 1950s to the relative experimentalism of Martin Bax's *Ambit*, which published, among others, Alexander Trocchi, B.S. Johnson, Jeff Nuttall, William Burroughs, Giles Gordon and George MacBeth, and Michael Horovitz's *New Departures,* publisher of Burroughs, Beckett and Stevie Smith. Both were founded in 1959. The 1960s saw Jeff Nuttall's underground *My Own Mag* - cheaply-produced so he did not have to deal with publishers - Michael Moorcock's editorship of the literary science fiction magazine *New Worlds* and B.S. Johnson as poetry editor of

[1] See Jeff Nuttall's *Bomb Culture* and Nigel Fountain's *Underground: The London Alternative Press, 1966-74.* London: Routledge, 1988

Transatlantic Review[1]. In the 1970s, Ian Hamilton's *New Review*, 1974-1979 and Emma Tennant's *Bananas*, 1975-1979 continued to encourage new writing, which was so popular that even a fashion and style magazine like *Nova*, 1956-1975, could publish Ann Quin in the 1960s.

> Gloomy prophecies that a magazine of this type could only find a limited readership proved false. Once *Bananas* was made available in newsagents and bookshops all over the country, people started to buy it. Subscriptions went up, from people and libraries. Manuscripts came in in large numbers. The magazine began to be attacked in critical quarterlies, always a good sign, and Auberon Waugh called it pretentious rubbish. Meanwhile people went on writing stories and more people went on reading them.[2]

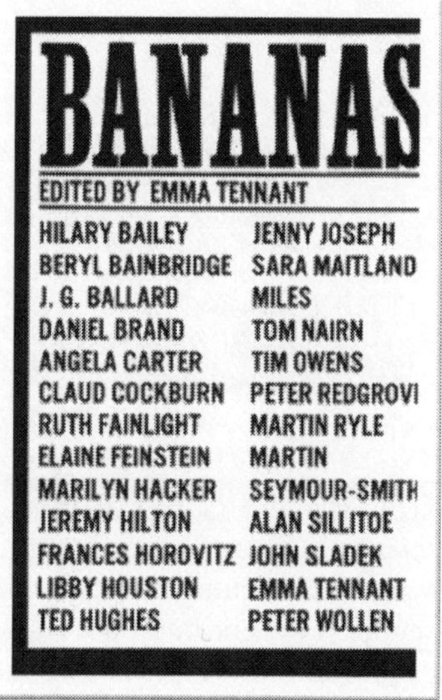

In France in the 1950s there was Alexander Trocchi's *Merlin* and its spin-offs *The Paris Review* and the American *Evergreen Review*, all publishing literature that pushed the boundaries of style and taste. By the mid-1960s French literary theory was becoming available in English[3] as were most of the *nouveaux romans* that inspired and were inspired by it, largely thanks to John Calder, who had also made available in the UK Beckett, Burroughs and Hubert Selby. Rayner Heppenstall's English study of Raymond Roussel was published in 1966. Barth and Pynchon had been published by this time, with Barthelme soon to come.

---

[1] Closed down in 1977

[2] Introduction to *Bananas,* ed. Emma Tennant. Colchester, Essex: Blond & Briggs, 1977

[3] Some dates of first publications in English of key works of French literary theory are: Nathalie Sarraute's *The Age of Suspicion; Essays on the Novel*, 1963; Alain Robbe-Grillet's *Pour un nouveau roman*, 1965; Roland Barthes' 'The Death of the Author' and *Writing Degree Zero*, both 1967, Jacques Derrida's *Speech and Phenomena*, 1967; Guy Debord's *The Society of the Spectacle,* 1970; Jacques Lacan's *The Language of the Self: The Function of Language in Psychoanalysis*, 1968; Michel Butor's *Inventory: Essays*, 1968; Michel Foucault's *The Order of Things,* 1970 and *The Archaeology of Knowledge*, 1972; Julia Kristeva's *Desire in Language*, 1980. Anaïs Nin's *The Novel of the Future* was written in English and published in 1968, but only in America.

In 1962 John Calder organised a conference on 'The Future of the Novel' at the Edinburgh Festival which introduced some contemporary American writers and pitted them against some well-known, traditionalist British novelists. 'Different writers outlined the future as they envisaged it, but the big sensation of the day was William Burroughs. He had earlier been described by Norman Mailer as 'possibly the only living American writer of genius." The conference was organised into panels, who argued passionately with each other, and with the speakers on subjects such as commitment and censorship; 'the climax was Henry Miller, long banned in Britain and still the subject of prosecutions in different American cities and states'.

> This was the way to put over new writing to the public and to create an interest in the writers: by putting their ideas and personalities in conflict with each other. Novelists work on their own, and the blank white paper is a challenge, but it is a lonely one. The chance to meet one's public and become for a while an actor could make all the difference. This did not apply to the shy or withdrawn. L. P. Hartley, Henry Williamson and one or two others who [*sic*] had not said a word. But it had made stars of [Eric] fried and [Khushwant] Singh, of the two tough ladies [Mary] McCarthy and [Rebecca] West, of Miller and Burroughs, of [Alexander] Trocchi, Mailer and Angus Wilson.[1]

---

[1] John Calder. *Pursuit: The Uncensored Memoirs of John Calder*. London: Calder Publications, 2001.

Calder subsequently repeated the conference idea, and other festivals copied it; Calder also held the conferences at the Harrogate Festival, which included the science fiction conference described in the next section. These not only brought together writers and audiences but exposed British writers to what was going on in other countries and what was possible in the novel.

stevie smith

Stevie Smith (born Florence Margaret Smith, 1902 – 1971) is now more well-known, and well-loved, as a poet than as a novelist. Although she was born after Anna Kavan, all her novels were written relatively early in her life and all but one are outside the scope of this study of mostly post-war experimental fiction. However, they are all unconventional, to say the least. Smith was brought up, along with her sister, by her feminist aunt Madge Spear, whom she called 'The Lion Aunt' and with whom she lived all her life. 'Dear Auntie Lion, I do so hope you will forgive what is written here. You are yourself like shining gold. When I think of what some women are like, I am full of humble gratitude and apprehension that I have you to live with.'[1] Smith lived a creative and intellectual life largely independent of men. She knew personally many artistic and creative women and corresponded with many others. However, she did not make a living from her writing and worked in the very male world of publishing; like Ann Quin a generation later she worked as a secretary, from 1923 to 1953. Smith had been writing poetry for ten years when she first submitted her poems to an agent, who suggested she should write a novel instead; *Novel on Yellow Paper*, 1936, was the result. After that she published her first volume of poetry, *A Good Time Was Had By All*, 1937, which was followed by more poetry and two more novels. Her last novel was published in 1949 and after that she concentrated on her poetry. Having left her secretarial job in 1953 she reviewed books, published sketches and read her poetry in public, becoming well-known especially for the poetry collection *Not Waving But Drowning*, published in 1957.

Smith's three novels[2] are all decidedly internalised and autobiographical: the world of externals only seems to exist through the narrator's rather eccentric view of it and her flowing, rambling chatter, which seems to have no ordering principle other than that of the association of ideas. The narrator of the first two novels,

[1] *Novel on Yellow Paper,* Penguin edition, 1951, p. 191

[2] *Novel on Yellow Paper; or, Work It Out For Yourself* (London: Cape, 1936; repr. Virago, 1980); *Over The Frontier* (London: Cape, 1938; repr. Virago, 1980); *The Holiday* (London: Chapman & Hall, 1949; repr. Virago, 1979)

Pompey Casmilus, is a thinly-fictionalised version of Smith herself; in the first novel she talks entirely about herself, her opinions and her life at work and in her small social circle. *Over The Frontier* starts in similar vein but Pompey then goes to Germany and the novel (which was published just before the Second World War) turns into a parody of a certain kind of jingoistic thriller written by John Buchan and others. Whereas *Novel on Yellow Paper* had been concerned with anti-Semitism, *Over the Frontier* is concerned with German militarism. Smith's third novel, *The Holiday*, published more than ten years later, is more conventional and though it has characters – the central figure Celia is in many ways like Smith herself – and a frustrated love story, it is mainly concerned with post-war Britain and its role in the world and many of the characters speak as if merely voicing Smith's own views.

Novel on Yellow Paper is so titled because the narrator is said to be composing it on office paper while she is at work:

> I am typing this book on yellow paper. It is very yellow paper, and it is this very yellow paper because often sometimes I am typing it in my room at my office, and the paper I use for Sir Phoebus's letters is blue paper with his name across the corner 'Sir Phoebus Ullwater, Bt.' and those letters of Sir Phoebus go out to all over the world. And that is why I type yellow, typing for my own pleasure[1]

The narrator, who, like Smith herself, is a private secretary who lives with her aunt, says: 'this book is the talking voice that runs on, and the thoughts come, the way I said, and the people come too, and come and go, to illustrate the thoughts, to point the moral, to adorn the tale'. Smith makes it clear that this is going to be an experimental novel:

> But first, Reader, I will give you a word of warning. This is a foot-off-the-ground novel that came by the left hand. And the thoughts come and go and sometimes they do not quite come and I do not pursue them to

[1] p. 13

> embarrass them with formality to pursue them into a harsh captivity. And if you are a foot-on-the-ground person I make no bones to say that is how you will write and only how you will write. And if you are a foot-on-the-ground person, this book will be for you a desert of weariness and exasperation. So put it down. Leave it alone. It was a mistake you made to get this book. You could not know.[1]

Despite the apparent frivolity and lightness of tone of most of the book, Pompey (and therefore Smith) are well aware of world politics and have serious things to say, especially about German fascism. Pompey has been to Germany and stays in the house of Jewish friends in Berlin. 'Oh how I felt that feeling of cruelty in Germany, and the sort of vicious cruelty that isn't battle-cruelty, but doing people to death in lavatories.'[2] It is important to remember that this was at a time when the British government and monarchy still had full diplomatic relations with Germany and that the policy of appeasement would continue for several years. No one had yet predicted the horrors of war or the Holocaust and, although a few committed writers like George Orwell, Christopher Caudwell and Ralph Fox were leaving to fight fascists in Spain just as *Novel on Yellow Paper* was being published, Smith's political insight in this novel is far in advance of the great majority of the writers of the time.

> But then see what they did this time to the Jews and the Communists, and later than this right nowadays to the Jews and the Communists, in the latrines, and the cruel beating and holding down and beating, and enjoying it for the cruelty.
>
> Oh how deeply neurotic the German people is, and how weak, and how they are giving themselves up to this sort of cruelty and viciousness, how Hitler cleared up the vice that was so in Berlin, in every postal district some new vice, how Hitler cleared that up all. And now look how it runs with the uniforms and the swastikas. And how many uniforms, how many swastikas, how many deaths and maimings, and hateful dark cellars and lavatories. Ah how decadent, how evil is Germany to-day.[3]

But despite the seriousness of this message, the novel keeps its lightness and its constant reminders that it is indeed a novel, addressing the reader and talking about literary technique. Pompey discusses her friend Harriet who is a poet but wants to write a book about fashion. Harriet does not know how to keep the book to a reasonable length.

---

[1] p. 16
[2] p. 87
[3] p. 88

But with me, I shall have no such difficulty. I shall know when to stop. And whatever I write then will be Volume Two.

But Harriet in her writing form has a very exact and precise sense of form. And that is a thing I am not able to come by. Reader, it is a fault.

People have said to me: If you must write, remember to write the sort of book the plain man in the street will read. It may not be a best seller – but it should maintain a good circulation.

About this I pondered for a long time and became distraut [*sic*]. Because I can write only as I can write only, and Does the road wind uphill all the way? Yes, to the very end. But brace up, chaps, there's a 60,000 word limit.

Oh how irritated I am by this funny idea of keeping your feet on the ground. Spoken like an officer and a gentleman, Sir People. Spoken like a prig and a nincompoop.[1]

[1] p. 197

norman hidden

Norman [Frederick] Hidden, 1913-2006 was primarily a poet, and his only novel, *Dr Kink and his Old-Style Boarding School,* 1973 is in fact an illustrated, autobiographical collage of verse and prose fragments about his time at Hereford Cathedral School from 1926-32. He later attended Brasenose College, Oxford, 1932-1936 where he obtained his MA in education. At the outbreak of the Second World War he was teaching in America and remained there until 1943, when he returned to Britain to join the armed forces and stayed on as an education and liaison officer until 1947. After this he taught English at schools and at Middlesex University until 1973.

Hidden founded and edited the Workshop Press's *New Poetry* Magazine, which ran for 52 issues from 1967-1981 and published many leading poets, with several distinguished guest editors. He also edited and compiled *The State of Poetry Today: a survey sponsored by New Poetry magazine*, 1978. From 1968 to 1971 he was the chairman of the General Council of the Poetry Society of Great Britain and was a member of the Executive Committee of the English Association, the Council of the National Book League and the Advisory Council of the English Speaking Board.

Hidden's work as an editor produced other anthologies[1], including one of poets from around the world[2] and two of poems to be read aloud[3], but seems to have prevented him from releasing many of his own solo volumes: he only published two volumes of his own verse[4], one of stories[5] and one of 'straight' autobiography[6]; despite this he did publish a manual for poets on how to get their work accepted[7].

Hidden described *Dr Kink*[8] as 'a literary experiment presenting a complex picture of a boy's love-hate relationship both with father and with school.' The book contains an assortment of styles and literary forms, in verse and prose and provides an entirely convincing portrait of life in an English public school at the time. The eponymous Dr Kink is the headmaster, also known by the boys as King and the Corpse. The school is governed by a combination of strict rules – 'There were fifty seven of them written out. And a lot of unwritten rules too.'[9] – and the arbitrary, capricious decisions of Dr Kink, which inevitably lead to corporal punishment. Anyone of a certain age who has been to an English boy's school will recognise these and other features of the book: the freezing corridors; the primitive lavatories; the headmaster's matronly and kindly wife (Queen); the prurient school masters seeing the dark shadow of sex everywhere.

---

[1] A Workshop Press anthology was also edited in his honour by Dick Russell on his 80th birthday: *Hidden talent: the Workshop poets. An anthology in celebration of the 80th birthday of the founder of the Press, Norman Hidden (edited by Dick Russell).* Russell Hill Press, 1993 Workshop Press

[2] ed. with Amy Hollins. *Many People, Many Voices: poetry from the English speaking world.* London: Hutchinson, 1978

[3] *Say It Aloud.* London: Hutchinson, 1972; *Over to You: a collection of poems for speaking aloud.* English Speaking Board, 1975

[4] *These Images Claw.* London: Outpost, 1966; *For My Friends.* Workshop, 1981

[5] *Caravan Summer and other stories.* London: Citron, 1999

[6] *Liaison Officer: Germany and the Anglo-US occupation*, 1946-47. Frinton on Sea: Clydesdale, 1993

[7] *How to Get your Poems Accepted: a guide for poets.* Workshop, 1981

[8] The novel is illustrated with line drawings – of which the cover design is a collage – by a 'Jhaan Machesney', about whom I can find no information; I presume this is a pseudonym.

[9] p. 1

In one of the more experimental sections, Hidden lays out two 'episodes' on facing pages with the following instructions:

> NOTE: In the incident which follows, episode A and episode B may be read in any or all of three ways:
> (1) by reading all the sections of section A consecutively and then continuing in the same manner with episode B;
> (2) by allowing the eye to traverse *of its own accord* from left to right, the two episodes thus forming an impressionistic whole;
> (3) by reading the pages consecutively as in the normal convention.

EPISODE A

"You are a heathen and a barbarian", said the Corpse. "You shall be punished accordingly."

The boy watched a spasm of unidentifiable emotion throw itself against the bars and walls of the Corpse's gaunt face, its skin tight and quivering. His nostrils were stained brown, and he smelt of snuff tinged with the faint clinging odour of incense. His study contained a small glazed statue of the Virgin Mary; a miniature crucifix, its ivory tinged with sepia, hung on a side wall. Whenever the Corpse spoke the name of Jesus Christ he crossed himself. These associations made him terrifying in the dimly-lit room with its thick brown curtains drawn tightly together. The boys called it the Tomb.

EPISODE B

The sky was blue-black, like a policeman's uniform. Its bulk spread like the jet hair of a dying God falling over the bruised, stained forehead of the day. It hung thick and dense and at its edges raggedly stretched into the last blue of hopeless dusk. It closed over the thick silhouette of the cathedral tower, merging its vast mass into the cloud of night. To Philip, standing by the dormitory eaves' window, narrow as a fortress-prison's look-out slit, midway between his bed and Percy's bed, it was a giant warder rearing itself against the one small aperture of obvious escape. A summer's night devoid of illumination: no stars, no moon, no street lighting. Only the blackness of the cathedral precincts, barring him in.[1]

[1] pp. 12/13. In the book these are facing pages not facing columns as I have represented them here for convenience.

After the disappearance of the classics master Kink's grip on reality begins to loosen and he takes to carrying around his cricket bat at all times. The sound of a mouse – actually the fingernails of a pupil – drives him over the edge.

> Kink leapt out of his seat and swung his bat, with a kind of chopping action, at a hole in the skirting. Crash, went the bat in maniacal fury onto the floor; crash it descended again, crash. Down and down came the bludgeon. The veins stood out on his forehead; his neck was red with bending and with the exertion. Saliva formed little drips at his mouth. We stood, or sat, petrified. Somehow we too could see and feel the splash of blood and mash of flesh as each stroke fell. It was as though *we* were being smeared and ground into the floorboards, battered out of existence forever. Suddenly he stopped and stood erect. His eyes were steel-blue and glinted with the same excitement they had at the nets when he had skied some impossible catch.
>
> "Queen won't disturb our cricket practice any more," he announced. Then he turned and went out into the corridor, saying "She won't need to lock her door again."
>
> They came and took him away, and it was a nine days' wonder. He was confined in a hospital which stood in some very pleasant grounds, and there he was able to play plenty of cricket through the long summer afternoons.
>
> We never saw him again; and of course we all felt sorry for Queen.[1]

Apart from Dr Kink, the other figure looming large in the boy's life is his father. Three of the book's sections are about him; the first, which opens the book, is an ambivalent poem of love, hate and awe.

> Father was a lucky man
> 99% of him knew his luck
> He could join the army and prudently
> keep bullets at long range.
>
> Battalion cook, he didn't think much
> of officers and getting killed
> After all, he'd got an infant son

---

[1] pp. 45/46

to think on.

. . .

I was in love
with mother, of course. He wouldn't
stand for that. At eight
he packed me off to boarding school.[1]

A self-made man, who talked of 'the historic pioneers of the socialist movement, whom as old men he had seen in his youth', his father is summarised for the boy, and for us, by his collection of books.

> An odd collection : *Darwin's Origin of the Species* in two volumes; *Darwin's Origin of the Species* in one volume, *A Guide to Gardening*, Thomas a Kempis' *On the Imitation of Christ*, the Plays of William Shakespeare, the poems of Lord Tennyson, Beatrice Potter's *History of the Co-operative Movement*, J. R. McDonald's *Socialism*, Annie Besant's *Theosophy*; *The Excursion* by William Wordsworth, *The Rubaiyat of Omar Khayyam*, Ruskin's *Unto this Last*, Fabian Essays, one or two novels by H. G. Wells, somebody's translation of the poems of Heinrich Heine, somebody else's pocketbook on *Gardening for Pleasure – and Profit*; William Morris's *News from Nowhere* and *The Earthly Paradise*, the novels of Jack London; and eight strongly bound volumes of *A New Popular Educator*.
>
> He was a self-educated man; like my mother, he had left school when he was twelve.

This is all we need to know about his father: a life summed up in books. After he leaves school, his father's working-class respect for the upper classes grates on him as they go together on a winter cruise to Madeira and the Canary Isles; a very fashionable thing to do at that time for people of a certain class, which his father is really not. He says 'you've got to admit they know how to live. Winter in Madeira, then back to England to live in the spring.' but his 'tone was half-envy, half contempt', his socialist heritage battling his middle-class aspirations. They meet a couple from the higher orders.

[1] no page number

> The round-cheeked woman in a tweed costume, the thin-faced man in pinstripe grey. Their voices as they passed had an affected tone that was instantly recognisable. A voice and a language made for each other. Pitched high to over-ride all others, asserting unchallengeable authority. The vowels drawled casually out over the rack to the limits of their exquisite torture.
>
> Such voices grated in the ear of Mr. Fredericks, the self-made man. "Public school types," he was about to say, but checked himself, remembering that he had sent his son to one of these same 'public' schools.[1]

Forced to have dinner with the self-made man and his son, the upper-class couple see the father's eating habits as vulgar and his attempts to make friends as embarrassing. Eventually their breeding and reserve break down as the lady says to the father: 'All I can say is that I feel sorry for that poor boy of yours.' The boy himself is 'awed by the extent of his father's hurt. And yet it was exactly what he had known would be the result of his father's attempts to be sociable, to ingratiate himself, to mingle with this brittle other world, who were shocked by burps and belches, by aitches dropped and soup sucked noisily in and the visible signs of masticated food.'[2] But despite his intense embarrassment at his father the two end the book sitting in a café in the sun, laughing at nothing in companionable and conspiratorial mirth.

> To the momentarily curious local inhabitants at neighbouring tables, they were a coarse, jolly, red-faced man and a young boy with struwelpeter hair and pale white face – sitting at a bare café table on which an empty glass was helplessly rocking to the vibration of their inexplicable and unabashed laughter, beneath the heaped-up flames of a fiery sun. Foreigners of course; but distinctly, yes one could tell, distinctly, they were father and son.[3]

---

[1] pp. 89/90
[2] p. 97
[3] p. 108

philip toynbee

Philip Toynbee, 1916 – 1981, the son of historian Arnold Toynbee and father of journalist Polly Toynbee, was a prominent left-wing intellectual who was the first communist president of the Oxford Union, visited Spain during the Civil War and wrote for the Observer newspaper. He wrote memoirs, two volumes of autobiography and books on nuclear policy and religion. In 1947 he published the highly experimental *Tea with Mrs Goodman,* reprinted in America the same year as P*rothalamium: A Cycle of the Holy Graal*, whose format B.S. Johnson utilised in *House Mother Normal.* The novel is constructed around a grid consisting of a number of narrators on one axis and a number of 'time units' on the other. (See Toynbee's explanation on the next page.) The narrators' names are given as:

A Max Ford
B Tom Ford
C Daisy Tillett – Tom's 'bonny bride'
D Charley Parsley
E Billy
F Miss Black
G Noel Tillett

The tone of the various narratives is generally portentous and deliberately difficult; although the characters are only having tea their thoughts are along the lines of Greek epics.

> Oh, I know you Mrs. Goodman, my old bitch, whore and familiar; harlot of the afternoon in Islington, of the night in Genoa and the night at Colwyn Bay. Damp from the last client, your bust-bodice is split by giant udders, thighs are swollen to bounce on, and a wooded hell's cut deep for my concealment. Chthonic lady of the back streets, under your German mountain, I'll sin for a thousand years, my armour rusting.[1]

[1] A3, Max Ford, p. 18

Notation of the Book Everything which appears in italics is overheard by the narrator, but said neither by him nor to him.

The pages are numbered both according to the period and events described (by the number itself), and according to the narrator (by the letter attached to the number). Thus page A7 covers the same period as pages B7, C7 and so on, but each is the experience of a different person. A narrator always begins at the point of his entry into the room, and concludes at his departure from it. Thus narrator F's account opens on a page marked F6 (and not F1) because it is not until time-unit 6 that she enters the room. Thus narrator B's account is numbered from B1 to B12, because he is present throughout the whole twelve pages covered by the book.

The following plan should make the notation clear:

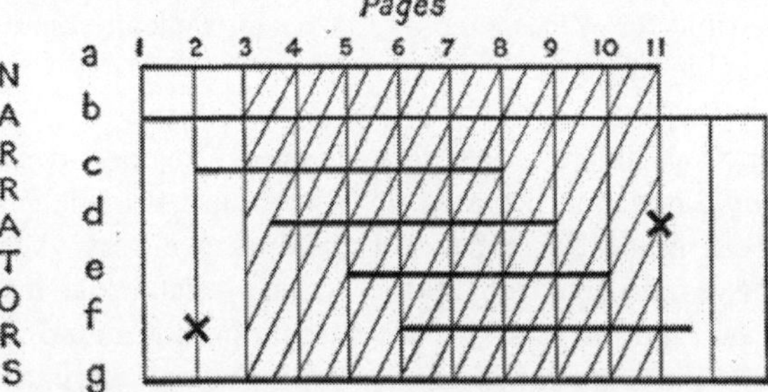

The book progresses along the horizontal lines from left to right and downwards, as in reading. Pages A1 to A10 are followed by pages B1 to B12, followed by pages C2 to C7, and so on. The faint vertical lines represent simultaneous moments of time. There is no page F2 (point crossed above) because narrator F is not yet in the room at page 2. Similarly there is no page D11 because narrator D has left the room by time-unit 11. The meaning of the shaded portion should become apparent in the course of the book.

In 1961 Toynbee published *Pantaloon; or, the Valediction*, a novel-length poem or poem-novel (Toynbee made no pronouncement as to how it should be categorised), the first in what turned out to be a series of four similar works, the last one appearing in 1968[1]. This may have been the book B.S. Johnson had in mind when he said, ostensibly in relation to Walter Scott: 'You will agree it would be perversely anachronistic to write a long narrative poem today?' Stephen Spender, reviewing it in *Encounter*[2], and referring to it as a 'poem-novel', said: 'So what is *Pantaloon?* It is really, I suggest, a rag-bag of memories and reflections held together by a character strenuously repudiating the idea that he is Philip Toynbee'. Spender judges it as poetry rather than as a novel, and is in fact very impressed by it.

> I have said so much *against* the book because these kind of criticisms have to be faced. The faults they refer to stick out a mile. But I entreat the reader to disregard them, and to read this book from beginning to end, overcoming all the protests which will make him, from time to time, want to throw it out of the window. For poets, it will come as something of a revelation; for it may well be the beginning of a break-through from the dreary academicism into which poetry has sunk in the day of the triumph of those Wagnerian dwarfs of criticism who are responsible for works such as the recent Pelican volume of essays on modern literature.

In the introduction to *Two Brothers* in 1964 Toynbee described how its predecessor *Pantaloon* was narrated; it is very hard to deduce from the book itself: 'a very old Anglo-Norwegian was talking to a very young Norwegian-American in the year nineteen-ninety-nine . . . in a small pension on a Norwegian river'. He also said that he was 'virtually suspending the sound of the narrator's voice' because 'I find myself increasingly anxious to eliminate all sense of narrative form in what I write.'

> Any honest attempt to adopt a new literary method springs in the first place from a sense that "life escapes" when methods are used which have become too familiar and unconsidered . . . the proper motive for trying to write in a new way is an urgent desire to represent the writer's

[1] *Two Brothers: The Fifth Day of the Valediction of Pantaloon*. London: Chatto & Windus, 1964; *A Learned City: The Sixth day of the Valediction of Pantaloon*. London: Chatto & Windus, 1966; *Views From a Lake: The Seventh Day of the Valediction of Pantaloon*. London: Chatto & Windus, 1968

[2] December 1961

> experience of life more fully and more realistically than any existing method would allow.[1]

Despite their differences, this sounds almost like it might be B.S. Johnson speaking.

[1] Two Brothers, p. 13

paul ableman

Born in Leeds, Paul Ableman (1927 -2006) grew up in New York and went to the prestigious Stuyvesant High School. Returning to England at age 18 he did national service and read English at King's College, London. (Both of which B.S. Johnson also did; Ableman appears in Johnson and Drabble's *London Consequences* but not in his *All Bull: The National Servicemen.*) Ableman never completed his studies but went, like many of his generation, including Alexander Trocchi, to Paris where he met Maurice Girodias, who published his first novel *I Hear Voices* in 1958 in the Travellers Companion series[1], where Trocchi's pseudonymous pornography had first appeared.[2]

Ableman wrote three further original novels: *As Near as I Can Get*, 1962; *The Twilight of the Vilp*, 1969; *Vac*, 1971 and *Tornado Pratt*, 1977 but was also active as a playwright. His first play was *Green Julia*, which was produced at the 1965 Edinburgh Festival and he combined fifty very short plays into the work *Tests*, which was first performed in 1966. But at the same time he was working in commercial television and radio, producing scripts for popular programmes. Later he came to specialise in the 'novelising' of British TV series such as *Shoestring*, *Porridge* and *Minder*. These were also written to order to subsidise his creative writing but did not do anything to help his career as a serious novelist and playwright.

His name was brought before the public in 1970 when he published *The Mouth and Oral Sex* (*The Sensuous Mouth* in America) through the small Running Man Press. No doubt influenced by his time with Girodias, this was a how-to manual illustrated by European and Japanese erotic art. The owner of Running Man was prosecuted for obscenity at the Old Bailey in 1971, in one of the last obscenity trials in Great Britain; many well-known figures supported the publisher. The book itself was acquitted but the brochures advertising it were ruled obscene under the 1953 Postal Act, leaving the publisher with a fine and heavy legal costs.[3]

---

[1] Reissued in England by New English Library in 1966 as number 102 in the series.

[2] It has been suggested that Ableman himself may also have written pornography to order for Girodias, but this is not confirmed by John de St. Jorre's definitive history of Olympia: *The Good Ship Venus : the erotic voyages of the Olympia Press*. London: Pimlico, 1994

[3] Jonathon Green, Nicholas J. Karolides. *The Encyclopedia of Censorship*. New York, 1990, p. 364

I Hear Voices was published by Maurice Girodias' Olympia Press in his Travellers Companion Series, alongside William Burroughs, Frank Harris, Samuel Beckett and both Alexander Trocchi's 'straight' novels and his pseudonymous pornography.[1] However, it has no erotic content; Girodias counted Ableman as one of the Olympia authors 'whose works did not contain any sexual provocations. I am thinking now of . . . Paul Ableman, whose novel (*I Hear Voices*) is perhaps the one which gave me the greatest pride and pleasure to publish'[2] High praise from the publisher of the above authors, not to mention Georges Bataille, Jean Genet and Raymond Queneau. In Britain *I Hear Voices* gained an approving review from Philip Toynbee in *The Guardian*.

> The spate of novels from the English publishers is so thick and full that it seems hard to believe that any writer of the least talent should be rejected. This brilliant and terrible little book shows that we have no grounds for such complacency. After hawking his typescript around London Mr. Ableman at last resigned himself, two years ago, to accepting the generous services of The Olympia Press in Paris. Thus English readers have been largely deprived of a strikingly fresh and original work of art which happens, by an accident of the times, to be well outside the current fashion. *I Hear Voices* is recounted by an imaginary schizophrenic; and this device is used to present a marvellous entanglement of different levels of reality. 'In reality' the hero is lying in a room; he tries to eat his breakfast; receives occasional visits. But by means of his madness, he can constantly get up and leave the house to encounter a wonderful series of dreamlike adventures. The writing is brilliant, Mr. Ableman can be both terrifying and hilariously funny; yet his book has not been thought worthy of publication in this country.[3]

---

[1] *I Hear Voices* was number 102 in the series; Trocchi's forged *The Fifth Volume of Frank Harris's My Life and Loves* was republished under his real name as number 108 and his *Young Adam* was number 109. William Burroughs' *Junkie* was 114

[2] Introduction to *The Olympia Reader*. New York: Grove, 1965, p. 19

[3] 16 October, 1960

who called it a 'brilliant and terrible little book'; Toynbee also expressed his dismay at the fact that it had not been brought out by a British publisher. A later review said:

> If the history of the postwar British *avant-garde* ever comes to be written one suspects that Paul Ableman will find a place in it as one of those useful shadow figures who are remembered less for their original talent than for reflecting the movements of their time.[1] . . Although his work spans a wide stylistic gulf it has all appeared in under ten years on all the narrow platforms available to British experimental writers. The novel I Hear Voices was published in Paris in 1958, thus attracting the kind of esteem previously accorded to such Parisian imprints as *The Rock Pool* and *The Ginger Man*.[2]

I Hear Voices is narrated, like some of the stories in Anna Kavan's *Asylum Piece* and Ann Quin's *The Unmapped Country* by an inmate in an institution of some kind. However the narrator is probably closest to Malone in Beckett's *Malone Dies*, 1951, first published in English in 1956, two years before *I Hear Voices*[3], though Ableman's tone is much lighter than Beckett's and closer to Flann O'Brien. Like Malone the narrator here does not seem to realise where he is[4]; he addresses the nurses as if they are friends and relatives and he refers to his doctor as the professor. Any or all of them may just be the voices of the title. 'They don't hear me, but I hear them. They must be near me. They must be discussing me. I must be the *third person* they're discussing. And yet they don't sound near, nor even very real, not like the voices of humans rooted to the earth, heavy and intangible.'[5] Although he seems to be confined to his bed, or at least to the institution, in his mind he is wandering the streets. He is also, like a Kavan character, slightly paranoid:

> I see the usual city scene. I see the people streaming on the pavements, the vehicles streaming in the streets. I see the lights and glass and feel how friendly it is this afternoon – how human. We are all –
>
> But what *are* my plans? Can I hold the Government responsible? I'm sure they understood. They had my brief. I concealed very little and listed all the vital aspects. My official side, perhaps, has always been

---

[1] Although I would not claim in this book to be the writing of a history of the postwar British avant garde, this is roughly how I have positioned Ableman.
[2] Irving Wardle 'The Ticket that Imploded' *Times Literary Supplement* June 9 1966
[3] Olympia had published Beckett's *Watt* in 1953, *Molloy* in 1955 and the trilogy of *Molloy, Malone Dies* and *The Unnameable* as Travellers Companion Series number 71 in 1959).
[4] Wardle assumes he is at home and Arthur is his brother 'so far as one can be sure of anything in this book.'
[5] p. 9

> somewhat underdeveloped but I took great pains. I feel sure that I itemized and listed. I shan't visit them yet, though I may minute them or dismiss them. I may move amongst them before long. But that's a minor part of it. First I must eat this egg.[1]

The eating of the egg becomes a recurrent topic; it almost becomes a character in the book. There may be multiple incidents involving it or the novel may in fact all take place on the same day and there is only one egg. 'Cousin Susan', who seems to be his nurse continually tells him to eat it but it he never does. 'the egg is cold and viscous now. However it expects to be eaten and has poised itself cleverly towards me, drooping over the cracked tray. The room is shivered too and I hardly believe in the light.'[2]

Susan tells him the professor has come to talk to him about his 'personal condition.

> "As reflected in this egg?" I suggest.
>
> "It's not reflected in the egg," he insists. "That's half your trouble. Look at that object once more. It's only a bit of shell, an ovoid of shell, calcium and so forth, with yolk and albumen inside. It comes from a hen."
>
> "So do I."
>
> "Now that's hardly likely, is it?"
>
> He smiles at me, a pleasant, winning smile, and attempts to attach a large meter to my throat.
>
> "Well, I haven't got a mother," I protest, knocking the meter to the floor where it whines and flickers feebly.
>
> "But you must have", says the professor. He looks thoughtfully but also, I am convinced, with a concealed impulse to fury, at the ruins of his meter on the floor. "I wish you hadn't wrecked that meter", he complains mildly. "They're fearfully expensive. . ."
>
> "I'm no friend to meters," I warn him. "And you haven't really proved that I have a mother.!
>
> No – well, I can hardly do that now. It's a long, complicated proof – but I *am* interested – Tell me, why do you imagine you haven't got a mother?"
>
> "I never see her."
>
> No. No, but you can remember her can't you?"
>
> "Memory's my best subject," I warn him. "I don't want to sound glib – but I'd beware of bringing up memory."[3]

---

[1] p. 18

[2] p. 24

[3] pp. 75/76

Of course, memory is exactly what he has lost. 'Susan then hands me my egg, draws my curtains and goes away. I am left with the impression of tramps on a bridge, basement windows and refreshments. The refreshments retain a magical quality in my memory. The incident to which the memory refers is a trivial one connected with my mother. unfortunately I cannot remember exactly how my mother was connected with the incident.'[1]

The 'professor' says he is connected with the 'Institute', in a parody of institutionalised mental health, where people are only 'subjects' to be studied.

> We have a great many fine men there, fine and humane men, all bundled together. They huddle together over their extracts and distillates, and exchange ideas. Later they commit these ideas to paper and they put out these papers to be soaked in the juices of life. When the papers have acquired a rich and savoury smell – "
>
> "Like ooze?"
>
> "No, like what they are. Like life-soaked papers – they read them to each other, sometimes straining their eyes badly as they try to pick out the words from amongst the fatty stains and tear-marks."[2]

But in the end the narrator lives inside his own head and everything or nothing around him may be real.

> I lie back and close my eyes. Is this my dark world? How deep shall I find it? How deep dare I descend? Whose hand waves in those dark mists? Is this my dark world? Is this my destiny?[3]

[1] p. 153
[2] p. 78
[3] p. 35

The Twilight of the Vilp, 1969 is an anomaly, at least in this book: a comic experimental novel; absurdist and again reminiscent in some ways of Flann O'Brien. In its science-fiction section it also bears comparison to the much later novels of Terry Pratchett and Douglas Adams. But even though it dates from the time of British New Wave Science Fiction and was published in paperback by Sphere Science Fiction it is not really a science fiction novel; it is a self-referential novel about the writing of a novel. In fact the narrator is quite scathing about science fiction. 'Science Fiction must still be regarded as a junior or ancillary department of literature incapable of providing a foundation for that delicate exploration of character and lofty moral edification which is the essence of the matter.'[1] The narrator, Clive Witt, who lives in a large household with an indeterminate number of children is a novelist looking for a hero for his next novel and advertises for one. Of the 73 replies he receives only three seem suitable: a professor of Literary Agronomy, an Irish-Burmese peasant and the inventor of the Earth Borer. He meets the three candidates one at a time and starts to write absurd drafts of a possible novel featuring them; the drafts for the novel themselves become the novel. But none of them work and he starts again on a completely different novel called *The Silver Spores* featuring all three of them and the erotic fantasy figure Sonya Guildenkrantz. This is an equally absurd science fiction story featuring the Vilp, an ancient race of beings; it is going well until the professor writes to him withdrawing from the novel. Witt continues anyway and gives us four alternative versions of the last chapter of *The Silver Spores*, which is called *The Twilight of the Vilp*. However, before he can quite finish it he receives a letter from Glebe, the inventor of the Earth Borer, which completely ruins his plans.

> It was no good. The game was lost. The whimsical unreliability of my characters amounting, I felt almost convinced, in the case of Glebe to certifiable lunacy, had wrecked the project. *The Silver Spores* would never drip from the presses, never grace the shelves of the libraries,

[1] p. 14

never comfort the nocturnal pillow. How many months had gone by on this abortive project? I could barely guess. Indeed after forty-five minutes of concentrated guessing I had abandoned the attempt. Still, there were consolations. I was still rich, respected and famous. Next time I would vet my applicants more carefully, subjecting them to a full range of emotional stability tests.[1]

[1] p. 139

peter redgrove

Peter Redgrove[1] (1932-2003) was one of the most prolific, talented and well-loved British poets of the twentieth century; he published over thirty books in his lifetime, including several novels. Redgrove studied natural sciences at Cambridge and worked as a chemist, scientific editor and journalist; he always kept an interest in science, but balanced by an interest in the occult. He was visiting poet at a number of British and American universities and taught at Falmouth School of Art in Cornwall, where he lived with his second wife Penelope Shuttle, whom he met in 1969. They jointly published two novels, a volume of poetry – *The Hermaphrodite Album*, 1973 – and a study of the importance of the female menstrual cycle.[2]

The preoccupation with magic and the supernatural which is present in all of Shuttle's works is strongest in her fourth solo novel, *The Mirror of the Giant*[3], described as a 'ghost story' though it is more of a love story (but with a quincunx of lovers rather than the trio of the first two novels) and the ghosts are really just memories. This preoccupation also pervades Shuttle's two collaborative novels with Redgrove - *The Terrors of Dr. Treviles: A Romance,* 1974, and *The Glass Cottage: A Nautical Romance,* 1976 - and even more Redgrove's own later solo novels *The God of Glass,* 1979; *The Sleep of the Great Hypnotist*, 1979; *The Beekeepers,* 1981 and *The Facilitators*, 1982.

Despite his interest in magic and the supernatural, Redgrove sees his work as having a political dimension. Like R.D. Laing, he recognises the importance of poetry to psychoanalysis, but works from the poetry end rather than the analytic. 'Psychotherapy and poetry are the same thing. The good psychotherapist finds the man's image of himself from the dream and gives it back to him perfected'[4], which is also what the poet does: if it is true poetry it accustoms us to the life of dreams, and dreams are life talking back to itself[5]. However, Redgrove does not see this self-discovery as solipsistic but essentially political. 'The goal is for inner and outer to become the same thing'; through greater self-awareness people can change not only their private but also their social and political lives: 'I think it's socially very important for people to know about their inner selves', and the poet can be the catalyst: 'If your art wakens them, they will not be taken in by the half-

[1] For a full biography see Neil Roberts. *A Lucid Dreamer: The Life of Peter Redgrove.* London: Jonathan Cape, 2012. Roberts has also posthumously edited Redgrove's *Collected Poems*. London: Jonathan Cape, 2012

[2] London: Routledge, 1981

[3] London: Marion Boyars, 1980

[4] Interview with Hugh Herbert in 'Faust and Foremost', *Guardian* 30th Nov. 1973, p.12

[5] ibid.

lives that society offers so many of them. Any art that wakes people is a political art'[1].

The eponymous Gregory in *The Terrors of Dr. Treviles* is a 'dream-therapist' and the novel satirises conventional therapists who are referred to as 'clergyman'; Redgrove's *In the Country of the Skin,* published in 1973[2], before either of the Redgrove/Shuttle collaborations, is an attempt to help people learn more about their real selves. The narrator of *Treviles* refers to *In the Country of the Skin*, which is described as being like Zen practice, where 'the aspirant would imagine very vividly and with every sense some object and event, and then with a stroke of the mind cancel it, saying 'not this, not this'. In doing so he or she found the true self, the user, behind the appearance.'[3] The novel is also said to have 'consisted of small, rapidly created universes which the poet then destroyed by creating another such universe as rapidly, and again, and so on, until he discovered the users of the universe'.[4] Whether the novel actually does achieve this effect is doubtful, but in its use of surrealistic imagery and mystical and mythological references it seems to be trying to capture and recreate the common human imagination, the Joycean uncreated conscience of the race. The narrator says: 'The novel flows from all my pens . . . I am the world telling its story to itself.'[5] This is what Redgrove thinks that both poetry and psychotherapy should do: reunite dream and imagination, which have become separated in the modern world. The psychotherapist, according to Redgrove, tends to treat people as objects in its attempt to be scientific, and only the poet can encompass and recreate the whole individual, which, in turn, will lead to a recreation of society. Explaining the background to the novel, and its portrayal of a split personality, the front cover says 'This novel is a true story. There are two men in one man, held together by their mutual skin'; the back cover then says:

---

[1] ibid.

[2] It won the Guardian Fiction Award for that year.

[3] op. cit. p. 45

[4] op. cit. p. 45

[5] *In The Country of the Skin*. London: Routledge, 1973, p. 4

> Peter Redgrove had fifty insulin shock comas, fifty deaths, for what his doctors perfunctorily classified as 'incipient schizophrenia', in 1950, when he was eighteen. It was this, together with his first experience of sexual love that turned him from science, that understands neither of these things, to poetry, which celebrates everything. He believes that 'neurosis' is initially the honest creative response of a hurt psyche to a dishonest world, and therefore to unwind a neurosis is to unwind truth. If he has unwound it truly in his poetry he believes that the latter may lead others as well as himself into the neurosis-free world that many pine for, though it may be stranger and more wonderful than we expected.

The novel is indeed strange and wonderful, a series of prose poems interspersed with sections of blank verse, but without the note from *Dr Treviles*, warning us not to try to make sense of it, and instead to constantly think 'not this, not this', it is also frustrating, despite the beauty of its language. From the start it is self-referential: 'My novel flows quietly from the spawn-tip of my frog-pen in black lines of yolk. . . The novel flows from all of my pens.'[1] And at the end: 'The book is . . . It is not a book it is a struggling bird I hold it by outstretched wings and it almost gets away but it is a book.'[2] This is a book that aspires to be more than a book: a healing process, certainly for Redgrove, and in his ambition, for the reader also. There is little doubt that the split characters Silas and Jonas are both aspects of Redgrove himself: 'Nobody could say why the treatment worked in cases of incipient schizophrenia, which is how Silas-Jonas had been diagnosed, but it did, they said. It didn't for long, apparently, because they later dropped insulin in favour of antidepressant drugs, and other psychotropics.'[3] The healing intention may even extend to Redgrove and Shuttle's relationship; she may be the Teresa of the novel.

> And Silas must do his magic, and be called Jonas; and Teresa does her magic because she loves Silas, but not Jonas; and she instructs Silas without knowing it; and Silas discovers Jonas with his magic; and Jonas does not love Teresa, and she knows it.[4]

---

[1] p. 4
[2] p. 146
[3] p. 38
[4] p. 14

PETER REDGROVE
THE BEEKEEPERS
A NOVEL

Peter Redgrove
The Sleep of the Great Hypnotist
The Life and Death and Life After Death of a Modern Magician

THE FACILITATORS
or Mister Hole-in-the-Day, a novel by
PETER REDGROVE

THE GOD OF GLASS
by Peter Redgrove
A Morality

george macbeth

Like Peter Redgrove, and born in the same year, George Macbeth (1932-1992) was one of Britain's best-loved, most distinguished and prolific poets. Like Redgrove he also wrote several novels. Born in Scotland, he lived most of his life in England. He studied classics at Oxford and joined the BBC in 1955, where he stayed for over twenty years as a producer of poetry programmes until he resigned in 1976 to write full time. His second wife was the novelist Lisa St Aubin de Terán (his second wife of three as he was her second husband of three); with his third wife he moved to Ireland, where he died of motor neurone disease, which he describes in his late poems. Macbeth was a teacher on one of the first creative writing programmes in the UK, at the London outpost of Tufts University, beginning in 1967.

Macbeth produced a very large number of books in his lifetime, mostly poetry but including several anthologies; of these, twelve books of his own poetry and six anthologies preceded his first novels, two of which, *The Samurai* and *The Transformation* first appeared in 1975. *The Samurai* introduces the seductive female spy Cadbury, who reappears in two further novels: *The Seven Witches* and *Cadbury & the Born Losers*. Cadbury's role is to seduce men for the British Secret Service in a spoof of James Bond and other similar spy fiction. She is reminiscent of other attractive female spies and secret agents of the 1960s like the television characters Cathy Gale (*The Avengers*, 1962-64), Emma Peel (*The Avengers*, 1965-68), Sharron Macready (*The Champions*, 1968-69), Pussy Galore (Ian Fleming's *Goldfinger:* novel, 1959, film, 1964) and comic strip, novel and film character Modesty Blaise (1963 onwards; the original film was made in 1966). These characters were reflected in the pop art of the late 1960s, such as Alan Jones' 'erotic' sculptures like *Chair*, *Table* and *Hat Stand*, 1969. As *The Avengers* has Steed, *The Champions* have Tremayne, and the slightly later *Charlie's Angels* (started 1976) had Charlie, Cadbury has Valerian, though in this case the sexual relationship is explicit. Like the above characters, Cadbury dresses for sexual attraction and seems more of a late 1960s than 1970s character.

> She knew she was worth looking at. She was wearing a chamois leather skirt from Skin, on the Kings Road, and a matching chamois shirt, with sleeves close-fitting on the upper arms and flaring at the wrists. The neckline was cut very low and laced across with chamois strips. Her boots were skin-tight matching suède, zippered to the knee. Underneath these she wore nothing except a pair of black silk panties specially cut to fit her.[1]

Already old-fashioned when it appeared and highly sexist, it was nevertheless a successful franchise, no doubt due to the regular, explicit sex scenes, which Cadbury is described as enjoying. Subtitled 'An Entertainment' it had two successors, and the first two novels were republished and rebranded as '*Cadbury and...*'

The Survivor, 1977 also has a Japanese theme: during the Second World War a Japanese pilot has crashed on a Pacific island and survived. Ashamed to be still alive and ashamed at the death of his daughter, he lives in a lighthouse and in a fantasy world within his own head. Interspersed with passages where his fellow officers search for him are scenes from his imagination, where fantasy, especially sado-erotic sexual fantasy, takes over from reality.

> It was the first time, and he came very quickly, feeling the strange jerking like a source of fear, as he left the girl unsatisfied, writhing in a kind if agony, as it seemed, on the stalks of hay.
>
> He had struck her across the face, then over her breasts, finally thrashing her with his open hand across the reddening buttocks, amazed by the insane desire she seemed to have for such punishment, and by his own increasing wish to go back in again to that squelching place he had been in before.
>
> This time he entered her from behind, more expertly than before, until she relaxed with a sudden convulsive jerk, and he felt his own hot

[1] p. 32

> semen surge again through the inward channel he was coming to understand.
>
> They lay for hours in the sun, his half-clothed body covering hers in the warm hay.
>
> That was the first time he had made love to his daughter.[1]

Like Michel Butor's *La Modification*[2], 1957, Georges Perec's *Un Homme Qui Dort*, 1967, Giles Gordon's *Girl With Red Hair*, 1974 and other novels from the period, *The Transformation*, 1975 uses a second-person narrative, in this case throughout. It creates a disturbing effect: who is the narrator? The novella is divided into three parts: Morning, Afternoon and Evening; the narration in the first part is in the past tense, in the middle section it is in the present and in the last section the future and future perfect; nevertheless, the time and location seem also to move, including scenes in Sebring's mansion and a zeppelin and timescales that seem to waver between the 1930s and the turn of the 19th century. In this short, poetic fantasy the addressee – the 'you' - is a man who has woken up to find he has become a woman, the woman he loves, Alcestis (who, in Euripides, faces death to save her husband).

> You felt paralysed. For a long time you lay rigid, feeling both of your legs change gradually into a pulpy mass of cold. You wanted to move more than anything in the world, but you couldn't.
>
> Then you could. In a sudden fit of movement, you flung back the black sheets and felt yourself lifted in one long running swoop towards the cheval-glass beside the dressing-table.
>
> You looked at yourself.
>
> From head to foot you were naked. It took you a moment to realise why you had screamed, and what had happened.
>
> Then you tried very hard to forget all about yourself. [3]

---

[1] p. 9

[2] published in English as *Second Thoughts* in 1958

[3] p. 12

The man, Guy Sebring, is now in the body of the woman he desires sexually; he has become his own sexual desire: 'you stared again at your new self, the familiar exquisite body you had stood and studied so often.'[1] 'In the sweat of your armpits, you began to smell what had always excited you, the odour of a girl in heat.'[2] This particular transformation obviously brings to mind Ovid's *Metamorphoses* and the myth of Narcissus, whose name is mentioned in the text, though never explicitly explored. The mysteries of identity are never fully solved; everyone has multiple aspects to their personality. 'You were stepping outside yourself, or perhaps back in, or perhaps between the twin selves the preliminaries to the act of love set up as antagonists or contestants.'[3] Is all love narcissistic? Are we always making love to an ideal that is just a projection of ourselves? And what defines our self? Not the places we inhabit.

> You have begun to realise that you are what you are. Your great house and its desolate corridors are your solitary environment, whatever that has to be. They are not the spell of your new being, any more than the carriage or the park. They are only the specialised context of what has taken place.
>
> You are what you are. Even in this dank, removed summer-house, a mile or more from the formal garden, your heavy, soothed thighs lie together around the absence of what you believe you were once desired for, and have come to desire. There is no magic that will lift the burden of being yourself.[4]

In another experimental device, self-reference, Alcestis sees on the dressing-table a book called *The Transformation*, the novel s/he is in. 'Lord Peter likes only boys' he reads there. Lord Peter later appears in the story, along with Alcestis' friend and possible lover Madeleine. To further deepen the gender ambiguity, and the feeling of decadence, Madeleine/Alcestis and Guy/Peter (will) seem to be coupling.

> You will dance with Madeleine beneath the great hanging chandeliers as they sway, watching the million lights wink in their little glass cups like the candles burning in a mosque. You will feel more happy than you have done all day.
>
> As you turn in the close music of the waltz, you will feel the room change. You will dance with Madeleine in a smaller group, in a little room all decorated in black lacquer.

---

[1] p. 17

[2] p. 24

[3] p. 35

[4] p. 45

> You will rest your head on her shoulder, watching the green eyes of the peacocks trailing their tails in gold along the dado. You will breathe in the heavy odour of incense, watch lazily the smoke drifting from a stick smouldering in a vase.
>
> You will know that elsewhere in the ship Lord Peter is dancing with Guy, perhaps already with one hand in the white buttons of his flies. You will rub your belly on Madeleine, enjoying the thought.[1]

The two women will make love and merge both physically and in terms of identity: 'two girls beside the lake in the park. You are one of them, but which one you hardly know.' But at the same time, Alcestis both fantasises about having sex with Guy and is still him, also fantasising about being penetrated by Lord Peter as both Guy and Alcestis. 'You will feel the steady pressure as the organ pierces you, the riven skin of your orifice as the brutal head rolls in and out. You will spread your arms wide, feeling for some hold on the slippery iron, taking whatever is thrust upon you in the crucifixion of your new identity.'[2] At the end, there is the suggestion that it has all been a fantasy, including Madeleine, and that 'you' are simply Guy, all the time in his own body and house, watching Alcestis.

---

[1] p. 83
[2] p. 90

stuart evans

Stuart Evans (1934-1994) was one of the few British novelists who could match Nicholas Mosley in both experimental form and intellectual seriousness; he was likewise not afraid to tackle the 'big questions'. Born in Swansea, Wales, Evans was brought up in a mining village in Glamorgan. He studied at Oxford University and worked, like so many novelists and poets of his generation, at the BBC. His work is not wholeheartedly experimental, though his first two novels[1], which are impressionistic and rather cerebral, do contain reflections both on their own status and on the nature of art in general. Evans's third novel, *The Caves of Alienation*[2], concerns the impossibility of ever adequately portraying or defining the individual; a collage of fictitious materials about an imaginary author, this can certainly be counted as an experimental novel.

In his next two novels, Evans again mixes narrative methods within a novel: in *Centres of Ritual*[3] third person narrative is juxtaposed with first person narratives and journals by various characters, and records of speech with no narrative to create a shifting, uncertain perspective on political and personal events; in *Occupational Debris*[4] the same techniques are employed to create, as in *The Caves of Alienation*, a confused and confusing portrait of a character who has

[1] *Meritocrats*. London: Hutchinson, 1972; *The Gardens of the Casino*. London: Hutchinson, 1974. See also the collection of verse *The Function of the Fool*. London: Hutchinson, 1977

[2] London: Hutchinson ,1977, reprinted in the Library of Wales series, Cardigan: Parthian, 2009

[3] London: Hutchinson, 1978. This is the first in a promised sequence under the general title *Windmill Hill* which is concerned with various aspects of present day liberal intellectual life. *Centres* accurately predict the Social Democratic Party, even naming Roy Jenkins and Shirley Williams.

[4] London: Hutchinson, 1979

died.[1] Before his first novel, Evans had published two volumes of poetry: *Elegy for the Death of a Clown*, 1955 and *Imaginary Gardens with Real Toads*, 1972. He then published another volume of poetry – *The Function of the Fool*, 1977 – before embarking on the Windham Hill series of novels. In addition to all his Evans wrote thrillers with his wife Kay under the pseudonym Hugh Tracy.[2]

Like Julian Mitchell's *The Undiscovered Country* and Emma Tennant's *Bad Sister* Evans' huge work of 1977 *The Caves of Alienation* – far longer than most experimental novels, which tend to be very short – purports to present the life and work of a writer who has died but is in fact imaginary. But where both the above works present a single text purporting to be by the 'author', *The Caves of Alienation* gathers together a collage of materials by and about the dead 'author' Michael Caradock -possibly a reference to the Welsh writer Caradoc Evans (1878-1945) - which, taken together, form a portrait of the man; however, even given such a huge collection of writing, this is necessarily an incomplete portrait and would always be, however much material was presented, and this is presumably Evans' point. It is interesting to compare Evans' 'biography' of Caradock with biographies of real people constructed in this manner:[3] from the traces left by

[1] These became the first two of a five-novel sequence under the series title Windham Hill; the others are: *Temporary Hearths*, 1982; *Houses on the Site*, 1984; *Seasonal Tribal Feasts*, 1987

[2] *Death in Disguise*, 1969; *Career with Death*, 1970; *Death in Reserve*, 1976.

[3] Jonathan Coe's biography of B. S. Johnson is an obvious parallel.

fragments of their lives without an explicit overarching view by an author. All the fragments are just windows into a black box that we can never enter.

It is difficult to know how much irony Evans intended as, on the evidence, Caradock was a mediocre writer and by no means worthy of such a serious volume. It is also difficult to say to what extent Caradock is Evans' alter ego: both were born middle-class in working-class Wales; both went to Oxford and became writers. Caradock had a penchant for older women, but we do not know if this was also true of Evans.

Throughout the text are placed italicised passges which are not credited but appear to be the random, unstructured thoughts of Caradock himself; where everything else is indirect these appear to be direct. Whether they are meant to be scribblings, transcribed tape recordings, or thoughts from inside Caradock's head we do not know; is this the 'real' Caradock? If so, it does not help us to understand him as the thoughts are vague and rambling.

> *The idea that pain ennobles is absurd. Who said that? The question is why suffer bravely.* Gemissez, pleurez, priez. *The stoics were fools like Elizabethan lazars using ratsbane and spearwort and crowfoot to fester small wounds into ugly and noisome sores the better to receive the alms of admiration. Do not suffer reticently. Howl, howl, howl.*
>
> *There is no dignity and all the works of this universe are a mockery of the idea of dignity and decency. Death is not an insult: the wanton childish gods cannot conceive that we are intelligent life and that therefore even when we proclaim the meaninglessness of existence, we should nevertheless say that Death is an insult. How can it be? Death can only be a relief. The inexorable logic of becoming or the blind illogical accident? What matter? Oedipus is blind, Lear mad. The brightness in the Western sky is the red light of burning civilisations yet unborn. Howl: because if you do not howl, the soul grows in upon itself and festers more corrosively than ratsbane applied to a scratch on the fleshed areas of the body. The wanton*

immortal gods understand nothing of our feeble notion that we have souls....[1]

The 'howl' injunction seems to relate to Lear more than Ginsberg but also calls to mind a work by another Welsh writer: Dylan Thomas's villanelle containing the lines 'Do not go gentle into that good night/Rage, rage against the dying of the light'. In some ways these are the most satisfying parts of the work: even though they are meaningless when examined, they have far more poetic strength than the quoted sections of his published work, with echoes of aphoristic and nihilistic philosophers like Schopenhauer, Nietzsche, and E. M. Cioran, as well as the dark mood of *Maldoror* and *Notes from Underground*. Again, it is impossible to know how much this was intended by Evans as deliberate bathos.

In another of many examples of nested commentary, we have one critic discussing another critic's criticism of Caradock: 'Kastner tries to find in him an amalgam of affirmation and nihilism based on Caradock's own interest in the divine, heroic, human cycle broadly after Vico, which is catalysed by the voice of God breathing over chaos.'[2] This is part of a highly pretentious radio broadcast which is presumably intended to typify the worst kind of academic discourse; we presume Evans is satirising this but if so the satire never draws attention to itself. Compared to these high-flown analyses of Caradock's work, his novels themselves, in the 'excerpts' we are given can be highly banal; this could almost be from a 1940s pulp novel.

> 'I suppose,' Roberta Calloway said, 'that you're too high-minded to understand: which is why that silly little alley-cat is giving you such hell. All I wanted was someone to want me. Really want me. I wasn't proving anything to *him*. Who the hell cares? I wanted to prove something to me. I suppose it was silly going for you...'
>
> 'I'm not quite sure what I should say...'
>
> 'What should you say?'
>
> 'Well, there were certainly others who... admired you...'
>
> 'Yes. And I was never quite sure that their socks were clean. If you know what I mean,'
>
> I suppose I should be flattered.'
>
> 'Yes. You should be! It doesn't matter. I don't think I'm oversexed, but I'm thirty-one and I've got a lot of... oh for God's sake, it sounds ridiculous. But I have ordinary female urges. I want physical sex. And if there are any substitutes, I'm not getting those either.'[3]

---

[1] p. 130

[2] p. 374

[3] p. 274

The banality of this and other passages contrasts strongly, and presumably ironically with the high academic seriousness of Caradock's commentators and of his 'official biography' by 'David Hayward'. In the appendix to this biography, Hayward lists and summarises all Caradock's works. The above quote is said to be from a posthumously published novel called *Laocoön*, 1971, whose portentous description in the appendix belies the triviality of the quoted sections.

> *Laocoön* is a dense and rather difficult novel which describes the last year in the life of a philosopher, Landgrave, once an academic, and an unsuccessful creative writer. He has spent much of his life thinking about the problem of mortality, about the future of civilisation and about the function of individuals in an inscrutable universe.[1]

The writer Evans is writing about the writer Caradock writing about the writer Landgrave who is drawing on classical mythology and the poet Spenser. These layers of irony recur throughout the book but raise the question: why are we reading this very long work (Evans' work, that is)? There is very little humour in the irony, deliberately no narrative structure and, unlike most biographies, we are not reading it because we know and are already interested in the person. It is (again, presumably deliberately on Evans' part) difficult to like or even be interested in Caradock. He, his friends and commentators seem mostly pompous and self-centred.

Compared to, say, Borges' short story 'Pierre Menard, Author of the *Quixote*', 1939, another portrait of a fictional author, *Alienation* very much outstays its welcome. The Borges story appeared in English in 1962, the same year as Nabokov's *Pale Fire*, another metafiction involving an imaginary author; unlike *Alienation, Pale Fire* presents only one work by its fictional author, a 999-line poem, and the whole work purports to be the work of a single editor, which gives it a tighter structure; not only is *Pale Fire* wittier and more wicked than *Alienation*, its fictional author was a much better writer and it is also half the length.

---

[1] p. 588

julian mitchell

[Charles] Julian [Humphrey] Mitchell was born in Essex, England, in 1935. He was educated at the prestigious Winchester College and He served in the navy before going to Oxford University, where he took both a BA in history and later an MA, which he completed in 1962 after he had travelled to America on a Harkness Fellowship. He became a freelance writer at this time and has remained one. In the late 1960s he was head of the Arts Council's literature Panel at a time when several of the authors in this study were receiving grants from that body.[1] He published six novels from 1961 to 1968[2] but turned to drama and became well known for his 1981 play *Another Country*, which later became a film. He has subsequently become a prolific writer for theatre and television; Mitchell has adapted many works for stage and screen and won a large number of awards. His first five novels were well-received, being skilfully-constructed novels of English manners and he was variously compared to Graham Greene and Angus Wilson, winning two major awards for *The White Father*.

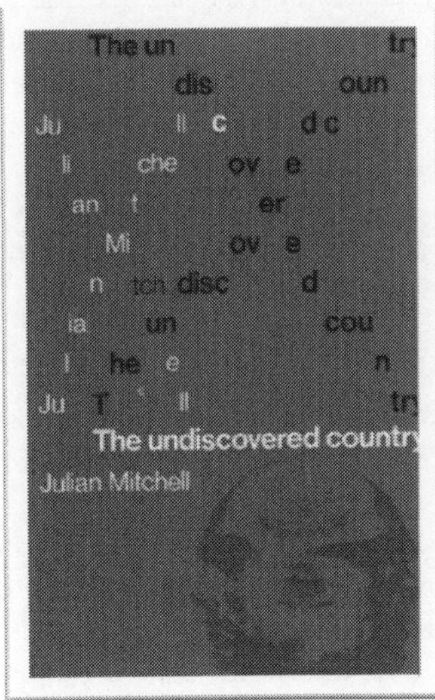

[1] As we have seen, John Calder blamed the Arts Council for giving out grants in a single payment, giving some unstable writers more money than they could handle.

[2] *Imaginary Toys*, 1961; *A Disturbing Influence*, 1962; *As Far As You Can Go*, 1963; *The White Father*, 1964; *A Circle of Friends*, 1966; *The Undiscovered Country*, 1968

Like Stuart Evans' *The Caves of Alienation* and Emma Tennant's *Bad Sister*, Mitchell's sixth and last novel before he turned full-time to play-and screenwriting, *The Undiscovered Country*, 1968 purports to present the work of an author who is in fact fictional. It is not only a novel within a novel but an experimental novel within a novel. In the first part, the narrator, called Julian Mitchell, recounts memoirs of his childhood and youth, where he meets and re-meets his childhood friend, Charles Humphries (more or less Mitchell's two other forenames), who is in some ways his alter ego and the person he desires to be: 'he's my oldest friend, my alter ego, my doppelganger, my secret sharer, my - '.[1] In an interjection the narration flashes forward to Charles' death; the narrator reflects: '*I am a minor novelist, telling the literal truth. I am a character in one of my own books. Yet I feel I am really a character in one of his. He never wrote it, and I don't know what to do or say.*'[2] The novel plays this game of mirrors: is the character Julian Mitchell an invention of the novelist Julian Mitchell, or merely an aspect of the character Charles Humphreys? Though both characters are obviously inventions of the novelist Mitchell, he is asking us to consider the possibility that the novelist himself is the product of his own imagination: the Humphreys side of his personality may be to some extent his creative force.

The novel was published in 1968, the year in which homosexual acts between consenting adults became legal in England; there is an obviously sexual side to their relationship though they never actually have sex together and Charles in fact seems to have a series of girlfriends. There is a hint of the bisexuality usually said to be prevalent in both public school and the navy while Julian is on leave. He reflects on the limited opportunities for sexual relief while on shore:

> if you gave a lift to an escaping Borstal boy, said our engineer officer, he might give you a quick one, but that was about it. Quite soon, though, I told myself, I would leave the navy's obscenities behind and go to Oxford, where the girls would form an orderly queue to enjoy the embraces of a mature amorist who also wrote some of the most passionate love-lyrics of his or any other time.[3]

Julian in fact has no real relationships with either sex, at least as presented in these memoirs, but seems to have always had ambiguous sexual feelings about Charles which he has never fully resolved, even after Charles's death. '*Yet it is still hard to tell the truth. Not to admit that, had you asked me, I would have followed you into the bedroom; not to confess that I was throbbing and aching with hope and fear.*'[4]

---

[1] p. 130

[2] p. 79

[3] p. 50

[4] p. 80

The facts and dates of the memoirs closely parallel Mitchell's real life: they form a 'self-portrait with imaginary friend'. Like the real Julian Mitchell, the narrator Julian Mitchell goes to Winchester public school and Oxford, serves in the submarine corps and wins a Harkness Fellowship to travel in America before returning to Oxford to complete his MA. The narrator has also written novels with the same titles as Mitchell's actual novels. He meets Charles at all of these key stages of his life and these form a series of snapshots of an upper-class literary life from the mid-1950s to the early 1960s. One of these snapshots is of his trip to Los Angeles in 1959, which makes him see 'both the hothouse academic life of Oxford and the refrigerated literary life of London as extraordinarily provincial. Not before time I realized that there were other standards of value besides those of All Souls and the *New Statesman*.'[1] However he does not entirely approve of American West Coast culture either.

> At that time Venice was full of beatniks, bearded, self-consciously dirty men and carefully sloppy women who talked without humour about the horrors of the American way of life and quoted cryptic Zen Buddhist injunctions in the translations of Allen W. Watts and D. T. Suzuki. Poets and novelists were their heroes – Ginsberg, Corso, Kerouac, Burroughs – and they smoked marijuana almost on principle and were extremely pleased when people made offensive remarks about them in the street. Their refusal to join in conventional American life was, I suppose, theoretically admirable; but the beats I knew were too muddled or lazy to enunciate anything approaching an alternative philosophy. They seemed to be sleep-walking through life, to be living only as symbols of revolt, never as revolutionaries.[2]

Whenever they meet as adults, Julian and Charles discuss literature; Julian has always wanted to be a poet though he has not produced much but the verses Charles shows to him are very bad indeed. It is not until after Charles's death that Julian has any knowledge of the manuscript of his (experimental) novel *The New Satyricon*. Charles has always encouraged Julian as a novelist; and a certain type of novel at that.

> Charles wished I'd stick to the novel, and the contemporary novel at that. Now that philosophy had abdicated its traditional role as explicator of the mysteries of life, the novel had taken over. Novels were written and read for what sense they made of the world: that was their true

[1] p. 95
[2] p. 96

> importance. They were immediate; if they survived, that was because certain features of the society to which they were relevant survived also.[1]

In their discussions 'Charles was always caustic about novelists' 'unscrupulous lying'. I used to argue for the illusion of realism through the elimination of the author from his work; Charles said the only honest thing for a writer to do was to display himself in and through his book.'[2] The book Charles left for Julian, *The New Satyricon* forms the second part of the novel *The Undiscovered Country*. It is certainly not a conventional novel; it makes no sense of the world but creates a strange new sexually-charged world, or series of worlds, a foreign land through which the bisexual and later transsexual Henry travels in a picaresque journey like a Tristram Shandy or a Gulliver (or, perhaps, in his female aspect a Fanny Hill). The text is fragmentary, not because it is incomplete but because this is how Charles intended it. The narrator Julian introduces the text and intersperses it with his own italicised, rather disingenuous interpretations. The introduction relates the work to its model, the *Satyricon* of Petronius, a Latin work which is already a satire of earlier works. The central character, Encolpius ('crotch') is 'a crook, a lecher, a pervert, wicked, witty and delightful'; presumably how Charles has seen himself, though Julian warns us against identifying Henry too closely with Charles. What we have of the Petronius text is fragmentary:

> The fragmentariness itself undoubtedly appealed to him. He once said to me that the traditional narrative line of the novel was of no interest to him. 'Why bother with all those boring explanations?' he said. 'Why tell people how A got from B to C? Why not just have characters and scenes?' When I protested that people would get lost or bored without some thread of plot, he agreed. 'Of course one must have connections between scenes,' he said. 'But if the same characters keep reappearing, that's all you need.'[3]

The narration jumps from one scene to another and even within scenes there are cinematic cuts and jumps in the middle of sentences; we are never told how 'A got from B to C'.

Arriving in a strange new country Henry catches sight of the back of a person – he does not even know if it is male or female – whom he falls in love with and spends the rest of the book pursuing. He first encounters the Encolpians, a society dedicated to 'the scholarship of the sexual appetite, and relates scenes that might have come from *The 120 Days of Sodom*. After Henry attends a strange theatre performance, there is a section which, according to

---

[1] p. 138
[2] p. 177
[3] p. 175

Julian's note, is a parody of James Bond where Bond is Jewish and the villain a Nazi; the Bond figure represents both Christ and Isaac, son of Abraham. Following this scene, Henry is suddenly a spectator at the Ideal Mother competition.

> . . . death for at the end of this hideous rite, Milo said, the sons were stripped and paraded before the mothers, then sacrificed on the naked belly of the Ideal Mother herself, after which the judgers were blinded, their tongues cut out, their hands looped, and their. . .
>
> Then, for the first time in my life, I gave solemn thanks to the inventor of television, whoever he may have been, a matter on which there is still, I believe, some international contention.
>
> . . . a familiarity which I could not explain, for I felt at once a stranger, as of course I was, and yet an old inhabitant, perhaps one who, having lived here many years earlier, was now returning to his native place, though this was naturally not so, for it was my first visit to the country, and the manners and customs of the people, in some ways superficially similar to those of my homeland, proved on closer inspection extremely strange and baffling, so that I felt almost as though the walls which I had taken to be solid might in fact yield to my touch if I pressed them with my fingers, and I found myself walking with exaggerated care along the corridor, keeping studiously to the dead centre of the thick pile carpets whose colours changed from bend to bend.[1]

After this Henry puts on a woman's dress and becomes a woman, staying female (or hermaphroditic) for the rest of the work. '. . . vanished utterly, and their proud place now gaped with an astounding openness, even though I could not even then help noticing that there were certain advantages as to the arrangement of . . .'[2] Henry tells a fable about ducks which Julian calls '*an extraordinary tour de force*', and which Julian says he wishes he had written (another reminder that this is a metafiction). Towards the end, to add the possibility of incest to the bisexuality, Henry begins to realise that the object of his love and pursuit 'strongly resembled my elder sister and brother, the twins who had given me a deep sense of isolation in my earliest childhood' as well as his mother. Then, at the very end, as Henry calls 'Come to me, my bride and groom, my beloved!' he hears 'the voice of the man I most loathed in all the world, my own father'.

---

[1] pp. 235/236. Elisions and spacing in the original

[2] pp. 238/239 Elisions in the original

I let him pick me up and lay me on the marble slab like a ram on an altar, let him draw from beneath his towel a gleaming blade, let him hold it, as though to bless, above me. As he did so I became aware of many familiar faces about him, though how in my blindness I knew . . .

. . . all whom I had ever loved, rank upon rank of them like angels, each with the face of my beloved, and my mother, praying at my head, and my brothers and sisters at my side and all the company of . . .

. . . mixing piety and love and detestation, pride and humility, indifference and care, the face of my beloved never changing as the hands raised the knife, nor when it fell with great force upon me, to the sweet lamentation of my abandoned loves, who . . .

. . . suspended between life and death, changing from gender to gender, no longer mine but the fluid shape of their imaginations, as they followed that first mortal assault with their own grave and loving farewells, each and none my beloved, my expiring self ready at last to give what . . .

. . . coughing and sighing . . .

. . . no trumpets, no clarinets, neither trombone nor bassoon, nor any singing. . .

. . . black . . .

. . . black . . .

. . . black . . .

BLACK
BLACK
BLACK[1]

---

[1] pp. 305/307

d.m. thomas

Like Penelope Shuttle and Peter Redgrove[1], also strongly associated with Cornwall, D[onald] M[ichael] Thomas was primarily a poet who turned to writing poetic novels[2]. Born in Cornwall in 1935 he took a degree in English at New College, Oxford and then worked for fifteen years as a lecturer in English, becoming head of English at Hereford College until he gave up teaching to become a full-time writer. Having learnt Russian while he was doing national service he returned to Oxford in 1978 to do research in verse translation. By this time he had already translated one volume of Anna Akhmatova and subsequently translated another.[3] Up to 1981 he had published several volumes of verse[4] and a children's book[5] and edited three books of Cornish poetry; he also had stories and poems published in Michael Moorcock's *New Worlds* magazine in the late 1960s and early 1970s[6].

His first novel, *The Flute Player,* 1979 was published by Gollancz's Fantasy imprint, which also published Angela Carter, Philip Pullman, Thomas M. Disch,

[1] Thomas and Redgrove appeared together in Penguin's *Modern Poets 11*.
[2] From 1983 onwards he continued to publish novels on an almost annual basis until 2000.
[3] *Requiem* and *Poem without a Hero,* 1976; *Way of All the Earth,* 1979. He would subsequently translate Yevtushenko and Pushkin.
[4] *Personal and Possessive*. London: Outposts, 1964; Penguin *Modern Poets 11*. London: Penguin, 1968; *Two Voices*. London: Cape Goliard, 1968; The *Lover's Horoscope*. Laramie, Wyoming: Purple Sage, 1970; Logan *Stone*. London: Cape Goliard, 1971; *The Shaft*. Gillingham, Kent: Arc, 1973; *Lilith Prints*. Cardiff: Second Aeon, 1974; *Symphony in Moscow*. Richmond, Surrey, Keepsake, 1974; *Love and Other Deaths*. London: Elek, 1975; The *Rock*. Knotting, Bedfordshire: Sceptre, 1975; Orpheus *in Hell*. Knotting, Bedfordshire: Sceptre, 1977; *The Honeymoon Voyage*. London: Secker & Warburg, 1978; *Dreaming in Bronze*. London: Secker & Warburg, 1981
[5] *The Devil and the Floral Dance*. London: Robson, 1978
[6] *New Worlds* 193, August 1969; *New Worlds* 5, 1972 (which also included Brian W. Aldiss and an early version of Emma Tennant's *The Crack*); *New Worlds* 6, 1973 (which also included a story by Giles Gordon); also in Langdon Jones' *The New S.F.: An Original Anthology of Modern Speculative Fiction*. London: Arrow, 1970

Ursula Le Guin and Emma Tennant's *The Bad Sister*. Thomas' novel won the Gollancz and Pan/Picador Fantasy Competition. It is dedicated to Akhmatova, Osip Mandelstam, Boris Pasternak and Marina Tsvetaeva and set in an unnamed and chaotic city not unlike St Petersburg in a country not unlike Russia, where there is 'luxury for the few and hunger for the many.'[1] The central characters are Michael, a poet, and a group of artists and musicians who are sometimes persecuted by the authorities but at other times are seen as valued members of society. The 'flute-player', Elena is an artists' model but becomes a prostitute to please her sick husband and to enable her to feed him; she can 'only endure her clients by trying to love them – in the spirit – however briefly. It was very difficult. They made it so. It shocked her at first to find out how odd people were – men anyway – how few of them wanted normal sex.'[2] There is a lot of strange sex and Elena drifts through the novel and the disintegrating society as a sort of angel of sexual and social service, always submissive to the needs of others.

The next novel, *Birthstone,* 1980, also published by Gollancz Fantasy is basically a gently comic Cornish tale, but becomes more of a fantasy when a visiting American couple go through a local stone formation and the woman begins to grow younger and changes personality. There is again much writing about strange sex and gender confusion by the narrator, who may be Jo, Joe or Joanne.

[1] p. 102
[2] p. 28

The White Hotel may be the best-selling of all British experimental novels: it was the number one seller in Britain for six weeks and number two in America; it has since been translated into thirty languages. Like many experimental novels it purports to present a series of documents relating to a real individual. In this case they purport to be case notes on and original documents by 'Anna G' a patient of Sigmund Freud's; he forwards them with a covering letter, dated Vienna 1931.

> I hope you will not be alarmed by the obscene expressions scattered through her poor verses, nor by the somewhat less offensive, but still pornographic, material in the expansion of her phantasy. It should be borne in mind that (a) their author was suffering from a severe sexual hysteria, and (b) the compositions belong to the realm of science, where the principle of *nihil humanum* is universally accepted and applied.[1]

The documents take several different forms: verses for Freud concerning her fantasised relationship with his son, which she is said to have written between the lines of the score of Don Giovanni[2]; a journal kept by Anna in Gastein, though narrated in the third person; case notes kept by Freud and a section about the Babi Yar massacre in the Ukraine in 1941, which draws heavily on (some people have said it plagiarises) Anatoly Kuznetsov's *Babi Yar: A Document in the Form of a Novel*, 1966[3]. The 'Don Giovanni' verses set the tone for her sexual fantasies:

> I have started an affair
> with your son, on a train somewhere
> in a dark tunnel, his hand was underneath
> my dress between my thighs I could not breathe
> he took me to a white lakeside hotel
> somewhere high up, the lake was emerald
> I could not stop myself I was in flames
> from the first spreading of my thighs, no shame
> could make me push my dress down, thrust his hand
> away, the two, then three, fingers he jammed
> into me though the guard brushed the glass[4]

In the middle of the 'Gastein Journal' section there are a series of 'postcards' from the white hotel, apparently sent by a variety of guests. They describe a fire which

---

[1] p. 15

[2] First published as a separate poem in *New Worlds*, 1979

[3] It was first published in a heavily-censored form in a Soviet magazine; Kuznetsov later defected to the West and the whole text was published in English in 1970.

[4] p. 19

consumes the hotel and during which a number of people have died. But the 'young couple' continue to have constant, graphically-described sex. Later, in the 'Health Resort' section 'Anna' now seeming perfectly lucid and having got over her fantasies, indeed denying she ever had them, tells Freud that she wrote the verses while snowbound and bored at Gastein; she was actually there with her aunt rather than any lover. 'I wanted it to be shocking; or rather, I wanted it to be honest to my complicated feelings about sex, and I also wanted my aunt to know what I was really like. I left it lying around and she read it. You can imagine how horrified she was.' She does admit, however that she had been 'crazy': 'when you suggested I write something, I thought I'd try you with the verses. So I copied them out in my score of *Don Giovanni*. I don't know why I did that. It shows I was crazy.' She tells Freud that the reason she had written the Journal in the third person was in response to his request. 'When you asked for an interpretation I thought I'd turn it into the third person to see if that would help me make sense of it. But it didn't. I needed *you* to do that.'[1]

In the sections attributed to Freud himself, he discusses the Journal:

> I now had the ludicrous sensation that I knew absolutely all there was to know about Frau Anna, except the cause of her hysteria. And a second paradox arose: the more convinced I grew that the "Gastein Journal" was a remarkably courageous document, the more ashamed Anna became of having written so disgusting a work. She could not imagine where she heard the indelicate expressions, or why she had seen fit to use them. She begged me to destroy her writings, for they were only devilish fragments thrown off by the "storm in her head" – itself a result of her joy at being once more free from pain. I told her I was interested only in penetrating to the truths which I was sure her remarkable document contained; adding that I was very glad she had evaded the censor, the train guard, on her way to the white hotel![2]

In the 'Sleeping Carriage' section, the heroine, whose real name turns out to be Lisa Erdman, an opera singer, is caught up in the Babi Yar massacre, which happened in real life on September 29th and 30th 1941, the largest of the Nazi massacres, in which over 33,000 Jews were killed.[3] 'The thirty thousand became a quarter of a million. A quarter of a million white hotels in Babi Yar.'[4] Lisa is killed but 'a part of her goes on living with those survivors'. In the final section, 'The Camp', Lisa appears again, in what seems to be both a transit camp and a

---

[1] p. 164

[2] pp. 106/107

[3] In addition to Kuznetsov's book, it was the subject of Shostakovich's 13th Symphony, first performed in 1962

[4] p. 221

Jewish heaven, though 'it seemed you did not have to be Jewish to be here; for her mother was on the lists.'[1]

> "Well, it's over," said Lisa, taking her mother's hand. Gradually the woman became calm.
>
> "Anyway," continued Lisa, "I think wherever there is love, of *any* kind, there is hope of salvation." She had an image of a bayonet flashing over spread thighs, and corrected herself hastily: "Wherever there is love in the heart."
>
> "Tenderness."
>
> "Yes, exactly!"
>
> They strolled further along the shore. The sun was lower in the sky and the day cooler. The raven came skimming back, and a shiver ran up Lisa's spine. She stopped. "Is this the Dead Sea?" she asked.
>
> "Oh, no!" said her mother, with a silvery laugh; and explained that it was fed by the Jordan River, and that river, in turn, was fed by the brook Cherith. "So you can see the water is always pure and fresh." Her daughter nodded, greatly relieved, and the two women walked on.[2]

[1] p. 228
[2] p. 238

tom phillips

Born in 1937, Tom Phillips is an artist not a novelist, though he has also written an opera and collaborated on a film with Peter Greenaway. He is a member of the highly prestigious Royal Academy, the highest honour for a British artist. In 1966 he set out to find a novel that he could buy for threepence (then roughly equivalent to a US dime) and 'treat.' He found *A Human Document* by the obscure Victorian author W. H. Mallock and turned it into *A Humument* by painting over all its 367 pages, creating 367 artworks and leaving visible small selections of text, which tell an altogether different story. The resulting works were first published, unbound, in 1973 and then as a bound book in 1980; Phillips has continued to work on it ever since.[1]

> Like most projects that end up lasting a lifetime this had its germ in idle play at what then seemed to be the fringe of my activities. A liking for words plus the related influences of William Burroughs and John Cage with their use of chance had led me into casual experiments with partly obliterated texts, mostly in the columns of *The Spectator*. By the date of the encounter with Mallock I had already begun to toy with the idea of treating a book in the same fashion. . . It was while I was experimenting with ways of combining pages that the book's christening took place, again by a chance discovery. By folding one page in half and turning it back to reveal half of the following page, the running title along the top abridged itself to A HUMUMENT, an earthy word with echoes of humanity and monument as well as a sense of something hewn; or exhumed to end up in the muniment rooms of the archived world.[2]

The resulting novel is a philosophical and poetic treatise, with elements of a love story, even containing a hero, or perhaps anti-hero: Bill Toge; Bill is short for William, the W in W. H. Mallock and 'would provide a good matey name for his more humdrum alter ego. When I chanced on 'bill' it appeared next to the word 'together' and thus the distinctly downcast and blokeish name Bill Toge was born.' Phillips introduced strict rules into his novel-game: wherever the words 'together' or 'altogether appeared in the original text, Toge would appear; the words of the original text are never 'shunted around opportunistically: they must stay where they are on the page. Where they are joined to make some poetic sense or meaningful continuity, they are linked by the often meandering rivers in

[1] It is now in its fifth edition as of 2011. The latest edition contains a page referring to 9/11 in New York, and one that contains the words 'facebook' and 'app'; the work is in fact now available as an app for iPhone and iPod, surely the ultimate aim for any experimental novel.
[22] 'Notes on *A Humument*', fifth edition, no page numbers

the typography as they run, with no short cuts.' Other characters appear, particularly Irma, and at one point there is even mention of the Unauthor.

Phillips has talked about his attempt to create a Wagnerian *Gesamtkunstwerk;* obviously *A Humument* has no music or staging, though he has created an opera, *Irma*, based on the text and one of the characters from the book. In that sense *A Humument* is closest to Jeff Nuttall, if only in the sense of integrating words and images, though Nuttall builds up from nothing where Phillips and Burroughs (also Robert Rauschenberg in his John Cage-influenced *Erased de Kooning*, 1953) strip away what is already there to create new works. Out of context, some of the 'poems' Phillips creates from the existing text do work very well by themselves. There is the almost Zen-like:

words
in winter.
cold
like
the other side of the
mother-
star[1]

This could almost be a translation of a poem by Paul Celan, a Sappho translation by Anne Carson, or a fragment of Ann Quin.

[1] p. 226

after the
Unauthor
end
ship
into endship. The virtual
language fusal
in
characters peraments of
the character
of ossib
time dang
anquil
tomary anquil
bling[1]

---

art
took
ornament
as water
found
desert
and
love
night[2]

---

[1] p. 113
[2] p. 130

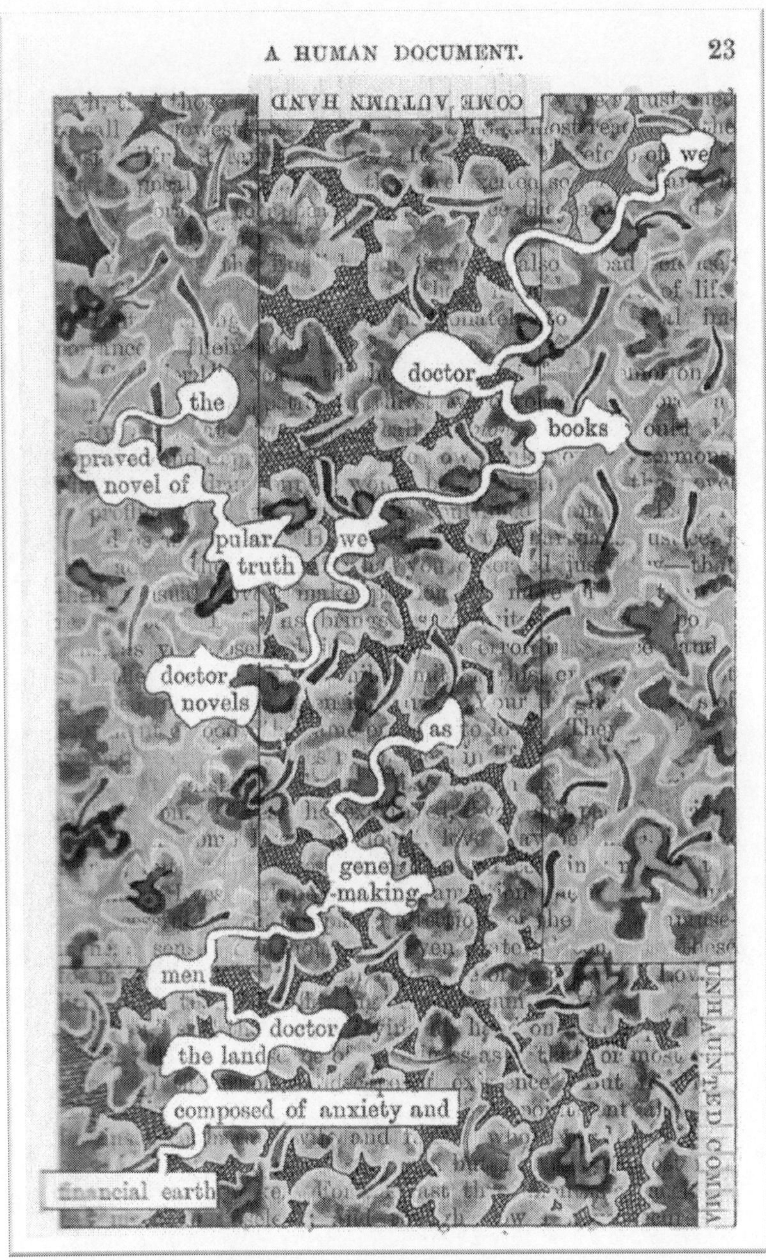
A HUMAN DOCUMENT.
23
COME AUTUMN HAND
of we
doctor
books
the
praved
novel of
pular
truth
we
doctor
novels
as
gene
-making
men
doctor
the land
composed of anxiety and
financial earth
UNHAUNTED COMMA

emma tennant

Bananas began in January 1975 with a specific aim. This was to introduce to as many readers as possible a selection of lively new writing by known and unknown writers, and to prove, in a country where 'little magazines' are virtually unread and undistributed, that people do take an interest in fiction of a high standard if they can get hold of it. The appearance and attitude of most of the magazines of writing and criticism seemed dreary and academic, despite the often excellent contents, and it was for this reason that we chose to make *Bananas* a newspaper: you could read stories as if they were the latest reports from the writer's brain rather than 'timeless' literature, and have the space for big, arresting illustrations and original drawings as well.[1]

Bananas was intended to capture 'the mix of irreverence, excellence in writing and sheer wackiness that seems right nowadays'[2]. As founder and editor, Emma Tennant, born 1937, was at the centre of the alternative literary scene. Basing *Bananas* in a house with a 'façade painted a bright psychedelic design and thus unmissable, as far as mad poets and would-be contributors are concerned'[3] in the then seedy, bohemian Notting Hill area of London, Tennant was a neighbour of Michael Moorcock and friend of J. G. Ballard, Angela Carter, Elaine

[1] Introduction to *Bananas*, ed. Emma Tennant. Colchester, Essex: Blond & Briggs, 1977

[2] *Burnt Diaries*. Edinburgh: Canongate, 1999, p. 22

[3] *Burnt Diaries*, p. 24

Feinstein and many other novelists and poets.'[1] Although closely connected with emerging writers she had never been part of the post-structuralist, French-influenced avant-garde; describing her time in the Paris of 1968, during the 'second French Revolution', she recalls:

> We walk on, to the rue St-Sévérin, where we have a room not far from the falling trees and burning cars of this new Paris, and we go out again, to the Joie de Lire, to buy Althusser, Barthes, Fanon and Foucault: I understand very little of these, and my comrade, who makes light of his role as an intellectual of the *New Left Review* brigade, seems to grasp them as little as I, in the original French at least.[2]

Not long before starting *Bananas* Tennant had started to publish novels. Her first, *The Colour of Rain*, was published under the pseudonym Catherine Aydy and the first under her own name was *The Time of the Crack*, 1973, part of which had previously been published in Michael Moorcock's *New Worlds*. Appropriately, it is an apocalyptic novel like much of the New Wave Science Fiction Moorcock published, but in this case it is also a social satire. London cracks along the River Thames and the 'clairvoyant and palmist' Medea Smith leads a group of women south of the river to a promised new world, followed by the Playboy Bunny girl Baba. Medea shows them her vision, in a 'black voice that filled the church'. 'Sisters, we are preparing ourselves to reach the Other Side. There will be tribulations, as our oppressors will try to stop us. But let me tell you what awaits us there. A matriarchal society.'[3] Medea's voice fills the air across London: 'The river is exhausted, the banks are wide, A new life for women on the other side.'[4] And later: 'I speak to you of the other side. None of the troubles of the old life are to be found there. Harmony, peace and pleasure will be ours. The goddess will be restored to her throne.'[5] But Medea fails and the dream

[1] She also, according to *Burnt Diaries* had a close relationship with Ted Hughes.

[2] Emma Tennant. *Girlitude*. London: Jonathan Cape, 1999, p. 213

[3] p. 42

[4] p. 85

[5] p. 95

of a new sisterhood vanishes; the women are again 'prisoners: wives and mothers'[1].

The Last of the Country House Murders, 1974, also combines social satire with a post-apocalyptic setting: England after the Revolution. Jules Tanner, the last survivor of the old upper class, who lives in the last country house, is to be murdered by the government as entertainment for the people. The government agent Haines has to select the murderer and arrange a suitably entertaining crime. Showing him round the house, the aesthete Jules tells Haines: 'This is the room where Gertrude Stein and I discussed *Tender Buttons*. Oddly enough the very room where Edith Wharton told me she was in love with Henry James'[2]. But identities become blurred and confused, the wrong man is murdered and the rebel army overturn the new order.

Hotel de Dream, 1976, is also a comedy of manners, not totally unlike Muriel Spark's *Memento Mori*, but as the dreams of the characters – residents in a boarding house – merge and conflict with each other, it also turns into an apocalyptic metaphor of a disintegrating society. The residents enter each other's dreams and the dreams eventually escape into the outside world and cause chaos. There are stories within stories and dreams within dreams: in Mrs Houghton's Fable, the characters in the story listen to the tale and watch as the scene changes around them. 'The characters held hands briefly, and as they did so the scene changed again'. They listen to the voice of their author dictating their

[1] p. 108
[2] p. 62

actions while trying to imagine alternatives.

> "I thought we were going to be free," Melinda cried. "That's the whole point Johnny, surely."
>
> "Yes. But I have doubts." Johnny gave a shamefaced smile. "Suppose we weren't free after all. We'd be stuck forever just before the end of the book. In the traffic jam on the motorway . . . for eternity. Think of that."
>
> "Yes," Melinda considered. "And if we were fee it might not be the kind of life we wanted. If we made her change the end . . ."[1]

They go to see Mrs Houghton and as ''the travel-stained characters stood pale in front of the author' she writes their parting and Melinda's suicide. '"The End," Mrs Houghton said snappily when she had finished. "Now are you both satisfied?"'[2]

The Bad Sister, 1978 is in the form of the novel in a novel, where the narrator purports to have inherited or discovered a journal or work of fiction which they are introducing; like Stuart Evans' *The Caves of Alienation* and Julian Mitchell's *The Undiscovered Country.* Tennant said of the writing of it:

> I've been lying low, trying to write The *Bad Sister*, a novel which takes as its inspiration [Scottish writer] James Hogg's Confessions of a Justified Sinner [1824]. It's a book of doubles, of female doubles, and has as its centre the belief held by ultra-feminists that they are above moral judgement. It was Heathcote [Williams] who told me that somewhere in Notting Hill there is a large, dilapidated house full of ferocious women with their love-children, all of whom are given the surname Wild. From this comes the name of my anti-heroine: Jane Wild.[3]

---

[1] p. 164
[2] p. 175
[3] *Burnt Diaries*, p. 117

Tennant herself rejects the sisterhood of witches: talking about her relationship with Ted Hughes, she says 'I am caught in the spell cast by Ted, the master magician, and there is no way out.' But she rejects the 'hermeneutics' he offers her; the 'School of Witches he would have me join leads, I know, to madness, despair, suicide.' She refuses to make a pact with the devil – with whom Hughes 'plays', even if 'the words I wrote were suddenly lit by genius.' She relates these feeling to the novel she has just finished:

> I see my novel, *The Bad Sister,* as a terrifying portent of the schizophrenic world into which I am drawn. 'Bathed in magic' is Angela Carter's epithet when I send it to her, and this will appear on the cover. It sounds as cosy as the box of chocs and crackling autumn fire it conjures up. In fact, my examination of the female double is already surrounded by inexplicable coincidences and an aura which is 'magical', but not in any fashion-word sense.[1]

The first and last parts of the novel purport to be editor's notes by a person who is making a documentary about the unsolved murders of the Scottish landowner, Dalzell and his daughter. The 'editor' believes the murders were committed by Jane, the landowner's other, illegitimate daughter who had been living in a community of women led by the mysterious, witch-like Meg. We are then presented with 'The Journal of Jane Wild', a poetic, sometimes hallucinogenic account of events by Jane herself. Meg appears in the journal, with mysterious powers, as does Gil-Martin, the shape-shifter in James Hogg's novel. However the ending note also presents a report by a psychiatrist who believes Jane is schizophrenic, and therefore may have invented the whole thing. The editor speculates as to whether this is really an example, as some women would have it now, of the inherent 'splitness' of women, a condition passed on from divided mother to divided daughter until such day as they regain their vanished power?'[2] Jane does see herself as one half – the 'bad sister' – of a pair.

> I am the bad throw of the dice. I am the double, now it's me who's become the shadow. Where I was haunted, now I will pursue. And the world will try to stamp me out, as I run like a grey replica of my vanished self – evil, unwanted, voracious in my needs. I will be outcast, dodging the steps of stronger women, fastening myself onto them at nights, trailing as their lying shadow in the day. Unless . . . bringing the world to rights . . . bringing to Meg's red altar the essential sacrifice . . . I

[1] *Burnt Diaries,* p. 138

[2] p. 216

> am restored to life and greenness and in tearing out the simulacrum need no longer live like one myself.[1]

Meg urges her to get rid of her alter ego: 'inside you day and night, enemy or friend, enemy shadow . . . or sister . . . I've seen her . . . she dogs you day and night. Oh yes . . . I know. And only when you are rid of her will you go to the port again.' But Meg will always demand something in return for her help.

> I could feel, now, that my shadows had been removed and that I was allowed to sample, for a while, the feeling of completeness. It was as if she had given me something else in place of the bad sister, something that made me as strong and round as the beginning of the world. For this feeling I would do anything she asked. I was an addict already, dreaming on the white-grained step, emptiness blocked out. My sisters had been nightmares. Meg would help me drive them away, black bats of uncertainty and loneliness and despair. . . I knew Meg wanted to take, in return for this, everything I had: my salvation would be paid for in blood, but never hers.[2]

If she takes Meg's help she will become 'a living shadow, a walking, living being without a shadow, a drinker of blood, a nightwalker in perpetual and thwarted search of day, a white skin without blood, a dark predator, a victim.'[3] At the end of her journal, in which she never confesses to killing her father or even mentions him, she does appear to kill Miranda, her boyfriend's former girlfriend, whom she has come to see as her half-sister (whose name we are never told by the 'reliable narrator' the editor). She appears to see herself as the vampire she has imagined: 'I close in on her . . . my teeth go into her smooth neck. Miranda . . . these are the hours . . . when it's so dark outside that I can fly the streets without dread of the stake, ravenous, insatiable!'[4] At the end of her journal, Jane goes out to meet the spectre of Hogg's novel. 'Gil-martin comes towards me. The ship sails through the deep folds of the hills. I knew he would be there waiting for me!'[5]

---

[1] p. 148

[2] p. 120

[3] p. 121

[4] p. 209

[5] p. 211

Wild Nights, 1979 and *Alice Fell*, 1980 are very different: both mythopoeic novels about small family situations become epic through the eyes of a young person (though in third person narratives). At the time of writing them Tennant was the friend and publisher of Angela Carter, whose *The Company of Wolves* was first published in *Bananas*, and they have something of Carter's magic realism, while being completely distinctive. In an Autumn 1979 note, Tennant says. 'Back from Scotland, where I gave a huge party to celebrate the publication of *The Bad Sister* and *Wild Nights*, the latter a fantastical account of my family here in the past – so both books are Scottish in origin.'[1] In the fantastic world of *Wild Nights*, the past and present coincide in a magical imagination and the seasons have personalities of their own. As the novel begins the narrator's Aunt Zita, a magical, mystical, mythical creature in the narrator's description, arrives at their house, with her imaginary retinue of 'courtiers, dwarfs, turbaned merchants' and her yellow diamond[2], summoning up 'long dead relations'[3].

> When my aunt Zita came, there were changes everywhere. The days outside, which were long and white at that time of year, closed and turned like a shutter, a sharp blue night coming on sudden and unexpected as a finger caught on a hinge. The house shrank; the walls seemed to lean inwards; my mother's shoulders grew hunched, as if she were trying to ward off some weight that was bound to descend from above. The people in the house were as sensitive as oysters.[4]

---

[1] *Burnt Diaries*, p. 209

[2] p. 34

[3] p. 30

[4] p. 5

As in *The Time of the Crack* and *Alice Fell*, the worlds of men and women are completely separate; women have magical powers not understood by men.[1] But the women never succeed in forging a completely separate, independent world. In *Alice Fell*, the Old Man is disturbed at the birth of Alice, which, despite the novel's mythic quality, is specifically set in the year of the Suez Crisis, as an old age of empire and certainty is disappearing.

> The Old Man went to the furthest room, and looked at the Blue Women and then out of the window at the downs. The sudden arrival of Alice in this house filled him with unease and misgivings. He no longer knew if the women in the tapestry, his tormented idols, had also fallen, from lack of fulfilment, lack of love or ambitions realised, into their attitudes of woven despair. He saw, for a moment as the clouds danced like buffoons before being blown away altogether to the valleys beyond the downs, that Molly and Pam had fallen too in their effort to be independent, to be new.[2]

The women are the servants of the house and they wait 'for the house to accommodate to them in return for their obedience to it. . . The more respectful the women were, the more the house became a tyrant to them.'[3] Alice escapes to a seedy London and a pimp, but returns to marry, unhappily. 'The photographer tried to make Alice smile a little more, with her eyes which were sad and dull. But she only frowned at him, as if his reflection of her on the day of her marriage was an unimportant one.'[4]

Tennant has continued to write novels prolifically, including *Woman Beware Woman*, 1983; *The House of Hospitalities*, 1987; *The Magic Drum*, 1989; *Sisters and Strangers: A Moral Tale*, 1990; *Faustine*, 1992 (a female re-imagining of the

---

[1] In 1979 Penelope Shuttle and Peter Redgrove's *The Wise Wound*, about the centrality of menstruation had appeared. Tennant knew and published the couple, whom she called the 'wizards of Cornwall'.

[2] p. 33

[3] pp. 71/72

[4] p. 121

Faust legend); *The Harp Lesson*, 2005 and *Seized*, 2008. She has also written several 'sequels' to classic novels by women: *Pemberley*, 1993, (a sequel to *Pride and Prejudice); An Unequal Marriage*, 1995 (a sequel to Pemberley); *Elinor and Marianne*, 1996, (a sequel to *Sense and Sensibility*); *Emma in Love*, 1997 (A sequel to *Emma*); *Felony: The Private History of "The Aspern Papers"*, 2002; *Adele: Jane Eyre's Hidden Story,* 2003 (a sequel to Jane Eyre); *The French Dancer's Bastard: The Story of Adele from Jane Eyre*, 2006; *Thornfield Hall: Jane Eyre's Hidden Story*, 2009 (another sequel to *Jane Eyre*); *Two Women of London: The Strange Case of Ms Jekyll and Mrs Hyde,* 2011 (another female re-imagining of a masculine story); *The Beautiful Child*, 2012 (a completion of a Henry James short story). Tennant has also published autobiographies, including the novel-as-autobiography *Strangers*, 1998 and its two successor volumes *Girlitude*, 1999 and *Waiting for Princess Margaret*, 2009; *Burnt Diaries*, 2000 (mainly concerned with the founding of *Bananas* and her affair with Ted Hughes); she also wrote the biography *Sylvia and Ted*, 2003 and A *House In Corfu*, 2002.

giles gordon

Although born in Scotland, Giles Gordon, 1940-2003 was at the centre of the London publishing scene for many years, as a publisher, editor and literary agent. He started as a trainee at the Edinburgh publisher Oliver and Boyd at the age of 19 before moving to London to join Secker and Warburg. After that he was an editor at Hutchinson and then the editor of Penguin's formidable drama list. In 1967 he became an editorial director at Victor Gollancz, after which he became an independent literary agent. He was a member of the Arts Council's Literature Panel during its first four years and was a member of the management committee of the Society of Authors.

Gordon knew all the novelists on the London scene and edited the anthologies *Factions: Eleven Original Stories*, 1974 which included Michael Moorcock, Rayner Heppenstall and Brian W. Aldiss and *Beyond the Words: Eleven Writers in Search of a New Fiction*, 1975, which included Alan Burns, Eva Figes, B.S. Johnson and Ann Quin. (This book was to have been edited by B. S. Johnson but he died before work on it started and Giles Gordon took it over.) Gordon also published his own short stories,[1] some of which are quite experimental, or at least use non-standard typography, and several novels,[2] of which all but one – *Girl With Red Hair* – are basically conventional stories of relationships and marriage. By the end of the 1970s he had almost stopped writing his own fiction and began to edit a stream of multi-volume collections of stories including several volumes of *Best English Short Stories* and collections of ghost stories, Scottish stories and Scottish ghost stories.

In fact Gordon seems to have been ambivalent about experimental fiction; in the introduction to *Beyond the Words* he explicitly denies the value, even the possibility, of the experimental novel.

> I would not want to suggest that there is, in itself, any virtue in the writing of fiction being 'experimental', assuming that were possible, which I don't believe to be the case if the author is serious about his art. If a novel is labelled experimental or avant garde by a reader, then it seems to me that the book has failed in its primary function, at least in terms of that one reader: to be a novel.

---

[1] *Pictures from an Exhibition*. London: Alison & Busby, 1970; *The Umbrella Man*. London: Alison & Busby, 1971; *Farewell, Fond Dreams*. London: Hutchinson, 1975

[2] *The Umbrella Man*. London: Alison & Busby, 1971; *About a Marriage*. London: Alison & Busby, 1972 *Girl With Red Hair*. London: Hutchinson, 1974; 100 *Scenes from Married Life*. London: Hutchinson, 1976; *Enemies*. London: Harvester, 1977; The *Illusionist*. London: Harvester, 1978; *Couple*. Bedford: Sceptre, 1978

> If content and form in fiction are inseparable, both essential aspects of a single artefact, a novel which with skill portrays its author's individual contemporary vision cannot be experimental or avant garde. It can only be itself, a work of fiction.

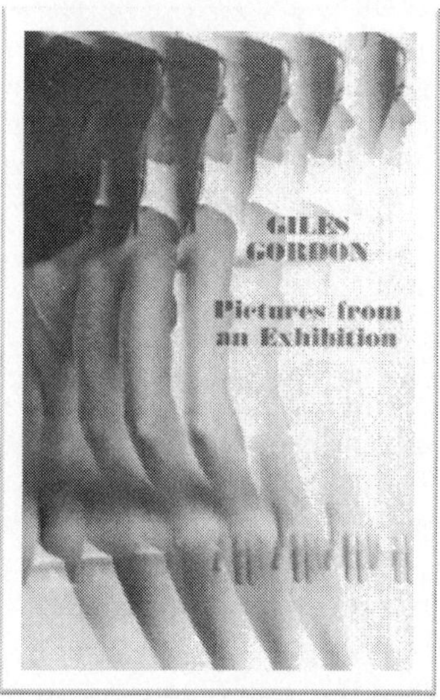

Nevertheless his first solo publication was the collection of experimental stories *Pictures from an Exhibition,* 1970. The first five stories are Called 'Pictures from an Exhibition' and numbered 1 through 5. The sequence is continued in the collection *Farewell, Fond Dreams,* 1975 which collects stories going back to 1969 and includes 'Pictures from an Exhibition' 6 through 33. This brings to mind J.G. Ballard's *The Atrocity Exhibition*, also originally a collection of stories, and indeed some of Gordon's 'Pictures', like some of Ballard's stories were originally published in *New Worlds* from 1969 to 1973. Also, the title of the story 'An attempt to make entertainment out of the war in Vietnam', which was also published in *Factions,* is reminiscent of Ballard's 'The Assassination of Kennedy Considered as a Downhill Motor Race', first published in 1967. Most of the stories do 'describe' or at least start from actual pictures, which are noted at the beginning or end of each story.

Pictures from an exhibition 4.

Two torsos fragments of two torsos
in a row / sitting together / standing together, that is together
male, female man, woman
a man and a woman, probably / back view
bottom view
one part is head / back of head
neck / back of neck
shoulders / back of shoulders, shoulder blades
This applies to both figures, both torsos

end of first fragment

other bit is waist / back of waist / both torsos
buttocks / four buttocks
arse / both arses
thighs / top part of thighs

end of second fragment

Their back views are back: head to shoulders / waist to thighs
man and woman complete completely
man and woman complete not dis in te grate ing
standing together, sitting together / together
together
watching something, watching
to gether
together
together

Pictures from an exhibition 14

Genealogy

a man a woman a man and a woman lovers a coupl
e a son a family a man a woman a man and a wom
an lovers a couple a son a family a man a woman
a man and a woman lovers a couple a son a family
a man a woman a man and a woman lovers a coup
le a daughter a family a woman a man a man and
a woman lovers a couple a son a family a man a
woman a man and a woman lovers a couple a son
a family a man a woman a man and a woman lovers
a couple a daughter a family a woman a man
a man and a woman lovers a couple a son a family
a man a woman a man and a woman lovers a co
uple a son a family a man a woman a man and a
woman lovers a couple a daughter a family a wom
an a man a man and a woman lovers a couple a s
on a family a man a woman a man and a woman
lovers a couple a son a family a man a woman
a man and a woman lovers a couple a son a family
a man a woman a man and a woman lovers a coupl
e a son a family a man a woman a man and a wo
man lovers a couple a son a family a man a wo
man a man and a woman lovers a couple a daughter
a family a woman a man a man and a woman love
rs a couple a son a family a man a woman a ma
n and a woman lovers a couple a son a family a

57

Giles Gordon's novel *Girl with Red Hair,* 1974 (dedicated to Rosalind Belben as her 1974 novel *The Limit* is dedicated to him) is his only real attempt at a thoroughly experimental novel. It uses a second person narrative, like George MacBeth's *The Transformation* and, as in a Robbe-Grillet novel like *Les Gommes* or *Le Voyeur* we have a kind of detective story in which it is not clear whether the central character (the 'you') is the murderer or even if there has been a murder. We are not even sure of the identity of 'you', who may be George (though 'you' say this is not your name) or Henry Haversham Godwen-Austen (who died in 1923 and whose biography is taken from the *Dictionary of National Biography*). There is an index at the back of the novel, in which You is an entry. The novel has a variety of sections and digressions, including a section titled 'PLOT' which reads like a novelist's summary of a planned novel, with headings such as *Stimulus; Mental Disturbance; Reflective Period* and *Decision.* However this is not the summary of the novel we are reading, though the characters in it do crop up elsewhere, including 'your' wife Francisca, who is one of the few constants. There is also a section entitled DEATHS, with obituary notices for all the characters in the book, mostly in the future, though 'YOURSELF' had died on '23 May 1940, in a nursing home in Edinburgh, husband of Francisca. Funeral already taken place.'[1] However, as Henry. 'you' died in 1923. 'You' are only physically described once, towards the end of the novel:

> you walked down the stairs, not aware that the thirty, forty people in the room were watching your progress, less out of interest than of idleness.
>
> Your image (the descending young(ish) man, thirties, forties, the long, expensive raincoat, brown or red or gold depending upon the light, or lack of same, or on the degree of red-green blindness of the observer) was caught, silhouetted against a white surface, between the fifth and sixth steps.
>
> Below, in the room you were already entering, were already in, the faces froze.[2]

---

[1] p. 109

[2] p. 147

At the start 'you' have gone to see Michael Thompson, who is an authority figure in some kind of mysterious agency, and may be investigating a murder. The scenes where 'you' meet him are rewound and repeated several times, as if on film. Pictures recur throughout the novel as clues: Thompson has pictures of twelve suspects (including 'you'), any of whom could also be the victim. As 'you' are waiting to meet Thomson:

> You bent forward, picked a magazine up from the glass surface. You flipped through it, glancing at the pictures.
>
> Your attention was held by one. Men in uniform standing about, as if looking for something, as if waiting for something to happen. There would be movement a few seconds after the photograph had been taken. Thirty seconds after the photograph had been taken – with a telescopic lens – the action would have progressed considerably. The men in uniform would have made their intentions clearer. Six or seven of them would have moved towards the door of a farmhouse (not seen in this particular picture). A man in jeans and a sweatshirt (or in a business suit, or in his pyjamas and a paisley dressing-gown, or his head covered with a blanket) would have been escorted out of the building towards a car. Someone running across a field, trailing a heavy spade behind him, encrusted with leaves and mud. A pile of leaves, burning. A deep hole, dug in the field, but the earth from the hole not beside it. A body, uncovered. Covered. A field with a body lying in it. A large empty field, ploughed up. You look again at the photograph, challenging the people in it to revert to their original – as you looked at it – positions. They had not moved.[1]

Are 'you' remembering this, imagining it, or is this a novelist planning a scene? The narration occasionally reverts to third person, as 'you' remember 'him'. 'Remember: picture the man, the body falling through an arc beautifully. On the grass. The man holding the gun looked around him'. He thinks that 'as he had not touched the man, had not shaken hands with him (one witness later was to dispute this point), his fingerprints would be nowhere on the body.' And if there were no fingerprints, 'he had not killed the man. A man. Therefore no one was dead.'[2] But at another point: 'You stood over the body on the immaculate lawn, the immaculate body. . . The grass was red. They had taken the body away, or it had not yet fallen. There were men there, with measuring tapes, calculating distances from particular positions to other particular positions.'[3] 'You' watch the

[1] pp. 18/19
[2] p. 47
[3] p. 133

lawn and see the place where 'the body would fall beautifully and lie, shot dead. It would not be appropriate for you to say how you knew that would happen before the event took place, before the action happened.'

> Had you been drinking with the victim, and the murderer? If so, did that make you the witness? Had you known they were to be victim and murderer? But the glasses were empty. There was no one at the table for you to talk to, or to listen to. The only people to be seen on the lawn were the men measuring, pacing out distances. You stood up, moved to another vantage point.[1]

The eponymous and mysterious girl with the red hair only appears late in the novel and her relationship to 'you' or the other characters is never explained, though according to the DEATHS section she dies on Christmas Day 2018 'peacefully in her sleep, beside her sixth husband, Brian Dickens. Funeral service at St Paul's Cathedral, London.' In successive scenes at the end of the novel, Thompson lays out for 'you' the pictures of the possible victims/suspects. Each time there are fewer pictures until at the end there are just twelve photographs of the girl with red hair. In the first scene only the twelfth picture is of her.

> 'And what about that one?' He asked, indicating the final picture.
>
> It was of a red-haired girl. She was simply, very beautiful.
>
> 'I haven't met her yet,' you said.
>
> 'So your work on the case isn't completed?' questioned Godwen-Austen, rather than commented.
>
> And Thompson:
>
> 'If you haven't met her yet, my dear chap, how do you know that her hair is red?'
>
> You blushed, you knew you blushed. You knew they'd seen you blush. They knew that you knew that they'd seen you blush.
>
> 'Ah . . .' said Godwen-Austen.
>
> Now he would be able to blackmail you.[2]

'You' meet the girl at a party and she calls you Benedict, though this name has not occurred before, and refers to 'you' as 'the mystery man at the other end of the telephone.'[3] She is 'savoury, delectable, toothsome, wholesome, appetising, lickerish, delicious, exquisite, exotic, rich, luscious, voluptuous.' But despite Thompson's apparent belief that the girl did it (not that we ever know what it is)

---

[1] p. 134

[2] p. 115

[3] p. 150

'you' are put on trial and several witnesses speak against you. Before the verdict, Thompson comes to see 'you'.

> 'Look, old chap, this is damn silly. I know as well as you do that you didn't kill anybody. Just because you've fallen in love with that red-head, you're in danger of being sentenced to life. It's no good, the likes of us, falling for the enemy.'
>
> 'But Michael, as I've said to you before, I'm not convinced she did it.'
>
> 'If not her, then who? Somebody did it.'
>
> Somebody is a lot of people. Millions.'
>
> 'By using our professional abilities, we deduced that she did it.'
>
> You did, Michael. You had twelve photographs of her. One of them had to be the murderer, one of them had to be . . .'
>
> 'I know all that.'
>
> 'The photographs being found in your possession merely indicate what good taste you have in women.'
>
> Thompson stood up, and without another word walked the full length of his room, left you. You were alone in his office. The light began to go but you didn't move out of the armchair to switch on a light. You didn't feel it was your business.
>
> Eventually, the man in uniform who had previously taken you to Thompson's presence escorted you from the room, down the corridor, and saw you out of the front door.[1]

[1] p. 161

new wave science fiction

> In my writing I am acting as a map maker, an explorer of psychic areas, to use the phrase of Mr Alexander Trocchi, as a cosmonaut of inner space, and I see no point in exploring areas that have already been thoroughly surveyed – A Russian scientist has said: "We will travel not only in space but in time as well." That is to travel in space is to travel in time – if writers are to travel in space time and explore areas opened by the space age, I think they must develop techniques quite as new and definite as the techniques of physical space travel – certainly if writing is to have a future it must at least catch up with the past and learn to use techniques that have been used for some time past in painting, music and film.[1]

William Burroughs was a major influence on both mainstream experimental fiction and what would become known as New Wave Science Fiction, a mid-1960s British movement[2]. Mary McCarthy had said of *Naked Lunch* that it 'must be the first space novel, the first serious piece of science fiction – the others are entertainment.'[3] With *Nova Express*, 1963, Burroughs had moved into science fiction territory and joined a growing number of writers who were using the techniques of experimental fiction with some of the tropes of science fiction: not the traditional concerns of space travel, galactic empires and aliens; not outer

---

[1] William Burroughs. 'The Future of the Novel', speech at the 1962 Edinburgh Conference, to which Burroughs had been invited by the publisher John Calder, also attended by Norman Mailer, Henry Miller and Mary McCarthy, and early, though unlikely champion of Burroughs. The speech was reprinted in *The Third Mind*, 1964.

[2] Barrington J. Bayley's 'The Four Colour Problem', *New Worlds Quarterly* 1972, was one of several British SF stories explicitly influenced by Burroughs, and Burroughs in turn admired Bayley's novel *Star Virus*.

[3] *New York Review of Books,* Feb 1963

space but inner space; not life on other planets but the possibilities for life on this one.

> On the whole, the props of SF are few: rocket ships, telepathy, robots, time travel, other dimensions, huge machines, aliens, future wars. Like coins, they become debased by over-circulation . . . in the fifties, . . . writers combined and recombined these standard elements with a truly Byzantine ingenuity . . . but there were signs even then that limits were being reached. By the sixties, the signs could not be ignored.[1]

As early as 1962 J.G. Ballard had introduced the idea of 'inner space' which Alexander Trocchi would take up and pass to Burroughs (though the phrase was actually used first by J.B. Priestley, in *They Came from Inner Space*, 1953).

> I've often wondered why s-f shows so little of the experimental enthusiasm which has characterized painting, music and the cinema during the last four or five decades, particularly as these have become wholeheartedly speculative, more and more concerned with the creation of new states of mind, constructing fresh symbols and languages where the old ceases to be valid. . . The biggest developments of the immediate future will take place, not on the Moon or Mars, but on Earth, and it is *inner space*, not outer, that need to be explored. The only truly alien planet is Earth. In the past the scientific bias of s-f has been towards the physical sciences – rocketry, electronics, cybernetics – and the emphasis should switch to the biological sciences. Accuracy, that last refuge of the unimaginative, doesn't matter a hoot. . . It is that *inner* space-suit which is still needed, and it is up to science fiction to build it.

The origin of the phrase New Wave, probably borrowed from the French cinema's *nouvelle vague* is usually attributed to Judith Merril, an American writer and editor who briefly lived in England. Merril brought out *England Swings SF* in America in 1968, introducing new British writers and their new kind of fiction to an American audience.[2] Never a formal movement, and with no manifesto or agenda, the New Wave's lifespan is usually identified with the period of the

---

[1] Aldiss, Brian W. and Harrison, Harry eds. *Decade the 1950s*. London: Pan, 1977, pp. 305/306

[2] Judith Merril. *England Swings SF: Stories of Speculative Fiction*. New York: Doubleday, 1968. Harlan Ellison's slightly earlier anthology *Dangerous Visions*, also published by Doubleday, in 1967, is also credited as a key work in the genre and introduced Aldiss and Ballard to Americans. It was a huge anthology and each story was preceded by an introduction to its author by Ellison himself. It was followed in 1972 by a sequel: *Again Dangerous Visions*.

magazine *New Worlds* from when it was edited by Michael Moorcock, starting in 1964 to its closure in 1970[1].

New Worlds had originated in 1946 and went through several unsuccessful incarnations under various owners before it was bought out in 1964 by the publishers Roberts and Vintner, who had previously published violent pulp thrillers; they appointed Michael Moorcock[2], already a well-known science fiction author, as editor. Moorcock immediately started to publish work that was not in the classic science fiction mould, while trying to keep the traditionalists happy. He said in an early editorial that he wanted to encourage 'prose that, given a sympathetic reading, will be explicit . . . in a form that is not necessarily conventional in construction or use of language'.[3] The first issue under Moorcock's editorship contained work by J. G. Ballard, Brian W. Aldiss, Barrington J. Bayley and John Brunner, and included a book review of William Burroughs. By 1966 the money had run out and Moorcock elicited help from a number of the great and good in British literature.[4]

> As many readers doubtless read in the press, the national economic restrictions led to the collapse of our chief distributor making us fear that we should be forced to cease publication. Brian Aldiss decided to write to the Arts Council and apply for a grant. Others lent their support to this proposal, among them Bruce Montgomery, Anthony Burgess, J. B. Priestley, Kenneth Allsop, Peter Redgrove, Professors Geoffrey Tillotson, Kathleen Tillotson and Roy Fuller, and Marghanita Laski, and we wish to thank them most warmly for doing so.[5]

The first issue after the Arts Council grant also included works by two of the New Wave's most prominent writers: the complete novel *Report on Probability A* by Brian W. Aldiss and the story 'The Assassination of Kennedy Considered as a

---

[1] It was subsequently revived several times.

[2] Born 1939

[3] Changes Coming' in *New Worlds* Vol. 50, no. 171, March 1967

[4] See Colin Greenland. *The Entropy Exhibition: Michael Moorcock and the British "New Wave" in Science Fiction*. London: Routledge and Kegan Paul, 1983

[5] ibid.

Downhill Race' by J. G. Ballard that would later become part of his experimental novel *The Atrocity Exhibition*. It is hard to imagine any other outlet through which these could have been published at that time. The choice of material was too much for many science fiction readers and there were never enough sales to make a profit. It was also too much for the main booksellers in Britain: W. H. Smith and John Menzies were offended by the sexual content and refused to distribute it. By 1970 Moorcock, who had been largely funding the publication through his own extremely prolific writing, had run out of money and *New Worlds* closed with issue 200, bringing, not an end, but a steep decline in this kind of writing. Although science fiction after 1970 has been irrevocably changed by the New Wave there have been few experimental science fiction novels since then and most novelists – and science fiction novelists tend to be very prolific – have largely returned to the traditional concerns of the genre in the outpouring of novels since then, the main permanent change being perhaps the splitting off of the fantasy novel as a separate genre. However, the innovations of the New Wave undoubtedly affected mainstream experimental novelists like Alan Burns, Christine Brooke-Rose and Ann Quin. Emma Tennant has also written about how much Michael Moorcock had influenced not only her early novels (part of her first novel was originally published in *New Worlds*) but her influential literary magazine *Bananas*.[1]

In the middle of this period, in 1969, a major literary conference in England brought together experimental novelists, science fiction writers and scientists. The publisher John Calder, who published Ann Quin, Eva Figes, Alan Burns, Alexander Trocchi, as well as Burroughs, Hubert Selby and most of the *nouveaux romanciers*, held the conference in Harrogate, along the lines of his previous conferences at the Edinburgh Festival in Scotland, which was devoted to science fiction:

> my idea then was to bring together scientists, particularly those who were planning our futures in terms of innovative practices, , inventions and planning, and those who were imagining possible futures in their writings. I . . . brought novelists Alan Burns, Eva Figes, Norman Spinrad, Brian Aldiss, J. G. Ballard, Margaret Drabble, Michael Moorcock, B. S. Johnstone [*sic*], and among others Erich Fried, Robert Jungk, G. W. Targett (who wrote largely for religious publications from a liberal perspective) Chris Evans, Walter Perry, D. L. Jayasuriya, Charles Marovitz [*sic*: Marowitz], Robin Blackburn, Christopher Priest, A Mr. jones (first name unfindable), Jeff Nuttall, a Professor Todcroft and a few others. . . They were a mixture of creative writers, journalists and scientists in different disciplines and the two-day conference was

[1] *Burnt Diaries*. Edinburgh: Canongate, 1999, p. 11

> lively. From the start there was obvious hostility between science fiction writers and psychologists and psychiatrists.[1]

There were several elements and themes that distinguished New Wave Science Fiction:

Post-apocalyptic settings: Burroughs had said in 1962: 'I am primarily concerned with the question of survival – with nova conspiracies, nova criminals, and nova police – A new mythology is possible in the space age where we will again have heroes and villains with respect to intentions toward this planet.'[2] Like Anna Kavan's *Ice* and *Mercury*, Alan Burns' *Europe After the Rain* and Christine Brooke-Rose's *Out*, many New Wave novels and stories were concerned, not with life on other planets or the far future of the Earth, but the imminent possibility of the destruction of life as we know it, which, as examined in detail by Jeff Nuttall in *Bomb Culture*, deeply affected many artists and writers in the 1960s, in the period between the Cuban Missile Crisis of 1961 and the build-up of the Vietnam War. In this category are almost all of Ballard's early novels; Aldiss's *Earthworks, Hothouse* and *Barefoot in the Head*, 1969; Michael Moorcock's *The Jewel in the Skull*, 1967; M. John Harrison's *The Committed Men* and *The Pastel City*, both 1971[3]; Brian W. Aldiss's *Hothouse*, 1962 (which had previously appeared as five novelettes); John Brunner's *Stand on Zanzibar*, 1968 and *The Sheep Look Up*, 1972[4]; Christopher Priest's *Indoctrinaire*, 1970, *Fugue for a Darkening Island*, 1972 and *Inverted*

---

[1] Calder, John. *Pursuit: The Uncensored Memoirs of John Calder*. London: Calder Publications, 2001, p. 312

[2] op. cit.

[3] Harrison, born 1945, was literary editor of New Worlds from 1968 and reviewed works under the pseudonym Joyce Churchill

[4] Brunner, 1934 – 1995 was an extremely prolific author of science fiction,, publishing over 100 novels, starting in 1951. He had already published over 50 novels when he started to experiment with form in *Stand on Zanzibar,* which won both the Hugo Award and the British Science Fiction Authors' Award in 1968

World, 1974[1]. Unlike, say, Anna Kavan's *Ice* and *Mercury*, these ruined landscapes are not metaphorical: they are predictions of real, potential disasters. But nevertheless, Ballard felt that they were representations of the authors' inner worlds.

> As an author who has produced a substantial number of cataclysmic stories, I take for granted that the planet the writer destroys with such tireless ingenuity is in fact an image of the writer himself. But are these deluges and droughts, whirlwinds and glaciations no more than over-extended metaphors of some kind of suicidal self-hate? . . . On the contrary, I believe that the catastrophe story, whoever may tell it, represents a constructive and positive act by the imagination rather than a negative one, an attempt to confront a patently meaningless universe by challenging it at its own game.[2]

As Alain Robbe-Grillet said in 1963[3], the world is neither meaningful nor absurd, it is simply there: the task is to know what to do about it.

Politics: where most traditional science fiction (and most experimental novels) are apolitical, the message of post-apocalyptic fiction is highly political: something needs to be done. Humanity has to change its ways before it is too late or change will be imposed, either by nature or by the misuse of technology. M. John Harrison was an avowed anarchist and all his works are critiques of late capitalism; Judith Merril, having lived in England, left America for Canada to avoid being involved in the Vietnam War; Ballard's *Atrocity Exhibition* and *Crash*, like Burns' *Dreamerika!* and J.M.G. Le Clézio's *The Giants*, are all political critiques of the lack of affect in modern society, all around the time of, and illustrating, Guy Debord's *Society of the Spectacle*.[4] Ballard's titling of his stories 'Why I want to Fuck Ronald Reagan' and 'The Assassination of John Fitzgerald Kennedy Considered as a Downhill motor Race' must be considered deeply political and he explicitly equates the pornographic elements of *Crash* with politics: 'Throughout *Crash* I have used the car not only as a sexual image, but as a total metaphor for man's life in today's society. As such the novel has a political role quite apart from its sexual content.'[5]

---

[1] Priest, born 1943, has also written radio plays and won several awards

[2] J. G. Ballard, 'Cataclysms and Dooms', in *The Visual Encyclopaedia of Science Fiction*, 1977; already quoted in the Alan Burns section.

[3] *Pour un Nouveau Roman*

[4] First published in France in 1967; first English translation published 1970.

[5] 'Introduction to the French Edition of *Crash* (1974)', reprinted in *Crash*. London: Panther, 1975

Fractured identities: like many experimental novels, New Wave Science Fiction is often concerned with split or multiple personalities or with the whole question of what identity means. Michael Moorcock's character the secret agent, assassin and rock star[1] Jerry Cornelius appears in multiple guises[2], with multiple names (usually with the initials JC, possibly referring to Jesus Christ) like Jherek Carnelian, and even different genders (s/he appears as Una Persson[3]) in different aspects of Moorcock's Multiverse. He has also been used by other authors: in 1971, Hutchinson published a collection of stories featuring Cornelius by a range of different authors, including Aldiss and Harrison, which had previously appeared in the underground magazine *International Times*[4]. Other New Wave authors played with the idea of divided or shifting personalities and the question of identity: in Christopher Priest's *The Affirmation*, 1981, the central character tries to pin down his identity by inventing a fictional self, but the two identities begin to merge, and in His *Dream Of Wessex*, 1977, the characters create a virtual reality future and forget their true identities; in Ballard's *The Atrocity Exhibition*, 1970[5] the central character changes his name in each chapter, and his girlfriend may be an invention and in Aldiss's *Report on Probability A*, 1967, the characters in the main story are simply called 'G who waits' and 'S the Watchful', but they are only the possible results of one probability and may not exist at all.

Sex: the 1960s was not only the decade that separated the Cuban Missile Crisis and the Vietnam War; it was also the Swinging Sixties that brought in sexual liberation. In Britain, 1960 was the year of the obscenity trial that finally allowed

---

[1] Moorcock himself was closely associated with the band Hawkwind.

[2] The main sequence of Jerry Cornelius novels, known as the Cornelius Quartet, is: *The Final Programme*. London: Allison & Busby, 1969; *A Cure for Cancer*. London: Allison & Busby, 1971; *The English Assassin*. London: Allison & Busby, 1972; *The Condition of Muzak*. London: Allison & Busby, 1977.

[3] Una even has her own novel with Jerry's sister: *The Adventures of Una Persson and Catherine Cornelius in the 20th Century: A Romance,* 1976

[4] *The Nature of the Catastrophe*. London: Hutchinson, 1971. For a history of the magazine *It*, see Nigel Fountain. *Underground: The London Alternative Press, 1966-74*. London: Routledge, 1988

[5] Some of the sections had previously been published as short stories.

mainstream publication of *Lady Chatterley's Lover,* originally published in 1928 but banned in Britain; as late as 1955 a bookseller was sent to jail for selling it. Thousands of books had been banned in Britain – including *Madame Bovary, Moll Flanders* and *The Decameron;* 1,500 novels had been banned between 1953 and 1955 alone. The Obscene Publications Act of 1959 had opened up a defence of literary value, though the police could still confiscate books they considered obscene and prosecute booksellers, as happened for instance with Alexander Trocchi's *Cain's Book* and Ballard's 'Why I want to Fuck Ronald Reagan'. However, by 1968 the last bastion of censorship had been swept away as the Lord Chamberlain's office, which had held, and widely used, the power to ban theatre productions, lost that power. Writers in all genres started to include sex scenes and they now started to intrude into science fiction, which had previously ignored sex in favour of technology. In *New Worlds*, Moorcock published Langdon Jones's 'I Remember, Anita ...' in the Sep/Oct issue of 1964 and in March 1968 the third part of Norman Spinrad's *Bug Jack Barron,* whose sex scenes led to complaints by British Members of Parliament that the Arts Council was sponsoring pornography and the dropping of the magazine by W. H. Smith and John Menzies. J. G. Ballard did not see the need to abandon technology for sex: in both *The Atrocity Exhibition* and *Crash*, he merged the two. Ballard said he would like to think that *Crash* was the 'first pornographic novel based on technology'; he was probably right: although Brian Aldiss had already combined the two in *The Primal Urge*, 1961, where people wear an Emotion Indicator on their foreheads to indicate if they are sexually aroused, this is hardly a pornographic book. Whereas Aldiss in 1961 is producing a gentle satire that harks back to the 1950s, by 1969 Ballard is equating machinery and sexual desire to illustrate the lack of affect in modern society.

Fragmented narratives: like many mainstream experimental novels, the New Wave used fragmented narratives to disorient the reader and question the nature of reality and the omniscient narrator. Many science fiction novels were originally published in magazines like *New Worlds* as short stories or novellas that were subsequently worked up into longer pieces to be published as novels, and some were serialised novels written in sections to meet deadlines, exactly as Dickens wrote, and changed along the way. Aldiss's *Hothouse* had originally been published as five novelettes and parts of *The Atrocity Exhibition* had been previously published as separate short stories. *Stand On Zanzibar* mixes many different kinds of narrative: newspaper cuttings; fragments of songs; snatches of conversation and advertising copy to build up a multi-layered narrative with no consistent voice; *Barefoot in the Head* contains songs, poetry and even concrete poetry; *The Atrocity Exhibition* has short paragraphs that present no overarching narrative and *The Adventures of Una Persson* has two narratives that merge at the end. Ballard said of fragmented narratives:

> In the conventional novel, there are limits to how much you can jump around: you've got to maintain the stretched skin of the narration or the whole damned thing begins to sound funny. With the fragmented technique, you can move about in time, you can move from realism to fantasy, and you can play on the fact that it is sometimes difficult to tell what is "real", what is being presented as a piece of realistic narration and what is being presented as, say the interior fantasy of one of the characters. And this reflects a characteristic ambiguity of everyday life today[1]

---

[1] Interview in Alan Burns and Charles Sugnet, eds. *The Imagination on Trial*. London: Allison & Busby, 1981, p. 24

brian w aldiss

Born in 1925, Brian Aldiss served in the Second World War, part of which he spent in Burma. After the war he worked in bookshops and began to write articles for trade journals about the bookselling trade; his first novel, in 1955, was in the form of a journal about a bookshop assistant and was published by the prestigious Faber and Faber. However, his first love was science fiction and he published his first short story collection in 1957 and his first novel *Non-Stop* in 1958 in the genre. Successful from the start, Aldiss has been one of the world's leading science fiction writers for most of his career; he has now published over 50 novels and story collections, as well as editing a large number of anthologies. Aldiss has won all the major science fiction awards and was awarded the Order of the British Empire in 2005. As we have seen, he encouraged Anna Kavan towards the end of her life, promoting her and her last novel, *Ice*, showing that he has an inclusive rather than exclusive idea of what science fiction should be.

His 1965 novel *Earthworks*, like J.G. Ballard's early novels, Alan Burns' *Europe After the Rain* and Christine Brooke-Rose's *Out*, and going back to H.G. Wells' *The Time Machine*, and Aldiss' own *The Hothouse*, 1962,[1] was a post-apocalyptic work where, after a disaster a fragmented society has arisen with classes at war with each other; in this case the powerful 'Farmers' who control the police state and the 'Travellers' who live outside society until they are caught and imprisoned by the Farmers.

Report on Probability A first appeared complete in *New Worlds* 17, March 1967, the first issue after the Arts Council grant. Though not exactly experimental it does play with ideas of identity and reality; especially the vertiginous idea of infinitely regressive or even circular layers of reality. The novel switches between narratives: that of the watchers, with sections on G who waits and S the watchful, interspersed with italicised sections describing beings who are watching them, and considering the various probabilities they are seeing, and a higher level of beings, who may be human, watching the watchers watching.

> *"Well, that's how it seems to be. Our robot fly has materialised into a world where it so happens that the first group of inhabitants we come across is studying another world they have discovered – a world in which the inhabitants they watch are studying a report they have obtained from another world."*
>
> *"I'd say we've run into some kind of mental reflection - distortion effect – hitherto unknown, as they say in the Sunday supplements."*
>
> *"Maybe so. Or maybe the key to it all lies in that report. Hey! – Suppose that report comes from the real world! Suppose the guys reading it, and the guys on the hillside watching them, and us watching* them *are* false *worlds, phase echoes. . . . Makes your flesh creep, doesn't it?"*
>
> *The Congressman said, "All we are after is facts. We don't have to decide what reality is, thank God!"*[2]

[1] Some of the stories that comprise the novel had been published in *The Magazine of Fantasy & Science Fiction*, 1961. Published in a shortened version in America as *The Long Afternoon of Earth*.

[2] pp. 70/71

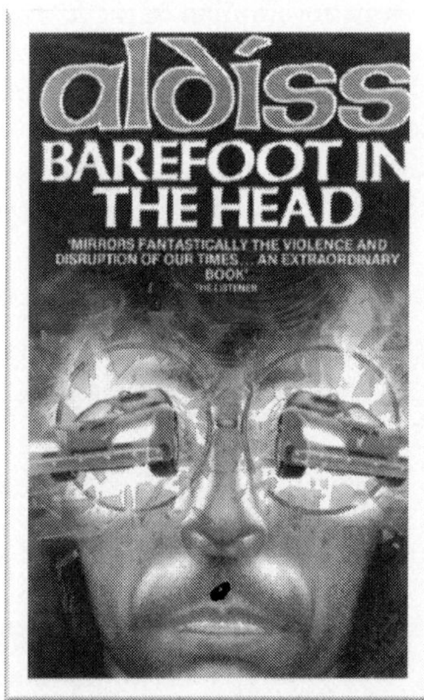

Barefoot in the Head was published by Faber and Faber in 1969 but had previously appeared 'differently fashioned – in chunks in NEW WORLDS over two years, thanks to the encouragement of its editor, Michael Moorcock, although the original chunk 'Just Passing Through', appeared in IMPULSE for February 1967.'[1] Very much of its time, the novel as it is constituted in its full version is decidedly experimental and highly psychedelic[2]: Aldiss acknowledges both P. D. Ouspensky and Procul Harum's track 'Whiter Shade of Pale' as influences. Even though at its heart there is a fairly conventional post-apocalyptic story, with a hero figure – Colin Charteris – trying to save the world, the novel contains several kinds of narrative, including poetry and even concrete poetry; The following is a representation of 'acid head'.[3]

DACIDAC
DACIDACID
ACIDACIDA
ACID ACI
HEAD
CI ID DA
ID DA AC
ACIDACIDAC
IDACIDAC
DACIDACI
CIDACI
DACI
ACID

[1] Acknowledgements in the Grafton paperback edition, 1979

[2] In his 1967 novel *An Age,* a future civilisation have developed 'mind travel'; using a drug called CSD [*sic*] they can time-travel in their minds.

[3] p. 70

As the world around him becomes more destabilised, so does the narrative, sometimes reminiscent of Burroughs and sometimes approaching *Finnegans Wake*-style wordplay.

> Those whore not for me are against me just a bit more punchy fallacy in westrun style there's a newtrality to cultivate to be more receptive look for shades patterns where this goodevil stuff cant rise he startled too many hares for Man the Drover.
>
> The shins of the flesh mere alimbic fantasy
>
> Don't be for or against anyone only the waking thing that lies in sleep
>
> Hold firm to dreamament
>
> It's the pattern of perceptivity
>
> Awakes the greater sleep
>
> Don't think we're too well made or permanent
>
> You are more merged each than you believe
>
> Better sensuous than sensible
>
> All you must have within is outside among verdance Christ and the westering thing supposited the inside out
>
> Never imagined where all roads would lead
>
> Here
>
> The eternal postion
>
> You have to have been there first
>
> Many theres
>
> For the here no multernatives
>
> His thought chewed deeper and deeper into the ruralities as the herding greentides lipped them
>
> Other thought impacted two thousand years
>
> Driver man became pedestrian. Be not do[1]

---

[1] p. 216

j. g. ballard

Few novelists of any generation have become adjectival – Dickensian and Kafkaesque being notable exceptions, but the adjective 'Ballardian' is now an accepted term, denoting a bleak, dystopian, post-industrial landscape where technology is threatening and perverted sexuality has replaced relationships and romance. Ballard, as quoted above, regards the writing of catastrophe novels as a 'constructive and positive act by the imagination rather than a negative one' in a world where the traditional novel has no place.

> The dominant characteristic of the modern mainstream novel is its sense of individual isolation, its mood of introspection and alienation, a state of mind always assumed to be the hallmark of the 20th century consciousness.
>
> Far from it. On the contrary, it seems to me that this is a psychology that belongs entirely to the 19th century, part of a reaction against the massive restraints of bourgeois society, the monolithic character of Victorianism and the tyranny of the paterfamilias, secure in his financial and sexual authority.[1]

> I was dissatisfied with science fiction's obsession with its two principal themes – outer space, and the far future. As much for emblematic purposes as any theoretical or programmatic ones, I christened the new terrain I wished to explore 'inner space', that psychological domain (manifest, for example, in surrealist painting) where the inner world of the mind and the outer world of reality meet and fuse.
>
> Primarily, I wanted to write a fiction about the present day. To do this in the context of the late 1950s, in a world where the call-sign of Sputnik 1 could be heard on one's radio like the advance beacon of a new universe, required completely different techniques from those available to the 19th century novelist.[2]

Born in Shanghai, China in 1930[3], which was under Japanese occupation after 1941, Ballard spent some of his youth in an internment camp and saw the horrors

[1] 'Introduction to the French Edition of *Crash* (1974)', reprinted in *Crash*. London: Panther, 1975

[2] ibid. See also the quotes from Ballard in the Anna Kavan and Alan Burns sections of this book

[3] died 2009

of war at first hand.[1] Returning to England he later studied medicine at Cambridge University with the intention of becoming a psychiatrist. Realising he wanted to be a writer, he enrolled at the University of London to study literature but did not complete the course. After working as an advertising copywriter he joined the Royal Air Force and was posted to Canada, where he first encountered American science fiction. After *The Wind from Nowhere,* 1961 his second novel, *The Drowned World*, 1962 quickly established his reputation as a leading science fiction writer; it was followed by a series of post-apocalyptic novels, mostly conventional in form,[2] and a number of collections of short stories, many of which had been published in science fiction magazines like *New Worlds* but some were published in the avant-garde literary magazine *Ambit*[3], of which he was prose editor from 1967, having first published a section of *The Drought* there in 1965. Ballard was also a contributing editor to Emma Tennant's *Bananas* magazine and published stories in every issue. Tennant recalled Ballard telling her of the extremity of his war-time and subsequent experiences:

> At dinner, Jimmy has told me of the privations of his years as a prisoner of war. I begin to realise how far he is from being a conventional Englishman, despite the brisk and slightly alarming air – of family doctor or solicitor – which he presents to the outside world. This is a man who was snatched from luxury and put behind barbed wire for four long years – and the pain suffered then was compounded when, happily married with three young children, his wife Mary died suddenly on holiday in Spain. He tells me he thinks the world is going through a death of affect – of feeling, of ability to love, I suppose he means – but of course he refers to himself, and it would be impossible to give a spontaneous hug to the man who writes of atrocities, of light aircraft crashing in overgrown tourist resorts, of despair disguised as revelry.[4]

Like Burns' *Dreamerika!*, Quin's *Tripticks*, Brooke-Rose's *Thru*, Le Clézio's *The Giants* and Burroughs' cut-ups, Ballard's mid-period works, especially *The Atrocity Exhibition* and *Crash* realise affect is dead and that the spectacle has become reality; advertising, TV, war reporting are not reflections of reality, they

---

[1] He subsequently wrote about this in *Empire of the Sun*, 1984, which was made into a film by Steven Spielberg.

[2] *The Burning World*, 1964; *The Drought*, 1965, *The Crystal World*, 1966, (whose first edition used a painting very like the Magritte on the cover of Alan Burns' *Europe After the Rain) The Atrocity Exhibition,* 1970 (with a Dali as its first edition cover), *Crash*, 1973, *Concrete Island*, 1974, *High Rise*, 1975, *The Unlimited Dream Company*, 1979, *Hello America,* 1981

[3] Founded in 1959 by Martin Bax

[4] Emma Tennant, *Burnt Diaries*, p. 30

are reality, and the modern novel needs to encompass this. Ballard was already a novelist in Guy Debord's *Society of the Spectacle* before it was published in 1967.

> I feel that the balance between fiction and reality has changed significantly in the past decade. Increasingly their roles are reversed. We live in a world ruled by fictions of every kind – mass-merchandising, advertising, politics conducted as a branch of advertising, the instant translation of science and technology into popular imagery, the increasing blurring and intermingling of identities within the realm of consumer goods, the pre-empting of any free or original imaginative response to experience by the television screen. We live inside an enormous novel. For the writer in particular it is less and less necessary for him to invent the fictional content of his novel. The fiction is already there. The writer's task is to invent the reality.
>
> In the past we have always assumed that the external world around us has represented reality, however confusing or uncertain, and that the inner world of our minds, its dreams, hopes, ambitions, represented the realm of fantasy and the imagination. These roles, too, it seems to me, have been reversed. The most prudent and effective method of dealing with the world around us is to assume that it is a complete fiction – conversely, the one small node of reality left to us is inside our own heads.[1]

[1] 'Introduction to the French Edition of *Crash* (1974)', reprinted in *Crash*. London: Panther, 1975

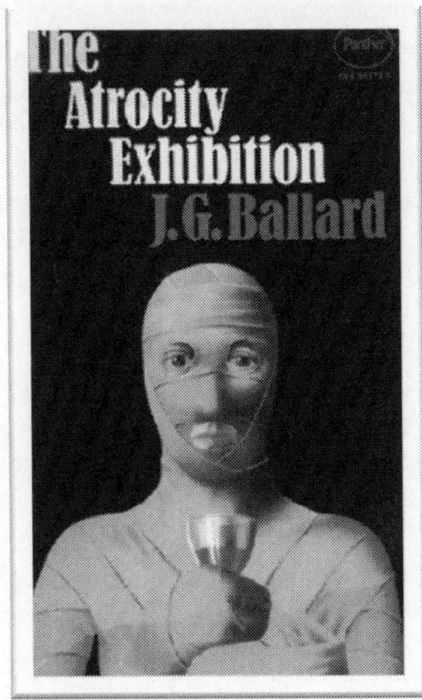

Like many science fiction works, much of *The Atrocity Exhibition* was originally published in magazines[1]. This raises the question of whether it is a novel or a collection of linked stories. The paperback edition explicitly calls it a novel but it is sometimes listed in Ballard's *oeuvre* as stories. Ballard himself said of it: 'In the strict, conventional sense of the term, it's not a novel. It doesn't have that self-conscious continuity that we tend to expect from a novel, but at the same time it's much more than just a collection of stories.'[2] Considered as a novel it has separate chapters, though each is titled as it had been as a separate story, and consistent characters, though the principal character changes his name each chapter: Travis becomes Talbot, Traven, Tallis, Trabert, Talbert, Travers, though sometimes he is just 'he'. Considered as a novel, it is certainly experimental. Ballard said of it:

> Needless to say, I'm constantly getting people who say: "*Atrocity Exhibition*, oh, couldn't understand it, couldn't read it, impossible to read." I don't think it's a very difficult book; it's written in a very easy and open style. It's not difficult, but unfamiliar. This is where the experimental writer (it's not a term I like, but there doesn't seem to be any other) has the cards stacked against him. People are so lazy or rooted in established conventions in their reading that they won't make the effort.[3]

Like *Crash* after it, the novel equates death and disfigurement, especially through automobile accidents, with sexual desire. Jayne Mansfield, James Dean and J. F. Kennedy are constants; not as characters but as 'spectacle'. Ballard started writing the stories after his wife's tragic early death, which left him with three children to bring up and, as in *Crash*, all the sex is affectless and related to technology, machinery and concrete; ther are no relationships on a human level. 'Now that sex is becoming more and more a conceptual act, an intellectualization

---

[1] Published in book form by Jonathan Cape in 1970

[2] Interview in Alan Burns and Charles Sugnet, eds. *The Imagination on Trial*. London: Allison & Busby, 1981, p. 23

[3] op. cit., p. 25

divorced from affect and physiology alike, one has to bear in mind the positive merits of the sexual perversions.'[1] Neoprene is equated with 'the obscene sculptures of Bellmer' with which the female body can 'coalesce, giving birth to deformed sections of her lips and armpit, the junction of thigh and armpit.' In this misogynist, depersonalised fetishist world, any part of the anatomy can be erotic. The female character Karen Novotny may even be a fantasy object rather than a person, a substitute for Elizabeth Taylor, with whom Dr. Nathan believes Talbert wants to have 'sexual intercourse. . . though needless to say not in the literal sense of that term'. Karen can be reduced to a series of sexual constituent parts:

> one may regard this as a kit which Talbert has devised, entitled "Karen Novotny" – it might even be feasible to market it commercially. It contains the following items: (1) Pad of pubic hair, (2) a latex face mask, (3) six detachable mouths, (4) a set of smiles, (5) a pair of breasts, left nipple marked by a small ulcer, (6) a set of non-chafe orifices, (7) photo cut-outs of a number of narrative situations – the girl doing this and that, (8) a list of dialogue samples, of inane chatter, (9) a set of noise levels, (10) descriptive techniques for a variety of sex acts, (11) a torn anal detrusor muscle, (12) a glossary of idioms and catch-phrases, (13) an analysis of odour traces (from various vents), mostly purines, etc., (14) a chart of body temperatures (axillary, buccal, rectal), (15) slides of vaginal smears, chiefly Ortho-Gynol jelly, (16) a set of blood pressures, systolic 120, diastolic 70, rising to 200/150 at onset of orgasm.[2]

However, it was not the genuinely subversive idea of the affectlessness of modern society in the book that caused The Unicorn Bookshop in Brighton to be prosecuted (successfully – despite poet and BBC producer George MacBeth's defence testimony) for selling it in 1968, but the playful and ironic individual story 'Why I Want to Fuck Ronald Reagan' that forms the last chapter of the novel. Fundamental and devastating criticism of society was not considered as outrageous as the word 'fuck', especially in the same title as the name of an American president.

---

[1] p. 68
[2] pp. 66-68

In *The Atrocity Exhibition* Ballard had explicitly equated sex and automobile crashes: 'it is hard to tell whether the positions are those of Miss Novotny in intercourse or as an auto-crash fatality – to a large extent the difference is now meaningless.'[1] In *Crash*[2], 1973, he expanded the idea in a novel that is not experimental in form but revolutionary in content, a 'pornographic novel based on technology', and a political statement about modern society.

> I feel myself that the writer's role, his authority and licence to act, have changed radically. I feel that, in a sense, the writer knows nothing any longer. He has no moral stance. He offers the reader the contents of his own head, he offers a set of opinions and imaginative alternatives. His role is that of the scientist, whether on safari or in his laboratory, faced with a completely unknown terrain or subject. All he can do is to devise various hypotheses and test them against the facts.
>
> *Crash!*[3] is such a book, an extreme metaphor for an extreme situation, a kit of desperate measures only for use in an extreme crisis. If I am right, and what I have done over the past years is to rediscover the present for myself, *Crash!* takes up its position as a cataclysmic novel of the present-day in line with my previous novels of world cataclysm set in the near future – *The Drowned world, The Drought*, and *The Crystal World.*[4]

The narrator, named Ballard, has had a friend, Vaughan, die in a car crash. They had both created erotic fantasies about accidents. 'Around the deaths of James

---

[1] p. 33

[2] *Crash* was made into a film by David Cronenberg in 1996

[3] The exclamation mark only seems to appear in this introduction by Ballard to the French edition, and is not used elsewhere; perhaps Ballard thought, belatedly, that it improved the title, or perhaps it was an editor who changed it, knowingly or otherwise. Like the exclamation mark in *Dreamerika!* it certainly changes the mood.

[4] 'Introduction to the French Edition of *Crash* (1974)', reprinted in *Crash*. London: Panther, 1975

Dean and Albert Camus, Jayne Mansfield and John Kennedy he had woven elaborate fantasies. His imagination was a target gallery of screen actresses, politicians, business tycoons and television executives.'[1] These figures are all part of the spectacle, of which the author-narrator is part. 'I thought of being killed within this huge accumulation of fictions, thought of my body marked with the imprint of a hundred television crime serials, the signatures of forgotten dramas which, years after being shelved in a network shake-up, would leave their last credit-lines in my skin.'[2] Ballard meets and has sex with Gabrielle, crippled in a car accident and in leg braces in a series of long, fetishist, pornographic scenes. 'As I unshackled the left leg brace and ran my fingers along the deep buckle groove, the corrugated skin felt hot and tender, more exciting than the membrane of a vagina.' Ballard himself has scars from an accident. 'Her fingers found the small scars below my left collar bone, the imprint of the outer quadrant of the instrument binnacle.' They explore each other's scars, 'deciphering together these codes of a sexuality made possible by our two car crashes. . . For the first time I felt no trace of pity for this crippled woman, but celebrated with her the excitement of these abstract vents let into her body by sections of her own automobile.' His orgasms from now on are in the 'sexual apertures formed by fragmenting windshield louvres and dashboard dials in a high-speed impact.'[3]

Ballard the author, as opposed to Ballard the narrator, does not try to avoid the charge of pornography and in fact celebrates it; the world is pornographic, the spectacle makes us all fetishists and voyeurs. At the end of the introduction to *Crash*, he has a disclaimer:

> Needless to say, the ultimate role of *Crash!* is cautionary, a warning against that brutal, erotic and overlit realm that beckons more and more persuasively to us from the margins of the technological landscape.[4]

But this is either disingenuousness, of which Ballard could never be accused, or an ironic and cynical counter to the anti-pornography lobby. *Crash* is profoundly attuned to the malaise of its time; not a caution against it but a celebration of it, and one of the key novels of the second half of the twentieth century.

---

[1] p. 17

[2] p. 50

[3] p. 137

[4] p. 9

afterword

In discussing Ann Quin, B.S. Johnson, Rosalind Belben and especially Anna Kavan and Rayner Heppenstall the question was continually present of the relationship of autobiography to fiction. Heppenstall particularly seems to have been unable to express his deepest feelings and relive his painful, personal memories except through fiction and the mask of the narrator, as if this exorcised or pardoned his sins vicariously. B.S. Johnson said: 'I write especially to exorcise, to remove from myself, from my mind, the burden [of] having to bear some pain, the hurt of some existence: in order that it may be over there, in a book, and not here in my mind.'[1] Ann Quin too seems only to have been able to write about her experiences in distorted and disguised forms, and Rosalind Belben did not feel able to share her explicit sexual fantasies/experiences except in the form of a novel, but said 'how can I imagine what I do not know?'[2] Jeff Nuttall presented his near-death in hospital as part of a fictionalised collage in *The Patriarchs*, a novelised autobiography just the other side of the line from his *Bomb Culture*, a semi-autobiographical social history and *Performance Art*, a completely autobiographical one. And, following his wife's tragic death, J.G. Ballard confronted his (and possibly our) darkest fantasies in *Crash*. When asked for a factual rather than fictional autobiography by B.S. Johnson for *All Bull,* Alan Burns could not bring himself to do it and wrote about his brother's experience instead. He then fictionalised his own life in *Buster*. The character in *Cain's Book* is undoubtedly Trocchi himself. Even Christine Brooke-Rose, one of the least internal writers in this study tried later in life to confront her younger self in *Remake*, an attempt to 'remake' her earlier life by fictionalising it. Perhaps alone of all the novelists in this study Stefan Themerson never fictionalised his own life but instead novelised his personal and idiosyncratic philosophical ideas. Having said this it must be admitted that several of these novelists, including Heppenstall, Mosley, Figes and Tennant have also written 'straight' autobiographies.

With increasing internalism in writing, when identity and fixed, shared norms and values are called into question, as they have been for so many modern writers, the only subject matter about which the writer may have any confidence may be her/himself, and even this confidence may be limited, so that the writer does not even feel able to write factual autobiography. The modes of fiction and

[1] *Aren't You Rather Young to be Writing Your Memoirs,* pp. 18/19
[2] *Dreaming of Dead People*

autobiography thus tend to merge, and the distinction to become blurred; this has happened in many modern works.[1]

The writer Caradock who is the subject of Stuart Evans' *The Caves of Alienation*, is said to have written an 'essay in autobiographical fiction', and this is an apt description of the works, not only of Quin and Heppenstall, but of several others. B.S. Johnson wrote three avowedly autobiographical novels: *Albert Angelo*; *Trawl*; and *The Unfortunates*.[2]

> The publisher of *Trawl* wished to classify it as autobiography, not as a novel. It is a novel, I insisted and could prove; what it is not is fiction. The novel is a form in the sense that the sonnet is a form; within that form, one may write truth or fiction. I choose to write the truth in the form of a novel.[3]

Also, Johnson's planned trilogy, of which, at his death he had only completed *See the Old Lady Decently*,[4] was highly autobiographical in intent. The first volume, which is a collage of poems, letters, stories and so on (and covers the period up to his own birth), being similar in this respect to another collage autobiography/fiction, whose promised subsequent volumes never appeared either: Norman Hidden's *Dr. Kink and his Old-Style Boarding School*.[5] Also autobiographical/experimental and about a boy from boarding school is Julian Mitchell's *The Undiscovered Country*, which, like Ann Quin's *The Unmapped Country* could be an umbrella title for this kind of novel. Emma Tennant's *Alice Fell* and *Wild Nights* both mythologise her childhood and of course all of Anna Kavan's works are attempts to come to terms with her upbringing (*Who Are You?* being another possible umbrella title). Johnson's *Trawl*, like Heppenstall's *The Woodshed* (from which, as I suggested earlier, the metaphor of trawling memory may have derived) juxtaposes present perceptions with the memories they evoke, and reflects on the nature of memory. Like Heppenstall, Johnson felt that writing down his memories in a partially disguised, fictional form, helped to ease the pain of them: 'Why do I trawl the delicate mesh of my mind over the snagged and broken floor of my past?'[6]; 'I have found few reasons in analysis of my past, so the benefit must have come from the rehearsal of the experiences themselves, like

---

[1] The earliest modern example may be e.e. cummings' *The Enormous Room*, 1922, published in the same years as *The Waste Land*, *Ulysses* and *Jacob's Room*.

[2] Respectively: London: Constable, 1964; London: Secker & Warburg, 1966, repr. Panther 1968; London: Secker & Warburg, 1969. Interview in Burns and Sugnet.

[3] *Memoirs*, p. 14

[4] London: Hutchinson, 1975

[5] London: The Workshop Press, 1973

[6] *Trawl* p. 21

writing an experience down, it fixes it, takes the hurt out of it: one remembers that one was hurt, but not the hurt itself.'[1]

Johnson realised that for a writer 'one always starts with I . . . And ends with I'[2]. A similar attempt at self-discovery in the merging of fiction and autobiography, by a writer with a similarly expressed concern for honesty and reaching the truth, is Alan Sillitoe's *Raw Material* (one of the few British novels Johnson approved of[3]), which is 'part novel, part autobiography'[4]. This contains reflections on the nature of truth, the relationship of fiction to reality, and the story (or *a* story, since it is at least partially invention) of Sillitoe's past. The reflections on fiction are not abstract theorising for its own sake, but arise from Sillitoe's desire to tell the truth about himself (to himself as much as to the reader) combined with the knowledge that this is ultimately impossible. It is this paradox that led him to write his autobiography in this way, rather than claiming it as an objective record of his life, and to call it a novel rather than an autobiography:

> No matter what I call this book, everything written is fiction, even non-fiction - which may be the most fictional non-fiction of all . . . Fiction is a pattern of realities brought to life by suitably applied lies, and one has to be careful, in handling the laws of fiction, not to get so close to the truth that what is written loses its air of reality.[5]

So the 'reality' of a narrative is a contrived effect, not necessarily directly related to its 'truth'; hence making a novel out of one's life rather than trying to present unmediated truth is an attempt to be more truthful, or at least more honest, not more fictional. For Sillitoe, the attempt to discover his own reality, through his own past, is an essential prerequisite to writing about other people truthfully: 'Before a novelist comes into the open he must find some trick of getting inside himself, and there is no other way to do it but to go backwards, which is the only direction left if one is to rediscover the fictional truth that sprawls behind one's spirit.'[6] For Sillitoe, as for Johnson, writing begins and ends with 'I':

> A writer's reality is other people. His hell is himself, whom he is continually trying to get away from, or explain into extinction. But he cannot escape, because the long exploration which lasts all his life from *alef* to *tav*, takes him deeper into that skin-enclosed world of visionary

---

[1] ibid. p. 180
[2] ibid. p. 183 (elision marks in the original)
[3] See his list in *Memoirs* op. cit.
[4] *Raw Material* (London: W.H. Allen, 1972), p. 10
[5] ibid. p. 11
[6] ibid. p. 14/15

> shade and colour, badger-runs of memory, and all inventions of the soul. He goes to find out what is there, and organize it into any sense he can. From such material he creates his *golems* and sends them on to the sidewalks.[1]

The writer's past and his personality are the raw material which, shape and distort it how he will, are an the writer has to work with.

Another writer from Nottingham who emerged around the same time as Sillitoe, and who also at one time seemed to be part of the 'angry' movement, but who has since moved far away from this type of novel, is Philip Callow, all of whose novels have been intensely autobiographical and personal. Callow's novels too pose the question of the separability of fiction and autobiography, and has no desire to try to achieve any objective, impersonal style:

> Who believes in a book cut away from its writer with surgical scissors? I don't, I never did. I don't believe in fact and fiction, I don't believe in autobiography, poetry, philosophy, I don't believe in chapters, in a story . . . In the end you find out what a prison a book is, no matter how you go at it.[2]

It is not only novelists who feel that a book cannot be cut away from its writer, and I would mention particularly two British writers who, though not novelists, share Callow's and the others' mistrust of impersonal objectivity, and have interwoven personal elements into their non-fiction works. I have already mentioned R.D. Laing, and it is natural, given his humanistic and individualistic views that he should renounce the pursuit of a (spurious) scientific detachment when dealing with people rather than objects. His *The Facts of Life*[3], like the books I have just mentioned, is a fictional autobiography, motivated by the same concerns as those of the novelists I have been discussing. All his later work similarly discards scientific methods, and tries to discover new ways to express the complexity and paradoxicality of human experience, which, like Mosley, he feels cannot be expressed in normal, discursive, scientific language. Apart from his own experiments with expression, he often quotes from literature to show that artistic perception is related to schizoid perception, and that people who may seem to be mad merely cope with the world in different ways to the rest of humanity, as do artists and writers. As writers have had to go outside realism to

---

[1] *Raw Material* p. 180

[2] Quoted in *Contemporary Novelists* op. cit. p. 240

[3] London: Allen Lane, 1976; repr. Penguin 1977. See also *The Politics of Experience* and *The Bird of Paradise* (Harmondsworth: Penguin, 1967); *Knots* (London: Tavistock, 1970; repr. Penguin, 1971) and *Sonnets* (London:
Joseph, 1979)

express the complexities of identity, so Laing has gone outside the dominant discourse in his own profession for the same purpose.

Laing's aim is the same as that of the novelists discussed in this study: 'The requirement of the present, the failure of the past, is the same: to provide a thoroughly self-conscious and self-critical human account of man'[1]. But this will not come from the pursuit of scientific detachment:

> It is tempting and facile to regard 'persons' as only separate objects in space, who can be studied as any other natural objects can be studied. But just as Kierkegaard remarked that one will never find consciousness by looking down a microscope at brain cells or anything else, so one will never find persons by studying persons as though they were only objects.[2]

Jeff Nuttall was associated, like Laing, with the individualism and self-expression and development of the underground movements of the sixties, and his *Bomb Culture* is something of an official history of the movements, arguing for the existence of a 'post-Hiroshima' generation, who have no belief in the future and no trust of politicians or institutions. True to this dislike of objectivity and impersonality, Nuttall's social history is never comprehensive, well organised and distanced, but is always opinionated, rambling and polemical. Furthermore, it continually intersperses autobiographical fragments with the history. Nuttall's history of the performance art movement in Britain, of which he was an important part, does not attempt to separate the personal from the historical, and he says in the preface that: 'This isn't a history book, it's a piece of autobiography'[3]. Nuttall's *Snipe's Spinster*[4] is on the one hand a novel, but is also, like *Bomb Culture* a combination of social history and reminiscence. Nuttall also often straddles the other border we have examined, as does Penelope Shuttle in a completely different style, that between poetry and prose. Nuttall sometimes alternates the two, but mainly uses a vigorous, rhythmic, often obscene prose poetry, whose strength seems to owe more to Dylan Thomas than to the American Underground poets he admired, though it also owes much no doubt to his interest in modern jazz: Nuttall was a jazz trumpeter as well as an artist in several media and he had written of his 'wish to create a literary adventure-labyrinth as dense and interpenetrative as a Pollock or a Shepp ensemble'.[5] Shuttle on the other hand, and perhaps uniquely in this study, saves her most

---

1 *The Politics of Experience* op. cit. p. 11

2 ibid. p. 20

3 *Performance Art: Memoirs* (London: John Calder, 1979), p. 9

4 London: Calder & Boyars, 1974

5 *The House Party* (Toronto: Basilike, 1975), unnumbered pages. He has also said: ' The-rhythmic figures owe much to Parker's saxophone phrasing' (*Contemporary Poets* p. 1114)

personal and private utterances for her poetry and the characters in her novels are more symbolic and distanced than personal

Like Laing, Nuttall believes that man is 'radically estranged from the structure of being'[1], but Nuttall believes that this is a permanent and necessary condition, rather than a historical phenomenon. However this should be seen as neither tragic nor absurd, and should be a cause for joy and a source of inspiration and strength rather than a cause for pessimism and despair: 'man is naturally un-natural and . . . this is an absolute enrichment rather than a psychic tragedy'[2]; 'If human life is defined by its separateness from nature, from vision, from eternity, it is precisely in that separateness, that alienation, that the richest rewards of human living lie.'[3] Instead of bemoaning the alienation which defines man's very condition, man should celebrate and explore this separateness and, unlike what he calls the 'mystics' - the solipsistic individualists - should continually work against the border between man and nature, and not retreat into the centre of his being, especially in his art:

> the conscious, the self-conscious mind, the ego, the *identity* is an obstruction to one's union with the cosmos . . . [But] there is a purpose, and a *divine* purpose, to the human alienation from the cosmos. The recognition, definition of Being, in wonderment and ecstasy can only be carried out by a conscious entity alienated from the eternal totality . . . Self-consciousness is, then, the faculty which (a) divides human beings off from Being and thus (b) bestows upon humanity that sense of *otherness* from Being, that distancing from the cosmos whereby the worshipping, *identifying* reaction of wonderment becomes possible.[4]

If man, and especially the artist, retreats into solipsism, which is the danger for internalised writing, and especially for that which is highly autobiographical:

> the individual will experience nothing but man, will lose sight of any comparative identity, will lack any ontological other, any spike against which he can scratch his back, any weight against which to exercise his strength. His muscles will slacken, his self will grow uncertain, his potency will drain away and he will become afflicted with a number of violent neuroses.[5]

---

1 *Politics of Experience* p. 24

2 *Bomb Culture* op. cit. pp. 252/3. This is the opposite view to Eva Figes'.

3 *Man, Not Man* (Llanfynydd, Carmarthen: Unicorn, 1975), p. 17

4 *Bomb Culture* op. cit. p. 251

5 *Man, Not Man* p. 18

The dangers of solipsism have not always been avoided in internal writing, even though Beckett has shown that it is possible to make the most powerful art out of it. Nuttall, however, advocates its opposite: using the edge of human existence, the barrier separating man from 'not man' as a wall against which to hurl oneself, 'a taut barrier of conditions and facts against which you can carry out exercises, confirming and perpetually celebrating your muscle of selfhood and humanity.'[1] The artist, avoiding both the solipsism which autobiographically based writing can entail, and the aesthetic nihilism of the seventies, can still use his own experience. S/he can still start with 'I', but does not have to end there. Even with

> the world falling away to reveal Laing's No Thing. I'm a naïve optimist. Rather than sit in meditative prayer with my mind blown as clear as Leary's I attempt to continue to build. In this building, myself and my comparatively unremarkable sexual predicaments are not so much a field of study or a point of argument, more bricks and mortar, construction materials, fuel.[2]

I have previously tried to define a trend in British novel writing, which I have classed as broadly experimental and internalised, mainly in opposition to other types of avant garde novel, and to the realist novel; I should now try to define some features which the novelists I have discussed have in common with each other.

I have already said that the novelists I have considered do not in any sense constitute a coherent, and certainly not a conscious movement; they would (and did) disclaim any important cross-influence, though at one time Quin, Figes, B.S. Johnson and Alan Burns were friends and part of a circle introduced by Heppenstall, John Calder and others. Whether they unconsciously and unintentionally exemplify a common trend is another matter, and I think that what I have already said shows that they do, and I will try to draw together the strands to make this even clearer.

There are serious critical problems when talking of literary or any artistic movements, and these should perhaps first be considered. Firstly, artistic movements are often, perhaps usually, defined ex post facto by critics who perceive certain similarities between certain, usually contemporaneous artists, sometimes in different media, and then may stress these similarities at the expense of the differing features of the works, and regardless of the intentions of the artists. (Some movements, such as Cubism and Futurism, are of course based on ideas or theories formulated in advance of most of the work, and possibly expressed in manifestoes, to which the movements followers adhere. Others, such as the Pre-Raphaelite Brotherhood or The Group, are more like societies formed

---

[1] ibid.

[2] *The House Party* op. cit. unnumbered pages

by like-minded individuals with a similar approach rather than a set of theoretical principles.) The danger of this critical practice, useful and perhaps inevitable though it is, is that the individuality of the artist and of individual works may be neglected, and they may be judged by the extent to which they instantiate the features of the movement concerned rather than by their own unique achievements.

In the case of the novelists I have discussed, the differences not only between each novelist, but also between the works of individual novelists' bodies of work are at least as important as the similarities between them, and I have tried not to lose sight of this nor to reduce these differences in any way. I have, in my treatment of each novelist, tried to bring out the implicit common themes and techniques, however, since this is an important critical task when the novels are ostensibly so different. In comparing different novelists, rather than different works by the same novelist, the procedure is necessarily more tenuous, since there are no *a priori* connections between the novelists, except their nationality (though even this is fraught, as I said in the Preface), and the literary tradition they inherited. To thus classify these novelists then is necessarily to some extent arbitrary and reductionist, and this should be borne in mind even though it cannot be eliminated.

I realise that these remarks are out of line with the notions of intertextuality as found in Kristeva, Barthes and others, of the author as producer as outlined by Macherey, or of the idea of the transindividual subject of Goldmann, and I have considered the authors as largely creatively autonomous, even though my thesis that the British novel has largely retained its humanism and individualism, paradoxically does seem to support the existence of Goldmannesque transindividual mental structures, and its anti-humanist implications. However, I think that, in the case of intertextuality and the author as producer rather than creator, even if one accepts the epistemological and ontological premisses of these ideas, this does not necessarily entail the methodological reductionism which usually accompanies them, and that one can consider authors as though they were discrete individuals and bracket the ontological questions. In the case of Goldmann, I think that his idea of similar mental structures in members of the same social group is simply disproved by the two facts that, as is shown in this study, artists from very similar backgrounds and social groupings can produce entirely different types of works, and, conversely, that novelists such as the ones I have grouped together can come from entirely different social *milieux* yet produce works which have many similarities.

This is not, however, meant to be an argument against French literary theory or post-humanism in general; my point is simply this: whether or not one accepts the theoretical premisses of post-humanism, each individual thinks and feels *as* an individual, so that not only can authors be treated as unique individuals (and this does not entail ignoring their background altogether) but the characters they create can be treated as expressions of these individuals, and as representing the thoughts and feelings of individual readers as well as their authors. I have tried to treat the characters in the novels I have considered in this study, not as though they were real people, but as though they were expressions and representations of powerful and important human feelings. I think that, in an age of increasing dehumanisation, the novelist needs more than ever to remain the investigator par excellence of individual uniqueness, and that the critic needs to help in this as much as possible.

The novel remains important, for the disciplines of sociology and psychology, which may at one time have looked set to replace the novel as a means of investigating human conduct, now tend to operate with a post-humanist perspective in which the individual is decentred, notwithstanding the efforts of anti-psychiatrists such as Laing and Szasz, and humanistic psychologists like Maslow, Erikson, Fromm and Rollo May.

I have tried to show that the British novel in this period had preserved these individualistic concerns while abandoning the naïve realist view of character as definable in external terms and unambiguously, and that there is a critical position which follows the same procedure. I have tried to maintain this position in this study, and I think that this fits in with the then British critical outlook, which seems to match in general the stance of the novelists with whom I have been concerned, and which, as I have argued, is so different from prevailing continental and American attitudes.

Having said all this, I must try to define the common features of the novelists I have considered not in terms of structural homologies or literary devices, as if the novels were devoid of human concerns, nor in terms of ethical enquiry, as if the characters in the novels were real people. Nor, as I have said, can the novels be considered as being parts of a coherent movement.

The overriding feature common to them is the combination of the desire to express in the novel the concerns of the contemporary individual with the feeling that the traditional, realist, techniques of the novel are inadequate for this purpose in this age. Within this, and despite their many and obvious differences, there are specific concerns and approaches which the novels do seem to have in common. These are neither necessary nor sufficient conditions for belonging to the overall tendency I am trying to define, but rather Wittgenstinian family resemblances, so that any two novels may have no obvious features in common, but they will both have features in common with other members of the family.

First of all I must consider in what sense these novels are experimental, a word I have used loosely though sparingly. There are certainly no shared techniques or styles which these novels have in common, and which are usually associated with experimental writing, but it is this lack of uniformity between the authors and within each author's works which is precisely what makes them experimental. Each one is an experiment, a new start, an attempt to express the complexity and paradoxicality of the individual. Because of this paradoxicality, no book can ever definitively sum up the individual, and the search for a means of expression can never be fully satisfied. Virginia Woolf foresaw that the novel which tried to express the individual would be likely to be part of a continual struggle, which would not produce a stable and coherent form without sacrificing the quest for truth:

> we must reconcile ourselves to a season of failures and fragments. We must reflect that where so much strength is spent on finding a way of telling the truth, the truth itself is bound to reach us in rather an exhausted and chaotic condition . . . [we must] Tolerate the spasmodic, the obscure, the fragmentary, the failure.[1]

But this failure should not be a cause of despair for either novelist or reader, and no method of striving for the truth should be ruled out: 'Any method is right, every method is right, that expresses what we wish to express, if we are writers; that brings us closer to the novelist's intention if we are readers.'[2] 'There is no limit to the horizon . . . nothing - no 'method', no experiment, even of the wildest - is forbidden, but only falsity and pretence.'[3]

I think that all of the novels I have considered is an experiment in this sense of searching for a form of expression, and that none of them uses unconventional technical devices for their own sake, but always at the service of an attempt to render the complexity of life more closely. Indeed, some of the novels are quite conventional in technique, and very few use any devices more radical than those used in the earlier, modernist period. Heppenstall's *The Blaze of Noon*, for instance is technically a straightforward first person narrative, but is undoubtedly experimental in that it tries to convey a radically different set of perceptions of the world.

It is, perhaps, more useful to think of the novels as non-realist rather than experimental since, if realism is taken in the sense I outlined in the Introduction - the presentation of the individual in society and society in the individual - it is the break from this which characterises these novels, as it characterised the modernist novel. Characters are not well defined and with a place fixed in an ordered and stable society which, whether they conform to it or rebel against it, provides them with an identity, a framework and an outline. In the novels I have discussed, there is no such ordered and stable society, and the characters are consequently only outlined by their own memories, perceptions and emotions, which are often confused or contradictory. Indeed, it is the search for a stable and

---

1 'Mr. Bennett and Mrs. Brown' op. cit. p. 110
2 'Modern Fiction' op. cit. p. 108
3 ibid. p. 110

coherent identity, which is a given in the realist novel, which forms the strongest motif in these novels, as in the modernist novel.

In fact it is possible to regard these novels as modernist or neo-modernist as opposed to postmodernist, in line with David Lodge's schema of modernist, anti-modernist and postmodernist; the authors are certainly 'moderns' rather than 'contemporaries'. This would imply that these British novelists, instead of breaking decisively with previous tradition as the postmodernists did, went back to an earlier period, rejecting anti-modernism in favour of its predecessor, modernism, rather than its successor, postmodernism. However, not all critics are agreed that postmodernism did in fact break radically from previous tradition, and Gerald Graff, for instance, has argued that there was no such decisive break.[1]

My arguments in my Introduction tend, I think, to show that there has been such a break, though it may have been as much with the humanistic and individualistic basis of the novel rather than in any technical or stylistic area that the change was decisive. Christopher Butler, like Lodge, believes that there was a break from modernism in the fifties, and extends an analysis of this to cover visual art and music as well as literature.[2] However, the examples he gives are of artists who are very conscious of their immediate predecessors as well as their inherited tradition, which they consciously sought to throw off. (Whether they succeeded or not is not necessarily the point: the important thing here is that they defined themselves in relation to a tradition, an oppositional relation.) The novelists I have been examining seem to have had no desire to break out of any aesthetic tradition: their struggles have been towards a means of expression rather than away from previous means. Indeed, it is characteristic of them that they are relatively uninterested in contemporary developments either in theory or creative writing, and Heppenstall, Mosley and Figes all made this point to me in conversation. Further, none of them had read the novels of the others to any great extent, and were certainly not influenced by any contemporary British or American writers. Their interests and influences were almost entirely from an earlier age (An exception is Mosley's interest in contemporary philosophy and psychology, and even this does not extend to French structuralism and post-structuralism; Brooke-Rose's did however.) All had read Beckett, and some contemporary French writing, in Heppenstall's and Brooke-Rose's case in the original – both had translated French works –and through Gaberbocchus the cosmopolitan Stefan Themerson was closely connected with Dada and surrealism. Eva in Figes spoke and translated German and D.M. Thomas Russian. A strong common influence seems to have been early existentialism: Dostoevsky was important to Quin and Mosley; Nietzsche to Heppenstall and Mosley, and Kierkegaard to Heppenstall. Literary influences seem to go along

---

1 See 'The Myth of the Postmodernist Breakthrough' in *Literature Against Itself* op. cit.

2 *After the Wake*: Oxford U.P., 1980

with these philosophical ones, as with Quin's love of Camus. On a purely literary level, Heppenstall's influences were primarily French novelists of an earlier generation - Montherlant, Céline, Jouhandeau - and Americans Miller and Saroyan. In writing techniques, Quin was most influenced by Virginia Woolf (especially *The Waves*) and Figes by Faulkner (*The Sound and the Fury*). Nuttall and Trocchi both inevitably fell under the spell of Burroughs (and he of them) as Johnson fell under the spell of Beckett.

I think that all this tends to show that the struggle for form on the part of these novelists is not a purely aesthetic move, but an attempt to forge a synthesis between the novel as it has been handed down, and an irrationalist, individualist, even perhaps solipsist, outlook, in the light of a dehumanised and dehumanising world, where the individual seems to have no place. For this purpose they have taken any techniques that would serve them from wherever they could, with no aesthetic theory to justify them, no body of critical or theoretical writing to adhere to for support, nor any immediate predecessors to rebel against.

One thing that all the very different novels which have resulted from this struggle have in common is that they all tend to undermine the objectivity of conventional narrative (first person as well as third: first person narratives can seem to be objective when the word of the narrator is accepted without question). Heppenstall has the blind Dunkel, who does not always know what is going on around him, the fantasising Leckie/Frobisher, who relates his fantasies in the same 'objective' tone as his normal experiences, and the juxtaposition in *The Shearers* and *Two Moons* of the cosmological perspective and the limited, personal one, pointing to the impossibility of any omniscient and all-inclusive presentation of all events. Also in *The Shearers* the narrator's objectivity is undermined both by the variety of narrative styles (which draw attention to the fact that this is a narrative, not the ultimate truth, and that there are many other possible narratives based on the same events but using different techniques) and the fact that the reader is never told the truth about the murders, despite access to the characters' thoughts, or even the verdict of the court. Similarly, in Mosley's *Accident* we really know what happened to William, or in *Assassins* to Mary. Mosley's Jarvis, Greville, Mary and Bert also have a very limited knowledge of what is going on around them, and the narratives share this limit, giving only glimpses of the action on the periphery of their characters' perceptions. In *Impossible Object* all this goes a step further: not only do neither the narrators nor the characters know fully what is happening, but it is, literally, impossible to describe. Figes, like Mosley, is interested in defective and partial perception, and this applies to Nelly and Beard as well as to Stobbs: the latter's perceptions are defective because of his age, but Beard and Nelly are equally, if not more out of touch with the real world (in so far as there can be said to be a real world: a concept the realist novel never questions, but which Figes calls into doubt, especially in her treatments of the relationships between fictional reality and 'real' reality). The two women of Rosalind Belben's *Bogies* are also unaware of what is happening to them, and Miss Dark is like not only Nelly, but also Leckie/Frobisher in her inability to tell fantasy from reality, as also are Anna Kavan's narrators and the character in Paul Ableman's *I Hear Voices*. Berg is also in this position, and all Quin's books contain other elements of uncertainty: S in *Three* is always a mystery; to herself as well as to Ruth and Leon (and the reader); the identity of the narrator(s) in *Passages* is always in doubt, as it is, though in a different way, in Mosley's *Accident*, which may be written by Charlie, and Figes' *B.* which may be written by B. The sense of the impossibility of ever defining, at least verbally, any person, on which *Three* is based, or of ever arriving at the 'truth' of any situation underlies all these novels. Novels-within novels like Tennant's *The Bad Sister,* Evans' *The Caves of Alienation*, Mitchell's *The Undiscovered Country* and Paul Ableman's *The Twilight of the Vilp* proclaim their fictionality as they claim to be 'real'. Sillitoe's paradoxical insistence that the truth can never be told by simply trying to tell the truth, and B.S. Johnson's claim that telling stories is telling lies are matched by Trocchi's statement that 'there is no story to tell'.

The impossibility of pinning down the truth about any situation surfaces in these novels in the frequent undermining of detective or murder stories: *The Shearers* clearly does this, as do *Accident*, *Assassins* (where Mary's kidnapping is never explained) and, even more obviously *Imago Bird*, where Bert compares the shot in his uncle's study to a shot offstage in a murder mystery. Both *Berg* and *Three* refer to detective stories, but, in both cases the reader is trying to discover, not the identity of a murderer, but whether any murder has been committed, and in *Berg* the central character is not a detective, but the potential murderer. *Nelly's Version* too is structured like a thriller, with hints and clues throughout, but here, as in all the other novels I have mentioned, but unlike the traditional detective story, there is no possibility of any revelation of the 'truth', no 'reading' of the situation. The same is true of other inverted, exitential crime novels like Trocchi's *Young Adam*, Giles Gordon's *Girl with Red Hair*, Themerson's *Special Branch*, Redgrove and Shuttle's *The Glass Cottage* and Nuttall's *Pig*, *The Gold Hole* and *What Happened to Jackson*.

Perhaps the most striking theme - stronger than a theme, a structural device - is that of the individual alone and powerless. Anna Kavan named herself after one of her characters who, like herself, had been alone and isolated since early childhood; all the characters Anna Kavan – herself an invented character –wrote are as alone as she was. Heppenstall's Dunkel is, almost literally, in a world of his own, a world of darkness, but the Frobisher/Leckie/Atha of the other novels is hardly less so: in *Saturnine* and *The Greater Infortune* he is alone in his unreal, fantasy world; in *The Lesser Infortune* he is isolated by his intelligence, as he is as a boy in *The Woodshed*, where, as an adult, he is alone with his memories; in *The Connecting Door* he is alone, not with himself but with his 'selves', and in

Two Moons he is alone with his guilt. In none of the books does he have any close emotional relationships (except to his son in *Two Moons*, but one of the reasons for his guilt feelings is precisely that he has not been close enough to him), not even to his wife, except at the end of *Saturnine*, and then the novel ends at the point at which he grows close to his wife.

Also alone with his guilt is Mosley's Jarvis, while his Greville seems to have no real contact with anyone, neither in his personal life with his wife, secretary or Natalie/Natalia, nor in his political life. Mary in *Assassins* is as much alone at home with her father as she is with her kidnapper, perhaps even more so, and her father is seen as having to bear alone the responsibility for the decisions in his dealings with Korin. Like Mary and Greville, Bert is shown against both the establishment and the anti-establishment, which he has contact with but without belonging to either, and Jason in *Serpent* like Mosley himself in *Catastrophe* emphasises the essentially solitary nature of the individual.

In *Impossible Object* we have several unhappy and uncommunicative relationships - not only the Mostyns' inability to express their feelings to each other, but everyone's inability to express their ambiguous and contradictory feelings because of the inadequacies of language. Likewise in Figes there are no relationships in which two people can really communicate their feelings, not even those between mother and daughter. Figes' women, though trapped in a recurrent cycle of imprisonment common to them all, are unable to communicate their sense of this to each other, let alone to men. Nelly seems to break out of the cycle temporarily, but is thereby all the more isolated by her lack of identity. Figes' men are also alone: Stobbs in his solitary journey to death (which everyone has to face alone) has lost his wife, whom he did not understand in any case, and is resented by the younger generation; Konek is the homeless, stateless and classless product of war, and Beard has been left by two wives and his son, and even B. comes to seem less real to him when he has been deserted by the real world and has only the fictional left. All of Rosalind Belben's women are also alone; even the married ones as in *Reuben Little Hero* and *The Limit* gain no real comfort and support from their husbands, even though they are well-meaning, and Penelope Shuttle's lovers are similarly isolated from even those they love. And Anna Kavan's characters' fictional marriages, like her own real one, leave her more isolated than she was before, without even a mother or sister to confide in, and the men in their lives a constant disappointment. Kavan gives us several versions of the glass-girl, the transparent *femme fragile* she felt herself but also shows us the hard, bright rock-like being she wants to, but never can be: free but alone.

In Ann Quin's work, Berg is not only alone, but tries to make himself even more so - a unique individual and existentialist hero, and S in *Three* is at least as alone while living with Ruth and Leon as when by herself; the presence of a couple makes her own isolation stand out even more, even though they hardly communicate with each other, and then only on a superficial level, and are really as isolated as S. In *Passages* there may be two people, but if there are they are alone in a strange land and have fleeting love affairs with no emotional contact. The narrator of *Tripticks* has had three wives but is now alone and trying to escape, and Sandra in *The Unmapped Country*, like Paul Ableman's narrator in *I Hear Voices* is alone in the mental hospital, isolated by her madness from the outside world; similarly in Such the narrator occupies a world between dream and reality. Trocchi's narrators in *Cain's Book* and *Young Adam* are isolated by their needs, sexual and chemical.

Alienation has been a persistent theme in modern literature, but I do not think that the isolation of the individuals in these novels is the result of alienation, either in the general or the strictly Marxian sense. It is true that Figes shows, as does Jeff Nuttall, that man is radically estranged from nature, but this is not the cause of the isolation of individuals from each other. Mosley's ideas on self-alienation are very different from alienation from society, and show it as, potentially, a great benefit; it is that which, as with Nuttall's alienation from Being, defines man and makes him separate and worthwhile. While alienation has been so variously used as to now be almost meaningless, it probably always implies a society or group from which the individual for some reason - or for no apparent reason - is excluded; Anna Kavan would always feel excluded from any society and Ann Quin never found a place where she felt she belonged. Multilingual, uprooted authors like Themerson, Brooke-Rose and Figes would always feel distanced from their environment - always, in Brooke-Rose's novel 'between', though some places, like Shuttle, Redgrove and Thomas' Cornwall, Belben's Dorset or Nuttall's Yorkshire could provide a physical and symbolic home.

But in these novels there is rarely any sense of a society at all from which to be alienated, and into which the individual could possibly be incorporated. It is true that Heppenstall's adolescence as shown in *The Woodshed* was marked by his social ostracism, but the older man, who narrates the book, and all Heppenstall's others, has few contacts to be isolated from, and his resentment of the middle classes seems to be merely an aspect of his dislike and distrust of other people in general. It is also true that Mosley's individuals exist in recognisable social *milieux,* but the point here is not that the society rejects or is closed to them, indeed Jervis, Greville and Hann at least are ostensibly members of the establishment of the society, but that the individual can never be fully a social being, since his inability to express himself linguistically leaves part of him essentially private.

In some of these novels society has broken down, usually after some apocalyptic tragedy - *Europe After the Rain*; *Ice*; *Mercury*; *Out*; *The Survivor*; most of J.G. Ballard – and the individual has no defined place in an undefined society. In others society has become the 'spectacle' – *The Angry Brigade*; *Babel*;

Dreamerika; *Between*; *Tripticks*; *Thru*; *Crash* - inhabited by affectless, powerless unindividual individuals.

Most modern novels of isolation show the individual set against mass society, but this is not the case in any of these novels, and nor are their characters romantic heroes isolated from the common people by some spiritual or intuitive superiority (Mosley's new type might be thought of in this way, but this type is not present in any of his novels; even Jason only describes rather than exemplifies it). Although this is the way Frobisher/Leckie sees himself, as do Beard and Berg, they are all deluded, and inadequate rather than superior. These, then, are neither sub- nor superhuman individuals; they are neither crushed by society nor transcend it. They are, precisely, individuals, and their essential solitariness is seen neither as the result of the loss of some community, a move from *Gemeinschaft* to *Gesellschaft*, nor due to some inherent difference or special quality in themselves, even though some of them are outsiders in the Colin Wilson or Camus sense. As are their authors: Kavan, born in France to British parents was given to a wet-nurse at birth by her mother who then went to America without her; Heppenstall was separated by his going to grammar school both from his poorer friends and his family, and from the boys he met there, who were mostly from a different background; Mosley was in a very isolated position just before and during the war (in which Anna Kavan's only child died) when his father was interned and generally reviled; in something of a reverse of this, Figes came over from Germany just before the outbreak of war, and spent her childhood feeling separated by her language, her religion, and her nationality, hating Germans and being German; Themerson was similarly forced to leave Poland, went to France and then because of the war had to leave there without his wife; Brooke-Rose, born in Geneva to an English father and a Swiss-American mother grew up speaking three languages and went to school in England; Trocchi was Scottish/Italian but never settled in Britain after national service, like many other rootless expatriates he knew in Paris; Quin's sense of not belonging had no such obvious causes, but seems to have been no less deeply felt, and she never seemed to find any home or any relationships of circles of friends into which she could fully absorb herself; in a similar way B.S. Johnson, who like Alan Burns was separated from his family as an evacuee during the war, despite, or perhaps because of his aggressive networking and self-promotion, never felt truly part of any social group.

The situation of the individual characters is neither meaningful nor absurd (to paraphrase Robbe-Grillet); they are simply there. And, being there, they need to find some way to make sense of, and to live through their lives, without any social, ethical, religious or genetic guidelines to help them. That is, they need to find a self which they can become, but do not know where to look for it. Anna Kavan literally invented herself; Figes' women seek it in the mirror, in their image as presented to them, but cannot fully adapt to the shape of it; Heppenstall's narrators seek to create a self through memory, and S in *Three* 'in the domestic mindlessness of Ruth and Leon, while Berg and Jervis, and to some extent Greville, try more to escape imposed identities than fine new ones, as does Stefan Konek.

The gap between the social self as presented to other people, and the inner self - if any - which is such an important theme in most of these books, leads to a common interest in roles, masks, facades and theatre as metaphors for these two aspects of character: the actor and the role. The comparison of life with drama occurs in *Nelly's Version* and *On Stage*, throughout Quin's work; in Mosley's *Imago Bird* and Greville's feigned illness and Jervis's assumption of different roles for different occasions, and in Heppenstall's use in *The Shearers* of the different types of ritual which people resort to in order to absolve them of individual responsibility for their actions. This comparison with roles in the theatre and in life is made explicitly in a non-fictional work in Erving Goffman's *The Presentation of Self in Everyday Life*[1], and in Alan Kennedy's *The Protean Self*[2], which is an application of Goffman's theories to the analysis of literary characters. Goffman maintains that everyone acts out several roles, which consist of a 'front' (the surroundings and background), and a 'performance' (speech, dress etc.). The roles vary with the situation, and may be played individually or, more usually, as a 'team' performance (as in Sartre's example of the waiter acting as a waiter and Jervis's acting like a don when with other dons), but the individual is always playing some role or other. The problem Goffman does not tackle is whether there is any self behind the role, and if so what sort of thing it is. Presumably Goffman would reply that it is impossible to tell, since no person can completely drop all their roles, but, nevertheless, this is what many of these novels do implicitly investigate. The title of Kennedy's book implies that he at least thinks that there is a self behind the roles, even if it has no 'shape' of its own, and the novels I have discussed all seem to assume this also. Indeed, they often take a case where the roles are breaking down, as with Mosley's Greville, or in conflict, as with Quin's Jervis and Berg (son/avenger), and the characters rarely have any 'team' with which to perform as a result of their isolation. Figes' Nelly's role has broken down completely, and her loss of memory, like an actor's forgetting not only his lines, but even what play he is in, leaves her not knowing what sort of role to play. Some characters do not even have names: Ableman's narrator for instance, or Belben's prisoner, whose identity is confused even to herself and may or may not be the person the authorities think she is. Even more unsettling are the novels written in the second-person, like MacBeth's *The Transformation* and Gordon's *Girl with Red Hair*. Both these show however that as readers we try to construct character from the thinnest of evidence, as with Bill

[1] London: Allen Lane The Penguin Press, 1969
[2] London: Macmillan, 1974

Toge in Tom Phillips' *A Humument* or the teeming mass of names in Alan Burns' *Babel.*

In an earlier age, the realist novel could assume that the social role and the self were the same, as the question of people even thinking in ways outside the limitations of their social sphere hardly arose (it arises in the Brontes, but then they hardly wrote realist novels). It was assumed that to describe a person's external situation and circumstances was to describe the whole person. In the modern period, this ceases to be seen as valid, and this is precisely Virginia Woolf's criticism of Wells, Bennet and Galsworthy. In the post-war period, especially with increased social mobility, the individual does not always know her/his 'place' or 'who' s/he is or is supposed to be, and does not know how to go about finding out. The change in this century has been noted, in relation to psychoanalysis, by Erik H. Erikson: 'the patient of today suffers most under the problem of what he should believe in and who he should - or, indeed, might - become; while the patient of early psychoanalysis suffered most under inhibitions which prevented him from being what and who he thought he knew he was.'[1]

Nevertheless, there is always a sense in these novels of some underlying self, and, indeed, this is precisely the basis of internalised writing, to try to penetrate the role, get behind the mask, and separate the mirror image from the real. This split between persona and person manifests itself in the novels not only in the emphasis on roles, but in various splits and dichotomies in the novels themselves, such as the juxtapositions of fantasy and reality in *Saturnine*, *Accident*, *Nelly's Version*, *Berg*, Belben's *Bogies*, Shuttle's *The Mirror of the Giant*, Tennant's *Wild Nights* and *Alice Fell* and Redgrove and Shuttle's *The Glass Cottage*; of present and memory in *The Woodshed* and *The Connecting Door*; personal and cosmological in *The Shearers* and *Two Moons*; public and private in *Imago Bird*, *Assassins* and *Accident*, and the schizophrenia of *Passages* and *The Unmapped Country*. Sometimes the opposites represented by these dichotomies are contradictory or incompatible; in Mosley nearly always so. In *Impossible Object* the man both wants his lover to stay and to go, and Jervis both wants to be fully alive in the existentialist sense, and to sink into his role and surroundings, which is almost exactly the situation of Leckie/Frobisher, who at the same time wants to be free of constraint, and to believe in Catholicism and astrology, which tend to deny individual freedom. Similarly, Berg wants both to belong to society and to transcend it, and the man in *Passages* wants both madness (the Dionysian) and security (the Apollonian). Liz Winter wants both freedom and the sense of identity that goes with lack of freedom, as do Nelly and Konek. Janus Stobbs wants and fears death and life[2] (the contradiction implied in the Romantic Wanderlust) and Beard, in order to capture life in his writing feels he must cut himself off from life as much as possible. In Belben's *The Limit*, Ilario is both

[1] *Childhood and Society* (New York: Norton, 1950, 2nd ed. 1963), p. 279

[2] This may be related to Otto Rank's 'life fear' and 'death fear'.

repulsed by and in love with Anna, and the narrator of *Dreaming of Dead People* both wants to be free and feels an almost intolerable loneliness.

These contradictory wishes and desires cannot always be held in a rational mind, and result. in what is normally called madness. Contradictory desires, or pressures on the individual can put them in what Laing calls 'untenable positions', from which there is no escape by rational means, and this is the reason for Leckie's self-imposed 'death'. There is certainly a good deal of mental instability in the novels I have mentioned, and in the stories of Anna Kavan. Leckie's hallucinations, Greville's ostensible state of mind and Jervis's real one; Nelly's and Belben's Miss Dark's lapses of memory or schizophrenia and Beard's mental decline; Berg's strange delusions, S's state before meeting Ruth and Leon and Sandra's stay in a mental hospital in The *Unmapped Country*; Redgrove's interest in psychiatry and 'dream-therapy' and Mosley's parody of psychiatrists in *Imago Bird* are all aspects of this concern to show that 'madness' is only one way of coping with pressures and desires which cannot be reconciled in any 'normal', rational way.

Another aspect of these contradictory desires and pressures is the way the characters tend to feel both powerless to affect events, and yet guilty for whatever happens. This applies especially to Anna Kavan, to all Figes' women, Leckie and Atha in *Two Moons*; Berg, Leon and the man in *Passages*; Belben's Ilario and the mother in *Reuben, Little Hero*, as well as Mosley's Jervis.

There may be other common elements between the books I have been discussing, but I think I have said enough to show that my grouping of them together has a firm basis, and that, if there was no coherent movement represented here, there were at least enough writers in Britain at that time with similar outlooks both in their humanistic intentions and in their approach to developing and extending the form of the novel, who are also very different from the majority of experimentally-minded continental and American novelists, to claim that British novel-writing was both flourishing and highly distinctive.

In 1820, Sidney Smith wrote that America had contributed nothing to civilisation and culture, and challenged: 'who reads an American book?'[1] But then came an explosion in American literature, and thirty years later Melville, reviewing Hawthorne, foresaw the emergence of a purely American literature superior to its British counterpart, and replied to the challenge: "Believe me, my friends, that men not very much inferior to Shakespeare are this day being born on the banks of the Ohio. And the day will come when you shall say, Who reads a book by an Englishman that is a modern?'[2] This change may have taken longer to come about than Melville thought, and perhaps was not so complete, but there is no

[1] *The Edinburgh Review*; repr. in *The Native Muse* ed. R. Ruland (New York: Dutton, 1976), p. 156

[2] *The Literary World* repr. in Ruland, op. cit. p. 321

doubt that, in regard to contemporary fiction at least, American and French authors were taken far more seriously at this time than British ones, to the extent that even informed opinion would often deny the existence of a British experimental novel, let alone question its ability to stand comparison with its foreign counterparts. This seems to have happened after the growth of American postmodernism and the *nouveau roman*: several articles in a series in the *Times Literary Supplement* in 1959[1] called for an increase in, and a more serious attitude to American studies in this country, but by 1968 Karl Miller, looking back over the previous fifteen years in English writing, said: 'The fever for American literature which succeeded the 'French flu' in this country has resulted in a philistine condescension towards native writers'[2]. And, writing in the same year and reviewing much the same period, Jeff Nuttall challenged:

> It is surely time we turned away from the Americans, a nation of agoraphobic neurotics whose only native excellence lies in the skill and grace of their movement (the benefit of which the world has felt) who are, in any case in an irrecoverable state of civic rot, and called upon the native European sense of classic form and rational serenity.[3]

Meanwhile, those people who were worried about the posthumanist march of the American and continental novels looked to realism, and the British novel, to preserve a traditional humanism, ignoring as far as possible the decline in aesthetic quality which had resulted in general from the attempt to treat contemporary reality in the form of the nineteenth century novel. But, as I hope to have shown in this study, realism and humanism are not inseparable in the novel, even if the humanism I have been examining is of a different, more individualistic kind than the traditional one.

Lukacs' criticism of modernism, and specifically of Kafka[4], was that, although Kafka was pointing to genuine terrors of the modern world, and to a genuine alienation, he was showing it as universal and inevitable rather than historically specific and changeable by political means. For Lukacs, realism would always be critical of society (and a socialist realism would show not only the problems of a society but the answers too). The answer to this (which was given by Ernst Fischer, Adorno, Marcuse and Brecht) is twofold: the problems have become so horrific that they cannot be adequately described but can only be alluded to; and the historical optimism of a Marxist is not shared by everyone. To this one could add, in defence of the move from realism, that the complexities

---

[1] All repr. in *The American Imagination* (London: Cassel, 1960)

[2] *Writing in England Today* (Harmondsworth: Penguin, 1968), p. 26

[3] *Bomb Culture* op. cit. p. 254

[4] In 'The Ideology of Modernism' in his *The Meaning of Contemporary Realism* (London: Merlin, 1963)

and contradictions of modern life, as Mosley tries to show, simply cannot be formulated in normal, discursive, realist writing. Also, in terms of political criticism of literature, in addition to Brecht's insistence that any art which would change society must first be shocking and disconcerting, there is the point that the 'literary myth of a rigidly ordered self contributes to a pervasive cultural ideology of the self which serves the established order.'[1]

Internalised writing, as I have tried to show, explodes this myth without subscribing to the other myth of the self as merely a product of converging lines of social, political, ideological and cultural forces; a place in a linguistic grid rather than a unique individual. Raymond Williams, regretting the passing of a humanist realism which showed the interaction of individual and society, describes how realism has split into two main trends: the 'social' and the 'personal'[2], which are obviously similar to my 'internal' and 'external'. Williams admits that this split is due to a genuine loss of community[3], but feels that a return to realism would help to recreate this community by showing this interaction at work again. But, leaving aside the rather optimistic nature of this plea, surely, if in humanism it is the individual who is the basis of all value (though this may not be true for a Marxist humanism), an internalised 'personal' novel, which investigates the individual, may be the best way to preserve humanism when, as Williams admits, there is no 'knowable community'.

The novelist is not a prophet, and seeing the loss of community may look elsewhere for her/his inspiration, perhaps inwards, inside the individual. The artist who seeks to express the plight of the individual must portray the isolation, fragmentation and loss of identity which are so typical of contemporary society, and must change as the situation changes if s/he is to remain true to the subject. The contemporary

> fiction writer is faced by breakdown on so many levels, without the compensatory idea of communities explored by the nineteenth century novelist, that he annually finds his material changing. After the Second World War, the traditional sense of community became outmoded, and will remain outmoded until the novelist discern new formations.[4]

---

1 Leo Bersani, *A Future for Astyanax* (New York: Little, Brown, 1976), p. 56

2 'Realism and the Contemporary Novel' in his *The Long Revolution* (London: Chatto, 1961; repr. Penguin, 1965)

3 See *The English Novel from Dickens to Lawrence* (London: Chatto, 1970) For criticism of Williams see Terry Eagleton, *Criticism & Ideology* (London: New Left Books, 1976), and Peter Ackroyd, *Notes for a New Culture* (London: Vision, 1976), pp. 106-119

4 F.R. Karl, *A Reader's Guide to the Contemporary English Novel* (London: Thames & Hudson, 1963; 2nd ed. 1972), p. 325

That things *were* changing annually is illustrated by the fact that an earlier edition of the same book had said:

> The greatest temptation the English novelist must resist in the succeeding years is his natural desire to withdraw from the large world into the little one. Dismayed perhaps by the buzzing confusions of a society in which no solutions are possible, in which the artist or layman cannot even recommend a way out, he may in self-defence retreat into a world of minor issues.[1]

But the fact is, as Virginia Woolf showed, and in which all the novelists I have discussed agree, to shrink the novel's world to the domestic may be to limit and narrow it, but to shrink it further, inside the individual, is to be open to the inexhaustible; as Dorothy Richardson said: 'everyone, every single soul, has all potentialities'[2]. The internal approach to the novel, far from constraining it, sets it free and along with it, potentially, the reader. This type of novel, which 'repeatedly depicts an extreme solipsism, affects us not with a sense of constriction but of release. For though the subject-matter is death and loss and degradation of the self-enclosed in its private world, the act of following through and articulating these things brings with it a powerful sense of joy and release.'[3] Josipovici is here talking about Robbe-Grillet, whose anti-humanism I have already discussed, but I think this comment applies to the novels I have considered, which, as I have argued, seem to me to extend the form of the novel without abandoning its humanist tradition. This seems to me important, and I agree with David Lodge that the

> function of the avant-garde is to win new freedom, new expressive possibilities for the arts. But these things have to be won, have to be fought for; and the struggle is not merely with external canons of taste, but within the artist himself. To bend the existing conventions without breaking them - this is the strenuous and heroic calling of the experimental artist. To break them is too easy.[4]

Despite poststructuralist doubts about the novel having any expressive possibilities to extend, and even if language cannot ultimately refer beyond itself,

---

1 1st ed. p. 294

2 Quoted by John Rosenberg in *Dorothy Richardson: The Genius They Forgot* (London: Duckworth, 1973), p. 71

3 Gabriel Josipovici, *The World and the Book* (London: Macmillan, 1971; repr. Paladin, 1973), p. 254

4 David Lodge, 'Objections to William Burroughs' in *Innovations* op. cit.

and 'this "I" which approaches the text is already a plurality of existing texts'[1], novels can surely open up new worlds of experience for the reader, regardless of their ultimate lack of reference, for once

> it is in a condition of literature, language behaves exponentially. It is at every point more than itself . . . All language . . . stands in an active, ultimately creative relationship to reality. In literature, that relationship is energized and complicated to the highest degree. A major poem discovers hitherto unlived life-forms and, quite literally, releases hitherto inert forces of perception.[2]

1 Roland Barthes, *S/Z* (New York: Hill & Wang, 1974), p. 10
2 George Steiner, 'The Language Animal' in *Extraterritorial* (London: Faber, 1972), p. 90

chronology

Novels discussed in the book; dates of first British publication.

1939	Rayner Heppenstall	*The Blaze of Noon*
1943	Rayner Heppenstall	*Saturnine*
1947	Philip Toynbee	*Tea with Mrs Goodman*
1948	Anna Kavan	*Sleep Has His House*
1949	Anna Kavan	*The Horse's Tale*
1951	Stefan Themerson	*Wooff Wooff*
1953	Stefan Themerson	*Professor Mmaa's Lecture*
	Rayner Heppenstall	*The Lesser Infortune*
1956	Anna Kavan	*A Scarcity of Love*
1958	Anna Kavan	*Eagle's Nest*
	Paul Ableman	*I Hear Voices*
1960	Rayner Heppenstall	*The Greater Infortune*
1961	Alan Burns	*Buster*
	Alexander Trocchi	*Young Adam*
	Stefan Themerson	*Cardinal Pölätüo*
1962	Rayner Heppenstall	*The Woodshed*
	Rayner Heppenstall	*The Connecting Door*
1963	Alexander Trocchi	*Cain's Book*
	Anna Kavan	*Who Are You?*
	B.S. Johnson	*Travelling People*
1964	Ann Quin	*Berg*
	B.S. Johnson	*Albert Angelo*
	Christine Brooke-Rose	*Out*
1965	Alan Burns	*Europe After the Rain*
	Alan Burns	*Celebrations*
	Stefan Themerson	*Bayamus*

1966	Ann Quin	*Three*
	B.S. Johnson	*Trawl*
	Christine Brooke-Rose	*Such*
	Eva Figes	*Equinox*
	Nicholas Mosley	*Accident*
	Nicholas Mosley	*Assassins*
1967	Anna Kavan	*Ice*
	Brian Aldiss	*Report on Probability A*
	Jeff Nuttall	*Isabel*
	Eva Figes	*Winter Journey*
	Penelope Shuttle	*An Excusable Vengeance*
1968	Christine Brooke-Rose	*Between*
	Jeff Nuttall	*Come Back Sweet Prince*
	Julian Mitchell	*The Undiscovered Country*
	Nicholas Mosley	*Impossible Object*
1969	Jeff Nuttall	*Oscar Christ*
	Paul Ableman	*The Twilight of the Vilp*
	Alan Burns	*Babel*
	Ann Quin	*Passages*
	Brian Aldiss	*Barefoot in the Head*
	B.S. Johnson	*The Unfortunates*
	Eva Figes	*Konek Landing*
	Jeff Nuttall	*Pig*
	Penelope Shuttle	*All the Usual hours of Sleeping*
	Rayner Heppenstall	*The Shearers*
1970	J.G. Ballard	*The Atrocity Exhibition*
1971	B.S. Johnson	*House Mother Normal*
	Eva Figes	*Waking*
	Nicholas Mosley	*Natlie Natalia*
1972	Jeff Nuttall	*The Foxes Lair*
	Alan Burns	*Dreamerika*
	Ann Quin	*Tripticks*

	Eva Figes	*B.*
	Rosalind Belben	*Bogies*
	Stefan Themerson	*Special Branch*
	Stefan Themerson	*General Piesc*
1973	Alan Burns	*The Angry Brigade*
	B.S. Johnson	*Christie Malry's Own Double Entry*
	J.G. Ballard	*Crash*
	Penelope Shuttle	*Wailing Monkey Embracing a Tree*
	Peter Redgrove	*In the Country of the Skin*
	Rosalind Belben	*Reuben, Little Hero*
	Norman Hidden	*Dr Kink*
	Tom Phillips	*A Humument*
1974	Eva Figes	*Days*
	Rosalind Belben	*The Limit*
1975	Anna Kavan	*My Soul in China*
1975	Ann Quin	*The Unmapped Country*
	B.S. Johnson	*See the Old Lady Decently*
	Christine Brooke-Rose	*Thru*
	George MacBeth	*The Transformation*
	Jeff Nuttall	*Snipe's Spinster*
	Jeff Nuttall	*House Party*
1976	Jeff Nuttall	*Krak*
	Jeff Nuttall	*Fatty Feedemall*
	Eva Figes	*Nelly's Version*
	George MacBeth	*The Survivor*
	Penelope Shuttle	*Rainsplitter in the Zodiac Garden*
1977	Rayner Heppenstall	*Two Moons*
	Redgrove/Shuttle	*The Glass Cottage*
	Stuart Evans	*The Caves of Alienation*
1978	Emma Tennant	*The Bad Sister*
	Jeff Nuttall	*The Gold Hole*
	Jeff Nuttall	*What Happened to Jackson*

1979	Jeff Nuttall	*The Patriarchs*
	Emma Tennant	*Wild Nights*
	Nicholas Mosley	*Catastrophe Practice*
	Rosalind Belben	*Dreaming of Dead People*
1980	Emma Tennant	*Alice Fell*
	Nicholas Mosley	*Imago Bird*
	Penelope Shuttle	*The Mirror of the Giant*
	Stefan Themerson	*Tom Harris*
1981	Alan Burns	*The Day Daddy Died*
	Nicholas Mosley	*Serpent*
1982	Jeff Nuttall	*Muscle*

bibliography

Ackroyd, Peter. *Notes for a New Culture*. London: Vision, 1976

Adams, Robert Martin. *After Joyce*. New York: Oxford U.P., 1977

Adelman, Irving and Rita Dworkin. *The Contemporary Novel: A Checklist of Critical Literature on the British and American Novel Since 1945*. Methuen, New Jersey, 1972

Aesthetics and Politics. London: New Left Books, 1979

Aiken, Conrad. *Time in the Rock*. New York: Scribners, 1936

Aldiss, Brian W. *Report on Probability A*. in *New Worlds* 171, 1967

_____ *Barefoot in the Head*. London: Faber and Faber, 1969

_____ 'The Impossible Puppet Show' in *Factions* ed. Giles Gordon and Alex Hamilton, London: Joseph, 1974

Aldiss, Brian and Harrison, Harry eds. *Decade the 1950s*. London: Pan, 1977

Allen, Walter. *Tradition and Dream*. London: Dent, 1966

Allsop, Kenneth. *The Angry Decade*. London: Peter Owen, 1958

Alvarez, AL *The Shaping Spirit: Studies in Modern English and American Poets*. London: Chatto & Windus, 1958

_____ (ed.) *The New Poetry*. Harmondsworth: Penguin, 1962

_____ *Under Pressure: The Writer in Society: Eastern Europe and the U.S.A*. Harmondsworth: Penguin, 1965

American Imagination, The. London: Cassell, 1960

Amis, Kingsley. *New Maps of Hell*. London: Gollancz, 1960

_____ The James Bond Dossier London: Cape, 1965

Amis, Martin. *Other People*. London: Cape, 1981

Antonini, Giacomo. 'Il Padre del Nouveau Roman' (on Rayner Heppenstall). *La Fiera Letteraria* (Milan), April 1962

Ash, Brian, ed. *The Visual Encyclopedia of Science Fiction*. New York: Harmony, 1977

Atkins, John. *Six Novelists Look At Society*. London: John Calder, 1977

J. G. Ballard. *The Wind from Nowhere*. Berkley Books, 1961

_____ *The Drowned World*. Berkley Books, 1962

_____ 'Time, Memory and Inner Space' in *The Woman Journalist*, 1963

_____ *The 4-Dimensional Nightmare*. London: Gollancz, 1963

_____ 'Myth Maker of the 20th Century' in *New Worlds* no. 142, May/June 1964

_____ *The Drought*. London: Jonathan Cape, 1965

_____ *The Crystal World*. London: Jonathan Cape, 1966

_____ *The Atrocity Exhibition*. London: Jonathan Cape, 1970

_____ *Crash*. London: Jonathan Cape, 1973

_____ *Concrete Island*. London: Jonathan Cape, 1974

______ 'Cataclysms and Dooms' in Ash, Brian, ed. *The Visual Encyclopedia of Science Fiction*. New York: Harmony, 1977
______ Interview with Alan Burns in Burns, Alan and Sugnet, Charles ed. *The Imagination on Trial*. London: Alison & Busby, 1981
Barth, John. 'Title' in his *Lost in the Funhouse*. London: Seeker, 1969
______ 'The Literature of Exhaustion' in The Novel Today, ed. Malcolm Bradbury. Glasgow: Fontana/Collins, 1977
Barthelme, Donald.. 'The Emerging Figure'. *Forum*, Summer, 1961
______ 'The Various Isolated: W.C. Williams I Prose'. *New American Review*, 15, 1972
Barthes, Roland. *Writing Degree Zero*. London: Cape, 1953
Barthes, Roland. 'Objective Literature: Alain Robbe-Grillet'. *Evergreen Review*, 5, Summer 58
______ *Elements of Semiology*. London: Cape, 1967
______ *S/Z*. New York: Hill & Wang, 1974
______ *The Pleasure of the Text*. London: Cape, 1975
______ *Image, Music, Text*, ed. and trans. Stephen Heath. Glasgow: Fontana/Collins, 1977
Bayley, John. *The Characters of Love: A Study in the Literature of Personality*. London: Constable, 1960
Belben, Rosalind. *Bogies*. London: Hutchinson New Authors, 1972
______ *Reuben, Little Hero*. London: Hutchinson, 1973
______ *The Limit*. London: Hutchinson, 1974
______ *Dreaming of Dead People*. Brighton: Harvester, 1979
______ *Is Beauty Good*. London: Serpents Tail, 1989
______ *Choosing Spectacles*. London: Serpents Tail, 1995
______ *Hound Music*. London: Chatto & Windus, 2001
______ *Our Horses in Egypt*. London: Chatto & Windus, 2007
Bellamy, Joe David ed. *The New Fiction*. Illinois U.P., 1974
______ *Superfiction*. New York: Vintage, 1975
Berger, Harold L. *Science Fiction and the New Dark Age*. Bowling Green U.P. 1976
Bergonzi, Bernard ed . *Innovations*. London: Macmillan, 1965
______ *The Situation of the Novel*. London: Macmillan, 1970, 2nd ed. 1979
______ 'Fictions of History' in *The Contemporary English Novel*, Stratford-Upon-Avon Studies 18, ed. Malcolm Bradbury and David Palmer. London: Arnold, 1979
Bersani, Leo. *A Future for Astyanax*. New York: Little, Brown, 1976
Bigsby, Chris. 'The Uneasy Middleground of British Fiction'. *Granta*, 1, 3, 1980
______ and Heide Ziegler. See Ziegler, Heide
Bisztray, G. *Marxist Models of Literary Realism*. Columbia U.P., 1973
Bloom, Harold. *The Anxiety of Influence*. New York: O.U.P., 1973

______ 'The Native Strain: American Orphism'. in *Literary Theory and Structure: Essays Presented to W.K. Wimsatt*. ed. Frank Brady et al. Yale U.P., 1.973

Boundary, 2. Issue on Postmodernism

Bowen, John. 'One Man's Neat'. *Times Literary Supplement*, 7 Aug 59

Bowers, Frederick. 'An Irrelevant Parochialism'. *Granta* 1,3, 1920

Bradbury, Malcolm. *What Is a Novel?* London: Arnold, 1969

______ 'The State of Criticism Today' in *Contemporary Criticism*, Stratford-Upon-Avon Studies 12, ed. Malcolm Bradbury and David Palmer. London: Arnold, 1970

______ *The Social Context of Modern English Literature*. Oxford: Blackwell, 1971

______ 'The Postwar English Novel' in his *Possibilities*. Oxford U.P., 1973

______ ed. *The Novel Today*. Glasgow: Fontana/Collins, 1977

______ 'Putting in the Person: Character and Abstraction in Current Writing and Painting' in *The Contemporary English Novel*, Stratford-Upon-Avon Studies 18, ed. Malcolm Bradbury and David Palmer. London: Arnold, 1979

______ and David Palmer, eds. *The Contemporary English Novel*, Stratford-Upon-Avon Studies 18. London: Arnold, 1979

Brecht, Bertholt. *Brecht on Theatre*, ed. John Willett. London: Methuen, 1974

Brooke-Rose, Christine. *A Grammar of Metaphor*. London: Secker & Warburg, 1958

______ *The Languages of Love*. London: Secker & Warburg, 1957

______ *The Sycamore Tree*. London: Secker & Warburg, 1959

______ *The Dear Deceit*. London: Secker & Warburg, 1960

______ *The Middlemen: A Satire*. London: Secker & Warburg, 1961

______ *Out*. London: Michael Joseph, 1964

______ *Such*. London: Michael Joseph, 1966

______ *Between*. London: Michael Joseph, 1968

______ *Go When You See the Green Man Walking*. London: Michael Joseph, 1970

______ *A ZBC of Ezra Pound*. University of California Press, 1971

______ *Thru*. London: Michael Joseph, 1975

______ 'Where Do We Go from Here?' *Granta* 1, 3, 1980

______ *A Rhetoric of the Unreal: Studies in narrative and structure, especially of the fantastic*.

______ *Amalgamemnon*. Manchester: Carcanet, 1984

______ *Omnibus*. Manchester: Carcanet, 1987

______ *Xorandor*. London: Avon Books, 1988

______ 'Illiterations', in Friedman, Ellen G. and Fuchs, Miriam. *Breaking the Sequence: Women's Experimental Fiction.* Princeton University Press, 1989

______ *Verbivore.* Manchester: Carcanet, 1990

______ *Textermination.* Manchester: Carcanet, 1991

______ *Stories, Theories, and Things.* Cambridge University Press, 1991

______ *Remake.* Manchester: Carcanet, 1996

______ *Next.* Manchester: Carcanet, 1998

______ *Subscript.* Manchester: Carcanet, 1999

______ *Invisible Author: Last Essays.* Ohio State University Press, 2002

______ *Life, End of.* Manchester: Carcanet, 2006

Brophy, Brigid. 'The Novel as Takeover Bid'. Broadcast, B.B.C. Third Programme, Aug 63. repr. in *The Listener*, Oct 63. repr. in her *Don't Never Forget.* London: Cape, 1966

______ 'The Economics of Self-Censorship'. *Granta* 1, 4, 1981

Bryant , Jerry H. *The Open Decision: The Contemporary American Novel and Its Intellectual Background.* New York: Free Press, 1970

Bryden, Ronald. "British Fiction 1959-1960' in *International Literary Annual No. 3* ed. John Wain. London: John Calder, 1961

Buchanan, George. *Passage Through the Present: Chiefly Notes from a Journal.* London: Constable, 1936

______ *Words for Thought: A Notebook.* London: Constable, 1936

Bullock, Michael. *Rudolph Cranstone and the Glass Thimble.* London: Marion Boyars, 1977

Burgess, Anthony. *The Novel Now.* London: Faber, 1967

Burns, Alan. *Buster*, in *New Writers 1.* London: Calder & Boyars, 1961

______ *Europe After the Rain.* London: Calder & Boyars, 1965

______ *Celebrations.* London: Calder and Boyars, 1967

______ *Babel.* London: Calder and Boyars, 1969; New York, Day, 1970

______ *Dreamerika! A Surrealist Fantasy.* London: Calder and Boyars, 1972

______ *The Angry Brigade: A Documentary Novel.* London: Allison and Busby, 1973

______ 'Essay' in *Beyond the Words*, ed, Giles Gordon. London: Hutchinson, 1975

______ 'Wonderland' in *Beyond the Words*, ed, Giles Gordon. London: Hutchinson, 1975

______ *The Day Daddy Died.* London: Allison and Busby, 1981

______ and Charles Sugnet, eds. *The Imagination on Trial.* London: Allison & Busby, 1981

______ *Revolutions of the Night.* London: Allison and Busby, 1986

Butler, Christopher. *After the Wake.* Oxford: OUP, 1980

Butor, Michel. *Inventory*: Essays. London: Cape, 1968

Byatt, A.S. 'People in Paper Houses' in *The Contemporary English Novel*, Stratford-Upon-Avon Studies 18, ed. Malcolm Bradbury and David Palmer. London: Arnold, 1979
Calder, John. *Pursuit: The Uncensored Memoirs of John Calder*. London: Calder Publications, 2001.
Camus, Albert. *The Rebel.* Trans. A. Bower. Harmondsworth, Penguin, 1971
Cary, Joyce. 'The Sources of Tension in America'. *Saturday Review*, 23 Aug 52. repr. in his *Selected Essays*, ed. A.G. Bishop. London: Joseph, 1976
Chase, Richard. *The American Novel and its Tradition*. New York: Doubleday, 1957
Cockburn, Claude. *Bestseller*. London: Sidgwick & Jackson, 1972
Coe, Jonathan. *Like a Fiery Elephant: The Story of B.S. Johnson*. London: Picador, 2004
Colmer, John. *Coleridge to Catch 22*. London: Macmillan, 1978
Conquest, Robert ed. *New Lines: An Anthology*. London: McMillan, 1956
_____ *New Lines II: An Anthology*. London: McMillan, 1963
Cooper, William. 'Reflections on Some Aspects of the Experimental Novel' in *International Literary Annual No. 2*, ed , John Wain. London: John Calder, 1959
Creeley, Robert. *Mabel: A story and Other Prose*. London: Marion Boyars, 1976
Crosland, Margaret. *Beyond the Lighthouse: English Women Novelists In The Twentieth Century*. London: Constable, 1981
Culler, Jonathan. *Structuralist Poetics*. London: Routledge, 1975
Curtis, Tony 'The Poetry of B. S. Johnson' *Anglo-Welsh Review*, Autumn 1976
Declaration. London: McGibbon & Kee, 1957
Derrida, Jacques. *Speech and Phenomena*. Evanston: Northwestern U.P., 1967
_____ 'Structure Sign and Play in the Discourse of the Human Sciences' in *The Structuralist Controversy*, ed. R. Macksey and E. Donato. Baltimore: Johns Hopkins U.P., 1972
_____ 'The Supplement of Copula: Philosophy *Before* Linguistics' in *Textual Strategies,* ed. J. V. Harari. London: Methuen, 1980
Dickstein, Morris. *Gates of Eden: American Culture in the Sixties*. New York: Basic Books, 1977
Duffus, R. L. *Books, Their Place in a Democracy*. Boston: Houghton, 1930
Durrell, Lawrence. 'No Clue to Living'. *Times Literary Supplement*, 27 May 60
Eagleton, Terry. *Criticism and Ideology*. London: New Left Books, 1976
Ehrmann, Jacques, ed. *Game, Play, Literature*. Boston: Beacon Press, 1968
Eliot, T. S. Introduction to Djuna Barnes, *Nightwood*. New York: Harcourt, Brace & Co., 1937
Ellison, Harlan. *Dangerous Visions*. New York: Doubleday, 1967
_____ *Again Dangerous Visions*. New York: Doubleday, 1972
Erikson, Erik H. *Childhood and Society*. New York: Norton, 1950, 2nd ed. 1963

Escarpit, Robert. *The Book Revolution*. London: Harrap, 1966
Evans, Stuart. *Meritocrats*. London: Hutchinson, 1972
______ *The Gardens of the Casino*. London: Hutchinson, 1974
______ *The Function of the Fool*. London: Hutchinson, 1977
______ *The Caves of Alienation*. London: Hutchinson, 1977
______ *Centres of Ritual*. London: Hutchinson, 1978
______ *Occupational Debris*. London: Hutchinson, 1979
Evenson, Brian and Howard, Joanna. *Ann Quin*. Review of Contemporary Fiction. vol XXIII #2, Summer 2003
Eyre, John. *The Pursuit of the Chimaera*. London: The Research Publishing Company, 1978
Faulkner, Peter. *Humanism in the English Novel*. London: Elek, 1975
______ *Angus Wilson: Mimic and Moralist*. London: Secker & Warburg, 1980
Federman, Raymond. *Cinq Nouvelles Nouvelles*. New York: Appleton-Century-Crofts, 1970
______ ed. *Surfiction: Fiction Now and Tomorrow*. Chicago: Swallow, 1975
______ *Double or Nothing*. Chicago: Swallow, 1971
______ and Ronald Sukenick, 'The New Innovative Fiction'. *Antaeus* 20, Winter, 1976
______ 'Fiction Today or the Pursuit of Non-Knowledge'. *Humanities in Society* 1, Spring 1978
Feldman, G. and M. Gartenberg. *Protest*. London: Souvenir, 1959
Fiedelson, C. S. *Symbolism and American Literature*. Chicago U.P., 1953
Fiedler, Leslie. 'Glass War in British Literature'. *Esquire*, Apr 58. repr. in his *No! In Thunder*. New York: Stein & Day, 1972
______ *Love and Death in the American Novel*. New York: Criterion, 1960
______ *Waiting for the End: The American Literary Scene from Hemingway to Baldwin*. London: Cape, 1965
______ 'The New Mutants'. *Partisan Review*, Fall 65. repr. in his *A Fiedler Reader*. New York: Stein & Day, 1977, and in *Innovations*, ed. B. Bergonzi. London: Macmillan, 1978
______ *The Return of the Vanishing American*. London: Cape, 1968
______ *Collected Essays*. 2 vols. New York: Stein & Day, 1971
______ 'Cross the Border - Close That Gap: Postmodernism' in *American Literature Since 1900*, ed. M. Cunliffe. London: Sphere, 1975
Figes, Eva
______ *Equinox*. London: Secker & Warburg, 1966
______ *Winter Journey*. London: Faber, 1967 and New York: Hill & Wang, 1968 (winner of the Guardian Fiction Prize)
______ *The Musicians of Bremen*: Retold. London: Blackie, 1967
______ *The Banger*. London: Deutsch and New York: Lion Press, 1968
______ 'The Writer's Dilemma', *Guardian* 17 Jun 68 p. 7

_____ *Konek Landing*. London: Faber, 1969
_____ *Patriarchal Attitudes*. London: Faber and New York: Stein & Day, 1970 repr. London Panther, 1972 and London: Virago, 1978
_____ *B*. London: Faber, 1972
_____ *Scribble Sam*. London: Deutsch and New York: McKay, 1971
_____ *Days*. London: Faber, 1974
_____ 'Note' in *Beyond the Words*, ed, Giles Gordon. London: Hutchinson, 1975
_____ 'On stage' in *Beyond the Words*, ed, Giles Gordon. London: Hutchinson, 1975
_____ 'Obligato' in *Signature Anthology*. London: Calder & Boyars , 1975
_____ 'Bedsitter' in *Signature Anthology*. London: Calder & Boyars, 1975
_____ Letter on modern fiction, *Times Literary Supplement* 7 Mar 75, p.253[1]
_____ "Battle of the Books', *Guardian* 9 Nov 76, p.9
_____ *Tragedy and Social Evolution*. London: John Calder Platform Books, 1976
_____ *Nelly's Version*. London: Secker & Warburg, 1977
_____ Letter on writers' unionisation, *Times Literary Supplement* 8 Sep 78, p. 994
_____ *Little Eden: A Child at War*. London: Faber, 1978
_____ *Waking*. London: Hamish Hamilton, 1981
_____ 'Holiday' in *Bananas*, Apr 81
_____ Interview with Alan Burns in Burns, Alan and Sugnet, Charles ed. *The Imagination on Trial*. London: Alison & Busby, 1981
_____ *Sex and Subterfuge: Women Writers to 1850*. London: Macmillan, 1982
_____ *Light*. London: Pantheon, 1983
_____ *The Seven Ages*. London: Hamish Hamilton, 1986
_____ *Ghosts*. London: Hamish Hamilton, 1988
_____ *The Tree of Knowledge*. London: Minerva, 1991
_____ *The Tenancy*. London: Sinclair-Stevenson, 1993
_____ *The Knot*. London: Minerva, 1997
_____ *Tales of Innocence and Experience: An Exploration*. London: Bloomsbury, 2004
_____ *Light: With Monet at Giverny: A Novel*. London: Pallas Athene, 2007
_____ *Journey to Nowhere: One Woman Looks for the Promised Land*. London: Granta, 2009
Figes, Eva, ed. *Classic Choice I*. London: Blackie, 1965
_____ *Modern Choice I and 2*. London: Blackie, 2 vols, 1965 and 1966

[1] Only a selection of articles is included: Figes has written many letters and articles, both in her former capacity as secretary of the Writer's Guild, and, on general topics in various journals. These have included particularly: *The Guardian*; *New Humanist* (monthly from Mar 72 to Jan 74 and occasionally thereafter); and *Nova* (London) between 1972 and 1975.

Figes, Eva, translator. *The Gadarene Club*, by Martin Walser. London: Longman, 1960

_____ *The Old Car*, by Elisabeth Borchers. London: Blackie, 1967

_____ *He and I and the Elephants*, by Bernhard Grzimek. London: Deutsch, 1967

_____ *Little Fadette*, by George Sand. London: Blackie, 1967

_____ *A Family Failure*, by Renata Rasp. London: Calder & Boyars, 1970

_____ *The Deathbringer*, by Manfred von Conta London: Calder & Boyars, 1971

Firchow, P. *The Writer's Place*. Minnesota U.P, 1974

Fischer, Ernst. *The Necessity of Art*. Harmondsworth: Penguin, 1963

_____ *Art Against Ideology*. London: Allen Lane, 1969

_____ 'Lukacs and the Theory of Reflection'. *Philosophical Forum* vol. 3 1972

Fitelson, D. Article on Heppenstall's *The Fourfold Tradition* and *The Greater Infortune*, New Leader 19 Mar 62, p. 28

Fletcher, John. *New Directions in Literature*. London: Calder & Boyars, 1968

_____ *Claude Simon and Fiction Now*. London: Calder and Boyars, 1975

Foucault, Michel. *The Order of Things*. London: Tavistock, 1970

_____ *The Archaeology of Knowledge*. London: Tavistock, 1972

Fountain, Nigel. *Underground: The London Alternative Press, 1966-74*. London: Routledge, 1988

Fox, Ralph, *The Novel and the People*. London: Martin Lawrence, 1937. repr. Lawrence and Wishart, 1980

Freedman, Ralph. *The Lyrical Novel*. Princeton U.P., 1963

Friedman, Ellen G. and Fuchs, Miriam. *Breaking the Sequence : Women's Experimental Fiction*. Princeton University Press, 1989

Freud, Sigmund. *Collected Works*. London: Hogarth, 1957

_____ 'Dostoevsky and Parricide' in *Dostoevsky*, ed. R. Wellek. New York: Prentice-Hall, 1962

_____ *Totem and Taboo*. London. Routledge, 1950

_____ *The Interpretation of Dreams*. Harmondsworth, Penguin, 1976

Frye, Northrop. *The Anatomy of Criticism*. Princeton U.P. 1957. repr. 1971

Fuentes, Carlos. 'Central and Eccentric Writing'. *American Review* 21, 1974

Gardner, John. *On Moral Fiction*. New York: Basic Books, 1978

Gass, William H. *Fiction and the Figures of Life*. New York: Vintage, 1973

Gedin, Per. *Literature in the Market Place*. London, 1977

_____ 'A Hand-Made Art.' *Granta* 1, 4, 1981

Gee, M.M. (Diss , Oxford, 1973) 'The Influence of Surrealism on English Writers of the Thirties and Forties'

Gindin, James. *Postwar British Fiction: New Accents and Attitudes*. Cambridge U. P., 1962

_____ 'Taking Risks'. *Granta* 1, 3, 1980

Goffman, Erving. *Behaviour in Public Places*. Glencoe: Free Press, 1963
_____ *Interactional Ritual.* New York: Doubleday, 1967
_____ *The Presentation of Self in Everyday Life*. London: Allen Lane The Penguin Press, 1969
_____ *Strategic Interaction*. Philadelphia: Pennsylvania U.P., 1969
_____ *Relations in Public.* New York: Basic Books, 1971
Goldmann, Lucien. 'Ideology and Writing'. *Times Literary Supplement* 28 Sep 67
_____ 'Criticism and Dogmatism in Literature' in *The Dialectics of Liberation.* ed. David Cooper. Harmondsworth: Penguin, 1968
_____ *The Human Sciences and Philosophy*. London: Cape, 1969
_____ *Towards a Sociology of the Novel.* London: Tavistock, 1975
Gordon, Giles. *Pictures from an Exhibition*. London: Alison & Busby, 1970
_____ *The Umbrella Man*. London: Alison & Busby, 1971
_____ *About a Marriage*. London: Alison & Busby, 1972
_____ 'An Attempt to Make Entertainment out of the War in Vietnam' in *Factions* ed. Giles Gordon and Alex Hamilton, London: Joseph, 1974
_____ *Girl With Red Hair*. London: Hutchinson, 1974
_____ *Farewell, Fond Dreams*. London: Hutchinson, 1975
_____ Entry in *You Always Remember the First Time*. ed. B. S. Johnson. London: Quartet, 1975
_____ *100 Scenes from Married Life*. London: Hutchinson, 1976
_____ *Enemies*. London: Harvester, 1977
_____ *The Illusionist*. London: Harvester, 1978
_____ *Couple*. Bedford: Sceptre, 1978
Gordon, Giles, ed. *Beyond the Words: Eleven Writers in Search of a New Fiction*. London: Hutchinson, 1975
Gordon, Giles and Alex Hamilton, eds. *Factions*. London: Michael Joseph, 1974
Graff, Gerald. *Literature Against Itself*. Chicago U.P., 1979
Granta. Editorial Introduction 1, 1, 1980
Greenland, Colin. *The Entropy Exhibition: Michael Moorcock and the British 'New Wave' in Science Fiction*. London: Routledge & Kegan Paul, 1983
Guignery, Vanessa. *Ceci n'est pas une Fiction : les romans vrais de BS Johnson*. Paris: PUPS, 2009
Hall, John, 'Landscape With Three-Cornered Dances'. *Guardian*, 29 Apr 72, p.8 (article and interview with Ann Quin)
Halperin, John ed. *The Theory of the Novel: New Essays*. New York: O.U.P. 1974
Hansen, Arlen J. 'The Celebration of Solipsism: A New Trend in American Fiction', *Modern Fiction Studies* 19, Spring 73
Hansford Johnson, Pamela 'Literary Style' in her *Important to Me*. London: Macmillan, 1974
Harrison, Jane. *Prolegomena to the Study of Greek Religion*. Cambridge, 1903, repr. Meridian, 1959

Hassam, Andrew. *Writing and Reality : a Study of Modern British Diary Fiction*. Greenwood Press, 1993

Hassan, Ihab. *Radical Innocence: Studies in the Contemporary American Novel*. Princeton U.P., 1961

_____ *The Dismemberment of Orpheus*. New York: O.U.P., 1971

_____ ed. Liberations. Wesleyan U.P., 1971

_____ *Contemporary American Literature, 1945-1972*. New York: Frederick Ungar, 1973

_____ 'The New Consciousness'. *Literary History of the United States*, ed. R.E. Spiller et al. London: Macmillan, 1974

_____ 'A re-Vision of Literature'. *New Literary History* VIII, 1976/7

_____ *Paracriticisms: Seven Speculations of the Times*. Illinois U.P. 1975

_____ Prometheus as Performer: Towards a Posthumanist Culture?' in *Performance in Postmodern Culture*, ed. M. Benamou and C. Caramello. Madison, Wisconsin: Coda Press, 1977

Havemann, Miriam. *The Subject Rising Against its Author : a Poetics of Rebellion in Bryan Stanley Johnson's Oeuvre*. Hildesheim: Georg Olms Verlag, 2011

Hawkes, John. 'John Hawkes: An Interview'. *Wisconsin Studies in Contemporary Literature*. Summer, 1965

Hayman, Ronald. *The Novel Today: 1967-1975*. Harlow, Essex: Longman for the British Council, 1976

Heath, Stephen. *The Nouveau Roman*. London: Elek, 1972

Hendin, Josephine. *Vulnerable People: A View of American Fiction Since 1945*. New York: O.U.P., 1978

Henri, Adrian. *Environments and Happenings*. London: Thames & Hudson, 1974

Heppenstall, Rayner[1]. *Patins. The Literary Guild, 1932*

_____ *Middleton Hurray: A Study in Excellent Normality*. London: Cape, 1934

_____ *First Poems. London: Heinemann, 1935*

_____ *Apology for Dancing*. London: Faber, 1936 (Ballet criticism)

_____ *Sebastian. London: Dent, 1937*

_____ *Proems: An Anthology of Poems, with others*. London: Fortune Press, 1938

_____ *The Blaze of Noon*. London: Secker & Warburg, 1939 (preface by Elizabeth Bowen); New York and Toronto: Alliance, 1940; Revised

[1] Only relevant articles are included: Heppenstall wrote regular pieces and reviews for many periodicals throughout his career, including particularly *New Statesman* (and, formerly, *New Statesman and Nation*); *New English Weekly*; *Twentieth Century*; *London Magazine* and *Times Literary Supplement*. Only plays entirely written by Heppenstall are listed: he collaborated on and edited many others while at the BBC.

(several textual changes and nine pages removed) and reset, London: Secker & Warburg, 1947 (no preface)

______ Reset, London: Barrie & Rockliff, 1962 (preface by Rayner Heppenstall)

______ *Blind Hen's Flowers Are Green*. London: Secker & Warburg, 1940

______ *Saturnine*. London: Secker & Warburg, 1943

______ 'English Nightmare' in *Partisan Review*, Sep/Oct, 1944

______ 'The Wild Man of the Woods' in *Penguin New Writing*, 1944

______ 'How I came to Have This Scar on My Top Lip'; 'I Am Not in Favour of the Working Class' in New Road 1944, ed. Alex Comfort and John Bayliss, London: Grey Walls Press, 1944

______ *Poems 1933-1945*. London: Secker & Warburg, 1947

______ *The Double Image: Mutations of Christian Mythology in the Work of Four French Writers of Today and Yesterday*. London: Secker & Warburg, 1947 (on Bloy, Bemanos, Mauriac and Paul Cladel)

______ *The Fool's Saga* in *Three Tales of Hamlet*, with Michael Innes. London: Gollancz, 1950

______ *The Lesser Infortune*. London: Cape, 1953

______ *Léon Bloy*. Cambridge: Bowes & Bowes, and Yale U.P., 1954

______ 'The Shooting Stick' in *Twentieth Century*, Apr 1955

______ 'Orwell Intermittent'. *Twentieth Century*, May 55 pp. 470/483

______ 'Outsiders and Others'. *Twentieth Century*, Nov 55, pp. 453/7; incorporated into *The Fourfold Tradition*

______ 'The Shooting Stick'. *Twentieth Century*, Apr 55, pp. 367/73; incorporated into *The Fourfold Tradition*

______ 'Leeds 1929-1934'. *Twentieth Century,* Feb 56, pp. 169/77

______ 'John Middleton Murray'. *New Statesman,* 23 Mar 57, p. 374

______ 'That Dreadful Girl'. *Twentieth Century*, Feb 58, pp. 112/21; incorporated into *The Fourfold Tradition*

______ 'Jocasta'. *Twentieth Century*, Aug 58, pp. 170/7 ; incorporated into *The Fourfold Tradition*

______ 'Morel'. Twentieth Century, May 59, pp. 482/92; incorporated into *The Fourfold Tradition*

______ 'Two Voices: English and the Rest'. *Times Literary Supplement* 7 Aug 59, p. supp. xxvi; incorporated into *The Fourfold Tradition*

______ *My Bit of Dylan Thomas*. Privately circulated, London, 1957

______ *The Greater Infortune*. London: Peter Owen, 1960; Reissued, London: Riband Books, 1961

______ *The Fourfold Tradition*. London: Barrie & Rockliff, and New York: New Directions, 1961

______ *The Woodshed*. London: Barrie & Rockliff, 1962

______ 'The Anatomy of Francophobia'. *Twentieth Century*, Mar. 61, pp. 238/45

______ 'Pain in Pleasure'. *The Times* 11 Aug 61

______ 'The Novels of Michel Butor'. *London Magazine*, 2, Jul 62, pp. 57/63
______ 'The Need for Experiment'. *The Times*, 13 Dec 62
______ *The Intellectual Part*. London: Barrie & Rockliff, 1963; Reset, London: Calder & Boyars, 1968
______ *The Connecting Door*. London: Barrie & Rockliff, 1962
Four Absentees. London; Barrie & Rockliff, 1960 and Philadelphia: Dufour, 1963
______ 'Speaking of Writing' (number 5 in a series by different authors). *The Times*, 19 Dec 63
______ 'Raymond Roussel: A Preliminary Study'. *London Magazine*, 3, Aug 63 pp. 18/25
______ *Raymond Roussel*. London: Calder & Boyars, 1966 and California U.P., 1967
______ 'Inside Broadcasting House', *London Magazine* 6 Oct 66 pp. 90/96
______ 'Two Pubs', *London Magazine*, 6, Nov 66, pp.5 6/63
______ "Laurence D. Gilliam, O.B.E.'. *London Magazine* Dec 66. pp. 69/761
______ 'A Demise of Poets'. *London Magazine*, 6, Jan 67, pp. 57/65
______ 'A Head and Three Controllers' London Magazine 6 Mar 67 pp. 80/86
______ 'In Pursuit of Sterne'. *London Magazine*, 7, Nov 67, pp. 38/44
______ *The Shearers*. London: Hamish Hamilton, 1969
______ *Portrait of the Artist as a Professional Man*. London: Peter Owen, 1969
______ *A Little Pattern of French Crime*. London: Hamish Hamilton, 1969
______ 'On Translating Balzac'. *Encounter*, 33, Sep 69, p. 71
______ 'Mauriac: Man of Anguish'. *Sunday Times* 6 Sep 70 p.12
______ 'The Light Touch'. *Encounter*, 34, Jun 70, p. 50
______ *French Crime in the Romantic Age*. London: Hamish Hamilton, 1970
______ 'Tables Speak'. *Hudson Review*, Summer 71, pp.2 47/6:)
______ *Bluebeard and After: Three decades of Murder in France*. London: Peter Owen, 1972
______ *The Seventh Juror*, 1972 (play for television)
______ *The Sex War and Others: A Survey of Recent Murder, Principally in France*. London: Peter Owen, 1973
______ 'Connections' *London Magazine*, 12, Feb/Mar 73, pp.105/110
______ 'Balzac's Policemen'. *Journal of Contemporary History*, 8, Apr 73, pp. 47/56
______ *The Bells*, 1974 (play for television)
______ 'The First Generation' in *Factions* ed. Giles Gordon and Alex Hamilton, London: Joseph, 1974
______ *Reflections on the Newgate Calendar*. London: W.H. Allen, 1975
______ *Two Moons*. London: Allison & Busby, 1977
Heppenstall, Rayner, ed. *Existentialism*, by Guido de Ruggiero. London: Secker & Warburg, 1947 and New York: Social Science Publishers, 1948 (with long introduction by Heppenstall)

_____ *Imaginary Conversations*. London: Secker & Warburg, 1948 (radio scripts commissioned and produced by Heppenstall, with introduction by him)

Heppenstall, Rayner, translator. *Architecture of Truth*. London: Thames & Hudson, 1957

_____ *Atala and René*, by F.R. de Chateaubriand, Oxford V.P., 1963

_____ *Impressions of Africa*, by Raymond Roussel. (with Lindy Foord) London: Calder & Boyars, and California V.P., 1966

_____ *A Harlot High and Low*, by Honore de Balzac. Harmondsworth: Penguin, 1970

_____ *When Justice Falters*, by René Floriot. London: Harrap, 1972

Hewison, Robert. *Under Siege: Literary Life in London 1939-1945*. London: Weidenfeld & Nicholson, 1977. repr. Quartet, 1979

_____ *In Anger: Culture and the Cold War*. London: Weidenfeld & Nicholson, 1980

Hidden, Norman. *These Images Claw*. London: Outpost, 1966

_____ *Dr. Kink and his Old-Style Boarding School*. London: The Workshop Press, 1973

_____ *For My Friends*. Workshop, 1981

_____ *How to Get your Poems Accepted: a guide for poets*. Workshop, 1981

_____ *Liaison Officer : Germany and the Anglo-US occupation*, 1946-47. Frinton on Sea: Clydesdale, 1993

_____ *Hidden talent : the Workshop poets. An anthology in celebration of the 80th birthday of the founder of the Press, Norman Hidden* (edited by Dick Russell). Russell Hill Press, 1993

_____ *Caravan summer : and other stories*. London: Citron, 1999

_____ ed. *Say It Aloud*. London: Hutchinson, 1972

_____ ed. *Over to You : a collection of poems for speaking aloud*. English Speaking Board, 1975

_____ ed. with Amy Hollins. *Many People, Many Voices : poetry from the English speaking world*. London: Hutchinson, 1978

Hillegas, Mark. 'Dystopian Science Fiction: New Index to the Human Situation'. *New Mexico Quarterly* 31, 1961

Hoggart, Richard. *An English Temper*. London: Chatto & Windus, 1982

Holquist, Michael. 'whodunnit and other questions: Metaphysical Detective Stories in Post-War Fiction'. *New Literary History* III, 1, Autumn 1971

Horovitz, Michael. 'Afterwards' in *Children of Albion*, ed. M. Horovitz. Harmondsworth, Penguin, 1969

_____ *Introduction to New Departures*, nos. 7-8 and 10-11, 1975

Houédard, dom Sylvester. *Op and kinkon poems and some non-kinkon*. Writers Forum Poets number 14, 1965

_____ *Vienna Circles*. Cleveland, Ohio : Renegads [*sic*] Press, 1965

_____ *Between poetry and painting: chronology*. England: s.n., 1965?
_____ *12 dancepoems from the cosmic typewriter*. Wiltshire: Compton Press, 1969
_____ *Like Contemplation*. London: Writers Forum, 1972
_____ *Begin again: a book of reflections & reversals*. Brampton, Cumbria LYC Museum and Gallery, Banks, Brampton: LYC Publications, 1975

Howe, Irving. "Literature and Liberalism' in his *Celebrations and Attacks*. London: Deutsch, 1979

Irigaray, Luce 'Women's Exile: Interview with Luce Irigaray'. *Ideology and Consciousness* 1, May 1977

Jackson Bate, W. *The Burden of the Past and the English Poet*. London: Chatto & Windus, 1971

Johnson, B. S. *Travelling People*. London: Constable, 1963
_____ *Albert Angelo*. London: Constable, 1964
_____ *Poems*. London: Constable. 1964
_____ *Trawl*. London: Seeker & Warburg, 1966. repr. Panther, 1968
_____ *The Unfortunates*. London: Secker & Warburg, 1969
_____ *House Mother Normal*. London: Collins, 1971. repr. Quartet, 1973
_____ *Poems 2*. London: Trigram Press, 1972
_____ *Poems '72*. Llandysul: Gwas Gomer, 1972
_____ *Christie Malry's Own Double Entry*. London: Collins, 1973
_____ *Aren't You Rather Young to Be Writing Your Memoirs?* London: Hutchinson, 1973
_____ *Everybody Knows Somebody Who's Dead*. London: Covent Garden Press, 1973
_____ *See the Old Lady Decently*. London: Hutchinson, 1975
_____ *Fat Man on a Beach* (excerpt). in Gordon, Giles, ed. *Beyond the Words: Eleven Writers in Search of a New Fiction*. London: Hutchinson, 1975
_____ Introduction to *Aren't You Rather Young to Be Writing Your Memoirs?*, in Bradbury, Malcolm ed. *The Novel Today*. Glasgow: Fontana/Collins, 1977

Johnson, B. S. and Ghose, Zulfikar. *Statement Against Corpses*. London: Constable, 1964

Johnson, B. S. and Oman , Julia Trevelyan. *Street Children*. London: Hodder & Stoughton, 1964

Johnson, B. S. and Drabble, Margaret. *London Consequences*: A novel. London : Greater London Arts Association for the Festivals of London 1972

Johnson, B. S. et al. *Gavin Ewart, Zulfikar Ghose, B S Johnson*. Harmondsworth: Penguin Books, 1975

Johnson, B. S. ed. *The Evacuees*. London: Gollancz, 1969
_____ *All Bull: The National Servicemen*. London: Quartet, 1973
_____ *You Always Remember the First Time*. London: Quartet, 1975

Jones, Langdon. *The New S.F.: An Original Anthology of Modern Speculative Fiction*. London: Arrow, 1970
Jorre, John de St. *The Good Ship Venus : the erotic voyages of the Olympia Press*. London: Pimlico, 1994
Josipovici, Gabriel. *The World and the Book*. London: Macmillan, 1971. repr. Paladin, 1973
_____ *The Lessons of Modernism*. London: Macmillan, 1977
Jung, Carl G. *The Psychology of the Unconscious*. London: 1933
_____ *Collected Works*. London: Routledge, 1971
Kaplan, S. J. *Feminine Consciousness in the Modern British Novel*. Illinois U.P., 1974
Karl, F. R. *A Reader's Guide to the Contemporary Novel*. London: Thames & Hudson, 1963, 2nd ed. 1972
Kavan, Anna (as Helen Ferguson) *A Charmed Circle* London: Jonathan Cape, 1929, republished as by Anna Kavan: London. Peter Owen, 1994
_____ *The Dark Sisters*. London: Jonathan Cape, 1930
_____ *Let Me Alone*. London: Jonathan Cape, 1930, republished as Anna Kavan: London: Peter Owen, 1974
_____ *A Stranger Still*. London: John Lane, 1935
_____ *Goose Cross*. London: John Lane, 1936
_____ *Rich Get Rich*, London: John Lane, 1937
Kavan, Anna. *Asylum Piece and Other Stories*. London: Jonathan Cape, 1940, republished: London: Peter Owen, 1972
_____ *Change the Name*. London: Jonathan Cape, 1941, republished: Peter Owen, 1993
_____ *I am Lazarus: Short Stories*. London: Jonathan Cape, 1945, republished: London: Peter Owen, 1978; title story originally published in *Horizon*, May 1943
_____ *Sleep Has His House*. London: Jonathan Cape, 1948, republished: London: Peter Owen, 1973, published in America as *House of Sleep*, New York, Doubleday, 1947
_____ *The Horse's Tale* (with K. T. Bluth). London: Gaberbocchus Press, 1949
_____ *A Scarcity of Love*. Southport: Angus Downie, 1956, republished: London: Peter Owen, 1971
_____ *Eagle's Nest*. London: Peter Owen, 1958, republished: London: Peter Owen, 1976
_____ *A Bright Green Field*. London: Peter Owen, 1957
_____ *Who Are You?*. Lowestoft: Scorpion Press, 1963, republished: London: Peter Owen, 1975
_____ *Ice*. London: Peter Owen, 1967, republished: Macmillan, 1973

_____ *Julia and the Bazooka and Other Stories* (Introduction by Rhys Davies). London: Peter Owen, 1970, title story published in *Encounter*, March 1969

_____ *My Soul in China: A Novella and Other Stories* (Introduction by Rhys Davies). London: Peter Owen, 1975

_____ *Mercury*. London: Peter Owen, London: Peter Owen, 1994

_____ *The Parson*. London: Peter Owen, 1995

_____ *Guilty*. London: Peter Owen, 2007

Kennedy, Alan. *The Protean Self*. London: Macmillan , 1974

Kenner, Hugh. *A Homemade World: The American Modernist Writers*. New York: Knopf, 1975

Kermode, Frank. *Puzzles and Epiphanies: Essays and Reviews 1958-1961*. London: Routledge, 1962

_____ *Continuities*. London: Routledge, 1968

_____ *Modern Essays*. London: Collins, 1971

Ketterer, David. *New Worlds for Old: The Apocalyptic Imagination, Science Fiction and American Literature*. Indiana U. P., 1974

Klinkowitz, Jerome and Roy R. Behrens. *The Life of Fiction*. Illinois U.P. 1977

_____ *Literary Disruptions: The Making of a Post-Contemporary American Fiction*. Illinois U.P., 2nd. ed. 1980

Kristeva, Julia. 'The System and the Speaking Subject'. *Times Literary Supplement*, 12 Oct 73

_____ 'The Subject in Signifying Practice'. *Semiotext(e)*. New York: Columbia U.P., vol. 1, no. 3, 1975

Lacan Jacques. *The Language of the Self*. ed. A. Wilden. New York: Delta 1968

Laing, R.D. *The Divided Self*. London: Tavistock, 1959. repr. Penguin, 1965

_____ *Self and Others*. London: Tavistock, 1961. repr. Penguin, 1971

_____ *The Politics of Experience and The Bird of Paradise*. Harmondsworth: Penguin, 1967

_____ *Knots*. London: Tavistock, 1970. repr. Penguin, 1971

_____ The Facts of Life. London: Allen Lane. repr. Penguin, 1977

_____ *Sonnets*. London: Joseph, 1979

Langbaum, Robert. *The Mysteries of Identity: A Theme in Modern Literature*. New York: O.U.P., 1977

Larsen, Egon. 'A View from Outside' in *Motives* ed . R. Salis. London: Oswald Wolff, 1975

Lash Jennifer. *Get Down There and Die*. Brighton: Harvester, 1977

_____ *The Dust Collector*. Hassock, Sussex: Harvester, 1979

Lawrence, D.H. *Studies in Classic American Literature*. New York, Selzer, 1923. Repr . Doubleday, 1953

le Guin, Ursula. 'Science Fiction and Mrs. Brown' in *Explorations of the Marvellous* ed , P. Nicholls. London: Gollancz, 1976

Leavis, Q.D. *Fiction and the Reading Public*. London: Chatto, 1932. repr. Harmondsworth: Penguin, 1979

Lehmann, John. 'The Heart of the Problem'. *Penguin New Writing 18*, Jul/Sep 1943

_____ *I Am My Brother*. London: Longman, 1960

_____ *The Ample Proposition*. London: Eyre & Spottiswood, 1966

Levi-Strauss, Claude. *The Order of Things*. London: Pantheon, 1970

Levin, Harry. *The Power of Blackness*. New York: Knopf, 1958

Lewis, R. W. B. *The Picaresque Saint: Representative Figures in Contemporary Fiction*. London: Gollancz, 1960

_____ *Trials of the World: Essays in American Literature and the Humanistic Tradition*. Yale U.P., 1965

Lewis, Wyndham. *Enemy Salvoes*. ed. C. J. Fox. London: Vision, 1975

Lodge, David. 'Objections to William Burroughs' in *Innovations* ed , Bernard Bergonzi. London: Macmillan, 1975

_____ *The Language of Fiction: Essays in Criticism and Verbal Analysis of the English Novel*. London: Routledge, 1966

_____ *The Novelist at the Crossroads*. London: Routledge, 1971

_____ *The Modes of Modern Writing: Metaphor, Metonymy and the Typology of Modern Literature*. London: Arnold, 1977

_____ 'The Novelist at' the Crossroads' in *The Novel Today* ed. Malcolm Bradbury. Glasgow: Fontana/Collins, 1977

_____ 'Modernism, Antimodernism and Postmodernism'. Inaugural Lecture, Birmingham University. repr. in his *Working With Structuralism*, London: Routledge, 1981

Lowenfeld, Viktor. *The Nature of Creative Activity*. trans. O.A. Oeser. London: Routledge, 1939, 2nd ed. 1952. repr. 1965

Lowry, Malcolm. 'Across the Panama' in his *Hear Us O Lord From Heaven Thy Dwelling Place*. London: Cape, 1962

Lukacs, Georg. 'Intellectual Physiognomy in Characterization' in his *Writer and Critic*. London: Merlin, 1970

_____ 'The Ideology of Modernism' in his *The Meaning of Contemporary Realism*. London: Merlin, 1972

_____ Introduction to his *Studies in European Realism*. London: Merlin, 1978

McCormick, John. *American Literature 1919-1932*. London: Routledge, 1971

McEwan, Neil. *The Survival of the Novel*. London: Macmillan, 1981

MacBeth, George. *The Samurai*. New York: Harcourt Brace Jovanovich, 1975; London: Quartet, 1976, reprinted as *Cadbury and the Samurai*. London: New English Library, 1981

_____ *The Transformation*. London: Gollancz, 1975, repr. Quartet, 1977

_____ *The Survivor*. London: Quartet, 1977

_____ *The Seven Witches*. London W. H. Allen, 1978, reprinted as *Cadbury and the Seven Witches*. London: New English Library, 1981

_____ *Cadbury & the Born Losers*. London: New English Library, 1981

Macauley, Rose. 'The Future of Fiction'. *New Writing and Daylight VII*. London: John Lehmann, 1946

Macherey, Pierre. *A Theory of Literary Production*. London: Routledge, 1968

Malamud, Bernard. *The Tenants*. London: Eyre Methuen, 1972

Mallin, Tom. *Knut*. London: Allison & Busby, 1971

_____ *Dodecahedron*. London: Allison & Busby, 1970

Mann, Peter H. 'The Library and the New Novel'. Lecture, Association of Assistant Librarians. Holborn Public Library, 1 Oct 80

_____ *The Literary Novel and its Public*. London: The Arts Council, 1980

Manning, Olivia. 'Notes on the Future of the Novel'. *Times Literary Supplement,* 15 Aug 58

Marshall, Peter. *Ancient and Modern*. London: Hutchinson, 1970

Merril, Judith. *England Swings SF: Stories of Speculative Fiction*. New York: Doubleday, 1968

Miller, David. "Language of Detective Fiction: Fiction of Detective Language'. *Granta* 1, 2, 1980

Miller, Henry. *The Air-Conditioned Nightmare*. New York: New Directions, 1945

Miller, K. ed. *Writing in England Today: The Last Fifteen Years*. Harmondsworth, Penguin, 1968

Miller, W. *The Book Industry*. New York: Columbia U.P., 1949

Mitchell, Adrian. *Wartime*. London: Cape, 1973. repr. Picador, 1975

_____ *Man Friday*. London: Futura, 1975

Mitchell, Julian. *Imaginary Toys*. London: Hutchinson, 1961

_____ *A Disturbing Influence. London: Hutchinson,* 1962

_____ *As Far As You Can Go*. London: Constable, 1963

_____ *The White Father*. London: Constable, 1964

_____ *A Circle of Friends*. London: Constable, 1966

_____ *The Undiscovered Country*. London: Constable, 1968

Monod, Sylvère. 'Rayner Heppenstall and the Nouveau Roman' in *Imagined Worlds*. London: Methuen, 1968

Moorcock, Michael. *The Final Programme*. London: Allison & Busby, 1969;

_____ *A Cure for Cancer*. London: Allison & Busby, 1971;

_____ *The English Assassin*. London: Allison & Busby, 1972;

_____ *The Condition of Muzak*. London: Allison & Busby, 1977.

_____ *The Adventures of Una Persson and Catherine Cornelius in the 20th Century: A Romance,* 1976

_____ Interview with Alan Burns in Burns, Alan and Sugnet, Charles ed. *The Imagination on Trial*. London: Alison & Busby, 1981

Morrison, Blake. *The Movement*. Oxford U.P., 1980

Moorcock, Michael & Jones, Langdon (editors). *The Nature of the Catastrophe.* London, Hutchinson, 1971

Morris, Robert K. Old Lines, *New Forces: Essays on the Contemporary British Novel 1960-1970.* London: Associated Universities Press, 1976

Mosley, Nicholas. *Spaces of the Dark.* London: Rupert Hart Davis, 1951

_____ *The Rainbearers.* London: Weidenfeld and Nicholson, 1955

_____ *Corruption.* London: Weidenfeld & Nicholson, 1957 and Boston: Little, Brown, 1958

_____ *African Switchback.* London: Weidenfeld & Nicholson, 1958

_____ *Meeting Place.* London: Weidenfeld & Nicholson, 1962. Trans. into French as *Aux Quatre Vents de Londres* by J. le Beguec, with preface by Henri Thomas. Paris: Gallimard, 1965

_____ *The Life of Raymond Raynes.* London: Faith Press, 1961. reissued, London: Hodder & Stoughton, 1963

_____ *Accident.* London: Hodder & Stoughton, 1965 and New York: Coward McCann, 1966 repr. London: New English Library, 1967. Trans. into French by J. le Beguec and Henri Thomas. Paris: Gallimard, 1968

_____ *Experience and Religion: A Lay Essay in Theology.* London: Hodder & Stoughton, 1965 and Philadelphia: United Church Press, 1967

_____ *Assassins.* London: Hodder & Stoughton, 1966 and New York: Coward McCann, 1967. repr. Harmondsworth: Penguin, 1969. Trans. into French by Louise Servicen. Paris: Gallimard, 1969

_____ *Impossible Object.* London: Hodder & Stoughton, 1968 and New York: Coward McCann, 1969. repr. Harmondsworth: Penguin, 1971

_____ *Natalie Natalia.* London: Hodder and Stoughton and New York: Coward McCann, 1971. repr. Harmondsworth: Penguin, 1975. Trans. into French by Laure Casseau. Paris: Michel, 1974

_____ *The Assassination of Trotsky.* London: Michael Joseph, 1972. repr. London: Abacus, 1972

_____ *The Assassination of Trotsky,* (screenplay), 1973

_____ *Impossible Object,* (screenplay), 1975

_____ *Julian Grenfell: His Life and the Times of His Death 1888-1915.* London and New York: Holt, Rinehart and Winston, 1976

_____ 'Julian Grenfell: War as story'. *London Magazine,* 16, Apr/May 76, pp. 53/61

_____ 'The Coming of Wit'. *Spectator,* 18 No v 78, pp. 16/17

_____ 'Rhodesia on the Rack: The Blacks'. *Sunday Times* 19 Nov 78 pp. 4/5

_____ *Catastrophe Practice.* London: Secker & Warburg, 1979

'Human Beings Desire Happiness' in *Lying Truths,* ed. R. Duncan and M. Weston-Smith. London: Pergamon, 1979, pp. 211/7

_____ *Imago Bird.* London: Seeker & Warburg, 1980

_____ *Serpent.* London: Secker & Warburg, 1981

_____ *Rules of the game Sir Oswald and Lady Cynthia Mosley 1896-1933*. London: Secker & Warburg Ltd, 1982

_____ *Beyond the Pale: Sir Oswald Mosley and Family, 1933-1980*. London: Secker & Warburg Ltd, 1983

_____ *Hopeful Monsters*. London: Secker & Warburg Ltd, 1990

_____ *Efforts at Truth*. London: Secker & Warburg Ltd, 1994

_____ *Children of Darkness and Light*. London: Secker & Warburg Ltd, 1996

_____ *The Hesperides Tree*. London: Secker & Warburg Ltd, 2001

_____ *Inventing God*. London: Secker & Warburg Ltd, 2003

_____ *Look at the Dark*. London: Secker & Warburg Ltd, 2005

_____ *Time at War: a Memoir*. London: Weidenfeld & Nicholson, 2006

Mosley, Nicholas, ed. *Prism* (a Christian periodical), 1957 - 1960

_____ *The Faith*. London: Faith Press, 1961 (on Raymond Raynes)

Nairn, Tom. 'The English Literary Intelligentsia' in *Bananas* ed. Emma Tennant. London: Blond & Briggs, 1977

Neumann, Erich. 'Creative Man and Transformation'. in his *Art and the Creative Unconscious*. London: Routledge, 1959

New Literary History vol. 3, no. 1. Issue on Postmodernism

Nin, Anaïs, *The Novel of the Future*. New York: Macmillan, 1968

Nuttall, Jeff with Keith Musgrove. *The Limbless Virtuoso*, London: Writers Forum, 1963

Nuttall, Jeff. *Poems I Want to Forget*. London, Turret, 1965

_____ *Pieces of Poetry*. London: Writers Forum Poets number seventeen, 1966

_____ *The Case of Isabel and the Bleeding Foetus*. London: Turret, 1967

_____ *Bomb Culture*. London: McGibbon & Kee, 1968

_____ *Come Back Sweet Prince: A Novelette*. London: Cuddon's Cosmopolitan Review, 1968

_____ *Oscar Christ and the Immaculate Conception: Another Novelette*. London: Writers Forum Poets number twenty three, 1968

_____ *Mr. Watkins Got Drunk and had to be Carried Home*. London: Writers Forum Poets number twenty four, 1968

_____ *Journals*. Brighton: Unicorn Bookshop, 1968

_____ *Penguin Modern Poets 12*. Harmondsworth: Penguin, 1968

_____ *Songs Sacred and Secular*. Indica Books: 1968

_____ *Pig*. London, Fulcrum: 1969

_____ *Poems, 1962-1969*. London: Fulcrum, 1969

_____ *Love Poems*. Brighton: Unicorn, 1969

_____ *Anthology: Poems By Members of the Faculty of Art & Design, Leeds Polytechnic*. Leeds: The Art & Design Press, 1970

_____ *The Foxes' Lair*. London: Aloes, 1972

_____ Entry in *All Bull: The National Servicemen*. ed. B. S. Johnson. London: Quartet, 1973

______ *Snipe's Spinster*. London: Calder & Boyars, 1975
______ *Man, Not Man*. Llanfynydd, Carmarthen: Unicorn, 1975
______ *The House Party*. Toronto: Basilike, 1975
______ *The Anatomy of my Father's Corpse*. Toronto: Basilike, 1975
______ *Krak*. Bradford: Jack Press, 1975
______ *Fatty Feedemall's Secret Self*. Bradford: Jack Press, 1975
______ Entry in *You Always Remember the First Time*. ed. B. S. Johnson. London: Quartet, 1975
______ *Objects*. London: Trigram, 1976
______ *Sun Barbs*. Hayes: Poet and Peasant Books, 1976
______ *Common Factors, Vulgar Factions*. London: Routledge, 1977
______ *The Gold Hole*. London: Quartet, 1978
______ *The Patriarchs*. London: The Beau & Aloes Arc Association, 1978
______ *What Happened to Jackson*. London: Aloes, 1978
______ *King Twist: A Portrait of Frank Randle*. London: Routledge, 1978
______ *Grape Notes, Apple Music*. Bradford: Rivelin, 1979
______ *Performance Art: vol. 1, Memoirs* and *vol. 2, Scripts*. London: Calder, 1979
______ *Muscle*. Bradford, Rivelin Press, 1982
______ *The Pleasures of Necessity*. Colne: Arrowspire, 1988
______ *The Bald Soprano: Portrait of Lol Coxhill*. London: Art Data, 1989
______ *Art and the Degradation of Awareness*. London: Calder, 2001
______ *Selected Poems*. Cambridge: Salt, 2003
______ *Jeff Nuttall: A Celebration*. London: Arc, 2004
______ *Jeff Nuttall's Wake on Paper*. ed. Michael Horowitz, London: New Departures #33, 2004
Olderman, Raymond M. *Beyond the Waste Land*. Yale U.P., 1972
Percy, Walker. *Love in the Ruins*. London: Eyre & Spottiswood, 1971
______ 'Notes for a Novel About the End of the World' in his *Message in the Bottle*. New York: Farrar, Strauss and Giroux, 1981
Petersen, Clarence. *The Bantam Story*. New York: Bantam, 1970
Pinter, Harold. *Five Screenplays*. London: Methuen, 1971
Poirier, Richard. *A World Elsewhere: The Place of Style in American Literature*. New York: O.U.P., 1966
______ *The Performing Self: Compositions and Decompositions in the Languages of Contemporary Life*. New York: O.U.P., 1971
______ 'The Aesthetics of Contemporary Radicalism' (Lecture). New York: Humanities Press, 1972
Priest, Christopher. *Indoctrinaire*. London: Faber, 1970
______ *Fugue for a Darkening Island*. London: Faber, 1972
______ *Real-Time World*. London: New English Library, 1974
______ *Inverted World*. London: Faber, 1974

_____ *The Space Machine*. London: Faber, 1976
_____ *A Dream of Wessex*. London: Faber, 1977
_____ *An Infinite Summer*. London: Pan, 1980
_____ *The Affirmation*. London: Faber 1981
Pritchett, V. S. 'The Future of Fiction' in *New Writing and Daylight VII*. ed. John Lehmann. London: John Lehmann, 1946
Pütz, Manfred. *The Story of Identity: American Fiction of the Sixties*. Stuttgart: Metzler, 1979
Quin, Ann. *Berg*. London: Calder & Boyars, 1964 and New York: Scribners, 1966. repr. London: Quartet (with Afterword by Dulan Barber), 1977. Trans. into French by Anne-Marie Soulac. Paris: Gallimard, 1967. Trans. into German by Elisabeth Fleitscher. Insel, 1966
_____ *Three*. London: Calder & Boyars, 1966 and New York: Scribners, 1968. Trans. into French as *Trio* by Lola Tranec. Paris: Gallimard, 1970. Trans. into German as *Drei* by Marie Bosse-Sporleder. Insel, 1967
_____ 'Leaving School'. *London Magazine*, 6, July 1966, pp.63/68
_____ 'Every Cripple Has His Own Way of Walking'. *Nova*, London, December 1966 pp. 125/35
_____ 'Never Trust a Man Who Bathes with His Fingernails'. *El Corno Emplumado* #27, Mexico City, June 1968, pp.8/16
_____ 'Motherlogue'. *Transatlantic Review*, 32, Summer 1969, pp.101/105, reprinted in Stevick, Philip, ed. *Anti-Story: An Anthology of Experimental Fiction*. New York: Simon & Schuster, 1971
_____ *Passages*. London: Calder & Boyars, 1969
_____ *Tripticks*. London: Calder & Boyars, 1972
_____ *The Unmapped Country*. (Incomplete) in *Beyond the Words*, ed. Giles Gordon, London: Hutchinson, 1975
_____ 'Eyes That Watch Behind the Wind'. *Signature Anthology*. London: Calder & Boyars, 1975, pp.1 33/49
_____ 'Ghostworm'. *Tak Tak Tak* number 6. London, 1993
Rabinovitz, Rubin. *The Reaction Against Experiment in the English Novel 1950-1960*. Columbia U.P., 1968
Redgrove, Peter. Interview with Hugh Herbert, 'Faust and Foremost'. *Guardian*, 30 Nov, 73
_____ *In the Country of the Skin*. London: Routledge, 1973
_____ *The God of Glass*. London: Routledge, 1979
_____ *The Sleep of the Great Hypnotist*. London: Routledge, 1979
_____ *The Beekeepers*. London: Routledge, 1981
_____ *The Facilitators*. London: Routledge, 1982
_____ and Penelope Shuttle. *The Hermaphrodite Album*. London: Fuller d'Arch Smith, 1973

_____ and Penelope Shuttle. *The Terrors of Dr. Treviles: A Romance*. London: Routledge, 1974

_____ and Penelope Shuttle. *The Glass Cottage: A Nautical Romance*. London: Routledge, 1977

Rahv, Philip. ed. *Modern Occasions*. London: Weidenfeld, 1966

Remington, T. and D. Miller. 'Science Fiction to Superfiction'. *Granta*. 1, 2

Robbe-Grillet, Alain. *Introduction to Last Year in Marienbad*. London: Calder, 1966, repr. 1977

_____ *Snapshots and Towards a New Novel*. London: Calder & Boyars, 1965

Roberts, Neil. *A Lucid Dreamer: The Life of Peter Redgrove*. London: Jonathan Cape, 2012

Rosenberg, John. *Dorothy Richardson: The Genius They Forgot*. London: Duckworth, 1973

Roth, Philip. 'Writing American Fiction' in *The Novel Today*, ed. Malcolm Bradbury. Glasgow: Fontana/Collins, 1977

Rutlan, R. ed. *The Native Muse: Theories of American Literature vol. 1*. New York: Dutton, 1976

_____ ed. *A Storied Land: Theories of American Literature vol. 2*. New York: Dutton, 1976

Sarraute, Nathalie. *Tropisms and the Age of Suspicion*. London: John Calder, 1963

Scholes, R. and R. Kellogg. *The Nature of Narrative*. Cornell U.P., 1966

_____ *The Fabulators*. New York O.U.P., 1967

_____ 'Metafiction'. *Iowa Review* I, 4, Fall 1970

_____ 'The Illiberal Imagination'. *New Literary History* V, 2, Winter 1974

_____ *Fabulation and Metafiction*. Illinois U.P., 1979

Schulz, Max. *Black Humor Fiction of the Sixties*. Ohio U.P., 1973

Schwarz, Barry. *The New Humanism*. London: David & Charles, 1974

Scott, A. and D. Gifford. *Neil M. Gunn: The Man and the Writer*. Edinburgh: Blackwood, 1973

Seymour-Smith, Martin. 'A Climate of Warm Indifference' in *Bananas* ed. Emma Tennant. London: Blond & Briggs, 1977

Shuttle, Penelope. An Excusable Vengeance. in New Writers Six. London: Calder & Boyars, 1967

_____ *Nostalgia, Neurosis and Other Poems*. Aylesford: Saint Albert's Press, 1968

_____ *All the Usual Hours of Sleeping*. London: Calder & Boyars, 1969

_____ *Branch*. Rushden: Sceptre Press, 1971

_____ *Jesusa*. Falmouth: Granite Press, 1971

_____ *Wailing Monkey Embracing a Tree*. London: Calder & Boyars, 1973

_____ *Moon Meal*. London: Sceptre, 1973

_____ *Midwinter Mandala*. London: Headland, 1973

_____ *The Dream*. Knotting: Sceptre Press, 1974
_____ *The Songbook of the Snow and Other Poems*. Ilkley: Janus Press, 1974
_____ *Photographs of Persephone*. Feltham, Middlesex: Quarto Press, 1974
_____ *The Dream*. London: Sceptre, 1975
_____ *Webs on Fire*. London: Gallery, 1975
_____ *Four American Sketches*. Knotting: Sceptre Press, 1976
_____ *Period*. London: Words Press, 1976
_____ *Rainsplitter in the Zodiac Garden*. London: Marion Boyars, 1977
_____ and Peter Redgrove. *The Wise Wound: Menstruation and Everywoman*. London: Gollancz, 1979
_____ *Prognostica*. Knotting: Martin Booth, 1980
_____ *The Mirror of the Giant*. London: Marion Boyars, 1980
_____ *The Orchard Upstairs*. Oxford: OUP, 1980
_____ *The Child Stealer*. Oxford: OUP, 1983
_____ *The Lion from Rio*. Oxford: OUP, 1986
_____ *Adventures with my Horse*. Oxford: OUP, 1988
_____ *Taxing the Rain*. Oxford: OUP, 1993
_____ and Peter Redgrove. *Alchemy for Women: Personal Transformation Through Dreams and the Female Cycle*. London: Rider, 1995
_____ *Building a City for Jamie*. Manchester: Carcanet, 1996
_____ *Selected Poems 1980-1996*. Oxford: OUP, 1996
_____ *A Leaf Out of His Book*. Manchester: Carcanet, 2001
_____ *Four Poems*. Redruth, Cornwall: Palores Publications
_____ *Redgrove's Wife*. Northumberland: Bloodaxe, 2004
_____ *Sandgrain and Hourglass*. Northumberland: Bloodaxe, 2010
Sillitoe, Alan. 'Both Sides of the Street'. *Times Literary Supplement* 8 Jul 60
_____ *Raw Material*. London: Allen, 1972
Smith, Stevie. *Novel On Yellow Paper: Or, Work it Out for Yourself*. London: Cape, 1936. repr. Virago, 1980
_____ *Over the Frontier*. London: Cape, 1938. repr. Virago, 1980
_____ *The Holiday*. London: Chapman & Hall, 1949. repr. Virago, 1979
Solotaroff. 'Silence, Exile and Cunning. *New American Review* 8, 1970
Sontag, Susan. *Against Interpretation*. New York: Farrar, Strauss and Giroux, 1967. repr. Delta, 1978
_____ *Styles of Radical Will*. London: Secker & Warburg, 1969
Spender, Stephen. *The Destructive Element: A Study of Modern Writers and Beliefs*. London: Cape, 1935
_____ *The New Realism: A Discussion*. London: Hogarth, 1939
_____ *The Creative Element: A Study of Vision, Despair and Orthodoxy Among Some Modern Writers*. London: Hamish Hamilton, 1953
_____ *The Struggle of the Modern*. London: Hamish Hamilton, 1963

_____ *The Imagination in the Modern World: Three Lectures*. Washington D.C.: Library of Congress, 1966

_____ *Love-Hate Relations*. London: Hamish Hamilton, 1974

_____ *The Thirties and After*. London: Macmillan, 1978

Stanford, Derek. *Inside the Forties*. London: Sidgwick & Jackson, 1977

Stein, Gertrude. *On Narration*. Chicago U.P., 1935

Steiner, George. *The Death of Tragedy: Essays on Language, Literature and the Inhuman*. London: Faber, 1967

_____ *Extraterritorial: Papers on Literature and the Language Revolution*. London: Faber, 1972

_____ *In Bluebeard's Castle: Some Notes Towards the Redefinition of Culture*. London: Faber, 1971

_____ *After Babel: Aspects of Language and Translation*. Oxford U.P. 1975

Stevick, Philip, ed. *Anti-Story: An Anthology of Experimental Fiction*. New York: Simon & Schuster, 1971

_____ 'Voices in the Head: Style and Consciousness in the Fiction of Ann Quin', in Friedman, Ellen G. and Fuchs, Miriam. *Breaking the Sequence : Women's Experimental Fiction*. Princeton University Press, 1989

Sturrock, John. *The French New Novel*. Oxford U.P., 1969

Sukenick, Ronald. *The Death of the Novel and Other Stories*. New York: Dial Press, 1969

Sutherland, J. A. *Fiction and the Fiction Industry*. London: Athlone, 1978

_____ *Bestsellers*. London: Routledge, 1981

_____ 'The End of a Gentleman's Profession'. *Granta* 1, 4, 1981

Swinden, Patrick. *Unofficial Selves: Character in the Novel from Dickens to the Present Day*. London: Macmillan, 1973

Sypher, Wylie. *The Loss of the Self in Modern Literature and Art*. New York: Vintage, 1962

Tanner, Tony. *The Reign of Wonder: Naivety and Reality in American Literature*. Cambridge U.P, 1965

_____ *City of Words*. London: Cape, 1971

Tennant, Emma. *The Time of the Crack*. London: Jonathan Cape, 1973

_____ *The Last of the Country House Murders*. London: Jonathan Cape, 1974

_____ Entry in *You Always Remember the First Time*. ed. B. S. Johnson. London: Quartet, 1975

_____ *Hotel de Dream*. London: Gollancz, 1976; reprinted by Penguin, 1978

_____ *The Bad Sister*. London: Gollancz, 1978

_____ *Wild Nights*. London: Jonathan Cape, 1979

_____ *Alice Fell*. London: Jonathan Cape, 1980

Tennant, Emma, ed. *Bananas*. London: Blond & Briggs, 1977

Tew, Philip. *B.S. Johnson : a critical reading*. Manchester: Manchester University Press, 2001

_____ *Re-Reading B. S. Johnson.* London: Palgrave Macmillan, 2007
Themerson, Stefan. *The Adventures of Peddy Bottom.* Editions Poetry, 1951; republished London: Gaberbocchus, 1954
_____ *Wooff, Wooff, or Who Killed Richard Wagner?* London: Gaberbocchus Press, 1951; republished Gaberbocchus 1967; included in *On Semantic Poetry.* London: Gaberbocchus, 1972
_____ *Professor Mmaa's Lecture.* London: Gaberbocchus Press, 1953
_____ *The Life of Cardinal Pölätüo with Notes on his Writings his Times and his Contemporaries.* London: Gaberbocchus Press, 1961; reprinted with *Bayamus.* Boston, Exact Change, 1997
_____ *Semantic Divertissements.* London: Gaberbocchus Press, 1962
_____ *Bayamus and the Theatre of Semantic Poetry.* London: Gaberbocchus Press, 1965; (previously published as *Bayamus* in 1949 reprinted with *Cardinal Pölätüo.* Boston, Exact Change, 1997; original, shorter version London: Editions Poetry, 1949
_____ *Apollinaire's Lyrical Ideograms.* In *Typographica*, 1966; republished London: Gaberbocchus, 1968
_____ *Tom Harris.* London: Gaberbocchus Press, 1967; New York: Alfred A. Knopf, 1968
_____ *St Francis & the Wolf of Gubbio, or 'Brother Francis' Lamb Chops' An opera in 2 acts Text & music.* London: Gaberbocchus, 1972
_____ *On Semantic Poetry.* London: Gaberbocchus, 1972
_____ *Special Branch: A Dialogue.* London: Gaberbocchus, 1972
_____ *Logic, Labels and Flesh.* London: Gaberbocchus, 1974
_____ *General Piesc, or, The Case of the Forgotten Mission.* London: Gaberbocchus Press, 1976
_____ *The Mystery of the Sardine.* London: Faber, 1986; reprinted by Dalkey Archive Press, 2006
_____ *Hobson's Island.* London: Faber, 1988; reprinted by Dalkey Archive Press, 2005
Thomas, D.M. *Personal and Possessive.* London: Outposts, 1964
_____ *Penguin Modern Poets 11.* London: Penguin, 1968
_____ *Two Voices.* London: Cape Goliard, 1968
_____ *The Lover's Horoscope.* Laramie, Wyoming: Purple Sage, 1970
_____ *Logan Stone.* London: Cape Goliard, 1971
_____ *The Shaft.* Gillingham, Kent: Arc, 1973
_____ *Lilith Prints.* Cardiff: Second Aeon, 1974
_____ *Symphony in Moscow.* Richmond, Surrey, Keepsake, 1974
_____ *Love and Other Deaths.* London: Elek, 1975
_____ *The Rock.* Knotting, Bedfordshire: Sceptre, 1975
_____ *Orpheus in Hell.* Knotting, Bedfordshire: Sceptre, 1977
_____ *The Honeymoon Voyage.* London: Secker & Warburg, 1978

______ *The Flute Player*. London: Gollancz, 1979
______ *Birthstone*. London: Gollancz, 1980
______ *The White Hotel*. London: Gollancz, 1981
______ *Dreaming in Bronze*. London: Secker & Warburg, 1981
Toynbee, Philip. *Tea with Mrs Goodman*. London: Horizon, 1947; reprinted as *Prothalamium A Cycle of the Holy Graal*. New York: Doubleday, 1947
______ *Pantaloon; or, the Valediction*. London: Chatto & Windus, 1961
______ *Two Brothers: The Fifth Day of the Valediction of Pantaloon*. London: Chatto & Windus, 1964
______ *A Learned City: The Sixth day of the Valediction of Pantaloon*. London: Chatto & Windus, 1966
______ *Views From a Lake: The Seventh Day of the Valediction of Pantaloon*. London: Chatto & Windus, 1968
Triquarterly 26, Winter 1973, issue on Postmodernism
Tredell, Nicholas. *Fighting fictions : the novels of B S Johnson*. West Bridgford: Paupers, 2000
Trocchi, Alexander. *The Outsiders*. [Contains *Young Adam* and four short stories.] New York: Signet, 1961
______ *Young Adam*. London: Pan Books, 1963; repr. London: New English Library, 1966
______ *Cain's Book*. New York: Grove Atlantic; London: John Calder, 1963
______ *The Fifth volume of Frank Harris's My Life and Loves: An irreverent treatment by Alexander Trocchi*. London: New English Library in association with the Olympia Press, 1966
______ *The Carnal Days of Helen Seferis*. North Hollywood: Brandon, 1967
______ *The School for Wives*. North Hollywood: Brandon, 1967
______ *Helen and Desire*. Paris: Olympia, 1971
______ *Man at Leisure*. London: Calder Signature Series no. 15, 1972
Trocchi, Alexander (as Frances Lengel). *Helen and Desire*. Paris: Olympia, 1954
______ *The Carnal Days of Helen Seferis*. Paris: Olympia, 1954
______ *Young Adam*. Paris: Olympia, 1954
______ *White Thighs*. Paris: Olympia, 1955
______ *The School for Sin*. Paris: Olympia, 1956
Trocchi, Alexander (as Carmencita de las Lunas). *Thongs*. Paris: Olympia, 1956
Trocchi, Alexander (as Frank Harris). *My Life and Loves* (fifth volume). Paris: Olympia, 1958
Tynan, Kenneth. *A View of the English Stage*. London: Davis-Poynter, 1975
Vidal, Gore. 'American Plastic: The Matter of Fiction'. in his *Matters of Fact and Fiction*. London: Heinemann, 1977 repr. Panther, 1977
Vinson, James ed. *Contemporary Novelists*. London: St, James Press and New York: St. Martins Press, 1972, 2nd ed. 1976

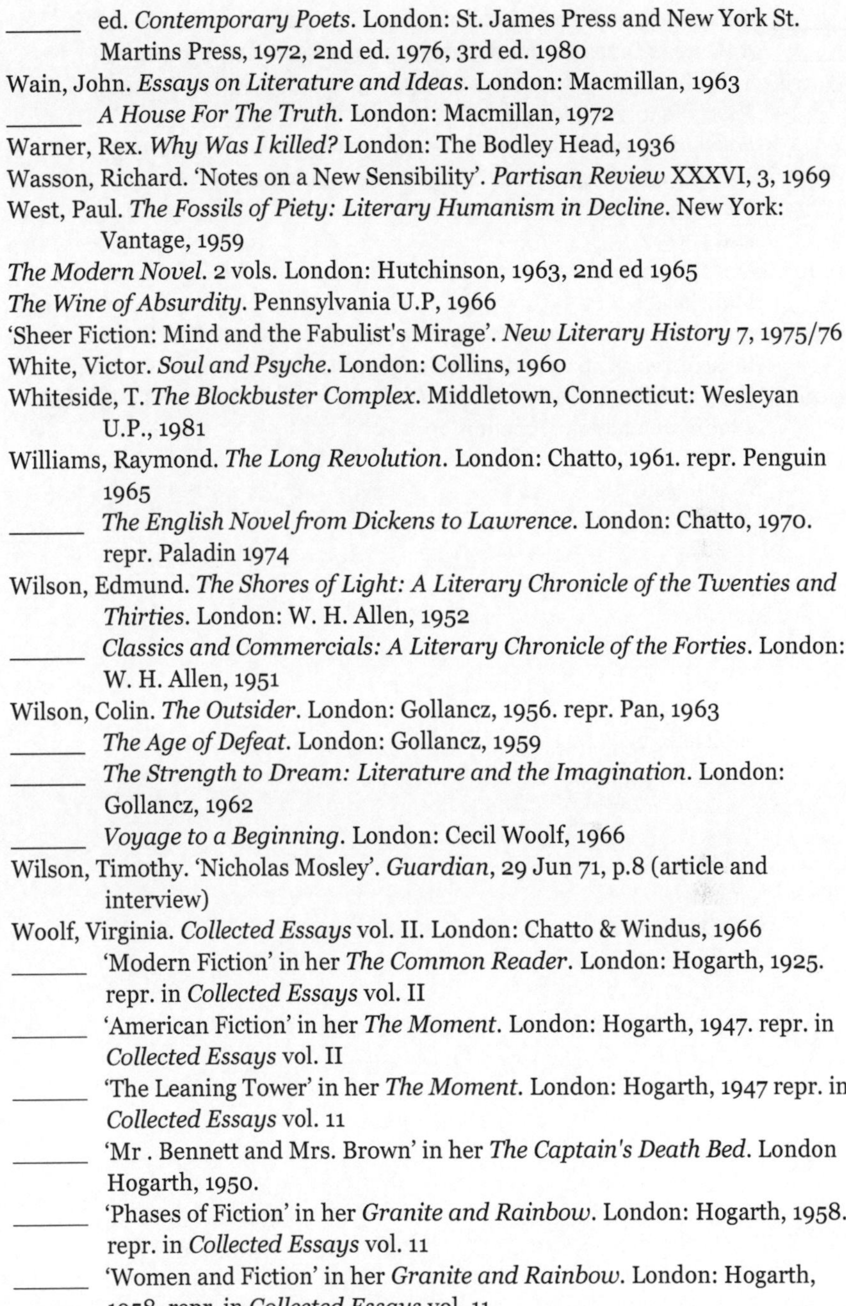

______ ed. *Contemporary Poets*. London: St. James Press and New York St. Martins Press, 1972, 2nd ed. 1976, 3rd ed. 1980

Wain, John. *Essays on Literature and Ideas*. London: Macmillan, 1963

______ *A House For The Truth*. London: Macmillan, 1972

Warner, Rex. *Why Was I killed?* London: The Bodley Head, 1936

Wasson, Richard. 'Notes on a New Sensibility'. *Partisan Review* XXXVI, 3, 1969

West, Paul. *The Fossils of Piety: Literary Humanism in Decline*. New York: Vantage, 1959

The Modern Novel. 2 vols. London: Hutchinson, 1963, 2nd ed 1965

The Wine of Absurdity. Pennsylvania U.P, 1966

'Sheer Fiction: Mind and the Fabulist's Mirage'. *New Literary History* 7, 1975/76

White, Victor. *Soul and Psyche*. London: Collins, 1960

Whiteside, T. *The Blockbuster Complex*. Middletown, Connecticut: Wesleyan U.P., 1981

Williams, Raymond. *The Long Revolution*. London: Chatto, 1961. repr. Penguin 1965

______ *The English Novel from Dickens to Lawrence*. London: Chatto, 1970. repr. Paladin 1974

Wilson, Edmund. *The Shores of Light: A Literary Chronicle of the Twenties and Thirties*. London: W. H. Allen, 1952

______ *Classics and Commercials: A Literary Chronicle of the Forties*. London: W. H. Allen, 1951

Wilson, Colin. *The Outsider*. London: Gollancz, 1956. repr. Pan, 1963

______ *The Age of Defeat*. London: Gollancz, 1959

______ *The Strength to Dream: Literature and the Imagination*. London: Gollancz, 1962

______ *Voyage to a Beginning*. London: Cecil Woolf, 1966

Wilson, Timothy. 'Nicholas Mosley'. *Guardian*, 29 Jun 71, p.8 (article and interview)

Woolf, Virginia. *Collected Essays* vol. II. London: Chatto & Windus, 1966

______ 'Modern Fiction' in her *The Common Reader*. London: Hogarth, 1925. repr. in *Collected Essays* vol. II

______ 'American Fiction' in her *The Moment*. London: Hogarth, 1947. repr. in *Collected Essays* vol. II

______ 'The Leaning Tower' in her *The Moment*. London: Hogarth, 1947 repr. in *Collected Essays* vol. 11

______ 'Mr . Bennett and Mrs. Brown' in her *The Captain's Death Bed*. London Hogarth, 1950.

______ 'Phases of Fiction' in her *Granite and Rainbow*. London: Hogarth, 1958. repr. in *Collected Essays* vol. 11

______ 'Women and Fiction' in her *Granite and Rainbow*. London: Hogarth, 1958. repr. in *Collected Essays* vol. 11

_____ *A Room of One's Own*. London: Hogarth, 1929. repr. Panther, 1977.
_____ *A Writer's Diary*. London: Hogarth, 1953. repr. Triad/Panther, 1978
Worringer, Wilhelm, *Abstraction and Empathy: A Contribution to the Psychology of Style*. London, 1953
_____ *Form in Gothic*. London, 1927. repr, London: Alec Tiranti, 1957
Writers Directory, 1980-1982, The. London: Macmillan, 1979
'Writer's Situation, The': (Symposium). *New American Review*, nos. 9,10 (1970) and 11 (1971)
Young, Alan. *Dada and After: Extremist Modernism and English Literature*. Manchester U.P., 1981
Young, Dudley. *New York Times Review* 24 Oct 71 (overview of Nicholas Mosley's work up to and including *Natalie Natalia*)
Ziegler, Heide and Chris Bigsby eds. *The Radical Imagination and the Liberal Tradition*. London: Junction, 1982

Printed in Great Britain
by Amazon.co.uk, Ltd.,
Marston Gate.